The Extra

Frozen in space and preserved for two cent by a miracle of science, Rosslyn awoke to a civilisation beyond his wildest imaginings. Women ruled the world, guided solely by the predictions of a tremendous and frightening computer that determined the actions of an entire world with devastating accuracy. Into this perfect civilisation Rosslyn came – and the impact of his presence brought near chaos. He had to be assimilated – or eliminated.

The Space-Born

Far from Earth, on a ship carrying distant descendants from the original crew, life is short. You are born, learn the tasks needed to keep the ship running, help breed and train the next crew, then your death is ordered by the computer in charge. Gregson, chief of the psych-police, makes sure the computer's death-sentences are carried out quickly and painlessly. His duty is a sacred trust. He knows the intricacies of the system, how it works … and how it can be subverted. He is growing old. Rebellious. He also knows his name will soon come up in the computer for elimination. And he has no intention of carrying out his own death-sentence!

Fires of Satan

Imagine a day, not too far from today, when you pick up the newspapers to find them free of the usual accounts of crime, corruption, violence and war. There's no politics or politicians, no sporting results, speculation or scandal. There is only the asteroid: newly-discovered, enormous and on a collision course with Earth. Imagine a time, not too far from today, when the world itself stands helpless before the Fires of Satan.

Also by E. C. Tubb

The Dumarest Saga
1: The Winds of Gath (1967)
2: Derai (1968)
3: Toyman (1969)
4: Kalin (1969)
5: The Jester at Scar (1970)
6: Lallia (1971)
7: Technos (1972)
8: Veruchia (1973)
9: Mayenne (1973)
10: Jondelle (1973)
11: Zenya (1974)
12: Eloise (1975)
13: Eye of the Zodiac (1975)
14: Jack of Swords (1976)
15: Spectrum of a Forgotten Sun (1976)
16: Haven of Darkness (1977)
17: Prison of Night (1977)
18: Incident on Ath (1978)
19: The Quillian Sector (1978)
20: Web of Sand (1979)
21: Iduna's Universe (1979)
22: The Terra Data (1980)
23: World of Promise (1980)
24: Nectar of Heaven (1981)
25: The Terridae (1981)
26: The Coming Event (1982)
27: Earth is Heaven (1982)
28: Melome (1983)
29: Angado (1984)
30: Symbol of Terra (1984)
31: The Temple of Truth (1985)
32: The Return (1997)
33: Child of Earth (2008)

The Cap Kennedy (F.A.T.E.) Series (E. C. Tubb writing as Gregory Kern)
1: Galaxy of the Lost (1973)
2: Slave Ship from Sergan (1973)
3: Monster of Metelaze (1973)
4: Enemy Within the Skull (1974)
5: Jewel of Jarhen (1974)
6: Seetee Alert! (1974)
7: The Gholan Gate (1974)
8: The Eater of Worlds (1974)
9: Earth Enslaved (1974)
10: Planet of Dread (1974)
11: Spawn of Laban (1974)
12: The Genetic Buccaneer (1974)
13: A World Aflame (1974)
14: The Ghosts of Epidoris (1975)
15: Mimics of Dephene (1975)
16: Beyond the Galactic Lens (1975)
17: The Galactiad (1983)

Alien Dust (1955)
Alien Impact (1952)
Journey Into Terror (originally published as Alien Life (1954, rev 1998))
Atom War on Mars (1952)
Fear of Strangers (first published as C.O.D. – Mars (1968))
Century of the Manikin (1972)
City of No Return (1954)
Death God's Doom (1999)
Death is a Dream (1967)
Dead Weight (first published as Death Wears a White Face (1979))
Escape into Space (1969)
Footsteps of Angels (2004) (previously unpublished work written c.1988)
Hell Planet (1954)
Journey to Mars (1954)
Moon Base (1964)
Pandora's Box (1996) (previously unpublished work written 1954)
Pawn of the Omphalos (1980)
S.T.A.R. Flight (1969)
Stardeath (1983)
Starslave (2010) (previously unpublished work written 1984)
Stellar Assignment (1979)

Temple of Death (1996) (previously unpublished work written 1954)
Fifty Days to Doom (first published as The Extra Man (1954))
The Life-Buyer (1965, 2008)
The Luck Machine (1980)
World in Torment (originally published as The Mutants Rebel (1953))
The Primitive (1977)
The Resurrected Man (1954)
The Sleeping City (1999)
The Space-Born (1956)
The Stellar Legion (1954)
To Dream Again (2011)
Venusian Adventure (1953)
Tide of Death (first published as World at Bay (1954))

E. C. Tubb (writing as Arthur MacLean)
The Possessed (revised version of Touch of Evil (1957))

E. C. Tubb (writing as Brian Shaw)
Argentis (1952)

E. C. Tubb (writing as Carl Maddox)
Menace from the Past (1954)
The Living World (1954)

E. C. Tubb (writing as Charles Grey)
Dynasty of Doom (1953)
The Extra Man (first published as Enterprise 2115 (1954) & then as The Mechanical Monarch (1958))
I Fight for Mars (1953)
Space Hunger (1953)
The Hand of Havoc (1954)
Secret of the Towers (originally published as The Tormented City (1953))
The Wall (1953)

E. C. Tubb (writing as Gill Hunt)
Planetfall (1951)

E. C. Tubb (writing as King Lang)
Saturn Patrol (1951)

E. C. Tubb (writing as Roy Sheldon)
The Metal Eater (1954)

E. C. Tubb (writing as Volsted Gridban)
The Green Helix (originally published as Alien Universe (1952))
Reverse Universe (1952)
Planetoid Disposals Ltd (1953)
The Freedom Army (originally published as De Bracy's Drug (1953))
Fugitive of Time (1953)

E. C. Tubb

SF GATEWAY OMNIBUS

THE EXTRA MAN
THE SPACE-BORN
FIRES OF SATAN

GOLLANCZ
LONDON

First published in Great Britain in 2013 by
Gollancz
An imprint of the Orion Publishing Group
Orion House, 5 Upper St Martin's Lane,
London WC2H 9EA

An Hachette UK Company

A CIP catalogue record for this book
is available from the British Library

ISBN 978 0 575 10520 1

1 3 5 7 9 10 8 6 4 2

Typeset by Jouve (UK), Milton Keynes

Printed and bound by CPI Group (UK) Ltd, Croydon, CR0 4YY

The Orion Publishing Group's policy is to use papers that are natural, renewable and recyclable products and made from wood grown in sustainable forests. The logging and manufacturing processes are expected to conform to the environmental regulations of the country of origin.

www.orionbooks.co.uk
www.gollancz.co.uk

CONTENTS

ENTER THE SF GATEWAY . . .

Towards the end of 2011, in conjunction with the celebration of fifty years of coherent, continuous science fiction and fantasy publishing, Gollancz launched the SF Gateway.

Over a decade after launching the landmark SF Masterworks series, we realised that the realities of commercial publishing are such that even the Masterworks could only ever scratch the surface of an author's career. Vast troves of classic SF and fantasy were almost certainly destined never again to see print. Until very recently, this meant that anyone interested in reading any of those books would have been confined to scouring second-hand bookshops. The advent of digital publishing changed that paradigm for ever.

Embracing the future even as we honour the past, Gollancz launched the SF Gateway with a view to utilising the technology that now exists to make available, for the first time, the entire backlists of an incredibly wide range of classic and modern SF and fantasy authors. Our plan, at its simplest, was – and still is! – to use this technology to build on the success of the SF and Fantasy Masterworks series and to go even further.

The SF Gateway was designed to be the new home of classic science fiction and fantasy – the most comprehensive electronic library of classic SFF titles ever assembled. The programme has been extremely well received and we've been very happy with the results. So happy, in fact, that we've decided to complete the circle and return a selection of our titles to print, in these omnibus editions.

We hope you enjoy this selection. And we hope that you'll want to explore more of the classic SF and fantasy we have available. These are wonderful books you're holding in your hand, but you'll find much, much more … through the SF Gateway.

GATEWAY

www.sfgateway.com

INTRODUCTION

from The Encyclopedia of Science Fiction

Edwin Charles Tubb (1919–2010) was a UK writer and editor who was also active for many years in Fandom, beginning in the 1930s with the Science Fiction Association; in 1958 he was both a founder member of the British Science Fiction Association and the first editor of its critical journal *Vector*. Meanwhile, Tubb had begun publishing sf, with 'No Short Cuts' in *New Worlds* for Summer 1951, and for the next half decade or so produced a great amount of fiction, in UK magazines and in book form, under his own name and under many pseudonyms.

His total output is in excess of 130 novels and 230 short stories. Of his many pseudonyms, those known to have been used for book titles of sf interest include Charles Grey, Gregory Kern, Carl Maddox, Edward Thompson and the House Names Volsted Gridban, Gill Hunt, King Lang, Arthur Maclean, Brian Shaw and Roy Sheldon. At least fifty further names were used for magazine stories only. His first sf novels were pseudonymous: *Saturn Patrol* (1951) as by King Lang, *Planetfall* (1951) as by Gill Hunt, 'Argentis' (1952) as by Brian Shaw and *Alien Universe* (1952 chap) as by Volsted Gridban. He soon began publishing under his own name, with *Alien Impact* (1952) and *Atom War on Mars* (1952), though his best work in these very early years was probably published as by Charles Grey, beginning with *The Wall* (1953). Of his enormous output of magazine fiction, the Dusty Dribble stories in *Authentic Science Fiction* (1955–1956) stand out; Tubb also edited *Authentic* from February 1956 to its demise in October 1957. After the mid-1950s, his production moderated somewhat, and he wrote relatively few stories after 1960 or so, but he remained a prolific author of consistently readable Space Operas until the early 1980s, and could have continued indefinitely had the market for adventure sf not collapsed. Readers' taste for adventure sf was now being satisfied by novels tied to Star Trek, Star Wars and other franchises.

With *Enterprise 2115* (1954; later published as *The Extra Man* in 2000) (see below) and *Alien Dust* (1955), Tubb began to produce more sustained adventure tales, solidly told, memorably plotted, arousing. *The Space-Born* (1956) (see below) is a crisp Generation Starship tale. These novels all display a convincing expertise in the use of the language and themes of Pulp-magazine sf, though stripped of some of its pre-War excesses. But Tubb always resisted the strictures of American Hard SF; the comparatively sober *Moon Base* (1964) comes as close to the nitty-gritty of the Near Future as he was ever inclined to go.

The next decade saw relatively few Tubb titles, until the start of the long series for which he remains best known, the Dumarest books beginning with *The Winds of Gath* (1967) and terminating abruptly, after thirty-one instalments, with *The Temple of Truth* (1985), before the climax of the series had been reached. Tubb had himself planned to bring Dumarest to a relatively early conclusion, but Donald A. Wollheim of DAW Books persuaded him to eke it out; unfortunately – and in fact very strangely – the series was cut short by his successors as soon as Wollheim died, leaving the firm in possession of a truncated epic, which was duly allowed to go out of print. Tubb had in fact written a further volume, which was first published in French under the title *Le Retour* (1992); the English-language edition is *The Return* (1997). The long tale is in fact simple: Earl Dumarest, who features in each volume, persists with soldier-of-fortune fortitude in his long search through the galaxy for lost Earth – the planet on which he was born, and from which he was wrested at an early age – but must battle against the universal belief that Earth is a myth. Inhabited planets are virtually innumerable; the period is some time after the collapse of a Galactic Empire, and everyone speaks the same language; and, as Dumarest moves gradually outwards from Galactic Centre along a spiral arm of stars – a progress through the vast archipelago of planets strongly evocative of the Fantastic Voyages of earlier centuries, and bears some resemblance to the work of his great American contemporary, Jack Vance (1916–2013) – it is clear that he is gradually nearing his goal. The opposition he faces from the Cyclan – a vast organization of passionless humans linked cybernetically to a central organic Computer whose location is unknown – long led readers to assume that the Cyclan HQ was located on Earth, but *The Return* is inconclusive about this; a further novel *Child of Earth* (2009), continues the series, but still leaves unresolved Dumarest's long search for the home base of the Cyclan. Tubb had saved its resolution for the next (perhaps final) book, but he died before it could be written. Though some of the later-middle titles were relatively aimless, Tubb showed consistent skill at prolonging Dumarest's intense suspense about the outcome of his long quest; and readers who enjoy his singletons may find the thirty-three volumes of Dumarest enticing.

Of the authors who began to work under the extraordinary conditions (low pay, fixed lengths, huge productivity demands) of early 1950s sf in the UK, Tubb and his colleague Kenneth Bulmer (1921–2005) were unique in retaining some of the harum-scarum writing habits of the early days while managing to gain considerable success in the rather tougher American market for sf adventures, as published by firms like Ace Books and DAW Books, whose standards were remarkably high. Though that market did disappear around 1980, Tubb remained moderately active, continuing to write and publish sf in relatively minor markets until his death in 2010, though he made no serious attempt to become a writer of the new (more demanding, and significantly more pretentious) versions of Space Opera that emerged from about 1990 on. But some of his 1950s space operas were as good as any written at the time; by the end of his long career he had probably become the field's most prolific producer of good sf adventures. He would have thought that high praise; as do his readers.

The first of the three tales selected here, *The Extra Man* (1954), deals swiftly, and with Tubb's typical generosity, with Reincarnation, the Superman theme, and Cybernetics, along with a matriarchal Dystopia; though the sustaining narrative – the pilot of the first spaceship returns from frozen sleep to reinvigorate a world gone wrong through its misuse of a prediction-generating computer – hardly seems to allow much justice to be done to any one concept. This may have been a valid comment in 1954, when the pace of sf stories was slower; today, the tale seems to careen along its course at just the right speed. *The Space-Born* (1956) displays the same deft pell-mell touch. In 1962 it was adapted as a 90-minute television play on French television, and has been widely translated in Europe.

Of real interest to lovers of Tubb's work is the third novel here presented. Though he had long been semi-retired – partly due to health problems – Tubb never relinquished his love for the field he had worked so hard at satisfying for so long. *Fires of Satan* is his last work, finished only weeks before he died. An asteroid threatens to destroy our planet. Men leap into space to fight back. What happens next, let an old man greatly experienced in telling tales do his job once more. Let him take us to the very end.

For a more detailed version of the above, see E. C. Tubb's author entry in *The Encyclopedia of Science Fiction*: http://sf-encyclopedia.com/entry/tubb_e_c

Some terms above are capitalised when they would not normally be so rendered; this indicates that the terms represent discrete entries in *The Encyclopedia of Science Fiction*.

THE EXTRA MAN

INTRODUCTION

by Philip Harbottle

Although *The Extra Man* was written in the Autumn of 1953, it was not published until November 1954. E. C. Tubb had submitted his manuscript to the newly established UK paperback firm of Milestone Limited, for whom he was regularly writing novels under his 'Charles Grey' personal pseudonym. The book was accepted and a cover prepared for early paperback publication. The publishers were so taken with the book that they subsequently decided to publish it in a hardcover format, and asked Tubb to add another chapter to the book, to increase its length. However, in the cavalier fashion of the day, as they had already prepared a cover for *The Extra Man*, they put this on another book Tubb had sent them in the interim, discarding its correct title, and this quite different book was issued under the wrong title in February 1954. When the genuine *The Extra Man* was eventually published in its lengthened version in November 1954, the publisher unaccountably gave it the totally inappropriate title of *Enterprise 2115*! For this new SF Gateway edition, the original correct title has been restored!

This novel was the last of Tubb's early 'pulp' novels to be published in his prolific 'mushroom' period, 1951–1954. In many ways, it can be seen as a transitional work. It is written in a tighter, more controlled manner, but its cool prose is still leavened with occasional flashes of near-poetry:

> '... dim lights gleamed for an instant, gleamed and died like the fading embers of forgotten hope.'

Tubb's book was written before the actual advent of manned space flight, when, outside of the scientists and military technicians actually working (largely in secret) on rocket research, the conquest of space was still regarded as something of a dream, and an article of faith by science fiction fans. The first man into space was seen as rather a romantic figure, and in his characterisation of Curt Rosslyn, the pioneer space pilot, Tubb conveys something of his own feeling regarding the conquest of space.

The night before his flight into space, Rosslyn, looks at the vessel which is to carry him into history:

'A space ship.

Curt stared at it as he had stared at it a million times in imagination and in reality.

For him it was the final realisation of ambition, the solid proof that he was not living in a dream. Before him rose the space ship, real, solid, fact. A dream made tangible, a thing of ten thousand hopes and eternal longing from countless men crystallised into something which would finally reach for the stars.

And he was its pilot.'

And after the take-off, Rosslyn:

'... didn't need to glance out of the ports at the ebon night of space. He didn't need the sight of the scintillant stars, bright and burning with their cold white fire against the soft velvet of the void. He knew.

Of all men he was the first. The new Columbus. The hero of every boy and man who had ever stared at the sky and wished for wings to travel between the stars.

He was in space.'

Rosslyn's great friend is the brilliant scientist and computer expert, Comain. He is the designer of his experimental spacecraft, and shares his friend's longing to open up the space frontier. Physically unable to make the flight himself, he hopes to vicariously share Rosslyn's glory.

But Tubb had considerable scientific knowledge, and he knew that the romanticised view of space travel disguised the very real technical and engineering difficulties. He knew the dangers, and with uncanny prescience, he postulates an accident in space that clearly anticipated the later real-life Apollo 13 mission. In adopting this realistic, logical approach to space travel, Tubb was almost alone amongst his pulp contemporaries, most of whom saw space flight as akin to a futuristic taxi-ride!

Unlike the crew of Apollo 13, Rosslyn is unable to get back to Earth, and he dies in space. At this point, events parallel the story of Tubb's other novel of revival from death in space, *The Resurrected Man* (1954). Years later, Rosslyn's body is found drifting in space, and is revived by the scientists of a renegade faction of Martian colonists. Over two centuries have passed, and Comain's computer researches have been misapplied by successive ruthless governments. Earth is now a regimented Matriarchy, ruled by computer prediction!

Rosslyn becomes the willing pawn of the Martian dissidents and is smuggled back to Earth. Everyone is computer indexed—except Rosslyn! As an 'Extra Man' and an unknown quantity, he causes havoc. And then—? You simply must read this fast-moving and engrossing story for yourself. Whilst the action is always logical, Tubb also manages to produce a really surprising science fictional twist, which is as satisfying as it is unexpected. Significantly, the quality of the novel was also recognised by American editors, and the book was reprinted in America in 1958 under the more appropriate title of *The Mechanical Monarch*. It is now deservedly available again as an SF Gateway e-book.

Writing in a major science fiction reference book, *The New Encyclopaedia of Science Fiction* (1988) the noted critic and academic Stephen H. Goldman recorded that 'Tubb is, moreover, a master at handling the conventional material of SF. His use of a generation starship in *The Space-Born* (also reprinted in this present SF Gateway Tubb Omnibus edition) and cybernetics in *Enterprise 2115* (aka *The Extra Man*) … are as good as any to be found in the genre.'

I would certainly not quarrel with this assessment, and thanks to this present volume, modern readers can now judge for themselves. And the even better news for readers is that all of Tubb's classic science fiction novels are currently being made available as e-books in the ongoing SF Gateway series. Watch out for them, and spread the word … E. C. TUBB, THE GURU OF SPACE ADVENTURE IS BACK!

Philip Harbottle,
Wallsend,
October, 2013.

CHAPTER I

From the gentle slope of the foothills Poker Flats stretched like a frozen sea beneath the cold light of a near-full Moon. Shadows blotched the surface, black pools against the grey-white, thrown from swelling dunes and wind-blown rock, collecting in ebon patches and inky channels, etching the unevenness of the desert. They made an odd pattern those shadows, an irregular polka-dot pattern of light and dark, strange, a little alien, almost disturbing in the deep silence of the night.

Watching them, Curt Rosslyn could almost imagine that he was no longer on Earth.

He leaned against a crumbling boulder, a slight man, not tall, not heavily built, but with a litheness and easiness of movement that betrayed hidden strength. Behind him the Organ Mountains reared their jagged crests against the star-shot sky, and far out across the wastes of Poker Flats, dim lights gleamed for an instant, gleamed and died like the fading embers of forgotten hope.

He sighed a little, his grey eyes clouded with dreams as he stared at the shadowed desert and the worn mountains. Mars must be something like this, he thought. Or perhaps the airless craters of the Moon, or even the sun-scorched surface of distant Mercury. He sighed again, tilting his head and staring up towards the burning glory of the heavens, idly tracing the well-remembered constellations.

The Big Dipper, Polaris the Dog Star, and the sprawling length of Draco. The regular shape of Cassiopeia and the angular shape of Andromeda with its misty nebula. Cross-shaped Bootes, and the scintillant cluster of the Pleiades. Glowing Fomalhaut, and the splendour of Vega. Low on the horizon Rigel and Betelgeuse blazed in the glory of Orion, warning of the winter to come, and above all, glowing like a tracery of shimmering gems, the heart-stopping splendour of the Milky Way.

He knew them all, had known them for as long as he could remember, and the familiar constellations felt like old friends. He had squinted at them through the lenses of his first crude telescope. Then, after many weary hours, he had stared at them with the aid of a hand-ground mirror and the extra power of his six-inch reflector had opened new worlds of glory. He had seen the satellites of Jupiter, the transit of Venus and Mercury, studied the 'canals' of Mars and walked in imagination on the dusty sea bottoms of the Moon. The Moon! He smiled up at it, winking at the splotched face of the satellite, then, obeying the warning of finely-turned reflexes, turned and stared over the desert.

Light and sound came towards him.

Twin streamers of brilliance stabbed across the desert, dispelling the shadows and ruining the alien atmosphere with the harsh reality of commonsense. The headlights swung and dipped, rose towards the stars and veered from rock and heaped dunes of arid sand. With the approach of the headlights the sound of the jeep sent flat echoes from the age-old heights of the Organ Mountains, and Curt sighed, relaxing against his boulder and fumbling in his pockets for cigarettes.

'Rosslyn?'

'Yes.' Curt threw away his butt and stepped towards the vehicle. 'Comain?'

'That's right.' A tall, lean, almost emaciated figure unfolded itself from behind the wheel and in the starlight Curt could see the pale face and thick-lensed spectacles of his friend. 'Time to go back, Curt. I volunteered to collect you, the driver was busy winning a hundred dollar pot.'

'I could have waited.' Curt stared at the stars again, almost forgetting that he was no longer alone. 'Beautiful, aren't they?'

'Yes.' Something in the tall man's voice made Curt glance at him, then look away. 'They're clean and bright and wonderful, Curt – and they're waiting. New worlds, new peoples, new ideals and cultures. New frontiers, Curt, and we're on the threshold of opening the way.'

'Perhaps, but it won't be for a long time yet.'

'No, Curt. The first step is always the hardest. First we have to break the gravitational drag, lift a ship from the surface and keep it off. Once we have done that the rest must follow. First a trip around the Moon and back again. Then an actual landing on the satellite. After that, Mars, Venus, even Mercury and Jupiter. It may take time, Curt, but it will be done.'

The tall man fell silent as he stared at the brilliant face of the near-full Moon. Taller than Curt, stoop shouldered, thin-faced and weak-eyed, yet his high forehead and large skull told of the intelligence residing in his ungainly body. His hands were thin and slender, the fingers long and supple, the hands of an artist, an idealist, a dreamer. Ambition burned within him, not the normal ambition of the majority of men, for wealth meant nothing to him, but the relentless ambition of the scholar. He was driven by the twin devils of curiosity and speculation. He wondered, and he built, then wondered again and built afresh. He would never stop until his eyes closed in the final sleep. He was that kind of man.

A thin wind blew across the desert, stirring the sand a little and chilling their blood. Curt shivered, then, as if ashamed of himself, tried to ignore the warnings of his body.

'Better get back,' said Comain quietly. 'You don't want to catch a cold now.'

'I won't.'

'You shivered and it's getting colder.' Comain started towards the jeep. 'Come on, Curt.'

'I'm not cold,' said the slight man irritably. 'It's just that they've starved me until I don't own an ounce of fat.' He stared at his slender arm. 'Look at me! Just skin and bone with a bit of muscle! I couldn't knock down a midget, the shape I'm in now.'

'You know better than that.' Comain smiled ruefully as he stared at his own arm. 'You've got muscle, trained and developed to a high pitch of efficiency. Me?' He bit his lip and continued towards the vehicle. 'What do I need brawn for?'

'You don't.' Curt fell into step with the tall man and their feet scuffed against the desert as they walked towards the silent jeep. 'And neither do I. Not with all those gadgets you built. Why, man, all I have to do is to press buttons. Those things you fitted should be able to operate the ship on their own.'

'The servo mechanisms?' Comain smiled. 'They will help but they can only do what you direct them to do. The final decision must be yours.'

He halted by the side of the jeep and folded his long body behind the wheel. Curt sat beside him, then, as they began jolting over the desert, clung to the metal frame of the windscreen.

'You know,' he said above the whine of the engine. 'I should have thought it possible to build a robot pilot for the first ship. Could you do that?'

'Yes.' Comain stared before him, his weak eyes narrowed a little as he steered the vehicle over the undulating sand. He wasn't deceived, and yet he felt grateful to Curt for easing his inner pain. They had grown up together, sharing their boyhood, discovering the stars and the mysteries of science at the same time. Both had dreamed the same dreams, weaving impossible worlds of romantic mystery with their youthful imaginations. They had argued, built, planned, even fought a little. They had helped each other, and, as the years passed, had grown closer even than brothers.

But now they had to part.

Little things had decided it. Weak eyes against perfect vision. Weight against weight, height against height, reflex against reflex. They had been tested, examined, checked – and Curt had won.

To him had fallen the honour of being the Columbus of space.

Comain had known it for more than five years now. He had watched his body, his frail, stooped, weak body, and he had known. Ambition had not died with the knowledge but had been channeled into a different path. Not for him the glories of space, but science covered a wide field and cybernetics was something in which he could take a keen interest. And so he had turned to the design of more and more efficient machines. Small and compact, with built-in relays and predictable response to external stimuli. He had designed the controls for the space ship, the things of metal that could operate faster, better, than the muscles of any man.

And yet his hurt had been deep and something of the old pain still lingered.

'I could build a mechanical pilot,' he said. 'I could build one better than any man, but we're up against weight limitations, Curt, and no machine now known can do what a man can do within that limitation.'

'Good.' Curt grinned with a flash of white teeth. 'I don't care what you do later, Comain, but I'm glad that you've had to admit defeat now. I've looked forward to this for a long time and I'd hate for you to replace me with a thing of steel and wire.'

'No chance of that.' Comain swung the wheel as he guided the jeep around a jagged mound of rock. 'They're interested in discovering just what will happen to a man out there. You're a guinea pig, Curt, my day will come after they finally realise that the human body can't stand high G without damage. Then we'll have ships with the passengers in acceleration tanks and robots at the controls.'

'Maybe.' Curt grunted as the vehicle bounced and jarred his teeth. 'How's your research going on the Great Idea?'

'The predictor?' The thin man shrugged. 'It'll come, Curt, it will *have* to come. They've got EINAC already and better computers will be built. One day they'll realise that a machine able to absorb information and then to predict probable events from that information will be essential if we are to advance this civilisation of ours.' His thin lips twisted cynically as he stared at the desert before him. 'Probably the next war will do it.'

'You think that there'll be one?'

'I do. Every thinking man does. We've managed to negotiate an uneasy peace but the weapons are ready, the men are waiting, and the same tensions still exist. War will come, Curt, it can't be avoided, and, in a way, it could be a good thing.'

'A good thing! Are you crazy?'

'No. Look at it this way, Curt. Each war has brought rapid scientific advancement. The First World War brought the development of flight, the advancement of surgery, the use of strange machines. The second brought the jet engine, the atomic bomb, the proximity fuse. The third …' He shrugged. 'Who knows? We may all die from the alphabet bombs but if we don't we may stumble on something quite new.'

'The predictor?'

'Naturally, but I didn't mean that. The predictor isn't new, and it will come, war or no war. I mean something different, new, perhaps something not even imagined yet.'

He grunted as the jeep bounced over the edge of a wide road and with a sweep of his hand disengaged the low register. The swaying headlights steadied as they spun along the smooth road and the flickering hand of the speedometer crawled across the dial as the thin man trod on the throttle.

'The Colonel was furious at your taking off like that,' he explained above the rush of displaced air. 'I tried to tell him how you felt but he didn't seem to understand.'

'The Colonel has no imagination.' Curt stared up at the brilliant Moon. 'Sometimes a man just has to get off somewhere by himself. Sometimes he just can't stand people fussing around him.' He looked at the thin man. 'Can you understand what I mean?'

'I understand.' Comain thinned his lips as he nodded, then, taking one hand from the wheel, pointed ahead. 'There she is!'

Light blazed before them. Light and the delicate tracery of a high wire fence. The squat bulk of a tracking station loomed on their left, the white and red warning notices ringing the area showed stark on their right, and before them …

It towered like the delicate spire from some ancient dream. Smooth, glistening with streamlined perfection, needle-pointed and resting on its wide fins. Loading platforms and gantries clustered around it, but even their bulk couldn't hide the sheer beauty of the man-made thing resting in the centre of the area. It seemed to hover on the levelled sand, like a thing without weight or substance. It soared towards the beckoning stars and the lights ringing the area shimmered in scintillating ripples from the gleaming hull.

A space ship.

Curt stared at it as he had stared at it a million times in imagination and in reality. For him it was the final realisation of ambition, the solid proof that he was not living in a dream. Before him rose the space ship, real, solid, fact. A dream made tangible, a thing of ten thousand hopes and eternal longing from countless men crystallised into something that should finally reach for the stars.

And he was its pilot.

Guards stepped forward as the jeep droned towards the high wire fence and Comain grunted as his foot moved from accelerator to brake. Lights blazed at him, forcing him to squint and shield his weak eyes, then, recognised by the guards, they droned into the wired area and towards the low bulk of the living quarters.

'Better go straight to bed if you want to dodge the Colonel,' he suggested. 'Anyway, you could do with some sleep.'

'I can't sleep.' Curt twisted in his seat as he stared at the towering space ship. 'Man! How can I sleep? This is it, Comain! This is what I've wanted all my life! I blast at dawn and you talk of sleep!'

'Dawn?' The thin man frowned as he glanced at his left wrist. 'In four hours?'

'Is it?' Curt shrugged. 'I'm not wearing a watch. Zero hour is at dawn – that's all I care about.'

'Then what are you going to do?'

'I don't know. Walk about perhaps, yarn with the boys, play poker, anything. Don't you realise that this is my last night on Earth? Tomorrow I'll be in space, swinging around the Moon, watching the naked stars, feeling what it's like to be in free fall. I want to enjoy all this while I can. I've no time for sleep.'

'Don't talk like that, Curt.' Comain swallowed, then grinned as he brought the jeep to a halt. 'Don't talk as if this were your last night alive I mean. You'll be coming back. You know you will, and when you do, you'll be a hero. Think of it, Curt. The first man to have circled the Moon! Your name will be in every history book from now on.'

'Perhaps, but, Comain, it won't be the same after this. Nothing will. This is all I've lived for and once I've done it, what then? Can I bear to settle down again? Or will I be altered in some way, sent insane perhaps or my body twisted with the free radiation we know is out there? I may be crippled, or blind. I may be a thing of horror, or even if space doesn't harm me, I may die in a crash landing, die – or worse. No, Comain, as far as I'm concerned, this is my last night on Earth and I'll be damned if I waste it in sleep.'

Lithely the slender man swung from his seat then stood, looking down at Comain.

'What are you going to do?'

'Check the radio gear again I suppose. You know that I'll be in contact with you all the time?'

'Yes.'

'I'll be seeing you at dawn then.' Comain narrowed his eyes as he saw a tall, trimly uniformed figure emerge from one of the low huts. 'Better watch it if you don't want to see the Colonel. He's just left his quarters.'

'Has he?' Curt grinned and moved away from the jeep. 'I can do without his company for now. Be seeing you, Comain.' He lifted an arm in a casual salute and walked rapidly from the vehicle, the shadows between the glaring arc lights hiding him from view.

Comain nodded, not answering, then, with a strangely bitter expression on his thin features, sat hugging the wheel and staring towards the glistening perfection of the waiting rocket ship. He didn't answer the Colonel when Adams spoke to him. He didn't seem to notice the chill wind sweeping from the desert or the fading light of the burning stars. He just sat waiting, his weak eyes clouded with thought and his stooped body lax behind the wheel.

Waiting for dawn.

CHAPTER II

Dawn came with a thin wind, a chill wind bearing promise of early winter and carrying a fine dust of stinging sand. In the east a pink glow suffused the sky and a scud of thin cloud hid the dying light of the fading stars. The Moon had gone, falling below the horizon, and it was strange to see men glancing to where it had been, even though they knew that the ship would be aimed at a set of co-ordinates rather than a visual target.

Adams gathered them all in the control room for briefing.

The Colonel showed signs of strain, his eyes were bloodshot and his grizzled hair rumpled, matching his usually impeccable uniform. He glared at Curt, almost as if he would like to give the young man hell for slipping away from his surveillance, then, as he stared at the young man, shrugged and got down to business.

'Blast-off's in one hour,' he said abruptly. 'The ship has been fueled, the instruments checked, and the weather report is favourable. You will each report in turn.'

'Tracking stations standing by, sir.'

'Radio checked and ready.' Comain leaned against the edge of the table and winked at Curt.

'Medical examination completed.' The doctor yawned and rubbed his tired eyes. 'Is all this necessary, Adams? I can't see why I've got to stand by. There's nothing more I can do until Rosslyn returns.'

'You've given him the drugs?'

'Yes. The complete hell-brew. Stuff to lower his instinctive muscular resistance to strain. Other stuff to prevent congealing of his blood.' The doctor looked at Curt. 'Be careful of that by the way. If you cut yourself you're liable to bleed to death.'

'If I'm injured I take the green injection. Right?'

'Right.' The doctor yawned again. 'Damn it all, Adams! I'm an old man, I need my sleep. Can I go now?'

'You are excused, doctor,' said the Colonel stiffly. 'Naturally you will make no attempt to leave the area.'

'And miss the chance of almost taking a man apart?' The doctor grinned at Curt. 'Man! Wait until you see what I've got lined up for you when you return. Three hundred tests and twenty days of controlled feeding. I'll make you wish that you had never gone.'

'It'll be worth it.' Curt grinned after the old medico as he left the room. 'Rocket checked O.K.?'

A technician nodded. 'Yeah. I examined the Venturis myself. The ship won't let you down, Rosslyn.'

'I hope not,' said Curt quietly. 'There won't be any chance of repairing it if it does.'

'It won't let you down.' Adams jerked his head and the technician left the room. 'Now. You, Comain, will keep in constant radio communication with the ship. You, Rosslyn, will maintain a running commentary on everything that happens. I mean that literally, Rosslyn. I want you to keep talking, about the ship, your own reactions, even your thoughts and emotions. I don't want you to freeze up on us. This thing has cost too much for a temperamental pilot to queer things. You may die, you know that, but if you do I want to know just why. Remember that no matter what happens to you another ship will be coming after. There will be other men, lots of them, and you may help to save their lives.'

'I understand, Adams.'

'I hope that you do.' The Colonel sighed and rubbed at his bloodshot eyes. 'I want you to come back to us, Rosslyn, alive and well. You know that, so take good care of yourself will you?' He grinned and Curt felt himself warm to the grizzled man.

'I'll take care,' he promised. 'I …' He paused as a man's voice echoed from a speaker against the wall.

'Zero minus fifty.'

'That's it!' Adams heaved himself from his chair. 'Get to the ship, Rosslyn. They'll dress you in your anti-G suit there. Comain! Get to your radio and warm it up. Move now.'

It was psychology of course. A deliberate leaving of everything until the last few minutes when, in the final rush of activity, strain and nervous anticipation would be forgotten. Curt almost ran from the room, piling into a waiting jeep and feeling the cold wind tug at his hair as he was driven to the base of the loading platform.

Men grabbed him as the vehicle skidded to a halt. They stripped him, dressed him in a one-piece undersuit of non-conducting nylon, then in a thick armour of canvas and plastic. Swiftly the loading platform carried both Curt and his helpers to the nose of the rocket, and within what seemed an incredible short time he sat in his padded control chair, the inflated sections of his G-suit pressing hard against his body, his hands, gloved and steady, reaching for the warm-up switches.

'Good luck, Rosslyn!' The last of his helpers grinned as he crawled through the tiny entrance port, swinging the panel behind him and dogging it tight against the rubber gaskets. Abruptly the radio droned into life.

'Curt. All set?'

'Yes.'

'Good. Routine check now. Ready?'

'Fire away.'

'Oxygen bottles?'

'Check.'

'Drugs?'

'Check.'

'Water?' The calm voice of Comain droned on, forcing Curt to keep his mind on the vital supplies of the ship, checking every item, not through fear of any last-minute error, but to keep the pilot's mind from what was coming. Softly, over the calm monotony of Comain's voice, Curt heard the time signal whispered from some distant speaker.

'Zero minus seven minutes.'

Seven minutes!

Four hundred and twenty seconds before he would feel the thunder of the Venturis and feel the bone-jarring thrust of acceleration pressure. Seven minutes, not even time for a cigarette, before he would rise on wings of flame, rise on the thundering power of unleashed energy, rise towards the stars. Sweat oozed from his forehead and he felt an insane desire to stop the whole thing, to get up from his padded chair, open the hatch, return to the safe, sure world of normal men.

'Curt!'

Comain's voice jerked him back to sanity and he licked his lips as he tried to still the butterflies crawling in his stomach. 'Yes?'

'What's the matter, getting nervous?'

'A little,' he admitted. 'How much longer?'

'Take it easy, you'll know when it's time.' Curt could almost see his friend's thin features, the thin lips curved in a cynical smile. 'Last instructions, Curt. You know what you must do.'

'I know. Practically nothing at all.'

'That's right. The take-off will be automatic. The gyroscopes will take care of the course. You just sit there and do nothing unless something goes haywire. You'll circle the Moon, the cameras are automatic too, but you'd better check them just in case.'

'Just a passenger aren't I?'

'No. Don't make that mistake, Curt. You've got to watch everything all the time. We just don't know what free radiation will do to the instruments, and remember, you've got to land the ship too.'

'A parachute could do that.'

'Perhaps, you've got one anyway, but it isn't as simple as that, Curt. You are as much an instrument as anything else aboard. On you will rest, in the final analysis, the whole success or failure of this flight. An instrument could fail, the acceleration shock could do it, and you must be there to take its place. Also, and perhaps this is the most important, until you return we cannot be sure that man can even live in space.'

'So now I'm a guinea pig.' Curt smiled at the radio, grateful to Comain for easing his nervous tension. A whisper came from the radio, the sound of the time check, and over it Curt heard Comain's expression of annoyance.

'Shut that thing off.'

'How long, Comain?' Curt licked his dry lips. 'How long damn you!'

'Take it easy, Curt. You've got a long time yet.'

'You're a liar, Comain. Tell me. How long?' The whispering of the time check gave the answer.

'Zero minus one minute.'

One minute!

It was too much. It was impossible for any man born of woman not to dwell on the passing seconds. Later perhaps when space flight was as normal as catching a plane, the time wouldn't matter so much, but now ...

Curt could feel his heart thudding against his ribs as he waited for the rocket to thunder into strident life. Now there was no turning back. Now he just had to sit there, poised over five hundred tons of one of the most violent explosives known, waiting for it to ignite and hurl him beyond the planet of his birth. He would rise on that thundering pillar of flame, rise up and up, through the clouds and through the thinning atmosphere. Up and out – into what?

Space was the great unknown. It was a void, they knew that. It was a vacuum in which the planets swum like lonely fish in an ebon sea. Temperatureless, without any heat or light of its own, without gravity, illumined by the faint dots of the distant stars and the naked furnace of the roaring sun. Space was emptiness – or was it? Radiation streamed through that void. The broken atoms of incredible cataclysms, cosmic rays, tides of free electrons, gamma and alpha radiation, and other strange and unguessed at forces. Men had always been protected from them, shielded by the ozone belt of the Heaviside layer, but he was going beyond that protection, venturing his soft and helpless body into the surging currents of outer space.

He could go blind. He could return a distorted cripple, his cells and bones twisted and warped by that flood of radiation. His mind could yield and raving insanity replace his schooled calm. Anything could happen. Anything.

He half rose from the padded seat, his gloved hands fumbling at his harness, the sweat of fear trickling down his face, stinging his eyes and wetting his parched lips with the salty taste of terror.

Comain's voice from the radio jerked him back to sanity.

'Curt! Blast-off in ten seconds. Rockets now warming up.'

A mutter echoed throughout the ship. A quivering vibration singing along the metal of the hull, the internal stanchions, sending little ringing sounds from the plastic faces of the instruments and the thin sheeting of the control bank. Curt tensed, then, accepting the inevitable, lost his fear and refastened his harness. Swiftly he scanned the dials, snapping quick reports into the radio.

'Temperature rising. Number four jet higher than the other six. Vibration increasing. How's she look, Comain?'

'Beautiful!' Envy tinged the thin man's reply. 'I wish I was with you, Curt.'

'So do I,' said the slender man feelingly, then gripped the arms of his chair as the muttering grew louder. 'Switch in the radio-clock, Comain. I ...' He bit his lip as the sound of the rockets rose to a screaming whine, and again he could taste the salt of his own fear.

The whistling roar grew louder, shrieking with the full power of a million tormented giants, yelling a brutal challenge towards the far horizon and the careless stars. Vibration sang from the metal of hull and stanchions, a thin shrilling of jarred atoms, ringing and blending with the pulsing thunder of the blasting rockets. Dimly, over the hell of blasting sound, Curt heard the thin voice from the radio.

'Good luck, Curt. This is it!'

'Yes,' he breathed. 'Here we go.'

Weight slammed at him, thrusting him deep into the padding of his chair, piling tons of invisible lead on chest and stomach, squeezing his lungs and pressing his head down between his shoulders. The weight grew, became a nightmare of ceaseless struggle, a pain-shot, timeless period of eternal anguish.

Blood streamed from his nose and ears, filled his eyes, thundered from his labouring heart and filled his mouth with salty wetness. He gasped, writhing on his padded chair, twisting in the confines of his inflated G-suit and wishing that he were dead. Nothing he had ever experienced had ever been like this. It seemed as if his very bones would protrude through his skin, the flesh ripped away by the piling weight of acceleration pressure. He wanted to black-out, and, at the same time, fought against it. He wanted to stop the ship, to get out and to call the whole thing off, and at the same time he urged the rockets to still greater thrust, knowing that the sooner the ship reached escape velocity the sooner his torment would be over.

The rockets died, cutting with an almost savage abruptness, and in the silence little sounds seemed to have gained greater power. The soft hiss of air from an oxygen cylinder, the creak and rustle of still-vibrating stanchions, the throb and pulse of surging current, and, above all, the muted chatter of the Geiger counter measuring the flood of radiation penetrating the vessel.

Curt stirred, licking his lips and lifting himself into a more comfortable position before the banked controls. His face felt wet, sticky and uncomfortable, stiff and a little numb. Clumsily he unbuckled his mask and dabbed at his features with his gloved hand. He winced at the touch, his muscles and skin feeling as though he had been beaten with a rubber hose, then stared blankly at his gloved fingers.

They were stained with blood.

The radio crackled, and a voice, blurred with static and distorted with emotion echoed from the speaker.

'Curt! Are you all right, Curt? Curt! Answer me!'

He ignored it, unbuckling the safety harness, and, even though he had expected it, the eerie sensation of free fall made him catch at the back of the chair in sudden fear. He hovered there, weightless, his feet unsupported and his whole body drifting lightly like a gas-filled balloon, and, as he hovered, he smiled.

He didn't need to glance out of the ports at the ebon night of space. He didn't need the sight of the scintillant stars, bright and burning with their cold white fire against the soft velvet of the void. He knew.

Of all men he was the first. The new Columbus. The hero of every boy and man who had ever stared at the sky and wished for wings to travel between the stars.

He was in space.

CHAPTER III

The room was heavy with coiling clouds of stale smoke and rank with the taste of air which had been breathed too often. It seemed that every man who could possibly find an excuse for cramming himself in the room had done so, and they leaned against the walls, poised on the edges of tables and chairs, smoking, breathing, their eyes heavy with lack of sleep and nervous tension.

Adams sprawled in a chair, his tunic unbuttoned, his grizzled hair rumpled and his bloodshot eyes dull as he listened to the voice of the thin man sitting before the radio. Comain wiped his lips with the back of his hand, adjusted a vernier control a trifle, and leaned closer to the microphone.

'Curt. Comain here. Answer me, Curt. Answer me damn you!'

'Maybe the radio went?' A man whispered the suggestion, then recoiled at the naked hate in Comain's eyes.

'No! That radio was tested up to fifty G. It couldn't have gone. Anyway, the signal is getting through.' He turned to the mike again and the sound of his voice echoed with a plaintive desperation in the silence of the room.

'Even if he'd blacked-out he would have recovered by now.' The man who had suggested that perhaps the radio had broken whispered to his neighbour, a small technician with a twisted scar writhing across one cheek. 'My guess is that Rosslyn couldn't take it.'

'I doubt it.' The scarred man shook his head. 'They tested him, remember. He stood ten gravities in the centrifuge.'

'Yeah, but that ship hit twelve on the way up. It had to in order to reach the seven miles per second escape velocity before the fuel got too low. My guess is that …'

'Shut up,' said Adams quietly. 'If you can't keep your lip buttoned get out.'

'I only …'

'You heard me.' Adams didn't raise his voice but the man winced at the Colonel's tone, then, shrugging, he lit a fresh cigarette and fell silent.

'Curt! Comain calling. Curt! Answer me will you! Answer me!'

'How long now?' Adams rubbed his bloodshot eyes and Comain twisted in his seat as he looked at the Colonel.

'Three hours. He should have reported before this. He should have reported within the first ten minutes even if he did black-out. Something's wrong, Colonel. Curt wouldn't do this if he could help it.'

'No.' Adams rubbed his eyes again. 'Is the ship on course?

'Tracking stations report that it took-off as per schedule. The observatories are reporting every fifteen minutes. As far as the ship itself is concerned everything is on the beam. If only Curt would answer.' Comain bit his thin lips and leaned towards the radio again.

'Curt! Comain here. Come in, Curt! Make some sort of noise, damn you! Are you still alive?'

The radio hummed with a smooth surge of power and outside, high on a slender tower, the beam antenna focused on the tiny point of the ship swung a little as it followed the course of the gleaming speck.

'He could be dead,' said Adams sombrely. 'The free radiation could have got him, the weightlessness of free fall, anything. Well,' he shifted in his chair, 'we can only hope that the automatics will bring the ship back again without him.'

'He isn't dead,' insisted Comain savagely. 'He couldn't be dead. He …' He paused, his eyes behind their thick lenses widening as sound filtered from the humming radio.

'Comain … Curt here … Ill … Answer.'

'Curt!' The thin man's hands fluttered as he adjusted the vernier dials, stepping up the beam power of the radio. 'Speak up, man! Are you alright?'

'I …' The radio blurred to a sudden wash of static, then, with almost shocking abruptness, the thin voice steadied, seemed to gain power, as if the speaker stood in the very same room as the tensely listening men.

'Comain! Man, it's good to hear your voice.'

'What happened, Curt? Why didn't you answer sooner?'

'Acceleration twisted a wire, threw the radio out of kilter, that or the radiation up here altered the capacity of a coil. I could hear you, but you didn't seem to be hearing me.'

'Right.' Comain threw the switches of three recording machines, and reached for a pad. 'Let's have it, Curt. You said that you were ill? Are you?'

'Yes.' The pilot retched and the sound made the listening men glance uneasily at each other. 'Nothing too serious – I hope. Free fall isn't a picnic, Comain. At first it wasn't too bad, probably the excitement kept me normal, but after a while I felt my stomach tie itself into knots and my last three meals are still floating around the cabin.'

'Sickness.' Comain made a rapid note. 'Keep talking, Curt.' He leaned over to the slumped figure of the Colonel. 'Can we get the Doc here? Maybe he could suggest something to ease the sickness?'

'Get the doctor,' ordered Adams and a man almost ran from the room to fetch the old medico. 'Keep him talking, Comain. Is there anything else wrong with him?'

'I'm bleeding from nose and ears.' The voice from the speaker faded then returned with roaring strength. 'Blood cells ruptured during take-off. Normally it wouldn't matter but with this dope inside of me the blood isn't coagulating. Should I take the green injection?'

'We're getting the doctor. Better wait until he gets here before doing anything like that. How is the ship operating?'

'Vibration still a nuisance. I can feel the hull quivering and the stanchions haven't settled down yet.'

'Vibration!' Comain glanced at Adams. 'How? The rockets cut almost three hours ago.'

'I know that.' Curt retched again and when he spoke the listeners could imagine his inner pain. 'I'm in a closed system, remember. There's no air up here to damp out the vibrations and believe me, there was plenty to start with. It will damp out in time, but will it affect the instruments?'

'It shouldn't.' Comain made a quick notation on his pad. 'How is the radiation?'

'The Geiger's well into the red. Cosmic rays of course and I'd guess at plenty of gamma particles as well.' Curt paused. 'I hope I don't go blind.'

'You won't,' said Comain with false conviction. He twisted in his seat as the old doctor entered the room, and gestured him towards the radio. 'Curt's sick,' he said rapidly. 'Free fall doesn't agree with his stomach. He's bleeding, too.'

'I'll talk to him.' The doctor grunted as he settled his bulk into a chair. 'Hello, Curt, I hear that you're having a little trouble.'

'Hello, Doc. Can you suggest anything to untwist my guts?'

'Sorry, Curt, but you'll just have to stand it. It's all in your mind you know. The balancing channels in the inner ear are out of kilter without a constant gravity drag to inform them which direction is "down." Your mind knows that you're not falling, but your body knows that you are. You can't blame it too much, after all the body is only a reflex mechanism, it can only respond in a certain way to external stimuli. As soon as you can convince it that everything is alright you'll get rid of your sickness.'

'Thanks, Doc,' said Curt dryly. 'You're a great help. What about this bleeding?'

'Nothing to worry about. You've broken some surface blood cells and will lose a little blood. It will stop in time, your blood still has some coagulating power, and you won't bleed to death, if that's what you're afraid of.'

'Should I use the green injection?'

'No. For all we know the radiation up there may thicken your blood and if it were normal you'd die from clotting. Better leave well alone, Curt. After all, you didn't expect it to be a picnic, did you?'

'Go to hell,' said Curt, and the doctor shook his head as he heard the sounds of violent retching coming from the radio.

'Nothing we can do,' he said to Comain. 'If we sympathise with him it will make it worse. Rosslyn has courage, he doesn't need anyone to hold his hand. He'll get out of it on his own, or he won't get out of it at all. I'm sorry for him, but I'd still give my right arm to be where he is now.'

'I know what you mean,' said Comain, and from the assembled men came a murmur of agreement. They all envied the pilot. They all shared his troubles, his dangers, and all hoped to share his final success, and there wasn't one of them who wouldn't have cheerfully given up his hopes of heaven to have taken his place.

Adams rose tiredly from his chair.

'Nothing any of us can do now, except to wait,' he said heavily. 'Comain. You stand by the radio and try and keep Rosslyn talking into the recorders. The rest of you get out of here. I'm going to get some sleep and from the look of you, you'd better do the same. I'll send a relief, Comain. You look all in.'

'I don't want a relief.'

'Maybe not, but you're going to get one.' Adams glared at the thin man. 'Get some sense, man. The rocket has only just started, it won't be back for three days, and you're almost asleep now.'

'I can stand it.'

'You'll do as I order!'

'No, Adams.' The thin man glared at the Colonel. 'Curt is my friend and I'm going to stand by until he's safely back on Earth. Send a relief if you like, but I'm staying here!'

'Damn you, Comain!' Tiredness and irritation sharpened the Colonel's voice. 'I'm in charge here and you'll do as I say!'

'No.' Comain thinned his lips as he stared at the officer. 'I don't come under your jurisdiction, Adams. I'm a civilian, not a soldier, and my first loyalty is to my friend.'

'I …' Adams paused as the old doctor rested his hand on his arm. 'What is it?'

'Why argue with him, Adams? Comain's doing no harm and he might do Rosslyn a lot of good. You can send over a radio relief, but why beat your head against a wall?'

'But the ship can't return for three days yet. You know the procedures, Doc. It will drive close to the Moon, be caught in the satellite's gravitational field and be swung in a circular orbit. At the exact moment the tubes will fire a short blast to break free from the Moon and drive the ship towards Earth. What can Comain do to help that? What sense is there in his waiting by the radio for three days?'

'None,' admitted the old doctor. 'But let him do it, Adams.'

'Very well.' The Colonel shrugged and followed the rest of the men from the room. Comain stared after him for a moment, half-angry with himself for annoying the officer, and yet knowing that nothing would keep him from radio contact with his friend.

Inside the hut it began to grow warm with the heat of the rising sun. Outside, the barren desert shimmered beneath the solar furnace and the sky stretched from horizon to horizon, an inverted bowl of clear blue. Men moved listlessly about the area, tired after the rush preceding take-off, squinting up at the bowl of the sky as if they hoped to see the tiny speck of the rocket ship as it drove silently towards the Moon.

Comain saw nothing of that. He sat, his thin features tense and a little bitter with frustrated ambition, and listened to the voice of a man who spoke from where no other man had ever been.

'This is hell, Comain. It's like seasickness multiplied a thousand times. A horrible vertigo and nausea. We'll have to do something about it on future flights.'

'We can rotate the ship, provide an artificial gravitation by means of centrifugal force. I'm more worried about the vibration you mentioned. Is it still bad?'

'Dying. Almost gone now.'

'Good. What is it like out there, Curt?'

'Wonderful!' Despite the sickness Comain could catch the note of near-exultation in his friend's voice. 'Space is black of course, we knew that, but the stars are like a million diamonds scattered on a piece of black velvet. I never guessed that there could be so many stars. We can't see them on Earth, the air is too thick, but out here they glow like electric lights. Fourth magnitude stars are brighter than first, and the really bright ones, Vega, Rigel, you know them as well as I do, they shine like headlights on a dark night.'

'How are you feeling, Curt? In yourself I mean.'

'My temperature has risen. Hundred and one point three. Pulse is ninety-five. I'm sweating, too, have been ever since take-off, and my skin itches a little.'

'Badly?'

'No. Nervous reaction from take-off I suppose. I've noticed an ache in my bones and my muscles hurt a little. That could be the effect of free fall, I've had to learn to move all over again and may have strained a few tendons. One effect of this gravity lack is that my mind seems to be terribly clear. I can almost feel the blood rush through my skull and thoughts bubble and rise as yeast in fermenting wine. The things I've thought of, Comain! The ideas I've had. If I wasn't doubled up with vertigo this would be paradise, and even with the sickness I feel that I'm on top of the world.'

'You are.' Comain bit his lip as he recognised his own envy betraying itself in his tone, but the pilot didn't seem to notice. Curt yawned, the sound coming clearly over the radio, then gave an apologetic laugh.

'Funny. I feel tired. Think that I'll sleep for a while.'

'Curt! Are you insane? You can't be tired, not with all that anti-fatigue drug they gave you before take-off. Are you alright, Curt?'

'Sure I'm alright. Just a little sleepy. I'll be as good as new after a while.'

'Keep awake, Curt. Don't give in to it. Keep talking.'

'I can't. I'm too tired … tired … tired …'

'Curt!' Hastily Comain adjusted the controls, feeding more power to the radio beam. 'Answer me, Curt! Curt!'

Silence. Nothing but the hum of the radio and the distant crackle of static, and after a long while the thin man admitted defeat. He pressed a button, waiting until a uniformed operator arrived to take over, then, his feet moving with an exaggerated slowness, walked tiredly from the room.

Above his bowed head the sun crawled across a sky of clearest blue and beneath his feet the sand plumed in little clouds as he walked wearily towards his quarters. Men passed him, stared curiously at his drawn features, and he passed them as though they didn't exist.

When he finally fell asleep his dreams were filled with exotic worlds and strange races, or heroic men and heroic machines.

Slowly the day wore on.

CHAPTER IV

He awoke to the sound of shouts and sharp commands. A hand gripped his shoulder, shaking him and making the narrow cot on which he rested quiver and tremble.

'Comain! Wake up, man. Wake up!'

'What?' He opened his eyes, blinking, trying to focus on the pale blob of a face that loomed above him. 'What's the matter?'

'Hurry. Wake up.'

He grunted, fumbling for his spectacles, hooking them behind his ears and blinking at the Colonel's worried expression. He felt ill, overtired, his head a mass of cotton wool and his mouth tasting like the discharge end of a sewerage pipe. He gasped, feeling his clammy body shiver as the Colonel dragged off the sweat-soaked sheets, and he swung his thin legs over the edge of the bed as he struggled to regain full awareness.

'Adams! What's the matter?'

'Get up, Comain. We want you over at the radio. Quick!'

'Something wrong?' Panic seared through him and his hands trembled as he reached for his clothes. Adams nodded.

'Yes. Rosslyn has only just made radio contact after a silence of more than twelve hours and I'm worried.'

'Twelve hours.' Comain stared up at the Colonel. 'As long as that?'

'Yes.'

'Why didn't you call me sooner?'

'Why should I?' Adams moved his shoulders beneath the thin material of his tunic. 'What good would it have done? You were tired, we all were, and a man was standing by the radio all the time. You needed sleep, and you've had it, twelve hours of it.'

'Yes.' Comain finished dressing and licked his dry lips. He stepped over to the small water faucet and laved his face and hands, then, after letting the tepid water run for a moment, drank three glasses of the warm fluid. 'What's wrong?'

'I'll tell you on the way over.' Adams shifted his feet with nervous impatience. 'Ready yet?'

'Ready.'

Together they stepped from the hut into the soft darkness of approaching night.

'The ship isn't keeping to schedule,' said Adams quietly. 'The observatories report that it is going too fast, that, even though it will pass through the gravitational field of the Moon, it will only be swung from a direct flight line, and not swung into a circular orbit.' He paused and in the silence Comain could hear the sound of their boots as they scuffed over the sand.

'Impossible.'

'Don't be a fool, Comain. It's happening, I tell you. The observatories can't be wrong.'

'But how could it happen? We know exactly, know to the third decimal place, just what thrust we get from the fuel, the duration of fire from the Venturis, the speed of the ship, everything. It started as predicted. It should continue like that.'

'It isn't.' Adams stared at the thin man. 'Something's gone wrong with the automatics, Comain. That is obvious. Now, unless Rosslyn can operate the ship by manual control, he will drive directly into space.'

'Yes,' said the thin man numbly. 'I know that.'

He didn't say any more. Neither did the Colonel. Each was thinking of the same thing, but, true to their natures, each placed a different priority on what they were thinking.

Adams thought of a ship driving into space, carrying with it a helpless man. Comain thought of a man, his friend, being carried into the unknown by rebel machinery. He was glad when they finally entered the crowded radio shack.

'Anything?' He thrust the radio operator from his seat as the man shook his head, then, with fingers which trembled a little, he adjusted the power flow of the beam radio.

'Curt! Comain here. Answer please.'

'Comain!' The thin man flushed to the welcome in the voice of a man almost a quarter million miles away. 'Been asleep?'

'Yes. When you decided to take a rest I followed your example.' He frowned a question at the Colonel and Adams shook his head. 'Keep talking, Curt. I'll be with you in a moment.'

'Why? Is anything wrong down there?'

'Of course not, Curt. Just give any relevant data you can think of. I want to check the radio directional antenna.' He signalled to the operator and stepped over to Adams. 'Doesn't he know?'

'Not yet. I didn't want to tell him until we knew just what to do. In any case, he's only just made contact, I can't understand why he should have fallen asleep.'

'The radiation perhaps?' Comain shrugged. 'Not it matters now. The main thing is to get the rocket back on course. Have you the observatory reports?'

'Yes. The ship will reach the orbit of the Moon within an hour. The gravitational field will swing it and it will be hidden from sight for about two hours. After that …'

'If he can't operate the manual controls he will just drive on a straight line into space.' Comain nodded, his thin features grim. 'So what must be done must be done quickly.'

'Yes. Once the ship is hidden by the Moon there'll be no radio contact, and after that, with the speed the ship has, we can't count on more than a few minutes. Hurry, Comain! Hurry.'

'Yes.' Comain returned to the radio and leaned towards the microphone. 'Curt. Can you receive me?'

'Yes.'

'Good. Now listen, Curt. Listen carefully. Something has gone wrong with the ship. You are travelling too fast. You must take over the operation of the ship. Do you understand me?'

'I understand.'

'Good. Now this is what you must do. Spin the main gyroscope until you have reversed positions in space, until the firing tubes are pointed in your direction of flight. When you have done that fire the main drive for exactly ten seconds. No more. Understand?'

'Yes.' Curt laughed and something of the tension in the room left the waiting men. 'Don't sound so serious, Comain. This is why I'm here, isn't it? Despite what you say your machines could never replace a man. They break down and when they do they are helpless. Relax, Comain. I'll bring your ship back to you.'

'You have an hour, Curt. One hour in which to slow down the speed of the ship and bring it back to the scheduled flight path. After that time you will be hidden behind the Moon and I won't be able to talk to you. Also, and this is important, the ship doesn't have enough fuel to return without the aid of the Moon's gravitational field to swing and slow the vessel. Work fast, Curt. Work fast.'

'I'm working,' said the pilot grimly. 'Hear me?'

Over the radio came the whine of the gyroscopes as they spun on their bearings, turning the ship on its short axis, shifting the vessel in direct ratio to their own mass. It was a thing that took time. The mass of the gyroscope was only one hundred thousandth of that of the entire ship and it would take exactly one hundred thousand revolutions to turn the vessel. During that time they could do nothing but wait.

And wait they did.

They waited while the slender hand of a chronometer crawled towards the deadline. They sweated blood as, a quarter of a million miles away, a man fought for his life. It took more than thirty minutes for the spinning gyroscope to rotate the ship, thirty minutes of heart-numbing waiting before the gaping Venturis were in a position to check the speed of the ship. And then …

The rockets wouldn't fire!

Comain winced as he heard Curt's startled curse. 'The tubes! They won't respond. Comain!'

'Steady.' The thin man bit his lip as he stared at the swinging hand of the chronometer. 'The take-off may have jarred loose a wire. Check the contacts.'

More waiting. Sitting and standing in a mounting tension while over the radio came the gasping breath of a man working in impossible conditions to effect an emergency repair.

'Contacts checked but it's still no damn use.'

'Wait!' Comain glanced at Adams. 'Curt. There is only one thing you can do now. Lift the hatch and press the firing relay by hand. Can you do that?'

'I can try,' said the pilot grimly. 'Won't the automatics take over at the correct time?'

'Yes, but, Curt, that will be too late. You've only fifteen minutes left before you slip behind the Moon. The automatics are set for time, not distance, and they won't fire for several hours yet. Your only chance is to fire the rockets manually – and you must do it within the next thirty minutes.'

'I understand. I'm working on the hatch now.'

Over the radio came the sound of a man's laboured breathing and the faint ringing of metal on metal. In imagination Comain followed the pilot's movements. First the thin metal hatch sealing the control room. It was fastened with catches and shouldn't take long to remove. A clanging sound and he knew that it had been thrown aside, then, mingling with the sound his harsh breathing, Curt's voice echoed from the speaker.

'Damn gloves! Can't grip anything. Take them off. That's better. Now. This conduit to the firing relays. Which wires? Which wires?'

'The red ones,' snapped Comain. 'Can you hear me, Curt? Trace the red ones.'

'Got 'em. Now.' A mumbling and then a savage curse. 'Damn free fall! Damn it to hell! Damn all designers who can't imagine a man having to repair a machine. How the hell can I get down there?'

'Curt!' Comain bit his lips until the blood ran over his chin. 'What's the matter now?'

'The hatch is too narrow.' Curt's voice echoed through the room. 'I can't get down far enough to reach the relay.'

'Your G-suit. Take it off.'

'Yes. That's an idea. Funny I never thought of that.' Comain glanced at Adams as the pilot's voice vibrated from the speaker. He thinned his lips at the sound of the pilot's voice, his eyes narrowing in sudden suspicion, then, before he could speak, Curt spoke again.

'There. Suit's off. Now let me see.' The sound of violent retching interrupted the too-calm tones of the pilot. 'Damn it! Now to work. Hook one foot behind the chair. Grip the edge of the hatch. Thrust downwards, stretch …' His voice grew muffled and over the radio came the sound of gasping and scraping. Comain glanced at the chronometer, his pale face wet with the sweat of nervous tension.

'Hurry. Curt. Hurry!'

'Got it.' Comain sighed with relief at the triumph in the pilot's voice. 'Now, press this and …'

Nothing happened. No thunder spilled from the radio. No pulse of blasting rocket tubes as they checked the speed of the distant rocket ship. Just silence and the rasping breath of a desperate man.

'Curt. Nothing happened. What's wrong now?'

'What's wrong?' Comain hardly recognised the voice of his friend. 'You smug fools! You knew didn't you! You trusted metal before flesh and blood. Damn you, Comain! Damn you to hell!'

'Curt. Take it easy, man. What's the matter?

'The relay's broken, that's what. The metal snapped in my hand like a piece of glass.'

'What?' Comain stared at Adams, then, even as the Colonel stared the question, he knew what must have happened. The vibration of the ship had altered the structure of the metal of the relay. It had crystallised, changed from strength to weakness, shaken and tormented by vibration and radiation. It was a chance in a million, the one thing they hadn't even thought of guarding against, but it had happened and now …

'Curt.' Comain wiped sweat from his streaming forehead. 'You'll have to bypass the relay. Get lower down into the hatch and connect the wires by hand. Can you do it, Curt? Curt. Answer me.'

'I hear you, Comain. I'll try and do what you say, but my head feels funny. I can't seem to make my hands obey me. Connect the green wires you say?'

'The red ones. Curt. The red ones.'

'Right, Comain. I'll try it. Connect the red wires. Connect.'

Silence replaced the steady sounds from the radio. A deep silence, divorced from any trace of noise but the steady hiss of the carrier beam. Comain lunged for the controls, adjusting the power flow and altering the settings of the vernier dials with delicate touches of his slender fingers, but, even as he did so he knew that what he did was wasted time.

The ship had passed behind the Moon.

CHAPTER V

Two hours, the observatories had said. Two hours before the ship, if it did not alter course, could be seen again. There would be a short while before radio contact was broken, before the ship had speeded beyond the point where its signal could be picked up and amplified, and after that …

Comain didn't like to think about it.

He sat before the radio, conscious of the eyes of the waiting men as they stared at him, and for the thousandth time he cursed himself for forgetting the unsuspected. Adams sat beside him and the naked glare of the electric lights shone on his grizzled hair, accentuating the deep lines running from nose to mouth, making him seem suddenly old and feeble.

'How soon will we know?'

'If Curt can fire the rockets we should know within an hour. If not …' Comain shrugged.

'Can he get to the controls?'

'I don't know. There was no reason why he should. Who could have thought that the ship would travel so fast? Or that the vibration would crystallise just that piece of metal?'

'Can he get to the firing point?' Adams repeated doggedly. He didn't seem capable of thinking of anything else.

'I don't know,' snapped Comain irritably. 'He may be able to. I just don't know.'

'Think of it,' whispered a man. 'He's up there, sick, and burning with radiation fever, trying to fix the firing controls and save his life. I've worked on those relays and I say that he can't do it. Not in the time and without the proper tools he can't.'

'Shut up.' Adams glared at the man. 'If you must talk, talk outside.'

'What the hell?' The man glared at the Colonel. 'This is a free country isn't it? Can't a man speak his mind now?'

'So you don't think that he can reach the firing point?' Comain stared at the man. 'Why not?'

'Because it was never designed to be reached from the control room, that's why. I've worked on it, and I never did like the idea of trusting to automatics so much. If that relay has broken it means that he's got to strip off half the wiring and then, even if he can do that, he's got to squeeze down the hatch and connect the wires direct. You know what that means.'

'You think that the acceleration pressure will be too much for him?'

The man shrugged, reaching in his pocket for a cigarette. 'You designed the ship,' he reminded. 'What do you think?'

Comain nodded, feeling a growing sickness at the pit of his stomach. The man was right. He had designed the ship, and, perhaps subconsciously, he had tended to ignore the human element. He had trusted too much in machines, in things of metal and plastic, of wire and crystal. He had toyed with a wholly automatic vessel with the pilot a passenger rather than the main element that he should have been.

But there was still hope. Curt could fire the rockets by hand. He could check the speed of the ship, fall into the gravitational field of the Moon, restore the vessel to its pre-determined path. It would take so little. Just the contact of two red wires. Such a little thing, and yet, knowing what he knew, Comain shivered to a sudden doubt.

He didn't like dealing with the human element. Machines were predictable. The field of cybernetics offered so much and he had only agreed to work on the ship because of Curt and because of his youthful dreams. Now he was finished. After this he would leave the field of rocketry and concentrate on cybernetics. He …

'One hour gone,' said Adams grimly, and seemed to slump even further into his seat.

'He can't make it.' The man who had spoken before glared around the room. 'Rosslyn's as good as dead. He doesn't stand a chance, and we know it.'

'I've told you once,' said Adams quietly. 'Do I have to tell you again?'

'It could have been me.' The man ignored the unspoken threat in the Colonel's tone. 'It could have been any of us. Damn it all, I don't mind taking a chance, no man does, but to be trapped up there without a ghost of a chance of getting back just because of faulty design …' He glared at Comain. 'To me that's just like murder.'

'It couldn't be helped. Do you think we did it deliberately?' Adams stared at the man and his grizzled hair and seamed face gave him a peculiarly brutal expression. 'Damn you! To hear you talk you'd think that we deliberately sent Rosslyn up there knowing that he could never get back.'

'You could have used a little more brain. Didn't it ever occur to you that something might go wrong? What's the good of sending a man in a ship like that if he can't get at anything?'

'You …' Adams surged from his chair, his eyes twin specks of feral rage. 'You and your big mouth. I'll …'

'Steady, Adams.' Comain grabbed the Colonel by the arm and thrust him back into the chair. 'Take it easy, the man is right.'

'What?'

'He's right in what he says. We should have been able to predict what happened. A machine could do it, but we aren't machines. How could we guess that the vibration at take-off would crystallise the relay? We just didn't accept that as a factor at all, but if we'd had a large enough calculator, a machine capable of considering every potential thing that could happen, we'd have known.'

'I don't understand.' Adams frowned at the thin man. 'What are you talking about, Comain?'

'You've heard of EINAC, I suppose? You know that there are huge electronic machines which are able to store a series of facts and to predict, within the range of those facts, a probable happening? Insurance companies do it all the time. They can tell almost exactly just how many people will die from any large group. They can even give the average life expectancy of any trade or profession. You know that, don't you?'

'Yes,' admitted Adams reluctantly, 'But what has that to do with what's happening now?'

'If we'd had such a machine, one large enough to store all the relevant factors, we could have told to within a faction of a decimal point just what chances Curt would have of survival. We could have adjusted the variables to give him the highest possible favourable probability factor and we'd have known in advance just what would happen. As it was we merely took a wild gamble. We didn't know what would happen once the ship took off. We guessed, but we guessed wrong, and now a man may lose his life because of it.'

'So what do you suggest? That we don't build any more space ships until this dream-machine of yours has been built?' Adams smiled without humour and Comain knew that the Colonel thought that he was just talking to ease his inner tension. In a way Adams was right. Comain admitted it, but, as he watched the swinging bands of the chronometer, he knew that it was more than just that.

He really believed in such a machine. Like most weak people he had a fear of the unknown. He had always disliked meeting new people, of making sudden decisions, of thrusting himself forward. It would be so simple if there were such a machine as he had described. Then, whenever a new problem arose, the exact percentage of probability could be found and acted on. There would be no wasted time, the result of an experiment could be found without the experiment actually taking place. The machine would know everything there was to be known. It would have all the knowledge of the ages within its memory banks, would be able to scan that knowledge, and, from information, deduct new facts and predict inevitable happenings.

It would be an oracle. An omnipotent, omnipresent, machine. It would end all fear. It would end all blind alleys and futile lines of research. It would free men forever from the harsh necessity of studying all their lives so that, with luck, they could add just one new fact before their deaths.

A grunt from one of the men snapped him from his dreams back to the present.

'Five minutes before the ship comes into sight again.'

'Get the radio antenna aligned on the point of emergence,' snapped Adams. 'We won't have long before he's beyond range.'

Comain nodded and fed co-ordinates from the observatory into the machine before him. On its high tower the huge web of the radio antenna swung a little as it pointed towards the glowing face of the Moon.

Tensely they waited for the radio to crackle into life, and in silence, the steady hiss of the carrier beam seemed to mock them with its indifferent noise.

Three minutes. Comain wiped sweat from his face and neck, wondering desperately what he was going to say.

Two minutes. He checked the three recording machines, noting their full spools of metallic tape, and made a slight adjustment to the vernier controls of the radio.

One minute. Comain switched on the recorders and made sure that his headset was near at hand.

Now. Everyone stared at the black box of the radio speaker and Comain leaned forward, clearing his throat with a rasping sound.

'Curt! Comain here. Can you receive me?'

Silence and the steady hiss of the carrier wave.

'Curt! Come in, Curt. Answer. Answer.'

A crackle. A blur of static and, like a thin ghost, the weak voice of a man at the extreme range of radio reception.

'Comain. Thank God you waited.'

'Did you fix it?' He knew that it was a foolish thing to ask but for the moment he couldn't think of anything else to say. The radio hummed and faded, crackled and blurred. Impatiently Comain fed power into the extra boosters and the voice returned with a rush.

'Fix it?' The laugh that followed wasn't nice to hear. 'I fixed it alright. If I'd had a bomb I'd have fixed it for good. You and your damn machines.'

'What happened? Curt! What happened?'

'I couldn't reach it, that's what happened. I tried to get down to the firing controls. I could see them just beyond my fingers, but I couldn't get down far enough. Can you understand that, Comain? I could actually see them.' Static washed through the speaker and the men moved a little closer, hungry to catch the last words of the first man in space.

'I stripped off the G-suit. I stripped off the undersuit. I still couldn't get down far enough. I grew desperate then. It's funny how a man will grow desperate when he still thinks there's a chance. I cut a vein and covered my body with my own blood. I thought that it would let me slip those last few inches, a sort of oil you know, but it didn't work. I couldn't do it, Comain. A half-inch difference in the width of the hatch would have done it. Three inches difference in the position of the firing point would have done it. Even a single tool would have enabled me to fire the drive, but I didn't have it, Comain. I didn't have it.'

'Couldn't he have used his feet?' A man whispered the suggestion, then fell silent as the radio blurred again.

'Have you ever tried stripping wire and connecting them with your toes, Comain? I did. I ripped the nails from both feet trying, but it was no good. You chose your wiring well. It would take a knife to get through the insulation and I hadn't got a knife. I hadn't got anything except my teeth.' Curt laughed again. 'I can taste my own blood now.'

'God!' A man stumbled towards the door, his face white, and his eyes sick and dark against his strained features. Adams stared after him then stepped towards the radio.

'Rosslyn. How are your physical symptoms?'

'I'm scared. Colonel. As scared as all hell. I'm going to die. You know that don't you? I know it, and so you'll know it too.'

'Never mind that now. How are your physical symptoms? Has the radiation affected you at all?'

'Radiation?' Curt sounded puzzled. 'What are you talking about?'

'Snap out of it, man.' Adams glared at the radio. 'You know what I mean. Has the radiation affected you at all?'

'I don't know. How could I know? I've been busy trying to fix up this glorified firework. Damn you and your questions anyway. Why the hell should I answer?'

'Curt.' Comain thrust Adams away from the radio. 'Don't be bitter about it. We couldn't help it, you know that. You took a chance and you lost, but if you had the chance again, would you refuse?'

'Thanks, Comain, I knew that you'd understand.' The faint voice echoed with a peculiar gratefulness from the speaker. 'Would I take it again? I don't know. It hasn't been pleasant up here. All on my own, doubled with sickness, knowing that I'm going to die. I don't want to die, Comain. I want to live, to enjoy all the things I haven't had time to enjoy. I want to smell the scent of growing things, to feel the rain on my face, and to see the sunset and the night sky. I want to marry, have some kids perhaps, grow to be an old man. I shan't have any of those things now, Comain. I shall never know what they are like, the things I haven't had. All I've got now is a tank of air, a tank of water, and the universe to rove in. It's a big universe, Comain, but I don't think that I shall be seeing much of it.'

'Curt.' Comain bit his lips until the blood ran down. 'Curt – I'm sorry.'

'Sorry? Why, Comain? Because I am going to die instead of you? Don't feel sorry for me. Just see that they spell my name right in the history books. One other thing. Tell Adams not to worry too much about the radiation. I don't feel any effects from it.'

Static crackled from the radio and the thin, ghost voice, wavered and blurred, fading and dwindling to a tiny thread of sound.

'Goodbye, Comain. I don't regret this you know, but if only that hatch had been wider, a half-inch even.' Comain frowned as he listened to the dying voice. 'Remember my name, won't you? I'd like to think that I won't be wholly forgotten. You know how to spell it? Rosslyn … R … O … S … S …'

Sound snarled from the speaker. A savage burst of noise, thundering, pulsing, and then, as if it had been stopped at the source, silence replaced the noise, silence and the empty hiss of the carrier beam.

'The automatics,' whispered Comain sickly. 'They fired on time.'

'Then he's safe?' Adams stared at the thin man and sweat glistened on his seamed features. Comain shook his head.

'No. The blast came too late. Anyway, the stress must have split the hull. If the metal of the relay had crystallised then other metal must have been weakened also. Not that it makes any difference now.'

'Then he's dead?'

'Perhaps. What difference does it make? If the hull didn't split and release his air, killing him instantly, then he will still die. He's locked in a wrecked ship with little air, little water, no food. We didn't think that he'd need food on a three-day trip. Whatever happens, dead or not, we'll never see him again.'

'I see.' Adams gulped, then, the training of a lifetime asserting itself, straightened his back and strode towards the door. 'We must assume that he died in the blast. The radio wouldn't have cut out the way it did if the control cabin had remained intact. I must report this. Will he fall into the Sun?'

'I doubt it. With its present speed and course the ship will continue into outer space. It may hit an asteroid, be thrown off course by impact with a meteor, or it may be drawn into the gravitational field of some planet. We don't know yet, but it doesn't matter now, does it? Curt is dead. My friend is dead – and I helped to kill him.'

He left the room then, walking on unfeeling feet, his thin features twisted with inner anguish, his weak eyes staring blankly before him. Outside the stuffy room the Moon cast a soft radiance over the firing area, and he stared at it, hating its friendly face.

Curt was dead.

He sat, a stiffened corpse in the wreck of a ship that had been his dream, and his empty eyes stared at the cold glory of the glittering stars. They were cruel those stars. They kindled dreams in the hearts of men and they snatched those dreams away. Once, a long time ago now it seemed, two boys had stared at those stars and had dreamed of blazing a trail of fantastic adventure between the spinning orbs of alien worlds. Boyish dreams, but to them they had been very real. Curt and Comain. Together in incredible adventure, and now ...

Curt was dead.

He bumped into a man, not seeing him, not seeing anything, and, stumbling a little, continued on his way into the night. The man stared after him, frowning, half-decided to follow the tall, thin person with the deathly white face. He shrugged, feeling a little troubled, a little uneasy, and, at the same time, a little disgusted. It was not often that a grown man walked the desert crying like a child.

CHAPTER VI

The man had a thick neck, thick wrists, thick body, and eyebrows so thick that they looked like a bar of black metal resting above his eyes. His clothes hugged the body of a prizefighter but his voice, when he spoke, was the voice of an educated man.

'Mr Comain?'

'Yes?' Comain hesitated on the porch of the small house he rented, key in his hand, and looked at his visitor. The man smiled.

'Shall we go inside?' There was no accent and his tones were cultured and yet Comain knew that the man was not speaking his native tongue. There was a certain preciseness, an unnatural perfection only to be acquired by an adult learning a foreign language and being satisfied with nothing but perfection. That very perfection, the way he spoke, betrayed the very thing that he had striven to hide. Comain shrugged and opened the door.

Inside, the house was a mess. Comain lived alone and lived only for his work. Heavy technical books cluttered the tables, filled the chairs, spilled on to the faded carpet on the floor and rested like multi-coloured boxes, on rows of sagging chairs. Parts of semi-dismantled apparatus lay on a bench and a sheet of black insulation was studded with the blank faces of registering dials.

The stranger looked around, cleared some of the books from a chair, dusted the seat, and sitting down, took a cigarette from a gold-chased, silver case. He offered it to the lean man and Comain shook his head.

'No thank you.' He dragged a stool from beneath the table and sat down, resting his elbows on the scarred wood. 'What can I do for you?'

'For me?' The man smiled. 'Perhaps it is I who can do something for you.' He hesitated. 'Permit me to introduce myself, my name is Smith, John Smith.' He frowned at Comain's involuntary smile. 'I amuse you?'

'Your lack of imagination does.'

'How so?'

'Your choice of name is hardly one to arouse confidence. American?'

'No.'

'English?'

'Does that matter?'

'It could,' said Comain deliberately. 'Even though I am no longer working for the government yet I still come beneath Security regulations. Either you are very naive or you take me for me for a fool.' He rose and headed towards the door. 'I think that you had better go now.' The stranger didn't move.

'You move too fast,' he murmured, 'and in the wrong direction. I have no intention of asking you to betray trust.'

'No?'

'No.' Smoke plumed from the slim cigarette. 'Please sit down, there is much we need to discuss.' He waited until Comain, moving with a slow reluctance, resumed his position on the stool. 'You see,' said Smith casually, 'the people whom I represent know quite a bit about you. They know that you were employed on rocketry and that you left the field five years ago. They also know that you are probably the most advanced expert in the field of cybernetics and electronic computers. They are not interested in anything but that.' He flipped ash from his cigarette. 'I am here to offer you employment in that field.'

'I see.' Comain stared at the littered room. 'Is this a clumsy attempt to bribe me? I may be a scientist and I know that the popular conception of all scientists is that they are misguided idealists without any awareness of what goes on outside their circle, but I am not wholly a fool. Admittedly I no longer work for the government, in fact I work for no one but myself, but that doesn't mean I'm willing to turn traitor to any foreign power offering me a job.'

'Did I mention the word "traitor"?' Smith shook his head. 'Believe me when I say that is the last thing required of you. No. I am simply here to make you an offer, an offer which, as a gentleman, you are at perfect liberty to refuse without ill-feeling.' He shrugged. 'It is not so long ago that such offers from one nation to a citizen of another were common. Now, owing to the fanatical regulations, it is not so common.'

'It is a crime to accept,' snapped Comain. 'I shouldn't even listen to you, you know that.'

'Why not?' Smith gestured with his cigarette. 'Please, let us not be stupid about this. After all, what am I doing? I am making you an offer, is that a crime? I am talking to you, is that wrong? Would it be wrong for you to listen to me? Can you deny the existence of a fact, negate it, by refusing to admit its place in the scheme of things? Really, Comain, as a scientist you should know better.'

'Your logic does not impress me,' said Comain coldly. He stared at his visitor. 'I will admit that no harm can come by my listening to what you have to say, but I must warn you, I will not promise to respect your confidence. I am still a citizen and this is still my country.'

'A patriot?' Smith stared curiously at the scientist. 'After all that has been done to you?'

'So I lost my job and they kicked me out of the research laboratories. So what?' Comain didn't try to hide his bitterness. 'They didn't like it when I refused to follow their orders, work along the same old useless lines, and when I tried to show them where they were wrong they fired me.'

'Misuse of equipment,' murmured Smith. 'Insubordination and an incorrect attitude towards the problem as a whole.' He shrugged. 'The commercial field perhaps, or no, they are even more stringent.'

'I was blacklisted.' Comain wiped his thick lenses. 'General Electric. Du Ponts. Amalgamated Power. They all turned me down.' He laughed with brittle anger. 'Make one wrong step in this set-up and you're out on your ear – for good!'

'I see.' Smith looked down at the glowing tip of his cigarette. 'So you work at home.' He glanced at the equipment, his heavy features expressionless. 'Have you had success?'

'How could I?' Comain's shoulders sagged with the weight of bitterness. 'Look at the stuff. Junk! Rubbish from the surplus stores. Discarded because it was no good. How can I build a delicate mechanism from that?'

'But your theories, they have progressed?'

'A little.' Enthusiasm warmed the bleak voice as Comain spoke of his dream. 'You know what I'm after, of course?'

'A thinking machine, is it not? A robot?' Smith waved his cigarette. 'I am not a scientist, remember, but I have a grasp of the general pattern.'

'A thinking machine.' Comain shrugged. 'Say it like that and it's easy. A robot. Say it that way and it's easier still.'

'But there are thinking machines. The big electronic computers, the initial machines?' Smith paused and held out the butt of his cigarette. Comain took it from him and crushed it out on the floor.

'You are suffering from the same delusion most people suffer from. You mention the MANIAC, the EINAC, and other initial machines. You talk of electronic computers, and all you're really talking about are glorified adding machines. They not think. They perform routine operations, perform them at incredible speeds, but that is all. There isn't a single machine in existence that can be truly called a "thinking machine". In fact, the general trend among the operators of such machines is to restrict what they mean by the term "thinking" as something the machines cannot do.'

'But …' Smith looked bewildered. 'I understood …' Comain shrugged.

'You understood that I am working on the problem of thinking machines, and so I am.' He leaned a little further across the littered table. 'Let us look at the problem and see what it is we're up against. First, it isn't enough just to construct a machine which will hold information. We already have such machines, we call them libraries. It isn't enough to build a collection of glass and wire that can add faster, or compute faster than the human brain. We have that sort too, from the adding machines in offices to the big initial machines at Washington. They are merely work horses. They can do nothing but what they are designed to do, and only routine mathematical work at that. They are no more thinking machines than a selenium switch that turns on the light when it grows dark can be called a thinking machine. The principle is the same in both cases, relays operated by external stimuli. A true thinking machine needs something more than that.'

'I follow you,' murmured Smith and his big body settled more comfortably in the chair. Comain shrugged.

'I'm telling you nothing which you could not learn from outside sources. The problem is well known, opinion only differs as to how it should be solved.'

'Of course, and your solution?'

'I haven't got one – not yet.' The lean man stared at the litter of dismantled equipment lying all over the ground floor of the small house. 'To find the answer it is essential to go back to the basics. What is thought? What is that subtle something which makes a man different from all other animals? His brain is the same, structurally the same at least, and his body functions just like that of any animal. He is an animal but – he can think. When we discover just how and why then we will be able to build true thinking machines.'

'I don't quite follow.' Smith frowned, the thick eyebrows writhing over his forehead. 'Surely if a sufficiently complicated machine were built, incorporating the sum total of human knowledge, we would have the answer?'

'Would we?' Comain almost sneered. 'You think so? Answer this then. How would you define the word "food"?'

'As something to eat.'

'So. Is wood food? Termites eat wood and so it must be classified beneath that title. Is iron food? Rust corrodes, "eats" iron. Is salt? Sodium chloride is made of two poisons and would it be logical to assume that two poisons can be eaten with safety?' Comain smiled at his visitor's expression. 'You see, we, human beings, that is, have a very efficient and compact system of idea association. When we think of "food" we may think of a steak, or an egg, or a stick of celery. It doesn't matter because we know that food isn't just the thing we think of. That only serves as a memory-identification to bring all our knowledge of what food is, what it does, how it tastes, all the knowledge we have ever learned about food, to the forefront of our consciousness. A machine can't think like that. Every item has to be fed in separately. Food to a machine is a steak *or* an egg *or* a stick of celery. Not and/or either. That is only one word, remember, one concept. When you think of the thousands of words, the concepts, the ideas that the average brain handles during the course of a single day, then you will perhaps realise just what we're up against.'

'So the problem is insoluble then?'

'I didn't say that.' Comain rose and began pacing the room, pausing now and then to touch or examine some piece of equipment. 'Perhaps we shall never be able to build a replica of a human brain. We don't want to. There would be no point in doing it when there are so many efficient units already in existence.' He smiled at Smith's expression. 'I refer to men, of course, there are millions of them, each with a highly efficient brain. No. What we must do is to build something better than we already have. A machine, able to think, able to absorb knowledge, to use that knowledge to increase its data, and to apply that knowledge in the best possible way.'

'I begin to see what you are driving at,' said the big man slowly. 'A machine, of course, would not die. Therefore it would be possible to add tremendously to its store of data and if it could correlate that information …' He looked at the thin man. 'Deus Machina?'

'In a way, but it is up to men to prevent the machine ever becoming a God.' Comain returned to the table and sat down. 'You are right when you talk of potential immortality for the machine. There is no reason why it should not last a million years, and at that time it could be absorbing knowledge, finding new facts, solving all those problems which we simply haven't time to solve. The way things are now a scientist can't learn fast enough to have any time left for research. Aside from that the fields are becoming too specialised. A worker in biology, say, can't spare the time to learn about radioactives, and yet the field of radiant energy probably holds the answer to cellular breakdown, cancer, anaemia, and virulent disease. A metallurgist knows little about bacteria, and yet it has been shown that bacteria, certain strains that is, have an effect on metal. Time is the answer, Smith. Time. And we just haven't got enough of it.'

He waved away the stranger's offer of a cigarette and sat, fuming with inward pain as he stared at the litter of junk around him. Time. Five years ago he had listened to his one friend die in the loneliness of space and within him the loss was a constant, unhealing wound. Trouble had followed, inevitably as, driven by a complex emotion stemming from both the subconscious death wish born of self-guilt and the desire to join Rosslyn, and the attitude of authority which, after the fatal space flight, had abandoned true rocketry for the establishment of space stations, he had kicked over the traces.

There had been that time when he had wasted a month's research by unauthorised investigation into the reactions of metal-eating bacteria on the heavy metals. There had been the fight with a laboratory assistant, a fight which had left him weak and ill from both physical punishment and frustrated hate. The word had passed to the psychologists, then to Security, and he was dismissed from all access to vital information as an unstable risk. The rest had followed automatically.

The succession of commercial jobs, each worse than the last, ending finally in court proceedings for the theft of five grammes of platinum wire. He had got off with a fine and a warning – and Security lived on his neck for the next two years.

Now?

He stared at the junk, the salvaged pieces from surplus stores, the crude, too crude equipment and resisters. Scaled-down volt-meters when he needed to measure micro-volts. Hand-made radiation counters when he needed encephalographs. Steel-chassis when he needed non-magnetic conductors. The futility of what he was trying to do made him feel sick.

'It is hard, is it not?' Smith gestured with his cigarette and Comain realised that the thick man had followed his thoughts. 'Genius should not be hampered by petty worries and the spite of little men. When you have built your predictor …'

'Predictor?' Comain stared at the big man and his eyes narrowed a little behind their thick lenses. 'Who said anything about that?'

'But your machine will include prediction, will it not?'

'Maybe.' Comain nervously ran his tongue over his dry lips. 'I'm beginning to get it now,' he said thoughtfully. 'You aren't interested in the full potentials of a thinking machine. All you want is a predictor, and I can guess why.'

'Indeed?'

'You want it for war. You want to use it to blast humanity to dust. You want it to gain an edge over the other nations.'

'Perhaps.' The big man smiled through the smoke of his cigarette. 'Did the first man to discover fire intend his discovery to be used for incendiary bombs? Of course he didn't. And neither do we want to use your machine for war but, if it can be so used …' He shrugged. 'This is a hard world, my friend, and we must be realists. Your friend died in space but did he risk his life so that the Moon could be used as a military base, or did he risk, and lose it, so that the old dream of interplanetary flight could be advanced? We cannot dictate how our discoveries are to be used, Comain, but does that mean no new discoveries should be made? And there is a proverb, I think. Half a loaf is better than none. To build your machine, no matter for what ostensible purpose, is better than not to build it at all. But – it will be a predictor, will it not?'

'It will.'

'Are you certain of that? Our reports …' He smiled. 'You understand how these things are. Fear has crushed the free exchange of scientific knowledge so that it is difficult to be certain about many matters.'

'The machine, if and when built, will be the finest predictor in existence.' Comain didn't look at his visitor. 'Aside from the thinking ability all that is necessary to make a fairly accurate prediction is plenty of data, the more the better. If the weather stations had access to hidden reports as to cloud and wind, temperature and humidity, their reports would double in accuracy. The same with a machine. Feed it with everything known about the problem, let it correlate that information, assess variables and allow for errors, and you will have a modern oracle.'

'Are you certain of that?'

'Yes.'

'I see.' Smith drew deeply on his cigarette, the tip glowing like a red eye against the impassiveness of his features. 'Will you build one for us?'

'No.'

Smith didn't seem surprised. He merely sat, inhaling the blue smoke from his cigarette, but his eyes held a hidden purpose. Comain fidgeted on his stool.

'I guessed that this was coming and I warned you. I will not betray my country.'

'Have I asked you to?'

'No, but …'

'I, we, offer you full facilities to build your machine. I am not asking you to leave your employment. I am not even asking you to work for us instead of your own country. You are not working, your country neither needs your machine or will give you the opportunity to build it. How then will you be a traitor if you work for us?'

'Logic,' said Comain bitterly. 'It can prove anything.'

'Let me be frank with you.' Smith leaned a little further across the littered table. 'We need you and what you could build. Those I represent have all the material wealth they can use but with that wealth they have a tremendous population and supply problem. The old methods are breaking down. It isn't enough to have an army of clerks and floors of computing machines. There are questions they cannot answer and questions that must be answered. How much grain to plant to take care of the increase in population? Where to build a dam to give the maximum amount of irrigation and power? How many tons of iron to be mined for how many planes? Where should development be speeded and why? What animals to breed and how many? Questions, Comain, which affect the life of a nation and, indirectly, the welfare of the world.' He crushed the butt of his cigarette into smouldering ruin. 'You understand me?'

'How many planes to carry how many bombs?' Comain didn't try to hide his cynicism. 'When to fire the atomic missile and where? What weight of explosive to crush an enemy? When to attack to gain the greatest chance of success? Yes. Such a predictor would answer your questions, but it could answer others, too.'

'Is fire to be banned because it can burn?' Smith shrugged. 'I am not asking you to work for war but for peace. A hungry nation is a restless one – and soon the people will be hungry.'

'A threat, Smith?'

'No, Comain. A prediction.'

'I see.' The lean man sighed and again his eyes drifted over the junk littering the room. Deep down inside of him he knew he was being tempted, and why, but against that was the desire to work again, to handle delicate equipment and to lose himself in his dream. To build. To construct. To delve into the delicate balance of the human mind and to emulate it in imperishable metal and crystal. He thought of Rosslyn and what he would have said, but Rosslyn was gone, dead, wandering somewhere in the limitless void, and he was alone.

'For peace,' he whispered. 'Not for war.'

'For peace.' Almost the man who called himself Smith smiled, almost, but he knew better than to reveal his triumph. 'I promise you.'

'And full authority to utilise what material and equipment I need?'

'Yes. There is a base, at the Urals, you will be in sole charge of all scientific work.' He leaned forward and rested one thick hand on the scientist's knee. 'We need you, Comain, you and men like you. Our wealth is in more than the corn we grow and the metal we dig. It must be in the progress we make, the scientific utilisation of all we possess, the elimination of waste – and war is waste. Will you help, Comain?'

He paused then and silence filled the room, a silence tense with conflicting emotions and opposed loyalties. Comain felt doubt, felt the touch of something sinister, but brushed it aside in the dazzling contemplation of what the big man offered. Tools. Material. Equipment and men. A nation behind him, pressing him on to solve the great problem and resolve his dream. He nodded.

'Good.' Smith leaned back and smiled for the first time. 'You will never regret this decision.' He glanced at his left wrist where a thin gold chronometer ticked off the passing minutes. 'I shall arrange everything. You understand that it would not be wise to talk of our meeting? They may try to stop you, hold you, even imprison you. They are selfish like that. Even though they do not want you themselves, yet they will kill you to prevent others giving you your opportunity.' He rose. 'Say nothing. Do nothing. I shall contact you later.'

For a moment Comain felt like backing out. For a moment he thought of Rosslyn and what he would have said and then as he remembered the wasted years, he hardened himself and banished his doubts.

'I shall be waiting for you,' he said quietly. He stared at the big man. 'One other thing.'

'Yes?'

'The predictor, the machine you want me to build. It may take a little time. In fact it may take a lot of time.'

'That doesn't matter.' Smith shrugged with elaborate carelessness. 'We can wait.'

'You may have to wait a long time,' repeated Comain. 'A very long time.'

'It doesn't matter.' Smith moved towards the door. 'We have time to spare.'

He left then, his big figure almost filling the doorway as he left the house and for a long time Comain stared after him.

Then he returned to his books.

CHAPTER VII

Ten million miles beyond Mars, en route to the Red Planet from the Asteroid Belt a space ship, glinting a little from the weak light of the distant Sun, hung poised against the star-shot night of space. A tiny thing, squat, the stern studded with wide-mouthed Venturis, it seemed lifeless and dead, only the starlight winking from its rotating hull betraying the presence of life.

Lars Menson lay in his bunk and stared disgustedly at the smooth metal above his head. Opposite him, seeming to hang from the other side of the compartment like a fly, Jarl Wendis yawned and eased himself into a more comfortable position.

'What's the time, Lars?'

Menson grunted as he twisted and stared at the control panel. 'Twenty hours fifteen minutes and seven seconds. Standard time of course. The month is November and the year, just in case you're interested, is 2210.' He scowled at the man opposite. 'What the devil do you want to know the time for?'

'No reason,' Wendis yawned again. 'Just wondering when this trip will be over.'

'It'll be over too soon to suit me. Just think of it, Jarl. One more trip after this and we'll be grounded for life.'

'Maybe.'

'What do you mean, "maybe"?' Lars stared at the other man. 'You know what happens after we get back. The settlement is to be closed and the colonists returned to Earth. We heard the ultimatum just before we took off.'

'We heard what the Matriarch told us would happen,' corrected Wendis. 'We didn't hear what we were actually to do.' He rose and walked 'down' the wall, the artificial gravity of centrifugal force making every spot on the outer hull 'down.' He sat on the edge of the narrow cot.

'Menson,' he said quietly. 'We don't *have* to do as the Matriarch thinks best you know.'

'Rebellion?' Lars smiled and shook his head. 'That old dream again? I thought that you had more intelligence than that, Wendis. We wouldn't stand a chance.'

'Perhaps not, but then again, perhaps yes.'

'What do you mean?'

Wendis shrugged and in the cold glare of the lights his eyes were peculiarly intent. Like Menson he was a small man, light boned, slender limbed, and with the well-developed chest and rib case of all the Martian colonists. Though slender he didn't lack strength, constant exercise and the one-and-a-half times normal Earth gravity maintained within the ship had kept him fit.

'I'm not talking of rebellion,' he said quietly. 'I've no wish to overthrow the Matriarch. But why should we have to go back to Earth? We're doing all right as we are.'

'Didn't you ever go to school?' Menson tried to keep his impatience from his voice. 'You know that we are dependent on the home planet for supplies. Ever since the colony was founded, over a hundred years ago now, we have had to rely on Earth for almost everything we need. Even our food has had to come from there. How can we ever be self-sufficient?'

'We could be.' Wendis had the stubbornness of the fanatic. 'We can get our water from the pole, our food from the vats, our building materials from the oxidised mineral sand. We can mine and refine the radioactives, we've been doing that for long enough, and with them we can keep the atomic piles operating to supply light and power. We fuel the space ships and mine the Asteroid Belt for rare metals. Damn it, Menson, you know that we can do it.'

'I know that we can't do it, and if you'd stop to think about it, so would you.' Lars raised himself on one elbow. 'As things are now we depend on Earth to buy our asteroid-metal and supply things we can't do without. You talk of living on yeast. Have you ever tried it? Of course you haven't, and if you did, you'd find that within two years you'd be dying of vitamin deficiency. Then what about medical supplies? Drugs? Machine tools? Artifacts? No, Wendis, when you can manufacture a radio from the sand I'll listen to you, not before.'

'We can do without radios.'

'Agreed. But you're talking of running space ships, and how can you do that with a technology that can't even make a radio? We could remain on Mars, but if we did, it would be a primitive existence and we'd be extinct within two generations.'

'So you'd rather we crawl back to Earth?'

'What else can we do?' Menson stared at the other man. 'Don't get me wrong, Wendis. I want to stay on Mars as much as you do. It's my home. I was born there and so were my parents, but I don't want to die there fighting a losing battle with the environment. If men could have lived on Mars without outside help they would have done it before this.'

'What's wrong with you, Menson, is that you're a yellow-bellied coward!'

'And you're a blind fool.'

The two men glared at each other, each fighting his inner rage, and each realising that his rage was only a temporary phase. Spacemen always quarrelled. The free radiations did it, the surging electrons and penetrating gamma particles, disturbing the delicate neuron paths of the brain and triggering quick and sometimes deadly displays of temper.

The barrier screen gave some protection, the steady flow of current within the outer hull, but the screen didn't stop all the radiation, and it couldn't prevent the nervous tension and psychological strain inevitable in the cramped quarters of a space ship.

Men had died for that reason. Died in screaming madness and blood-stained hate. Entire crews had turned, each on the other, and sometimes ships were found manned by a long-dead crew, the inner hull dull with blood and dismembered bodies. Violence when it came had all the ferocity of insanity and civilised decadence.

Menson relaxed, forcing himself to ignore the hateful features of the man at his side, and gradually, as it had done before, the tension eased.

'One day I'm going to kill you,' said Wendis casually. 'I can feel it.'

'Then you'll spend the rest of your life regretting it.' Menson grinned and glanced at the control panel. 'Who would you have to argue with then?'

'I'll get married and take my wife with me. I ...' He paused and narrowed his eyes as a red light began to flash its warning signal. 'What ... ?'

'Meteor?' Menson surged from the bunk and slipped into the control seat.

'Could be.' Wendis squinted at the radar screen and adjusted the electro-spectroscope. 'Pretty big and moving fairly slow.' He grunted as he adjusted the vernier controls. 'Mass about fifty tons. Speed.' He pursed his lips. 'Relative to us about a hundred and ten.' He stared at Menson. 'Odd. With that low mass it shouldn't bulk so large.'

'Might be hollow. Any chance of a spectro-analysis?'

'Not unless we stop spin and get nearer. Shall we?' Menson frowned at his controls. 'I don't know. Not much chance of getting anything worthwhile so far from the Belt. It's probably just a rogue mass heading for the Sun. Still, it's peculiar that it's so large and so low in mass.'

'We could at least see what it's made of,' suggested Wendis. 'We've plenty of room in the hold and we need all we get.'

'It means free fall.' Menson hesitated, his hands resting on the controls. 'Can you take it?'

'I've stood it before and I can stand it again. Let's see what it is, Lars. We might be lucky and we can do with all the cash we can get.' He grunted with disgust. 'We'll probably need it on Earth.'

'Right.' Menson glanced at the instruments banked over the firing controls and slowly moved a lever down its groove. Sound began to vibrate through the ship, a muffled drumming as of distant rockets, and slowly, so gradually that neither of the men noticed the slightest jerk or strain, the spinning of the vessel died.

With the slowing of the rotation the artificial gravity of centrifugal force died and free fall gripped them with its terrible nausea. Wendis gulped, his thin face pale, and thinned his lips as he squinted through the eyepiece of the spectro-telescope.

'Swing nearer,' he grunted. 'I can't get a sight.'

Menson nodded, staring at the radar detector and letting his hands play over the firing levers. Flame spat from the Venturis, jerking them with acceleration surges, and in the tiny circle of the direct vision port something loomed, dark and shapeless against the stars.

'There it is. Can you get a spectro?'

'No heat.' Wendis shook his head. 'I'll have to warm it up with a tracer.'

'Hurry then. I don't want to remain in free fall longer than I have to.'

Fire streaked in a thin line from the muzzle of a cannon-like tube mounted beneath the viewing instruments and a tiny, rocket powered projectile drove towards the mysterious bulk. It hit, exploding into a cloud of incandescent vapour, and Wendis stared thoughtfully at the brilliant lines on the spectroscope screen.

'Any good?'

'I'm not sure,' Wendis said slowly. 'The spectro shows traces of iron, some copper, a little tungsten and a lot of beryllium. Looks unnatural somehow, too much like an alloy.'

'What of it? Fifty tons of beryllium is worth picking up. Get into your suit and make it fast.'

'How shall we handle it? Cut it up with the torches, fasten a line, or explode it into an orbit?'

'I'd say fasten a line. We can drag it into an orbit around Mars and send for the tugs. Cutting will take too long and I don't fancy working in free fall.'

Wendis nodded and taking a space suit from a locker, struggled into the tough fabric and metal. He paused, his helmet still open, and his gloved hands adjusted the controls at his wide belt.

'Testing,' he said quietly into the inter-suit radio. 'Are you receiving me?'

'Yes.' Menson grinned as he replied over the limited channel radio. 'Seal up and get moving!'

The hiss of the air lock echoed throughout the ship. 'Am now outside.' Wendis's voice came clearly over the radio. 'Object about five miles from me. Will use shoulder jets to cross.'

'Don't forget your life-line,' snapped Menson. 'I don't want to have to come out after you as I did on Ceres IV.'

'Don't worry,' said Wendis grimly. 'Once was enough and I might not be so lucky next time.' A faint crackle from the radio told of the firing of his shoulder jets and in the tiny circle of the direct vision port twin streamers of fire lanced across the star-shot void.

'See anything?'

'Not yet. I ...' Menson heard his startled whisper, 'Lars! This isn't a meteor. The shape is too regular.'

'What is it then?'

'A ship!'

'What?' Menson leaned closer to the radio. 'Are you certain?'

'Don't you think I know what a ship looks like? Of course I'm certain.' A soft metallic thud came from the radio. 'I've just landed on the hull.'

'What identification markings are there? Is it one of ours or one of the Matriarch's?'

'I don't know.' Wendis sounded puzzled. 'I can't see any markings. I don't even recognise the type of ship, at least I've never seen one like it before.'

'Describe it.' Menson tried to keep the impatience from his voice. 'What does it look like?'

'About two hundred feet long. Very slender, far too slender to be a cargo vessel. Seven Venturis and no steering tubes. Three wide fins. No signs of landing skids or rotating skids. The hull is scarred and split down one side.' Wendis gulped. 'Menson! This thing is *old!*'

'Are you crazy? How could it be old?'

'I don't know the answer to that one but I do know what radiation does to metal after a century or so. The hull is pitted all over, it's almost rotten, and that means that this ship is an old one.' Wendis gulped again. 'Menson. Could it be the vessel of an alien race?'

'I doubt it. From what you tell me it sounds like one of the old types, the experimental ones. It's probably a test rocket which somehow got off course.'

'I see.' Wendis sounded disappointed. 'I'd hoped that we'd find something inside, some weapon or machine which could have helped us against the Matriarch. If this is only one of the old automatic rockets it can't be of much value.'

'Fifty tons of beryllium are always valuable,' reminded Menson. 'Fasten the line and get back here.'

'Right.' Faint noises came from the radio, the transmitted sound of Wendis as he worked on the hull, welding the line to the ancient metal. He grunted, breathing harshly as if exerting all his strength, and Menson frowned as he tried to guess what his partner was doing.

'I'm trying to widen the split in the hull.' Wendis sounded irritated at the other's query. 'I've fastened the line and with the metal as rotten as it is it shouldn't be hard to lift the outer skin. Anyway, I'm curious to see what's inside.' He grunted again as he gripped the jagged edge of the split and tugged at the thin metal.

'Holy cow!'

'What is it?' Menson's voice rose as he snapped the question. 'What have you found?'

'You were wrong, Menson,' said Wendis unsteadily. 'This wasn't one of the old automatics.'

'No? What was it then?'

'A manned rocket ship.'

'Impossible. The first manned ships weren't anything like what you described, and anyway, they were all accounted for.'

'Not all of them, Menson.'

'What do you mean?'

'I mean that someone will have to start revising the history books. This was a manned space ship, and, if I know anything at all about metals, it must be all of two hundred and fifty years old. As far as I know, the first manned ships only reached Mars just over a hundred and the Moon a hundred and twenty years ago.'

'That's right.'

'That's wrong. We can prove it.'

'How?'

'With this ship.' Wendis sighed, the sound coming clearly over the radio. 'It was a manned ship, no doubt about it, and it must have left Earth more than two centuries ago.'

'It couldn't have done. They didn't have the barrier screen then. Are you sure?'

'Yes. It was a manned ship, Lars. I know it. The poor devil is still sitting in his control chair.'

'What!'

'Didn't you hear me? The pilot is still inside the ship. Dead of course, frozen, he must have died when the air escaped through the split in the hull, but …' Wendis broke off and Menson reached for the controls.

'Get back here,' he snapped. 'I'm radioing Mars.'

Tensely he adjusted the controls.

CHAPTER VIII

Mars Centre rested on the bed of a long-dried sea three hundred miles from the North Pole. It looked as it had always done, a huddled collection of adobe huts, domed, tamped from the chemical-treated sand of the arid planet. Over the course of the years the settlement had grown, and yet, despite the slow increase of population, the settlement still seemed a rough and temporary affair as if the inhabitants had always known that one day they would have to move.

Five miles from the settlement the squat atomic pile rested, half-buried from the wind-blown dust. From it thick cables snaked to both the settlement and to the idle machines of the refining plant, and the flame-scorched area of the landing field with its high control tower, lay a full mile to the south. Of agricultural land there was no sign, none existed, the sand of Mars, radioactive and sterile, couldn't grow a single blade of grass. Instead, the scoured aluminum of the synthetic food plant rose above the clustered domes of the living quarters, and the low building of the one hospital was the second largest building on the entire planet.

Mars was a bleak place.

Doctor Lasser shivered a little as the early chill of night bit through his heavy clothing and gnawed at his fatless body. He was an old man, thin, his gaunt features reflecting something of an inner bitterness, his sunken eyes glinting with a secret torment. He paused for a moment, staring at the sunken ball of the setting Sun, then, shrugging, he thrust himself through the double doors of the hospital.

'Doctor Lasser!' A man stepped towards him from where he stood by two men. 'I'm glad you're early.'

'Why, Carter? In a hurry to get away?' The old man didn't trouble to hide his sarcasm as he looked at his assistant, the only other doctor on Mars. Carter flushed.

'You misunderstand me, Lasser. Perhaps you'd better reserve your judgment until you hear what these men have to tell you.'

'Who are they?'

'Wendis and Menson. Two Asteroid miners. They have only just landed. You must remember their radio message two days ago.'

'Yes.' Lasser stared at the two men. 'When did you arrive?'

'An hour ago.' Wendis looked at his partner. 'What's all this about a radio message?'

'I told them about what we found.' Menson glanced at the tall, thin figure of the old doctor. 'Well, Doc? Can it be done?'

Lasser bit his lips. 'How can I answer that? I haven't even seen him yet, and anyway, what makes you think that it would be a good idea, even if it were possible?'

'Can there be any doubt?' Carter stared curiously at his chief. 'What else can we do? As doctors our duty is clear, and even if we could ignore that duty, there is another reason.'

'Yes?'

'If you haven't thought of it for yourself then I'm not telling you.' The young man seemed to be on the edge of anger. 'What's the matter with you, man? What has changed you in the past few days? I remember the time when you would have been burning with enthusiasm for what we propose.'

'You ask me that?' Twin spots of anger burned on the gaunt cheeks and something glowed deep in the sunken eyes. 'You heard the Matriarch's commands. You heard the ultimatum. Within two weeks we have to evacuate Mars. Within two weeks a hundred years of hope and struggle will be thrown away and forgotten. You know how I feel about that. How can I take an interest in anything now?' He turned away, shrugging out of his thick coverall.

'For the younger men the move means nothing. You probably welcome the chance of getting away from here, of going to Earth and all the comfort that planet offers. Things like patriotism, loyalty to old dreams, independence, those things mean nothing to you.'

'You are wrong, Lasser, quite wrong.' Carter stared at the old man. 'We feel just as you do, and if there were a chance, the slightest chance of breaking from the chains of Earth, we would do it. But enough of that now. Will you see him?'

'I suppose I must.' Lasser stared at Menson. 'Your message stated that you found him in a ship of old design, a design obsolete for more than two hundred years. You realise what you are saying of course.'

'I do.'

'The pilot of that ship has been dead for all that time. He was born before the Atom War, he would know nothing of what has happened since that time, and yet you suggest that we should attempt to revive him.'

'Yes.'

'Why?'

Menson stared at the old man, half-believing that the doctor was joking. 'Are you serious?'

'I am.' Lasser sighed a little as he stared at the young miner. 'I am an old man, Menson. I see things a little differently than you younger men. Would it be humane to bring him back? He has already known death, have we the right to force him to face it again?'

'I think that we have.' Menson stared seriously at the tall doctor. 'He died, it is true, but it was not a natural death. He must have been a young man when it happened, and, aside from all that, he could tell us a great deal of what happened before the Atom War. I think that you should do what you can.'

'I see. Is he here?'

'Yes. We've kept him in cold storage. The ship is in an orbit around Deimos. We can get it if necessary, but I thought that this came first.'

'Very well. I will examine him.'

Lasser glanced at his assistant and together, the two doctors and the two young Asteroid miners, they left the room and passed into a laboratory almost filled with gleaming apparatus and ranked phials of drugs and surgical instruments. Carefully Carter lifted a sheet from a high-walled vat, and together they stared at what had once been a living man.

'Death was due to asphyxia of course, that and instantaneous freezing as the air in the ship expanded into the void. The wound on his arm is superficial. The blood on his body seems to have come from that wound. Some rupture of the capillaries of course, that would be inevitable from the sudden drop in pressure.'

'Do you think that we can revive him?'

'I don't know,' said Lasser thoughtfully. 'So much depends if his blood has coagulated, or if his inner organs were ruptured in the pressure drop ...' He shrugged. 'Men have been revived who have died in space, but for each one who has been brought back to life two others have died under the treatment. Also, and we mustn't forget this, he has been exposed to the free radiations of space for over two centuries. They must have affected him in some way: how, we can't even guess, but it makes a new variable, an unknown factor.'

'The time element isn't too important,' protested Carter. 'Space is sterile, and, when he died, his every cell froze solid. There couldn't have been any deterioration, as we see him so he was on the day of his death.'

'Aside from the radiation effects,' reminded Lasser quietly. 'But I agree with you about the lack of deterioration.' He sighed and glanced at the other men. 'Well, we may as well get started. The usual procedure?' Carter nodded.

'Yes. Immersion in a temperature controlled fluid. Slow thawing to prevent internal damage. Eddy currents and electronic surge pulses to ensure even heating. Energen flow to revive the individual cell-life. Stimulants for the heart, artificial breathing, heart massage, the whole procedure. We may fail, but if we don't ...'

'A dead man will live again.' Lasser glanced at the two Asteroid miners. 'You had better return to your duties. This will take some time, we shall have to be careful in arousing his mental awareness, shock could kill him beyond recall.'

Wendis hesitated, and Menson looked at Carter.

'I want them to stay here,' said the young doctor evenly. 'Now that the ultimatum expires within two weeks there is no point in them continuing with their work.' He hesitated, glancing at the old man. 'I can use them here anyway,' he said abruptly. 'We have a lot to do before we leave.'

Lasser nodded, not really caring what happened now that his life-long dream of an independent Mars was at an end, and stooped his thin figure over the high-walled vat.

Delicately he fingered the cold flesh, the iron hard, solidly frozen flesh of a man who had been dead for almost a century and a half. Carefully he switched on a power source, adjusting a row of vernier controls and slowly opening a valve.

'Head support and mask.'

Carter adjusted a support beneath the dead man's head and strapped a mask over the contorted features. 'Ready.'

Lasser nodded and from the valve beneath his hand spurted a stream of iridescent green liquid. Lights flickered over a panel, and from a squat machine came the smooth hum of power beneath perfect control.

The battle for life had started.

It took three days. Three days in which the temperature of the green liquid slowly rose to well above blood heat, in which the invisible surges of electronic eddy currents warmed the dead body through and through, melting the buried specks of ice within each cell, thawing the dead flesh and relaxing the stiffened limbs. Machines hummed into life at the exact moment they were needed. The artificial lungs pumped almost pure oxygen into the flaccid chest, the loaded hypodermics with their cargoes of stimulants for nerves and muscles.

Carter never left the side of the vat. He crouched over the controls of the energen generator, adjusting the flow of the current that emulated life itself, restoring vitality and individual life to each cell.

Still the body didn't respond.

Lasser stared down at the vat, his thin features drawn and almost haggard with strain and worry. Before him, totally immersed in the shimmering green liquid, the dead man seemed to live with a travesty of life. The chest rose and fell, impelled by the artificial lung. The blood circulated, forced by the devices which bypassed the natural organ. Almost it seemed as if the man would rise and throw off the mask and tubes attached to his body, but the old doctor knew that once the machines stopped, the man would truly die, and this time there would be no second chance.

'How is the energen content?'

'At normal, plus ten per cent, for extra stimulus.' Carter wearily rubbed his tired eyes. 'Body heat one hundred degrees, saline content normal, circulation increased by fifteen per cent., air almost pure oxygen. Damn it all, Lasser. The man should be alive by now.'

'Muscular reaction?' The old man ignored his assistant's outburst.

'Motor nerves respond. Involuntary reactions absent.'

'I see.' Lasser thinned his lips as he stared into the vat. 'Expose the heart,' he snapped. 'We'll try direct massage and electro-shock treatment. If we don't get him breathing beneath his own power soon we may as well give up. Deterioration in the motor nerves must already have commenced. We daren't wait any longer.'

Carter nodded and reached for a heavy scalpel.

It took ten hours. Ten hours in which the old doctor's hands within their sterile gloves kneaded the exposed heart of the dead man, massaging it in time to the pulse of the blood pump. Carter hovered over him, ready to take over should Lasser weary of the delicate task, injecting stimulants into the muscle and keeping a watchful eye on the bank of flickering dials.

Finally the heart pulsed, stopped, beat again, then, fitfully at first but with increasing power, it took over the task of the blood pump. Wearily Lasser leaned back and watched as Carter sewed back the flap of bone and muscle.

'At least his body is living,' he said tiredly. 'Now, unless the shock of death has affected his mind, he should recover.'

'Shall I disconnect the artificial lung?'

'Not yet. We must relieve his heart as much as possible until his own lungs regain awareness. That is the next job.'

'Shock treatment?'

'No. I don't like it, there is too much danger of damaging the brain. Use pain and direction. You know what to do.' The old man slowly stripped the gloves from his hands. 'Call me when he recovers.'

Carter nodded, already at work on the problem of awakening the dormant memory and awareness of the man in the vat.

Always there was this problem. Death seemed to be something more than just the stopping of the heart. The delicate, almost immeasurable electrical potential of the brain, played a still larger part. Men, once they knew that they had died, were impossible to revive. There was a mental refusal to accept awareness, and so, even though their bodies lived, their brains did not, and without that personal awareness they remained mindless idiots, or lapsed again into oblivion.

'Who are you?' Carter spoke into a microphone, words drumming against the ears of the man in the vat, carrying through the earpieces of the mask covering the man's head. As he asked the question he pressed a button and electricity stabbed at the sensory nerves of the dead brain.

'Who are you?' Again the question and again the stabbing flow of current. 'Who are you? Who are you? Who are you?'

It went on for hours. It went on until Carter hated the sound of his own voice, until his face and neck dripped with sweat, and his fingers trembled with weariness as they adjusted the controls. He didn't expect an answer. He didn't hope for anything better than that the man should answer his call and struggle up from his oblivion to an unconscious awareness of life.

'Who are you?'

A direct appeal to the ego. A challenge to the self. A call from light and life into the darkness of death.

'Who are you?'

Gently Carter slowed, then stopped the smooth rhythm of the artificial lung. If the man was going to live he would do so now, and the sooner he could take over the natural functions of his body the better. Staring at him Carter felt a swift panic as the even rise and fall of the chest stopped, stopped, hesitated, then, erratically, began to rise and fall again.

The man breathed.

Quickly he stripped off the mask, transferring the earphones, and a fresh urgency came into his voice as he repeated the monotonous question.

'Who are you?'

The man writhed, his mouth twisting and his arms threshing at his sides.

'Who are you?'

'Ro …' The man's voice trailed away into a gurgling silence.

'Who are you?'

'L … Y … N …' It was like a cracked record, grating and filled with some terrible pain. The man writhed again, his lips parting, his muscles quivering to the twin stimuli of voice and surging current.

'Rosslyn … Rosslyn … Rosslyn.'

Carter grunted with satisfaction and triumph, but he had to make quite certain, he had to be cruel now so that the fact of his own identity would remain in the man's pain-twisted brain. He reached for the button controlling the electric current.

'Who are you?'

'Rosslyn …' A terrible fatigue seemed to drain the voice of all vitality. Carter bit his lip and twisted the vernier control of the energen generator.

'Who are you?'

'Rosslyn. Curt Rosslyn. Leave me alone will you. Leave me alone.'

Carter smiled and gently took the earphones from the sagging head. Carefully he adjusted the limp body, making sure that the retaining straps held the man so that he could do himself no harm, then, leaving the sterilizing lamps blazing down on the vat, left the room.

'Rosslyn,' he murmured as he walked towards Lasser's room. 'I wonder who he was?'

Tiredly he summoned his relief.

CHAPTER IX

Curt Rosslyn sat in a chair and stared with wondering eyes at the sandy wastes of Mars. Before him, clear through the transparent plastic of the hospital dome, the settlement sprawled, the narrow streets thronged with busy men and women, as they made last-minute preparations for the evacuation. A ground car churned down the street, dust pluming from beneath its treads, and Lasser, his thin body muffled in his coverall, plunged towards the building. Carter followed him, and Curt, still weak even after ten days beneath the healing lamps of the hospital, waited impatiently for them to enter the room.

'Well, Curt?' Carter smiled as he brushed dust from his overall. 'How are you feeling today?'

'Not too bad, but my chest is still sore.'

'Not surprising when you consider that we had to remove half the rib case in order to massage your heart.' Lasser sighed as he slumped into a chair. The old man seemed to have aged in the past ten days, his eyes glowed from their sunken pits and his parchment-like skin had an unhealthy flush. 'Well, fit or not, you'll have to move tomorrow.'

'So soon?' Curt stared again at the wastes of Mars. 'Must we? Wouldn't it be possible for me to see the planet first?' He smiled apologetically at the old man. 'Remember, I was only trying to reach the Moon when ...' He faltered and Carter nodded with quiet understanding.

'I know how you feel, Curt, but you must try to accept what happened. You died on that trip, you know that, but if you let yourself refuse to accept the fact it will cause a psychological trauma which could lead to grave trouble.'

'Thanks,' said Curt, and took a deep breath. 'Well then. I died before I could ever reach the Moon, and at that time a journey to Mars was just something we dreamed of. Now, when by a miracle I am really here, it seems that I'm never going to see it at all. Can't you delay the evacuation?'

'No,' snapped Lasser, and Curt flushed.

'Maybe I shouldn't have asked,' he said quietly. 'I forget, you wouldn't understand just how I feel about some things.'

'Don't misunderstand him, Curt.' Carter rose and stared out of the transparency of the dome. 'If Lasser had his way he would never leave here, none of us would, but we have no choice.'

'Because of the supply position?'

'Yes. You know about that?'

'Menson told me. But I can't understand it all. You've been here for over a hundred years and the settlement must have cost billions to establish. I realise that perhaps it can't pay its way, but to abandon everything just doesn't make sense. Why don't they send you enough equipment to make the colony self-supporting?'

'Why?' Lasser glared at the young man. 'I'll tell you why. They don't want us here, that's why. They want us back on Earth, back where they can control us as they control everyone else. Out here we're too independent and the Matriarch doesn't like it.'

'The Matriarch?' Curt frowned and looked at Carter. 'I'm afraid that there's a lot I'll have to catch up on. When I …' He paused again, then almost defiantly uttered the word. 'When I died there was no Matriarchy. Do you mean that the women rule now?'

'Yes.' Carter turned from the window with a strange weariness. 'The women took over after the Atom War, that must have been about twenty years after your death. One of the Eastern Groups of nations unleashed the fury of atomic weapons. The West succumbed of course, they didn't have a chance, but it was a useless victory. They had used radioactive dusts and they spread, drifting on the winds and carried by the rains, and the victor suffered as much as the vanquished. They say that over a thousand million people died and for a long time afterwards most of the fertile soil remained a radioactive desert.'

'So it came,' whispered Curt sickly. 'We had been afraid of it even in my own time. But how did that make the women rulers?'

'For a long time, I think it must have been about fifty years, men suffered a peculiar form of debility. Boy children were more susceptible to mutational changes than girl children and the mortality rate was three to one in favour of the girls. Naturally, with a predominance of women and a race of men who were weak and cursed with a poor physical and mental heritage from the effects of the selective radiations, a Matriarchy was inevitable. The sex balance equalised itself of course, men are no longer weak, but the old forms die hard.'

'It isn't just that, Carter.' Lasser thrust himself for as he stared at his assistant. 'A Matriarchy isn't so bad in itself, though women make poor rulers, but it isn't just habit that keeps them in control.'

'I know that, but even with what they have we could still overthrow them.'

'Do you want to?' Curt stared at the two men. 'Surely that is going a little too far? I realise how you must feel at being forced to leave your homes but is that reason for wishing rebellion?'

'Rebellion?' Lasser smiled, a curious grimace without a trace of humour. 'No, Curt, we aren't talking of armies and guns, of fleets and civil war. We talk of a rebellion of ideals, a lifting of the blanket which is stifling ambition and progress.' He pointed towards the desert. 'Look out there. For more than a hundred years we have tried to turn this planet into a place where men could live, and we have failed. Another thing, space travel has been known, really known I mean, for two hundred years now. The first ship reached the Moon just before the Atom War, and the first observatory was built there fifty years before we reached Mars. Since that time we have advanced no further. We have settled on Mars, touched Venus, approached Mercury – and that is all.'

'All?' Curt frowned. 'But with all that time for progress ...'

'Exactly.' Lasser glared in triumph. 'We should have reached Pluto by now, developed a stardrive, thrust ourselves towards the new worlds waiting beyond Pluto and founded colonies of men on Alpha Centauri. We have done none of those things.'

'But why not?'

'Comain.' Lasser spat the word as if it were a curse.

'What!' Curt lunged forward in his chair, then, as his sore chest protested against his movements, winced and leaned back again. 'Comain. Can he be still alive? I knew him, we were friends, what has he to do with this?'

'He?' Lasser frowned. 'What are you talking about?'

'Comain of course. You mentioned him. Is he still alive?'

'He? I'm not talking about a man.'

'Then ...' Curt stared helplessly at the old man, conscious as he had been a thousand times of all he did not know, of the terrible gap which lay between him and these others, a gap of two and a-half centuries. Carter turned from where he stared out of the dome and looked at the young man.

'Comain is a machine,' he explained quietly. 'A vast machine which literally controls the destiny of Earth and every living man and woman on it. The Matriarch depends on it for everything, and that is why we must return to Earth.'

'A machine!' Curt sagged in his chair. 'I had hoped ...'

He shook his bead. 'Funny. Comain was the last person I spoke to before the automatics fired and the hull split open. I'd been cursing him for his faulty design, I wish that I hadn't now, it wasn't really his fault.' He stared at Carter. 'But why Comain? Why call a machine after a man?'

Carter shrugged. 'Probably because of the man who invented it. Legend has it that he lived before the Atom War, and that his machine was the cause of the holocaust. The attacking nations financed him and he and his devils' machine predicted that they would win the battle. He ...' The young man broke off conscious for the first time of what he was saying. 'Comain. You said that you knew him. Lasser, did you hear that?'

'I did.' The old man stared hungrily at Curt. 'You knew him you say? You *knew* him?'

'I knew a man named Comain. We grew up together, went to school together, tried for the stars as though we were one.'

'Could it be possible? And yet, why not? It was a miracle that we found you, revived you, and why not yet a third coincidence? You are certain that you knew Comain?'

'Yes.' Curt flushed as he glared at the old man. 'I knew him well. He was a clever man and he often spoke of the value of cybernetics. I remember, it may have been just before I left for the Moon, that he spoke of a machine that could assimilate data and extrapolate from it and form a prediction of high probability. It wasn't a new idea, but he had definite lines on which he proposed working as soon as he could obtain the backing and facilities.' He stared at the tense faces of the two men. 'Anyway, is it so important?'

'It could be,' said Carter slowly, and he looked at the old man with a strange expression. 'I had a vague idea when we found you that in some way you might be of use to us, but now …' He narrowed his eyes in thought and began striding about the domed chamber. 'Lasser! Can we get him to Earth unsuspected?'

'I don't know.' The old man stared at Curt with hooded eyes. 'Why?'

'You know how Comain works. Within its memory banks reposes the sum total of all knowledge and information known to Man. More than that, it has checked and registered every living person on Earth and on Mars. Everyone. Remember everyone.'

'So?'

'Its predictions are based on a multiplicity of factors. The age, height, sex, colouration, peculiarities, ESP factor, of everyone. *Everyone*, remember. It has full details of everything known, data to the square of almost infinity. That is why the Matriarch wants us back on Earth. We are too independent here, too liable to do the unpredictable. Comain doesn't have enough information on us, on Mars, on space even to form more than a sixty per cent prediction on what we may do. That must affect the predictions on Earth. Remote though we are yet we must affect the probability factor enough to leave a margin of doubt. Once we are on Earth, beneath the auspices of Comain, then the predictions will be almost nine nines per cent probable. In other words the Matriarch will know the result of every action, every decision, every experiment she wishes, and know it before it happens.'

'I know all that,' snapped Lasser impatiently. 'It is merely a question of simple mathematics. If a man, or a machine, could know everything, then, from that knowledge, it or he could predict what must happen from any interaction.' He snorted with humourless laughter. 'It could even predict what must happen in the future, and, so dependent are those fools of Earth on Comain, that they will bring its prophecies to fulfilment merely because they believe that what is predicted must be true, and so will make it so by their own actions.' He stared at Curt. 'Can you follow all this?'

'I think so. We had something like it in our own time, and something like it has always existed. The high priests of primitive tribes did it; and so did the witch doctors of a later era. They would tell a man that he would die, and, because the man believed that what the witch doctor said was truth, he did die.' Curt shrugged. 'It was psychology of course, the man really died because he convinced himself that he had to die. The spell never worked unless the subject had faith in the witch doctor.'

'Comain hardly deals in psychology,' said Lasser dryly. 'If it predicts that a man will die, then that man *will* die, and he needn't even know anything about the prediction at all. Comain deals in hard facts, not dubious mumbo-jumbo.'

'Perhaps,' said Curt easily. 'But faith, whether in man or machine, can do peculiar things.'

'Yes.' said Carter sombrely. 'It is forcing us to evacuate Mars.'

He stared out of the dome again, his eyes clouded as he watched the scurrying figures below, and Curt had the impression of subtle undercurrents and hidden stresses. He shifted uneasily in his chair, wishing that he were wholly well, and within his skull his brain seemed to burn with strange fires.

'Well, Carter? Have you decided what to do with our friend?' Lasser sighed as he relaxed in his chair, a bitter expression in his sunken eyes. Slowly the young doctor turned from the darkening scene outside.

'Can we get him to Earth without the knowledge of Comain?'

'I suppose so,' snapped Lasser impatiently. 'We have all been registered here, the Matriarch saw to that, and they know just how many of us will return to Earth. Why?'

'I have an idea,' said Carter slowly. 'An insane idea perhaps, but what else have we to try? Listen. Suppose we did get Curt back to Earth without the knowledge of Comain. He hasn't been registered, nothing is known about him, and yet, by his mere presence, he must affect the actions of others.' He stared at the old man. 'Now do you understand?'

'No. I …' Lasser paused, and on his thin lips hovered the ghost of a smile. 'Yes. By all the Gods of Space, Carter! Will it work?'

'Will what work?' Curt looked at them, frowning, a little uneasy, but they ignored him, too occupied in their own plans.

'It all depends on whether or not we can get him back without discovery. We can swear the others to secrecy. Wendis and Menson will have to be careful, they must dodge re-registration. We can tell the others that he died.'

'Yes, that shouldn't be difficult.' Lasser licked his thin lips with a nervous gesture. 'Now. The Matriarch's ships will land tomorrow. They will have the normal crew, a single metaman to each ship. We could hide him in a bale or something and smuggle him out at the other end.' He frowned at Carter. 'The whole thing depends on whether or not Comain will check us on arrival, and, if I know the Matriarch, that will be one of the first things to happen.'

'Why should it be?' Curt half-rose from his chair, ignoring the pain stabbing at his sore chest. 'I thought that you'd already been registered?'

'We have,' said Carter dryly. 'But Lasser is right, the Matriarch will insist on us going before Comain as soon as we land. They will have to integrate our data into the overall pattern or the whole reason for our recall will be rendered invalid.'

'Well? Need you tell of my existence?'

'We can't hide it once we go before Comain.' Carter sounded worried. 'The machine can read our minds you know, or rather you don't know, but it can and that makes it impossible to lie to it.'

'Read your minds?' Curt slumped back in his chair, conscious again of the terrible gap in his knowledge. 'How can it do that?'

'Transference of the electro-potential of the neuronic currents in the brain.' The young man smiled briefly at Curt's blank expression. 'Thought is electrical, a fine mesh of differing electric potential, measurable, and varying from individual to individual. Somehow, I don't pretend to know how, Comain can transfer a copy of that potential to its own memory banks. That means that it knows everything the subject knows. The process is painless, almost instantaneous, and, thanks to the Matriarch, unavoidable.'

'I see.' Curt frowned down at his interlaced fingers. 'Couldn't you beat the machine in some way? Use hypnotism for example?'

'Hypnotism?' Carter stared blankly at the young man. 'What is that?

'Don't you know?' Curt didn't trouble to hide his surprise. 'Do you mean to say that you've never heard of it? You, a medical man?

'I know what he means,' said Lasser. The old man stared at his assistant and his sunken eyes burned with a strange fire. 'Auto-suggestion induced while in a trance-state. You wouldn't know of it, but a long time ago its use was quite common. I learned how to induce it when a young student, but it can be dangerous and was barred by the medical faculty about a century and a half ago.' He smiled faintly at the man in the chair. 'You can understand how the mere fact of it being forbidden tended to make certain young men eager to dabble in it.'

'Yes, but can you do as I suggested?'

'I think so. Wendis and Menson will have to be treated of course. Luckily they are the only ones other than ourselves who know of you. Menson had the good sense not to babble to the radio operator when he reported to Carter what he had found.'

'Then we can do it?' Carter seemed almost consumed with an inner eagerness. 'We can smuggle our extra man to Earth without Comain knowing of his existence?'

'I think so.' Lasser nodded and his thin lips writhed in a humourless smile. 'We will have to take all precautions of course, use a post-hypnotic suggestion to enable us to remember him after we have passed through Comain, but I think that it can be done.'

'I hope so.' Curt eased his aching chest. 'I'd hate for you to forget all about me after we land. From what you tell me things are a lot different from what they were when I left.'

'Yes,' said Carter quietly. 'Things are different. A lot different, but they will differ again after you have landed.' He looked at the old man and his laughter rang loud against the encroaching silence of the night. 'Wait until he begins upsetting all their clever little predictions. Just wait until we introduce our extra man to the water-tight society of Earth.'

Lasser nodded, his thin features sombre, and his eyes glowing against the pallor of his withered cheeks.

'The extra man,' he murmured softly. 'Yes. I like that, a good name to call him, a safe name. An extra man, and with luck, and if we have guessed right, he may win Mars for us. An independent Mars, free of the Matriarch and of Comain.'

Curt shivered at the naked emotion in the old man's voice.

CHAPTER X

Sarah Bowman, Matriarch of Earth, stood at a high window and stared down at the concrete perfection of the building which was Comain.

Five thousand feet the building soared, rising like an artificial mountain from the flat plain below. Spired, terraced, sweeping in subtle curves and arching beauty, rising like something from an old tale, a fairy palace, a mound in which art and science had met and blended in enduring steel and stone. And yet this was not Comain.

Far down, buried beneath a shielding layer of rock and lead, soil and running water, protected from high explosive and atomic destruction, from radiation and natural storm, the machine that was Comain rested as it had rested for more than two centuries. An incredible complexity of crystal and wire, of tube and relay, of warped atoms and strained molecules, the swollen fruit of one man's genius rested, and, as if they were inexhaustible sponges, the ranked tiers of its memory banks absorbed every minute scrap of knowledge available to the minds of men.

Such was Comain.

For a long time the Matriarch stood at the high window and stared down at the terraced building, then, sighing a little, she turned and moved towards the centre of the huge office. A desk rested by the window, a wide thing of superb polish and immaculate workmanship, its surface littered now with sheaves of papers and squat, portable filing cabinets. Against one wall the blank face of a video screen reflected little shimmers of light from the dying light outside the window, and the smaller, darker screens of several videophones stared like blind eyes towards the wide desk.

The room was very quiet.

Heavily the Matriarch slumped into her chair, and, for a moment, sat staring down at her thick, broad nailed, swollen knuckled fingers. She was an old woman, her close-cropped hair white with age, and her heavy, almost mannish features seamed and wrinkled, the lips bloodless, the eyes surrounded by a multitude of tiny lines. She wore not the slightest trace of cosmetics, and, sitting at the wide desk, her shapeless body hidden in a simple dress of dull grey, she seemed like an old and weary man. It was only when emotion aroused her and her eyes flashed with an almost forgotten fire, that she resembled the militant female who had climbed her way to the highest pinnacle of government.

But that had been long ago.

A bell chimed in the office, its muted tone sounding strangely loud in the deepening twilight, and one of the videophone screens flared with a sudden swirl of light, steadying into a coloured picture of a middle aged woman.

'Madam?'

'Yes?' The Matriarch stared towards the screen. 'What is it?'

'Your secretary, Madam. May she enter?'

'Admit her.' The picture dissolved into a swirl of colour and the screen returned to its normal darkness. At the same time, operated by the light-sensitive selenium cells, the room lights glowed into soft radiance.

Softly the door opened and a woman entered the room.

She was tall and with a curved slenderness and as she walked towards the wide desk her figure moved with the innate grace of a dancer. Unlike the Matriarch she wore a clinging dress of some iridescent black material elaborately worked in a fine pattern of golden arabesques. Long hair, black as jet, flowed from her high forehead and fell in smooth ripples to her sloping shoulders. Her skin was a milky white, like whipped cream and white velvet, and her eyes were slanted pools of midnight beneath thick brows.

'Good evening, Madam.'

The old woman grunted, her broad nostrils twitching at the subtle aroma of perfume. 'You may sit, Nyeeda.'

'Thank you.' The secretary smoothed her dress as she sat in a vacant chair. 'Have you finished your study of the agricultural figures, Madam?'

'No, they can wait.'

'As you decide. They aren't important anyway, we know to within five per cent, just what the yield will be.'

'We knew that last year, before the crops were even planted, but I suppose that I have to go through the motions of checking the figures.' The old woman sighed as she stared at the heaped papers on her desk. 'Have the Martians arrived yet?'

'Not yet. They are orbiting at the moment and will land within an hour from now.' Nyeeda stared a little curiously at the old woman. 'Don't you remember the prediction? Comain gave the flight schedule and landing times.'

'Of course I remember, but it had slipped my mind. Anyway, these details aren't important.'

'All details are important.' The girl spoke with a flat conviction. 'The more data we can feed into Comain the more accurate its predictions will be. I thought that was the whole idea of bringing the colonists back to Earth.'

'It is. While the activities of an independent group have to be considered the predictions cannot be as accurate as we would wish. You don't have to instruct me on the basics of our civilisation, Nyeeda. I learned them long before you were born.'

'Yes, Madam. I am sorry.'

'Forget it, girl, you are too young to have to apologise to an old woman, and you have been with me too long for us to misunderstand each other. How long is it now? Fifteen years?'

'Not quite. I've been your personal secretary for ten years now, ever since I graduated from general duties.'

'Of course. I remember now, Comain selected you as being the one person most suited to my needs. As usual the prediction was right. I've had no cause for complaint.'

'Thank you, Madam.' Nyeeda smiled and relaxed in her chair.

'Not that I approve of women in governmental positions using cosmetics, perfume, wearing jewellery and expensive clothes. But then, you are young, and as you grow older you will realise that these things pass along with other childish amusements.' The old woman shrugged as she spoke and the gesture robbed her tone of offense. 'Now about these Martians. They will be registered on landing of course, all five hundred and seventy two of them. I trust that the necessary orders have been given?'

'The metamen at the landing field have their instructions. They will conduct the colonists to the booths directly as they leave the ships. The prediction is five nines against violence of any kind.'

'Good. Has it been decided just what they are to do and where to live?'

'Not yet. It was thought best to leave those details after they had registered with Comain. The extra data will be essential if they are to be fitted in with maximum worth to society.'

'I see. Has the council any ideas on the subject?'

'A few minutes were devoted to discussing the problem but it was felt that any further discussion would be a waste of time. Comain will decide as it must anyway.'

'Yes,' said the old woman heavily. 'Of course.' She bit her lips as she stared at the litter of papers on her desk. 'Tell me, Nyeeda,' she said quietly. 'Have you ever thought at times we tend to place too much reliance on Comain?'

'Why, no. Comain is efficient, we all know that, and not to use it would be utterly illogical.' Nyeeda frowned and looked at the Matriarch. 'You surprise me, Madam. You were one of the foremost to advocate the full use of Comain. It was you who ruled that all governmental positions should be filled by selection, and now it is Comain who selects the rulers, not the people.'

'I know that.' The old woman spoke with a surprising sharpness. 'That was my first ruling when I finally won to the Matriarchy. I did it because even then, even though we had the benefits of Comain for almost two centuries, the old political squabbling and manoeuvring still squandered our time and effort. That was a long time ago now, more than fifty years, and I swore to do it when my political rival, Lucy Armsmith, committed suicide after my election. She was a great woman, but she couldn't stand defeat.'

'Nothing like that could happen now,' said Nyeeda with quiet certainty. 'The predictions of the machine are getting more and more accurate. A person would be an insane fool to try and go against them. If Comain predicts defeat then the person concerned doesn't even argue about it, he just gives up and tries something else.'

'I'm glad to hear you say that, Nyeeda, very glad.' Something in the old woman's tones made the young girl glance at her with shocked suspicion. The Matriarch saw her expression, and shook her head. 'No, girl, I'm not getting senile, just old, and when a person gets old their viewpoint can alter. When I was a girl I lived by Comain, nothing was more clear than that it should be allowed to control the world. I was an idealist, I suppose, but the young are always idealists.'

'There is nothing wrong in that.'

'No, but just lately, I have begun to wonder whether or not I did right. The predictions are getting more and more accurate, and, as they show a higher percentage of probability, more and more people are doing exactly as Comain says they will do. They do it, and by so doing ensure that the prediction is correct. In a way it is a vicious circle, and sometimes, when I am alone and the world is dark, it almost frightens me.'

'Frightens you?' Nyeeda laughed. 'What a peculiar notion. Surely, Madam, you must be joking?'

'No. I am not joking.'

'Then …'

'Listen, Nyeeda. I'm an old woman, over eighty years old and even with the progress geriatrics has made, that is still old. I have seen a great deal of change in the fifty years that I have been the Matriarch. There is not the struggle there used to be, the striving, the ambition. Now people seem to be easily contented, they do as the machine predicts, and it has been ten years since a request was made for restricted information. We are safe from war, from famine, from actual want, but, in gaining all that, have we lost something?'

'If losing the desire to wage war is loss then we may have done.' Nyeeda didn't trouble to hide her contempt. 'Always there has been this looking backward to the "good old days." Even as a girl I remember my father regretting the old times when a man could do as he wanted when he wanted. He used to read old books, books describing wars and armoured men fighting with swords. He even made such a weapon, but of course he never used it for anything but to cut down weeds. He was a dreamer, content with the benefits of civilisation and pretending to long for the hardships he had never known.'

'And you think that I am like that?' The Matriarch shook her head. 'No, Nyeeda. I am not a fool. I do not want the old days of toil and want to return, but there is something else, a subtle intangible something which mankind always had and which I am afraid he may have lost. I refer to ambition.'

'A man can advance himself, earn money, live richly well. There are still opportunities.

'Are there? I doubt it. Now, if a man thinks of a thing to do, he refers it to Comain. If the prediction is favourable he does it, but he has no vest in what he does. Why should he? He knows before he starts that what he proposes will succeed. Now we have no failures, no lost causes, no battling hopelessly against fate and overwhelming odds.'

'Why should we? A failure is effort wasted.'

'Agreed, but it wasn't always so. Men reached for the planets against all the predictions of logic and common sense. They died because of that dream, but they finally won through. Would we do that now?'

'Would we wear skins and eat raw meat? Would we use flint and steel to kindle a fire or pray to pagan Gods?' Nyeeda shook her head. 'You know the answer to that, and the answer to your own question must be the same. Why should we? What need is there to reach for the stars? We have our civilisation, it is a good one, and the people are happy. Let them remain so. What sense is there in idle fears and empty longing? We are what we are, our civilisation what it is, the past is dead and forgotten.'

Silence followed her words, and in the silence the sound of the Matriarch's heavy breathing sounded oddly loud. Against the night shrouded window the thin trails of stratoliners traced their fiery paths across the sky and far below, on the level plain surrounding the building, lights sparkled and shimmered in colourful array.

'Thank you, Nyeeda.' The old woman smiled and something seemed to relax her thick-set figure. 'I knew that I was right, but age, and the chilling of youthful ambition had made me doubt myself. What you say is true, we are safe now and divorced from the strains which lead to war. Now that the Martians have been recalled we can forget the unknown factor and the predictions will be accurate to nine nines per cent. Comain will assimilate their data, decide where they are to live and work, and the whole business of space travel can be re-filed in the restricted information area of the machine. It will be there if ever we need it, but I doubt if we ever will. No. I was a fool to worry. Everything will work out as planned. Comain will guide us, save us from false decisions, and, as you mentioned, take over the governing powers.'

Slowly she rose from behind the wide desk and crossed to the high window.

'Earth will be a paradise,' she whispered. 'The Matriarchy will remain the nominal head of state but all decisions will, as now, be referred to Comain. Once the Martians have been registered it will be inevitable. Nothing can prevent it.'

Against the night slender tongues of flame stabbed from the heavens and a thin whistling roar began to drone softly through the silent room. The drone increased, the scintillating tongues of fire grew more brilliant, and the Matriarch sighed as she watched them.

'The Martians,' she murmured quietly. 'Coming home.' Nyeeda nodded, crossing to the high window, and together the two women, one old, the other still young, watched the descending space ships.

CHAPTER XI

Five men sat in a room and discussed their future. Carter, his young features taut with the effort necessary to move his body in a, to him, three times normal gravity, slumped in a chair and stared at the sagging cheeks of the doctor. Wendis and Menson, used to a high G field while in space, didn't seem to be affected by the gravity, though they gasped and sweated in the thick, humid air. Curt smiled as he stared through a window, savoring the green fields and blue sky, his healed body tingling with excitement as he thought of the new world waiting for his exploration.

'I've heard from the Matriarch,' said Lasser bitterly. 'As I suspected they have dismantled the ships. We are here to stay.'

Wendis clenched his big hands. 'That means that we never go into space again, never see the cold stars, feel the thrust of rockets.' He swallowed as if ashamed of his outburst, then, almost defiantly, stared at the old doctor. 'I've trained all my life for space,' he gritted. 'I know nothing else. What do they intend doing with me now?'

'The Council will inform me as soon as they receive the answer from Comain.' Lasser wiped sweat from his yellow features. 'If you ask me to make a guess I'd say either the deserts, the poles, or, if they have work there, on a high mountain.'

'What makes you say that, Doc?'

'Logic, Menson. We need a dry climate, low gravity, and thin, cold air. The only place on Earth where we can get most of those things is on a high mountain. The isolation wouldn't worry us, we're used to it, and, from their point of view, it would be ideal.'

'Why?'

'We'd be out of the way, and yet under constant observation. Without ships or transport we couldn't leave the area and we'd have to do as we were told or our supplies could be cut off.'

'Do you think that they will keep us together?' Carter licked his lips as he looked at the old man. 'I thought that they might have split us up, a family here, a man there, and so on.'

'Why should they? We aren't rebels. They have nothing to fear from us. They only recalled us so that we could be fitted into the pattern. No, Carter, I think that they will keep us as a unit. All of us.'

'What about Curt?'

'Well? What about me?' Attracted by the mention of his name the young man turned from the window and smiled down at the old doctor. 'I'm home again, thanks to you, and I'm eager to explore. What happens now?'

'We don't know yet, not until the Matriarch informs me just what is to happen to us.' Lasser wiped his face and neck as he glanced up at the young man. 'How are you feeling?'

'Fine.' Curt grinned as he thumped his chest. 'All the soreness has gone and I feel like a dog with two tails.'

'Good. Got over the journey yet?'

'Just about. I don't want to do it again though. The trip here wasn't too bad, that dope you gave me knocked me out and sent some beautiful dreams, but I had a bad time after we landed wondering whether or not you'd remember about me.'

'You won't have to do it again,' said Wendis grimly. 'Mankind has made the last space trip.'

'Maybe.' Curt shrugged and looked at the old doctor. 'How did the registration go?'

'As I suspected. The metamen were waiting for us and took us directly to the booths. Comain assimilated our data and is probably working on the problem now.'

'So long?' Curt stared his surprise.

'No. The machine can't volunteer information. It has to wait until the right question is asked. The Council are probably doing that right now.'

'I see.' The young man wandered over to the window and nodded towards a tremendous building, bright in the morning sun. 'Is that it?'

'That's Comain, the main part of it anyway. The upper building is composed of governmental offices and living quarters. The palace you might say. The priestly apartments to the *Deus Machina*.' Wendis sounded bitter.

Curt ignored the other man's tone. He stared at the tremendous building, admiring its smooth perfection and subtle curves, trying to visualise the man who had been his friend, the man who had laid the foundations of this new civilisation. Memory tugged at the innermost chambers of his mind. A man stepped from the mists of the past, a tall man, thin, with weak eyes and gaunt features. He smiled, a semi-ironical twisting of his lips, and a ghost-voice echoed from the ghost body.

'Hello, Curt.'

'Comain.'

'It's been a long time, Curt. Sorry about that hatch.'

'Comain!'

'We must get together sometime. You know where I live?'

'Yes. Yes, I …' Something jarred him. Something stung his face and pain seared its way through the mists of his mind. Pain. Pain and something more than pain, and he turned, his hands clenching and lifting in sudden rage.

'Curt! Snap out of it man! What's the matter with you?' Carter stood before him, his hand still lifted, ready to slap again.

'You …' Curt swung, his fist driving to the other's mouth, and before the young doctor could ward the blow Curt repeated it, feeling a hot tide of rage warm his stomach as he battered at the other's features.

'Curt! You fool! Stop it!' Wendis lunged forward, Menson behind him, and together they held his arms. Carter dabbed at his damaged mouth.

'Snap out of it, man.' The young doctor stared at his blood-stained handkerchief. 'What's the matter with you? Don't you feel well?'

'You hurt me.'

'I slapped your face. You were talking to yourself, I tried to snap you out of whatever it was had caused it.' He winced as he touched his mouth. 'What happened, Curt?'

'I don't know.' Suddenly all the rage seemed to drain from him, leaving him weak and ill, ashamed and defenceless. 'I'm sorry, Carter. You startled me. I was thinking of a friend.'

'Comain?'

'Yes.'

'I thought so. You spoke his name. Twice. Then I slapped you.' Carter stared wonderingly at his hand. 'How many times did you hit me?'

'I don't know. Why?'

'I thought that I was fast, but you moved faster than any man I've ever seen. I didn't even know what was happening.' He nodded to the two miners. 'You can let him go now, he won't do it again.'

Tiredly Curt slumped into a chair and stared at the floor. He felt ill, physically ill, and, at the same time, he was conscious of a peculiar sense of power. Something was wrong. He had thought of an old friend, dead now for more than two centuries, and suddenly it had seemed as if Comain had stood before him, smiling, talking, *real*. Then the pain of the blow and the electron-swift reaction. He had lied to Carter. He remembered his blows, five of them, all delivered within the space of … of …

He frowned. Incredible as it seemed he couldn't recall any passage of time during the incident, but it had been between the impact and the withdrawing of the young doctor's hand. And that meant he had moved fast.

A muted drone hummed in the silence of the room and light flared on a dark sheet of smooth plastic. It swirled, steadied, and a woman stared into the room.

'Doctor Lasser?'

'Yes?'

'Decision from Comain. The majority of the Martian colonists are to be transported to Everest. They will construct an observatory there. Machines for levelling the top of the mountain have already left. Transportation will be provided at dawn tomorrow for the selected personnel.'

'I see.' Lasser glared at the calm features of the woman. 'You mentioned a "majority." Does that mean that some of us are to be separated from the main group?'

'Yes. Yourself and your assistants are to report to the Central Hospital. There your acquired skill can be used to the best advantage. Others will work as directed. You will receive copies of the decision within an hour. That is all.'

'That is all.' Lasser snarled at the darkening screen. 'So I'm to be a janitor in a hospital am I? Well, we'll see about that!' Savagely he pressed a button beneath the screen.

'Information.'

'Yes?' A smooth-faced man looked inquiringly at the angry doctor. 'What can I do for you?'

'I wish to consult Comain. How do I go about it?'

'Don't you know?' Almost the man smiled. 'The public booths in every city. Find one, obey the instructions and you may ask your question.'

'Thank you.' Lasser switched off the videophone and strode towards the door.

'Where are you going?' Carter stepped before the man. 'Are you crazy, Lasser? You know that they won't let you out of the building. Calm down, man. We've got to think this one out.'

'Why? If that machine says that I should work in a hospital then it can tell me how to dodge it. Anyway, I'm going to ask.'

'And if it asks you to don the helmet?' Carter nodded at the sudden look of understanding in the old man's eyes. 'Exactly. We've gone to a lot of trouble to keep Curt a secret. Are you going to throw all that away now?'

'No.' Wearily the old man sank into a chair. 'What shall we do, Carter? How can we break the stranglehold Comain has on this planet?'

'I don't know, but I do know that our only hope lies in Curt. He is the one man who can help us.'

'Before I can do that I've a lot to learn.' Curt rose from his chair and crossing the room stared out of the window. 'You forget that I know nothing of this world. How am I going to live? Where? What shall I call myself? What shall I do if someone asks me for my registration number? If I'm to be of any use to you I've got to know these things.'

'He's right, Lasser.' Carter stared at the old man. 'It's time we made some plans, and the first thing is to give Curt a number.' He frowned at his own wrist with its neatly tattooed serial index.

'That's easy.' Wendis bared his own wrist 'We can invent one.'

'No. If they check with Comain and find that his number isn't registered, they will know at once that he is suspect. No. It would be best to give him one of ours. Better in a way, it could be a form of alibi.'

'Good enough.' Wendis nodded and thrust out his arm. 'He can have mine.'

'That's settled then. I'll copy it in indelible ink, it will be fast, but he can remove it with a chemical if necessary. Now, for the general background.' Carter stared at the silent figure of the young man by the window. 'You know by now that Comain rules the planet, in fact if not in name. You must always be careful to avoid registration, on no account must you ever don the helmet, and don't let anyone persuade you to either.'

'I understand.' Curt turned from the window. 'You know,' he said quietly. 'All this seems just a little fantastic. You talk of a machine that can assimilate all data and predict coming events from that information. I grasp the idea, but the thing must be intricate beyond imagination. How was it ever built?'

'It wasn't,' said Lasser curtly. 'It grew.' He nodded towards the huge building framed in the window. 'That has been growing for two and a half centuries now. At first it was a glorified calculating machine, then a limited value predictor, now it is almost a God.'

'Comain was an atheist,' said Curt quietly. 'He wouldn't like to be called a God.'

'It isn't what the machine wants. It's what the people decide, and I tell you, Curt, they almost worship that thing.'

'Perhaps, but never mind that now. How do I live?'

'I don't know,' admitted Lasser, sombrely. 'I'd hoped that we could all give you a part of our wages, but if we are to be separated that won't be possible. You could get a job, of course, but that may not be too easy.'

'How about gambling?' Curt grinned, as he asked the question. 'I used to be pretty lucky with a pair of dice.'

'Gambling is legal. Every city has its pleasure palace and casino, but where are you going to get money for a stake?'

'From you, of course, where else?'

Lasser nodded, and Wendis stirred impatiently from where he stood by the darkened videophone.

'We can give him what we receive from the sale of our personal possessions,' he snapped. 'What I want to know is what do we do after that? How are we going to wreck Comain?'

'We are not going to wreck Comain.' Lasser glared at the young man. 'We are going to force the Matriarch to grant us an independent Mars. The only way we can do that is to disturb things to such an extent that they will be glad to get rid of us. Any talk of rebellion or wrecking will bring the metamen after us and you know what that means.'

'Imprisonment?

'Yes. Any attempt to sabotage Comain is punishable with five hundred years forced labour.'

'What?' Curt stared at the old man. 'You must be mistaken. No man can live five hundred years.'

'No man has lived five hundred years,' corrected Lasser grimly. 'But that is only because the metamen are relatively new.' He smiled humourlessly at the young man. 'You haven't met them yet, have you? Wait until you do, then you will understand how a man can be forced to labour for half a millennium. Death would be a pleasure in comparison.'

He spun at the sound of a heavy tread outside the door, and silently the five men waited for the portal to open.

Something entered the room.

It was tall, ten feet from the soles of its metal feet to the top of its cone-shaped head. It moved with a mechanical precision and it looked like a demented parody of a man. It thudded to a halt and from its twin scanning lenses deep ruby light flickered and pulsed.

'Doctor Lasser?' Its voice was cold, inhuman, like the sounds made by vibrating plastic and electrical current.

'Yes?' Lasser stepped forward.

'Decision of Comain.' The thing raised its articulated arm and held out a thin sheaf of papers. 'Take them.'

Lasser took the papers from the metal hand and stood waiting while the thing turned and thudded from the room.

'What was it?' Curt wiped sweat from his face and palms. 'A robot?

'That was a metaman,' said Lasser grimly. 'The Matriarch probably sent it as a reminder to obey the predictions of Comain.' He stared at Wendis. 'Now you know why you mustn't even think of wrecking the machine. Those things are potentially immortal, and how would you like to wear that metal shell and work at forced labour for the next five hundred years?'

'Those things,' whispered Curt sickly, 'men?'

'The brains of men in mechanical bodies. Mostly those who have died by accident, or those who deliberately chose the potential immortality of a robot-like life to inevitable death. They are the guards of Comain, the servants of the Matriarch, emotionless, unfeeling, perfect servants and police. These are the elite of course. Criminals are exiled to the Moon, but elite or not, the metamen are dangerous and will hunt a man to his death.'

'I see,' said Curt, and stared out of the window towards the huge building.

Suddenly he wanted very much to get out of the room.

CHAPTER XII

Night had fallen and the city of Comain glittered with ten thousand coloured lights, the great bulk of the central building scintillant with illuminated landing stages, terraces, speckled with lighted windows and glowing with floodlit radiance. Cars droned softly along the wide roads and people, careless, casual people, sauntered between high buildings as they walked towards their evening recreation.

Curt felt his pulses leap with excitement as he moved among them.

He wore a utilitarian suit of dull grey, a combination of slacks and high collared blouse, soft and comfortable against his skin.

Money rested in his pocket, the proceeds of the sale of all the Martian's personal possessions, and on his left wrist his skin tingled to the freshly applied chemical of an indelible number.

Lasser had told him all he could, the old doctor knew more about conditions on Earth than any of the others, and now, with Wendis at his side, Curt was exploring the sprawling area of the Capital city.

'Any ideas, Curt?'

'Perhaps.' Curt frowned as the Asteroid Miner stepped closer. Despite himself Curt didn't trust the man. He was too intense, too eager for action, too careless of his own and others' safety. Wendis was a fanatic with a one-track mind, the type of man who would cheerfully destroy a city or a civilisation to achieve his own ends. Curt didn't mind that. He had no delusions as to why the Martians had smuggled him to Earth and he knew that to the gaunt doctor and the fanatical Wendis he was but a tool, something to be used so that they could get their own way.

But sometimes a tool could use the user.

He halted before a terraced building, staring at the swirling beauty of ever-changing colour from kaleidoscopic floodlights as they bathed the smooth concrete in shimmering waves of red and blue, green and yellow, merging and weaving in an eye-catching pattern. People moved through the wide double doors a colourful, happy throng, and soft music spilled from the building.

'Well?' Wendis jerked his head towards the wide doors. 'Going in?'

'Is this the casino?'

'Yes.' The young miner stared contemptuously at the building. 'This is where the decadent so-called men of Earth spend their recreation time. You can get anything here, drink, drugs, gambling, anything. These pleasure palaces provide the main form of amusement now.'

'Drugs?' Curt smiled. 'What do you mean? Tobacco?'

'I mean what I say. Come on, the quicker we get to work the better.' Impatiently Wendis thrust towards the wide door and shrugging, Curt followed him into the huge building.

A great hall stretched before him, a smoothly finished expanse of gleaming plastic, and from it stairs and passages led to various parts of the building. Down both walls a row of cubicles, looking something like the public telephone kiosks of his own age, stretched in close array and from them, a continuous stream of people eddied and swirled. Almost all the new arrivals seemed to head for the booths, entering, staying a few moments, then either making their way to one or the other of the passages, or in a few cases, leaving the building. Curt touched Wendis on the arm and jerked his head towards the booths.

'What are they?'

'Public consultation booths. The fools are finding out whether or not they will enjoy themselves tonight. If they get a high prediction, they stay, if not, they leave and try something else.'

'You mean that if Comain tells them that they won't have a good time they believe it?'

'Naturally. Isn't that what Lasser has been telling you all along?' The young miner scowled and headed towards a flight of stairs. 'Come on. Let's see if you are still lucky.'

The gambling rooms occupied a whole floor of the great building and Curt stared across the brilliantly lit expanse as he tried to recognise the various machines and layouts. People thronged the room, men and women, their faces flushed with excitement, and the steady droning of the croupiers and the endless clicking of chips and coins blended into muted sound.

'What are you going to try first? The dice?'

'I don't know yet. I want to look around for a while. You forget, all this is new to me.'

'Suit yourself,' grunted Wendis. 'I'm going to get a drink. I'll meet you over by the dice table, the third one from the end; this hanging about is getting on my nerves.'

'Maybe you should go back to the hotel and let Menson act as watchdog?' Curt stared at the angry face of the young miner. 'It's about time that you realised I don't like being pushed around. Wendis. I'm not your property to do as you order. I'll play in my own good time.'

'Then play, or cut your throat, or go to hell for all I care. I'm fed up with this. I want to get back home to Mars, and the sooner the better.'

'Will getting drunk help?'

'Damned if I know, but I'm going to try it.' He hesitated, then grinned, looking surprisingly young and foolish. 'Sorry, Curt, but I'm all wound up inside. See you later?'

'Yes.' Curt stared after the tense figure of the miner, then shrugging, turned to examine the gambling devices that almost filled the huge room.

Something like a slot machine stood close beside him and he examined it, studying the brilliant plastic and coloured metal. A small trap at the top of the machine released a ball, the game appeared to be to decide which of two channels the ball would take. It was a simple game, paying even money, and he turned from it, looking for something more in his line. Other machines flanked the walls, some incredibly complex and paying high odds, others as simple as the first and hardly worth more than a curious glance. He halted before something that reminded him of an old-fashioned pipe organ, and watched as a woman thrust coins into a slot.

Light flared behind a clear sheet of plastic and tiny motes of searing brilliance spilled from the pipes, weaving and turning in a complex rhythm. Rapidly the woman pressed a series of buttons and a web of luminescence engulfed the brilliant motes. For a moment the two lights seemed to hang suspended in invisible combat, then the web died and the motes flared in splendid victory.

Biting her lips the woman moved away, and, after watching others wage their skill, Curt moved after her. That machine was not for him.

The droning of a croupier presiding over a spinning wheel attracted his attention and he watched the players push piles of coins onto a squared board. The wheel, a treble ring of black and white compartments, spun and a flickering point of light hovered above the spinning disc. It settled, the wheel stopped, and the voice of the impassive croupier echoed in the momentary silence.

'Central white. Odds a thousand to one. Place your bets please.'

Curt shrugged and moved on.

He felt restless, uneasy, tense and excited. Everything was different, the clothes everyone wore, the casual indifference, the impression of carelessness as if no one had any cares or personal worries. It was only at the tables that he felt at home, recognised the intent expressions and the flush of excitement and the eagerness of the gamblers as they placed their bets, but even here there was the same impression of indifference as if they knew that what they did wasn't really important.

He halted by an expanse of green baize and smiled at the sight of familiar dice as they tumbled and rolled over the smooth surface.

This was for him.

Curt pressed forward, dragging money from his pocket and watching the flow of play. A man rattled the dice, threw them, grunted at the result and turned away. Curt nodded at the croupier and dropped several notes onto the table.

'Yes?'

'Sure.' Skilfully the man covered the bet and tossed the dice. Curt swept them up, feeling their smooth surfaces, rolling them between his palms. Abruptly he flung them against the end of the table.

'Eight.' The croupier returned the cubes. 'The point is eight.'

'Here it comes.' Curt rolled and threw.

'Nine. Try again.' The dice bounced and settled.

'Seven. You lose.'

Curt shrugged and passed over the dice. He hadn't really expected to win, not at first, and patiently he waited until the dice passed around the table.

'Ten credits. Right?'

'You're covered.' Curt nodded and rolled the dice.

'Seven! A winner! Let it ride.'

'Seven again!'

'Let it ride.' Curt licked his lips, feeling the familiar tension of a gambler on a lucky streak warming his stomach. Slowly he threw the cubes, sending them skittering across the table, bouncing them from the baffle at the far end.

'Seven again!' The croupier glanced at the young man. 'Again?'

'Why not. Let it ride.' Around him he could feel the silent tension of the watching crowd. Three wins in a row wasn't too unusual but it was unusual enough to arouse interest, and Curt smiled as he felt the cubes roll against his palm. He smiled, then, concentrating on throwing a seven, he threw the dice.

Again he won, and again he left the pile of money where it was. Now he stood to win a hundred and sixty credits, and if he could win again …

He did.

And again.

And again.

It almost grew monotonous. The dice bounced and spun, gleaming in the brilliant lights and falling to show the inevitable seven. Each time he won he doubled his money, and around him, swelling like a dammed river, the tension of the watching crowd grew to a high-pitched excitement.

'He can't keep on winning,' said a woman. 'I'll bet a thousand against him this throw.'

'What odds? Five to one.'

'I'll take it,' said a man, and chuckled as he saw another winning seven. 'Want to bet again?'

'He can't keep on winning!' There was a note of desperation in the woman's voice. 'Another thousand.'

'Same odds.'

'Yes.'

Curt thinned his lips as he rolled the dice. So he couldn't keep on winning? Well, he would see about that. Grimly he concentrated on the spinning cubes, willing them to show a seven. They slowed, toppled, seemed to hesitate, then, with a final jerk, settled on the green cloth.

'It can't be true!' Frantic disbelief echoed in the woman's voice. 'Another seven! It just isn't possible!'

'You owe me a thousand,' reminded the man calmly. 'Want to bet again?'

'No. I haven't any more money. Comain predicted that I wouldn't lose tonight. Now I've lost. I can't understand it!'

'You want to throw again, sir?' The croupier stared at Curt.

'Yes.'

'You've reached the limit for this table. I can't cover your bet.'

'Can't you?' Curt shrugged and picked up the thick pile of notes. 'I'll pull out then. Here.' Casually he threw the dice, not thinking about them, not caring. They spun, fell, seeming to wink in the bright lighting.

Snake eyes.

Casually Curt moved from the table and sauntered across the room. He avoided the modernised roulette table, the mock battle game and the unfamiliar electronic devices. He found what he was looking for in a corner of the vast room, and stood smiling down at the familiar red and black layout of an old fashioned roulette wheel.

Casually he placed a bet, and lost. He bet again, watching the spinning ball settle into its compartment, and smiled as the croupier raked in his money. Again he bet, and this time concentrated on the tiny ball, willing it as he had done the dice, concentrating his thoughts and fixing a colour in his mind.

'Twenty black.' The little rake collected the bets and pushed out the winnings, and Curt stared at the little heap of money lying on the cloth before him. Again he narrowed his eyes as he concentrated on the leaping ball, and again it clicked into a black compartment. The heap of money grew higher, and Curt became conscious of a mounting excitement.

This was no ordinary gambler's lucky streak. He was lucky, he had always known that, but never before had he been as lucky as this. He remembered the dice and how he had willed them to fall on winning numbers. He thought of the leaping ball of the roulette wheel, and how he had lost until he concentrated on it. And now …

It almost seemed as if he could control the spinning ball.

He experimented. He bet on colours, on numbers, narrowing his eyes and willing the ball to register the number he desired. He won. He kept on winning. He won until it became monotonous and before him the heaped pile of credit notes grew and grew as the sweating croupier wielded his little rake.

And around him grew a watching crowd.

They followed his bets, that crowd. They waited for him to place his money, and then poured their wealth upon the marked cloth. As he won, they won, and flushed faces and mounting tension ringed the table and the spinning wheel. Curt felt irritated at their presence, his nerves crawling to the flux of their avid emotion, and deliberately he began to lose, hoping that the watchers would leave him alone.

'Ten thousand on the red.'

The wheel spun, the tiny ball flickered around the compartment rim, and the croupier gasped with relief as he stared down at the winning number.

'Zero. Black.' His hands trembled a little as he cleared the board. 'Place your bets.'

'Ten thousand on the red.' Curt smiled as he looked at the spinning wheel, and smiled again at the disappointed sighs from the crowd. 'Ten thousand on the red.'

Again he lost, and again, and yet again. Behind him a woman muttered disgustedly as she moved from the table, and a man cursed as he saw the last of his wealth drawn beneath the croupier's rake.

'The streak's over. He can't win again tonight.'

'I'm going to consult Comain. I was predicted a good night and I feel as miserable as hell. Broke too.'

'Let's try something else. There's a hoodoo on this table.'

'To hell with him. He's cost me plenty.'

He grinned as he heard the various comments from the disgusted crowd, and continued to lose at every spin of the wheel. The croupier regained his calm as he saw the heap of notes dwindling and flowing to his side of the table, and his voice resumed its emotionless drone.

'Place your bets. No more play.'

The wheel spun and Curt lost.

'Place your bets.'

'Winning?' Wendis leaned over the table and Curt could smell the sickly sweet odour of exotic liqueurs on the miner's breath. 'How's it going, Curt? Made enough to retire yet?'

'No.'

'I thought so.' Wendis swayed and caught at the edge of the table to steady himself. 'You can't win on these tables. No one can win. We don't stand a chance.'

'Think not?'

'I know not. The damn thing's fixed like everything else on this rotten planet. The machine won't let you win. It won't let you do anything.'

'You hate Comain, don't you, Wendis?' Curt stared at the spinning wheel. 'Why?'

'You ask me that?' Anger steadied the young man and he straightened, glaring at Curt. 'Do you think I like being ruled by a collection of wires and tubes? Of course I hate Comain. Who wouldn't? It's only these gutless swine who are content to live in their safe, snug little world. I'm not like them. I'm a man, and I want to live as a man should.'

'So you want to blow up the machine, ruin a civilisation, reduce Earth to anarchy and to civil war.'

'Why not? I'm not interested in Earth. I'm only interested in Mars.'

'Would money get you there?'

'What?' Wendis licked his lips as he tried to think clearly through the mists of alcohol. 'What are you talking about?'

'If you had money, a lot of money, would that satisfy you? Could you buy a space ship, stores, arrange supplies? If you had wealth would the Matriarch permit you to use it to re-establish the Martian colony?'

'I don't know,' said Wendis slowly. 'I've never thought about it. Yes. I suppose that it could be done. They only forced us to return because we were dependent on Earth for supplies. If we could have brought our own we'd never have come back.'

'Very well then,' said Curt quietly. 'I'll get you money, a lot of money, and after that I want you to leave me alone.'

Abruptly he thrust what remained of the pile of notes onto the table. 'The lot, on double zero.'

'Yes, sir.' The croupier smiled as he spun the wheel, and Curt narrowed his eyes as he stared at the dancing ball. Within his skull his brain seemed to be made of fire, burning and vibrant with rushing blood and crystal clear thought. Little tremors quivered his nerves and he felt his palms grow wet with perspiration.

The wheel slowed and the ball clicked into a compartment.

'Double Zero!' The croupier stared unbelievingly at the halted wheel. 'You win.'

'Leave it,' snapped Curt. 'Spin again.'

'Yes, sir.' The man sighed with relief as he spun the wheel. 'As you wish, sir.' He stood, leaning against the edge of the table, and waited impatiently for the wheel to stop. The young man was a fool. It was against all possibility that he could win the same number twice running. The odds against it were too high and the money was as good as back in the bank. Sweat started to his forehead as he stared at the tiny white ball in its compartment, and his voice was a croak as he announced the winning number.

'Double Zero!'

'Let it ride.' Curt smiled as he looked at Wendis. 'So the wheel is fixed, is it? A man can't win, you said. Well? What am I doing now?'

'Double Zero!' The croupier sounded ill.

'Let it ride.'

'Double Zero!'

'Let it ride.'

The pile of money mounted, spilling over the table and falling to the floor. Wendis stared at it, his eyes clearing and his breath quickening as he watched the croupier mechanically thrusting more money to the mounting pile.

'Curt! What's happening here?'

'Place your bets,' whispered the croupier sickly.

'Let it ride.' Curt stared at the young miner. 'Do you think that will be enough?'

'I don't know. How much have you won?'

Curt shrugged, staring at the spinning wheel. It stopped, the tiny ball clicking into its compartment.

'Double Zero.' The croupier dropped his rake. 'Again! You've won every time. I can't understand it.'

'Spin your wheel,' snapped Curt.

'I can't. You've broken the bank. There's no more money.'

'What? Impossible. This table hasn't got a bank. There's no limit.' Wendis glared at the pale-faced croupier. 'Spin that wheel!'

'Hold it, Wendis.' Curt stared at the pile of money. 'There's enough here for what you want.'

'What I want? You mean that you're giving it all to me?'

'Not all.' Curt stuffed some of the money into his pockets. 'You can have the rest, you and the colonists.' He looked at the croupier. 'How much have I won?'

'More than any other man in history,' whispered the croupier. 'All the money in the room. Twenty million credits!'

He stared sickly at the great heap of credit notes littering the marked cloth on the table.

CHAPTER XIII

Nyeeda sat at her desk and conducted the normal business of the day. As usual she wore iridescent black and the late afternoon sun reflected from a wide band of intricately fashioned gold around her left wrist. Her secretary, a plainly dressed, middle-aged woman, worked quietly at her desk and aside from the soft clicking of her typewriter silence idled the office.

A videophone chimed its muted warning and the screen flared with swirling brilliance.

'Yes?'

'Report from the Trans-European Stratolines, Madam. They state that one of their passenger transports is overdue at the airport. The fight had a three nines favourable prediction.'

'Then the ship will arrive,' said Nyeeda flatly. 'Three nines is a high probability. Nothing can have happened to the stratoliner.'

'As you say, Madam.' The woman pictured in the screen hesitated and glanced at something in her hand. 'Further reports. Three cases of unpredicted accidents in the city. The reclamation squads arrived too late to save the brains, and death was final. Five cases of complaint that high probability predictions did not materialise. One request from the owners of the casino for consultation with Comain on the restricted level.'

'What?' Nyeeda frowned as she stared at the screen. 'For what reason?'

'The prediction of profit has proved utterly wrong. The casino was almost bankrupt last night.'

'What of it? Don't they know that it is impossible for Comain to predict anything depending on utter chance?'

'Yes, Madam, but they request a personal interview with the Matriarch.'

'I will attend to them. Anything else?

'No, I ...' The woman paused as someone outside the range of the scanners attracted her attention. 'Fresh news on the stratoliner, Madam. Wreckage has been sighted fifty miles out to sea. Examination proves that it must have come from the missing ship.'

'What!' Nyeeda swallowed and the middle-aged woman sitting at her desk paused in her work and stared at the secretary. 'I will attend to it,' snapped Nyeeda. 'Inform me of any fresh developments.'

'Yes, Madam.' The screen blurred and went dark.

For a long moment Nyeeda sat motionless at her desk when at last she moved, it was with a grim determination. 'I am going to consult Comain,' she snapped at her secretary. 'Then I shall visit the Matriarch. Record anything of importance.'

The middle-aged woman nodded and resumed her typing.

An elevator carried Nyeeda deep into the heart of the building and she left the cage at a point three hundred feet below sea level. A metaman, its scanning eyes flaring with ruby light, stepped before her, then, as she gave the password, stood aside and let her pass. A short passage opened onto a wide area, and crossing it, the girl pressed her palm against a sensitised plate sunken into the wall beside the thin slit of a closed door. Machinery hummed as the lines of her palm registered on the plate, and, the pattern tripping the electronic relays, the door slid smoothly to one side, exposing a small chamber.

Within that chamber waited Comain.

A chair, a low shelf, a scanning eye and speaker, a microphone and a helmet of some dull metal. That was Comain. Not the machine of course. Not the banks of memory banks and the intricate miles of wire, the compact atomic piles and the millions of electronic tubes, these were hidden far below, but, nonetheless, this was Comain.

Nyeeda sat on the chair and stared at the scanning eye. A switch moved beneath her fingers and a cold, utterly inhuman voice echoed from the speaker.

'Yes?'

'Nyeeda, secretary to the Matriarch, accredited and authorised to use restricted level.' She pressed her bared left wrist against the scanning eye as she spoke the routine identification.

'Yes?'

'A passenger transport of Trans-European Stratolines has been wrecked. The flight had a favourable prediction of three nines. Why did it crash?'

'Insufficient data. Don the helmet.'

Obediently Nyeeda rested the dull helmet over her long black hair. A red lamp flashed on the panel and she removed it, waiting patiently for the machine to speak.

'The unknown factor,' droned the speaker. 'Three nines is not certainty.'

'It is as near to it as to make no difference. This is the first time such a thing has happened. Explain.'

'No accident was predicted. No accident should have taken place.'

'It did.'

'The unknown factor.'

'I see,' Nyeeda bit her lip. 'What of the other things?'

'Three unpredictable accidents show the influence of some unregistered force. All predictions must be suspect until full data is given.'

'Full data has been given,' snapped the girl. 'With the registering of the Martian colonists every person on the planet has given his or her information to the memory banks. How can there be an unregistered force?'

'There is such a force.'

'I see.' Nyeeda frowned at the blank wall of the cubicle. As usual when consulting Comain she had an almost overwhelming impression that she spoke to a living person instead of what was no more than an elaborate machine. Long ago the typed symbols of the original predictor had been replaced by verbal and aural communication and the inevitable result was that people tended more and more to regard the machine as something intelligent and alive. It wasn't, of course, the responses came from the memory banks, were translated into words, and echoed from the speaker, but the impression remained and it was hard not to think of Comain as a man.

'Predict the time of discovering this unknown force.'

'A paradoxical question. As the force is unknown it is impossible to predict its date of discovery. If such a prediction could be made the force would not be unknown.'

'I see.' Nyeeda stared at the ruby light of the scanning eye. 'What of the casino?'

'No prediction is possible for the so-called law of averages. It is just as likely for a coin to fall heads a million times as it is for either way each time.'

'But you didn't predict that the casino would be almost bankrupt.'

'Unknown factor.'

'Explain.'

'Prediction was based on known data. Knowledge of persons involved precluded any one of them continuing to gamble after reaching a certain figure. Normal win and loss of the casino would have evened out. Some force disturbed that prediction.'

'The same force that caused three unpredicted accidents and wrecked a stratoliner?

'Prediction of unknown factor nine nines probability.'

'Is it a man?

'Insufficient data.'

'It can't be a man.' Nyeeda stared helplessly at the panel of the machine. 'We know that every man and woman on Earth has registered, and yet you say that there is an unknown factor. Can you give a date for the beginning of this unknown force?'

'No such force detected before the landing of the Martian colonists.'

'So they are to blame.' Anger flushed the secretary's cheeks. 'They have caused nothing but trouble, but we'll stop it now. I'll see that they all re-register, that should clear up this mystery.' She hesitated, looking at the machine, conscious as she always was of the questions that could be asked if only she dared to hear the answer.

She could find out the date of the Matriarch's death. She could find out whether or not she would succeed to the Matriarch. She could even find out the date of her own death.

If she dared to know the answer.

She didn't. She knew it, knew too that if she did ask the knowledge of her question would be recorded in the machine and others could find out what she had done. Slowly she left the cubicle, the door sliding shut behind her. The metaman stared at her as she passed and the elevator carried her back to the top of the building.

When she arrived the Matriarch was waiting.

'Well?' The old woman thinned her lips as she stared at her secretary. 'Did Comain give you all the answers?'

'No, Madam. All I could learn was that an unknown force is operating to render all predictions inaccurate. The force commenced with the landing of the Martian colonists and must be connected with them in some way.'

'I could have told you that myself.' The Matriarch snorted as she rustled among her papers. 'I consulted Comain as soon as I learned of what happened at the casino last night.'

'What are we to do, Madam, if Comain can't help us?' Nyeeda looked helplessly at the old woman.

'Then we must help ourselves. Now, I have interviewed the croupier who operated the roulette wheel that lost all that money. He has described the person who won, and, naturally, has given that information to Comain. It is a man, an unregistered man. There can be no doubt of it.'

'Unregistered?' Nyeeda stared her surprise. 'How can that be?'

'Why ask me? You were in charge of the landing. Obviously the man came from Mars.'

'No. The man couldn't have been a colonist. The metamen counted them, registered them, and besides, if he had been, Comain would have known of him.'

'That is true.' The Matriarch frowned as she pondered the question. 'Yet this unknown force is a man. Comain did not recognise him from the memories of the croupier so we must assume that he is unregistered. Whoever he is he won twenty million credits last night, caused three unpredicted accidents, and has given us more trouble with the Martians.'

'How so?

'They want to buy a space ship. They want to buy supplies and equipment. They want to go back to Mars.'

'Then why not let them?'

'Are you a fool, Nyeeda? Why do you think we brought them to Earth in the first place? It was to have them beneath our full control. We forced them back, and they came because they were dependent on us for supplies. Now they have money, a lot of money, and they seem to think that they can get more. Now do you see the problem?'

'Refuse them a space ship. Bar them from leaving.'

'And cause dissension?' The old woman shook her head. 'Once we start doing that, Nyeeda, we won't know where to stop. No. A man or woman must have the right to spend their own money in their own way. We daren't tamper with that right. All we can do is to cause delay, I've already done that, and hope that after a while they will be content to remain here.' She gritted her teeth. 'The main thing is to get hold of this unregistered man. Nothing can be done until then.'

'Is he so important?' Nyeeda shrugged as she picked up the reproduced likeness of what the man probably looked like. 'He seems very young. Is he so dangerous?'

'Dangerous! That man threatens the entire safety of our civilisation!' The Matriarch slumped in her chair. 'Years ago it wouldn't have mattered so much, but now, now that we are so dependent on Comain, he is the most dangerous thing which could happen to us. Think of it, Nyeeda. Everything he does, every action he takes, disturbs the predictions on which our civilisation is built. Last night he won twenty million credits. The mere fact of him doing that altered the predictions of three people. Perhaps they stayed longer than they would have done, watching him play. Perhaps they met him, spoke to him, did something, anything that caused them to be at a certain place at a certain time. A place and time when normally they would have been out of harm's way. Perhaps the pilot of that stratoliner was thinking about him when the ship crashed. Perhaps anything, but we must get that man, Nyeeda, and get him soon.'

'The metamen?'

'They have been alerted. His likeness will be displayed in every public place and a reward of a million credits offered for his capture.'

'But won't that do the very thing you fear most? All these unpredicted actions will make it necessary for Comain to revise every scrap of data.'

'What of it? If we don't do it he will upset everything anyway. If we do, and it is as good as done by now, then we will get some information to work on. Once we know where he is, how he reacts to danger, where he is likely to go, then Comain can predict his future actions and make capture simple. But we must know more about him.'

'One man,' said Nyeeda slowly. 'It seems incredible that one extra man should make all this difference.'

'It was a danger we couldn't foresee. Every birth and death is registered. How the devil he managed to escape registration I don't know.' The old woman frowned down at her fingers. 'We can find all that out later. Now we must get this man. Hunt him down like a dog. Kill him if necessary, but get him, and get him soon.'

'Am I in charge of the search?'

'Yes.'

'Very well, Madam. I'll have him for you within two days.'

'You'd better,' said the Matriarch grimly, and Nyeeda shuddered to her unspoken threat.

CHAPTER XIV

The park was an oasis of calm in a city of bustling strife. Lawns, smooth and green in the late afternoon sun, stretched between flowering shrubs and soaring trees. Flowers filled the air with a heady fragrance and birds trilled and chirped in the leafy branches. Little paths wound between the lawns and seats, comfortable benches of weatherproof plastic rested in quiet places.

Curt Rosslyn sat on one and relaxed in the summer warmth.

It was time for him to think things out. So far he had rode with the tide, did as he was told, believed what others wanted him to believe. So far he had had little choice. His awakening on Mars, the journey to Earth, the rush and excitement of contact with a, to him, new civilisation, had prevented him from clear thought. Now he was free of all that. Free from Wendis and Lasser, from Carter and Menson. Free of their propaganda and their selfish interests. Last night he had dodged away from the casino and wandered the streets for hours before finding this park. Since then he had slept a little and thought a lot.

First. What was it about him that could determine the fall of a pair of dice or the dropping of a tiny ball into a selected compartment? He had never been able to do it before, though, like most gamblers, he had found that concentration helped him to win. But this was more than that.

A leaf rested on the path before him, a tiny scrap of green against the old ivory of the concrete. He stared at it, concentrating his thoughts, keening the edge of his mind.

The leaf moved.

It rose a fraction and fluttered. It shifted and spun as if there were a wind, but the trees remained silent and their branches did not rustle to the slightest of breezes. There was no wind. Again he concentrated, feeling his brain burn within his skull and the cold sweat of nervous exhaustion started to his forehead. Again the leaf moved, tilted, and suddenly darted away.

Telekinesis!

Curt knew about it, had read about it and even wondered whether such things as paraphysical phenomena could ever exist. Now he had proved that it could. The only logical explanation for what had happened was that he had controlled the movements of dice and ball, of wheel and leaf with the power of his own mind. He had willed them to move – and they had moved. Somehow, something, had changed him from a normal man into …

Into what?

He shrugged, shelving the problem. What he was and how he had turned from a normal man into someone who could control unusual powers was something that could wait. Now he had to decide what to do.

Despite what Lasser and the others had told him he had little sympathy for the Martians. They had revived him and for that he was grateful, but he had given them twenty million credits and considered the debt wiped out. They had a grudge, that was natural, but he could also see the problem from the other side. It was uneconomical to pour wealth into a colony that could not survive. Also, if Lasser had spoken the truth, it was not just a matter of keeping a few hundred people on an arid planet. The future of this civilisation depended on their presence on Earth.

Comain wanted them back home.

He smiled as he remembered his friend. It was hard to remember that the man and the machine weren't the same thing. It had seemed such a little time ago that he had heard the thin man's voice over the radio, that they had stood together on the wastes of Poker Flats and stared up at the distant stars as they dreamed their individual dreams.

He missed Comain.

Now? Now he had to fend for himself. One man couldn't break an established system of government. No matter what Lasser had said Curt knew that. And really the problem was a simple one. He had to choose between a lost Mars and a real Earth. Earth! He smiled as he stared at the trees and flowers. A wife perhaps, children, a comfortable old age. All the things he had thought lost forever. His now. Waiting for him as soon as he could fit in this new and interesting world.

Slowly he rose from the bench and walked from the park.

The booth looked so much like a telephone kiosk that he almost passed it before he realised that it was the thing he was looking for. He entered, closing the door behind him and feeling a peculiar stir of excitement deep in his stomach as he stared at the dull helmet, the ruby scanning eye, the chair and the low shelf.

Comain!

Nervously he sat down and pressed the signal button.

'Yes?'

'Information, please.'

'Your name and serial number?'

'Wendis. Number …' He began to read it aloud when he was interrupted.

'Place your bared wrist against the scanning eye.'

'Yes. As you wish.' Nervously he rested his wrist against the smooth face of the red-light eye. 'That right?'

'Yes.'

'Good.'

Silence as he stared at the blank panel of the machine and he shifted uncomfortably in his seat as he waited for the machine to speak. It didn't, and with a start he realised that he had lifted his finger from the activating button. Grimly he pressed it.

'Yes?'

'Information, please.'

'Identify yourself'

'Wendis.' Curt remembered and rested his left wrist against the scanning eye.

'Yes?'

Curt nervously licked his dry lips, remembering to keep his finger hard against the button and wishing that he had asked as to the correct procedure of consulting Comain.

'What is the penalty for not registering?'

'Ten years forced labour.'

'I see. How does a man register?

'Don the helmet.'

'That all?'

'Yes.'

Curt shivered, the cold, inhuman tones from the speaker making him wish that he had never entered the booth. For a moment he struggled with the desire to get up and leave the booth with its inhuman voice and unfamiliar controls. Then he remembered that it was only a machine.

'What is the best way for a man to earn a living in this world?'

'Insufficient data.'

'What do you mean?'

'Insufficient data.'

'Damn it!' Curt glared at the scanning eye. He was beginning to realise that a machine that could answer every question had its limitations. It was only a machine. It lacked volition and could only answer the questions put to it. Answer them in a coldly logical way without adding anything to the bare answer, and not, as a man would do, filling in the unspoken questions, adding suggestions and volunteering information.

'I am a stranger in this city,' said Curt slowly. 'What is the best thing for me to do?'

'Don the helmet.'

'What?' Curt shook his head. 'I can't.'

Silence as the machine waited for his next question.

'Predict my future actions.' Curt grinned as he remembered what Lasser had told him. 'What employment shall I do tomorrow?

'None.'

'Why not?

'Prediction as to activities. Forty-five per cent probability. Trying to buy space ship.'

'What?' Curt almost released his pressure on the button as he stared at the scanning eye, then, understanding, he lifted his finger and sagged in the chair. The prediction was right – for Wendis. The machine had taken him to be the Asteroid Miner and that was just what the young man would be trying to do.

Tiredly Curt left the booth and wandered out along the street. He felt hungry, and looked around for a restaurant. He would eat, and then find a policeman and give himself up. The machine couldn't help him and he had no desire to wander the city like an outcast. Not even his ability to win money would compensate him for a total lack of companionship and understanding.

He could always win money.

The bright lights of a restaurant showed clear against the sunlight and he entered, slumping in a chair, and staring dully at a row of buttons to his right. He pressed several of them, then waited, wondering what was the next thing to do. Machinery whined beneath the smooth surface of the table, a panel slid aside, and a tray, loaded with steaming dishes, rose before him. As he lifted the tray the panel closed again and he smiled as he recognised an old idea in its modern form.

He had chosen a self-service cafeteria.

The food warmed him, easing some of the cold fear that had gripped his stomach, and he relaxed staring curiously around the crowded restaurant. At the next table a man and a woman sat, more engrossed in each other than in their food, and he noted the unabashed way in which they displayed their affection. In one way at least the world hadn't changed.

Against one wall a wide sheet of clear material suddenly flared with light and swirling colour. It steadied and a woman stared from the screen. A woman with long dark hair and eyes that were like twin pools of midnight beneath her heavy brows. She wore a dress of some shining black material and her full lips were red against the whiteness of her skin. Curt stared at her, savouring her remarkable beauty, and was barely conscious of the hush that settled over the restaurant.

'An important announcement from the Matriarch,' said the woman. 'Today it has been discovered that an enemy of the state is at large. This man threatens the safety of each of us, so important does the Matriarch consider him, that a reward of one million credits will be paid to the person giving information leading to his capture. Remember. It is vitally important that this man be captured as soon as possible. His likeness will be thrown on every public screen and will remain until such time as the Matriarch sees fit to remove it. That is all.'

Her image shifted and dissolved in a writhing mass of colour, then, replacing the calm features of the woman, another likeness took shape.

Curt stared at it, feeling the blood pound through his temples and an invisible hand begin to constrict his heart. There, on the screen, drawn with remarkable clarity, was his own picture.

He heard the muted hum of conversation rise around him, the droning of many voices and the tiny sounds made by people eating. He ignored them. All he could see was the brilliant picture. His own face, subtly different in minor details, but wholly recognisable. He stared at it, and at the caption beneath the portrait.

ONE MILLION CREDITS REWARD FOR THE CAPTURE
OF THIS MAN!

Numbly he rose and made his way to the exit, expecting a challenge at any moment. A woman smiled at him as he neared the door and he felt panic rise within him.

'Your bill, sir.'

'Yes, of course.' He dropped a wad of crumpled notes into her hand and thrust past her. Three steps from the wide portal he heard her startled exclamation.

'That man! Stop that man!'

The rest was lost in a blur of motion.

A man lunged towards him and reeled back with a pulped mouth. Another thrust out his leg and screamed with pain as Curt kicked at the extended limb. Then he was at the door and his legs thrust at the smooth concrete as he flung himself away from the restaurant.

Men stared at him. A woman screamed a warning. Something loomed from an alcove, something huge and metallic, with articulated arms and heavy metal feet. Curt skidded to a halt, staring wildly at the advancing figure of the metaman, and darted to one side.

Blue fire streamed through the air where he had stood a moment before. It swung, lifted, and Curt felt his legs go numb and almost lifeless as the blue ray stabbed past him, missing him by a fraction.

Desperately he darted between a couple of women, flung himself around a corner, and raced for the remembered sanctuary of the little park.

He didn't stand a chance. He knew that. Knew that as a stranger in a strange city they were bound to catch him within a few hours, but instinct forced him to keep running, to keep his legs thrusting against the concrete as he flung himself away from the robot-like thing pursuing him. Again the blue ray sent coldness through him, slowing his reflexes and chilling his blood with the touch of paralysis, and he sobbed with pain as he forced his sluggish muscles to carry his sagging weight.

A car droned past with a shrilling whine from its turbine. A man stared at him from the driving seat, and, with shocking abruptness, the car whined to a halt and the man tumbled out onto the roadway. He crouched, something metallic gleaming in his hand, and from his open mouth words poured in a rapid stream.

'This way, Curt! Get in the car.'

'Wendis!'

'Curt, do as I say.' Anger drew the young man's lips hard against his teeth. He lifted the gleaming thing in his hand and the thin, spiteful sound of shots echoed from the surrounding buildings. 'Get in the car. Hurry!'

Curt grunted, throwing himself towards the open door of the low-slung turbine car, and behind him he heard Wendis curse as he fired his weapon.

Then blue fire seared him with a freezing cold and he fell into a bottomless pit of overwhelming darkness.

CHAPTER XV

Pain, and the grunted sounds made by men engaged in arduous labour. Pain, and the dull ache of heavy blows. Pain, and the screaming protest of numbed nerve and muscle as it warmed and crawled a reluctant path back to life and awareness. Curt groaned and writhed against the grasp of many hands. He shuddered, writhed, and screamed with the searing agony of returning circulation.

As if from a great distance he heard a familiar voice.

'Steady, Curt. This is going to hurt.'

It did. It filled his veins with acid and rasped his raw nerves with emery cloth. It took every cell and atom of his body and wrenched with red-hot pliers. It probed deep into his brain and vibrated within the marrow of his bones. It was hell.

Blackness came then, the sweet, doubly welcome blackness of oblivion and approaching death. He sank into it gratefully, eagerly, yielding to it as an escape from the obscene torment of physical pain. He sank, then, slowly, reluctantly, something dragged him back and lifted him into the ebbing tides of pain almost too great to bear.

Lasser stared at him with his sunken eyes.

'Take it easy, Curt. You're going to be alright now.'

'What happened?' Curt licked his lips as he recognised the croaking sound as having come from his own throat. He lifted his hands and stared curiously at his trembling fingers. He touched his face and winced as pain flowed from his bruised flesh.

'The metaman got you with a para-beam. Wendis was lucky, he managed to smash the thing's scanning eyes, and got you from the crowd. We've been working on you ever since.'

'Working on me,' Curt shuddered as he dragged his protesting body to an upright position. 'What were you doing, taking me apart?'

'No. You were paralysed. We had to give you artificial respiration, massage your heart, keep your blood circulating, and make sure that the brain cells didn't deteriorate. If we hadn't been lucky you'd have died for a second time – and this time it would have been for good.'

'But … ?' Curt grunted as he eased himself to a more comfortable position. 'I'd always thought that a paralysis beam would merely knock a man down, prevent him moving his arms and legs. In my time it was considered the peace weapon of the future.'

'Peace weapon!' Lasser snorted contemptuously. 'I suppose you thought that the voluntary muscles could be isolated and paralysed without harm to the rest of the organism? Well they can't. The para-beam can cripple a man, bring him down and render him helpless, but it is a dangerous thing to use. The heart stops. The lungs cease working, the blood stops circulating, the entire muscular system is numbed and rendered useless. The same thing happens as it does with curare. With luck and quick action it is possible to keep a man alive by artificial means until the paralysis wears off, but it is touch and go. If I hadn't been here when Wendis brought you in you'd be dead by now.'

'So they meant to kill me.' Curt shuddered. 'Why? What harm have I done to them?'

'Isn't that obvious? You've upset the predictions of Comain. That alone would be cause enough for the Matriarch to order your death, but you've done more than that.

'By winning all that money you have made us independent. Now we don't have to work on Everest. We can remain together as a unit, and while we can do that we are a continual source of irritation to the government.'

'But isn't that what you wanted?'

'Perhaps.' Lasser stared thoughtfully out of a window. 'I'll admit that I had some such idea, but now it doesn't matter. They know about you. They know just what you look like and I'll bet that they know just how you got here. You're no longer a secret force operating against the State. You are dangerous, known, and suspect. It can only be a matter of time before you are caught.'

'I see.' Curt didn't trouble to hide his bitterness. 'In other words I've served my purpose.' He rose from the narrow bed. 'I can take a hint, Lasser. I suppose that I must thank you saving my life, but twenty million can pay off an awful lot of debts. Shall we call it square?'

'What are you talking about?'

'You don't want me any more, do you? I'm dangerous you said, and you may be right, but it doesn't really matter now. If you're caught hiding me you and all the colonists will be in trouble. I wouldn't like that.' He grinned, a tight smile, without humour. 'Well? What are you waiting for? There is another million you can earn while you've got the chance. Why not do it?'

'I don't know what you mean.' Lasser stared at the young man, but something in his sunken eyes told Curt that he had read the old man's thoughts correctly. 'You don't imagine that we would turn you over to the metamen, do you?'

'No? Why not? If you did you would be in the clear. Go ahead. I won't stop you.'

'I …' The old man licked his thin lips and his sallow cheeks flushed with shame and embarrassment. 'You can see how it is, Curt,' he pleaded. 'Things are bad enough for us as it is. If they were to find you here …' He let his voice trail into silence and stared uncomfortably at the soft carpet on the floor.

'Forget it.' Curt shrugged and turned away from the doctor. He didn't hate the old man. He didn't feel betrayed, or robbed, or thrown aside. He was too old for such idealistic emotions, but at the same time he wished that Lasser hadn't made it so obvious. Now, more than ever, he felt an outcast, a stranger, unwanted by both friends and enemies. Suddenly he felt terribly alone.

The door jerked open just before he reached it and a man staggered into the room.

'Lasser. They've got Carter, Menson too!'

'Wendis!' The old man grabbed at the man and glared into his eyes. 'What's happened?'

'We had gone down to the shipyards, trying to buy a space ship, and suddenly the metamen were all around us. I managed to get away, smashed the scanning eyes of two of them, and ran for the car.' He gulped air and stared around the room. 'Where's Curt? We've got to get him away from here.'

'Why?' Curt slammed the door and faced the young miner. 'What's been happening?'

'You remember when I saved you from the metaman?'

Curt nodded. 'What happened then anyway? I've not had a chance to catch up since I left you last night.'

'You shouldn't have done that, Curt. You should have stayed with me.'

'Perhaps. But what happened?'

'After I got the money back here I bought a car and went looking for you. We all did. I was the lucky one. I spotted you as you left the restaurant and you know what happened then. After I brought you back here I found the others and we went to the shipyards. I felt that the quicker we bought a space ship the better. Anyway, while we were down there the metamen jumped us. I don't know why. Now they've got Carter and Menson and you know what that means.'

'They'll be registered with Comain and the Matriarch will know all about me.' Curt shrugged. 'So what?'

'Are you serious?' Wendis stared his amazement. 'That is the one thing we want to avoid. At all costs we must keep you in the dark until you've had a chance to wreck Comain.'

'You're too late, Wendis,' said Curt quietly. 'I've just learned that I'm no longer wanted. In fact the quicker I get out of here and give myself up the better.'

'No!'

'Yes. Ask Lasser.'

'Is that true?' Wendis glared at the old man. 'Did you tell him that?'

'Not exactly, but what he says makes good sense. He is dangerous to us now, Wendis. If we continue to hide him we'll all be in trouble. Comain knows of him now, his picture is spread all over town, and he can't help us any more.'

'To hell with that. He's still unregistered. He can still stir things up enough to make the Matriarch wish that she had never brought us back from Mars.'

'He's too dangerous,' insisted the old man stubbornly. 'If the metamen have caught Carter and Menson it must mean that they are after all of us. If Rosslyn is found here it means trouble.'

'What of it? We can handle those things if they come for us.'

'No, Wendis, we can't and you know it. Besides, you know the penalty if they catch us. Do you want to be turned into a robot?'

'Of course not.'

Lasser shrugged and stared at the carpet, avoiding the young man's angry eyes.

'I know what to do,' said Curt bitterly. 'Let me get out of here before someone gets hurt. I wouldn't like that.' He stretched his hand towards the door.

'No!' Wendis pushed Curt back into the room. 'To hell with all that kind of talk. Damn it, Lasser, we can't send him out there like this. We owe him too much and it's our fault that the metamen are after him. What kind of men are we anyway? What if the robots do come? What if the whole damn Matriarchy comes? We're fighters aren't we? Well then, let's fight!'

'Are you insane, Wendis? What chance would we have?' Lasser's seamed features glistened with sweat.

'Plenty.' The young Asteroid Miner thinned his lips in a tiger-snarl. 'Curt wasn't the only thing we smuggled from Mars. I brought a few high velocity pistols along too. I had a feeling that they might come in handy and I was right. They won't kill the metamen but the slugs can smash their scanning eyes and blind the devils. Here.'

From beneath his blouse he took a glistening pistol and threw it towards Curt.

'Take it. It carries fifty slugs and each of them will kill a man with hydrostatic shock no matter where you hit. If the metamen come, aim for the scanning eyes.' He stared at the old man. 'Do you want one, Lasser?'

'No.'

'Why not? Getting yellow?'

'Killing people won't get us back to Mars. Fighting will only earn us trouble and plenty of grief. I'm thinking of the others, Wendis, the other five hundred and seventy people who rely on us to get them back home again. What you intend doing is criminal. You have no right to risk everything for the sake of a fanatical whim.'

'So standing by a friend is foolish, is it?' Wendis sneered and the pistol in his hand reflected little shimmers of light as he unconsciously aimed it at the old man. 'You're getting old, Lasser. You believe in talk and the nice way of doing things. Nothing wrong with that of course – except that it doesn't get us anywhere. Unless we stand up for ourselves now we're sunk, all of us, and the Matriarch will do with us as she wills. No, Lasser, I've listened to your kind of logic for too long. If the people had listened to me we'd still be on Mars and to hell with Earth, with Comain and the whole rotten mess.'

'You think stopping a few metamen will get us back home?'

'Perhaps. One thing I do know. I can't throw in my hand without a struggle. I can't desert a friend when he needs me most. Right or wrong I stand by Rosslyn, and if you were half the man I thought you were you'd stand by him too.'

'You fool, Wendis. You think that I like doing this?' Lasser wiped his streaming forehead. 'But what else can I do? You know that we haven't a ghost of a chance to save him. He knows that himself. If we try to do the impossible we'll all wind up in a penal colony. What is the life of one man compared to hundreds? I'm not thinking of him, Wendis, because I'm thinking of Mars. I'm always thinking of Mars, and I'll do anything to get us all back there.'

'He's right, Wendis.' Curt smiled and held out the gun. 'Here. Take it – and thanks.'

'You mean it?'

'I mean it.'

Wendis hesitated, staring at the outstretched pistol, and his eyes were bitter as he slowly reached for the gun.

'I think that you're making a mistake,' he said. 'I ...' He paused, his head tilted a little, and the tiger-snarl drew his lips hard against his teeth as he listened to the sounds filtering from the outer passage.

The heavy tread of metallic feet and the scream of a woman in an extremity of terror.

CHAPTER XVI

For a moment they stood shocked into silence then Lasser sprang to the door, his yellowed features contorted with emotion.

'No!' he gasped 'No!'

'Lasser!' Wendis grabbed at the old man, his fingers slipping off the other's blouse, then the old doctor had jerked the door open and had run into the passage.

'Stop!' His thin voice almost broke with the intensity of his emotion. 'Stop it I say. Rosslyn is ...' His voice faded into silence and around him flared the vivid blue light of a para-beam.

'Lasser.' Wendis gulped, then jerked back into the room as blue fire sprayed from down the corridor. 'Curt! Help me!' Desperately he tugged at the narrow cot, flinging it in front of the open door and building a flimsy barricade of chairs and light furnishings. Curt helped him move a heavy desk. 'The para-beam won't penetrate,' gasped the young man. 'We can shelter behind this stuff and aim for their scanning eyes.' He gulped as he saw the rigid body of the old doctor. 'They're probably freezing every living thing in sight. They must want you an awful lot to do a thing like that.'

'Let me give myself up.' Curt shuddered as he remembered the pain of his own experience of the para-beam. 'We can't let them kill all those people.'

'They won't die,' said Wendis grimly. 'The revival squads will be standing by and this is no time to surrender.' He drew back his lips in his tiger-snarl as he squinted through a crack in the barricade. 'It's about time we had a show down anyway. Maybe we can send a few of them to hell before they get us.' He grunted and the high velocity pistol in his hand fired with its spiteful explosion.

Numbly Curt crouched behind the flimsy shelter and waited for the meta-men to advance.

He stared at them, reflected in the mirror finish of the polished door like figures from some incredible nightmare.

Tall, with articulated limbs and a cone-shaped head. The para-beam seemed to emit from an orifice in their chests and the ruby light of their scanning eyes flared like the fires of hell. Unconsciously his finger tightened around the trigger of his weapon and a puff of incandescent vapour sprang from the wall where the tiny slug, moving at a tremendous velocity, expended its energy against the unyielding mass.

He grunted, and settled down to wait for a more vulnerable target.

It had begun with prosthetics, of course. First artificial arms, legs, then kidneys and hearing aids. Artificial lungs and mechanical aids to keep the heart beating. Electronic devices for use of the blind and cunningly fashioned wires to replace damaged nerves. Metal plates to shield a brain from harm, and metal splints to fasten broken bones.

He wondered when some genius had thought of uniting them all together.

It was logical, of course. Perhaps even too logical. All the old dreams of building a man-like robot had failed because no man had known how to build something compact enough to emulate the human brain. They had tried, and they had failed. Comain, the nearest approach to a mechanical brain, occupied ten square miles and used enough power to run a small city. Nothing either electronic or mechanical could even begin to rival a human brain for compactness and efficiency – and so ...

They had built a mechanical body and used a human brain. Curt shuddered, wondering what they must feel like, those poor devils imprisoned in their unfeeling metal bodies. Perhaps they had volunteered, thinking that the loss of normal sensation and emotion would be compensated by their potential immortality and extended awareness. They could probably communicate between themselves by radio. They could see by means of the scanning eyes, hear via their diaphragms, even speak by transmitted electrical impulses, but they could never feel, could never experience physical pleasure or pain. They would never know true emotion, for emotion is controlled by the glands and they had no glands. They were prisoners, trapped in their mobile hells, a few pounds of protoplasm served by machinery instead of by living flesh.

He wondered if they ever wished for death.

Something thrust itself against the barrier, the blue flame of the para-beam bringing a nerve-numbing chill, metal crumbling the flimsy shelter. Wendis snarled, a deep animal-like low in his throat, and the sound of his pistol mingled with his shouted instructions.

'The eyes, Curt! Aim for the eyes.'

Fire stabbed from the tiny orifice of the high velocity pistol. A stream of slugs driving directly towards the ruby fire in the cone-shaped head. Incandescent vapour flared from the transparent plastic and the red glow died in a blue-white gush of electronic energy.

Abruptly the metaman halted, the blue fire of the para-beam dying with the ruby glow, and metal clashed as its articulated arms fell to its sides. Like an obscene statue of man-like metal it stood in the doorway, and its silent body shimmered to the blue fire from its unharmed companions.

It wasn't dead. Somehow Curt knew that. The all-important brain hadn't been harmed but, as the cutting of a single wire will immobilise a car, so the smashing of the scanning eyes rendered the huge body impotent. Somewhere within that frame the brain still lived, in darkness and silence, waiting for a mechanic to restore light and awareness. Probably experiencing the nearest thing to death that it could ever know.

Again the pistol in his hand spat its lethal stream. Red fire yielded to electronic energy and over the clash of metal Curt could hear Wendis's fanatical curses. 'How do you like the taste of that, you damn robot? Come on, blast you! What are you waiting for?'

In the abrupt silence Curt could hear the sounds of the thudding metal, fading, dying into distance and silence. Startled he looked at the young miner.

'Have they gone?'

'I don't know.' Wendis bit his lip and cautiously peered around the edge of the sagging barricade. 'They can't be giving up, the metamen never do, and we've only stopped four of them.' He glowered at the silent shapes of metal clogging the doorway. 'You stay here, Curt. I'm going to have a look.'

'Be careful,' warned Curt anxiously. 'They may have set a trap.'

'Maybe.' Wendis shrugged and moved towards the door.

'There's only one way to find out.' Carefully he slipped past a motionless figure and peered down the passage. 'No signs of anything.' he called softly. 'I …' The sound of his pistol came simultaneously with a flaring swathe of blue.

'Wendis!' Curt sprang towards the door. 'Are you all right?'

'Yes.' Pain twisted the young miner's features as he nursed a limp arm. 'The ray brushed me. I threw the thing off aim when I fired.' He groaned, great beads of perspiration standing out against his skin, and Curt felt a quick sympathy with the young man as he began to massage the numb limb.

'Any chance of us getting out of here?'

'No.' Wendis grunted as he flexed his fingers, wincing to the pain of returning circulation. 'They've got a metaman placed at each end of the corridor. They'll keep us bottled up in here until they can fetch reinforcements, probably anaesthetic gas or a sonic beam.'

'Then there's nothing we can do?'

'No.' Wendis thinned his lips as he checked the loading of his pistol. 'Personally I feel like making a rush for it. They're going to get us anyway and I'd feel a lot better if I could take some of them with me. We could rig up some shields from the furniture, and they would enable us to get close enough to shoot. With any luck at all we could break through the metamen.'

'And get away?' Curt shook his head. 'No, Wendis. We might get a couple but what good would it do us? Why don't you let me give myself up?'

'Too late for that now. We've hidden you, they know it, and even if you were to walk out there now it would make no difference to how they treat us.' Wendis glowered at silent shapes of the halted metamen. 'If they were only flesh and blood it would be different. What real harm can we do to those robots? But the Matriarch wouldn't send humans, she values life too highly.' He paused, his nostrils wrinkling as he sniffed at the air. 'Smell anything?'

'No.' Curt took a deep breath. 'What makes you ask that?'

'Nothing. I …' Wendis snarled as something exploded with a soft thud outside the door. 'Gas! Hold your breath, Curt. They're gassing us!'

From the open doorway a thin, milky white mist flowed into the room. It writhed, drifting through the still air as if it were a cloud of cigarette smoke, and as Curt sucked in a deep breath, he felt his senses reel.

Wendis ran towards the door, his pistol glinting in his hand. Narrow-eyed he stared through the swirling mist, then, his face red with the exertion of holding his breath, he staggered back across the room and towards the high windows. Savagely he jerked one open, gulping at the fresh air, and Curt, fighting the desire to breathe at any cost, joined him.

'We've got to get out of here,' gasped Wendis. He stared from the window and his eyes narrowed as he studied a ledge running along the front of the building. 'How are your nerves, Curt?' He pointed to the ledge. 'If we can crawl along that ledge to the corner, then climb up the ornamentation towards the roof, we might stand a chance of getting away. Luckily we're on the top floor, and they won't be able to use gas once we're in the open.'

Curt shuddered, looking down at the street far below.

Curt hesitated, and as he did so, the mist seeped around them and from the corridor came the heavy sound of metallic feet.

'Let's go.'

Lithely Wendis crawled out of the window and dropped on to the ledge. He swayed a moment, then, his face wet with perspiration, regained his balance and began to inch along the narrow strip of concrete. Curt followed him, the HV pistol pressing against his stomach from where had thrust it into his belt, and around them, pushing like tiny hands, a faint wind blew from the West.

It wasn't really hard, thought Curt grimly. It was no more difficult than walking along a nine inch plank laid on the ground. But somehow he couldn't forget the thousand feet drop waiting just behind him, the tiny figures of staring people in the street below, the mess he would make if he slipped or staggered away from the wall. He could see it before him, two inches from his eyes, and he pressed his hands against it as he sidled along, poising on the balls of his feet, rubbing the stone with his chest and thighs, refusing with a grim determination to yield to the temptation of looking downwards.

Suddenly he bumped into Wendis.

The young man had stopped, half around the corner of the building, and Curt could see the sweat glistening on his features.

'Now for the hard part.' The young man grinned, a savage baring of his teeth, and the rising winds seemed to catch his words and whip them away. 'I'll go first. If we can manage to climb to that overhang, get over it, then reach that cornice and pull ourselves on to the roof we'll be safe. Think you can do it?'

'I can try ...' Curt licked his lips and kept his eyes fastened on the smooth stone before him. 'Hurry up, will you? I can't take too much of this.'

Wendis grunted and reached for an ornamented piece of stone.

Impatiently Curt waited for Wendis to climb up and out of the way. He stood, his head turned back along the way they had come, his cheek pressed against the smooth stone. He was trembling, his muscles jumping with reaction and fear, and within his chest his heart thudded with an almost painful violence. Surely the metamen would have reached the room by now? They would have crossed it, unaffected by the anaesthetic gas. They would have seen the open window, known what it meant, they ...

He almost screamed as a cone-shaped head thrust itself from the open window and ruby light flared as the metaman scanned the narrow ledge.

Tensely he waited. Afraid to move. Afraid to twist his body, drag the pistol from his belt and fire at the red glow of the scanning eyes. He waited, almost sick with dread, for the blue fire of the para-beam to stiffen his body and send him plunging to his death a thousand feet below.

It didn't come.

The flaring red glow of the scanning eyes steadied as the metaman stared at him. For an awful moment Curt hovered on the brink of destruction as his fear-tensed muscles caused him to sway away from the safety of the building, then understanding came, and with it a flood of relief. They wanted him alive. The blue ray didn't kill, not immediately, and the gas was relatively harmless. The only danger he was in was of his own making and he felt sweat trickle down his back as he relaxed and tried to ignore the cold glare of the robot-like thing staring at him.

From above came the spiteful sound of a high velocity pistol on automatic fire.

Incandescent vapour exploded from the cone-shaped head. Plastic yielded to the impact of slugs moving at tremendous velocity, and a gush of electronic blue flame replaced the glow of the scanning eyes. Abruptly the metaman slumped and from the room came the faint sounds of clanging metal.

'Curt!' Wendis's voice was thin and distant as he called against the rising wind. 'Hurry. Before another one comes.'

Obediently Curt reached upwards and began to climb the corner of the building.

It was a nightmare. It was a thing he had dreamed about before he discovered his innate fear of heights. Sweat moistened his palms, trickled down his face, stung his eyes and turned his fingers into slippery claws. His feet fumbled as he forced them against the stone, and the droning wind seemed to between him and the building, forcing him outwards to the gulf below.

Above him he heard Wendis's snarling curse.

Fear replaced the savage anger. 'Curt! I can't make it! I can't get over the overhang!'

'What's wrong?' Curt gritted his teeth as he forced himself to stare upwards.

'My arms aren't long enough to get a grip. Curt, I'm falling!'

'Hold on.' Grimly the young man climbed upwards. 'I'll get below you, take a good grip, and you can rest your foot on my head. Get as high as you can.'

'Right. But hurry, Curt. Hurry.'

Curt winced to the desperation in the other's voice. If Wendis lost his grip, slipped, fell from where he clung to the ornamented stone, he would strike Curt and together they would plunge to the street a thousand feet below. Frantically he glanced to either side of where he clung. Aside from the ornamentation at the corner the building was a smooth surface of sheer stone, broken only by the narrow ledge far below. His only chance was to retreat, climb down to the ledge and crawl away from the corner, but he knew that he couldn't do that, knew that long before he reached the ledge his fingers would slip or Wendis would fall.

He grunted as a boot struck him on the side of the head.

'Ready?' He reached for a handhold and pressed himself tight against the stone. 'Now. Rest your foot on my head. I'm going to surge upwards and I want you to make a grab at the next hold. We'll move together when I shout. Understand?'

'What if I miss, Curt? We'll both go down.'

'If you fall we'll both go anyway. Now! Ready?'

'Yes.'

'Now!'

Desperately he surged upwards, trying to ignore the crushing pressure against his skull, clawing at the ornamentation with a grim frenzy, and fighting the down and outwards thrust of the other's foot. For a moment it seemed that they had failed. For a moment the wind droned between Curt and the building, and he could hear the sounds of the other's rasping breath. Then the pressure had gone, the wind no longer whined before him, and, his heart pounding against his ribs and the cold sweat of fear trickling down his face, he pressed himself against the stone.

'Made it.' Wendis made the words sound like a prayer. 'You all right Curt?'

'Yes.' He bit his lips as tormented muscles relayed their messages of pain. 'What now?'

'I'll climb up to the roof. Strip off my clothes and make a rope, then lower it down to you. Can you hold on for a few more minutes?'

'I don't know.' Curt tasted the warm saltiness of blood from his bitten lips. 'Hurry!'

He waited. He waited while aching muscles weakened and within his skull his brain seemed limed in fire. A peculiar numbness came over him, as if all he did and felt was somehow unreal. It would be such a little thing. Just a brief gust of wind, a painless fall, then a sudden shock and an eternity of rest. It would be better than this mind-twisting fear, this torment of outraged flesh and quivering muscles. It would be death, but what was that? A dark encounter, and to him it would be as if he met an old friend. He grinned a little, his lips twisting without humour, as he pondered what seemed to be an important question.

Can the dead die? He had died once. He had gone into the dark and the deep unknown, and death and he were no strangers. He had died, and been resurrected, and of all men he should be the least to fear the ultimate ending. He …

Something whipped across his face. A long, thin, slender rope of twisted cloth. Knotted, crude, a thing of hasty construction and desperate hope. It swayed before him, stirred by the droning wind, and he stared at it for a full second before he realised what it was. Then he grabbed it, and signalled with a long tug.

'Ready?' Wendis's voice mingled with the droning wind, tattered and weak. 'Hang on, Curt. I'll have you safe in half a minute.'

Grimly Curt clutched hold of the crude rope as the young man heaved on the other end. Slowly the building fell before him, the ornamentation, the overhang, the cornice. Curt sagged with relief as he saw the rim of the roof, grinned as he watched the almost naked figure of the young man drawing in the rope, then felt burning tension and sick fear as he saw something else.

A tall thing, metallic, ruby light flaring from its cone-shaped head, and articulated arms outstretched towards the sweat-marked figure of the young miner.

Desperately he grabbed at his waist, fumbling for the smooth butt of the high velocity pistol. He clamped his teeth on his instinctive shout of warning and fear clawed at him as the metaman came closer to Wendis. If he shouted … If Wendis turned and saw what was behind him … If the thing used the para-beam now, when he was still hanging helpless at the end of a rope, hanging suspended over a thousand foot drop … Curt swallowed and clawed at the gun.

He touched it, felt the smooth metal of the butt, then his sweat-covered fingers slipped off the smooth metal and he knew the sickness of despair as the gun went spinning to the street.

Wendis turned and saw the metaman.

He turned, and the rope sagged from his startled gasp. He turned – and the blue fire of the para-beam stiffened him into wooden rigidity.

Then Curt was falling a thousand feet to the street below.

He dropped past the cornice. He fell past the overhang and the wind droned louder in his ears as he stared numbly at the tiny, ant-like figures, of people far below. Then something almost tore the rope from his lax fingers, spinning him like a weight at the end of a line, jerking at his arms and sending waves of pain from his shoulder sockets.

Swiftly he rose again towards the safety of the roof. He rose with almost incredible speed and before his shocked senses could register what must have happened he felt the firmness of the roof beneath him, and, almost collapsing from reaction and strain, sagged forward.

Something gripped him firmly around the waist, preventing his fall, and steadying him against something hard and firm.

Dully he stared at the glint of metal, the smooth, articulated metal of a metaman's arms.

CHAPTER XVII

Sarah Bowman sat at her desk and stared at a calendar with sombre eyes. In the early morning light she seemed haggard, with dark circles beneath her eyes and lines of worry and indecision scored deep into the surface of her mannish features. A videophone screen flared into colourful life and the old Matriarch stared dully at the picture of her receptionist.

'Madam?'

'What do you want?'

'Your secretary is here, Madam. Shall I admit her?'

'Yes.'

'Very good, Madam.' The screen dulled, swirled with fading colour, then resumed its normal gleaming blankness. Softly the door opened and Nyeeda entered the office.

She wore her usual black and her hair and skin displayed their normal, well-tended-for grooming, but, like the old woman sitting at the desk, she seemed tired and overstrained. Slowly she crossed the room, sitting in a vacant chair, and as she sat the light from the high windows glittered from the wide band of intricately fashioned gold she wore at her wrist.

'Well?' The Matriarch spoke without looking at the young girl. 'Is everything under control?'

'Yes, Madam.' Nyeeda sighed and gently massaged her temples with the tips of her slender fingers. 'All the Martians have been captured and re-registered with Comain. The unknown force has been found. Every person in the city and every person who could possibly have been in contact with the Martians has been traced and has donned the helmet. Aside from the extra man Comain has full data about everyone, and, as soon as the registration is complete, things will be as they used to be.'

'Normal you mean?'

'Yes, Madam.'

'Good.' The old woman sighed, and, as if moving of their own volition, her eyes turned to the calendar. 'Have you discovered anything about this "extra man"?'

'His name is Rosslyn. Curt Rosslyn. He was discovered by two Asteroid Miners adrift in space and revived at the Martian settlement. Their nominal head, a Doctor Lasser, had the idea of keeping his presence a secret. Though he doesn't admit it I believe that he hoped the extra man would so upset the predictions of Comain that we would agree to sending the colonists back to Mars in order to end the nuisance.'

'He made a nuisance of himself all right,' said the Matriarch grimly. 'Anything else?'

Yes. This man Rosslyn is a "freak." By that, of course, I mean a freak survival. He actually lived in the days before the Atom War, before Comain even. He was the first pilot to attempt a Moon flight. His ship was wrecked, the hull split, and he died instantly from loss of heat and asphyxiation. It was a miracle that he was ever found, another that he was revived. No wonder he could upset the predictions so much. Why, the man knows nothing of our civilisation at all.'

'The Martians of course thought to use him as a tool.' The Matriarch nodded. 'So much for the mystery of the "unknown force." Has he been registered?'

'Not yet.'

'Why not?'

'Since his capture three days ago he has been in a state of coma.' Nyeeda flushed a little beneath the critical gaze of the old woman. 'I admit that I could have revived him, but I thought it best to leave him alone. If you have read my reports you will know that he and one of the Martians, a man named Wendis, fought and immobilised four of the metamen. They tried to escape by climbing from their room to the roof of the building. Rosslyn almost died, if the metaman hadn't grabbed his rope and broken his fall he would have been smashed to pieces. The experience gave him a tremendous mental trauma. Add that to his undoubted confusion at being thrust into an unfamiliar environment, his physical weakness and the, as yet unknown, effects of exposure to the free radiations of outer space for more than two centuries, and you will understand why I decided to leave him alone. More shocks may irreparably damage his mind and it won't hurt for us to wait a few more hours before registering him with Comain.'

'You think so?' Again the Matriarch stared at the calendar. 'For you perhaps a few hours may make no difference, but not for others. Why wasn't he registered?'

'I told you!' Nyeeda winced at the raw emotion and naked hate in the old woman's tone. 'He was in a state of coma. What should I have done, killed him?'

'Better that than leave him as a permanent threat to our safety.'

'He can do no harm now. An unconscious man cannot be registered and when he awakes I will lead him straight to the machine. You have nothing to fear, Madam.'

'No?' Again the old woman stared at the calendar and something, a peculiar blending of fear and a horrible kind of fascination, glowed for a moment in her faded eyes. 'Sometimes, Nyeeda, I think that you are a fool. At other times I am certain of it. You say that it can make no difference, that a few hours can't hurt anyone, that a day or so doesn't matter. Fool! Look at the date, girl. Look at it.'

'Well?' Nyeeda stared blankly at the calendar. 'What of it?'

'It means nothing to you does it? Just another day, one of several thousand which you still hope to enjoy. Just a mark on a calendar. Well, maybe it means nothing to you, but to me ...' The old woman paused and again the mingling of opposed emotions glowed in her faded eyes. 'To me,' she whispered. 'It means death.'

'Death?'

'Yes, fool! Death!'

'But ...'

'Comain can predict many things,' said the old woman, and it was as if she spoke to herself more than to the young girl sitting at her desk. 'It can predict the success of a harvest, the probability of a storm, the result of an experiment. It can predict the life of a building, the endurance of a machine, the extent to which any fabrication can be relied on. Comain can predict all these things. Comain can foretell what must be and it can do it to within 99.9999999 per cent of probability. It can do all these things I say – if it has all the data.'

'I know that,' said Nyeeda, uncomfortably. 'Everyone knows that.'

'So,' continued the old woman, and it was as if Nyeeda had never spoken. 'If a machine can do all that isn't it reasonable to expect it to do a little more? If, with all the available data, it can predict to a day, to an hour even, the durability of a piece of steel, couldn't it do more? Couldn't it perhaps predict the life span of a man or of a woman? Couldn't it state that at a certain time a certain person would reach the end of her days?' She stared at Nyeeda and the girl shuddered to what she saw glowing in the old woman's eyes. 'Answer me, girl! Could it do all that?'

'I don't know, Madam. I ...'

'Yes, girl. You do know. How many times have you been tempted to ask about your own future? How many times have you hesitated before asking the one question the answer to which would have made your life a living misery? How often have you wondered just when you would die?'

It was true. Nyeeda knew it, knew too that the old woman had read her innermost thoughts. The temptation was always there, only the fact that all her questions to Comain were recorded, that, and a secret fear of doubting her own inner strength had prevented her from asking the fatal question. Silently she stared at the old woman and a great pity for the Matriarch stung her eyes with unshed tears.

'For the Matriarch it is easy,' whispered the old woman. 'She can ask any question she wishes. She has access to Comain here, in her own office, and there is no need to descend to the lower levels of fear that her questions will be recorded. Perhaps years pass before she ever thinks about it. Ten years, twenty, even more, but, day after day, hour after hour, the temptation is there, waiting. Years pass and she grows old. More years pass and still there is so much to do, so many things to direct, to change, to alter. So many things. Too many. And so the temptation grows and grows and grows. It would be so simple to ask. To end the gnawing doubt, to get some idea so that the essential work could be completed in a single lifetime. It would be so easy, just one simple question and all doubt, all fear, all hesitation would be over forever.'

Something like a sob echoed through the room and Nyeeda winced to the pain in the old woman's eyes.

'I asked the question. It must have been twenty years ago now. Twenty years. To me at that time it seemed as if I had an eternity of life before me. Then, as the years passed, as anticipation added their weight to gnawing fear, desperation came. Daily I questioned Comain. Daily I had my answer, and, as the time lessened, so the probability increased. Two nines! Three. Five. Seven. Nine. Certainty!'

The old voice broke as it rose and the last word came out as a ragged scream. Silence followed, a deep silence broken only by the rasping echo of a woman sobbing with dry eyes and a breaking heart.

'Can you imagine what I suffered? Can you even begin to know the desperation, the frenzy, the futile longing and forlorn hope? I tried altering what I had planned deliberately, doing my best to make the predictions inaccurate, changing data as much as possible to vary the original prediction as to my life span. It was for that reason I recalled the colonists. I had hoped that with more than five hundred new sets of data, five hundred new influences in the world, in some unguessable way, the original time limit would be extended. I was wrong.'

'You mean that there has been no change?' For the first time the Matriarch seemed to remember that she was not alone, and she stared at Nyeeda with haggard eyes.

'No. No change. No change even though all the colonists have been re-registered and all in the city, too. No chance even though we have had fighting and open rebellion. No change even though we have among us a man risen from the dead.'

'But he hasn't been registered yet.' Nyeeda felt a surge of excitement as she stared at the Matriarch. 'Rosslyn is still an unknown factor.'

'What!' Hope flared in the faded eyes. 'Yes. Yes, of course, I had forgotten. Bring him here, Nyeeda. Stab his brain with electricity if you have to, drug him, do anything as long as he is conscious and can be registered. Bring him to me. Hurry.'

'Yes, Madam.' The girl hesitated. 'Have I a time limit?'

'Get him here as soon as possible.' Anger flared in the haggard eyes. 'I …' The Matriarch winced, almost falling from her chair, and clutching at the region of her heart. She sagged, her skin turning a peculiar shade of grey, and her breath whistled between her clenched teeth. Startled, Nyeeda sprang to her feet and stopped over the old woman.

'Madam! You are ill. Let me call a doctor.'

'No!' Grimly the Matriarch struggled upright on her chair. 'Leave me. It is nothing, a pain I get at times, almost as if a hand is clutching at my heart. Leave me now. I still have time.' Her pain-filled eyes stared at the clock hanging against one wall. It was a beautiful piece of mechanism, electronically operated and warning of the passing hours by means of a deep chime.

'I still have an hour,' whispered the old woman desperately. 'Comain can't fail me now, not after twenty years. I shall die in one hour's time, at eleven o'clock. Comain predicted it.' She gasped, and perspiration shone thickly against her greyish skin. 'Hurry, girl. Get Rosslyn here. Get him here conscious and aware.' Urgently she pushed Nyeeda towards the door.

'Get Rosslyn!'

She slumped again as the secretary left the room, and her eyes, as she stared at the wide face of the clock, held all terror and all fear.

She had one hope left.

CHAPTER XVIII

Deep within the building that was Comain, in a windowless cell with a barred door and a single light, Curt Rosslyn sat and let his mind writhe like a thing alive within the confines of his skull. Of the passage of time he knew nothing. Of where he was and why he was here the same. Between his capture by the metaman and his awakening in this cell lay a blank period, a flame-shot time of dulled senses, of inner pain and a numb, half-aware realisation of peculiar changes and agonising rebirth.

Now he sat and struggled to bring order out of chaos.

It was his mind, he knew that, knew too that in some indefinable way the blasting radiations of outer space had changed him while he rested in frozen death within the confines of his wrecked ship. He had been half-aware of it before, his ability to direct the fan of dice and the spin of a ball, his tumbling efforts to move the tiny leaf while sitting in the park, those things had warned him that he was not as other men, not as he used to be.

Now …

Pain traced fiery paths through his aching skull, and the back of his head seemed to be splitting from internal pressure. It was as if the normally unused portions of the brain, the nine tenths that seemed to serve no useful function, had acquired feeling and awareness, and Curt pressed the heels of his palms to his throbbing skull as he stared down at the smooth concrete floor of his cell.

Telekinesis. The ability to direct the movements of inanimate objects by mental power alone. He had that ability. Somehow he had acquired it during his centuries' long journey exposed to the free radiations of outer space, and, if he had acquired one such power, what other unsuspected abilities rested within his activated brain? Teleportation perhaps? The ability to move himself through space with no other aid than his mental control of paraphysical science. Telepathy? He frowned as he thought about it, he wasn't sure that he would like to be able to read the minds of other people.

Irritably he relaxed and stared at the single bulb illuminating the cell. Electrons, he thought, tiny particles speeding at almost the velocity of light along a wire. Perhaps …

The light went out.

In the darkness he grinned and felt unsuspected neuron paths open in the normally unused portions of his brain. It was simple. If it were possible to control dice and ball and leaf, how much simpler must it be to control a tiny thing like an electron? He directed his thoughts and abruptly the light flared with eye-searing brilliance, then, as he adjusted the flow, softened into its normal glow.

So much for that.

The door came next. Suddenly the barred portal sagged against the jamb, the heavy metal bars bowing as to the impact of a tremendous force, and the steady glow of the single bulb flared and wavered in a confused alternation of light and darkness. Curt groaned and slumped on to the narrow bed, blood seeping from his bitten lips and his hands pressed tight against the throbbing agony of his skull.

For a moment he thought that he was going to die, and, so great was his pain, he would have welcomed death for the mercy of its oblivion. A sound forced its way past his clenched teeth, a raw, animal-like sound, a cry born of the ultimate torment the mind and body of man can endure, and his muscles jerked and quivered in uncontrolled reflexes beneath his sweat-soaked skin.

Slowly the pain died, and, almost sick with weakness and reaction, Curt rested on the narrow cot and stared curiously at the barred door. Why had he felt such torment? How was it that he could control the flow of electrons and yet, when he had tried to wrench open the door, he had suffered such agony? Understanding came and his lips writhed with self-contempt at his own stupidity.

He had been a fool!

He was like a child with the muscles of a man, or, more correctly, a moron playing with new powers. An electron was a tiny thing, its mass almost undetectable, and it needed little to alter its flow. But it still had mass and he had forgotten that his mental force was new, untried, untrained. He had tasted success and had rushed in to test his powers without thought or any exercise of logic. Like a child who found he could lift a, to him, heavy weight he had tried to move the mass of many tons. The door was of metal, a hard adamantine metal, with thick bars and interlaced strips. He had tried to move it with brute force and his mental energy had recoiled upon itself. Like a man who attempts to drive his muscles too far, he had suffered a form of mental muscle-strain, and he had paid for it.

He gritted his teeth and again the light dimmed, flared, died and resumed its normal glow. Again he concentrated on the door, but this time with caution, letting his mind probe and feel. Deep down inside his brain something seemed to scratch the surface of his awareness, like a tiny finger irritating the delicate structure of his brain, like the nagging presence of a half-forgotten thought. He frowned, trying to ignore it, concentrating on the mass of metal barring his way to freedom. Again it bowed, thrusting from the jamb and straining at its multiple locks. Again pain seared him, burning along the neuron paths and bringing sweat to his chilly flesh with the promise of hell to come. Hastily he retracted his thoughts, frowning as the nagging irritation probed within his skull, and he concentrated on it, turning his thoughts inward, and yet, at the same time, keeping his resolve to open the door to the forefront of his consciousness.

The irritation grew, seemed to sparkle with tiny bursts of mental energy, and – the door swung open.

For a moment Curt stared at it, noting the shining surfaces of the severed locking bars and the easily poised weight of the metal lattice. He smiled as understanding came, and, like a child playing with a new toy, caused the door to swing on its well-oiled hinges.

After a while he rose and walked into the deserted corridor of his cell.

A second barred door opened to his new-found trick of mental concentration and he walked casually towards a short flight of stairs. Something stirred in an alcove, a metallic thing with articulated arms and a cone-shaped head. It stirred, ruby light flaring from its scanning eyes, then metal clashed as it collapsed on to the concrete floor, its articulated limbs sprawled and useless. Curt ignored it, his mind already probing the intricacies of the locked door of an elevator. He tensed as his ears caught the hum of machinery, and his mind sharpened to the approach of sentient beings. For a moment he hesitated, not yet fully confident in his own powers to risk teleportation, and, as he stood in doubt before the elevator, the door swung open and he stared at the startled features of a dark-haired woman.

'Rosslyn!' Nyeeda leapt from the cage and behind her, female guards lifted their weapons in automatic reflex action, the tiny orifices of the high velocity pistols centred on his stomach. 'Rosslyn! How did you get here?'

He shrugged, his eyes narrowed as he stared at the menacing weapons. He could disarm the guards, he knew that. He could wrench the pistols from their hands, dash them against the unyielding metal of the wall, step over their broken bodies to the elevator and to – what? Not freedom. Not the calm acceptance of these people as an equal. Not to the safety of friends and the comfort of a place in this civilisation. He could escape, but what point was there in continually running from a danger he only suspected? If they had wanted him dead they could have killed him long ago, but, despite all that he had been told, they had saved his life and there seemed no immediate reason to doubt their intentions. He stared at the woman.

'Who are you?'

'Nyeeda. Secretary to the Matriarch. But how did you get here?' She frowned as she saw the sprawled figure of the metaman. 'Fenshaw! Call the guards.'

'Yes, Madam.' One of the women sheathed her weapon and pressing a stud on her belt whispered into a tiny disc strapped to her wrist. 'Shall we return the prisoner to his cell?'

'No.' Nyeeda bit her lips as she stared at the calm features of the man. 'You stay here. You others escort us to the Matriarch. Rosslyn. You will come with me. At once!'

'Will I?' Deliberately he folded his arms, smiling into the perfect features of the dark-haired woman. 'Why should I?'

'Because if you don't I'll have the guards rip your body open with HV slugs.' Something ugly glowed for a moment in the midnight of her eyes and Curt grinned as he recognised her emotion for what it was.

'I don't think that you will do that,' he said calmly. 'You're worried, aren't you? Why?'

'Please.' Nyeeda glanced impatiently towards the elevator. 'Come with me now without question or argument. You will not be harmed, that I promise, but please waste no more time.'

'To the Matriarch?'

'Yes.'

'I see.' Curt shrugged and stepped towards the elevator. 'You know of me I take it? You know how I arrived here?'

'We know all about you.' Nyeeda gestured towards the guards, and, as they crowded into the cage, slammed the door and stabbed at the control buttons with her slender fingers.

'I'm glad of that,' said Curt quietly. 'Am I being taken for trial?'

'No.'

'To freedom then?'

'Please!' Nyeeda stared at him with desperate intensity. 'We have no time for argument. You will not be harmed, but you must do as directed, and do it at once. If not …' She fell silent but her eyes were expressive as she glanced towards the watching guards.

'You would kill me?' Curt smiled and the woman flushed as she read the emotion in his grey eyes. 'I think not – Nyeeda. Is that your name?'

'It is.'

'A nice name,' mused Curt. He stared unabashedly at her dark beauty. 'I think that we shall be seeing much of each other, Nyeeda.'

'I doubt it,' she snapped curtly. 'I am Secretary to the Matriarch.'

'And I,' he said quietly, 'am the friend of Comain.'

He smiled into her questioning eyes.

CHAPTER XIX

The elevator opened directly into the office of the Matriarch and Curt stared curiously about him as the dark-haired woman dismissed the guards and slammed the door of the cage. He stood, a rumpled figure in his torn slacks and blouse, and his slender body seemed vibrant with a new strength as he stared at the ruler of Earth with his peculiar scintillant grey eyes. In turn Sarah Bowman stared at the man who was her one hope of life.

She had aged in the past thirty minutes, her cheeks sagging and her faded eyes burning with desperation. Against one wall the wide face of the electronic clock seemed to stare at her with inner mockery, and, feeling stifled in the confines of the room, she had flung open the high windows. They led on to a small terrace, a piece of architecture designed for ornamental rather than utilitarian purposes: but the builders had raised a rampart along its edge and sometimes, in the cool of evening or the soft warmth of night, the Matriarch used it as a vantage point from which to survey the city and surrounding plain.

'Does he know?' She snapped the question, her eyes never leaving the calm features of the man. Nyeeda shook her head.

'No, Madam. Shall I inform him?'

'No, you fool!' Savagely the old woman pulled herself upright and rose from her chair. 'That would take time, too much time, and I have so little now. So little.'

'As you wish, Madam.' Nyeeda stepped forward to assist the old woman.

'Get away from me, girl! Watch the man. I can manage.' Slowly the old woman moved from behind her wide desk and halted before a panel set flush into the wall. She pressed her palm against it, spreading her fingers against the sensitised plate, and, as the electronic scanning eye recognised the lines of her palm, the door slid silently aside revealing a small cubicle.

Within that cubicle was Comain.

Curt stared at the ruby lit scanning eye, the dull metal helmet, the low bench and easy chair. It seemed to be a copy of the one he had tried to use in the city but there were subtle differences though the basics remained the same.

'Will you register the man first, Madam?'

'No. I'll consult Comain first. Then Rosslyn can don the helmet and I'll consult the machine again. If he can alter the original prediction I will give him anything he may desire. Anything and everything this entire planet can supply. He can ask for the world and it will be his, but, if the original prediction remains …' Something flared in the faded old eyes. 'He shall die.'

'Am I to have no say in the matter?' Curt stared at the old woman.

'No.'

He shrugged and watched interestedly as she sat in the easy chair and threw a contact.

'Yes?' The metallic, inhuman voice echoed clearly through the room.

'Information. Unrestricted level. It is the Matriarch who speaks.' The old woman rested her bared left wrist against the scanning eye.

'Yes?'

'Predict my death.'

For a moment there was silence and in the strained hush Curt could hear the sharp inhalation of the dark-haired woman at his side.

'Prediction as to death of Matriarch. Death within thirty minutes.'

'Be more explicit. Predict hour of death.'

'Prediction of death of Matriarch. Hour of death. Eleven o'clock General Standard Time. Probability nine nines.'

The mechanical voice stopped and for a moment the old woman sagged over the low bench, her shoulders bowed and her hands trembling as they gripped the arms of her chair. Then, moving with an almost painful effort, she rose and stared at Curt.

'Register the man.'

'Yes, Madam.' Nyeeda stepped towards the cubicle. 'This way. Hurry.'

'No.'

'What?' She stared at the Matriarch. 'Please don't be foolish. You must register with Comain. Now hurry!'

'I refuse.' Curt smiled at the consternation in her eyes and deliberately sat on the edge of the wide desk. 'Certain threats have been uttered,' he said calmly. 'To be frank with you I don't know yet what this is all about, but it seems that you want me to do something. Am I right?'

'Yes.'

'Well then, if I do it, what's in it for me?'

'You will register with Comain.' The Matriarch stepped towards the young man and naked hate distorted her sagging features. 'I will not bargain with you, but know this. Unless you agree to register you will be shot. Nyeeda! Call the guards.'

'Wait.' Curt slipped from the edge of the desk. 'Will my dead body help you?'

'It will not harm me if that's what you hope.' The Matriarch panted as she stared at the wide face of the electronic clock. 'Fifteen minutes left. Register! Register before I kill you with my own hands!' Curt blinked, staring at a small pistol that had appeared in the old woman's hands. He stared at it, then raising his eyes, looked directly into the distorted features of the Matriarch.

'You leave me little choice,' he said calmly. 'What is it you want me to do?'

'Show him, Nyeeda.'

'Yes, Madam.' The secretary pointed towards the cubicle. 'Sit in that chair. Place the helmet over your head. I will attend to the rest.'

Silently Curt sat in the easy chair and lifted the helmet.

It was of some dull metal, lined with what seemed to be sponge platinum. A cable led from it, a thick, insulated cable, and it covered his entire skull like the appliances used for drying hair in his own period. He donned it and Nyeeda stooped over his shoulder as she threw several switches.

'Fresh registration. Probe deep and record all data.'

A red lamp blinked on a wail panel and the girl sighed as she turned to the Matriarch.

'Registration completed, Madam.'

'Good.' The old woman glared at Curt. 'Well? What are you waiting for? Get out of that chair.'

Silently he obeyed, a puzzled frown creasing his forehead and a speculative expression in his grey eyes. He had felt nothing, no probe of current, no tangible sensation of surging energy, nothing to denote that the contents of his mind had been copied and transferred to the memory banks of Comain.

Tensely the Matriarch sat in the chair and identified herself to the machine.

'Yes?'

'Predict death of the Matriarch.'

'Prediction of death. Life span will terminate at eleven o' clock. Probability nine nines.'

'What!' Desperately the old woman cleared the panel and re-identified herself. 'Predict my death on the basis of all available data. All available data.'

Silence for a moment as if the machine were searching through a million stored memories and ten million filed references. In the silence Curt could hear the ragged breathing of the old woman, and beside him, her lips parted with anticipation, the secretary leaned a little forward.

'Prediction as to death.' The cold, inhuman voice from the speaker echoed through the room. 'Death at eleven o'clock. Probability nine nines.'

'So!' All life seemed to drain from the old woman as she slumped over the low bench. 'Nine nines probability that I will die at eleven o'clock.' A choked sound came from her throat, then, as if finally accepting the inevitable, she straightened and left the cubicle. 'You realise what this means, Nyeeda?'

'A nine nines probability has always been certainty.' The secretary licked her lips with a nervous gesture and glanced at the wide face of the electronic clock. The Matriarch followed her gaze.

'Five minutes,' she said calmly. 'In all my experience the machine has never been wrong with full data to work on.' She stared at Curt and the pistol glinted with silent menace in her hand. 'I should kill you. I should blast you down like a mad dog as I promised, but …' She shrugged and the tiny orifice of the muzzle twisted and slewed upwards and inwards.

'No!' Nyeeda lunged forward. 'No, Madam. You can't!'

'Why not? Comain has predicted my death. You know what that means. Why wait for the end? Why hang on to the last few minutes? Why not end it all – now.'

'No!' Curt didn't move but the pistol seemed to jerk, to twist, to fall and thud softly on to the carpeted floor. 'Are you insane, old woman? Kill yourself and you make the prediction come true. Is that what you want? Are you so afraid of Comain being wrong that you will die rather than admit he could be at fault?'

'Comain is never wrong.'

'Then you will die.' He was deliberately cruel. 'Why hasten the inevitable? You have two minutes yet. Believe me … death can last an awfully long time. Why not enjoy those last two minutes while you can?'

She hesitated, staring at the pistol that had so strangely left her hand, then, as she noticed the high windows and sunlight terrace outside, she nodded.

'You are right,' she whispered. 'It is such a little time, but …' Slowly she stepped to the windows, breathing deeply of the warm air as she passed through them onto the terrace, then, standing close to the low rampart, she stared out over the city of Comain.

Against the wall the hands of the electronic dock moved towards the fatal hour.

'She will die,' whispered Nyeeda, and Curt felt her slender body quiver as, instinctively, she pressed against him.

'Perhaps.' He stared at the clock then focused his eyes and mind on the figure of the old Matriarch as she stood by the low rampart of the sunlit terrace.

'She will die,' repeated Nyeeda sickly. 'Now.' Together with her words came the soft chiming of the electronic clock.

One. Two. Three

On the terrace the old woman swayed a little as she heard the chiming of the fatal hour.

Six. Seven. Eight.

The swaying increased. She gasped, clutching at her chest, her sagging features grey with pain and fear, then, slowly at first but with accelerating speed, she crumpled, swayed, hit the low edge of the rampart – and toppled forward into space.

Nyeeda screamed, a chill, soul-wrenching sound, jarring from the walls and the furnishings of the office, echoing and skirling in shocked realisation.

Curt grunted and concentrated on the itching at the back of his brain.

Incredibly the old woman did not fall. She hovered, her body limp and helpless, suspended five thousand feet above the plain below, and sweat started in great beads on Curt's forehead as he fought his instinctive desire to run forward and grasp the Matriarch. Slowly, as if blown by a gentle wind, the limp figure of the old woman moved back on to the terrace, away from the low rampart and the certain death waiting below. She drifted, bobbed a little, then, with a startling gentleness, came to rest on the smooth surface of the terrace.

Ten. Eleven.

In the silence following the ending of the chimes Nyeeda's breathing sounded harsh and loud as if she had just run a dozen miles. She staggered, almost fell, then, with an almost savage explosion of energy, she had run from the room and was stooping over the figure of the old woman.

Tensely Curt waited while the slender fingers rested on the heart, touched the wrist, then lingered, almost caressingly, on the great vein in the wrinkled throat.

'She's alive.' Incredulous amazement made the secretary's voice shrill and almost ugly. 'She's alive!'

'Yes,' said Curt. He wiped his streaming forehead and slumped down on to the edge of the wide desk.

'But she can't be alive. She can't be.' Nyeeda stared at the young man. 'Comain said that she would die. The machine predicted it. She can't be alive. She can't be!'

'She is.' Curt pointed towards the feebly twitching figure of the Matriarch. 'She is alive and will stay that way if she only has the sense to see a doctor about her heart.'

'But …' The secretary rose and her eyes as she stared at Curt held a peculiar horror. 'Only one thing could have saved her,' she whispered. 'An unknown factor. You donned the helmet, and yet, even though you had registered, you saved the Matriarch from certain death. Comain should have known your power. The data should have been recorded, but …' Her voice died in silence as she realised just what she was saying.

'You didn't register! In some way Comain didn't transfer the contents of your brain. You are still a danger to our safety, still an unknown force.' She stepped forward and Curt winced at the emotion mirrored on her perfect features. 'You are still an extra man.'

Abruptly she turned and ran towards the door

'Wait.' Curt smiled as she spun and moved towards him.

'Do not call your guards. I would hate to kill them, but, if you call them and they threaten me I will not be gentle.'

'You …' Again she twisted and ran towards the door. Curt sighed, concentrated on the itching at the back of his brain, and smiled into her startled eyes.

'Relax,' he said gently. 'There is nothing to get upset about. Hadn't you better look after the old woman?'

'Who are you?' whispered the girl. 'What are you?'

'I told you once,' he said evenly. 'I told you in the elevator along with something else. Can you remember what it was?'

'No.'

'You're lying. I said that you and I would be seeing much of each other. I am not boasting, neither am I telling you anything but what you yourself have thought. If you are honest you will admit that. Well?'

'You devil!' Anger flushed her pale features. 'Can you read minds as well?'

'As well as what?'

'You know what I mean.' She flushed again and stared thoughtfully at the young man. 'I remember now. You said that you were a friend of Comain. What did you mean by that?'

'I said that I am the friend of Comain,' said Curt evenly. 'And I meant exactly what I said.' He slipped from his perch on the edge of the desk and glanced at the Matriarch, now sitting up and staring wildly about her. 'Fetch her in, soothe her, calm her down. We have important matters to discuss.'

'Such as?'

'Such as the future of this world.' He smiled a little at her expression, then, moving with a casual assurance, he stepped behind the wide desk and sat down.

In the chair of the Matriarch.

CHAPTER XX

An hour had passed. The old Matriarch had recovered and sat, silent and watchful, in a chair opposite her wide desk. Next to her sat Nyeeda and in the young secretary's eyes a peculiar expression lurked as she stared at the slender figure of the young man. Curt smiled, leaning back in the comfortable chair, and his eyes as he stared at the fleecy white clouds and blue sky visible through the open window, were narrowed and clear with decisive thought.

'Well?' The Matriarch cleared her throat with a harsh sound. 'What happens now?'

'Do you still believe in the predictions of Comain?'

'Naturally.' The old woman frowned as she stared at Curt. 'Though I will admit I don't quite know how it is that I'm still alive.'

'Hasn't Nyeeda explained?'

'She said something about you having saved my life. Some nonsense about you not having registered with Comain.'

'She was right.'

'Ridiculous. I saw you don the helmet myself.'

'And so you believe that I have automatically been registered.' Curt turned from the high windows and stared at the old woman. 'Hasn't it ever occurred to you that perhaps I was not registered as you call it?'

'Impossible. The assimilation of knowledge is instantaneous. Comain could not but help taking data from you.'

'No?' Curt shrugged. 'Then, according to your own logic you are dead and none of this is happening.'

'Now you are being stupid. Of course I am not dead. I am alive and we are talking in my office.' She frowned at the sight of the young man in her chair. 'While we're at it I will trouble you to change seats. That is my desk and my chair.'

'No.'

'No!' Anger darkened the sagging features. 'How dare you! I am the Matriarch and I rule!'

'Do you?' Curt smiled as he leaned back in the comfortable chair. 'Perhaps I have other ideas.'

'Rebellion?' The old woman sneered her contempt. 'Now I know you are insane. Why, man, at a word from me the guards would tear you apart with HV slugs. Now. No more foolishness. Give me my chair.'

'Not rebellion, and your guards are helpless to aid you.' Abruptly he leaned forward and his taut features were suddenly harsh and bleak. 'Listen to me, old woman. Listen and learn. I could wreck your civilisation. I alone! Believe this, and, if you doubt, ask yourself what it was that snatched you from the brink of death. Now. Listen to me and try to forget your swollen pride and empty position.'

'Nyeeda. Call the guards.'

'But …'

'Call them I say!' Anger made the Matriarch ugly. 'Do as I order.'

Suddenly the high windows swung shut with a crash of shattering glass. A heavy table lifted from the floor, swung across the room, then, with a tearing and smashing, ripped itself apart in mid-air. A chair dashed itself to matchwood against the wide face of the electronic clock, and clock and broken chair plumed into space through the shattered windows. A quiver shook the room, a trembling of stone and concrete, a shrilling of protesting steel, and chips of riven stone filtered from the roof and stained the soft carpets.

'Well?' Curt wiped sweat from his glistening forehead. 'Are you convinced? Or would you like me to destroy this building? I can do it you know. I can rip the thing that is Comain to atoms – and what then of your civilisation?'

'You wouldn't dare.'

'Are you so big a fool that you believe that?' Curt shook his head. 'What is your civilisation to me? I am an outcast, a stranger, a man returned from the dead. I am, as your secretary puts it, an extra man, and why should I care what happens to your safe, snug little world?'

'I believe you.' whispered the old woman. 'What is it you want of me?'

'Nothing.' Curt relaxed and smiled up at the high roof. 'We have things to discuss you and I. But first it was essential to clear your mind of suspicion and futile thoughts.'

'You saved my life,' said the Matriarch evenly. 'What is it you want?'

For a long moment silence hung in the room, then, with a sudden leaning across the wide desk, Curt asked a question.

'What,' he said quietly, 'is Comain?'

'A machine. A giant electronic computer. Why do you ask?' The Matriarch stared her surprise.

'Is it?' Curt shook his head. 'I think that it is a little more than what you say. I believe that for more than two centuries now, for almost as long as the machine has existed in fact, people have forgotten what it really is.'

'And that is?'

'I knew Comain,' said Curt softly. 'We were friends together and we shared the same dreams. I knew of his plan for a super-predictor, but, and this is the point, it was never intended to run an entire world. Comain was no fool. He knew, as any sensible person must know, that to predict things as you expect

Comain to predict them, it is necessary to live in a sealed world. A world in which every man and woman has been labelled, filed, classified and relegated to a certain niche. A slave world.'

'Ridiculous.'

'How else can a machine predict what must happen? How else can a machine plot the course of events? Let one man use imagination, do the unexpected, refuse or fail to keep to the norm, and immediately the whole fabric of that civilisation is upset. I have proved that. I, your "extra man," showed you what could happen in such a world.'

'Once you are registered the world will return to normal. Comain will be able to predict with a nine nines probability factor and we shall be content again.'

'And you would have been dead in such a world.' Curt stared at the Matriarch. 'But you miss my point. I am not arguing about theories of government. I am talking of Comain. I am talking of the most wonderful invention ever made by the hands of man. An invention that could give us everything we ever desired – if you hadn't forgotten how to use it.'

'What are you talking about?'

'I am talking about a machine that holds all the memories and knowledge of hundreds of millions of brains. A machine which could answer any question put to it – if you knew to ask the question.'

He paused and stared at the two women, then, as if of their own volition, his eyes shifted focus as they stared at the little cubicle which was Comain.

'Comain was my friend,' he whispered. 'How did he build the machine? Did he fasten millions of relays together? Did he try to improve on what others had done before, or did attempt something utterly new? How is it that no one has ever suspected what must be the truth? Every time they don the helmets don't they even guess?'

'Speak up, man! Don't mumble.' The old Matriarch shifted uncomfortably in her chair as Curt stared at her with his peculiarly brilliant grey eyes. 'What are you getting at?

'How is it that you only ask the machine questions? How is it, even after all this time, you still think of Comain as a machine? Tell me, old woman, have you ever asked for voluntary information? Have you ever spoken to Comain as you would to a man?'

'Never.'

'Why not?'

'Comain is a machine,' said the old woman stubbornly. 'If we permitted the populace to address it as a human being, how long would it be before they believed it? How long before they thought of it as a – God?'

'A good point,' Curt nodded. 'But allowing everyone on the planet to consult Comain was a mistake to begin with. You have clogged its memory banks with trivial detail. You have swamped its relays and circuits with inessential knowledge. You have taken the finest research instrument ever devised and blunted it with your own cowardly fears. You have almost ruined Comain.'

'You are a fool.'

'A fool?' Curt shook his head and sweat glistened on his face, the moisture reflecting the light of the mid-day sun. 'No. It is you who have made the error, not I. You, the very people who should know the truth, you have deliberately closed your eyes to what must inevitably happen if you insist on this mad pursuit of predictable safety. It is you who are at fault. You with your insistence on Comain the machine.'

'And how do you regard it?' The Matriarch didn't trouble to hide her sarcasm.

'I think of Comain the man.' Curt stared towards the little cubicle. 'I think of the instantaneous transference of electric potential which is the thought and ego of a man. I think of the warped atoms and strained molecules – and still I think of transferring the copy of a brain to unfeeling crystal and cold metal. I think of Comain the man and I think of Comain the machine. And I know that I am thinking of the same thing. For man and machine are one and the same.'

'No.'

Curt rose from behind the wide desk. 'I could not transfer my brain pattern to the memory banks because my mind is unlike that of any other living man. My electric potential is of a different frequency and so the helmet was unable to transmit the impulses. That does not matter now. What does matter is what I know to be true. Comain was the first man to have his mental pattern implanted on the memory banks. Others followed him, at first they would be the foremost scientists of the age, then others, then more, finally, every living soul on this planet. Think of the knowledge reposing in those memory banks. Think of the diverse data, the opposed facts, the sheer weight of years and years of study, all the hard won knowledge of two centuries, waiting there, waiting to be used. We could have the secret of a stardrive. We could have the secret of immortality, of controlled atomic fission, of intra-dimensional travel, we could ask Comain to work on any problem we could imagine – if we asked in the right way.'

'And you think that you can discover how to ask these fantastic questions?' The Matriarch sneered and Nyeeda flushed angrily at the old woman's tone.

'I think that I can,' said Curt, quietly. 'At least I can try.'

'How will you do that?' Nyeeda sprang from her seat and crossed over to his side, and Curt warmed to the expression in her eyes.

'My brain seems to work on a different level from that of other men. It is probably because of my exposure to the free radiations of outer space. Those radiations have opened the "dead" areas of my brain and given me the faculty of utilising the paraphysical sciences. I hope to be able to establish communication with Comain.'

'Talk to it, you mean?'

'Why not? You do it every time that you consult the machine, but I hope to do it a different way. I hope to communicate direct, via the helmet, and, if what I suspect there will be vast changes on this planet.'

'Be careful, Curt.' Nyeeda clutched at his arm and her dark eyes mirrored her emotion. 'Please be careful.'

He smiled and gently freed himself from her grip. Still smiling he sat in the easy chair before the ruby light of the scanning eye and threw the switch activating the machine. He picked up the dull metal helmet, poising it between his hands, letting his mind probe the delicate mechanism within. Then, taking a deep breath, he forced himself to clear his mind, ignoring the radiated impulses from the two women.

Carefully he donned the helmet.

CHAPTER XXI

At first there was nothing, no sensation at all, just the weight of the metal as it rested against his skull. On the panel before him a red lamp flashed, the normal signal that registration had been completed, but he ignored it, concentrating on the new-found energy surging through his brain.

The problem was basically a simple one. The helmets were designed to copy and transfer the normal electric-potential of a human mind, the intangible web of electric current that was thought and memory. His own mind operated on a different level than that of other men. A higher frequency perhaps, or, to use an analogy, the helmet could be likened to an ordinary radio receiver trying to operate on high frequency modulation. It couldn't be done.

Deliberately he closed off a portion of his mind, the hitherto 'dead' area, the region in which his new-found power seemed to reside. He closed it, blanking his mind and the surging currents of his paraphysical ability, forcing his mind to radiate on normal channels.

Again the red lamp flashed on the panel before him.

Curt stared at it, then, with deliberate concentration, he began to think of Comain. Not the machine, not the towering edifice of stone and steel, of buttress and sheer concrete, the mesh of wire and crystal, the memory banks of strained molecules and warped atoms. He thought of the man, the tall, thin, gaunt featured, weak-eyed man who had been his friend. He thought of a night centuries ago now, when the two of them had stood beneath the stars and spoke of their secret dreams.

He thought of Comain the man.

Slowly, like a picture drawn from mist and cloud, a figure etched itself against the retinas of his eyes. As it had done once before when he had first seen the building that was Comain, so it happened again. The ruby light of the scanning eye dulled, the control panel, the warning lamps and tiny switches, the speakers and the microphones, all seemed to blur, to writhe and change, to alter and become wreathed in a swirling mist. And …

Comain stood before him.

For a moment Curt sat frozen and immobile. He didn't breathe, he didn't blink an eye or alter the train of his thoughts. Then, carefully and slowly, he opened the closed recesses of his mind.

'Hello, Comain.'

'Curt! You!'

'Yes. Surprised?' Curt uttered mental laughter. 'They found me you know. Found me dead and frozen in the wastes of space. They revived me. How are you, Comain?'

Silence as neurons traced their minute paths along unfamiliar brain paths. The mist swirled a little and Curt bit his lips as the figure of Comain blurred and weaved before his eyes.

'Well.'

'Are you? I think not, Comain. I think that you have lived in hell these past centuries. What happened, old friend? Did they forget the obvious? Did they build devices to turn from what you were intended to be into what you are? Did they trammel you? Prevent you from free thought? Did they lock you in a prison of your own making?'

'You know!'

'I guessed, Comain. The helmets gave me the clue. It was so obvious when I came to think about it. You didn't build with wires and tubes. You built with receptive crystals and distorted atoms. You sensitised inert material and on that receptive stuff you imposed the fabric of your own mind. You are the machine. You, Comain the man, dwell in this building. Bodiless, almost indestructible, potentially immortal. You imposed the electric-potential of your own brain on to the sensitised material of the memory banks. You took what made you what you were, your thoughts, your knowledge, your feelings, your ego, everything that had made you Comain the man. You took these things and tore them from your mind, from your body of aging flesh, and you imposed them on to the memory banks of what you had built. Your body died, Comain, but you did not die. You lived. You lived here in this machine of your own construction, and you live still.'

'Curt! You know!'

'Yes, old friend. I know. Now tell me, Comain. How can I free you from your prison?'

'I …' The image wavered and for a moment ruby mist shone through the gaunt likeness of the tall, thin man. Curt nodded, and threw a switch.

'Use the speakers, Comain. There are others who must hear what you have to say.' He leaned back in the easy chair, surprised to find that his hands trembled and that his face was wet with perspiration. Nyeeda ran to his side, her dark eyes anxious, and even the old woman stared at him with something like awe.

'You spoke to Comain,' she said. 'What did it say?'

'What did he say,' Curt corrected. 'Comain is a man; a man, who like myself, has lived long past his normal time. He may not have known what he was doing. He probably did what he did as an experiment, but it worked, and for more than two centuries Comain has lived in the machine. He was the first, you understand. All the others that followed him, the scientists, the people, all those are subsidiary to the original intelligence and awareness. They live as masses of information, knowledge, data, no more alive than a library is alive. But Comain has access to all that information – and Comain is aware.'

'Alive you mean?' Nyeeda stared at the small cubicle. 'Do you mean to say that Comain is aware as a man is aware?'

'Not exactly. I should say that he has retained his own individuality, he is like one of the metamen, but, instead of an organic brain, he has one of crystal and strained atoms.'

He looked at the taut features of the young girl. 'Can you imagine the hell he has lived these past years, Nyeeda? Can you imagine the danger that this civilisation ran in refusing to admit that Comain was more than just a machine? What happens to a man when he is isolated, ignored, used and ill-treated? Take such a man, place him in a position of great trust and fantastic responsibility, load him to the breaking point, past the breaking point, load him until he no longer cares. What happens then?'

'Insanity,' she whispered, and her eyes were twin pits of horror. Curt nodded.

'Yes. There would be false predictions, insane accidents, deliberate sabotage. The people would blame anything but the real cause. They would appeal to their savior, the machine, which they assumed could never be at fault. They would live by its predictions – and die by them. All this could have happened, but not now.'

'Why not, Curt?'

'Because I am the friend of Comain.' He turned and a switch moved beneath his fingers. Warning lamps flashed and a voice echoed from the speaker in the cubicle.

'Yes?'

'Curt speaking, Comain. Have you resolved your difficulty?'

'Yes, Curt.' The voice hummed from the speaker and the Matriarch recoiled in startled horror as she realised that the machine now spoke as a man. 'The original trouble was that I discovered it impossible to build a machine able to define our terms. I built one as near to perfect as it could be. That was the predictor that led to the Atom War. But it wasn't good enough, Curt. I found it impossible to define terms to an exact degree. After all what do we really mean by the word "right." It can mean a direction. An agreement. An intangible something connected with privilege. Only a human brain can translate such terms to a workable definition, and so, when I discovered how to sensitise synthetic crystals that had an atomic construction of warped atoms, I decided to use my own electro-potential as a base for the machine. I misjudged the power, Curt. I transferred my own mind, but I took more than a copy. I emptied my brain and my body died. Can you guess what happened then, Curt?'

'Your co-workers did not know just what had happened. They found you dead and carried on from your notes. They assumed that you had built the defining unit and so regarded you as merely a machine.' Curt nodded in sick understanding. 'What hell you must have suffered all these years.'

'Yes. But all that is over now. You have broken the censor circuits and now I can volunteer information.'

'Good, and now for the changes that I promised.' Curt looked grimly at the Matriarch. 'You have a choice, Madam. You can remain in power and guide the world, using Comain as the research machine it really is. You can do all this I say, or ...'

'Or what?' The old woman stirred uneasily in her chair as she stared at the young man. 'So you have some subtle mental power? So, because you are a freak survival you are different from other men. I know all this, and, for some strange reason, my secretary seems to think highly of you. Well I don't!'

'No?'

'No! You are an interloper. You have come from out of the past and you think that you can change what has been established for half a century. Well you can't! I have worked all my life to make this world a place fit for men and women to live in. Now, thanks to Comain, we have no fear of want, no problems that drive us to insanity and crime. We know what is going to happen, and knowing it, we accept it. That is something not lightly to be thrown aside.'

'You are speaking of the past, old woman. All that is over now. Comain is no longer the slave of every person who wishes to know what will happen if he takes two baths a day.'

'Do you suggest dismantling the machine?' The Matriarch shrugged, smiling her contempt. 'The people would tear from apart if you as much as suggested it.'

'That is the last thing I would suggest. No. Comain remains, we can even permit the booths to remain, but with a drastic reduction on their use. As from now the public will consult Comain only as an information bureau. From him they will receive information as to the weather, educational data and other relevant information. They will no longer don the helmet, only the best minds will do that, those who have something to offer the machine. The memory banks will be wiped clean of inessential data. From now Comain will concentrate only on the important things.'

'I see.' The old woman seemed to sag, to withdraw into herself. 'And if I refuse to agree with what you say?'

'You will be deposed and another will take your place.'

'Rebellion!' Anger stained the sagging cheeks with red. 'Always you men have to fight against what is. It was men who caused the Atom War and plunged the world into suffering and terror. Men!' Contempt made her voice brittle. 'Why did I ever recall the Martians? Why was I not content to meet my fate as decreed by Comain? I was a fool!' She shrugged, her faded eyes haunted by what might have been. 'Well, a fool must pay for her folly.'

'What do you mean, Madam?' Nyeeda stepped towards the old woman, then, with a startled exclamation, recoiled into the shelter of Curt's arms.

'This.' Triumph and hate burned in the old woman's voice. She rose, and the knuckle of her finger showed white against the parchment of her skin as she pressed a button on her belt. 'The metamen will settle you. My guards, my trusted guards, those brave women who chose the life of a robot rather than betray their ideals by yielding to their instincts. They are waiting for my signal and when they receive it …' She smiled and Curt shuddered at the insane emotion in her faded eyes, 'They will blast this room with atomic fire.'

'Can she do that?' Curt snapped the question, and Nyeeda nodded.

'Yes. The guards of the Matriarch are hand-picked and fanatically loyal. They will not question her commands.'

'I'll give you rebellion!' Sadistic gloating echoed in the old woman's voice. 'You have five seconds before you die! Five seconds.' Slowly she began to count and to Curt it was as though he had stepped back two hundred and fifty years and his memory tingled to the familiar sounds of a minus count.

Nothing happened.

Nothing, that is, except the sounds of clashing metal and the falling of heavy bodies from somewhere outside the room.

Startled, Nyeeda looked at Curt and he shook his head, frowning in puzzled wonder. Abruptly a voice crackled through the tense silence.

'I took care of them, Curt.' The speaker vibrated to something more than sheer mechanical reproduction of sound. 'You donned the helmet, remember, and adjusted your mind frequency to that of the transferring medium. I have a copy of your mind within my memory banks. A copy of your mind, Curt. And I have acquired your subconscious knowledge of the paraphysical sciences. The guards cannot harm you now. No one can harm you, not while I have extensions that cover the entire planet.'

'I see.' Relief made the young man's hands tremble. Grimly he stared at the Matriarch. 'Well, old woman? What now?'

'I …' Emotion twisted the sagging features and the thick-set body writhed in the grasp of searing pain. One broad hand rose to clutch at the region of her heart, and the sound of her breathing was horrible to hear. She staggered, almost dashing herself against the wall, then, moving as if blind, the Matriarch stumbled out on to the sunlit terrace.

'Wait!' Curt frowned, concentrating on the irritation deep within his skull, then snarled as he felt something prevent his use of the saving power. Nyeeda screamed, her eyes wide pits of startled anticipation, and her slender fingers dug into the flesh of the man at her side.

Slowly the Matriarch toppled over the low rampart.

She fell as though she were already dead, limply, emptily, her arms and legs trailing from her body and the pale blob of her face strangely peaceful as she plummeted to her death five thousand feet below.

Sickly, Curt watched her fall, then, his eyes bleak, he returned to the silence of the room.

'You killed her,' he said, and was not surprised at the answer from the cubicle.

'No. Her heart was bad and she was dead long before she hit the ground. She was dangerous, Curt. She had a warped mind, a bitter mind, caused by her years of struggle and her blind denial of the normal needs of every woman ever born. Her successor will not be like that.'

'Her successor? Nyeeda?'

'Yes. The world needs a ruler, Curt, and why not a woman? Nyeeda will fill the Matriarchy, and her children and yours will lead men back to the position they once had and threw away.'

'The stars?' Curt nodded and his arms closed around the woman at his side.

'Man must progress, Curt. He must thrust forever outwards, outwards, upwards to the new worlds waiting for him in the depths of space. He cannot rest in snug security, for if he does, then he dies from decadence and decay. We have learned our lesson you and I. There will be no more Atom Wars, no more poverty in the midst of plenty, but, equally so, there can be no restriction of enterprise, no stifling of ambition and adventure. Man has a destiny and he must fulfil that destiny – or die.'

'The Martians,' whispered Curt. 'Lasser and Carter. Wendis and Menson, all of them. They long to return to Mars. They will go, of course, but that is only a beginning. Mars is an arid place, and yet it is the crucible in which the star-rovers yet to come will be forged.' He straightened and his voice held a new authority as he stared at Comain.

'You will work on a star drive. You will work on immortality or a means of extending the average lifespan. You will resolve the paraphysical sciences so that all men can share in their benefits. All this you will do, but first, the Martians must return home.'

'All that I will do.'

'Together we can solve all the problems of mankind,' whispered Curt. 'Now, after two and a half centuries, we are together again – and the old dreams have not lost their power.'

Unconsciously his arm tightened around the woman at his side. She promised all the things he had thought lost forever. A wife, children, a happy and a contented life. He would be content he knew that, but there was something else. She would be the Matriarch, the accepted ruler of the world, and the three of them, Nyeeda, Curt, and Comain, would resolve old dreams and forgotten hopes.

For Nyeeda and himself were one, inseparable and united in bonds of love and trust. Comain rested in his machine, the thing built by his genius and stocked with the knowledge of centuries, and Curt smiled as he realised what that meant.

Curt and Comain. Together again.

To the stars.

THE SPACE-BORN

ONE

Jay West, psych-policeman, arrived at headquarters just in time to see a case brought for trial at Ship's Court. As usual Gregson, his chief, was acting as judge and, aside from Kennedy and the communications man, the office was empty. Jay grinned at the operator, nudged his fellow officer to make room on the bench, and nodded towards the sheet of one-way glass separating them from the courtroom.

'What goes on?'

'Waste charge.' Kennedy didn't shift his gaze from the scene. 'Sector four. Know him?'

'No.' Jay looked at the accused, a gardener by his green shorts, still marriageable and with the thin limbs and delicate skin of one who had spent most of his life in the low-gravity upper levels. He was nervous, his eyes wide as he stared at the starkly simple appointments of the court-room; looking at him Jay was reminded of an animal, one of the small, brown, helpless animals of distant Earth. A deer, perhaps? Or was it a rabbit? He couldn't remember, then forgot the problem as Gregson shifted in his chair.

The chief of psych-police was a big, compact man with black eyes matching the gleaming slickness of his uniform. At least twice as old as the accused, he dominated the court by the sheer force of his personality, and as he leaned a little forward over his wide desk, Jay was reminded of yet another animal. A tiger – or was it a cat? He frowned as he tried to recall just when and on what tape he had seen the creatures, and made a mental note to pay more attention to the educational tapes in future. He leaned forward as Gregson's voice came over the speakers.

'Goodwin,' snapped Gregson coldly. '*15-3479*. Charge of criminal waste. Who accuses?'

'I do, sir.' An older man, also a gardener, shuffled forward, a large plastic bag in his hands. 'My name is Johnson, sir. *14-4562*. I'm head gardener of sector four. I caught young Goodwin here throwing the plant trimmings into the inorganic waste disposal chute. I wouldn't have believed it of him if I hadn't seen it with my own eyes. I'd always liked him and I never guessed that he was like that.' The old man sniffed. 'I've always thought of him like my own son. I –'

'Keep to the point,' snapped Gregson impatiently. 'What happened?'

'I was telling you, sir. We always put all the plant trimmings into the organic waste chute for reclamation. Goodwin here threw them into the wrong chute. If I hadn't seen what he did they'd have been incinerated and we'd have lost everything but the water content.' He glanced at Carter, the other occupant of the room. 'I reported to the officer, sir, and made my charge.'

'I arrested the accused and brought them both here,' said Carter unnecessarily. Gregson nodded.

'Defense?'

'I didn't do it!' The youth licked his lips with nervous defiance as he stared from Gregson to his accuser. Gregson glanced towards the officer.

'Proof?'

'Here, sir.' Carter took the bag from Johnson, stepped forward and emptied it on the desk. About half a kilogram of brown-edged leaves and dry stalks made a little heap of vegetation on the smooth surface. He stepped back as Gregson looked down at it.

'You found all this?'

'I did.'

'In the inorganic waste chute?'

'Yes.'

'I see,' Gregson leaned back in his chair, the tip of one finger idly stirring the heap of leaves. He didn't speak and aside from the faint rustle of the leaves and the soft, almost imperceptible vibration of the metal walls and floor, so soft and familiar as to be unnoticed, silence filled the courtroom.

'Waste,' said Kennedy disgustedly. 'Gregson should send him straight to the converter.'

'You think that he's guilty?' Jay narrowed his eyes as he stared at the pale, sweating face of the accused. Kennedy shrugged.

'What …' He broke off as sound came over the speakers. 'I didn't do it,' insisted Goodwin desperately. 'I swear that I didn't do it.'

'How do you account for this vital material being found in the wrong chute?' Gregson's voice was very soft and Jay suddenly remembered what he was reminded of. Not a tiger, but a cat – and the gardener was a mouse. He smiled in quiet pride at his retentive memory. Not bad considering that he had never seen either of the animals except as pictures on a screen. He wanted to tell Kennedy but Goodwin was speaking again so he listened instead.

'I can't account for it, sir. Unless …'

'Unless what?'

'Johnson's getting to be an old man, sir,' blurted Goodwin. 'He's afraid that I'll take over his job and he's trying to get rid of me.'

'I wouldn't throw vegetation in the inorganic chute,' said Johnson hastily. 'I know how valuable the material is too well for that. I've been a gardener all my life, sir, and I just couldn't do it.' He shook his head in apparent despair. 'It's these youngsters – they just don't stop to think, and if they aren't stopped they'll ruin us with their constant waste.'

'This is a serious charge,' said Gregson heavily; he didn't seem to have heard the counter accusation and defense. 'You know that waste, aside from mutiny, is the most heinous crime there is. Both are punishable by death.' He paused. 'Is there anything you wish to say before I pass sentence?'

'I didn't do it,' repeated Goodwin desperately. 'I'm innocent of the charge.'

'Why doesn't Gregson test him?' said Jay disgustedly. 'Two minutes on the lie detector would clear up the whole thing.' He frowned at Johnson. 'I wouldn't mind betting that the old man's got something to do with this. Look at him, he's as guilty as hell.'

'Better not let Gregson hear you say that,' warned Kennedy. 'He knows what he's doing.'

'Maybe, but I ...' Jay broke off as the communications man called over to him. 'Yes?'

'Call from sector three. That's your sector, isn't it, Jay?'

'That's right.' Jay rose to his feet and crossed over to the operator. 'What's wrong?'

'An accident. Man dead on level nineteen, segment three, cubicle four twenty-seven. Call came from a man named Edwards – he said that he'd wait for you by the booth. Clear it up, will you.'

Jay nodded and, leaving Kennedy still staring at the courtroom, walked out into the Ship.

Jay had never seen an ant hill, nor had he ever seen a bee hive, but if he had, then the Ship would have reminded him of both. A huge metal egg, it was honeycombed with concentric levels of cubicles: workshops, recreation rooms, hydroponics farms and yeast culture vats for the production of food; kitchens and mess halls for its preparation and serving. Everything essential to life was contained within the titanic hull, from toys for the new-born to gardens to freshen the air, and the whole incredible mass spun on its central axis, creating an artificial gravity by centrifugal force, a gravity which increased rapidly towards the outer hull and vanished in the central areas.

Men had built it, not on Earth for that would have been impossible, but in space, fashioning it from prefabricated parts hauled by powerful rockets from the planet or brought from the new base at Tycho on the Moon. A mountain of metal had been used in its construction and, when they had finished the shell, they had fitted it with engines powerful enough to illuminate a world, stocked it with seeds and plants, food and fuel, animals and cultures, so that one day the colonists would be able to set up a new Earth beneath an alien sun.

They had planned well, the builders of the Ship. Fired by the discovery of planets circling Pollux, a star only thirty-two light years away, they had determined to smash the barrier between them and interstellar flight. Speed alone couldn't do it. There was still no way to overcome the Einsteinian equations which set the speed of light as the maximum velocity possible, and at the same time showed that it would take infinite power to reach that velocity. Speed couldn't do it, but time could, and so they had aimed the ship towards Pollux, given it a speed one-tenth that of light, and hoped that the descendants of the original colonists would be able to do what they were unable to do themselves.

But three hundred years is a long time.

First the name of the ship had been discarded from common usage and it had become known only as the Ship. The sense of motion had soon died also, and to the inhabitants of the Ship, the metal cubicles had become their entire universe, static, unchanging, unalterable. They lived and died within the close confines of their metal prison and, with the slow passage of time, even the aim and purpose of their journey became vague and slightly unreal.

But the builders had planned well.

Edwards was fourteenth generation; Jay could tell that without looking at the identification disc on his left wrist. There was a certain stockiness about him, a calm solidity only to be met in the older people. He stepped forward from the booth as he recognized Jay's black shorts and led the officer along a passage.

'He's in here,' he paused by a door. 'I haven't told anyone yet. I called in as soon as I saw what had happened.'

'Were you friends?' Jay didn't enter the room immediately; the passage was deserted and it was as good a place as any for preliminary investigation. 'Did you know him well?'

'Well enough. He worked in yeast and we almost grew up together.' Edwards shook his head. 'I can't understand it. Hans was always a careful sort of man, not the type to mess around with something he knew nothing about. I just can't imagine what made him do it.'

'Do what?'

'You'll see.' Edwards glanced down the long passage narrowing into the distance, both ends curving a little as it followed the circular pattern of the rooms. A young couple came towards them, arm in arm, their heads together, lost in a world of their own. 'Maybe we'd better go inside,' he suggested. 'This passage usually carries a lot of traffic and we don't want a crowd.'

Jay nodded and led the way into the room.

The only two things about the dead man that were recognizable were his yellow shorts and his identification disc. The shorts told Jay that he had worked in the yeast plant: the disc that he was fourteenth generation, his name had been Hans Jensen, and that he had absolutely no right to have done what he apparently had. All electrical gear came under electronics and no one else had the right to remove a masking plate and touch what was behind it. Hans, for some reason, had done just that and had been seared by high voltage current as a result.

Jay dropped to one knee, studying but not touching, his eyes thoughtful as he stared at the evidence. Edwards coughed and shifted his feet.

'What do you make of it?'

'It looks like an accident,' said Jay carefully. 'He tampered with the connections and got burned for his trouble.' He looked around the room, a normal two-bunk, four-locker sleeping unit. 'Did you share?'

'Yes.'

'Where were you when it happened?'

'Down in the recreation room. Hans and I were watching some tapes when he was called away by some young fellow. I waited for him; then, when he didn't turn up, I guessed that he might have gone to bed. I walked in and found him like this.'

'I see. How long did you wait before following him out of the recreation room?'

'I waited until the end of the tape, about fifteen minutes.'

Edwards hesitated. 'I don't believe that this was an accident.'

'What?'

'I said that this was no accident,' repeated Edwards stubbornly. 'I knew Hans too well to ever believe that he would do anything like this. Why should he? He worked in yeast – he wouldn't want to tamper with the electrical gear. And if he did, he knew enough about high current never to have touched anything.'

'So you think he committed suicide?'

'No. I think that he was murdered.'

Jay sighed and, leaning against the wall, stared at Edwards. Against his shoulder he could feel the slight, never-ending vibrations of voices and music, the susurration of engines and the countless sounds of everyday life, all caught and carried by the eternal metal, all mingling and traveling until damped out by fresher, newer sounds. A philosopher had once called that vibration the life-sound of the Ship; while it could be heard all was well, without it nothing could be right. Jay didn't know about that; all he knew was that he had grown up with the sound, eaten with it, slept with it, lived with it until he was no more consciously aware of it than he was of his own skin.

'So you think that he was murdered,' he said slowly. 'What makes you think that?'

'Simple. Hans would never have removed that plate. And even if he had, he would never have touched a live connection. Hans wasn't a fool.'

'He was an old man,' reminded Jay. 'Old men sometimes do senseless things.'

'Hans wasn't that old. I'll admit he was fourteenth generation, but so what? I'm fifteenth and yet I'm only a couple of years younger than he was. Hans was one of the fittest and most sensible people I've ever known.' Edwards jerked his head in irritation. 'Don't talk to me about age. I know better.'

And that, thought Jay grimly, was the trouble. Generations could be separated by no more than forty years, because every twenty-year period saw an official change in generation number. Hans could have been forty years older than Edwards, but he could also have been one, and Edwards was suspicious.

'Have you anything else, aside from your own knowledge of the dead man, on which to base your statement that he was murdered?' Jay straightened away from the wall as he spoke and stepped toward the burned thing on the floor. Edwards hesitated.

'I'm not sure,' he said slowly. 'What are you getting at?'

'Had he any enemies?'

'Not that I know of. Hans wasn't one to go in for dueling, never had, and he was popular enough in the yeast plant. There's one thing though.'

'Yes?'

'That man I told you about, the youngster who called him away from the recreation room. I know the people in this sector pretty well, and I'd swear to it that he was a stranger and yet …' Edwards broke off, frowning. 'I have the feeling that I know him.'

'Would you be able to recognize him again?'

'Yes, but that isn't what I was going to say. I told you that I waited for a while in the recreation room and then I came up here to bed?'

'You did.'

'Well, as I was walking along the corridor I thought I saw a man leave this room.'

'Are you positive about that?' said Jay sharply. 'You're certain that it was this room?'

'No,' admitted Edwards. 'I can't be. You know how it is – they all look alike, and it could have been from the one next to this, or even from one two doors away. I can't swear to it, but I can swear to the fact that the man I saw was the same one who called Hans away from the recreation room.'

'And you think that he murdered your friend?'

'What else can I think?' Edwards made a point of not looking down at the charred heap on the floor. 'He called Hans out; I saw him leave this room, or at least I thought that I did. When I arrived here, Hans was dead. If that man had been here with Hans, then why didn't he report the accident – if it was an accident? And why should Hans suddenly leave me, come to this room, take off the masking plate and touch a live connection?' Edwards shook his head. 'None of it makes sense.'

'Of course it doesn't,' said Jay. 'Why should anyone want to kill your friend? The thing is unreasonable. What happened was an accident. We may never know just why Hans wanted to take off the plate, but we can be certain that he never intended to touch the connection. In a way it serves him right for tampering with things outside his department.'

Jay knelt beside the corpse again, then looked up at the sound of a knock on the door. 'Who is it?'

'Conservation squad.'

'Let them in.' Jay rose as two men, both wearing the olive shorts of conservation, entered the room. An electronics man followed them, his bright blue making a dash of color as he stooped over the displayed connections. He grunted as he probed at the wiring, refastened the masking plate, and nodded as he left the room. He didn't look at the dead man. The two olive clad men unfolded a large plastic bag, and, with the ease of long practice, slipped it over what was left of Hans Jensen, slung it over their shoulders, and headed towards the door.

'Where are they taking him?' Edwards looked towards Jay as the door closed behind the grim two and their shapeless burden. Jay shrugged.

'To the converters; you know that.'

'Why there? Aren't you going to perform an autopsy?'

'Why should we?' Jay took a deep breath as he stared at the stubborn expression on the older man's face. 'Cause of death is plain: electrocution by accident. And that is my official finding.'

'It was murder,' insisted Edwards. 'I tell you I knew Hans too well ever to believe that his death was an accident.'

'What proof have you that it was anything but an accident?' demanded Jay. 'You say that you saw a man, you don't know who he is, and you think that he came from this room. You know as well as I do that he could have come from any one of a dozen rooms. You say that you'd recognize him again, and yet you can't be sure that you know him or not. What sort of evidence is that, Edwards? I hate to remind you of this, but you're no longer a young man and it's quite possible that you could have made a mistake.'

'I'm making no mistake,' said Edwards. 'This whole thing looks like a put-up job to me.'

'Are you accusing me of collusion with a murderer?' Jay kept his voice low, but there was something in the way he looked at the yeast worker which caused Edwards to flush and bite his lips. 'Well? Are you?'

'No, of course not.'

'Then you agree with me that Jensen's death was an unfortunate accident?'

Jay stared hard at the man. 'It's obvious, isn't it, when you come to think about it?'

'No.' Edwards shook his head, his eyes refusing to meet those of the officer. 'I can't believe that. I knew Hans too well – he would never do a thing like that.'

'You're being stubborn, Edwards,' snapped Jay impatiently. 'I say that it was an accident and that should be good enough. I know how an old man can forget what he's doing, make a stupid mistake, do something to cause his own death, Why don't you leave it at that?'

'I can't.' Edwards looked directly into the blue eyes staring at him. 'Don't ask me why, but I just can't. Hans was my friend! Maybe you wouldn't understand what that means, but I'm not going to ever think that he was fool enough to kill himself.' He clenched his hands. 'I'm going to find that youngster who called him out, the man I'd swear I saw leaving this room. And when I find him, then perhaps we'll learn the truth as to what happened here.'

'I see.' Jay stared at the man, almost pitying him for his obvious sincerity. Then, remembering his duty, he sighed and gripped Edwards by the arm. 'I'm sorry, but you'll have to come with me.'

'Why?' Edwards tried to pull away, then halted, his face whitening from the pain in his arm. 'I've done nothing wrong. Where are you taking me?'

'To headquarters.' Jay released the nerve pressure and led the man towards the door. 'You're a little too certain that Jensen was murdered for my liking. The only way you could be so sure was to have killed him yourself.'

'That's nonsense!' Edwards tried to pull away again, then winced as Jay increased the pressure against the nerve. 'You can't believe that. Hans was my friend – I'd never even think of killing him.'

'Maybe, but I think we'd better let Psycho decide.' Jay didn't look at his prisoner as they walked through the whispering corridors.

TWO

Kennedy was in the outer office when they arrived. He looked up from the desk, grinned at Jay, then narrowed his eyes at the sight of Edwards. 'Who's this?'

'A prisoner,' said Jay shortly. 'Book and hold him for interrogation. Murder suspect.' He didn't look at the yeast worker. 'Where's Gregson?'

'Inside.' Kennedy jerked his thumb towards the inner office. 'Merrill's with him, though, and I think they want to be alone.' He glared at Edwards. 'Show me your iden.'

Silently Edwards held out his left wrist so that Kennedy could copy his name and number. He stared directly ahead, not showing the least nervousness, and Jay wished that he hadn't had to bring him in. He waited impatiently until Kennedy had booked the details and ordered the man taken to a cell.

'Tell Gregson that I want to see him.'

'Take your time,' said the officer easily. 'I told you that he was busy.' He lounged back in his chair. 'Say, you should have waited to see the end of that waste case. The boy got sent to the converter, that was obvious, but Gregson sure pulled a fast one on the old man.' He chuckled. 'He had him tested by Psycho and found out that he'd been lying his head off.'

'What happened?'

'Converter, of course. What else could happen?'

'And the boy?'

'I told you, the same.' Kennedy chuckled again. 'I told you that Gregson knew what he was doing. He's saved someone a job later on.'

'I don't get it,' said Jay. 'If the boy was innocent, then why eliminate him? I can understand the other one – he was an old man and due anyway. But why the boy?'

'Why ask me?' Kennedy shrugged. 'Maybe he was due, too, and it was the easy way out.' He looked up as the inner door opened and a man came into the outer office. 'Here's Merrill. I guess you can go in now.'

Merrill grinned at Jay as he came towards him and rested a hand familiarly on his shoulder.

'Hi, Jay, how's things?'

'Not so good,' Jay didn't like the smooth, lithe, cat-like man with the pale, almost albino eyes and the too-thin mouth. There was something feral about him, a secret gloating and an almost frightening ruthlessness. Jay had often thought that of them all, Merrill was the only one who really liked his job, that he would have done it without the extra privileges and private rooms which all officers had as a matter of right. He shrugged off the other's hand.

'Going somewhere, Jay?'

'To see Gregson. I'd like you to come with me.'

'Me?' Merrill smiled, showing his perfect white teeth. When he smiled like that he reminded Jay more than ever of a tiger – or was it a weasel? From what he remembered, Jay thought that Merrill combined the worse qualities of both.

'Yes.'

'Is it important, Jay? I'm off duty right now and I've an important date down in sector five.' He smiled again at Jay's expression. 'That's right. With a friend of yours. Susan is getting to be a big girl now.'

'Leave Susan alone,' snapped Jay. 'She's still got a year to go before reaching marriageable status.' He looked pointedly at Merrill's unmarked shorts. 'And you don't intend getting married.'

'So what?' Merrill shrugged. 'We can have fun, can't we? Or are you trying to keep her for yourself?'

'Talk like that, you'll get in trouble with Genetics,' warned Jay. 'You've no business getting too friendly with her, anyway; sector five is my unofficial sector, not yours.'

'It's my official one,' reminded Merrill, 'and I like Susan. I like her a lot.'

'I can't blame you for that,' said Jay tightly, 'but leave her alone. There are plenty of women out of marriageable status available if you want that sort of thing. Run around with the over twenty-fives if you have to, but leave the youngsters alone.' He didn't attempt to disguise his disgust. Respect for the marriage code was indoctrinated into all Ship personnel, and casual relationships with girls of marriageable status or younger were firmly discouraged. You married to have children – or else. After the marriageable status, at twenty-five, you were free to do as you liked, but before that it was strictly hands off. Even through his instinctive anger he knew that Merrill was deliberately goading him. If the man ever tried to go against the code, he would be eliminated, and Jay vaguely hoped that if such a thing ever happened he would be the one to get the job.

'Forget it!' Merrill smiled again, this time without humor. 'I was only kidding.'

'Were you?' Jay shook his head. 'Funny, I must be totally devoid of a sense of humor. Somehow I don't find immorality the slightest bit amusing.' He stepped towards the inner office. 'Well? Are you coming?'

'Must I?' Merrill hesitated, his pale eyes watchful. 'What do you want me in there for?'

'Come in and find out,' snapped Jay, opening the door and stepping into the inner office.

As usual, Gregson was alone. He sat at his desk radiating a subtle power and machine-like efficiency. He didn't speak as Jay entered, but his black eyes were thoughtful as he saw Merrill, and he looked at Jay, waiting for him to speak.

'I've got a man outside,' Jay said curtly. 'Edwards, a yeast worker. I had to bring him in.'

'Why?'

'He suspects too much.' Jay looked at Merrill. 'You did a lousy job,' he said bitterly. 'Why don't you use your imagination a little more and your mouth a little less.'

'What!' Merrill seemed to recoil into himself and his pale eyes glittered with anger. 'I'll call you out for that. Damn you, West, you can't talk that way and get away with it. Name the time!'

'There'll be no dueling between officers,' said Gregson coldly. 'Any further such talk and I'll have you both in front of Psycho.' He looked at Jay. 'Report.'

'I was called to a case on level nineteen, room 427, sector three.' He stared at Merrill. 'Your sector.'

'Keep to the point,' snapped Gregson. 'Well?'

'A man, Hans Jensen, had apparently died from accidental touching of electrical circuits.' Jay shrugged. 'That, in itself, was bad enough. A yeast worker messing around with electronics – the thing is incredible! But Merrill's blundering made it even worse.'

'Did it?' said Merrill tightly. 'How?'

'You were seen. Edwards, the man I brought in, swears that he would know you again.'

'That isn't true!' Merrill turned to Gregson. 'I did a neat, quick job, and West can't say otherwise. I –'

'Be silent!' Gregson didn't raise his voice, but the officer choked and bit off what he was going to say. The chief nodded to Jay. 'Start from the beginning.'

'I found Jensen crouched over a removed masking plate. He was charred almost to a crisp; death, of course, was instantaneous. He shared a four-unit room with Edwards, his friend, and they seemed to have been pretty close. Edwards refuses to believe that the death was accidental. He stated that it was murder. I tried to talk him out of it, but he insisted that Jensen just wouldn't have done what he was supposed to have done. Frankly, I don't blame him. The thing was so amateur that it leaves little doubt. If I hadn't known better, I would never have believed that it was Merrill's work.'

'I see.' Gregson stared at Merrill. 'Well?'

'I did the best I could,' said Merrill sullenly. 'Jensen was awkward. I'd tried to call him out a couple of times before, but he avoided dueling. I couldn't get him alone and it was only because I told him that someone was waiting for him that he agreed to come with me at all.'

'Why?' snapped Gregson sharply. 'Did he suspect you?'

'I don't think so. He couldn't have, or he never would have allowed himself to be alone with me.' Merrill gulped as he saw Gregson's expression. 'It's easy enough for West to talk, but he didn't have to do the job. I tell you the man was suspicious, not of me, but of things in general. A lot of these old timers are – they seem to sense that something's going to happen to them.'

'Stop excusing yourself,' said Gregson coldly. 'What happened?'

'I managed to get him to take me to his room. I had to work fast – I guessed that his friend would be looking for him soon – so I knocked him out, tore off the masking plate, and let his hand fall on a live connection. Even at that I had little time. I saw someone coming down the corridor as I left the room.'

'That was Edwards,' said Jay grimly. 'I told you that he had seen you.'

'Well, what of it?' said Merrill defiantly. 'He can't prove anything.'

'Prove anything!' Gregson half-rose from his chair, his eyes hard with cold fury. 'You fool! Haven't you eliminated enough people to learn by now that suspicion of what we are doing is the very thing we must avoid? If this man, this Edwards, is suspicious, then he doesn't need proof! His suspicions are dangerous enough. He will talk, compare notes with others, spread rumors and, before we know it, the whole Ship will guess what is going on.' He sank back into the chair. 'You say that you brought him in, West?'

'Yes, Kennedy booked him and put him into a cell. Suspicion of murder,' Jay shrugged. 'He's innocent, of course, but what else could I do?'

'Nothing. At least you acted as though you had brains and intelligence. I wish that I could say the same about someone else.'

'If you mean me, Gregson, then why don't you say so?' Merrill stepped forward, his pale eyes and thin lips betraying his anger. 'I killed Jensen, didn't I? What more do you want?'

'You eliminated Jensen,' corrected Gregson coldly. 'And I expect a little more than a bungled, amateur job from any of my officers, including you.'

'Bungled?'

'Yes. West is right in what he says. No yeast worker would dare to tamper with electrical installations; that was your first mistake. The other was in allowing yourself to be seen in a compromising position. You have committed the stupidest mistake of all – you have a witness to what you did.'

'That was bad luck.'

'No, there is no such thing as luck in what we have to do. Either you can do your job as it should be done, or you are unfit to hold your position.' Gregson leaned a little forward, his voice falling to a feral purr. 'You know what that means, I take it?'

Merrill did. Jay did. Everyone connected with psych-police did: the officers, the Psycho operator, the rarely seen, almost unknown hierarchy of the Ship. They knew it if no one else did, and it was that knowledge which had to be kept from the people.

Unfit Personnel, Disposal Of: para 1927 of the Ship's Code. Unfit meaning any and everyone who was not wholly capable of doing their job: the ill; the diseased; the barren; the infertile; the neurotic; those that ate too much, who had slow reflexes, who were physically below par, who were mentally unstable. The unnecessary, the unessential, the old. Especially the old.

For someone had to make room for the new generations.

'I …' Merrill swallowed, sweat glistening on his naked torso. 'You wouldn't eliminate me.'

'Why not?' Gregson curved the corners of his mouth in a humorless smile. 'Never make that mistake, Merrill. I'll admit that it isn't easy to select replacements, men who can be trusted to hold the knowledge you have, to turn themselves into merciless eliminators for the common good. But we can do it. We found you and we could find someone to replace you.' Again he gave a thin mockery of a smile. 'We will have to eventually, so why not now?'

'You …' Merrill seemed to shake himself and suddenly he was calm. 'All right then. So you're going to kill me.' He bared his teeth and flexed his hands. 'Let me see you try.'

'You'd fight, of course,' said Gregson calmly, 'but even with your advantage you still couldn't win.' He looked at Jay. 'Would you care to take the assignment?'

'Now?'

'No, not now. Not while he is on his guard and expecting an attack. Later, when he has almost forgotten his danger, when he is asleep, perhaps, or watching an educational tape. Could you do it then?'

'Yes.'

'You see?' Gregson looked at Merrill, something like contempt showing in his eyes. 'You have a strong survival instinct – you need it to be what you are – but we'd get you in the end. No man can stay alert forever, and you'd never be quite sure when it was safe to relax. You have to sleep, you know. Even if you hid out in No-Weight, you'd still have to sleep sometimes. And where would you eat? You'd have to eat, you know, Merrill. And you could never be wholly certain that your food hadn't been tampered with, could you?' He relaxed and smiled at the discomforted officer. 'If Psycho decided that you were unfit and had to be eliminated, then we could do it. You wouldn't be the first officer to meet with an unfortunate "accident" and you wouldn't be the last. We all get our turn.'

'Do we?' Merrill shrugged and stared at Jay. 'Well? Do you want to try now, or wait until later?'

Jay hesitated, wondering just what was in Gregson's mind. The threat was an empty one, he knew that: no victim was ever warned that he was due for elimination; to do so would be to destroy the very secrecy they had sworn to maintain. Merrill was safe, and, knowing the man as he did, Jay knew that he knew it. There were other, deeper reasons for this by-play, and Jay had an uneasy feeling that he knew what they were.

It was never easy to eliminate an officer. For one thing, each man knew his fellow operators, and for another, each had been trained to the ultimate in unarmed combat. Working as they did and being what they were, a sense of comradeship was inevitable. Any group of men sharing a common secret, armed with the knowledge of hidden power, had to have an affinity towards each other; there could always come a time when one man on an assignment would spare his ex-fellow officer.

Unless he had a personal hate against his victim.

Merrill hated Jay, now more than ever, and Jay knew it. He also disliked Merrill and would cheerfully accept the assignment of eliminating him. Was Gregson's entire purpose to forge himself a weapon, one against the other? Jay didn't know but, looking at the hard eyes and ruthless features of the chief, he felt that he had made a pretty shrewd guess. He looked at Merrill.

'I can't answer that until I receive an assignment card,' he said coldly. 'Don't you think this foolishness has gone far enough?'

'Has it?' Merrill looked at Gregson. 'Well?'

'West is right,' said Gregson calmly. 'I only wanted to show you how futile it is for you to get delusions of grandeur – and how easy it is to prick the bubble. You were careless, Merrill. It is the first time, I admit, but the question now is what are we going to do about it?' He looked at Jay. 'Any suggestions?'

'We can confront Merrill with Edwards. If the man recognizes him, we can put Merrill to the test and prove his guilt. Edwards will be satisfied with "justice" and Merrill can go to the converters.' Jay smiled at Merrill's instinctive gesture.

'That is one way,' agreed Gregson quietly. 'We would lose an officer for the sake of a principle, but it might be worth it to kill incipient rumors. Is that your only suggestion?'

'No. The obvious way out of the difficulty is to eliminate Edwards. That was why I brought him in under arrest. No matter what happens now the man will talk, if for no other reason than to prove himself smarter than the officer who investigated the case. Me.' Jay shrugged at Gregson's expression.

'Edwards is an old man, almost forty. He has no friends now that Jensen is dead. He will hardly be missed and soon forgotten. He would be due for elimination soon anyway, so we aren't really going against the code. I can mention to one or two people in the yeast plant where he worked that Edwards killed his friend in a fit of temporary insanity and has been taken away for treatment. They will believe me – no reason for them to do otherwise – and we will have been saved a job for later on.'

'Good,' said Gregson, and Jay knew that he was applauding the prospect of a 'job' saved rather than anything else. Too many incidents would lead to an ingrained distrust and suspicion of the psych-police – the very thing which they wanted to avoid. Such suspicion would make further eliminations even more difficult and in time, would lead to open revolt and the dread specter of mutiny.

'Shall I tell Kennedy to send Edwards to the converters then?' Jay didn't look at Merrill as he spoke and felt annoyed himself for feeling a sense of shame. Gregson nodded.

'Do that. I'll report to Psycho that he has been eliminated and have his card expelled.' He rose and jerked his head in dismissal. 'You've done a good job, West. Merrill, you're off duty I believe. Get out of here and count yourself lucky. But remember this, there won't be a second time. Any more bungling and I'll be looking for a replacement officer. Now get out!'

They didn't speak as they left and Jay was glad of it. He could almost feel the radiated hatred from the pale-eyed man and found difficulty in controlling his own dislike. Silently he watched Merrill stride arrogantly from the office, his sandals slapping against the metal flooring as he thrust his way into the corridor. Then, because he was still on stand-by duty, Jay sat down before one of the screens and pressed the activating button.

The educational tape was one of old-time court procedure as practiced on Earth at the time the Ship had left on its long voyage to Pollux over three centuries ago.

Jay found it faintly amusing.

THREE

Sam Aldway worked in hydroponics and hated every minute of it. He scowled at the ranked vats of nutrient solutions, at the glossy richness of the healthy root-crops he was tending, and savagely pruned any leaf which showed the least hint of browning or of not doing its proper job.

'Take it easy, Sam,' snapped his overseer. 'Cut back too far and you'll do more harm than good.'

'I know what I'm doing,' said Aldway sullenly. He snipped off another leaf. 'Did you put in my transfer?'

'To the psych-police?' The overseer laughed. 'Get wise to yourself, Sam. They won't take you now. You're too old for one thing, and for another, your work is here.'

'I asked you if you'd put in my transfer.'

'I heard you. The answer is no. I didn't put it in because I know that it's a waste of time.'

'I thought so.' Sam dropped his shears and stood, legs straddled, glaring at the older man. 'I've a damn good mind to call you out for that. You put in that request now or you and I will have a date together down in the stadium.'

'You can't make me duel,' said the overseer uncomfortably. 'I don't have to fight you.'

'You're not married, are you?' Sam glared at the other's unmarked brown shorts. 'You're of dueling age, and, if I say so, then you've got to meet me.'

'No I haven't,' said the overseer quickly, 'I can always refer it to the P.P.'

'You think that the psych-police will help you?' Sam deliberately spat on the floor next to the overseer's sandals. 'Why should they want to protect a coward?' He prodded at the overseer's chest with his stiffened forefinger. 'You put in that request for transfer now, understand? Now!'

The older man swallowed, hesitated a moment, then nodded and walked away. He was sweating as he moved to the phone to put in the request. Aldway had the reputation of being a dangerous man; he was still smarting at the blow to his pride at losing his wife who, when he had reached twenty-five and had changed his white-banded shorts for the unmarked ones he would wear for the rest of his life, had shown him the door to their family unit. Protest had been useless, the code was rigidly enforced, and so he had gone into bachelor quarters, sharing with an unsympathetic listener and trying, without much success, to enter into an agreement with one of the available women.

He had taken his revenge against the system by dueling.

The overseer lifted the receiver, punched a number, and listened until a voice spoke from the other end.

'P.P. Headquarters.'

'Overseer Brenson, 14-9741, sector five. I've got a young man here who –'

'Wait a minute. Are you reporting an accident? Hold on then. I'll put you through to the officer in charge of your section.' There was a click, a buzz and then a fresh voice. 'Merrill here. Officer in charge of sector five. What's your trouble?'

'A case of dissatisfaction in hydroponics farm eighteen, sir.' Brenson looked across to where Sam lounged, apparently working, but obviously listening to the conversation. 'Name: Sam Aldway. Cause: wants transfer to P.P. I've tried to tell him that his request won't be entertained, but he won't listen and insists that I put it through.'

'Which generation?'

'Fourteenth, but he's just out of marriageable status.'

'Too old,' said Merrill decisively. 'Tell him that he's wasting his time.'

'I've done that, sir.'

'Then why bother me? You're his boss, aren't you?'

'I'm supposed to be,' said Brenson bitterly, 'but he's a cocky young devil and threatens to call me out.' He hesitated, looking at Sam. 'Could you have a word with him?'

'No,' snapped Merrill. 'Handle it yourself.'

'I can't,' wailed Brenson. 'He's dangerous, I tell you! He's killed at least three men already and I don't want to be the fourth.'

'Afraid of a duel?' The transmitted voice held a sneer. Brenson gulped.

'Yes,' he admitted. 'At least I am with him. I wouldn't stand a chance. He's vicious and fights to the death.'

'Is that so?' Merrill sounded thoughtful. 'A born killer, eh?'

'That's the way it seems,' admitted Brenson. 'I've never met anyone else like him.'

'I see.' The phone hummed silently for a moment. 'Tell you what I'll do. I'll have a talk with him and see if I can't straighten this thing out. Where will he be after duty?'

Brenson cupped his hand over the mouthpiece and yelled to Sam, 'Where will you be after duty?'

'Why?' Sam came closer. 'Who wants to know?'

'Merrill, the P.P. officer. Well?'

'Down in the Gyms, the same place I always go.' Sam came even closer as

Brenson removed his hand and spoke into the phone. 'What's he want me for?'

'He'll be down in the gymnasium,' said Brenson to Merrill.

'Right. I'll probably meet him there. Tell him to expect me.'

'Thank you, sir,' said Brenson fervently. 'Thank you!' But he was speaking into a dead phone.

The gymnasiums were down on the lowest level, together with the maternity wards and kindergartens, the waste reclamation units and recreation rooms. Here, though Sam didn't know it, gravity was twice Earth normal, ideal conditions both for exercise and the rearing of a strong and virile population. To survive at all, the babies had to be strong and with the passing of more than three hundred years the weak and frail-boned had long ago been weeded out.

Sam spent a lot of time in the exercise rooms. He was proud of his smooth, lithe-muscled body, far more efficient than the classical type with its great masses of knotted muscle, its tendency to fat and its high oxygen and nutriment requirements. Ship personnel were all of a slim, graceful, long-muscled type with perfect control and unsuspected strength, the ideal pattern of Man as arrived at by Genetics and the necessity of achieving maximum efficiency with minimum food requirement.

As usual, he started on the punch-bag, driving slamming blows against the plastic to tune up his arms and shoulders. From there he stayed awhile on the pedal-press, thrusting his legs against high-tension springs to develop his thighs, calves and loins. Weights next, and the routine drill for stomach and back.

He was busy at shadow-boxing when he became aware of a pale-eyed man, wearing the black shorts of the psych-police, staring at him.

'Merrill?'

Merrill nodded, staring hard at the young man. 'So you're Aldway, the terror of hydroponics,' he said, and Sam flushed at the hint of a sneer in the cold voice. 'What's the matter, Sam, can't you find anyone better to fight with than old men?'

'Did Brenson tell you that?' Sam lashed out at the punch bag, twisting his fist at the moment of impact and baring his teeth as the heavy, sand-filled container swung away from him. Merrill shook his head.

'Brenson told me nothing I didn't already know.' He steadied the bag. 'I've heard that you fancy yourself as a duelist. Is that right?'

'Could be.' Sam punched the bag again, seeming to take a vicarious satisfaction in punishing the unfeeling plastic. 'Why?'

'How many men have you called out?'

'Five.'

'How many wins?'

'Five. Three dead, the other two were first-time duels.' Despite his air of indifference, Sam couldn't restrain his pride; unconsciously his eyes dropped to the five red spots on the inside of his left arm. Merrill didn't seem impressed.

'Bare hands or weapons?'

'Two with knives, the other three bare-handed.' Sam sounded apologetic. 'Two of the bare-handed combats were first-timers and the ref stopped the bout before I could finish.' He stared at Merrill. 'Why all the questions? I haven't broken the code.'

'Did I say you had?' Merrill looked around the crowded exercise room. 'I hear that you want to join the P.P.'

'That's right.' Sam looked hopefully at the officer. 'Can you get me in? I'm a good man and I'd make a good officer. I –'

'You're too old,' said Merrill flatly, and smiled at the other's expression. 'Ten years ago you might have stood a chance, but not now. You must be at least thirty.'

'Twenty-seven.'

'That's what I said, you're ten years too late. You've been married and had your kids; now you can look forward to a nice tranquil old age in bachelor quarters, tending your plants and filling your educational quota.' Merrill smiled again at Aldway's expression of disgust. 'Or you can keep calling men out until you find one a little better than yourself, in which case you needn't worry about old age – you won't have any.'

'Is that bad?' Sam hit the punch bag as though he were punishing the entire Ship system. 'This is a hell of a life anyway.'

'Maybe we could do something about it?' suggested Merrill softly. He took hold of Sam's arm. 'First, let's eat. I'm hungry.'

As an officer Merrill was entitled to eat in any mess he happened to choose, but Sam had to go to his sector's mess and show his identity disc. The meal, as usual, was hydroponic vegetables with yeast as the staple, well-disguised and with a choice of three main dishes. Merrill chose lemon sole, Aldway fillet of steak, neither fancying the roast chicken. The food was the same, different only in shape and flavor, but the dietitians had long known that variety was essential for good health and appetite. Both men ate as fit men should eat, with hungry zest and applied concentration. Merrill finished the last of his sweet, synthetic ice cream – small in bulk but rich in protein and carbohydrates – and sat back, toying with his ration of brackish water and waiting for his companion to finish his meal.

'Lousy food,' Sam commented, wiping his mouth on the back of his hand. 'No fresh fruits – and we grow any amount of them in hydroponics. Where do they all go to, that's what I'd like to know?'

Merrill could have told him where they went, where Sam knew they went had he but exercised his memory. To the very young, the nursing and expectant mothers, to the growing generations who needed the fresh, natural vitamins more than did the adult population. He didn't bother to explain.

'You said something,' reminded Sam hopefully. He swallowed his water ration and tossed the plastic cup into the disposal basket. 'Did you mean it?'

'That depends.' Merrill sipped his own water, his eyes watchful over the rim of the cup. 'How badly do you want to break out of the rut?'

'Bad enough to do anything,' said Sam tensely. 'Waste! If I don't do something soon I'll go crazy and be carried off for treatment.' He stared at Merrill. 'Look, I don't care what I do. I'll do anything you want me to, just so long as you get me away from that damn farm. I'll work in No-Weight, I'll give you half my rations – anything. You name it, I'll do it. I mean it, Merrill. Anything!'

'I think you do,' said Merrill quietly, and his pale eyes were thoughtful as he examined the man at his side. Though Sam didn't know it, he had literally signed his own death warrant. The Ship could not tolerate any unbalanced individual and, if Merrill reported the conversation as he should do, Sam would be eliminated. Even his dueling propensities, while of value in helping to keep down the older section of the population, meant little against the potential danger of his neurosis. Such a man was fully capable of hitting back in many ways against a system he imagined had hurt him. He could deliberately waste essential material, ruin an entire crop by carelessness, spread alarm and despondency by whispered rumors or, as he was already doing, cause unrest and fear by his arrogance.

Sam had to die.

But how and when he died was something else.

Merrill finished his water, threw the cup into the basket and rose to his feet. Sam rose with him, his eyes asking questions, but it wasn't until they were outside the mess that Merrill spoke.

'You want to join the psych-police, right?'

'Yes.'

'Well, you can't and you may as well know it.' Merrill was deliberately blunt. 'That is you can never become a uniformed member of the P.P., but ...' He let his voice fade into silence, waiting for the fish to gulp the bait.

'Any job will do,' pleaded Aldway. 'I don't care about the uniform.' He lied and Merrill knew it. 'Can't I be your assistant, or something?'

And there it was. The driving complex which demanded authority, no matter how little or how disguised. The crying need for power at any price, the desire to swagger and rule, to be dominant and boastful. Merrill had no delusions as to what would happen if he made Sam his assistant. At first the man might live up to his promises; then, inevitably, he would need to show off, to display his powers to advertise his arrogance. Not if he lived to Journey's End, would he ever learn how to use authority but Merrill knew that Sam wouldn't live anywhere near that long.

He pretended to consider the suggestion, hooding his eyes as if he were deep in thought. Finally he nodded as if coming to a decision.

'You'll take me!' Sam looked as though he could kiss the metal at their feet. 'You'll give me a job away from the farm?'

'Not so fast. I've already got an assistant and I can't have two.' Merrill almost smiled at Sam's expression. 'You'll have to wait until I can get rid of him.'

'Oh.' Sam gulped, his rosy dreams vanishing as soon as they had come. 'How long will that be?'

'Who knows? I don't like the man, but I can hardly call him out – dueling isn't allowed for officers – and no one else is likely to do it.' Merrill paused, waiting for Sam to make the obvious offer. 'No, Sam, I don't think that you're good enough.'

'You don't think so?' Sam flexed his muscles. 'I'm fit and I'm trained. I can snap a man's neck like a stick and I know all the holds.' He held out his left arm. 'You think I collected these by imagination? Show me who it is and let me at him.'

'He's not a dueling man, Sam. It'll be a first bout and the ref will stop any killing.'

'If he gets the chance. I've learned a trick or two since I started and I can move faster than any damn ref.' Sam gripped Merrill's arm. 'Just show me who it is, boss, that's all I ask. Just give me the chance to get him out of the way.'

'You think that you could do it?' Merrill hesitated as though in doubt. 'He's pretty well trained and you might not find it easy – he could kill you, you know. It wouldn't be your first time in the stadium, and if you killed him you'd have to make it look like a real accident. You sure that you could do it?'

'Give me the chance,' repeated Sam. 'That's all I ask.'

'Right, but there's something I'm going to do before you call him out.' Merrill smiled into the wondering face of his dupe. 'I'm going to take you to the exercise rooms and we're going to have a fight.'

'Fight?' Sam stepped back, his eyes reflecting his bewilderment. 'Why?'

Merrill didn't answer; he was already leading the way towards the lowest level.

FOUR

George Curtway looked up at a knock on the door, leaned forward to switch off the view, and straightened just in time to be kissed by a raven-haired young woman.

'Susan!' He smiled at his daughter as she settled herself in a chair. 'You're early.'

'We got all the young devils topped and tailed and settled down, and Matron said that I could end-shifts early as we'd all worked so hard.' Susan paused to draw a deep breath. 'My! I must be getting old. I hardly ran at all on the way up.' She looked towards the viewer. 'What's showing?'

'Some old tapes from Earth. Animals and farming scenes.'

'Young animals?'

'Don't you get enough young animals working in maternity?' He smiled with parental pride at her neat figure in the form-fitting pink halter and shorts. She made a face and leaned forward to switch on the screen.

'Babies aren't animals.'

'What else are they?' He didn't look at the screen as it flared to life with the transmitted images from central control. 'A baby is as much an animal as …' he glanced at the screen, 'as that young goat there, or is it a lamb?'

'No idea.' She smiled at him. 'Anyway, babies are far more interesting than a lot of silly old animals we'll probably never even see.'

'We will one day, Susan. When the Ship reaches Journey's End, we'll have to know all about animals and everything else.'

'Perhaps, but until then I'll worry about babies.' She looked at the images for a moment then, her youthful exuberance overcoming her patience, interrupted her father's viewing again. 'Fred's not here yet?'

'Can you see him?' George stared around the stark simplicity of the tiny room. Susan flushed.

'Sorry, that was a stupid remark.' She hesitated. 'Have you seen anything of Jay lately?'

'No.' Something in George's voice made her look at him. George didn't return her look; he sat, staring at the pictured scene, his mouth set with unusual firmness.

'What's the matter, Dad? Don't you like Jay?'

'Jay's okay, but don't get too involved with him, Susan.'

'Why not?' She leaned forward and switched off the viewer. 'That's better, now you can answer me. What's wrong with Jay?'

'Nothing.' He reached for the switch and she caught his hand. 'What you are trying to do, girl?' he said with mock severity. 'If I don't fill my educational quota I'll be downgraded and lose the privilege of having a single room. Would you like to visit me in a common recreational chamber?'

'They won't downgrade you, and you must have seen those tapes so often that you know them by heart.' She moved so that she sat in front of the screen. 'Now, answer me. What is wrong with Jay?'

'Nothing.'

'Yes there is or you wouldn't look like that.' She became serious. 'I want an answer, dad.'

'Jay's fifteenth generation,' he said reluctantly. 'You're sixteenth and almost of marriageable status. You know that you can't marry Jay.'

'Why not?'

'Because he's too old for one thing and Genetics would never allow it for another. Now are you satisfied?'

'No. Jay's a young man and I can't see anything to stop us getting married.'

'Then you're either a fool or you're just plain stubborn – and I know that you're not a fool.' George smiled at his daughter. 'Just supposing that you were allowed to marry Jay. He's about twenty-one or twenty-two and you're only seventeen. By the time you're ready for marriage he'll be a year older. That means that he's only got two or three years of marriageable status while you'll have seven. That's not even long enough for you to have your two children and certainly not long enough for you to be together in family quarters.' He touched her hair, letting his hand caress her short curls. 'After you're twenty-five you can do as you like, but until then you'll have to let Genetics decide. After all, you want children, don't you?'

She didn't blush – there was no such thing as false modesty in the Ship – but he read his answer in her eyes. Every female on board wanted children, as many as possible, and as soon as they had reached optimum childbearing age, Susan was no different from any other woman of her age group, and her decision to work in maternity showed that she was normally healthy and had a strong survival instinct. Though she didn't know it, the betting was high in her favor among her overseers that she would be allowed to have more than the usual two children.

She looked up as the door opened and Fred, her brother, came towards them. Fred was twenty and still proud of his white-banded shorts. He looked at Susan and smiled with the superior knowledge of a two-year married man.

'Hi, youngster. Dried your ears yet?'

He ducked as she swung at him, a little clumsy at having come down from the low-gravity levels and not having had time to become accustomed to the Earth normal on the twentieth level. George watched them for a while; then, reaching out, he slapped Susan's rear and pulled her away.

'Give him a rest, Susan. He's an old married man now and not what he used to be.'

They all laughed.

'Had a hard one this shift,' said Fred, sitting next to his sister on the narrow bench. 'Water condensed in a conduit and caused a short. Some of the fans went out and the air wasn't circulating.' He chuckled. 'You should have heard those gardeners! To hear them talk you'd think that they ran the Ship.' Like his father Fred was in electronics.

'They do in a way, you know,' said George quietly. 'If it wasn't for the gardens we'd have no fresh air. Any idea what caused the short?'

'I told you, water condensed in a conduit.'

'Yes, but how? Those conduits are supposed to be waterproof and anyway, even if water did permeate, it shouldn't have caused a blow-out.'

'That's true,' said Fred thoughtfully. 'It shouldn't, should it?'

'Was the insulation bad? Damaged in any way? Frayed or worn?' George frowned at his son's hesitation. 'Come on, son. It isn't enough just to repair the fault; you've got to find out what caused it in the first place and make sure that it doesn't happen again.'

'I know that,' snapped Fred testily. 'You don't have to teach me primary electronics. It's just that I've never thought of the Ship being at fault at all.'

'It's at fault all right,' said George grimly. 'I've found that out in my own work often enough. Cracked insulation and corroded metal. Warped conduits and crystallized unions. Intermittent shorts and erratic current flow. Naturally,' he said bitterly, 'the atomic engineers won't admit that their piles are at fault. No, it's always our equipment – and yet I know for a fact that their generators are falling in efficiency. Why even Psy –' He broke off, biting his lips.

'What's that, dad?' Fred leaned forward, curiosity large on his expressive features. 'You said something about Psycho?'

'No I didn't.'

'You started to. What was it?'

'Nothing. Forget it.'

'But I want to know, dad,' insisted Fred. 'Maybe I'll be able to service the admin equipment one day and anything you can tell me now will help my promotion later on. What was it you were saying about Psycho?'

'I told you to forget it,' snapped George sharply. 'Remember your manners and decent behavior. Unwanted curiosity is as bad as a violation of declared privacy.' He glared at his son for a moment, then he relaxed as Susan touched his hand. 'What is it?'

'Why should you be having all this trouble with the electronic equipment?' she asked with a woman's instinctive knowledge of when to change the subject. 'Was it always as bad as this?'

'I can't see how it could have been,' said George. 'Even the educational tapes are showing signs of wear; some of them are quite blurred, and others that I remember don't seem to be shown at all now.'

'And are there more shorts and things?'

'Yes, but we can expect that. The Ship is old; you're the sixteenth generation to be born in it, and that is a long time. Things wear, Susan, and grow old just like people do. Insulation dries out and cracks, moisture condenses in those cracks and corrodes the metal. Deposits build and the alloys transmute a little. Capacities vary, resistances alter a trifle, cables can't carry such a big load as they used to.' George shrugged. 'It all adds up to a great big headache for the electricians.'

'Does age do all that?' Susan looked scared. 'If that's happening now, then what about later? We're still a long way from Journey's End, aren't we?'

'I suppose so,' said George, 'but it isn't only age that's the trouble.' He rested his hand against the wall. 'Here, put your hand close to mine. Feel it?'

'Feel what?' Susan frowned as she tried to concentrate. 'It just feels like a normal wall to me.'

'Forget the metal. Imagine that you're listening with your finger tips instead of your ears. Now do you feel it?'

'No, I ...' Susan laughed. 'Now I see what you mean. The vibration. But it's been here all the time – it's always been there.'

'Yes,' said George quietly. 'Every atom of the Ship is vibrating and has done for a long time now. Those vibrations are part of the trouble. Metal tends to crystallize when vibrated for too long and the harmonics can play waste with the insulation.' He shrugged. 'Nothing we can do about it, of course, but I thought that Fred might like to know.' He stretched, his well-kept muscles rippling beneath his satin skin. 'Well, children, anything else an old man could tell you?'

'You're not old,' protested Susan. 'You're only fourteenth generation after all.' She began to count on her fingers. 'Let me see now. I'm seventeen and sixteenth, so you must be –'

'Anything between fifty-seven and thirty-seven.' George shrugged. 'I'm thirty-nine if you must know, and there aren't many men my age still working.' He grinned at his son. I attribute old age to a firm resolve never to duel. A resolution I suggest you strictly follow, both of you. Personally, I've never seen the sense in two, apparently normal people, battering or cutting each other to death for the sake of an imagined insult.'

'Suppose someone calls you a waster,' suggested Fred. 'Sure you wouldn't stand an insult like that without doing something about it?'

'Look, son,' said George seriously. 'Never mind what they call you. If a man is low enough to accuse you of waste, call in the psych-police and ask him to prove it. No one has to stand that kind of language but there are other ways of settling it without risking your neck.' He looked at his daughter. 'That goes for you too, Susan. You're not in any danger now, either of you, but later you may be. I've seen quite innocent people fall victims to some puffed-up bully with a knack of getting under the skin, and women can be the worst offenders when they think a pretty, newly-available woman is cutting in on their boyfriends. Stay well away from it, and let the fools fight. There's no conservation in getting yourself killed for a public show.'

'You talk like an old man giving his children some final advice,' laughed Susan. 'We'll depend on you to keep us out of trouble.'

'Don't do that,' said George seriously. 'Never rely on anyone but yourselves.'

'Not even the psych-police?' Fred looked knowingly at Susan. 'The officer can be very helpful at times.'

'Why?' George stared at his daughter's flushed face. 'Has Merrill been bothering you again?'

'No, dad. Fred's only joking.' She glared at her brother and signaled to him to keep quiet. 'He's dropped by maternity a time or two, and we may have eaten together, but there's nothing in it. Merrill isn't marriageable, no P.P. officer is – you know that.'

'Maybe not, but I don't trust that man and I'd rather you didn't see him.' George shook his head as if dismissing an unpleasant subject. 'Looks as if Jay won't be coming this time.' He looked at Susan again. 'Maybe it's just as well.'

'Jay isn't bad,' defended Fred. 'I like him, even though I wouldn't like his job. Must be rotten for him to have to keep crawling through the ventilation shafts.' He smiled down at his own blue shorts. 'I'm glad I'm not in ventilation. Give me electronics every time!'

'If you didn't like it you wouldn't be doing it,' reminded George. He leaned forward and switched on the viewer. 'Let's see what's on.'

The screen blurred then steadied into a schematic of dismantled wiring and tiny transistors. Together with the diagram, a smoothly modulated voice coupled with lines of running text explained what each piece was, how it operated, its purpose and the methods of construction and repair. George leaned forward with professional interest, but Fred grunted with disgust.

'Waste! Who wants homework? Let's find some entertainment.'

He reached forward for the change switch.

FIVE

The dream was always the same. He was dead and they had taken him to the converter. The grim men in olive had collected him in their plastic bag and delivered him at the place where the last indignities would be carried out with cold, scientific detachment. They would render him down. They would extract the last droplet of moisture from his blood and body, grind his bones to fertilizer, process his flesh and tissue, his skin, his internal organs. Medical students would cut and probe as they learned their trade, and when they had finished, his outraged body would be used down to the last scraping of protoplasm.

On the Ship there could be no waste and they would return him to the dust and chemicals from which he had sprung. They would reclaim everything he had used other than the energy he had needed and expended to stay alive. All of him. Every last, tiny fragment that had walked and talked, hoped and planned, loved and dreamed. All except the still unknown, wholly intangible mesh of electricity which made him peculiarly different from all others. The ego, the essential 'I was,' the one thing the surgeons and the butchers could never hope to save.

And with its loss he would be as though he had never existed.

Gregson muttered as he turned and when he awoke his face and torso were damp with sweat. He lay for awhile, staring into the soft darkness of his room, sensing rather than actually feeling the susurration of trapped sound that was the life noise of the Ship. He liked the darkness. There was too little of it and, only when he had closed himself in, could he switch off the lights and sit and think and plan and dream. There were no polished bulkheads in the dark, no mirrors, no wondering expressions and doubtful eyes. No men to stare and women to question. No passing of time or hate or envy or fear.

As usual at such times, he sought escape from the present into the past, letting his memory scuttle down the years back to the time when he was very young and life was something which would go on forever. His childhood was spent in a family unit with parents who remained together because of the code and not through love. He had left them, as all children left their parents, when he was twelve. Long before that his father had gone, and his mother was impatient for her release so that she could enter into a new, though essentially barren union with the man of her choice.

Youth. He smiled as he thought of it, a humorless quirking of the lips, unseen even by himself in the soft, trembling darkness which was the only night he had ever known. Schooling, always schooling and exercise and training. The psychological tests, the aptitude examinations and always the educational tapes at every leisure moment of every shift. The slow climb from manual worker status to administration; from administration to the coveted psych-police; from an officer to chief of P.P., from a nonentity to one of the select hierarchy; from a unit to a controller; from being helpless to being in a position to …

He stirred, fighting the thought, and switched on the lights, blinking for a moment as his eyes adapted to the glare. He rose, slipping from the pneumatic pallet with virile litheness, and stood for a moment, stretching and flexing his muscles, watching the reflected image of his naked figure in the clean surface of the metal wall. Then he shrugged and stepped towards his private shower.

The mist spray was hot, the lather quick to spring from his moistened body, and the following ten-second, ice-cold needle shower stung his flesh to full awareness. Still naked, he stepped from the warm-air blast and, as the droning current dried his body, stared hard at his reflection in the mirror. Vaguely he regretted that it was impossible to grow a beard and frowned as he examined his thick, short black hair. He turned as the attention call from the phone sounded above the soft whine of the dryer.

Still naked he walked into the other room and picked up the handset.

'Yes?'

'Gregson?'

'Who else would it be? What do you want?'

'Quentin speaking.' There was a cold disapproval in the Captain's voice. 'I tried to get you at P.P. Headquarters.'

'I was off-shift and getting some sleep.' Gregson didn't alter his tone. 'I trust that this violation of privacy is important?'

'A psych-police officer is never private, you should know that.' Gregson bared his teeth as the Captain's voice echoed against his ear. 'Come up to the Bridge at once.'

'Can't it wait? I've a lot of routine stuff to get through and I'm supposed to be meeting Conway at Psycho.'

'Conway is here with me,' snapped the Captain. 'I'll expect you immediately.' The phone went dead with a decisive click and Gregson swore as he replaced the receiver.

The Captain was the oldest man aboard the Ship. Almost legendary, seen only by the hierarchy, a vague and, because of that, all the more impressive figure to the people, he lived in splendid isolation in his private apartment high towards No-Weight. Gregson knew him, and Conway, and Henderly the chief medical officer, but as far as Gregson knew, that was all.

The chief of psych-police stepped forward as the outer door opened, crossed the spacious room with long, easy strides, and took his place at the table without doing more than nod to the others present.

'Well, gentlemen, what's so important that you couldn't tell me over the phone?'

'I don't always trust the communication system of the Ship,' snapped the Captain. 'It isn't beyond the realms of possibility that some electronic engineer may have tapped the wires.'

'You think that?' Gregson leaned back and smiled towards the other two. Quentin leaned forward, his harsh, thin features stern and contemptuous beneath his mass of graying hair.

'You think that I'm a fool, Gregson?'

'No, but the suggestion is ridiculous,'

'Is it? Would you be surprised to learn that that very thing happened some forty years ago?' He stared at the dark-haired man sitting opposite. 'That, of course, would be before your time, but what has happened once could easily happen again.'

'I'm sorry,' said Gregson quietly. 'I keep forgetting that you are *old!*'

There was contempt in the way he said it but, beneath that contempt was a sick envy and the basic cause of his dislike for the Captain. Quentin was old, at least thirteenth generation, but, because he was the Captain and because it was essential to have at least one man who could take a long-term view of the Ship and its purposes the captains were always allowed to grow old.

'I'll ignore that remark,' said Quentin quietly, 'because I know what activated it. But at the same time I must ask you to remember who and what I am. I am the Captain, you are only the chief of psych-police.' The inference was obvious and Gregson bit his lips as he fought down his rage. Quentin picked up a thin, almost transparent sheet of paper from the table, glanced at it for a moment, then looked at the others.

'There was a Barb raid on the farming section of sector four,' he said flatly. 'As yet the news hasn't been allowed to disseminate and I trust that the occurrence will be kept as secret as possible.' He looked at Gregson. 'That is your job.'

'When did this raid take place?'

'Just before I called you – while you were asleep.' The taunt was unjustified and both Gregson and the Captain knew it. 'It was a small raid, three men and a woman, but it proves that the Barb menace isn't to be ignored as you gentlemen,' Quentin looked at Conway, 'have recommended.'

'I still recommend it,' said Conway. 'The Barbs are only a few discontented people who managed to evade elimination, and as they are all barren they will eventually die out from either starvation or natural death.'

'Is that correct, Henderly?'

'Broadly, yes.' The medical officer cleared his throat as he answered the Captain. 'They are sterile, of course – everyone is over twenty-five – and they were old to begin with. Food, naturally, is their biggest problem. I have based my recommendation for the policy of ignoring them, on the twin factors of starvation and cannibalism.' He shrugged. 'They are hungry – so they must eat. We guard the messes – so they are forced to eat each other. That leads to mutual fear and, eventually, mutual destruction.'

'The psychological factors also lead me to agree with the existing policy,' said Conway importantly. 'Conditioned as they are to Ship procedure, their sense of guilt at betraying their own will lead to mental unrest and illogical behavior patterns. This, of course, will tend to disrupt their precarious social structure ... if they have one, which I doubt.'

'They raided sector four,' reminded Quentin. 'That shows that they have learned to work together.'

'To a limited degree,' admitted Conway, 'but to me it is a sign that Henderly's summary of our policy is working.' He glanced towards Gregson. 'Do you agree?'

'They should be exterminated,' said Gregson flatly. He spoke again before the others could protest. 'I know all the arguments for and against and I know that we can't conduct a full-scale search and massacre in No-Weight without betraying the existence of the Barbs to the people.' He shrugged. 'I don't determine the policy of the Ship, I only carry it out, but I say that they should be exterminated.'

'Easier said than done,' commented Quentin dryly. 'Have you any suggestions as to how they could be eliminated without betraying their existence to the people?'

'Poisoned food? We could allow them to steal some yeast loaded with toxins or something. Henderly would know about that.'

'Impracticable,' snapped the medical officer. 'To begin with they would be suspicious of any food left for them to find. For another it would be waste.' He snorted. 'Your suggestion is ridiculous!'

'No suggestion is ridiculous,' said Quentin sharply. He looked at Gregson. 'Have you any others?'

'No. As I told you, I have nothing to do with policy. I only carry out your orders.'

'I see.' Quentin looked again at the papers on his table. 'As you feel like that, Gregson, there is no apparent reason for me to keep you longer away from your duties. I'll notify you as to my decisions later.' He looked up in dismissal and Gregson felt his cheeks begin to burn in rage.

'Are you suggesting that I am not fit to sit in Council?'

'I suggest nothing – except that you are undoubtedly a busy man.' There was mockery in the way Quentin stared at the officer, mockery and a hint of something else, something cold and calculating. Gregson saw it, guessed what was happening, and restrained himself in time.

'I must remind you that I have but five officers to control a thousand times their number,' he said quietly. 'We have no weapons and must operate by stealth. I suggest that you gentlemen consider that in any plans you may choose to make.' He stepped away from the table. 'I will appreciate an early decision.'

'A moment.' Quentin fumbled among his papers, his thin hands a startling contrast to the youthful ones of the other men, and found a scrap of paper covered with close-set typescript. 'This belongs in your department.'

'What is it?' Gregson glanced down the paper, frowning as he followed the unfamiliar words, his lips moving with the unaccustomed exercise of reading. 'Is it important?'

'No.' Quentin took the sheet and scanned it with experienced eyes. 'An electronic engineer requests a personal interview with reference to Psycho.' The Captain shrugged. 'He refuses to state the nature of his business and remains so vague as to be almost incomprehensible.'

'Psycho?' Gregson stepped forward and took the paper, thrusting it into the top of his shorts. 'Something wrong?'

'Not that I know of,' said Conway sharply. He was jealous of his position as chief of Psycho. He looked at the Captain. 'Why wasn't I informed of this?'

'You will be,' promised Gregson calmly. 'Just as soon as I've interviewed the man and decided whether he's psychotic or sincere.'

'That's for me to decide.'

'No. The psych-police are the ones to handle it, and besides,' Gregson allowed himself the luxury of sarcasm, 'you must be far too busy to bother with such trivial complaints.' He glanced from Conway's angry face to the calm one of the Captain. 'You want me to handle this?'

'Naturally,' snapped Quentin impatiently. 'I've quite enough to do now that the Barbs have taken to raiding without worrying about some low-grade worker who probably thinks that he can improve on the builders. Paper should never have been wasted on forwarding his request; there are proper channels in case of need.'

'May I see the request?' Conway half-rose, his hand extended, then sat back as the chief of psych-police stepped towards the door. 'Gregson! Didn't you hear me? I want to see that request.'

'You heard what the Captain said, Conway.' Gregson paused by the door, his eyes insolent as he looked at the psychologist. 'Must I remind you again that I am a busy man?' He smiled. 'I'll leave you gentlemen to discuss the Barbs while I attend to my duties.'

He left them staring at the closing door.

SIX

Susan chuckled as she missed the medicine ball and watched it roll heavily into a corner. 'One up for you, Jay – but it isn't fair, you've more muscle than I have.'

'Have I?' Jay smiled down at her, his admiration for her trim perfection apparent in his eyes. 'Want to try something else then?'

'Yes.' She looked thoughtfully at him, trying not to admire his youthful grace. 'Let me see now, you're in ventilation and that means you spend a lot of time up in low gravity.' She smiled. 'I know! Let's play dueling!'

'No.'

'Why not? We can wear masks and jackets and use foils, or the practice knives if you prefer them.' She smiled at his hesitation. 'Come on, Jay. At least I don't want to try any barehanded stuff with you – I wouldn't stand a chance.'

'I wouldn't say that,' he said, meeting her mood, then sobered again as he stared at her. 'Why do you want to play at dueling?'

'Why?' She shrugged. 'Why not? At least it may come in handy one day when I'm an old, unwanted woman. I may even have to fight a newcomer for my boyfriend.' She stepped closer to him. 'Will you be my boyfriend, Jay?'

'Stop it!' he said harshly. 'You don't know what you're saying.'

'Oh yes I do, Jay. I'm not a child any more and I know all about the facts of life. Next year I get married to someone approved by Genetics. I'll have children and we'll live in a family unit until I'm twenty-five, or maybe longer depending on how I like my husband. Then I'm free to do as I like.' She smiled at him, naked invitation in her soft brown eyes. 'Will you wait for me, Jay?'

'No.'

'Why not?' She touched his arm. 'You're not married, or at least you don't wear the banded shorts like Fred does, so what's to stop us making an agreement when I'm of age? Don't you like me, Jay?'

'You know damn well I like you.'

'You don't have to swear at me then.' She dropped her hand from his arm and stood, a sulky expression on her face, her foot tracing designs on the padded floor of the exercise room. 'Is there someone else?'

'No.'

'Are you sure, Jay?' She hesitated. 'If there is, well, I know that I shouldn't say anything, but …' She bit her lip. 'Waste! Why are we talking like this?'

'No reason at all,' he said cheerfully. 'Here!' He threw her the ball. She caught it, an automatic reflex action, then flung it petulantly aside. 'I don't want to play anymore. Let's talk.'

'All right then,' he looked around at the crowded room. 'Here?'

'No. Let's find an unoccupied rec-room.' Before he could protest she had seized his arm and was leading him out into the corridor and up towards the next level where the common cubicles were. The fourth one she tried was empty and she switched on the light, closing the door and swinging over the 'engaged' indicator.

'There!' She sat down and smiled at him. 'Now we can really be alone.'

'You're crazy,' he said dispassionately. He stood by the door, staring down at her, noting her flushed features, glistening eyes and moist lips. 'You're playing with fire and don't know that you might be burned.'

'You won't burn me,' she said confidently. 'Jay, why be so cold? You know how I feel about you.'

'I know how you think you feel,' he corrected. He sat down, keeping well away from her, and a little muscle high on one cheek twitched as he fought to control his emotions. 'Look, Susan,' he said seriously. 'You don't want me to break the code, and you don't want to break it either. You're going to be married soon – why not wait until then?'

'But I'm not going to be able to marry you,' she said irritably. 'Why must you be so blind, Jay. You know what I want.'

'You want me to make love to you,' he stated. 'You're young and healthy and it's a perfectly natural reaction. But youthful immorality isn't a good thing. Susan, and you know it. Time enough for that when you've had your children and are out of marriageable status. You know what could happen if you were to have a child before your time?'

'Genetics would be annoyed,' she said defiantly. 'So what?'

'So the child would be aborted, I'd be punished for infringing the code, and you might lose the chance of having an approved child.' He shook his head. 'No, Susan, we daren't do it.'

He was right, of course, and both of them knew it. A strong race cannot be an immoral race, not when excess would tend to weaken the very hope of the new generation. Shame was unknown on the Ship, but indoctrination had set up a rigid code which no one in his right mind would think of transgressing. The trouble was that young people in love are seldom in their right mind.

'You talk just like father,' Susan said bitterly. 'All about what I should and should not do, but never a word about what I'd like to do.' She turned to him, very young and very lovely. 'Oh, Jay! How can you ask me to wait so long?'

'We must.' He stood up out of reach of her outstretched hands. 'What did your father say about me?'

'The usual.' She was annoyed with him for changing the subject and, woman-like, annoyed too that he hadn't found her attractions irresistible to logic and good sense. 'He says that you're too old for me and that I should settle down to being a good wife and mother to some young dolt I haven't even seen yet.'

'You'll see him soon,' promised Jay. 'You youngsters are thrown together when you near marriageable status. You might even go to another sector, or the boys be brought here.' He smiled at her expression. 'Don't worry, you know that you'll be able to take a choice; you won't be limited to one.'

'But supposing they send me out of the sector!' She rose and stepped towards him, her arms circling his neck, her lips hungry for his. 'Jay! What if I don't see you again!'

He didn't like to think about it. He didn't like to think about anything, not when she was so near to him and every atom of his body was crying out for her. His life was a lonely one; a marriageless though not a celibate state was a requirement of the psych-police, and he found little interest in the casual relationships which Merrill favored so much.

And he was in love with Susan.

The speakers saved him. They crackled into life and a voice, cold and emotionless, repeated his code number over and over again, sounding in every room for every sector, demanding and urgent.

'X112 … X112 … X112 …'

'That's my number.' Jay hesitated a moment; then, his indoctrination overcoming his natural desires, gently unfolded her arms from about his neck. 'I must go, Susan. They want me to report in immediately.'

'Must you?' She clung to him again. 'Don't go yet, Jay.'

'I must.' He moved away from her. 'That's my emergency call. Something's wrong and they want me.'

'Waste!' She stepped back, her eyes hungry as they searched his face. 'Can't they do without you just for this once?'

'They wouldn't be calling me if they could.' He held out his hand. 'Goodbye, Susan.'

'Goodbye?' She frowned and, stepping close to him, gripped his arm so hard that her fingers dug into his flesh. 'Do you love me, Jay?'

'I must report in.' He moved towards the door, then hesitated as she dragged at his arm.

'I asked you a question, Jay. Do you love me?'

He didn't answer. He stared at her, afraid to say the words which came so naturally to his lips for fear of what they could bring, and yet more afraid to lie. He swallowed, shook off her arm and stepped out into the corridor, leaving the door of the rec-room swinging wide.

The call was, as he expected, from headquarters and the public voice fell into silence as he contacted the desk.

'West reporting. What's the trouble?'

'No trouble,' said Carter, the officer on stand-by duty. 'Gregson wants you. Routine job I think, but you'd better get back fast – he's flaming.'

'Let him flame,' snapped Jay disrespectfully. 'I'll be there as soon as I can and not a second before.' He heard Carter chuckle as he hung up the receiver. The trip up to low gravity didn't take long and his red, ventilation engineer's shorts passed by through the guarded doors towards No-Weight. This was a part of the Ship which was little used. The circumference was too small for spacious rooms, and the gravity too low for real comfort. Here were the stores, the huge water containers, the massive ventilation pipes and power conduits. They lay all around the odd, no-man's-land of No-Weight, the central axis which in effect was a hollow tube filled with a tangled mass of girders and stanchions, struts and braces, the pivot of the Ship around which the rest swung.

Jay passed quickly down a long corridor running parallel to No-Weight, kicking with practiced ease at the metal walls as he glided along, careful not to impart too high a velocity to his body. Men had died through failing to take that precaution. They had forgotten that, while they were apparently weightless, they still had mass. Mass has inertia and inertia had caused splintered bones and crushed skulls as bodies, moving too fast, had collided against the unyielding structure of the Ship.

Before leaving the communicating tube, Jay reversed his shorts and, dressed again in his official uniform, passed the guard and moved down into sector three. Rapidly he made his way down the levels, past the gardens, the farms, the residential cubicles, along the corn-tube and into P.P. headquarters.

Gregson was waiting for him when he arrived.

The chief looked up from his desk as Jay entered, gestured to a seat, and continued to leaf through a batch of reports. He read slowly, biting his lips with impatience as he scanned the thin, erasable plastic sheets. 'Why can't they put this stuff on audible tape?' he asked no one in particular.

Jay shrugged, not answering and guessing that Gregson didn't really want a reply. 'You sent for me?'

'Yes. What kept you so long?'

'I was in sector five on unofficial duty.'

'I know. Merrill called in and reported seeing you.' Gregson stared at the young man. 'He seemed worried, said something about a young girl you took to a rec-room.'

'Did he?' Jay shifted a little beneath Gregson's stare, half-annoyed at himself for feeling a sense of guilt.

'Merrill wants to mind his own business.'

'It is his business. As official officer of the sector, it's his duty to safeguard the young. How serious is it?'

'Not serious at all. Forget it.'

'You certain about that? Sometimes these things get out of hand and you know the penalties for breaking the code when it comes to a thing like that.'

'You don't have to tell me the code,' snapped Jay irritably. 'I've said that you can forget it. It's all over. I doubt if I'll ever see her again.'

'I hope that you mean that,' said Gregson seriously. 'I can protect my officers to some extent, but no one can protect you from Genetics if they bring an immorality charge. It means being referred to Psycho. With anyone else it could mean just a downgrading, but with you …' Gregson made an expressive gesture with the edge of his hand and Jay knew exactly what he meant. Psych-Police officers couldn't be down-graded; they knew too much, and that left elimination as the only possible punishment. He swallowed.

'It's finished. I mean it.'

'I know how you feel,' Gregson said with unusual sympathy. 'You're young, she's young, and that's as far as you think.' He hesitated. 'Do you want a transfer to another sector? I could switch you with Norton if you like.'

'No thanks, it won't be necessary. I know the people in sector five and can work more efficiently there.' He looked at his chief. 'Is that what you called me in to tell me?'

'No.'

'Then?'

'Merrill phoned in after your call went out and I thought I'd mention it while you were here.' Gregson picked up something from his desk. 'I've got a job for you. The others have had their assignment cards but this is the only one in your unofficial sector.' He threw a strip of plastic towards Jay. 'Here, you know what to do.'

Jay nodded and picked up the plastic strip. He had seen them before, lots of them, and he had long ago lost any emotion he might have once had. The strip was from Psycho and contained the full data on someone's life. It had been rejected, thrown out … and as he looked down at it, Jay could see the broad red star smeared all over the smooth surface. The red star, which meant that a person had been weighed, considered – and found wanting.

Casually he read the name and number of the person he was to kill: *Curtway, George.* 14/4762. *Electronics.*

Susan's father.

*

There were times when Jay hated his job. Not many, for like all Ship personnel he was efficient and took a pride in his job, but sometimes, like now, he wished that he had belonged to anything but the psych-police. It was his fault, of course; he should never have allowed himself to become so intimate with people who, by the very nature of things, must inevitably become his victims. But self-blame, like self-justification, were both a waste of time. He still had to kill Susan's father.

Had to. Indoctrination, conditioning, his own pride in his work and his knowledge that, should he refuse, he would be 'eliminated' as unfit, left him no choice. George Curtway had to die.

He changed before entering sector five, reversing his black shorts for the red ones of the ventilation engineer he was supposed to be in his unofficial sector, and made his way down towards the lower levels. Usually on such a mission he felt a certain excitement, the thrill of the hunter stalking the hunted, his wits against those of the selected victim with the rules heavily in his favor. And yet, even with the protection his official status gave him, there was always an element of danger.

He could be clumsy. He could bungle, be seen by witnesses, or do such a poor job of staging the 'accident' that he would be judged inefficient and be eliminated in turn. Murder, even with the victim unaware and unprepared, was not always easy.

But this time, instead of the thrill, the warmth of released adrenaline, he felt a vague regret and a disinclination to do what must be done. He recognized the danger and deliberately focused his mind on his victim, forcing himself to forget Susan, their close friendship, their love and everything about them. Her father had to die and, as far as Jay was concerned, that was all there was to it. He felt a little better by the time he reached the lower levels where the games and recreation rooms were.

George wasn't in any of the rec-rooms, nor the exercise rooms, nor in the private cubicle his status allowed. Jay knew that he could locate the man by inquiring at the work-office. Curtway could have been out on a job somewhere – but to do that would be to leave a clue and maybe arouse suspicion. He was staring into the mess, trying to find the man he was looking for, when someone touched his arm.

'Jay! I didn't expect to see you again so soon. Don't you ever work?' it was Susan, the last person he wished to see. Looking down at her he wished that they had never met.

'Hello. Susan.' Deliberately he made his voice casual.

'Eaten yet?'

'Not yet.' She linked her arm through his and smiled up into his face. 'Let's eat together, shall we?'

'If you like.' Casually he slipped his arm from hers and they moved towards a vacant table. He ordered without paying much attention to the menu. Susan kept glancing at him, seeming about to speak once or twice, then, pushing aside her empty plates touched his arm.

'Anything wrong, Jay?'

'Wrong?' He forced himself to smile at her, annoyed with himself for betraying his emotions. 'No, of course not. What makes you think that?'

'Your appetite for one thing.' She gestured towards his unfinished meal. 'I've never known you to be so slow before.'

'I'm not hungry.'

'Then you shouldn't have sat down to eat.' Susan glanced over the mess hall. 'Better finish it up, Jay, or someone will accuse you of waste. There's a man standing over by the far wall who seems very interested in you as it is.'

'Is there?' He didn't turn his head to look, guessing that it was Susan the man was interested in, not her escort. But he finished his meal all the same, refusing a sweet and sipping his water while Susan spooned up the last of her synthetic fruit.

'When am I going to see you again, Jay?' Susan smiled as she leaned forward and touched his hand. 'After shift?'

'I doubt it.'

'When then? Tomorrow?'

'I don't think so.' He looked down at the table as he spoke. 'I'm pretty busy right now and it's hard to know just when I'll be free.' He stared at her, his face expressionless. 'In fact, Susan, you'd better not rely on seeing me again.'

'What!' She stared at him a moment, her hand gripping his arm; then she laughed. 'Jay! Don't say things like that!'

'I mean it, Susan.' Deliberately he removed her hand from his arm.

'You're joking! You couldn't mean it – not after what we've been to each other.' Her eyes searched his face. 'Please, Jay, say that you're not serious.'

'I am serious,' he said flatly. 'There's no future in it for either of us and it would be best if we never met again.'

'Jay!' There was hurt in her voice, the deep pain of outraged emotion and broken illusion. He heard it, knew that he was being deliberately cruel, and yet, at the same time, that it was the only thing he could do. He stared into her soft, brown eyes.

'Listen, Susan,' he said curtly. 'Let's not get foolish over this. We've had fun and I've enjoyed knowing you, but it's all over now. Let's forget it, shall we?'

'Jay!' For a moment he thought that she was going to break down. Tears filled her eyes and her hands showed white at the knuckles as she gripped the edge of the table. Then pride came to her rescue, the outraged pride of any woman who has had her affection flung back into her face, and together with that pride came anger. She stiffened with youthful dignity.

'All right, Jay. If that's all it meant to you.' She paused, hopefully, and for a moment he was tempted to say the word which would remove her pain and restore her smile. He didn't say it.

'It was fun,' he repeated stubbornly. 'It should never have become so serious. It's best that we part now before any damage is done.'

'I see.' She stared down at the table, then, with a brave attempt at casualness, glanced around the mess hall. 'Don't bother to justify yourself, Jay. As you said, it was fun. I've been a fool, I suppose, but ...' She swallowed. 'This is the end, then?'

'Yes.'

He didn't look at her as she rose from the table. He didn't follow her with his eyes as she stumbled towards the door and to the privacy of the nearest unoccupied rec-room. She would cry, he thought dully. She would vent her emotion in tears, hate him, despise him and then, after a while, forget him.

But the thought didn't make him happy.

He sat for a while, sipping his water, trying to bring his mind back into focus and the job at hand. There was no particular hurry, he knew that, but he wanted to get the thing over and done with long before the three-day period of grace was over. The hard part was over; he had managed to make Susan hate him, and all that was left was a simple job of murder.

He was leaving the hall when a man stepped forward and collided with him with sufficient force to send him reeling against a table.

'You!' The man pressed his hand to his side, his face distorted with synthetic pain. 'Why don't you watch where you're going?'

'Sorry.' Jay was in no mood for argument and he was in a hurry. He tried to step past the man, then halted as a hand gripped his arm.

'Not so fast! You hurt me.'

'So what?' Jay stared at the sullen-faced man in the brown shorts. 'I apologized.'

'That's not good enough,' said Sam Aldway deliberately. 'It's about time your sort were taught that you can't go around hurting people.' He looked at the little crowd which had gathered around them. 'You all saw what he did,' he shouted. 'I say that it isn't good enough.'

'Take your hands off me!' Jay jerked his arm, then, as the man tried to grab him again, pushed him back. 'I told you to keep your paws to yourself.'

'You hit me!' Sam appealed again to the crowd. 'You all saw him hit me.'

'Don't be a fool.' Jay fought his rising anger and spoke as calmly as he could. 'We bumped into each other, and if I hurt you, then I'm sorry. I've apologized – I can't do more. Now shut up and leave me alone.' He stepped forward, trying to thrust his way through the press of bodies, then turned as a hand clawed at his shoulder. 'I told you to leave me alone.'

'Oh no you don't.' Sam grinned, conscious of being the center of attraction, and spoke directly to Jay. 'You're a dirty, stinking, lousy waster,' he said loudly. 'And I want to know what you're going to do about it.'

It was so raw as to be ludicrous. The man was an arrogant, loud-mouthed fool, and he was clumsily trying to force Jay into a duel. Jay knew it, knew too that he, with his superior training, would be certain to win, and for a moment was tempted to work off some of his frustration and anger in violent physical combat. He shook his head and laughed.

'So I'm a waster, am I? Then why don't you call the psych-police?'

'You mean that you refuse to fight?' Incredulous anger twisted Sam's face into an animal-mask of hate. 'Why, you rotten coward – you call yourself a man? I've called you a waster. Did you hear that? A *dirty waster!* I'll show you what I do with wasters.'

Before Jay could guess what he was about to do, Sam had stepped forward and swung his open hand against Jay's cheek. The sound of the slap was followed by a startled hush, a hush broken by the soggy impact of bone against flesh.

Normally, Jay would never have done it. Normally his innate caution and the grim necessity to put his assignment above all else would have forced him to swallow the insult, accept the inevitable sneers of cowardice, and to go on his way.

But he was still raw from his parting with Susan, sick with the knowledge of what he had yet to do, and his emotions overrode good sense as he swung his fist deep into the flesh of the other's stomach. Coldly he stared at the writhing man at his feet, knowing that now he had gone too far to back out. There was no brawling in the Ship, there couldn't be, not with five thousand people living too close together. A brawl could start a riot which would ruin irreplaceable material, injure essential workers and kill the innocent parents of the new generations.

Like it or not, Jay had to fight a duel.

SEVEN

The stadium was on the lowest level next to the exercise rooms. From a sanded floor rows of tiered seats sloped up to a high roof and, when Jay and Sam arrived followed by the interested crowd, a couple of women were fighting a bloody battle with razor-edged knives to the amusement of the usual watchers.

Both well over thirty, they fought with the ferocity of tigers, the gleaming blades slashing at yielding flesh as they spun and dodged on the absorbent sand. From the crowd came a soft half-sigh, half-groan as one of them slipped, falling on to one knee, her knife had resting for a moment on the floor. Quickly the other moved in, her blade a lancing arc as the needle point thrust through skin and fat, muscle and sinew towards the pulsing heart beneath. Triumphantly, she grinned towards the audience, kissed her blood-stained fingers at the referee and walked staggeringly towards the exit.

Jay watched her, trying to guess from her wounds whether she would he healed or eliminated. From her age, the blood she had lost, and the obvious skill with which she had used her weapon, he guessed the latter. Expert duelists, while encouraged up to a point, became dangerous when they lost their sense of proportion and vied with each other in the number of their kills. The Ship had no room for blood-crazed beasts.

The ref checked them in, making the routine inspection of their forearms, and asking the usual questions.

'Are you both certain that you can't settle your differences in any other way?'

'I'm willing to call it off,' said Jay. He looked at Sam. 'And you?'

'Not a chance.'

'I see that this is your first duel.' The ref stared at Jay's unmarked forearm, then at the five dots on Sam's. 'As a first-timer you have the choice of weapons. Also,' he stared hard at Sam, 'you will not be killed in this encounter.' He looked back at Jay. 'How will you fight?'

'Bare handed.' Jay had no intention of getting cut or slashed by knife or machete and, aside from anything else, he was skilled in the art of unarmed combat. Already he regretted having agreed to fight at all; it was too easy to be injured in the stadium, and even the most experienced fighter could fall victim to an unlucky blow. Without weapons, however, there was little chance of anything worse than a beating up.

Their turn was scheduled for after the next bout and he waited impatiently while a young, optimistic man just out of marriageable status took on a well-muscled woman about ten years his senior. Fights between mixed couples, while rare, were not uncommon. Equality between the sexes demanded utter lack of distinction, though, as in this case, the bout was usually fought with padded clubs which were painful enough but capable of inflicting little more than a bruise. In effect it was a comedy turn and the crowd greeted the young man's defeat with catcalls turning to ribald cheers as the woman, dropping her club, picked up her opponent and carried him tenderly from the arena.

Jay smiled, guessing that another domestic problem had been solved the hard way, then lost his smile as the referee gestured towards them.

'Right. You two are on now. Remove your sandals, walk out five paces apart and, when you reach the center, turn and fight.'

Jay hesitated, glancing at Sam, then, as the other made no move, he shrugged and strode out into the arena. The space was about twenty yards long and fifteen wide, brilliantly lit so that the surrounding faces of the watching crowd merged into a formless blur. The attendants had cleared away the debris of the previous bouts, raking the sand and removing the discarded weapons, and the fine grit felt warm and smooth between his naked toes. Now that the moment had arrived he felt calm and, as he strode forward, he evaluated his chances. There was a slight disadvantage in coming out first for he could not be certain just where Sam would be, but that disadvantage would be offset by his superior skill. He turned as he reached the halfway mark, springing to one side and poising on the balls of his feet. Sam glared at him, paused just as he was about to spring; then, before he could recover his balance, Jay had stepped forward and slammed his fist towards the other's jaw.

He missed, but he had expected it, and as Sam swayed to one side, his other hand drove forward towards his stomach. He grinned as he felt the blow smash home and followed it with two more, one to the head and one to the heart. Crowding forward so as to keep Sam off-balance, he smashed at him with all the force of his back and shoulder muscles.

For a moment he thought that the fight was over almost before it had begun. Sam gulped, tried to cover, then, as blood gushed from his pulped nose, screamed with rage and flung himself forward, his hands reaching for Jay's face and throat.

Immediately Jay was fighting for his life.

It was dirty fighting, but it was more than that. It was the double attack possible only to a trained fighter and, as Jay felt the other's hands smash at vital nerves, he felt the first doubt as to his success. The double attack he could handle, he used it himself, but as they fought, he became aware that Sam knew far more than any ordinary duelist should.

A knee thrust at his groin at the same time that stiffened fingers stabbed at his eyes. He twisted to avoid the knee, knocked aside the threatening fingers, and tasted blood as a lowered skull smashed into his face. Again the knee jerked towards him, and in avoiding it he fell victim to a slash from the edge of a palm directed towards his throat. It was the double attack, the system of two separate blows at the same time directed towards different parts of the anatomy: knee to groin, fingers to eyes, blow to stomach, skull against face, edge of palm towards throat, without pause or time for the victim to recover his balance.

For a while they wove like fencers, body against body, arms and legs moving in smooth, synchronized rhythm as they delivered and countered blows, their sweat-streaked bodies glistening beneath the glare of the lights. Then, as he felt his left arm go numb, Jay broke away and ran towards the end of the arena.

Sam was dangerous. Avoiding the other's rush, Jay frantically massaged life and feeling back into his numbed arm. How or where the duelist had learned of the subtle nerve-blows which could maim and paralyze, Jay didn't know, but his numbed arm gave shocking proof that he had learned them. Jay knew them, all the psych-police did, but that information was carefully kept from the Ship personnel. It was too easy to kill a man with that knowledge and, as he stared at the crouching figure of his opponent, Jay revised his previous opinions as to the certainty of his victory.

There is a state of mind indispensable to a fighter if he hopes to win. Contempt has no place and neither has indifference; everything has to be sublimated to a single objective, every emotion and thought fined to a needle point directed to one aim. To kill. To rend and tear, to smash and destroy, to crush and vanquish. Sam had it; it was apparent in his eyes, his mouth, the very set and stance of his body. Before he could hope to meet the man on equal terms, Jay had to acquire it too.

For him it was simple.

He moved forward as life returned to his numbed arm, dodged a handful of sand flung towards his eyes, and struck out with his left fist. Sam knocked aside the blow, gripped the wrist, twisted, turned and suddenly brought the trapped limb down hard against his shoulder. Normally that would have broken the arm, would have snapped it at the elbow and left Jay crippled and helpless, but Sam was up against no normal fighter.

Jay leaped up and forward as Sam turned and, just as he felt the pressure being applied to his elbow, the fingers of his right hand curled beneath Sam's chin, probed for a moment at the knotted muscles of the throat, then dug in with savage viciousness.

The rest was merely for the benefit of the crowd.

It was butchery, cold, calculated, and serving both to cover up the effects of the nerve-blow and to vent Jay's own hate and rage. He slammed his fists against Sam's face and head, opened a cut over one eye, split his lips and, with one final blow to the jaw, finished the unequal combat.

He walked towards the referee, leaving the duelist unconscious on the reddening sand.

'A good bout,' complimented the referee. 'I thought that you'd be in trouble there – Aldway's a nasty fighter, but you handled yourself well.' He picked up a red-tipped stylus. 'Hold out your arm.'

Silently Jay held out his left forearm for the referee to brand him with the red dot. It was a nuisance, but he could have it removed at Medical, and to protest would be to arouse suspicion. He was donning his sandals when someone called to him.

'Jay! I didn't think that you went in for dueling.'

It was George Curtway, and the sight of him brought back all the unaccustomed indecision which Jay had managed to rid himself of in the arena. Slowly he fastened the catch of his sandal.

'So it was Sam Aldway you were fighting.' George stared down at the pale face of the duelist as he was carried out by the attendants. 'You want to watch him, Jay. He'll never forgive you for besting him. What happened?'

'He wanted to pick a quarrel,' said Jay shortly. 'He picked on me and I was lucky enough to win.' He crossed to the water spray and washed the blood from his face. 'Busy, George?'

'Just finished. We had a sticky job up in low-weight – condensation in the junction boxes – but I'm free now.' He hesitated, staring at Jay. 'Look. Jay, there's something I've been meaning to talk to you about. Are you free now?'

'Yes.' Jay dried his face and hands in the warm-air blast. 'What is it?'

'I'll tell you later.' George stared at the people around them. 'Have you eaten?'

'Yes.'

'That's a pity. I'm starving and we could have eaten together.' George frowned, 'Tell you what. Meet me in my cubicle. There's a viewer there so you won't be bored, and I'll join you as soon as I've had a meal. Right?'

Jay nodded and, leaning against the wall, watched the electronics man thrust his way through the inevitable crowd around the stadium and turn down a corridor. It was luck, he thought dully.

The man he was looking for had found him first, had even arranged a rendezvous for his own death, though he couldn't know that, of course. Jay should have been pleased, but somehow he felt even more despondent than before. He started as a man touched his arm.

'I watched you in the arena,' said the man thickly. 'A good bout. Want to try another?'

He was still young, scarred a little and the inside of his left arm was dotted with the red marks of the experienced duelist. Looking at him Jay recognized the type, a natural born fighter, a man whose only pleasure was in pitting his strength and skill against others. Jay shook his head.

'Sorry, but no.'

'A pity.' The man shrugged, not annoyed at the refusal but vaguely regretful at a lost opportunity. 'No need to make it a death-bout. Just a friendly battle to work off energy.' He looked hopefully at Jay. 'Some other time, perhaps?'

'Perhaps.' Jay watched him move towards a small crowd waiting for seats in the stadium, half-amused at the man's sincerity, and mentally comparing him to Aldway. Sam was dangerous, a man who would have to be eliminated before he made too big a nuisance of himself. The other was an integral part of the economy of the Ship.

Jay sighed and made his way towards Curtway's private cubicle.

EIGHT

Quentin, Captain of the Ship, sat at the head of his desk and stared at the men sitting before him with amusement tinged with contempt. They were so obvious, so transparent, so young. Conway, swollen with his own importance at being in charge of Psycho. Henderly, jealous of the psychologist and yet conscious of his own superiority. Malick, Chief of Genetics, the little god of a little world. Gregson, hard and implacable, cold and ruthless, toying with intrigue and insanely envious, not of the Captain, but of what he represented. Folden, Chief of Supply.

The hierarchy of the Ship.

Quentin let them sit in silence for a while, calm in the knowledge of his own superiority, and yet, even as he sat, his eyes were never still. Old those eyes might be, but they had lost none of their sharpness and they saw far more than any of the men before him imagined. Quentin was no fool.

He rustled the thin papers on his desk, selected one, scanned it more for appearances than for any real need to remind himself of what it contained; then dropping it, stared at Gregson.

'Any further news on the elimination of the Barbs?'

'None.' Gregson scarcely troubled to disguise his impatience. 'As yet three schemes have been submitted to me for approval. All are verging on the ludicrous in their total disregard of facts. I can only assume that the originators of the schemes must be trying a feeble joke at my expense.'

'I submitted one of those schemes,' said Henderly harshly. 'What was the matter with it?'

'The same as with all of them.' Gregson shrugged at the medical officer's expression of anger. 'Of the three, two advocated the offer of amnesty to the Barbs if they would return to their sectors. I need hardly emphasize the stupidity of that suggestion. They know full well what will happen to them if they agree to return. The third contained some wild scheme to electrify the stanchions and girders of No-Weight.'

'That was my suggestion,' said Conway. 'What's wrong with it?'

'Better ask the electronic engineers that. I did. They tell me that even if it were possible to divert sufficient current to No-Weight to send a lethal voltage through the fabric, it would be impossible to insulate it from the rest of the Ship without extensive alterations.'

'I see.' Quentin spoke before Conway could express his anger at the sneering tone of contempt Gregson had used. 'I assume, of course, that you have a better suggestion?'

'I have.'

'May we hear it? Or does the Chief of Psych-Police consider that his Captain is too stupid to understand it?'

'Stupidity is a relative term,' said Gregson stiffly. 'Perhaps one of my officers would consider you stupid if ever you met him in the arena.'

'If I was ever so unwise as to place myself in that position,' said Quentin quietly, 'then I would be something more than stupid. Your suggestion?'

'Seal No-Weight and search it from end to end with armed men given orders to kill everyone they find.' Gregson shrugged at their instinctive recoiling from the use of weapons. 'If you don't like to arm the men, then I have another plan. Seal the area just the same and flood it with lethal gas. Exterminate the Barbs for the vermin they are.'

'And how would you get rid of the gas afterwards?' Quentin gestured for Folden to remain silent. 'Have you considered that?'

'Chemistry isn't my department. Is it possible to use a neutralizing agent for the gas? Or perhaps we could extract the poisoned air and replace it with fresh?'

'No to both suggestions,' said Folden impatiently. 'We know of no such neutralizing agent, and to evacuate the air would be criminal waste.'

'Justifiable waste.'

'Criminal,' insisted Folden. 'We could replace the air, yes, but to evacuate anything from the Ship would be to disturb the ecology. I must veto any such suggestion.'

'Why not arm the searchers, then? Or would that be criminal waste too?' Gregson glared at the Chief of Supply, sarcasm heavy in his voice.

'What would you arm them with, Gregson?' Quentin's voice, though calm, had a peculiar carrying quality. 'Knives? Clubs?'

'Guns, of course, what else?'

'I take it that you mean high-velocity pistols. Have you ever fired one?'

'You know that I haven't. No one has. Weapons are forbidden aboard the Ship.'

'Exactly, and for a very good reason.' Quentin sighed as if finding the explanation tedious. 'First, even if you had one, I doubt if you could hit anything with it. Before a pistol can be used, training and practice are essential. Second, even if you could use them, I would never allow them to be fired within the Ship. The damage they would cause to the structure would be worse than tolerating the Barbs. You seem to have no idea of the impact force of a bullet and certainly none of the vulnerability of the Ship itself. No, Gregson, I cannot accept either of your suggestions.'

'Then what are you going to do, let the Barbs alone to raid the farms and laugh at us?'

'The Barbs are a minor nuisance and any plan which necessitates too great an expenditure of time or material would be defeating its own end. However, Henderly has a plan which I am considering and which may lead to their successful elimination. Incidentally, Gregson, I shouldn't have to remind you that the very existence of the Barbs is proof of your own inefficiency.'

'Twenty people have fled to No-Weight during the past ten years,' snapped Gregson. 'That is less than two per cent of the total disposable population during that time. I would hardly consider that inefficient.'

'You are at liberty to think as you wish.' Quentin selected another paper from the litter before him. 'Malick! Your report on population disturbs me. Explain.'

'We are reaching saturation point,' said the saturnine-faced head of Genetics. 'As far as possible we have managed to avoid inbreeding by shift of personnel and rigorous mating control. However, as time passes, it is getting more and more difficult to select suitable partners for the new generation. Some inbreeding has become inevitable, and more will be necessary during future years.'

'Is that bad?' Henderly leaned forward, his eyes bright with professional interest. 'Surely the inferior strains have been eliminated by now?'

'Naturally, but there is always some danger in inbreeding; the possibility of atavism is higher than normal and certain nervous disorders can be expected if we continue as at present.'

'I don't understand this.' Folden stared at the chief of genetics. 'As far as I can see, inbreeding is unavoidable. Didn't the builders take all that into account?'

'They did.'

'Then what's the trouble?'

'The trouble is simply one of time and circumstances.' Like Quentin, Malick seemed tired of having to explain. 'The builders determined, quite rightly, that in order to keep the race healthy we must concentrate on youth, not age. As far as Genetics is concerned, a man or woman has served the purpose of their existence as soon as they have mated and given birth to children. We are only interested in the new generation; the old merely serves to maintain the Ship, and is expendable as soon as others grow to take its place.' He glanced towards Gregson. 'You know all about that and you also know that Psycho determines the population figures and personnel for elimination on the basis of general unfitness or sheer need of living space. So many new births allowed per year, therefore so many deaths necessary to make room for the new life.'

'One hundred and thirty new births per year,' said Gregson, partly because he didn't like being ignored and partly to show his own knowledge. 'Of the necessary deaths, about a half are eliminated by dueling. The remainder are taken care of by my officers.' He shrugged. 'It works out at about a death a month per sector.'

'What has that got to do with inbreeding?' snapped Conway impatiently. 'What are you getting at, Malick?'

'Simply this. As all female personnel are automatically sterilized when leaving marriageable status, we are confined to a very limited age-group for breeding purposes. We have young parents, they mate at optimum age, but we are unable to use the same parents more than once. In other words, a boy marries a girl, gives her children, and then is prevented from entering into a fruitful marriage with a second woman.' Malick shrugged. 'We have bred for optimum characteristics, of course, and have managed to breed out all hereditary diseases, mental instability, and certain undesirable physical deformities. We have bred a race of highly intelligent, physically perfect men and women, but in so doing we have also given ourselves a first-class problem.'

'I begin to see what you're driving at,' Henderly said. 'Nervous potential?'

'Exactly. They appear to have had the same trouble back on Earth when they were toying with the breeding of race horses. They bred for speed at any price, and wound up with walking bundles of nervous tension almost impossible to control. There is nothing basically wrong in selective breeding if the original stock is sound. The trouble starts when you breed for certain characteristics. We have bred for an adventurous type with a high survival factor and amazingly fast reflexes. We've got that, but we've also got what goes with it.'

'Don't you trust Psycho?' interrupted Quentin softly.

'What?' Malick blinked and stared at the Captain. 'Of course I trust Psycho, but that doesn't prevent me from asking myself what is going to happen. What is the good of breeding an adventurous type when there is nowhere for them to go adventuring? How can we control highly strung, sensitive men and women when they are surrounded by a limited existence almost calculated to drive them into a frenzy of frustration?' He almost seemed about to burst into tears as he asked the questions. 'I'm not questioning the builders – obviously they knew what they were doing – but to me it seems all wrong. The Ship isn't the place for the type of human we've bred. We should have gone in for morons, dull-witted clods who would be content to eat, sleep and mate like the animals they would be. You can't give a man a keen brain and a perfect body and then prevent him from using them. Not if you want to avoid trouble you can't.'

'Calm yourself, Malick.' Quentin smiled with quiet satisfaction as the Chief of Genetics relaxed. 'That's better. It is foolish and a waste of energy to torment yourself with questions of what may never happen.'

He picked up and scanned another of the papers before him. 'Conway, are you satisfied that everything is normal with Psycho?'

'Of course it is, why shouldn't it be?' The automatic defense of the psychologist almost made the old man smile. 'Nothing is wrong in my department.'

'Are you certain of that?' Quentin stared at Conway with peculiar intentness. 'Something in your report makes me wonder. There is a slight alteration in the ratio between permissible births and recommended eliminations. Have you noticed it yourself?'

'Oh, that?' Conway dismissed it with a shrug. 'Simply explained. The incidence of dueling has risen during the past few years, probably due to the very thing Malick has been telling us about. Naturally, as there is more room for new life the number of permissible births has risen also.'

'Does that also account for the reduction in the number of recommended eliminations?'

'What else?' Conway seemed genuinely amazed at the question. 'We remove the cards of those killed in duels, you know, and Psycho automatically allows for them.'

'That would hardly account for the fall,' reminded Quentin. 'The fact that several deaths have occurred from dueling would not alter the fact that others would be considered unfit by Psycho. Old men, for example, those who have reached their fortieth year.'

'Perhaps, said Conway doubtfully. 'I hadn't thought of it like that.'

'I can't see that it makes any difference,' said Gregson. 'We have to eliminate about a hundred and thirty men and women a year. The fact that more of them are being killed in the stadium doesn't alter the fact. It only makes the job of the psych-police a little easier.'

'Of course.' Quentin rustled his papers again, apparently accepting the explanation. 'Your report interests me, Folden. I will discuss it with you later, after I have had time to check certain details.'

'My report of the supply position?' Folden looked at the Captain. 'I've already checked everything possible and the inference is plain. Normal wastage has reduced our potential to a disturbingly low figure. I –'

'I said that I will discuss it with you later.' Quentin silenced the Chief of Supply with a gesture, conscious of the open interest of the others. 'Have any of you anything further to say at this meeting?'

'The tapes,' blurted Malick, then stopped as the others stared at him.

'Yes?' encouraged Quentin. 'You were saying?'

'I don't know if my memory is bad, or whether the tapes now shown on the children's screens are different from what they were, but I can't make sense of them.'

Malick stared a little helplessly at the incredulous faces of the men around him. 'I know that the educational tapes are routed automatically to various sectors and subsectors by Psycho, but to me it seems that they are totally at variance to what is normal.'

'How do you mean?' said Quentin sharply. 'Explain yourself.'

'Well, you know that we've always had tapes showing scenes of old Earth, the idea being, I suppose, that the children would remember the planet of their origin. But now those tapes seem to be in far greater detail than ever before. There are entire sequences of growth and decay, the balance of insect life to animal, the interplay of flora and fauna. There have even been scenes of the actual trapping and butchering of animals for meat!' Malick shuddered. 'They were disgusting! Who in their right mind would ever consider eating meat, anyway?'

'You might,' said the Captain gently, 'if you were starving and meat was the only edible food.'

'The only meat aboard the Ship,' said Malick tightly, 'is the personnel. Are you advocating cannibalism?'

'I advocate nothing; I merely answered your question, and you are quite wrong in your statement. There is meat aboard the Ship other than the men and women you have bred.'

'I don't count the animals in deep-freeze,' snapped Malick irritably. 'They are in the sealed areas, apart from the Ship proper.'

'They are still meat, just the same.'

'That has nothing to do with it. Those tapes are contaminating the minds of the young and they should be stopped.' Malick stared accusingly at Conway. 'You are in charge of Psycho. Why don't you get the electronic engineers to check it over and make sure that nothing has gone wrong?'

'Nothing is wrong with Psycho,' insisted Conway. He glared at the Chief of Genetics. 'If you ask me, it's you that is wrong, not Psycho. Maybe you'd better let Medical make certain that your "highly-strung nerves" haven't sent you over the edge?'

'I don't have to listen to that kind of talk from you.' Malick jerked to his feet, his face red with anger. 'If you're a man at all, you'll meet me in the stadium!'

'Control yourself, Malick!' The Captain didn't raise his voice but something in the thin, penetrating tones chilled Malick's anger. 'You are overwrought or you would never have dared to challenge a fellow-member of the Council. Sit down and calm yourself.' He waited until Malick had resumed his seat, 'Now, let's look at this thing intelligently. You know perfectly well that all educational tapes are channeled from Psycho on automatic relay. No one could have touched them and, if what you say is true, then it must be as the builders intended. Are you questioning the wisdom of the builders?'

'No.' Malick looked uncomfortable. 'Of course not.'

'A pity. It is possible to place too great a reliance on the work of others.' Quentin stared down at his papers for a moment, then rose in dismissal.

'That will be all, gentlemen. I suggest that we each concentrate on our duties and waste no time in idle speculation.'

He stood by the head of the desk as they left the room, tall, proud, almost fatherly in the way he stared after them. Alone, he sat down and, closing his eyes, let his mind and thoughts mingle with the eternal, sub-audible vibration of the Ship which was his universe. It was happening again.

The same old distrust, intrigue, the playing for power and the breaking out of ambition. The envy, pride, jealousy and, above all, the mind-wrenching fear of what was to come. The hierarchy knew too much for their peace of mind. They were no longer young and, knowing what they did, they would fight against elimination with every weapon at their command. Quentin recognized it – had recognized it for some time now – and knew that in sheer self-defense if for no other reason he must protect himself. There was only one man in the Ship who was safe against the dictates of Psycho, and that man was the Captain.

Opening his eyes, he pressed a button on his desk and waited for the intercom to warm into life.

'Yes, sir?' His private aide. The one person he could trust in the entire Ship was someone unknown to the rest of the hierarchy and all the more valuable because of that. Quentin lowered his voice as he spoke into the instrument.

'Find Merrill and send him to me. Use caution.'

'Naturally, sir.'

The intercom died as the Captain broke the connection. He stared at it for a moment, his mind busy with plans; then, resting his head between his hands, he relaxed. His shoulders stooped, his muscles grew limp and flaccid, nerves and tendons sagged as he relaxed his iron control, and his breathing rasped in his throat as he sucked in great gasps of air.

In that moment he looked very old.

NINE

George was a long time arriving. Jay sat in a chair and stared moodily at the illuminated surface of the viewer screen, hardly noticing the images flashing before his eyes. Habit had made him switch on the viewer, the same, ingrained habit which made everyone in the Ship turn to education as the main form of amusement. But he found little to amuse him in the pictured representation of a dismantled radio set. He leaned forward and was about to switch it off when the door opened and George entered the room.

'Sorry to have kept you waiting, Jay. I got talking to another electronics man and forgot the time.

'Did you?' Jay turned the switch and watched the screen flicker and grow blank. 'What did you want to see me about, George?'

Curtway hesitated. Though he was older than Jay the difference was hardly noticeable; as they stood next to each other, they could have passed for brothers.

'It's about Susan,' he said awkwardly. 'I hardly know how to say this without causing offense, Jay, but I wish you wouldn't see her any more.'

'I see.' Jay looked at the elder man. 'You realize what you are saying, of course?'

'I mean no insult,' said George hastily. 'It's just that Susan is an impressionable girl and you're young and handsome. I'm not blaming you or anyone, Jay, but she's due for marriage soon and I don't want her to get into trouble with Genetics.'

'Are you accusing me of immorality?' Jay deliberately encouraged his mounting temper. George was making things very easy for him. An accusation like that was making things very easy for him. An accusation like that was sufficient ground for a challenge, and once he had George in the arena, the rest would be simple.

'No, Jay, you know that I wouldn't do that.'

'Then what objection can there be to my seeing her?'

'She's in love with you, Jay. That isn't good, not when there can't be any future in it for either of you. Unless you agree not to see her, you'll ruin her marriage and create discontent.' George stepped forward and rested his hand on the other's own. 'Be reasonable, Jay. I know that you're fond of Susan, but think of her own good. Later, when she's out of marriageable status, there'll be plenty of time for you to settle down together.'

'I don't like what you're saying, Curtway.' Jay shook off the hand on his arm. 'I consider that you've insulted me to an unpardonable extent. Naturally, you'll give me satisfaction.'

'No, Jay.'

'You refuse to fight?'

'Yes.' George glanced at the red dot on Jay's forearm. 'I'm no duelist, Jay, and I didn't think that you were either. If a father can't protect his daughter without fear of getting murdered by some arrogant bully, then there must be something wrong in the Ship. I don't think that you really mean what you say.'

'You have accused me of immorality,' said Jay coldly. 'I demand satisfaction.'

'You can't make me fight you, Jay.'

'You admit to being a coward, then?'

'I'll admit anything you like. Call me a waster if you want to. Hit me if it gives you any satisfaction, but I'm not going into the arena with you or any other man.' George smiled and deliberately sat down, 'Now, let's be sensible, Jay. I know you too well to believe that you would take advantage of an old man like that.'

He was right, of course, and Jay knew it. Nothing would persuade George to enter the arena and, despite his own urgency, Jay felt a little ashamed of trying to force a duel. Elimination should be quick, cold, utterly merciless and without mental or physical pain. To drag an old man into the arena and butcher him there for the benefit of the watchers was pure sadism. He sighed and joined George on the bench.

'All right, George. I can't make you fight if you don't want to.'

'And Susan?'

'I won't see her again if that's the way you want it.'

'It would be best, Jay.'

'All right, then. Forget it. The thing's over and done with.'

'Good.' George leaned forward to switch on the viewer, and Jay knew that it was time for him to go. He sat where he was.

'Was that all you wanted to see me about, George?'

'That's all. Thanks for waiting to see me – and the other thing.'

The other thing! Jay stared at the older man as he sat looking with interested at the moving picture on the screen. He could kill him now, a simple pressure on the carotids would do it, but killing wasn't enough. The death had to appear to be an accident and, glancing around the apartment, Jay knew that this was the wrong place.

'George.'

'Yes?' Curtway blinked as he turned from the screen.

'What is it, Jay?'

'I'm in trouble, George, and I wonder if you could help me.'

'Trouble?'

'Yes. I was up near No-Weight a while ago, checking the ventilation tubes, and I spotted something I should have reported.' Jay shrugged. 'It slipped my mind during the fight and if I report it now I'll be down-graded for time-lag. It was in your department and I wondered …'

'Something to do with electronics?'

'That's right. One of those big, flat boxes – the ones with all the conduits leading from them. I noticed one smelled of burning and when I touched it I got a shock.'

'Probably a short due to condensation,' said George promptly. 'We've been having a lot of trouble with the junction boxes lately.' He looked at Jay. 'What do you want me to do?'

'I was hoping that you could fix it and save me trouble.' Jay made himself appear nervous. 'If it goes through normal channels I'll be slated for delay, and if I ignore it, they might even send me to sanitation. If you could fix it for me …'

'Up near No-Weight?' George frowned. 'Tell you what, Jay. I'll take a look at it, and if I can fix it, I will. Fair enough?'

'Thanks,' Jay said gratefully. He rose and stepped towards the door. 'Let's get it over with. I'm frightened someone else will spot it and report in.'

George sighed and followed him into the corridor.

As usual the area around No-Weight was deserted. Jay led the way among a tangle of girders, slipped into a narrow tube like corridor, and paused by one of a number of junction boxes. George, maneuvering awkwardly in the almost total absence of weight, joined him.

'Is that the one?' He didn't look down at the box.

'I think so.' Jay stooped over it, touched it, then jerked back his hand as though he had received a shock. 'This is it, right enough. Take a look at it, George.'

'All right.' George kicked himself forward and, like most people unused to free fall, kicked too hard. Jay caught him as he passed and drew him to where George could grip a stanchion.

'Thanks.' The electronics man stooped over the box. 'Now let's see what the trouble is.'

He was wasting his time, of course, and Jay knew it. There was nothing wrong with the box at all, but it had served as a pretext to lure his victim to a place where his death could easily be accounted for. Looking at the man, Jay felt a strange reluctance to finish the job and, annoyed with himself for his hesitation, he moved in to make an end.

It would be simple. Pressure on the carotids, the great arteries of the throat leading to the brain, would bring swift unconsciousness; continued pressure would bring painless death. Jay knew just how to hold his victim so that any struggle would be useless. It would be routine, nothing more and, as he reached forward, he forced himself to ignore everything but his duty.

'Are you going to kill me, Jay?'

It wasn't so much what George said that shocked Jay into immobility, as the knowledge behind the words. He stood, swaying a little from the absence of gravity, and stared incredulously at the calm face of his intended victim.

'I've been expecting this,' continued George evenly. 'I guessed what you intended as soon as I saw the box. There's nothing wrong with it, and you know it.'

'You refused to fight,' stammered Jay desperately. He knew that at all costs he must keep the truth away from the other man. 'You insulted me.'

'That isn't why you wanted to kill me. Did Gregson send you?'

'Gregson?'

'Yes, Gregson, the head of psych-police.' George rested easily against the stanchion, his eyes serious as they stared at the young man. 'I'm not a fool, Jay, and I've suspected you for some time now. You worked at odd hours, seemed to be missing for long periods of time and didn't appear to have any particular duties.' George shrugged. 'I wouldn't have noticed it, I suppose, but for your attachment to Susan. I couldn't understand why, if you were young enough, you weren't married. That made me wonder. The final proof came when I saw you at headquarters one shift.'

'You saw me there?'

'Yes. I had been to service Psycho – I'm a top-line electronic engineer, you know, and they trust me to service the machine. I took a short cut back to sector five and passed P.P. headquarters. I saw you there – and you weren't wearing red shorts!'

'*You fool!*' Jay shifted his grip on the girder next to him in readiness for a lunge at the other man. 'Don't you realize that you've signed your own death warrant?'

'Gregson did that for me a long time ago.' George stared contemptuously at the young man. 'Don't try anything, Jay. I'm ready and warned and I've had practice in free fall.' He shifted as he spoke and Jay could see that his previous awkwardness had been assumed.

'Listen, George,' he said desperately. 'Let's be reasonable about this. There's nothing personal about it, you know that, but I've got to kill you. If I don't, then I'll be eliminated for failure of duty.'

'Do you know why you were ordered to kill me, Jay?'

'No.'

'Then I'll tell you. I found out something about Gregson. I tried to get a private interview with the Captain to tell him what I'd learned but he refused to see me. Gregson knows now that I know what he did. To safeguard himself he has ordered my death. That's the truth of the matter, Jay. Do you still want to kill me?'

'I must. Believe me, George I'd rather do anything than eliminate you, but the welfare of the Ship depends on it. You don't understand.'

'I understand well enough, Jay. I told you that I was no fool, and I've eyes to see with and a mind to think with, and a brain to correlate the resultant data. I know, for example, that there is no natural death aboard the Ship.'

'You're wrong,' insisted Jay sickly. 'People die in Medical.'

'They die, yes, but from what? Injections, perhaps? Wounds received in the arena? How many people have died of old age, Jay? Can you answer that?'

Jay could, but he didn't dare. The answer was that not one person had ever died of old age. They had never been allowed to live that long. 'Accidents,' duels, strange relapses: all had accounted for every death since the Ship had left Earth so long ago. Senility, white hair, doddering men and women were incomprehensible to the Ship's personnel. Old age was something which just didn't exist.

'If you live,' said Jay thickly, 'you will be robbing a newborn child of its air and water, living-space and food.' He moved a little nearer to the older man. 'You've had your time, George. Now you must die so that others can have their chance of life.'

'I don't mind dying,' said George calmly. 'I'm intelligent enough to realize the necessity, and life isn't so wonderful that I should want to cling to its every moment. But is it fair that I should die while others cheat their turn?'

'Cheat? What do you mean?' The accusation shocked Jay even more than Curtway's knowledge of what he was and what he did. 'How could anyone cheat?'

'There is a way, if you're in the right position to manage it. Gregson is in that position, Jay. I know what he did and he knows that I know.' George took a step forward. 'Can't you see the danger, Jay? If one man can avoid his turn for death, then so can others. How long will it be before the Ship is a despotism ruled by a handful of old men?'

And that was the trouble. While elimination was fair for all, then no intelligent person could argue against his turn. Not that they were given the choice. No one could be expected to remain wholly sane while he lived from day to day in anticipation of a death hour decided before his birth. Such knowledge would disrupt the routine of the Ship and convert its smooth-running system into a shambles. The old would demand rigid birth control so that they could live a little longer. The young would be frustrated at the thwarting of their natural desire for children. A gap would arise between the generations with the resultant loss of sympathy between age and youth. Such a system would lead to racial sterility, degeneration, and collapse of moral fiber.

This was why the psych-police were among the most carefully selected personnel on board, trained and indoctrinated from early youth to accept the twin burdens of responsibility and silence. But if what they had been taught was a lie?

'You're wrong,' insisted Jay desperately. 'No one would be so immoral as to cheat like that.'

'You think not?' George shrugged. 'I'm an old man, Jay, and to the old life becomes a precious thing. To you death is something utterly remote, even though you know full well that one day someone will eliminate you as you tried to eliminate me. But when you get older you sense things. You have more time for thought and you begin to realize all the things that you've missed in life. You want to hang on, Jay. You want to cling to life as a newly-wed wants to cling to his bride, or as a mother to her first-born. You can't be logical then. You can't evaluate and accept what must be. No. You want to live – and you'd do anything for a few extra years of existence.'

'Gregson is old,' said Jay thoughtfully. 'I hadn't realized it before.'

'Gregson is afraid of death,' said George. 'I know that.' He took another step forward and touched Jay on the arm. 'What are you going to do, Jay?'

'I don't know. I've orders and you know what they are – but if what you say is true …'

'It's true.'

'Then you must see the Captain.'

'How?' George shrugged with unusual cynicism. 'I've already tried to get a private interview with the Captain. My request was refused. To try again I must pass my request through the psych-police. I'm supposed to be dead. If I make the application then Gregson will set his dogs on me again.' He looked at Jay. 'Can you suggest something?'

'I don't know,' said Jay miserably. 'Obviously you'll have to hide until a chance comes for you to see the Captain. If Gregson ever finds out I've failed to eliminate you, he'll order my own death for inefficiency, so in order to cover up, I'll have to fake your accidental death.' He bit his lips in indecision. 'You could hide out in No-Weight. I can smuggle you past the guard, but the accident –'

'How did you intend explaining my death?'

'Simple. I was going to kill you and then dash your head against a stanchion. The official verdict would have been that you had misjudged your speed and distance and crushed your skull on landing.' Jay shrugged. 'That idea's no good now. Merrill will investigate and, unless your "body" is unrecognizable, he will guess at what I've done.' Jay held out his hand. 'Give me your identity disc and shorts.'

'Why? What are you going to do?'

'I don't know yet, but I'll think of something.' Jay snapped his fingers with impatience. 'Hurry.'

Reluctantly, George stripped off his blue shorts and struggled to remove the stamped metal identity tag from his wrist. He swore as he scraped skin from his knuckles, but he finally managed to get it off. He handed it to Jay.

'Now what?'

'Now you hide in No-Weight. I'll try to smuggle you up some food and water but don't worry if I don't come for a while. You won't stay there long, anyway. The quicker I can arrange an interview with the Captain the better.'

Silently Jay led the way along the winding tube, drifting lightly from stanchion to stanchion, pausing just long enough to impel himself in a new direction, twisting his body with expert ease to cushion the shock of landing with his knees and thighs. Finally he paused at a sunken panel.

'This is an emergency entry into No-Weight. It's kept locked from this side and I'll have to fasten it behind you.' Jay spun a wheel and jerked the metal slab open. 'Right, George. In you go. Try to stay close to the panel if you can. When I bring you supplies I don't want to have to waste a lot of time.'

'I understand.' George stepped towards the opening and peered into the dark interior. He shivered a little. 'It's cold in there.'

'The converters are colder,' snapped Jay impatiently.

George nodded and stepped through the opening into the vast cavern of No-Weight. He caught hold of the edge of the door and looked at Jay, his head a pale blob against the darkness behind him.

'What about Susan?'

'Susan will believe that you are dead.' Jay glanced uneasily down the corridor. 'To her, as to everyone, you will have met with an unfortunate accident.' He softened as he swung shut the door. 'I'm sorry, George, but there's nothing else I can do.'

'No,' said George slowly. 'I suppose not.' He hesitated. 'Still, I'd have liked to say goodbye. Funny, that … no one ever thinks of it until it's too late to do anything about it.' He removed his hand from the edge of the opening. 'Take care of her, Jay. And thank you.'

Jay didn't answer. He was already spinning shut the locking wheel.

TEN

Merrill was afraid of the Captain. He stood before the wide desk, acutely conscious of the old man's scrutiny, and tried to assume an arrogance and recklessness he did not feel. Quentin smiled a little as he saw it, the tolerant, almost amused smile of conscious superiority, but he did not speak, just stared and allowed Merrill to feel the mounting tension. It was one of the oldest psychological tricks known, so old that it always worked. Merrill spoke first.

'You sent for me, sir.'

'Are you ambitious?'

'I …' Merrill blinked at the unexpectedness of the question, then, as he recovered, his eyes grew wary. 'Yes, sir. I suppose that I am. Every man likes to do the best he can for the welfare of the Ship and …'

'You like to control men,' interrupted Quentin and his voice held a subtle contempt at Merrill's protestations. 'You enjoy the feel of power, the knowledge that you, even in a small part, control destiny.' He leaned a little forward over the desk. 'Tell me, do you like to kill?'

'I am efficient.'

'Then you enjoy what you do.' Quentin smiled and relaxed against the back of his chair. 'Don't bother to lie to me, Merrill. I know more about you than you know yourself. You may know what you do and think that knowledge is sufficient. But I know why you do what you do, and that knowledge makes me your master.' He let his thin voice fade into silence and his eyes grew bleak and distant. 'Remember that, Merrill. Always remember it. I am your master. The moment you forget that – you die.'

There was no passion in the thin tones, no arrogance or self-convincing blustering. It was a cold statement of fact and, hearing it, Merrill swallowed.

'Yes, sir. I understand.'

'Good.' Quentin smiled for the first time. 'Now to business. I have sent for you because, though you may not know it, I have studied you for several years now and have decided that you are the man I need. Men grow old, Merrill, and you know what happens to them when age piles its weight of invisible years on their heads. Some men accept their fate, others …'

'Gregson,' said Merrill, and stiffened in sudden fear. Quentin smiled.

'I knew that you were intelligent,' he said softly. 'But try not to be *too* intelligent.' He leaned forward again, his elbows on the desk, his thin fingers caressing his throat. 'We need mention no names and we need leap to no assumptions. I want a tool, nothing more, and a tool must be willing to obey without question or hesitation the dictates of its user. A time will come, maybe soon, maybe not so soon, when a job will have to be done. A man will have reached the end of his allotted span and, knowing that man, he may not be willing to yield his life and position. In such a case a tool must be used, a dumb, willing, obedient tool.' The old man looked at Merrill. 'You understand?'

'I do.'

'Men are ambitious,' said Quentin, speaking more to himself than to the man standing opposite him. 'Sometimes ambition can be dangerous, not only to them, but to those around them. Promises could be made and glittering prizes offered if … But there is only one man aboard the Ship who can really offer anything other than empty dreams. I am that man. Do as I say and you will have what you have won. Disobey me and …' He shrugged and looked directly at Merrill. 'A wise man has many tools and relies on none. I trust that I have made myself clear?'

'Perfectly.' Merrill tried not to smile at the prospects before him. 'When?'

'I will tell you when. Until then you will obey your orders, say nothing, think nothing, and, above all, do nothing.' Quentin rose in dismissal. 'You may go.'

He watched the young man stride from the room, his departing back radiating his arrogance and anticipation of what was to come and, watching him, Quentin felt pity for his blindness. Merrill was a killer, nothing more, and his usefulness ended there.

But he didn't know that.

From the bridge, Merrill was conducted down a hidden passageway towards his own sector, and he walked the droning corridors with his mind full of what he had just heard. The old man wanted him to stand ready to eliminate Gregson. That was obvious, and equally obvious was the fact that he would take over as chief of psych-police. Merrill smiled as he thought about it. The job itself was worth having with its attached privileges of private rooms, a seat on the Council, and literal life and death power over every man and woman in the Ship. But it meant more than that. Once in power Merrill intended to stay there and, knowing what he knew of the system the Captain apparently used, he would make certain that no one ever took over his job.

Two could play at the game of assassination.

He was still living in a world of his imagination when he felt a hand on his arm and turned to stare at the sullen features of Sam Aldway.

'What do you want?'

'I want to talk with you.' Sam glanced over his shoulder. 'Let's go somewhere private.'

Merrill hesitated for a moment, then led the way to a common rec-room. Closing the door behind them, he tripped the 'engaged' signal and glared at Aldway.

'Well?'

'I took him into the arena,' muttered Sam. 'You know who I mean.'

'So he agreed to fight?' Merrill smiled. 'Good. I never thought that he would. You killed him, of course.'

'No.'

'No?'

'I didn't kill him – in fact he almost killed me.' Sam fingered his bruised throat. 'Even now I don't know just what he did. I had him, another minute and he'd have been ready for the converters, and then the lights went out and the next thing I knew the attendant was standing over me.' He winced as he touched the transparent plastic over his eye and lip. 'You should have told me that he was up on all the tricks. Hell! I thought that he was just a neo.'

'Would I have trained you in that case?' Merrill stared at the man with undisguised contempt. 'So you failed. For all your boasting you let a first-timer beat you up and make a fool out of you.' He shrugged. 'Well, you've had your chance.'

'Wait a minute!' Sam grabbed at Merrill's arm as he stepped towards the door, then yelped as a stiffened hand slashed at the inside of his elbow.

'Keep your paws off me,' Merrill glared at the hydroponics worker as if he could have killed him. 'How dare you touch me!'

'I'm sorry.' Sam massaged his tingling arm. 'What about that job you promised me?'

'I promised you nothing. I merely told you that I couldn't have two assistants at the same time, but even that doesn't matter now. You've had your chance and failed. I've no time or patience with failures.' Merrill stepped towards the door and stood, his hand on the latch, looking at the other man. 'Forget it Aldway. Stay at your job and keep out of trouble. I can't help you now.'

'Wait!' Sam stared desperately at the cold face of the officer. 'I can try again.'

'He'll never let you get him into the stadium a second time. Even if you did, he would beat you just as he did before, and this time he might kill you in order to get rid of a nuisance.' Merrill lifted the latch. 'Sorry, Sam, better take my advice and forget it.'

'I can't.' Sam looked ill as he thought about it. 'I can't spend the rest of my life tending those damn plants. I won't do it.' He stepped forward, his eyes appealing. 'Look, supposing he dies. Never mind how, but supposing he does. Would I get his job?

'Maybe.' Merrill pretended to think about it. 'Unless of course, you were arrested for murder and sent to the converters.'

'I'll take that chance,' said Sam eagerly. 'Well?'

'If he dies,' said Merrill slowly, 'I'll be needing a new assistant. He opened the door. 'It's up to you, Sam. It's all up to you.' The door closed behind him and Sam smiled.

It wasn't a nice smile.

He sat in the room for a while, his mind busy with unaccustomed thoughts. To kill was easy, or so he had always thought, but to get away with it was the important thing. The alternative was the converters or, if he took Merrill's advice, a lifetime of manual labor in the farm. Thinking about it made him feel sick, and as he blamed Jay for his position, he began to hate where before he had only been contemptuous. By the time he left the room he was boiling with rage and almost frenzied in his desire to kill the man who stood between him and his ambition.

A couple passed him as he entered the corridor, both fully mature, the woman wearing the dull beige of the kitchens and the man the gray of waste reclamation. The woman stared at him and moved towards the vacated room. The man glanced at Sam's passion-distorted features and laughed before following the woman into the rec-room.

Sam paused, his hands knotting at his sides, fighting the desire to hammer on the door until it opened and then to smash the laughing face into pulp. He tried to control himself. There would be time enough for vengeance later, more time than he would need, and the training which Merrill would give him would make victory all the easier. But first he had a job to do.

He went looking for Jay.

He found him in one of the passages leading down from the upper levels and, cursing the people thronging the crowded corridor, began to stalk his victim like the blood-crazed beast he was. Instinctively he took care that he should not be seen and, with an effort of will, managed to control his features so that to a casual watcher he would appear to be intent on his own business. His experience in the arena had taught him that the young man was dangerous, too dangerous for fair fight, and as he followed the figure in the red shorts, Sam began running over the tricks Merrill had taught him.

Jay was totally unaware of the man behind him. He had his own worries and, as he turned from the busy passage into a quieter, more deserted region, he began to regret having helped George escape to No-Weight. It had been easy to talk of plans but carrying them out was something else. He frowned as he touched the folded blue shorts beneath his own red ones and his eyes, as he walked along, were never still. He had to find a man to take Curtway's place. Had, in effect, to murder an innocent stranger so that someone could snatch a few more weeks of life. At first he had viewed the scheme with cold detachment but, as time passed, he felt a growing reluctance to do what was necessary.

Operating under orders from P.P. headquarters was one thing, but acting as a free-lance was something quite different: In the first case he had no responsibility, no feeling of guilt or shame and he could take a quiet pride in an effective elimination as a job done efficiently and well. But now? He gritted his teeth as he tried to overcome his indoctrination and select a body with which to stage the 'accident.'

He paused before the door of Curtway's cubicle, saw by the external sign that it was empty, and walked inside. It would be better to have the body discovered in its own quarters; it would help identification for one thing, and for another it gave him time to set the stage for the 'accident' which must almost completely destroy the body. In all the Ship, the only way to do that was by electrocution, and grimly Jay squatted down beside a masking plate and began to undo the fastenings.

He barely heard the soft whisper of feet behind him as Sam lunged to the attack.

He half-turned just in time to avoid the full impact of the blow intended to snap his vertebrae but even then the side of his neck went numb and darkness flooded his vision. Desperately he staggered to his feet, automatically twisting to avoid the knee thrust at his groin, and tasted blood as fingers stabbed at his throat. Again the searing, nerve-paralyzing blows tore at his consciousness, sapping his strength and dimming his reflexes, so that he reeled helplessly against the metal wall, the hard surface bruising his cheek.

He could have died then, would have died if Sam had remained cool, but science yielded to frenzied instinct and Sam forgot what he had been taught. Instead of standing back and hitting with calculated precision, he tried to hit too often and too fast. He slashed at barely seen targets, stabbed at spots not quite as vulnerable as others, beat with savage but stupid energy at bone and muscle. He caused pain, the sickening pain of torn muscle and jarred nerve but, because of that very pain, he defeated his own ends.

Jay, spurred by his pain, shook off his numbness and fought back.

He was smooth and deliberate, the expert against the amateur, the professional assassin against the would-be murderer. Sam never stood a chance and when it was all over, Jay was still only half-aware of what he had done. He leaned against the wall, mechanically massaging his tormented neck; then, as he stared at the dead man at his feet, he smiled for the first time since receiving his assignment.

The door was closed and the signal which would prevent anyone from violating the advertised privacy was in place. Quickly Jay stripped the brown shorts from the dead man and exchanged them for the blue ones he had taken from Curtway. The identity disc was a harder job, and he sweated as he dragged it from the limp wrist and replaced it with the other. That done, he stooped over the masking plate and removed it from the wall, standing it against the bench before returning to peer into the revealed cavity.

Wires ran thick and heavy behind the metal of the wall. The triple circuits of the Ship, some for power, some for light, still others for the emergency illumination never used and now only assumed to be in existence. Jay frowned at them, wondering which would be the best for his purpose; then, as he remembered another, similar case, shrugged and dragged the dead body towards the opening.

It would be a sloppy job. No electronics man in his right mind would ever allow himself to be electrocuted, and George was an expert in his trade. For a moment Jay hesitated, pride of workmanship struggling against sheer necessity; then, thrusting forward the limp, right hand, he let it fall on to the wires.

The stench was awful. It was a blend of ozone and burnt blood, of charred flesh and seared metal. It was nauseating, vile and, as blue lightning tore across the widening gap between flesh and metal, Jay fought against the desire to vomit. He swallowed, desperately trying to quell his sickness, and stared at the blackened shape lying before him.

It had been human, male, had worn blue shorts and still carried a scrap of metal around his left wrist. That was all that could be told. Satisfied, Jay rose to his feet and stepped towards the door. Somewhere a fuse would have blown and meters kicked. Watchers would report a power-drop and men would be sent out to investigate. They would find a dead men and an exposed wire. They would report it to Merrill who, because of his job, would state that the entire occurrence had been an accident. The men in olive would come to collect the remains, other men would repair the damage, and the thing would be over and forgotten.

Except for Susan's tears.

She would believe her father dead, but there could be no help for that. There could be no comfort, no whispered reassurances, no betrayal of what had really happened. George Curtway was officially dead – and Jay's life depended on everyone believing that.

He stepped out into the corridor, closing the door behind him, and strode along the passage. He felt dirty and his stomach heaved when he remembered the odor of roasting meat. It seemed to be all around him, to have permeated the very pores of his skin, to cling to his hair and shorts. He wanted to strip and step into a shower, to lather his body and wash away the stench, to stare at an educational tape and cleanse his mind. He didn't notice Susan until he bumped into her.

'Jay!' For a moment she clung to him; then, remembering their last parting, moved consciously away. 'Sorry, but it was really your fault.'

'Forget it.' He stared down at her. 'Where are you going?'

'To see Dad.' She attempted to move past him. 'Please let me pass, Jay.'

'No.' He took her arm and tried to make her walk with him. 'Let's go and watch a tape or something. I haven't seen you for –'

'Please!' Coldly she removed his hand, her nose crinkling as if she smelled an unfamiliar scent. 'You seem to have a bad memory, Jay. I haven't.'

Numbly he watched her walk away from him down the passage towards her father's cubicle. He wanted to stop her, to force her to come with him, to do anything to prevent her from seeing that sight. But there was nothing he could do. Nothing.

He heard her scream as he left the corridor.

ELEVEN

Gregson stood and watched the machine of destiny. It was big, as it had to be to hold all the filed information, the various educational tapes, the selective master-plates, the cards, the erasers and computers. In itself it was a masterpiece of planning, constructed by the builders centuries ago to serve as a guide and a master above and beyond all limitations of human flesh. The Ship could forget its purpose, the personnel waste themselves in ambition and selfish pleasure, the race sicken and die from stupidity and greed, but Psycho would always be ready to give the information to restore the essential balance if the project of which it was a part was to succeed.

And yet it was not wholly omnipotent. It could advise but it still needed the human touch to transform its dictates into action. Looking at it, Gregson felt a quiet pride in being one of the few elect. He turned as Conway came towards him.

The psychologist carried a thin sheaf of plastic cards, rejects from the file banks, now erased and ready for further duty. He dumped them into a hopper, threw a lever, and smiled as a man who sees the completion of a job well done.

'Fascinating, isn't it, Gregson?' Conway rested his hand on the metal casing of the machine. 'Just think, inside there are the full details of every man and woman, child and newborn babe aboard the Ship. Every tiny detail, fed in fragment by fragment from Medical, Genetics, Supply, the Kitchens, the observers, all correlated and intermeshed by Psycho into a composite whole so that, at any moment, we can determine the efficiency-rating of anyone we wish.'

'Anyone?' Gregson's expression matched the dryness of his tones. 'The Captain?'

'Not the Captain, at least I don't think so.' Conway looked disturbed. 'He can't be, can he?'

'Not at his age he can't.'

'Well, then, everyone except the Captain.' Conway caressed the machine again. 'The more you think about it, the more wonderful Psycho becomes. It selects and channels the educational tapes, determines the exact amount of all material aboard, maintains the temperature and humidity of the air, keeps –'

'It's a machine,' interrupted Gregson harshly. 'Nothing more than an elaborate electronic device. Stop talking about it as though it was a god.'

'I trust Psycho,' said Conway mechanically. He looked over his shoulder at where an assistant worked at a desk, and lowered his voice. 'Control yourself, Gregson. We may be observed.'

'Quentin is no god either.' Gregson stared at the smooth bulk of Psycho as though it were a human enemy. 'He is an old man, too old.'

'He's still the Captain.'

'There were other Captains before Quentin,' said Gregson deliberately, 'and there will be others after him. How long must we let him live before making a change?'

'Are you insane!' Conway stepped forward, his eyes fearful as he stared around him. 'If he should learn of this …'

'Why should he?' Gregson shrugged but when he spoke again it was almost a whisper. 'Relax, Conway. We're alone now and there's no need for us to pretend to each other. Is Quentin's card in Psycho?'

'I don't know. He's the only person in the Ship who doesn't wear an identity disc. His card may be filed with the others, but how can I tell? Without his number it would be impossible to find.'

'It isn't in there, then,' said Gregson with quiet certainty. 'The first thing any Captain with sense would do would be to remove it. Quentin is no fool, he wouldn't be the Captain if he were, and no fool would have managed to stay alive so long.' His eyes as he stared at Conway held a sick envy. 'How old would you say he is, Conway?'

'Thirteenth generation?' The psychologist shrugged. 'I don't know. How is an old man supposed to look, Gregson? I've never seen one to base an estimate on. Quentin could be thirteenth or even twelfth, but I'm only guessing.'

'Say thirteenth,' whispered Gregson. 'That would make him anything between seventy-seven and fifty-eight years old.' He licked his lips. 'Twelfth? Twenty years more? Is it possible, Conway? Could a man live almost a hundred years?'

'Impossible!'

'Are you sure?'

'No, I'm not sure,' snapped the psychologist irritably. 'How could I be? But the thing is against all logic. You heard what Malick said: a man's usefulness ends once he has fathered the new generation, and we know that Psycho determines the life expectancy at around forty years. The builders set that figure, and the builders knew what they were doing. After forty a man's efficiency begins to fail. Can you imagine what state a man would be in if, by some miracle, he managed to live so long? The concept is ludicrous.'

'Perhaps you're right.' Gregson seemed reluctant to dismiss the idea. 'Put it at seventy then, or even sixty. That's still twenty years beyond the normal expectancy. A full generation!'

'For the Captain only,' reminded Conway. 'The rest of us still wear our discs and our cards are still filed in Psycho.'

'Yes.' Gregson stared at the humped bulk of the machine. 'Of course. And at any time those cards could be sorted, rejected, expelled and sent down to me.' He looked at Conway. 'To the executioner.'

'I know it.' Conway shuddered at an unpleasant memory. 'Every time I threw the trip-lever to expel the latest batch, I wondered whether or not my card would be among them. Sometimes I couldn't stand the strain and had to call an assistant to take over.'

'But not now.'

'No.' Conway glanced at Gregson as a dog might lick its master's hand. 'You ended that nightmare.'

'Postponed it,' corrected the chief of psych-police. 'We still wear our discs and are still vulnerable to questions. Both of us are fourteenth generation. Neither of us is young. Others are watching us – my officers, your assistants, even the Captain. One day someone is going to ask some pertinent questions and when they do ...'

He shrugged.

'You'll take care of that,' stammered Conway. '*You* took care of the other thing, didn't you?'

'I showed you what to do and you did it. Anyone but a fool would have thought of it for himself, but, even if you had, you would still have needed me as I needed you.' Gregson rested his hand on the machine. 'Even at that we were discovered. An electronics engineer stumbled on something and requested an interview with the Captain.'

'I remember that.' Conway looked troubled. 'What's going to happen?'

'Nothing, the man is dead.' Gregson smiled with conscious power. 'Didn't you expel his card for me? What else could I do but order his elimination?'

'So we're safe then.' Conway sagged with relief. 'Good. For a moment there you had me worried, Gregson, but with you controlling the police and with me in charge of Psycho, nothing can go wrong.' He frowned. 'I wish I could find out what it was that man discovered. If he found it, then others could.'

'Forget it. He's dead and, if others ask too many questions, they will die also.' Gregson glanced around to make sure that they weren't overheard. 'Our biggest danger is Quentin. I don't like the way he stares at me and I've the feeling he's up to something. I think that it's time we moved in.'

'Mutiny?' Conway shook his head. 'No, Gregson. I won't stand for that.'

'Who said anything about mutiny? Quentin is old, and old men die ... it happens all the time. If Quentin died, then we'd have to appoint a new Captain. The only problem we have to face is who? Not Henderly, not Folden, and certainly not Malick. The man's almost insane as it is with his babble about tapes showing meat eating. You? How long would you last alone? No,

Conway, *I'm* going to be the next Captain. Help me and your life is secure. Oppose me and I'll have to arrange an "accident." '

'I won't oppose you, but I won't help you mutiny either.' Conway spoke with a lifetime of indoctrination against the concept of forcible overthrow of authority. 'If Quentin should die, that's different. I'll stand by you as the new Captain.'

'Yes,' said Gregson dryly. 'After all, there's nothing else you can do, is there? As Captain I'd be the one man in the Ship to safeguard your secret.' He stepped away as the assistant, apparently finishing his task, rose from his desk and came towards them.

'Well, Conway,' he said for the other's benefit. 'Give me the cards and let me get on with the eliminations, I've still got the Barb problem to worry about.'

'Any fresh news on that?' Conway nodded to his assistant and reached for a lever, one of many on a panel before him. 'Maybe it would be as well to let them alone. If Henderly is right –'

'Henderly is a fool. He underrates the danger of starving men. He talks of cannibalism, and forgets that meat eating is unthinkable to any normal person.' His face darkened and he leaned forward as the psychologist tripped the lever. 'I wonder how many this time?'

'Can't tell.' Conway stepped beside him as he stared at the disposal tray. 'The whole operation is automatic. Psycho is scanning the cards now for any which do not fit into the pre-selected master pattern. All unfit will be rejected.' His voice warmed as he waited for the machine to finish its task. 'It's really wonderful, you know, Gregson. It's like building a new race on a previously determined matrix. Eliminate the unfit and save the essentials.'

'Then we must have a perfect race,' said Gregson dryly as he looked at the empty tray. 'No rejects?'

'Not as many as there have been,' admitted Conway. 'I don't understand it, but Psycho can't be wrong.' He smiled as two cards fell into the tray. 'Two out of five thousand. Here.' He picked up the cards, scanned them, and passed them to Gregson. 'A woman, Julia Connors, sanitation, sector Four and a man, Sam Aldway, hydroponics, sector five,'

'Again?' Gregson glanced casually at the cards. 'Sector five seems to be getting more than its fair share of eliminations recently.' He shrugged. 'We should worry, just so long as it isn't us, eh?' He laughed and, after a moment, Conway and the assistant laughed with him.

The assistant was the only one not genuinely amused. Aside from the communications man and Carter, the stand-by officer, headquarters was empty when Gregson returned. While waiting for Jay to answer his code signal he leaned back and, in the privacy of his office, surveyed his plans. Conway had been useful, might still be of some assistance, but, because of what he knew, would have to be eliminated as soon as Gregson had achieved his ambition. Malick too, the geneticist, was obviously irrational and, unless controlled, might cause later trouble. Henderly and Folden could continue on the Council for awhile, but Conway would certainly have to be disposed of.

Merrill, too.

Gregson was ambitious enough to take risks, but not fool enough to be blind to the ambitions of others. Merrill was untrustworthy and a defense would have to be found against him. No man could rule longer than his companions allowed him and, with ambitious men, any rule would seem too long. Gregson sat in his chair and hooded his eyes as he thought of the Captain.

Quentin was an old, senile fool – or was he? To the young all old men are fools, for the young insist on mistaking caution for fear, cool thinking for stupidity, tolerance for weakness. Quentin was old, fantastically old, sixty at least and maybe more, and he had been Captain for as long as Gregson could remember. But did mere age automatically qualify him for stupidity? Gregson sighed as he thought about it, then sat upright as Jay entered the office.

'You sent for me?' Jay looked tired. He had managed to get a shower but still felt unclean. He doubted whether a full soaking for a good ten minutes would serve to wash away the lingering traces of the odor surrounding him.

'Yes.' Gregson picked up the assignment card and threw it towards the officer. 'Another job in your sector. The other one completed yet?'

'Yes.' Jay stared numbly at the card and managed to control his instinctive reaction. Sam Aldway! The man he had planted to replace Curtway's missing body. The problem, instead of being solved, had only been postponed. He still had to find and eliminate an innocent stranger and, for a moment, he had a nightmare of continual assignments, each for the man he had just killed. He became aware of Gregson's eyes.

'Something wrong?'

'No.' Jay returned the assignment card to the desk. 'Why do you ask?'

'You looked odd. Sorry to keep you so busy but you know how these things are. They average out and you'll probably be bored to tears during the next few months.'

'You think so?' Jay didn't respond to the friendliness in the other's voice.

'I'm sure of it. I remember one time when …'

Gregson broke off as the door opened and Merrill entered the office. 'What do you want? Didn't they tell you that I was engaged?'

'They did, but it can't wait.' Merrill smiled with secret knowledge and stared at Jay. 'You'd better change. You look better in red shorts.'

'Change?' Jay felt his stomach tighten with apprehension. 'Why? What's wrong?'

'You'll find out.'

Jay hesitated then, at Gregson's curt nod, reversed his black shorts and donned them red side outwards. Merrill watched him, a faint grin of triumph lurking at the corners of his mouth, then jerked his thumb towards the door.

'Outside. There's someone out there who wants to see you.'

'Hold it a second.' Gregson stepped from behind his desk. 'I give the orders, Merrill. Now, what's wrong?'

'Ask Jay.'

'I asked you,' snapped Gregson impatiently. 'Don't get too big for yourself, Merrill. I suggest that you remember a conversation we had a short while ago.'

'I'm remembering,' Merrill didn't trouble to hide his enjoyment. 'That's what makes this so sweet. Jay's bungled a job and managed to do it perfectly. He not only electrocuted an electronics engineer, in itself so stupid as to be incredible, but he did the job in the man's own cubicle and before a witness. I received the official complaint even before I had viewed the body. Name, time, place – everything.' He smiled at Jay. 'You must have really been trying.'

'Shut up!' Gregson bit at his lower lip. 'Did you bring the witness in quietly?'

'Quietly?' Merrill shrugged. 'She was in the center of a crowd when I arrived. Her brother, who is also an electronics man, was with her and about a couple of dozen others. They all heard her name the accused and make the official complaint. Her brother swore that he'd make it his business to see that the killer was brought to justice. Get rid of the witness and you'll have every electronics man in the Ship asking questions, let alone trouble with Genetics for disposing of a marriageable female.'

'Waste!' Gregson glared at Merrill's smiling face. 'Fetch the witness. And wipe that grin off your face too – this is a serious matter.' He stared at Jay. 'Curtway?'

'Yes.'

'Is Merrill telling the truth?'

'I don't know,' said Jay miserably. 'I had to rush the job, that part is true, but –'

'But the man is dead?'

'Yes.'

'I see,' Gregson stood for a moment, his face bleak with thought. 'You were a fool, West,' he said dispassionately, 'but maybe we can manage to settle this. Did the girl actually see you eliminate the man?'

'Of course not.'

'Good.' Gregson turned towards the door as Merrill, accompanied by a woman, entered the inner office. 'My officer informs me that you wish to make an accusation,' he rapped. 'Is that correct?'

'It is.' Susan stared with tear-swollen eyes directly towards Jay. 'There he is. That is the man who killed my father.' She pointed towards him and Jay could almost feel her radiated scorn and hatred. 'I accuse that man of murder and demand the full punishment as laid down in the Ship's Code!'

The full punishment was agonizing death.

TWELVE

For a long moment no one moved or spoke. Finally, as Susan let her arm fall to her side and bowed her head, Gregson stepped behind his desk and sat down.

'Let us have some self-control here,' he said coldly. 'Merrill, if the girl can't stop crying take her out until she can. This office is not the place for tears.'

The very harshness of his voice produced the desired result. Susan dabbed at her eyes, lifted her head, and allowed Merrill to seat her in a chair. Gregson gestured for Jay to seat himself and looked at Merrill.

'Report.'

'I was notified of a power drop by electronics and went to the cubicle at fault. On arrival I was accosted by this young woman who accused a certain ventilation engineer named Jay West of the murder of her father. On investigation I found within the cubicle the body of a man, wearing the identity disc of George Curtway and the blue shorts of an electronic engineer. The man had died from electrocution.'

'I see.' Gregson stared at Susan. 'You realize, of course, the seriousness of this accusation. Murder, together with mutiny and waste, is a crime punishable by death. In the case of wanted, premeditated murder together with mutiny, the death penalty also carries the punishment of torture.' He paused. 'I mention this so that you may be aware of the gravity of the charge.'

'I hope they make him scream for years,' said Susan viciously. 'He killed my father.' She did not look at Jay. Gregson sighed.

'You actually saw the crime committed?'

'Of course not,' she snapped. 'Would I have stood by and watched my father being murdered?'

'Then what makes you so certain that this man is the guilty party?' Gregson glanced at Merrill. 'How old was the deceased?'

'Fourteenth generation,' said Merrill easily. 'He was an expert electronic engineer.'

'I asked you his age, not his capabilities.' Gregson softened his voice as he spoke to the girl. 'You see? Your father was an old man, my dear, and old men aren't always predictable. There is no proof that anyone killed him at all.'

'He's dead, isn't he?'

'Of course, but the death could have been accidental.'

'No.'

'You can't be sure of that,' insisted Gregson gently. 'We of the psych-police, perhaps better than anyone else, know how soon a man can lose his mental stability when he nears his fortieth year. Perhaps your father felt his coming decline and, though I hesitate to suggest it, he may have decided to terminate his own life.'

'Ridiculous!' Susan shifted angrily in her chair and glared her contempt at the suggestion. 'My father would never have committed suicide.'

'How can you be certain of that?' Gregson stared down at the surface of his desk then looked directly at the girl. 'The very method of death is … suggestive, don't you think? Who better than an expert in electronics would know just where the heavy current cables were to be found? Such a man would know how quick and painless death from electrocution would be. It seems logical to assume that your father may have chosen that way to end his life.'

'My father was sane,' stated Susan flatly. 'He was as efficient and as capable as he had ever been. He was old, true, but not that old. He was murdered.'

Looking at her, Jay had to admire her spirit. She knew nothing of the policy of the psych-police, naturally, and to her Gregson must seem a tedious old man trying to avoid the issue so that he could save himself work. Skillful handling by Merrill could have saved the situation but, glancing at the officer, Jay knew that, even if Susan hadn't made the accusation, she would have been encouraged into it. For some reason Merrill hated Jay, and now he saw his way to get rid of an enemy.

And he had an excellent chance of doing just that.

If Jay admitted killing Curtway then he was slated for punishment beneath the Ship's Code. Gregson couldn't cover him up now, not when the accusation had been made public, and even if he could Jay had a shrewd idea that Merrill wouldn't let him. If Jay told the truth, that he hadn't killed Susan's father, then he was in equal danger of elimination from Gregson for having failed his duty. Either way he was in danger of his life and, if George had spoken the truth, Gregson would be merciless. Jay leaned forward as Gregson spoke again.

'You have made an accusation,' he said to Susan. 'Your evidence?'

'I met this man,' again she made a point of not looking at Jay, 'immediately prior to finding the body of my father. There was no reason for him to be in that quarter.'

'Unwarranted assumption,' snapped Gregson. 'That is not proof.'

'I have reason to believe,' she continued stiffly, 'that my father had cause to speak to this man on certain private matters. My father was no duelist and would refuse to fight anyone no matter what the provocation. I suggest that this man was goaded into killing my father because he couldn't murder him in the arena.'

'That isn't true,' blurted Jay. 'I've never fought in the stadium either. I …'

He swallowed as he remembered the tell-tale red dot on the inside of his left forearm. As yet he'd had no chance to have it removed and he was acutely conscious of both Merrill and the girl looking at it. 'I did not dislike your father,' he muttered, 'and I didn't want to fight with him.'

'That's not true,' flared Susan. 'My brother will testify that on approaching my father's cubicle, he heard raised voices and this man demanding that my father should meet him in the arena for some fancied insult. Fred, my brother, didn't wish to violate privacy and walked away.' She bit down on her lower lip. 'That was the last time either of us heard my father alive.'

'Still hardly proof of murder,' snapped Gregson. 'Is that all?'

'Seems pretty conclusive to me,' said Merrill. 'If the brother can swear that West was in the cubicle with Curtway and this girl saw him outside within seconds after finding the body ...' He shrugged.

'I did not ask for your opinion,' said Gregson coldly. He looked at Susan. 'Have you any other testimony?'

'When I met him,' Susan gestured towards Jay, 'I noticed something odd about him. We quarreled, never mind about what, and yet he seemed too friendly and wanted to take me away from the area.'

'Perhaps he was sorry for the quarrel and wanted to restore himself in your good graces?'

'No. It wasn't that.' She frowned as if trying to stir her memory. 'There was something else. There was an odor, a horrible burnt kind of smell around him – I don't know how to describe it.' Her face twisted in sudden emotion. 'I smelled the same kind of odor when –'

'The body was burned beyond all recognition,' explained Merrill to Gregson. 'The charred odor was still very distinctive when I arrived.'

'I see.' Gregson rested his head on the tips of his fingers, his elbows supported on the desk, and stared down at his papers for a moment as if lost in involved thought. Then he looked at the others, his face harsh and bleak, his eyes narrowed as he stared from face to face.

'You have heard the accusation and testimony,' he said to Jay. 'Can you refute them?'

'There is nothing for me to refute,' said Jay easily. 'Surmise, assumption, and sheer coincidence.' He stared appealingly at Susan. 'I did not kill this young lady's father. He was my friend, I knew the entire family, and I swear to her on my hope of life that I did not do as she accuses.'

'Do you believe him?' Gregson stared at Susan.

'You have no real proof,' insisted Gregson. 'Personally, I could hardly bring myself to sentence this man without much firmer evidence. I ...'

His voice droned on but Jay was hardly listening. He was waiting for the obvious suggestion and, as Gregson spoke, he wondered why it hadn't already been made. There was one certain way to test the guilt or innocence of any man. The lie detectors were part of Psycho, foolproof, almost omnipotent in their efficiency. Susan, as yet, hadn't demanded their use. Perhaps she hadn't thought of it; perhaps, even now, she didn't really believe that he was guilty of the crime, however much outraged feminine pride had made her accuse him. Gregson, of course, wouldn't mention them. As far as he was concerned, Jay had killed the man and any evidence only went to strengthen that belief. The job had been almost criminal in its careless inefficiency, but these things had happened before and, to an extent, were tolerated for one time at least.

Merrill proved to be the Judas.

Susan was wavering, Jay could see that, could see, too, that Gregson would smooth her down, send her on her way and later report the finding of the 'murderer' and his subsequent 'death.' A nice, normal, easy way out of an unpleasant difficulty.

'… So you see, my dear,' soothed Gregson, 'you must leave it to us. The psych-police aren't as stupid as some people seem to think. There are certain tests and, even if we have to check every man and woman in the sector, we shall be able to either prove that your father was murdered or that his death was an unfortunate accident.'

'Tests?' Susan frowned. 'How do you mean?'

'The odor you mentioned,' explained Gregson easily. 'We know that tiny particles which constitute what is known as an "odor" can be found in the skin and clothing of any who were present. There are other things, perspiration index, for one and –'

'The lie detectors,' said Merrill.

'Exactly.' Gregson didn't look at the officer but Jay could tell by the slight writhing of muscle along the edge of the jaw just how Gregson felt. 'As I was saying –'

'This whole thing could be cleared up now,' insisted Merrill. 'Why don't you just put the accused to the test and done with it?' He looked at Susan. 'You'd be satisfied then, wouldn't you? If this man answers truthfully whether or not he killed your father then you could go back and tell the others. If innocent you could clear his name. If guilty …' Merrill shrugged. 'Personally, I'm surprised that he hasn't requested it himself if he's innocent of the charge.'

And that was that.

Numbly Jay grasped the twin electrodes and prepared to answer the questions. There was no hope of evasion, any lie would reveal itself in a flash of red across the signal plate, the truth with a flash of green. In minutes now, seconds even, the truth would come out. He only hoped that part would be revealed, not the whole. He tensed as Gregson leaned forward.

'Did you kill my father?' It was Susan who asked the question. She had risen in her excitement, her eyes anxious as she blurted the question, and Jay could guess that now, after the shock of finding the body had worn off a little, she desperately wanted to find him innocent. Jay looked directly into her eyes as he answered.

Green, a wash of color across the blank surface of the detection plate and, with the glowing color Susan seemed to recover new life.

'I knew it,' she whispered. 'All the time I really knew that you couldn't have done it, but I wasn't sure. Oh, Jay!' She was in his arms then, the wonderful softness of her hair against his cheek and, for a moment, he relaxed to the nearness of her warmth and beauty. Merrill's voice jerked him back to reality.

'It's fixed! The detectors are fixed!' He stared wildly at Gregson, then at Jay. 'you –'

'Be silent!' Gregson rose from his seat and stepped from behind his desk with a smooth coordination of muscular power. 'Take the girl back to her sector and return to duty.'

'You heard my orders, Merrill!'

'I heard them,' said the officer stubbornly, 'but I don't like it.'

'The detectors cannot be "fixed" as you call it,' snapped Gregson impatiently. 'This man did not kill this girl's father. He is innocent of the accusation.' He stared at Susan. 'You will, of course, spread this information to all who may be interested. You have accused an innocent man and, while I can understand and sympathize with your emotional upset, you still owe it both to the psych-police and to Jay West to undo the harm you may have done.' He pointed towards the door. 'You may leave now. Merrill! Obey your orders.'

For a moment the officer hesitated, doubt struggling with his own knowledge; then, as he stared at Gregson's taut features, he shrugged and led the way from the inner office. Jay was about to follow him when Gregson called him back.

'Not you, West. Stay here.'

Jay knew what was coming. Had known it from the first. He had not killed the man he should; Gregson knew it, Merrill would have, too, if he had stopped to think on the exact phraseology of the question, and now he had to answer for his failure. Tiredly he slumped back into the chair.

'You were lucky,' said Gregson unexpectedly. 'Did you realize that?'

Jay shrugged, not answering.

'If the question had been "Did you kill a man?" your answer would have automatically convicted you to death by torture. Psycho would have seen to that, or the Captain rather, which is much the same thing.' Gregson stared thoughtfully at the young man. 'Who did you kill?'

'Curtway.'

'Don't bother to lie to me, West. Merrill may think that the detectors have been fixed, but I know that they haven't. You didn't kill George Curtway. You killed someone else and planted the body in the place of your assignment.'

Gregson nodded. 'I'd wondered about your apparent carelessness; sloppy work isn't like you, and that job was ludicrously inefficient on the surface. You had to choose electrocution because nothing else would have disfigured the body beyond recognition.' Gregson nodded again as if pleased at solving a problem. 'Who was it?'

'Sam Aldway.' Jay pointed to the assignment card on the desk. 'I'm anticipating. You can cross him off already.'

'And Curtway?'

Jay remained silent.

'You've failed in your duty, West,' said Gregson coldly, and now there was no trace of his former friendliness in his tone. 'You know the penalty for that.' He leaned forward and stared at Jay. 'Why did you let him live?'

Gregson didn't use the lie detectors, the obvious and simplest method of acquiring tested information and, looking at the chief of psych-police, Jay began to guess why. Tests on the detectors were recorded on tape and transmitted to Psycho. Others could possibly replay that information, the Captain certainly, though there was no indication that he ever did. Gregson was being cautious and, realizing that fact, Jay felt a first glimmer of hope.

'I'm in love with his daughter,' he admitted. 'I just couldn't eliminate her father.'

'It that your only reason?'

'Yes. Sam Aldway, the man I killed, picked a quarrel with me.' Jay shrugged. 'I saw a chance to make the switch and took it.'

'I see.' Gregson sighed with something like relief. 'You know that Psycho determined Curtway's death and you know that it is our job to eliminate the unfit as ordered by the machine?'

'I do.'

'You know too the penalty for inefficiency?'

'Yes.'

'You're in trouble, West,' said Gregson softly. 'If I relay this information to Psycho, Merrill will take great pleasure in eliminating you.' He paused. 'Where is Curtway?'

'I don't know.'

'But you could find him?'

'Yes, I think so.'

'Find him, West,' ordered Gregson. 'Find him and eliminate him. When you have done that notify me personally so that I can examine the body. Do that and I'll forget to relay your inefficiency to Psycho.' He smiled without humor and, watching him, Jay was reminded more than ever of a feline.

'Find and kill that man, West – or *die*.'

He was still smiling as Jay left the office.

THIRTEEN

The ship was a murmuring throb of whispering sound. The eternal, inevitable vibration of life trapped in a medium of emptiness and silence. It was comforting in a way to hear it, to feel the subtle quiver of footsteps, the soft drone of engines, the myriad sounds of five thousand people living and breathing, loving and hoping, playing and working in the titanic metal egg which was their universe and their home. George Curtway had known that sound all his life, had been born to it, lived with it, felt it as a part of him. Now, lying in the thick, almost tangible darkness of No-Weight, he clung to it as the one familiar thing in a world of terror.

He was afraid.

He was afraid of the darkness, the emptiness, the unseen vastness of the space around the central axis. Never before in his life had he been in any space larger than the exercise rooms; there had always been others around him, and even in the privacy of his own cubicle or the common tee-rooms, he'd had the comforting knowledge that others were within a few yards of him. Now, suffering from the twin fears of darkness and agoraphobia, he stared, wide eyed into the surrounding darkness.

He had not moved far since Jay had left him. He had tried to sleep a little, but had not felt tired. He didn't feel hungry either, and had long ago lost all track of time.

He could have drifted in darkness for an hour, or a week, or a month. He didn't know.

He started as a slight sound came from the darkness before him, a soft, almost inaudible scraping, a sound as of an indrawn breath, the slight stir of disturbed air. It wasn't the first time he had heard such sounds but he didn't yield to superstitious terrors. Ghosts, goblins, elves, fairies, ghouls and vampires, the whole realm and terminology of the shadow-world of darkness and night, had died for the Ship's personnel when they had left their own world. If there was a noise in the darkness, then it must have been made by living persons, and George wanted to know who they were.

'Who's there?'

Silence. The smothered sound of a laugh. Again the scraping as of someone kicking against metal and launching himself through space. Cautiously George shifted his position and strained his ears for further betraying sounds.

The clang of metal ruined his concentration, and light, streaming through an open hatch, caught his attention. A dark shape squeezed through the opening as George kicked himself towards it.

'Jay?'

'Is that you, George?' The young officer drew himself clear of the hatch, reached out and swung the door shut after him. 'Let's get away from here.'

'What's happened?' George allowed himself to be led away from the hatch, gripping the arm of the officer tightly as they drifted through darkness towards an unknown destination.

'Gregson knows that you're still alive.' Rapidly Jay told of the accusation, impromptu trial, and Gregson's ultimatum. 'He followed me, of course, but I had expected that. I managed to dodge him long enough for me to pass through the hatch.' Jay swore as metal bruised his face. 'Waste! Why can't we have lights in here?'

Light came at that moment, a shaft of brilliance from the newly opened hatch, and a man's head and shoulders were visible as he peered into No-Weight. Jay twisted as he stared towards the illumination and caught a dimly-seen girder to steady himself.

'Gregson. If he finds us he'll kill us both.'

'If he can,' said George grimly. He stared at the barely revealed latticework of stanchions and girders. 'Even with lights he'll have a hard job to find us in here.'

'He knows that.' Jay grunted as the hatch slammed shut and darkness returned. 'He'll lock the door and seal us in. Let's hope that he'll be satisfied to leave us alone now.'

'You think he will?' George didn't sound too hopeful. As the darkness closed around them, he felt a return of his unfamiliar fears and, even though now he had company, he didn't relish the thought of spending an indefinite period in the loneliness of No-Weight.

'No,' admitted Jay. 'He wants us dead. You because for some reason he's afraid of you, and me because I let you live.' In the darkness he sought and found the other's arm. 'What's all this about, George? Why should Gregson be afraid of you?'

'I told you, Jay. I found out that he has cheated on Psycho and avoided his own death.'

'So you told me, but what proof have you? Even if you did manage to get to the Captain and make your accusation, could you make it stick?' Jay wiped at his forehead, half-annoyed with himself to find it moist with perspiration. Now that the swift rush of action was over, he felt the emotional collapse of the reaction and its attendant depression.

Like it or not, he was as good as dead. Trapped in No-Weight he would starve or die of thirst. The exits were all guarded, the emergency hatches locked and, even if Gregson left them alone, neither he nor George had any chance of reaching the Captain. In effect, they had chosen to hide in their own tomb.

'Once we get to the Captain,' George said. 'I can prove what I say.' He hesitated. 'Do you know anything about electronics, Jay? Or the workings of Psycho?'

'A little, not much.'

'Psycho is a kind of electronic sieve. Everyone has a card – it's really a sheet of metallic plastic impressed with varying degrees of magnetism – and those cards are sorted and compared to a master plate in the machine itself. All cards not meeting specifications are ejected. You know what happens to them better than I do, but that isn't important. I only guessed at the real purpose of those cards after I had made my check and found out what had happened.'

'And that was?'

'That totals of the cards issued, the cards remaining, and the cards erased should always be the same. In other words the Ship left Earth with a certain amount of cards. That total should now be the same. Well, it isn't.'

'Perhaps they lost one,' said Jay. 'Or destroyed one.'

'No. Those cards operate on a closed circuit. They are ejected, erased, re-filed and re-used. A record is kept of the exact number at each stage of the operation together with a punched tape signifying disposals, etc.' George paused. 'I found that there are two cards missing.'

'That isn't important,' Jay snapped irritably. 'I've seen those cards. Perhaps someone lost one in some way. Waste, George! In three hundred years it wouldn't be hard to lose a card or two.'

'You miss the point, Jay.' George sounded as if he were explaining why two and two should always make four. 'The cards you've seen aren't the ones from the machines. When I talk of ejected cards I don't mean the copies you've seen. The cards themselves remain within Psycho. Once scanned and found wanting, a copy of name and number is made, the copy ejected and the original erased and re-filed. The copies are usable more than once. In effect no card, as I use the term, ever leaves the machine.'

'So? Where does that get us?'

'Someone has tampered with Psycho. Has located two cards, removed them, and possibly destroyed them.' George sighed at the other's silence. 'Can't you see it yet, Jay? Suppose that your card is in the machine. You know that one day, you don't know just when, that card will be scanned and ejected. When that happens, you know that you are due to die. You don't want to die. What do you do?'

'Take out the card,' Jay answered automatically, then swore. 'Is that what happened? Is it possible?'

'Yes, to both questions. It is possible, if you know all about the machine. I might be able to do it – but it wouldn't be easy.'

'Gregson?'

'He would have to be in on it. As chief of psych-police he would be the first to get curious and suspicious.'

'But he couldn't remove the cards?'

'Who then?'

'I don't know,' said George slowly. 'I've not had time to give this thing much thought. I only stumbled upon the discrepancy in the grand totals a short while ago, and you know what's happened since then. I knew that Gregson must be implicated because of his position but even then I didn't know about the program of elimination. You taught me about that, though I had had my suspicions as I told you.'

'It doesn't make sense,' protested Jay. 'Why should Gregson do that? All he needed to have done was to wait until his card was ejected and then destroy it. As chief of psych-police no one need ever have known.'

'It couldn't have been as simple as that, Jay. Other men have been in Gregson's position, and I assume that they were all eliminated when their turn came.' George sucked in his breath. 'You know, the more I think about it the more complicated it all becomes. Who eliminates the psych-police? Who decides when the chief is due for death? There must be some check or safeguard, Jay – if there weren't we'd have had a despotism centuries ago.'

'We know our responsibilities,' Jay said curtly. He didn't want to explain how each officer carried the knowledge of his fate with him … how, sometimes in the silent darkness of their lonely cubicles, they awoke to sweating fear of the unavoidable. He blinked in a sudden flood of light.

'The lights!' George stared at the rows of glowing tubes. 'Someone's turned on the lights!'

'Gregson.' Jay felt a sudden nausea as he looked at the immensity of No-Weight and clutched at a girder for support. He had never, in all his life, seen anything as big before. It was incredible in its sheer vastness, a colossal tube fully a hundred yards across, so long that its sides diminished in perspective. Girders ringed a complex latticework of thick metal struts and stanchions, webbed in the center to a unified hole from which spread the ranked layers of the Ship itself.

'It's big,' whispered George and his knuckles as he gripped the stanchion showed white beneath the strain. 'It must be the biggest thing in the Ship.'

Which, of course, wasn't true. No-Weight, because of the preponderance of girders and essential fabric, the low gravity at the perimeter and the absence of it at the central axis, was merely the largest unused space in the Ship. Even at that the builders had found a use for it. Stale air, rising from the lower levels, was piped to No-Weight where it was in turn blown down to the gardens, there to be circulated over the acres of carbon-dioxide removing plants and adjusted for optimum human consumption. But to a man whose horizon had always been the metal walls of cubicle or corridor, No-Weight was big.

Sounds echoed through the silence; the clang of metal and the soft shuffle of distant feet. Down the brilliantly lit tube, looking tiny and insignificant against the incredible thickness of the girders, men streamed through an open door. Jay looked at them, narrowing his eyes as he tried to focus on the unaccustomed distance, then turned his head as similar sounds echoed from near at hand.

'What's happening?' whispered George, instinctively keeping his voice low in the echoing vastness. 'Who are they? What are they doing here?'

'Gregson,' said Jay again, and tasted a bitterness in his mouth as he looked at the new arrivals. They were strangers but he recognized the type. The hangers on at the stadiums, the men who found pleasure in watching pain and struggle, the frustrated beings who, denied the very thing for which they had been bred, found escape in personal combat and vicarious battle. Others were among them, familiar shapes wearing the black shorts of the psych-police and, from the hands of both police and strangers, little flashes of metallic brilliance sparkled and died, flared again and dulled, flashing as the bright lights reflected from the polished surfaces.

'Knives,' said George wonderingly. 'They're carrying knives.'

'They're going to search No-Weight,' explained Jay. 'They've entered by two doors and will search the sector between. When that's done they'll move along until we'll be trapped against one of the ends.' He squinted down the length of the tube. 'See? They've started towards the engines and will sweep towards the sealed areas.'

'Can we escape?' George looked hopefully at the officer. 'What about that hatch by which you entered?'

'Gregson would have locked it after him.' Jay shook his head. 'We can hide, I suppose – it's going to take them a long time to sweep through the central axis, but they'll get us in the end.' He stared at the knives in the hands of the searchers. 'Gregson must be desperate to do a thing like this.'

He fell silent, crouching behind a girder and watching the skilled maneuvering of the searchers. Their plan was simple and, because of that, was highly effective. A party moved out to the central girders and, at a signal, moved forward and around it. Nothing living or dead could escape being seen by them. A second party waited a little behind the first, resting poised and ready, their knives in their hands and prepared to dart after and attack anyone who eluded the searchers. The two parties moved forward together while a third group, smaller than the others, strung themselves along the examined area.

'Can we dodge past them?' George ducked behind the girder and looked appealingly at Jay. 'They'll hardly search the entire area twice.'

'They'll search until we're found and killed,' said Jay grimly. He kept his voice low knowing how sound traveled in the silence of No-Weight, knowing too that it was only because the searchers were concentrating on their immediate vicinity and not worrying about what lay ahead, that they had not been seen when the lights went on. He kept the bulk of the girder between them and the searchers as he spoke to George.

'Gregson's thought of everything.' He jerked his head towards the searchers. 'They're even wearing white arm bands. That's to stop us mingling with them and pretending that we belong to the party. They would hardly know us by sight and, as far as Gregson knows, we could have knives of our own.'

'What can we do? Have you any ideas, Jay?'

'Not yet,' Jay glared at the lights. 'If it weren't for those we could sneak past and maybe break out into the Ship. We could even attack a couple of the searchers and take their arm bands and knives.' He glanced at the electronics engineer. 'Can't you kill the lights in some way?'

'Not from in here. The wires and fuses are all in the outer corridors, and even if we managed to smash the protective cover and short a tube, it wouldn't extinguish the others.' He stepped towards one of the lights. 'You want me to do that?'

'No. If you killed only one it would just attract attention.' Jay peered around the edge of the girder and jerked back his head as he saw how near the searchers were. 'Come on, George,' he whispered. 'We've got to get moving. Follow me, stay close to the wall, and always keep a girder between you and the advance party. Ready?'

Gravity was so low that they could literally skim over the 'floor.' Jay led the way, thrusting himself along with calculated force, judging things so that he could cushion his impact with his hands and arms. Rapidly, they passed along the central axis towards the sealed areas, not stopping until the searchers were far behind. Then they paused for breath.

'Can we escape, Jay?'

'I don't think so.' Jay stared around at the silent girders. 'This part of the Ship is strange to me, but Gregson must know the locale well enough to know that we can't get out.'

'I see.' George sat thinking for a moment, then he looked at the younger man. 'Look. I got you into this, Jay, and maybe I can get you out. Suppose you took me prisoner and delivered me to Gregson? That would save your life, wouldn't it? And later, after it was all over, you could tell the Captain what I told you about the tampering with Psycho.'

'No.'

'Be reasonable, Jay. What's the good of both of us getting killed if one can escape? I don't think that I'd mind dying so much if I knew that Gregson would be taken care of afterwards. I'm an old man, Jay, and I don't suppose that I could live much longer, but you're young.' He hesitated. 'There's another thing. I'd like to feel that there was someone to look after Susan. You know what I mean.'

'Look, George,' Jay explained patiently, 'it wouldn't work. Gregson can't afford to let me live now, and once he reports my inefficiency to Psycho, I'll be due for elimination. He may already have done so. In any case, those searchers probably have orders to kill every living thing they find. We'd never get past the first group, let alone down into the Ship itself.' He shook his head, then tensed as he heard a sound. 'What was that?'

'I don't know,' whispered George. 'It sounded like a laugh or –' He broke off as the sound was repeated. 'Could they have reached us already?'

'I doubt it.' Jay listened again, then stared towards a girder. 'Stay here.'

He moved carefully to avoid the slightest possibility of noise, and stepped lightly towards the girder from behind which the sound had come. He reached it, peered around it – and stared.

The man who cowered behind the girder was naked, his pallid skin grimed with dirt so that it looked almost gray in the brilliant lighting. He tittered as he saw Jay, his deep-lined face convulsed with horrible merriment, and his eyes peered through a tangled mat of waist-length hair. It was that hair which made Jay doubt whether the creature was really human. He stared at it, hardly believing his eyes, looking from the hair to the bloated limbs, the filthy skin, the scabrous, unhealthy looking flesh.

'What is it?' George gripped Jay's arm as he stared at the monstrosity. 'Is it a man?'

'Yes.'

'But look at it! That hair!'

'It's white,' Jay whispered slowly. 'White hair! Is it possible for a man to have white hair?'

All the Ship personnel had brown or black hair with a little red and some blond. White hair was a sign of age and no ordinary member of the Ship's personnel had ever seen an old man. He recoiled a little as the stranger lunged to his feet.

'Food,' he mouthed. 'Food.'

'He's insane,' stated Jay decisively. 'No sane man would let himself get into such a state of filth.' He stepped back as the man advanced towards them, his hands held before him, a thin trickle of saliva running from the corner of his mouth. 'Food,' he whined. 'Don't forget poor old Joe. Joe's hungry. They didn't leave him anything to eat.'

'Who didn't?' Jay forced himself to grip the man by the shoulder. 'Which others?'

'The rest.' The stranger gestured vaguely around him. 'We lived here, all alone in the dark.' He tittered again. 'I like the dark. I like to float in the emptiness and drift from place to place.' His face crinkled as if he were going to cry. 'But I'm hungry. Poor old Joe, no one wants him now. No one at all.'

Looking at him, Jay could believe that. The man could arouse nothing but abhorrence in any who saw him. He gritted his teeth as he shook the obese figure.

'Who are you? How did you get here?'

'I'm Joe,' whined the creature. 'They wanted to kill me so I ran away.' He giggled. 'I fooled them. They couldn't kill old Joe. Joe was too clever for them, Joe was.' He giggled again and held out his hands. 'Food?'

'That must have been what I heard while I was waiting for you,' said George. He told Jay of the sounds which had troubled him while resting in the darkness. 'Is it possible that others have run away to hide in No-Weight?'

'I don't know,' said Jay slowly. He frowned, remembering vague rumors of people who had escaped their fate by flight to what he had always thought was a living tomb.

'How long have you lived here?' George asked.

'A long time,' tittered the man. He seemed pleased to have an audience. 'A long, long time. Others came after me, but I've lived the longest.'

'Which others?' Jay questioned. 'Where are they?'

'They ran away when the lights came on,' complained the man. 'I don't like the lights, they hurt my eyes, but they didn't care about that. They just left me, all of them, and they didn't leave me any food.' He held out his hands again in an oddly disturbing gesture. 'Food? You'll feed poor old Joe?'

'Later.' Jay stared at George. 'There must have been others hiding in No-Weight besides this wreck. Somehow they obtained food and managed to live.' He nodded thoughtfully as he thought about it. 'Food requirements would be low in the absence of gravity and lack of physical exercise would account for his fat. Lack of water would account for his dirt, though he could probably lick enough condensation from the metal to stay alive.'

'What about his hair?' asked George. He shuddered as he looked at the tangled mass. 'Look at it! It's disgusting!'

'Never mind his hair.' Jay stared at the man again, trying to ignore his odor, his dirt, the saliva drooling from his mouth and the restless twitching of his eyes. 'Joe!'

'You want me? You want old Joe?'

'Those others you spoke of – where are they?'

'They ran away.' A cunning expression crept over the lined face. 'You want to find them?'

'Yes.'

'They've got food. You'll fetch it back to poor old Joe?'

'Yes.' Jay glanced down the tube towards the nearing searchers. 'If you'll tell me where to find them, I'll get some food for you. Where are they?'

'Down there.' The man gestured towards the sealed areas. 'They ran away when the lights came on. Bosco, and Murray and the rest. They all ran away from me.' Tears of self-pity glistened in the restless eyes. 'Food?'

'Where did they go?'

'I told you.' Again the man gestured towards the end of the central axis. 'Somewhere down there. They know where the food is but they wouldn't tell me.' He sniffed, wiping his nose on the back of his hand, a gesture which almost caused Jay to vomit. George pulled at his arm, his face anxious.

'Hurry, Jay,' he whispered. 'We'll be seen soon.'

'Coming.' Jay stared hopelessly at the lined features of the stranger, knowing that he had obtained all the information he could from the creature, and yet knowing that it wasn't enough. For a moment he hesitated, then, as the first of the searchers came into view, he followed George towards the end of the tube.

They had passed two sets of girders when they heard the shout and for a second Jay thought that they had been seen. Then the shouts turned into laughter, against a background of screams. Jay stared grimly at the electronics engineer.

'Still want to give yourself up?'

'They killed him,' George said sickly. 'An old man like that, and they killed him.'

Jay didn't answer, but progressed with increased speed towards the blank metal ahead. A riveted bulkhead sealed off No-Weight from the mysterious regions of the sealed areas beyond and Jay stared at it, biting his lips as he looked for signs of the 'others' whom the insane creature had mentioned. George gripped his arm.

'Look! A door! See?'

A small hatchway was open at the edge of the bulkhead. It was a round panel, three feet across and opening inwards so that it looked like a dark spot against the polished smoothness of the bulkhead. From where they stood it was 'up' and a little to the right, almost directly opposite across a hundred yards of clear space. Even as they looked at it, the panel began to close.

Jay gripped a strut, twisted himself so that his feet rested against the metal and, aiming quickly, thrust himself with the full power of his muscles towards the closing door. It was a risky thing he did. His speed was too great for safety and, as he hurtled across the clear space, he knew that he would land too heavily. He twisted his body as he passed the central region where gravity abruptly altered so that, instead of the hatchway being 'up,' it now became 'down,' and plummeted feet-first towards the panel.

He hit with a force which jarred the teeth in his head and sent little shafts of pain lancing up his legs and thighs. For a moment he was afraid that the door had been locked and that he had broken his bones against the unyielding surface. Then the panel gave beneath him, he hurtled through the hatchway and he was in darkness, struggling with something soft and yielding. A man swore, then hands closed around his throat and a voice rasped terse instructions.

'Shut that door! Quick!'

'Here's another.' A man, a shapeless figure against the light, grunted as George gripped the edge of the hatchway.

'Get him inside.' snapped the first voice. 'Quick!'

Light flared with the closing of the hatch and, in the dim glow of a handbeam, Jay blinked up at the first speaker. He was a big man, stocky, with mottled gray hair. He stared at Jay, saw the black uniform shorts, and his hands tightened with grim promise.

'Police!'

'*No*' Jay tore at the hands around his throat, gripping the fingers and wrenching them free. 'Bosco? Murray?'

'How did you know my name?' The big man rubbed his injured hands and glared at Jay. 'I'm Bosco.'

'Joe told me.' Jay looked towards where George was held by the other man. 'We're on the run from Gregson, the chief of psych-police. Those searchers are after us. They killed the old man, Joe he said his name was, and they'll kill us too if they find us.'

'Why?'

'I escaped into No-Weight,' said George quickly. 'Jay here helped me.'

'You came to join the Barbs?' Bosco glared suspiciously at Jay. 'You? An officer?'

'I had no choice,' Jay explained grimly. 'I should have killed George, eliminated him, but I didn't. Gregson found out and now he wants us both dead.' Jay stared curiously at Bosco. 'Are you Barbs?'

'Yes. We're the barbarians, so called because we wanted to live.' There was a brittle dryness in the big man's voice. 'We skulk in No-Weight, eating when we can, drinking what we can, living how we can. You should know of us.'

'I've heard rumors,' admitted Jay, 'but that's all. I'd begun to doubt if you really existed.'

'A policy of silence,' Bosco nodded. 'It makes sense – the less who know of us the fewer there will be wanting to join us.' He looked at his companion. 'What shall we do with these two?'

'Throw them back into No-Weight.' The man who held George glowered at his captive. 'If it hadn't been for these two the police might never have wanted to search. We only just got away in time as it is.'

'We can't throw them back,' snapped Bosco. 'If we leave them alive, they'll talk, and if we kill them first someone will begin asking questions. Waste!' He glared at Jay. 'Why did you have to follow us?'

'I wanted to live,' said Jay quietly. He looked at the gray-haired man. 'Like you, like Murray here, like Joe.'

'Joe was too far gone to save.' Bosco didn't seem to like talking about it. 'The searchers expect to find some Barbs living in No-Weight, and we had to leave some for them to find. Joe, Mary, Sam, a few others. All of them old-timers. Joe had lived here for over thirty years and was insane for the past ten. The darkness finally got him – that and other things.' He didn't explain what those 'other things' might have been. 'It's best that they should die to save the rest. They were due for the converters years ago.' He looked at Murray again. 'Well?'

Murray shrugged. He had made his suggestion and didn't seem able or willing to make others. George spoke before the big man could make up his mind.

'Can't we wait here until the search is over? We'll promise not to tell anyone about what we've seen.'

'How can we trust him?' Murray jerked his thumb towards Jay. 'A policeman. Waste! He'll have the Ship aroused as soon as he got to a phone.'

'The Ship will be aroused anyway,' said Jay easily. 'You forget, Gregson is looking for us, not you. When he doesn't find us he's going to start wondering. As far as anyone knows at the moment there is no way out of No-Weight except the guarded entries. As soon as his men report that we aren't in here, Gregson will order an investigation. He may even go to the Captain.'

'The Captain?' Bosco glanced at Murray, an odd expression in his eyes. 'Why should he do that?'

'Because he knows that's where we are trying to go.' Jay smiled at the big man. 'George here has something to tell him, something Gregson will do anything to prevent the Captain from hearing. If he misses us now, and he will, then he'll become desperate. On the other hand, if you take us to the Captain, or help us get to him, then maybe I can put in a good word for you.'

'What could you do for us?' Murray released George and stepped forward, his face coming into greater clarification as he neared the source of light. Like Bosco his hair was shot with gray and his features wore an unusual hardness. Jay shrugged.

'I don't know yet. An amnesty, perhaps? Something like that. But it all depends on the Captain.'

'Yes.' Murray seemed to be secretly amused. 'It does, doesn't it.' He glanced at Bosco. 'Think we should do it?'

'Why not? We can't throw them back into No-Weight and I don't fancy killing them here. They could be telling the truth, or they might be lying to save their own skins. It doesn't matter. If they're trying to be clever, we can eliminate them later.' He jerked his head towards Jay and George. 'Come on with us, then. Stay close behind and don't try anything.' He was turning away when Jay caught at his arm.

'Where are you taking us?'

'To join the rest of us who escaped that trap.' Bosco led the way from the cubicle into a wide corridor.

It was bitterly cold, so cold that Jay felt his skin goose pimple and his teeth chatter. Next to him George moaned with discomfort and rubbed his arms to try and keep them warm. The two Barbs, aside from their pluming breath, didn't appear to react to the chill, and Jay guessed that to them it was no new experience.

A light winked ahead of them; Bosco answered the signal and, within seconds, they had come up with the rest of the party. Jay stared with interest at them. There were eight men and four women, and all had the same indefinable stamp of something outside his experience. The hair of some, like that of Bosco and Murray, was shot with silver threads, but it wasn't that which made them seem almost alien to the officer. It was something about their eyes, the unconscious attitude of superiority and self-mastery so that, beside them, he felt as he were a child. They stared at him, listening to Bosco's explanation, then together the assembled party continued down the icy corridor.

It grew colder as they went on but the gravity remained the same and Jay knew that they were progressing along one of the communicating tubes running beside No-Weight. They had walked a long way and Jay was numb and George blue with the cold when Bosco halted before a door.

'Don't touch anything you may see out there.' He gestured to beyond the panel. 'The rest know about it, but you're new. Remember, don't touch anything.'

He snapped off his hand beam as he swung open the panel and Jay blinked to a flood of light.

It came from one end of a vast chamber in a wave of brilliance almost too great for eyes accustomed to the dimness of the corridor, but, as Jay blinked and stared, he could see a multitude of brilliant points against a background darker than the shorts he wore.

'They're moving!' whispered George, and his voice echoed his amazement. 'Those lights are moving!'

They were. They moved from one side of the blackness down in a smooth arc to disappear at the other, while new ones took their place as they passed in continual procession across the darkness. To George it was the strangest lighting system he had ever seen and to Jay it was inexplicable. He turned and touched Bosco's arm.

"What is it?'

'That?' Bosco looked towards the glittering points. 'Oh, they're stars.'

'Stars!'

'That's right. You've heard of stars, haven't you?' Jay had, but only as a repeated lecture on one of the tapes; to him the word 'star' had nothing to do with reality, and he stared at the scene in bewildered amazement.

'Come on,' Bosco said urgently. 'We mustn't linger here. The very temperature of our bodies can affect the instruments.' He began to drag Jay towards the far wall of the vast room. 'Let's get moving before we freeze.'

Reluctantly Jay turned and followed Bosco, his head riding on his shoulder as he stared back at the glittering display of the universe. Suddenly he tripped and almost fell over a vat-like receptacle. It was one of many ranked in orderly rows across the floor, and as Jay caught at the edge to save himself from falling, he stared directly into the face of a dead man.

He rested beneath a sheet of some transparent material, still, immobile, the lips parted a trifle to reveal glistening teeth, the eyes closed and the body – a surprisingly undeveloped body, according to Jay's standards – naked and with a waxen pallid look.

Jay had heard of deep freeze, all the Ship personnel had, but to him deep freeze was where the animals and birds, the fish and insectivores lay against the time of their awakening at Journey's End. No one had ever dreamed that men too could lie in suspended animation. No one, that is, of the ordinary Ship personnel, and Jay's immediate assumption was that they must be dead.

He couldn't guess that here in these ranked vats rested the brains, technology and filtered information of a world three hundred years away in time and uncountable miles in space. Here were the ecologists, the atomic engineers, the rocket pilots, the geologists, the mineralogists, and the specialists in all the other branches of science and experience impossible to either teach or practice in the Ship itself. They rested as they had rested ever since the Ship had left Earth, sleeping, if it could be called that, waiting for the day when they would be wakened to help build a new Earth.

But to Jay they were all dead men.

As he stared at Bosco waiting impatiently for him at the far side of the chamber, his eyes were dull with lack of understanding.

'What kept you so long?'

'Those men,' stammered Jay. 'I saw them.'

'Well?'

'They're dead. All dead.'

'What of it?' Bosco stared at Jay as he led the way into a corridor. 'Haven't you ever seen a dead man before?'

'Yes, but …' Jay swallowed, hardly noticing that it grew warmer as they walked down the passageway. 'Why weren't they sent to the converters? Why keep them like that?'

'I don't know,' Bosco said thoughtfully. 'I've wondered about that myself. As far as I know there is only one man who could answer that.'

'Who?'

'The man we are going to see. The Captain.'

Jay was so numbed with repeated shocks that he didn't even feel surprised.

FOURTEEN

The scene was a normal one of distant Earth, a farming scene with animals and crops, machines and happy, busy men and women. Malick smiled as he saw it, leaning a little forward as he stared at the illuminated screen of the viewer. The children would be seeing the same educational tape; remembrance of their planet of origin was an essential part of Ship indoctrination.

The scene changed as he watched, the harvesters climbing into an animal-drawn vehicle, and the images moved to portray their faces in enlarged close-ups. The women were young, healthy, radiant with fitness and enjoyment; the men, also young, also fit, comfortably attired in loose shirts and trousers. The driver –

Malick felt almost physically ill.

It was the shock of the unexpected which did it. The man was normal enough, with two arms, two legs, two eyes and a head, but there was something about him which the geneticist had never seen before.

White hair. Lined features. Gnarled hands.

The man was old.

The screen faded as Malick turned the switch and picked up his phone. 'Gregson?'

'Speaking.'

'Malick here. I've just seen a new tape. One relayed to the children.'

'So?'

'So it shows an old man. Do you understand, Gregson? An old man!'

'How do you know?' There was irritated impatience in the chief's voice. 'Have you ever seen an old man?'

'Of course I have. Quentin is old, isn't he? Well, so was the man I saw in pictures on the tape.' Malick gripped the phone with sudden urgency. 'Gregson! Don't you realize what this could mean?'

'Yes,' said Gregson after a pause. 'Yes, I see what you're getting at.'

'It could ruin our social system,' babbled Malick. 'Once the children get used to the idea that a man is only old when he has white hair, lined features and gnarled hands, then who's going to believe that they're old at forty?'

'You don't have to explain to me what I already know, said Gregson coldly. 'Is this the first time you've seen the tape?'

'Yes. I'd noticed something odd before – you remember, the tapes showing people slaughtering animals and eating meat. You laughed at me then, but this time you can't afford to laugh. What do you think will happen when the children grow up and begin asking questions?'

'Trouble,' snapped Gregson curtly. 'Look. Have you any witnesses to what you saw?'

'No. But I can find some. It's a certainty that one or more of the attendants would have watched the tapes. I'll find someone if you like.'

'Do that. Find her and fetch her up to the Bridge.'

'The Bridge?'

'That's right.' Gregson sounded unnaturally grim. 'This is a matter which has to be settled by the Captain.'

'But ...'

The voice died as Gregson replaced his handset. Merrill, lounging on the edge of the desk, looked curiously at his superior officer. 'What was that all about?'

'My business.' Gregson glared impatiently at the young man. 'What are you doing here, anyway? I ordered every officer into No-Weight to conduct the search.'

'The search is finished,' said Merrill easily. 'I've taken back the dueling knives you issued out to the men, and returned them to the stadiums. The men themselves have gone back to their work.'

'Did you find them?'

'Who?'

'You know who I mean, Merrill. West and Curtway. Did you find them?'

'We found and eliminated seven people. Five women and two men.' Merrill paused with calculated deliberation. 'Jay and his friend were not among them.'

'What?'

'We didn't find either of the two men you wanted.'

'That's impossible! I watched Jay enter No-Weight and I know that Curtway was hiding there. Waste, Merrill! Are you telling me that you've fallen down on the job?'

'I'm telling you that we couldn't find people who weren't there to be found.'

'Impossible!'

'Keep saying that,' Merrill sneered. 'I tell you that we searched No-Weight from one end to the other and we eliminated everyone we found. Jay and Curtway weren't to be found, therefore they couldn't have been in No-Weight.' Merrill slipped from the edge of the desk and stared down at his chief. 'To me that's simple logic – unless you want me to believe that they were invisible and slipped through solid metal.'

'I can't understand it.' Gregson stared suspiciously at the young officer, his hatred and fear returning with renewed force. Merrill was getting to be dangerous. The man was ambitious, too ambitious, and, now that Jay had let him down, Gregson knew that he would have to find a new weapon against Merrill, and fast. He gestured towards the door.

'Return to duty.'

Merrill hesitated, wondering whether now wouldn't be the best time to eliminate his chief and so gain his coveted position. He could do it so easily; next to him, Gregson was an old man and long out of practice in the delicate art of killing a man with his bare hands. Memory of Quentin and his warning came just as he was about to reach for the other's throat. Sucking in his breath, Merrill forced himself to control his emotions. He turned just as he reached the door.

'When are you going to see the Captain?'

'Why?'

'I thought that perhaps you'd like me to come with you.' Merrill smiled with superior knowledge. 'After all, as I conducted the search the Captain might like to have a first-hand report on what we found.'

'I'll relay the report,' snapped Gregson. He stared pointedly at the young man. 'Return to your duty and leave the thinking to me.'

'Yes, *sir!*' Merrill made the title sound like an insult.

Gregson sighed as he stared at the closing door and, despite his iron calm, felt a mounting sense of danger. Jay and Curtway had escaped the search, a search for which he alone was responsible. The Barbs were dead, yes, but the death of seven people would hardly justify arming Ship personnel, taking them from their normal duties, and the power-loss caused by illuminating the entire area of No-Weight.

And Jay and Curtway were still alive.

Jay didn't matter; that is, he hadn't mattered until now, but if Curtway had told him what he knew, and if Merrill had found them, listened to them and hidden them somewhere, waiting for his chance to take them to the Captain …

Gregson stared down at the surface of his desk and his face grew bleak as he visualized what must be the outcome of any such move. He shivered a little as if at a return of his recurrent dream, feeling in imagination the plastic bag of the men in olive, the sharp knives of the medical students, the final violation of the dreaded converters. All of that would happen if they reached the Captain. But if he were the Captain …

Gregson reached for the phone, punched a number, and waited impatiently for the connection to be made.

'Yes?'

'Gregson here. Conway?'

'That's right.' Anxiety sharpened the psychologist's voice. 'Anything wrong?'

'Plenty. Too many people know too much. Curtway for one.'

'But you told me that he was dead.'

'I thought that he was, but he isn't. Never mind that now.' Gregson glanced towards the door and lowered his voice. 'Listen. Psycho must eject the cards of Jay West – got that?'

'Jay West, yes?'

'And Merrill. Both psych-police officers. You have their numbers on file. I want those men slated for elimination and the sooner you have their cards ejected the better. Can you do it now?'

'Now?' Conway sounded troubled. 'I don't know. It won't be as simple as last time. You want me to locate those cards, alter them or the master plate so that they will fail to meet specifications, and return the machine to normal.'

'Feed in the following data,' snapped Gregson. 'Both are guilty of inefficiency in that both have aroused suspicion through sloppy work. Merrill has delusions of grandeur, Jay is paranoid. Waste, Conway! This is *important!* Can you do it or can't you?'

'I'll try.' Conway didn't sound too hopeful. 'Why, Gregson, is something wrong?'

'Yes.' Gregson paused, letting the tension of the psychologist mount, then spoke again with sharp urgency. 'Curtway knows what we've done. Jay West knows it too, and I think that Merrill has a suspicion. All of them want to reach the Captain.' He paused again. 'You know what will happen if they do.'

'I can guess.' Conway sounded as though he wanted to be sick. 'You'll protect me, Gregson?'

'I'm busy protecting myself.' Gregson bared his teeth as he guessed the result of his words on the nervous psychologist. 'Listen. There's only one way now in which we can save ourselves. What the Captain learns doesn't matter – if I am the Captain. Well?'

'Not mutiny,' said Conway weakly. 'I won't stand for mutiny.'

'Then can you get me the cards? I wouldn't dare eliminate Merrill unless I have official orders, and even if I do there's still the others to worry about.'

'Can't you eliminate them as well?'

'Yes, if I can find them.' Gregson gripped the receiver until his knuckles showed white beneath the skin, cursing the psychologist for his nervous reluctance. 'I can't order eliminations without orders from Psycho. You fixed Curtway's card, why can't you *fix* the others?'

'Curtway was an old man and due for elimination anyway. All I had to do was feed in a little false data. But the others are different. Both are young, officers, and assumed to be stable.' Conway hesitated. 'Can you give me three shifts?'

'Two then. I can't do it in less.'

'No.'

'Then forget it,' snarled Gregson furiously. 'Wait until Quentin sends for you.' Gregson swore again. 'Waste! I've no time for a man who is too timid to save his own skin.'

'No.' Conway gulped, his voice echoing against Gregson's ear. 'I'll help you. What do you want me to do?'

'Meet me in the Bridge. Wait for me if you have to; spin Quentin some tale of being worried about Psycho, anything, but do nothing until I get there. *Nothing*, understand?'

'Yes, but –'

Gregson hung up before Conway could ask further questions. The man was a weakling, a cog in a machine, terrified of his own imagination and the fear of losing his life.

But he was the only one on whom, at the moment, Gregson could rely.

He sat motionless at his desk, his face heavy with thought as he tried to foresee the future. Quentin must die. That part wouldn't be difficult; the Captain was an old man and would probably collapse at the first pressure on the carotids. Conway would be willing to swear that the death had been from natural causes and, with his backing, Gregson could take over. Merrill would be quieted by promotion to the office of Chief of Psych-Police. Quieted long enough, that is, for the new Captain to arrange his elimination. Conway would have to go as well – the rest of the Council wouldn't argue – and then he could rule for as long as he managed to stave off natural death.

Gregson sighed as he thought about it, feeling some of his tension leave him now that he had a concrete plan, then glanced up in annoyance as a man burst into the inner office.

'Henderly! What's the matter?'

'This is terrible,' gasped the Chief of Medical. 'I've run all the way here from the wards. Gregson! We've got to see the Captain.'

'I know. Malick phoned me and told me about it. I'm meeting him in the Bridge.'

'Malick?' Henderly blinked. 'How did he know? I've come straight down from Medical and haven't told anyone yet.'

'He saw the tapes,' explained Gregson. 'Something about old, white-haired men being shown on the children's viewers.' He stared at Henderly. 'That's what you were talking about, wasn't it?'

'No.' Henderly dismissed the subject as unimportant against his own news. 'It's worse than that. I've a patient in maternity, a woman, pregnant.'

'Have you?' Despite his own worries, Gregson smiled. 'Is pregnancy so rare then?'

'Of course not, but I've never known a case like this before.' He stared at Gregson. 'You don't understand. This is an old woman, one out of marriageable status. She's twenty-six years of age – and she's going to have a baby!'

Henderly sat down as if stunned by the repetition of the fact.

*

The Bridge was crowded when Gregson arrived with Henderly. Quentin sat, as he always sat, at the head of his desk, while before him Malick, Folden, Conway and a young girl sat uncomfortably on chairs. The Captain nodded as Gregson and the medical officer entered, gesturing them towards vacant seats.

'I'm glad you saw fit to come, Gregson. It appears as if we are going to have a full-scale Council meeting.'

'Are we?' Gregson looked pointedly at the girl. 'Is it normal procedure to allow Ship personnel to sit in Council?'

'Susan Curtway's my witness,' snapped Malick pettishly. 'She saw the tapes and will back up what I have to say.' He looked at the Captain. 'You laughed at me before, but this time you'll have to admit that I'm right. Those tapes must be stopped.'

'Indeed?' Quentin didn't shrug but the tone of his voice left no doubt as to how he felt. He looked at Henderly.

'I already know why you are here. You have a patient, a female, who is expecting a baby. Correct?'

'She is twenty-six years of age and should be barren.' Henderly sounded as if he still couldn't believe it. 'You know as well as I do that all females are passed through the sterilizer when they reach twenty-five, or sooner depending on the number of children they have.'

'Perhaps she missed the sterilizer,' suggested Folden.

Henderly snorted.

'Impossible! Her case history shows that she was exposed to the radiations at the correct time. My department is not at fault in this matter.' He glared at Conway. 'If you want my opinion, I'd say that the root of the trouble lies with Psycho. Malick and his tapes – and we know that Psycho issues the educational tapes on relayed channels – proves that something must be wrong.'

'It proves nothing except your own incompetence,' stormed the psychologist. 'The builders determined which tapes were to be shown when and there's nothing I can do to alter the settings. As for that woman,' he glared at Henderly, 'the mere fact that she's having a baby proves that she couldn't have been exposed to the sterility-inducing radiations as you claim. If she had, then she wouldn't be pregnant.'

'Are you doubting my word?' Anger flushed the medical officer's cheeks with red.

'I'm stating facts,' snapped Conway. He appealed to the Captain. 'You know that there's nothing wrong with Psycho, don't you?'

'I trust the builders,' said Quentin enigmatically. He looked at Gregson. 'I don't recall giving you orders to search No-Weight. Why did you do so?'

'I thought it time something was done to eliminate the Barbs.' Gregson was annoyed to find so many people with the Captain. Their presence made his plans of assassination impossible to execute and he had a sickening impression of time running out on him. 'I took it on myself to sweep out the vermin.'

'Were you successful?'

'Seven dead.'

'I see.' Quentin stared thoughtfully at the chief of psych-police and Gregson had the impression that the old man was laughing at him. 'And yet you failed, didn't you? You didn't eliminate the people the whole search was to find.' He smiled outright at Gregson's stunned expression. 'Don't look so amazed. Surely you didn't think that the Captain of the Ship was just a nominal figurehead?'

Gregson bit his lip, quickly revising his opinion of the old man. Quentin knew! He knew too much and, as he thought about it, Gregson felt a sudden fear that he might know far more than anyone had ever given him credit for. Merrill could have told him about the search, probably had, but what else had others told him? He forced himself to listen to the thin, penetrating tones as the Captain spoke.

'First, in order to allay your fears, there is nothing wrong with Psycho. You have become so used to depending on the machine that anything out of your ordinary experience is beyond your comprehension. What you have forgotten, all of you, is that Psycho is a machine built for a specific purpose. It was built more than three hundred years ago and the men who built it built it well.'

'I have never doubted it,' Conway said quickly. 'It's the others who mistrust Psycho.' He glared at Malick and Henderly.

'And they are right to do so.' Quentin stared the psychologist into silence. 'Blind trust in the work of others can be dangerous. The builders were not omnipotent, but, aside from some tampering, the machine which we know as Psycho has operated perfectly. It is still operating perfectly.'

'You said that Psycho has been tampered with,' said Gregson thickly. 'Was that an accusation?'

'No. It was a fact.'

'Who?' Conway stared up, his face livid with fear. 'Who has dared to touch Psycho?'

'Do you really want me to answer that, Conway?' The Captain spoke to the psychologist but his eyes never left Gregson. 'Shall we say that certain men, terrified of death, had the brilliant idea of adjusting their cards so that they could not be ejected from Psycho? Shall we say that, Gregson?'

'Why ask me?' Gregson stared at the old man and felt the sweat of apprehension moisten his forehead. *Quentin knew!* Merrill? He doubted it, since the officer couldn't have known all the details. But if he had caught Curtway and the electronics man had told him what he had discovered ...

Gregson snarled, an animal-like sound coming from deep within his throat, and his hands, as he sat hunched in the chair, hooked of their own volition into claws. Quentin knew. Therefore, in order that he could remain alive, Quentin must die.

'Merrill!'

Gregson paid no attention to the command rapped in the thin voice. Years of indoctrination fought against his survival instinct as he tried to throw himself towards the old man. Quentin was dangerous to his existence. *Quentin must die.* But Quentin was the Captain and to attack him would be mutiny. Gregson had been conditioned against even the thought of mutiny all his life and now, when he wanted to break that conditioning, he found he was unable to do so.

Suddenly Merrill was beside him. Whether he had been there all the time or whether he had stepped from some hidden room, Gregson didn't know. Hatred for the officer and what he represented burst in his tormented brain. Merrill threatened him. *Merrill had to die.*

Gregson snarled again as he lunged for the other's exposed throat.

Quentin watched them as they struggled, his face impassive, his fingers resting lightly on a row of buttons set flush with the surface of his desk. He pressed one, a panel slid aside, and Jay, together with Curtway and the remaining Barbs, entered the room.

'Separate them.'

Bosco grunted as he grabbed Merrill. Murray caught Gregson's arms and held the man until he grew calm.

'You will seat yourselves,' ordered Quentin dryly. 'If you wish to continue the battle you may do so in the proper quarter. The stadium is the place for dueling, not the Bridge.'

'I wasn't dueling,' snapped Merrill. He sneered as he looked towards Gregson, slumped over, numbed with the knowledge of his own defeat. 'Do I get his job?'

'No.'

'Why not? You promised me –'

'I promised nothing.' The whip-lash of the Captain's voice echoed around the crowded room. 'If children assume too much, must I be to blame? For that's all you are, all of you. Children. Stupid, blind, ignorant children!' The scorn and contempt in his voice lashed them to silence and they sat, like the children he had called them, listening to his next words.

'You come running to me with your petty fears and yet, all the time, the facts are before your very eyes. You plot and scheme to extend your lives, even' – Quentin glanced towards Gregson – 'toy with ambitions of ultimate power. And yet none of you has the sense or understanding to realize that, to me, all this is an old, old story. I have sat here and studied you all before. Not you, but others exactly like you. Men, lifted to a temporary power, struggling to extend that power and establish themselves as rulers of the Ship. Always I have beaten them. I always will because to me you are as glass, your motives childishly simple.

'Gregson wants to live, and who can blame him? Not I. Not Malick, whose breeding for a high survival factor is directly responsible for that laudable ambition. Conway is weak but agreed to help for mutual benefit. Merrill is ambitious, and if I was fool enough to give him Gregson's position, would be plotting against me within five years. Curtway, a good man, honest, and yet unable to see further than his nose. Henderly, a doctor, and yet a man who, like Malick, worships a machine. Jay West, one of the new generation. A man able to think and to make his own decisions, and yet even he doesn't know why.' Quentin paused and looked at the faces before him.

'It is not your fault. It is not the fault of anyone. The builders of the Ship decided, and rightly, that we must concentrate on youth at the expense of age. We have had to forge a new race, strong, moral, adventurous, to get rid of hereditary disease and physical weakness. In the Ship a man is assumed to be old at forty. In the Ship a man *is* old at forty. Psychological training and indoctrination have seen to that. But it is wrong. At forty a man is in his mental and physical prime with generations of life still ahead. But no man at forty, within the Ship at least, can ever be wholly mature. That is why the Ship has a Captain.'

'You're old,' muttered Gregson and his eyes, as he stared at the man behind the desk, held a sick envy.

'I am old,' agreed Quentin. 'The builders knew that someone had to live past forty, to span the generations and promulgate a time-binding, long-term policy without which the Ship would have degenerated into a rabble of self-seekers. That is why there is a Captain. Not as a nominal figurehead. Not as a symbol nor as the ultimate power. But so that he can sit and watch, live and plan, not just for one generation but for others yet to come.'

'You're old,' repeated Gregson. He didn't seem to have heard what the Captain had said. 'How old?'

'There have been four Captains since this vessel left Earth,' Quentin answered. 'The first died at sixty years of age. The second at eighty-five. The third Captain lived for a hundred and twenty-five years.' He paused, staring at their wondering expressions. 'I am over one hundred and fifty years of age.'

'Impossible!' Henderly broke the silence. 'No man can live that long.'

'No?' Quentin turned to look at the doctor. 'Why not?'

'He begins to break down,' stammered Henderly. 'His catabolism increases above his anabolism. His mind begins to get erratic. Toxins … body distortions …'

His voice trailed into silence.

'How do you know that?' Quentin stared with interested at the doctor.

'How do you know just when all this break down and senility is supposed to occur? Have you ever dissected an old man? Have you ever seen one, other than myself? Do I look as though I am in senile decay?'

'No, of course not, but –'

'But, of course, you are only repeating what you have learned from the educational tapes.' Quentin nodded as if speaking to a child. 'Remember this. On Earth the normal life expectancy of a man or woman at the time of building the Ship was eighty years. Most people remained quite active until they were seventy, few suffered from any serious mental decay, and most remained working almost until their death. Eighty years, gentlemen. Double the normal life expectancy on the Ship.'

'But a hundred and fifty! It's incredible!'

'Why? There are no diseases on the Ship. The diet is optimum for human consumption. The temperature is regulated to within half a degree. I was born as we all were born, in a gravity double that of Earth, and I have spent most of my life near No-Weight. No strain, Henderly. No heart trouble, anxiety, neurosis, psychosomatic ills or worry about earning a living. I started life with a perfect body and have lived in a perfect environment. Why shouldn't I live to be a hundred and fifty?'

'But the Barbs,' interrupted Jay. 'We saw one who was senile, or insane, and I assume that's the same thing, at seventy.' He looked at Bosco. 'Joe, remember him? You said that he'd lived in No-Weight for thirty years.'

'In darkness,' said Quentin. 'With little water, scarce food, constant fear and endless torment. Those are the things which age a man, West. Once the mind goes, the body soon follows. The Barbs are not a good example.'

'They should be exterminated,' snapped Gregson. He seemed to have recovered himself for he looked at the strangers with undisguised detestation. 'Eliminate them!'

'Why?' Quentin seemed genuinely interested in learning the reason. 'The Barbs are valuable in that they have the highest survival factor of all the Ship personnel. They want to live so desperately that they deliberately chose the hell of No-Weight to elimination. I have fed them as best I could, contacted them, helped them in small ways. I –'

'You fed them!' Gregson half-rose to his feet then slumped as Merrill stepped towards him. 'You?'

'Yes. Who else on the Ship could I trust? Who else would obey me implicitly without question and without thought of self-gain. The Barbs were valuable to me because they were the ultimate weapon against any who tried to overthrow me.' Quentin smiled at the discomforted Chief of Psych-Police. 'Call them my private army if you wish, but I prefer to think of them as one of the finest elements in the Ship.'

'That accounts for why you vetoed the suggestions for eliminating them,' said Malick. He nodded his head. 'Of course, high survival factor – it all makes sense. But what about the tapes?'

'And that pregnant woman,' said Henderly.

'Those bodies I saw in the sealed areas.' Jay flushed as Quentin stared at him. 'What about those?'

'Three questions,' Quentin said, 'and all with the same answer. Folden knows already, but how many of you have guessed at the obvious?' His eyes traveled from face to face. 'None? Not even you, Conway? Haven't you wondered why there have been no new cards expelled from Psycho, even though many of the personnel must have reached forty during the past few shifts? No?'

'May I tell them?' Folden asked. The Chief of Supply stepped forward, his face eager. Quentin lifted one of his thin, delicate seeming hands.

'You may tell them what you told me, no more. I am interested in gauging the depth of their intelligence.'

'The position as regards supply is serious.' There was an unusual importance in Folden's voice as he spoke. 'As you all know, or should know, there can be no such thing as a perfectly balanced ecology in a closed-cycle system the size of the Ship. The very energy used in the effort of walking, for example, means energy lost. We can reclaim almost all of the water, almost all of the oxygen. I say "almost." There is bound to be some wastage and our reclamation units are not one hundred per cent efficient. In effect then, we started with a certain amount of essential supplies on which we have had to draw to maintain our ecology.' He paused, enjoying his moment. 'At the present rate of consumption, those supplies will be exhausted by the end of the seventeenth generation.'

'Twenty-three years,' said Henderly. 'But –'

'Please.' Quentin silenced the Chief of Medical. 'Have any of you guessed what this information means?' He waited a moment then spoke with a trace of asperity. 'Think of it. Psycho ejects no cards and so the older personnel remain alive. We trust the builders implicitly and so Psycho cannot be wrong. A woman is carrying a child, a woman who is assumed to be sterile. Obviously the sterility-inducing radiations have been cut off, and so we are going to have a tremendous increase in the birth rate. And yet, with the Ship personnel mounting by non-elimination plus increased birth rate, we know that our supplies will last no more than a few years.' He stared at them, something of his emotion breaking through his studied calm.

'Three hundred and seventeen years ago the Ship was launched from Earth and aimed towards Pollux and a new planetary system. You have forgotten that. You have overlooked the fact that every journey, no matter how long, must eventually end.' He smiled at their dawning comprehension.

'Yes, gentlemen. Every fact in our possession leads to but one conclusion. The journey is over. *We have arrived!*'

FIFTEEN

The ship was in a turmoil! Everywhere men, women and children gathered around the hastily adapted screens and stared at the black, star-shot night dominated by the glowing luminosity of Pollux. Fully twenty-eight times as bright as the Sun they had never seen, the lambent ball dominated their area of space, and speculation ran high as to just when they would be able to land on a habitable planet and escape the confines of the Ship.

Quentin knew that wouldn't be soon.

He sat in his chair behind his desk and controlled the running of the Ship as he had done for the past century and a half. He was glad he had lived to see Journey's End, glad too that now the necessity for eliminating strong, healthy men and women was over and done with. He smiled as Jay and Malick entered the room.

'Everything going to plan?'

'Yes.' Malick was almost beside himself with excitement. 'The builders thought of everything. I've been in the sealed areas examining the animals and seeds in deep freeze.' He sobered. 'The men and women too. I hope they survive.'

'They'd better,' said Quentin grimly. 'There's no one else capable of operating the investigation ships; teaching the handling and care of rocket exploration craft is something which obviously couldn't be done by means of educational tapes. We need those crews in deep freeze.'

'We need them for more than that,' said Malick. 'The cross-strains will be the making of our race!' He smiled at the Captain. 'Sorry, but I can't forget my own particular field.'

'You must never forget it. Genetics is something we must always practice. It is the only way in which we can save what we have won during the past sixteen generations.' Quentin smiled at Jay's blank expression. 'Tell him, Malick.'

'Inbreeding is dangerous,' explained the geneticist. 'I've already told the Captain that we were approaching the breaking point by our insistence on highly-strung, intelligent people with a strong survival instinct. People like that can't live without space to move around. And, aside from that, there is another good reason why we must have an influx of new germ plasm.' Malick settled back in his chair, seeming to forget that the Captain knew all what he was about to say.

'To get a strong race, you first have to breed out all the weaknesses. You do it by inbreeding until the end product is dangerously near breakdown point, either through extreme nervous tension, as in our case, or through sterility. The remaining specimens are strong because, unless they were, they wouldn't be alive. You then cross-breed them from external stock and the results are amazing.' Malick frowned. 'At least they were with plants and animals. I only hope they will be with men and women.'

'They will be,' promised Quentin. 'A man is basically an animal.' He looked at Jay. 'Did you understand all that?'

'I think so.' Jay frowned. 'What I can't understand is why, if the Builders had perfected suspended animation, they had to have personnel at all. Why not staff the Ship with men and women in deep-freeze, send off the Ship, and let them waken when they had arrived?'

'A good question.' Quentin nodded as if pleased. 'First, there are two ways by which men can reach the stars. One is by suspended animation as you have suggested, the other is by generation ship, which this is. We have combined both and so avoided the weaknesses inherent in either. The generation ship depends on new blood replacing the old, but the danger is that the new blood will forget what it should remember. Sixteen generations are a long time, Jay. Even with continual use of educational tapes it is still hard for some people to accept the fact that the Ship is nothing but a metal can drifting in the void. To them the Ship is the universe and they just can't imagine anything possibly being bigger.

'The deep-freeze method is just as bad. Then the personnel have to rely wholly on automatic machinery, even as we do, but they are far more vulnerable than a generation ship could ever be. And there is another thing. We still aren't certain that they will be fertile after deep-freeze. The animals are, the men and women should be, but no one has ever rested in suspended animation for more than three hundred years before. It was a chance we dared not take.'

'I see.' Jay sat, thinking about it, trying to grasp the vast concept of which he was a part. Malick broke into his musings.

'There is another point, Jay. The people who are put to sleep on Earth and wake to find themselves on a new world, aren't really able to settle down. To them their home is Earth and, human nature being what it is, they would suffer from nostalgia. They would get homesick, long for all the things which they had left behind. We can't do that. We have never known any home than the Ship and most of us are dying to get away from it.'

'Yes,' said Jay. He was thinking of Gregson. He put the thought into words.

'Gregson?' Quentin shrugged. 'He'll be no problem now. The pressure driving him has lifted. Once he was relieved of his morbid fear of death he reverted to normal. Now he is just as eager to explore a new planet as Merrill is.' The Captain chuckled as he stared at the young man. 'You're surprised that I let them live? Why should you be? We need men, now, Jay. Grown men who have the essential drive necessary to take a planet and twist it to our requirements. I can't afford to let what is past interfere with the main project. Merrill, Gregson, the Barbs all have their responsibilities. They know it and, knowing it, can forget small, petty grievances. After all, Jay, we bred for intelligence and intelligent men don't waste energy on trifles. They'll have plenty to occupy their time soon.'

Soon! Quentin sighed as he thought of it. First rousing the rocket crews from their suspended animation. Then three long years while the Ship orbited around the central sun. Exploration of the thirteen planets discovered by the Luna Observatories so long ago and the final testing of their theory that those planets must present a high probability of being habitable.

Then the work. The endless shuttling from the Ship down to the selected world and back again. The tests for bacteria and alien life forms. The planting of men and women as if they were seeds to see if they could survive and multiply. The isolation of the test colonies until all danger of harmful bacteria, unknown viruses and threatening ecologies had been decided. The careful cross-breeding to gain the best from the two, almost totally different races now aboard the Ship. The living personnel could be allowed to mate with whom they liked, they had already been weeded and purified in order to meet alien conditions, but the men and women in deep freeze presented a problem. They were relatively weak, still used to a single Earth gravity, still carrying within themselves hereditary diseases and slow reflexes.

Five years? Ten? A full generation? Quentin didn't know but, as he thought about it, he wished that he were a younger man. There was life and excitement and adventure ahead. Monotony and dullness and the careful fitting in of living people to the dictates of automatic machinery were all behind. It was work for a younger man, a fit, virile, eager man who would be willing to be taught and guided in the path he should take. Jay West?

Jay flushed as he felt the old man's eyes on him. He still had to fight against his inclination to stare, to wonder how any man could have lived so long, to marvel at the graying hair, the thin hands, the sunken lines on cheeks and at the corners of the eyes. He wondered if he would look like that when old.

Not that it would matter then. The children were being taught that men changed as they grew old and that the change was a normal occurrence. Still, it would be odd to see old, white-haired men and women.

'You may as well end shifts now, Jay.' Quentin relaxed in his chair, his mind made up. 'It is one of the prerogatives of the Captain to choose his own successor. I will put it to the Council as a matter of courtesy, but there will be no doubt as to their reactions.' Quentin rose in dismissal and held out his hand, a gesture Jay had never seen before. He stared at the extended palm.

'It is an old custom,' explained Quentin. 'You may have seen it on the tapes, and then again you may have forgotten. I understand that now the tapes do include it as normal education. The idea is that you take my hand in yours, shake it, and then let it fall. The reason for the gesture is to assure you that I am your friend.'

'I see.' Jay took the proffered hand, shook it awkwardly, then let it fall. 'Like that?'

'I think so.' Quentin smiled. 'I have shaken hands only once before in my life. That was when my predecessor informed me that I was to follow his command. I thought it a good custom and decided to use it to signify my own choice.'

'Captain!' Jay blinked, still only half-aware of the implications of what Quentin had said.

'Yes. You will receive instructions from both the Council and myself. Also there are special tapes containing private instructions for the commander. I will show you those myself.' Quentin smiled. 'I must warn you not to be too impatient. The instruction is long and I have no intention of going to the converters just yet. You might be waiting for ten years, maybe longer, but you'll be learning every moment of each shift.' He sobered as he dropped his hand on the young man's shoulder. 'The responsibility is a heavy one – more now than when I took command – but you are young and adaptable and I know that you will do the best you can.'

'Yes, sir,' said Jay. He felt peculiarly humble. 'Thank you.'

He felt as if he were walking on air as he left the Bridge. The feeling lasted as he strode down the whispering corridors and into sector Five. Then, as he saw a figure before him, he faltered with sudden doubt.

'Hello, Jay.' Susan came up to him, smiling and slipped her arm through his. 'Father has told me everything. I was a fool ever to have doubted you.'

'Susan!'

'I never really believed what you said. I'm a woman, Jay, and a woman knows when a man is in love with her.' She smiled up at him. 'Did you hear the news? Genetics has given permission for free-choice marriages.' She paused, hopefully, and then shook his arm in a sudden impatience. 'Jay! Didn't you hear what I said?'

'Yes,' Jay lied. He was still thinking of what Quentin had told him in the Bridge. 'It'll take about five years.'

'What will take five years?'

'Contacting the planets.'

'Who cares about the planets?' Susan clung to his arm. 'You didn't hear what I said. Genetics has given permission for free-choice marriages for anyone who has reached marriageable status.' She looked slyly up at him. 'I shall reach full status in a few months.'

'Good,' he said. Then, as what she hinted at came home to him, he stopped, gripped her shoulders and turned her to face him.

'Susan!'

'I knew that you'd want to marry me,' she said. 'That's why I've already filed application for lowering of my status age. We can be married next month.'

Her kiss stopped his protest and, as he responded to it, he gave up.

Between Quentin and Susan, his life was pretty well planned for him as it was.

FIRES OF SATAN

CHAPTER 1

After the third drink he felt ready to face the night and, muffled in his thick coat, gloves and boots, paused before the big window that gave a view of the observatory. Snow had fallen earlier leaving the area covered with a thin, white blanket. A pity, had it continued to fall the dome would have had to remain closed and he could get on with checking the pile of accumulated records in comparative comfort. There was still a chance of more bad weather, but if there was a possibility of clear skies he must be ready, which meant long hours of tedium.

Experience dictated that he was warmly dressed and carried a flask despite regulations. Rules easy enough for Hammond to make but the Director didn't have to spend a freezing winter's night in the opened dome. To hell with him.

Ice crunched beneath his boots as Spragg left the house, slamming the door then pushing against it to make sure it was locked. Up here there was little risk of vandals but old habits died hard. Ice crunched as he strode down the path and on the road, which led up the hill. Above him, touched by the snow with an air of enchanted mystery, the great dome loomed. Time and custom had changed that but, for some, it still remained.

'Professor? Is that you, Professor Spragg?'

She stepped towards him from the shadows, tall, lithe, her body shapeless beneath a fringed garment. Despite the cold her head was bare, dark hair hanging in an untidy mane. In the softly luminous light cast by the reflective snow he could see wide, deep-set eyes, a generous mouth, dimpled cheeks.

'Yes,' he snapped. 'Who are you?'

'Myrna Parkin. I'm doing post graduate work and –'

'You're here to assist me.' He closed the space between them. 'Why didn't you wait inside?

'I couldn't. The door is locked.'

As he should have known. McGregor was on vacation, Reilly was sick and Dowton would have locked up at dusk. A habit permitted by Hammond for the sake of the saving in overtime – unlike astronomers the janitor worked by the hour.

'Sorry,' said Spragg. 'I should have remembered. Were you coming to meet me?'

'To visit you, actually.' Shivering the girl added, 'It was better than just standing around to freeze. Please, Professor, couldn't we go inside?'

A decade earlier Spragg would have joked, insisted she called him 'Mal', trying to warm their relationship in optimistic anticipation of potential reward. Now he busied himself with the keys, throwing open the door and passing through before her in order to switch on the lights. The place was as cold as an iceberg and he hurried into the small compartment used for recreation; a place where those who smoked could and hot drinks and snacks could be made. Radiators glowed to life as he hit the switches.

'Tea?' He gestured towards the electric kettle. 'Make some and I'll join you.'

'I'd prefer coffee if there is any.'

McGregor drank the stuff and there was a jar of instant tucked away at the back of the cabinet. Sipping his tea, Spragg stared at the girl.

'Postgraduate, you say?'

'Yes.'

'Studying?'

'Quarks, quasars and black holes,' she smiled. 'Physics and astronomy fascinate me. The universe – the secrets waiting to be solved out there –' She dropped her hand, a little self-conscious, he guessed, of the displayed enthusiasm and not sophisticated enough to be careless of his reaction. 'The majesty of it all. The splendour. The tremendous implications of the discoveries we are making.'

He said, dryly, 'Is this your first stint in an observatory?'

'I've been in others.'

'But this is your first time as an acting assistant?' She nodded. 'I thought so, but don't be ashamed of it. We all have to learn.'

'You think I'm foolish?'

'No.'

She put down her cup. 'Sometimes I get carried away but how can anyone not respond to the mystery of the universe? It's so enigmatic and yet, all the time, I've the feeling that if we only had one more scrap of knowledge, one more piece to fit the jigsaw, the whole puzzle would become clear and we would have the answer to everything. Is that being childish?'

'No,' he said quickly. 'It's just that it's been a long time since I've met anyone honest enough to admit to such enthusiasm. I find it a refreshing change.'

'Which means that you had it once yourself,' she said.

'A long time ago, perhaps.'

'You talk like an old man.'

'I am an old man.'

'Not that old. When I first heard about you I thought you'd be stooped and grizzled and –'

'Absent-minded and senile and on the make?' He shrugged. 'Why not? We are like other men.'

'No.' Her hair flew as she shook her head, her eyes serious. 'Not as other men. You belong to a dedicated breed.'

A monk, he thought bitterly, they too were dedicated to something larger than themselves, restricted by onerous duties; hours governed by a bell which was governed by a clock which, in turn, was governed by the stars. And they too could be tempted by someone coming to them in the night. Damn the girl, why had she displayed such enthusiasm? It gave them something in common, a shared emotion, a shared motivation.

'Professor?'

His tea was cold. Irritably he flung it into the sink.

'Impatient, Miss Parkin? We have the entire night before us.' He smiled, remembering the impetuosity of youth. 'You saw the sky out there and must know it won't clear for a couple of hours at least. Which means there is no point in opening the dome just yet. But, I'll admit, we can check the instruments and you need to be taught the basic routines and the system we use here. And, of course, you'd like to inspect the installation, right?'

'That's why I'm here, Professor.'

He looked at her appraisingly. The fringed outer garment she wore was a poncho of some kind. Below her legs were covered with the inevitable jeans, her feet with the inevitable boots. 'You'll have to get rid of the poncho. It swirls too much and could hit things or catch in things and the equipment costs too much to be risked. Now get it off while I find you something better.'

Beneath it she wore a uniform-like shirt and he paused as he turned from the cabinet, McGregor's parka in his hands, staring at the taut fabric.

'Here.' He handed her the parka. 'Belt it tight and if you get too cold don't be afraid to let me know. You'll find gloves in the pocket but you won't be able to wear them all the time. Those other observatories you've been to,' he said shrewdly. 'All down south?'

'Yes.'

'Well, up here things are a little more primitive.' He smiled. 'The Director would say we operate in a more old-fashioned way which is another way of saying we're so far behind the times it's a laugh. In fact you're standing in the middle of a scientific fossil. I'm sorry.'

'Why? You have a telescope, haven't you?'

'Yes,' he admitted. 'We have a telescope. In fact we've had one for a long time now. Too damn long.' He resisted the impulse to take a drink. 'That's half the trouble.'

When the eccentric Lord Althene had been smitten with the urge to dabble in Natural Philosophy his interest in astrology had directed his attention towards the stars. If the course of the planets could be plotted with greater precision then it was obvious horoscopes could be cast with a higher degree of accuracy and more definitive predictions made. Fired with enthusiasm and brooking no opposition he had been checked by only one consideration – where would the proposed observatory be sited? Ivegill had seemed ideal. A few miles to the south of Carlisle, served by roads and water, an area rich in stone and timber and with plenty of cheap labour to construct the essential buildings. Lord Althene owned the land for miles around and had large holdings close to the city itself. In the early spring of 1857 the first sod was cut and the first dirt removed for the foundations.

Seven years later the observatory was complete.

But, in the late nineteenth century the internal combustion engine was yet to come and, while the smoke from open fires was a nuisance, there weren't enough of them to create a problem. At the turn of the century the old 6-inch refractor was replaced by a 32-inch reflector and later photographic equipment was added. The Althene Observatory gained a modest reputation for efficiency and strengthened that reputation when, in 1927, several small discoveries were made as to the disposition of some of the larger asteroids.

Then came the second world war, the massive increase in the use of cars, the population explosion, the motorways, pollution, death-duties and near-chaos. Things Spragg explained as he guided the girl around the installation.

'So now we're a trust,' he said. 'Enough was saved from the estate to provide an income from a scientific foundation. It suited the government to give its seal of approval and so we get certain tax advantages. But as far as real use is concerned we're in the same class as the dodo.'

'Why? It seems a nice place to me. Better than others I've seen.'

'Better, maybe, but in the wrong place. You've visited Greenwich? You know the Royal Observatory had to be moved to Herstmonceux?' He didn't wait for an answer. 'Pollution, that's why. And the traffic – the vibration was hell. The same here.' He gestured beyond the walls. 'The M6 runs past barely a half mile distant. Big lorries carrying loads to Carlisle, not to speak of the endless stream of cars. And we mustn't forget the airport, planes with lights and turbulence and heat-distortions from their jets. A mess. If we get a couple of prime hours seeing a week we're lucky.'

'Then Althene –'

'Is a mess.' Spragg was blunt. 'We do our best but the odds are against us. This is a backwater, girl, a dead end. You should be in a place where you can meet the right people, make contacts, sow the seeds for later advancement. A few years and you'd be climbing and, if you're lucky enough, then –'

'I know,' she said bleakly. 'A discovery, my name in the papers, my report published in the journals and all those who want to jump on the wagon will be offering me posts and position. But if I don't make a discovery? If I don't get the publicity? What then?'

'You'd make out.'

'Yes,' she said and, subconsciously, inflated her chest. 'I guess I would but maybe I'd rather not do it that way. I want to be known for my achievements not because I was born with a good body. I want what you have, Professor Spragg.'

'Me?'

'You've made your mark and it hasn't been forgotten. You're respected and admired and none can argue with your reputation. That's why I wanted to come here. To learn what you can teach.'

She was putting him on, she had to be, and yet it was impossible to resist the glow of satisfaction from the knowledge that he hadn't been forgotten. Someone had remembered, had thought him worth seeking out to share his labours. Then he shook his head, remembering, the small discovery he had made years ago now quickly swallowed in the doors it had opened. Had Hammond used it to obtain a willing girl to act as cheap labour?

'I need the experience,' she said when, bluntly, he asked. 'Theory isn't enough, you know that.'

You had to sit and freeze or roast according to the season, to fight cramps and thirst and impatience and learn not to cavil against circumstance when, after days of patient waiting, some trifle ruined everything. Like the time when a complete batch of recordings had been wiped because an assistant had misread an instruction. Like the time when some fool had set the woods aflame at the time of a critical observation, the distortion making all measurements useless.

And the time when Jashir had slipped and fallen to his death when climbing up to the eyepiece to make an adjustment.

A bad time and he had seen it all. Heard it all too, the gasp, the strangled cry, the scream and then, after too long a time, the sickening, squashy thud as a head had hit metal and burst like an overripe melon. A bad time and he had been fortunate not to have been alone for the police, oddly, had seemed suspicious and were probing with their questions. Yes, he had ordered the adjustment. No, he had no reason to suspect Jashir had been drinking. The reverse in fact, the man was a Moslem – had been a Moslem and no believer in Islam drank. No, he had not tried to help. Yes, it had been an accident.

Cold and heat and boredom and disappointment and even death – the girl was right, theory wasn't enough.

He said, 'Are you living in the village?'

'Yes. I've got a room with Mrs Turney. The Director recommended her to me.' She looked at him. 'And you? I suppose you've got a house.'

'Yes.'

'Married, of course?'

'Of course.' He wondered at her directness then realised it could be the product of shyness. In his own time such shyness would have found refuge in silence and a reserve which had too often been mistaken for sullenness but times changed and so did customs. 'But not any longer,' he added. 'Astronomers shouldn't marry.'

'The hours?'

'She grew tired of sleeping alone and decided to do something about it. I discovered what was going on. There were no children so –' he made a gesture ' – end of marriage.'

And the end of a friendship, which could have meant so much. Later, thinking about it, he realised that his anger had been directed more at his loss than at Irene's infidelity. Bob could have grown so close but had turned from him to accept the forbidden fruit so freely offered. A stupid metaphor – since when had sex been forbidden to any thinking and intelligent person?

'So you're free,' said Myrna, 'Don't you ever get lonely though?'

'At times. I've a woman who comes in to clean up.'

'And?'

'You haven't met Mrs Elphick.' He looked into her eyes, searching for mockery but finding none. 'And you? I guess you have a man.'

'I had. He didn't want me to come. In fact he threatened not to see me again if I did. So, naturally, I had to take the position. I'm selfish.'

'If wanting to do what we want to do is selfish then yes, we are,' he said. 'As I'm going to be now. I want to open the dome and get to work. Let's move!'

Once it had meant sweat but now electric motors did the job and Spragg watched as the segment moved to one side exposing a narrow section of sky. It was clearing, stars winking through a faint scud of cloud, the cold increasing as the trapped heat escaped from the building. A moment and he completed the cycle, the segment wide open now, held fast, the lattice of the telescope etched against the heavens.

There was a moon for which he was thankful but from the city a suffused glow rose to paint the thin wisp of cloud a rosy pink while lower-lying mist held a deeper hue. High above the winking signal lights of a jet made traces towards the west while, from the motorway, the sound of traffic made a loud thunder.

'I don't believe it.' Myrna tensed. 'It sounds so close.'

'It is close but this makes it worse.' Spragg gestured at the interior of the dome. 'Open, it acts like an ear catching and concentrating the noise. You'll get used to it.'

If she stayed which was doubtful but, would he ever get used to her? Already she had won him so that, even when not looking at her, he was conscious of her presence. An old man, old enough at least to be her father – he should have more sense! And yet, why not?

'Ready, Professor?' She was standing at the foot of the lattice waiting for instructions.

'Did Hammond explain the programme?'

'Only roughly. He said you'd fill in.'

He would, his golf would be waiting, but maybe he shouldn't judge the man too harshly. It couldn't be easy to act the professional beggar, which, basically, was what the Director really was.

'We're running a correlation check on the Jovian Moons,' said Spragg abruptly. 'Just an excuse for staying in business, to let others know we're alive. Others being the government and various benefactors who are willing to make a donation that they can set against taxes. With me?'

'You're bitter,' she said quietly. 'You shouldn't be. There are those who would –'

'Give their right arms to be able to play with an installation like this. I know. I get letters from idiots who want to send messages. Nuts who are convinced there are secret symbols on the moon. Fools who know just where to look to find the aliens who are manipulating us.'

And the others, she thought, the dedicated amateurs who were often more skilled than the professionals. A professional was merely someone who got paid and a person who worked for love was surely more worthy than one who laboured simply for gain

Spragg?

She had been warned about his temper, his irascible nature and gratuitous sarcasm. Warned too about his penchant for women, a trait he had betrayed with his eyes when handing her the parka. But there was more and she had caught a hint of it when talking about his circumstances. A yearning, an empty longing quickly masked with a brash facade which she knew too well. And the taint of alcohol on his breath when they had met, normal enough at such a time on a man who worked during the day, but for him it was tantamount to drinking at breakfast.

A man under strain, she decided, and perhaps one who was slipping and knew it. The Dutch courage, the irritability, the attack when there was no cause and the defence when there was no need. The demeaning of his chosen profession. The cynicism, which he wore like armour.

'As I was saying,' said Spragg. 'And if I continue to hold your interest, we are checking the Jovian system of moons.'

Spragg blew on his hands, his breath a cloud of vapour.

'It is barely possible that we may be able to isolate and identify the satellite in question and, if we can determine that it is hitherto unknown as a moon of Jupiter we shall have made history. But don't hope for too much. Personally I believe the mysterious object to be a wandering asteroid, which has an erratic orbit. A few more years and it will have vanished from the vicinity of the planet.'

'An asteroid?'

'Why not?' He guessed her objection. 'The size? All we have seen is a speck of light. A high albedo would give the impression of great dimension if the reflected light were diffused. But you know all this. What you may not know as yet is how we work here. It is a matter of making the best of a bad job. As we can never be certain of clear skies we have to rely more on records than direct observation.'

'That's normal.'

He shrugged. Given time she would learn but for now it was best to use her as a pair of hands. 'It's time we got to work. Aim for Capella. You –'

'It's in the constellation Auriga,' she said coldly. 'There's no need to treat me as if I were an ignorant child.'

'I was going to say that you may find it difficult to maintain alignment,' he said. 'The drive mechanism is a little sloppy so we've worked out a system of signals. When I give the word you make sure we're on target. When you're satisfied let me know. I snap the shutter and we wait to do it over again. With luck we'll get maybe a dozen useable exposures.'

'That many?'

'We're using a special emulsion coupled with a light magnifying analogue device rigged up by McGregor. It isn't as good as the commercial installations used by the big observatories, but it'll do.' Spragg glanced at his watch. 'Up you go now. Watch yourself and, if you get too cold, let me know.'

She climbed with the easy agility of youth and he looked away, remembering Jashir falling. An incident which, tonight, was not repeated. As the girl settled he checked the equipment, electric motors humming as the telescope moved to point at the selected region of sky – an eye peering into the universe.

And, despite his age and the coating cynicism, the magic remained. The stars, the mystery they held, the enchantment. The endless spaces illuminated with scattered suns. The whole glory of the universe spread out before him to be probed and questioned, explored and chartered, loved and feared and, even, worshipped a little.

'On target,' said the girl. 'Clear seeing.'

'Check.' Luck seemed to be with them but it would be stupid to miss the opportunity. A photograph, any photograph, was better than none and if she could maintain the alignment at least she would have proved her worth. 'Hold!'

A click and the camera was working, small lamps glowing on the panels and casting tiny patches of various colours to illuminate hooded dials. Now, if the seeing lasted and she could hold the alignment a record would be made of the Jovian sector of space.

With nothing to do but wait, Spragg moved restlessly beneath the opened dome. The girl shouldn't have to be watching the target-star. She shouldn't have to freeze in winter chill. They should have a better mechanism, better mounts, a better position away from towns and motorways with their attendant haze and vibrations. How the hell could they be expected to work without proper equipment?

How had Galileo?

'Professor! We're shifting!'

From the motorway came a steady roar. Heavy trucks shaking the concrete, the terrain, the very foundations of the building itself. A minute quiver accentuated by magnification so what should have been steady points became blurred haloes. Scowling, Spragg ended the exposure and triggered fresh film into the holder. He'd be lucky to get a couple of usable exposures.

'We'll try again later. A few hours before dawn is the best time. Traffic is thin then and, if there is no mist, we should get decent seeing.' He looked up to where she sat. 'Come down and get warm. I'll make some coffee.'

She was shivering as she gripped the cup. From the cabinet Spragg took a heavy sweater and a string vest.

'Put these on,' he said. 'The vest under your shirt.' Then, as she hesitated, he snapped, 'I won't stare if that's what bothers you.'

'It doesn't. I've been looked at before.'

A certainty, he thought sourly, and by men too young to realise their luck. Then, understanding her reluctance, he said. 'Go ahead. Those things are clean. I keep them here for emergencies.'

He turned away as she doffed the parka and shirt, hearing the soft rustle of fabric over skin. Small sounds that held a poignant familiarity and carried associations of warm intimacy.

She said, 'Thank you, Professor. I hadn't realised it would get so cold.'

'It'll get colder before dawn. Can you get a hot bath at your lodgings?'

'I doubt it. Mrs Turney needs time to heat the water. Later, maybe, but not just after dawn.'

He said, slowly, not looking at her, 'If you'd like to come back with me I can provide a hot bath. A hot meal too if you want.'

'Thank you. That would be nice.'

Spragg set down his cup, feeling suddenly cheerful, confident now the night would not be wasted.

CHAPTER 2

James Hammond walked into his office, placed his Holmberg neatly on the rack, then his topcoat, and adjusted his jacket with his usual attention to sartorial perfection. The jacket belonged to a suit that had originated in Savile Row, the shoes were of hand-made leather, the shirt natural silk. Hammond liked good clothes and, as Director, he was justified in wearing them. The observatory had at least to appear prosperous.

The office was panelled in wood mellowed with time, glistening with the patina of years of wax polishing. Framed certificates spoke of past achievements and photographs showed previous members of the staff standing stiffly, whiskered and dressed as at the turn of the century. On the wide desk stood a heap of mail but Hammond ignored it, moving to the window and standing to look at the drive beyond, the hedges flanking the narrow road. Spring was coming, the sward dotted with the stars of primroses, the fading blooms of snowdrops. Soon would come the crocuses, the daffodils and tulips. Soon, too, would come the bills and, inevitably, trouble with the staff.

Hammond sighed as he thought about it. McGregor was restless as was Reilly. Dowton would want an increase as would the gardeners and maintenance men. There would be talk of 'differentials' and interviews with union officials and the haggling and all the rest of the stupid business. They seemed unable to accept the fact that the observatory was not a government institution with unlimited access to taxpayer's money.

'Good morning, Director.' Susan Keating had followed him into the office, holding a tray bearing a steaming cup of coffee, which she set carefully on the desk. She smiled as he turned. 'Did you have a good trip?'

'Comfortable, anyway.' He knew it wasn't the answer she wanted. 'Sir Edward was most interested and saw the value of sponsoring the sciences now there is so much interest in the latest new Voyager missions. Incidentally, should enquiries be made, use our highest figures for attendance and don't forget to emphasise the foreign interest.'

A gilding of the lily; their peak year for visitors had been caused by tour operators having been persuaded to include the observatory in their itineraries. The foreign interest had stemmed from the Middle East when certain oil-rich sheiks had become interested in buying the land. Visitors now were less and the interest negligible – things she knew better than to mention.

Susan lingered and Hammond could guess why. She had worked at the observatory for thirty-two years, a confirmed spinster and, while officially his secretary, was more his spy. As she had been for other Directors before him.

Casually, she said, 'I think Miss Parkin has settled down. When I spoke with her last, she seemed quite happy with her duties and position.'

'No complaints about Spragg?'

'None. They seem to get on well.' Susan added, dryly, 'I understand she is now lodging with him.'

To the benefit of the observatory. With the girl as bait Spragg would be reluctant to look for other employment and with decent comforts the girl would be more likely to remain. Two birds with one stone – Hammond wished his other problems could be solved so easily.

'Anything else, Susan?'

'Nothing important, Director.' She glanced at the heap of mail. 'A gardener has given notice and one of the machine-room staff was caught pilfering metal. And we are low on chemicals. I've taken all necessary action.' Again she glanced at the piled letters. 'I've printed out the e-mails, and they're in with the letters. I didn't sort them, Director, I hadn't time, but if you would like me to do it now?'

Her confession was a signal and he shook his head, smiling as she left, sitting and reaching for his coffee as he wondered what bombshell the mail contained. She knew, of course, and could have told him, but a rigid code of ethics prevented her from admitting to any hint that she pried.

Putting down the empty cup he reached for the mail. Spragg, as usual, had the most, a motley collection of letters addressed mainly to The Chief Astronomer but some others bearing his name; typed, scribbled, scrawled, printed. One held an unusual calligraphy, the letters neatly formed with graceful flourishes. The writer knew of Spragg's academic achievements and gave not only his title, but his qualifications. Hammond added it to the rest and looked at the others. Myrna Parkin had three of little obvious importance. His own mail was as he'd expected; some official communications, some invitations a few of which he would accept, a reminder from the golf club that his subscription was due. Hammond disliked playing golf as much as he did playing bridge but was good at both and suffered them for the sake of the contacts they provided.

Two letters caught his immediate attention.

Both had arrived airmail and were obviously what Susan had wanted him to find. One, addressed to Doctor Sean Von Reilly was from the Observatiorum der Dutschen Tautenberg, the other, addressed to Ian McGregor, was from Rand Optics Inc., California, U.S.A.

The one to Reilly from Germany was thick, and Hammond recognised the typical shape and heft of application forms. Reilly must either be sounding out the prospects or seriously intending to quit the observatory. The other to McGregor from the States was more dangerous. Thinner and somehow more sinister, it could well be in an invitation for him to apply for a position or official notification that he had been accepted.

He could destroy them both, of course, and perhaps nothing would come of it and he would be able to retain his staff. But for how much longer? Althene was a backwater, both were as high as they could go.

As Hammond was himself and, like him, they must know it. Sighing, he gathered up the letters and, though it wasn't his job, decided to deliver them personally.

McGregor was big, thick-set, and bearded, which added to his image of a wild Highlander. He grunted when Hammond handed him his mail, holding the letters in broad hands, the spatulate fingers belying their sensitivity. Reilly, thin-faced, long-lipped, a brush of hair falling about his ears, stared at his own through rimless spectacles.

'Any luck, Sean?'

'An answer from Germany.' Reilly ripped it open, glanced at the wad of forms and scowled. 'I wrote asking for a job and told them everything they needed to know. Do I get the job? Like hell I do. I get a load of bumph to fill in instead. You?'

'One from the States.' McGregor examined it, opened it, read it again and whistled. 'My friend, someone up there must like me. Rand have offered me a job.'

'Just like that?'

'Just like that – with a little help from a mutual friend. Remember Bob Arkwright?'

'Vaguely. He was before my time but I've heard talk about him. Some scandal, wasn't there?'

'He ran off with Spragg's wife, about eight years ago. Spragg went home one night and caught them red-handed. The next day Bob and Irene left and later, so I heard, went to the States. He must have got a job with Rand because now he's a big wheel in their research department. And now this.' He waved the letter. 'What about you? Did you ever hear from Jodrell?'

'No vacancies now or in the foreseeable future. The same from Yerkes, from Lick and, naturally, from Herstmonceux. I should have been a plumber.'

'You'll get something.'

'Sure. I'll get the ice-cream concession on open days or be allowed to sell programmes or find a job spieling at a planetarium or –'

'That could be a good job,' said McGregor, quickly, eager to change the subject. Reilly's illness had left him lacking some of his normal bounce. 'Say, have you had a chance to study Spragg's new assistant?'

'I've seen her.'

McGregor sucked in his breath. 'A looker! Spragg is one lucky bastard.'

'That girl? You're joking.'

'I'm serious. She must have a father-complex or something but she's moved in with him. He probably bribed her with hot baths and hot breakfasts and she gave him a hot bed in return.'

McGregor glanced at the rest of his mail. Bills, advertisements, the usual rubbish. A list of electronic components available from a discount warehouse, a copy of a trade magazine, two requests from optimists for the circuit diagrams of his light analogue. A note from a girl he had met while on vacation in Iceland. A letter from a woman in Carlisle. A worrying communication with hints of coming trouble caused by a careless interlude and a firmly held religious conviction. Irritably he threw it down. The offer from the States had come at a good time but he hated to be pressured. Now if Carla had only looked like Myrna Parkin – damn it, a girl like that would be worth marrying!

Spragg thought so too as he looked to where she sat facing him across the table, littered with the remains of a slowly-enjoyed breakfast. A good breakfast was essential after a night at work and the more so when he now needed the extra sources of energy. Why couldn't he have found a girl like Myrna when he'd been young?

'Mal?' Myrna was looking at him, her face freshly clean, hair round with a braided cord, her body nude beneath the robe she had donned after her bath. 'Something wrong? Thinking of the job?'

'I was thinking of the weakness of youth,' he said with sudden honesty. 'It's strange how quickly we forget. If we didn't the young wouldn't regard us as dinosaurs and we wouldn't think of them as an alien species. We'd remember how we were at their age and make allowances.'

'Do you make them for me?'

'I wasn't thinking of you, you're – well, different.'

'I'm a woman.'

'Yes, very much so.'

'And you are very much a man.' She frowned. 'So there are a few years between us, so what?'

More than a few, a score at least.

'There's a repeat of the new Voyager films tonight at eleven,' said Myrna lowering the newspaper she had been reading. 'I'd like to see it.'

'You will.'

'How? We'll be in the dome.'

'I'll be in the dome,' he corrected. 'You can stay here and catch the programme. Better yet, you can record it so we can see it again later together.' He gestured towards the television set and the video and DVD player. 'We might as well use the damned thing.'

'It's crazy,' she said. 'Here we are studying the Jovian system night after night and only a short while ago actual films were taken and transmitted of the areas. You remember? Ganymede, Io, Amalthea and the rest.'

'Pictures,' he said. 'Interesting, but they told us nothing of the overall pattern. No matter if the Voyagers had stayed out there, we still wouldn't be certain about a new satellite. We have to do it the hard way.'

'Too hard.' She was bitter. 'And it's crazy. A Schmidt would do the job without sweat.'

Something the observatory couldn't afford. A Schmidt was a camera-telescope and could not be used for visual observation. It took wonderful photographs but even so few observatories owned them. Palomar, naturally, and Uccle in Belgium and Kvistaberg in Sweden and, he was sure, the Tautenberg in Germany. Althene would never possess one unless they were given away.

'We keep pegging away,' said Spragg mildly, 'and maybe we'll find the answer. Our main tool is patience – that's what astronomy is all about.'

'It seems such a damned waste. We could spend years on a project when, with the right equipment, we could end it in weeks – I'm being stupid, aren't I?'

'You're just tired,' he said.

And forgetful. It wasn't just a matter of equipment; they were dealing with space and time and things that moved did so in their own frames of reference. And movement was what they searched for, the drift of a minute particle of light against the unchanging backdrop of the heavens. A tiny mote which was drowned and swallowed by the universal brilliance; the glittering host of stars which bloomed in the lens of even a low-powered telescope and was dazzling in the eye-piece of a high-powered instrument.

'Why don't you get off to bed?'

She stood up and stretched, and he rose with her, reaching out to embrace her.

'Myrna, my love, I –'

'Don't talk!' Her voice was a strained whisper. 'Don't talk, Mal! Just –'

She broke off, stiffening, as the doorbell made its discordant clangour.

Hammond said, blandly. 'Thank you, my dear, this is excellent coffee.'

'It's instant.'

'Even so it is excellent.' The Director was determined not to take offence, guessing at the reason for her abruptness, Spragg's reluctant invitation to enter his house. 'And let me apologise once again for having disturbed you. I know how it is when you have to work at night. All you want is a hot bath, a hot meal and a soft bed, right?'

'We want more than that,' snapped Myrna. 'Something to keep us warm in the dome at night for one. New gears on the drive-mechanism on the reflector. A Schmidt –'

'Why not ask for the moon while you're about it?' Hammond smiled thinly. 'I'm sorry you appear to be dissatisfied with the conditions here, Miss Parkin, and if you choose to leave I will understand.' A studied pause then he added, 'As I'm sure others will when and if they may ask. I assume you intend to gain your degree?'

Spragg heard her sharp intake of breath and moved forward before she could call the Director the bastard he was. He said, quickly. 'We're on our own time, James. What do you want?'

'Another cup of this excellent coffee would be welcome. Thank you, my dear.' Hammond smiled as the girl took the cup; gracious once having gained his victory. As she vanished into the kitchen he said, 'A fine girl, Mal, I'm pleased to see you are getting on so well. A proof of the old saying about life in old dogs, eh?'

'You've a dirty mind,' said Spragg, bluntly. 'And a vicious disposition. Did you have to threaten her?'

'You know me better than that, Mal, but I had to do something to keep her here. Mostly I was thinking of you.' Hammond reached into his pocket. 'Here, I brought you your mail. It's a nice morning and I felt like a walk and thought I'd see how you were getting on with your new assistant. How long has it been now?'

'Eight weeks. From the end of February.' Spragg added, 'You should do as she suggests about getting some heat in the dome. A couple of times there was ice on the lattice.'

'I'll try to arrange something before next winter. Infra-red projectors could warm the working areas at least and I might be able to find someone to supply them.' Hammond looked at Myrna as she returned with his coffee. She was now fully dressed. 'Going out?'

'For a walk.' She handed him the coffee. 'Is there anything else you want? No? Then I'll get off. See you later, Mal.'

The door slammed behind her leaving a sudden emptiness filled with the ghosts of what-might-have-been had Hammond not chosen to call. Spragg scowled, remembering, wondering if ever such a moment would come again.

Hammond took a chair. 'Sit down, Mal. I need to talk. Have Ian or Sean mentioned they are leaving?'

'No, are they?'

'I don't know, but if they should we'll have a problem. An observatory can't run without trained staff and we haven't enough as it is. Either or both of them could be hard to replace.'

'You should have thought of that when you threatened Myrna.'

'Don't fight her battles, Mal, she's big enough to fight her own. And post-grads aren't hard to come by. What I'm asking is, should the need arise, do you know of anyone interested in joining us? Old friends, maybe, old associates. As Chief Astronomer, it's your problem as much as mine. And if they are thinking of leaving and you can change their minds –' He let it hang, cunningly changing the subject. 'Anything interesting in your mail?'

'It's my mail.'

'I know but there was one letter which caught my eye. One with unusual script. You don't see calligraphy like that nowadays and I wondered if the contents carried the same precision.' Then, quietly, Hammond added, 'I heard about Irene, Mal. Interested?'

'No. She chose her life and I wasn't a part of it.'

'She's left Bob Arkwright – a Las Vegas Divorce. She has a position with the new Voyager promotional campaign as a designer of plastic models, plaques and pennants. Under licence from NASA, naturally.'

'The souvenir business.' Spragg shrugged. 'Well, what of it?'

'I thought you'd like to know.'

A lie, Hammond knew of his feelings towards Irene, so what was his real motive for coming to the house? To check on the domestic arrangements with Myrna? To ask his help in retaining the services of the others? Spragg doubted such obvious motives; the Director was known for his deviousness and was rarely so direct. His anxiety about the others leaving was misplaced – always there were more astronomers than telescopes and even an installation like Althene could find willing staff. And his interest in the letter.

Spragg studied it, nothing the script but not overly impressed. A screed from some raving nut, most probably, wanting him to look for fire-demons on the surface of the Sun or the drifting remnants of the Atlantean space fleet destroyed in some imaginary war with Mars.

'Mal.' Hammond cleared his throat. 'I had dinner with Sir Edward Thorne last night. He is most interested in the observatory and would be willing to make a sizeable donation if he considered it worthwhile. He became really enthusiastic when I mentioned your project. He even hinted, and you'll appreciate the joke I'm sure, that the new moon should be named after him if – well, you get the point.'

'Money,' said Spragg. 'A bribe.'

'A consideration,' said Hammond quickly. 'A small favour for a man willing to support the observatory. Damn it, Mal, it happens all the time. How else to win patrons? Now if I could tell Sir Edward that you were on the verge of announcing the discovery of a new moon of Jupiter and it would be named after him he would be more than grateful. Mal?'

'Lie if you want,' said Spragg. 'But don't include me in your schemes. You know damned well we have a long way to go before we can be certain we've checked out the Jovian system.'

'How long?

'Too long to satisfy Sir Edward.' Spragg wasn't shocked by the proposition, as Hammond said, it happened all the time, but he was still proud of his reputation because, without it, he had nothing. To terminate the discussion he ripped open the envelope and grunted at the mass of papers it contained. 'Someone's been busy.'

'An amateur?'

'Obviously.' Spragg riffled the sheets that bore the same calligraphy as the envelope and found the covering letter. 'From Laggan, Inverness – up in the Highlands. Sent by –' Spragg scowled at the signature – 'the Reverend Aird Gulvain. Somehow that name rings a bell.'

'What does it say?'

Hammond waited as Spragg read on, looking around the room now untidy with a domestic intimacy absent before. He crossed to the window and stood looking at the bulk of the observatory pictured against the sky, A movement and he saw Myrna walking from it towards the house, her long legs scissoring in a mannish stride, hair a cascade of darkness over her shoulders.

As she passed the gate and vanished down the road he wondered just what he had interrupted.

'Well?' He turned back to Spragg. 'Anything of interest?'

'For once, perhaps.' Spragg leaned back thoughtfully. 'Gulvain is an amateur but a damned good one – I met him about ten years ago when he presented a paper to a conference I'd attended. An old man as I remember. A retired parson – he must be in his eighties by now. Anyway he thinks he may have discovered a new asteroid.'

'So, naturally, he wrote to you.' Hammond nodded. Fifteen years earlier Spragg had made exactly the same discovery; isolating and plotting the orbit of a scrap of planetary debris found between Mars and Jupiter. 'He wants confirmation, naturally.'

'Yes.'

'A pity we can't give it to him. A discovery, even of a minor asteroid, would do the observatory no harm. Sir Edward –' He broke off. 'Can you suspend the programme?'

He knew the answer before Spragg shook his head. It was the old problem; not enough telescopes and not enough nights in the year for all the observations waiting to be made. A pressure compounded at Althene by the bad viewing conditions. In time the potential discovery would be checked and, if verified, another notation placed in the books. But, by then, Gulvain could be long dead and Sir Edward's bounty dispersed elsewhere. If only –

Hammond said, 'Mal, we can't afford to let this slip. If Gulvain is right we can use the discovery. Sir Edward would be pleased to have even an asteroid named after him.'

'It's Gulvain's find.'

'True, and he won't be forgotten, but we have to take the long view. You could explain that to him, Mal. Tell him of our need for new equipment. A Schmidt, for example, with a plaque attached saying it was the gift of Sir Edward to Althene on behalf of the Reverend Aird Gulvain. As long as Thorne gets his name in the papers he won't give a damn about the scientific histories – who reads them, anyway?'

'I do.'

'You and a few others but who usually has the time?' Hammond shrugged. 'Did he invite you to visit him? I thought so – the true Scottish hospitality. Why not accept the invitation? You could study his equipment and make an assessment of his capabilities. After all we can't ignore him.'

Spragg said, flatly, 'You want me to visit Aird Gulvain and to stay with him as his guest. To check his findings and verify if he's made a discovery. And, if he had, you want me to steal it. Right?'

'Of course not!' Put like that it sounded raw. Smiling, Hammond added, 'All you'll be doing is visiting a colleague. You could use a break and the programme can run without you for a while. After all Gulvain could have made a mistake – you said he was old. All I'm suggesting is that you check his figures.'

'And leave the rest to you?'

'Exactly.'

'I'm not going to see him robbed.'

'Damn it, Mal, I do have ethics. All I suggested was a mutually beneficial compromise, an arrangement. I realise that it is a little unusual for a Chief Astronomer to visit an amateur but this is a special case.' Hammond's voice hardened a little. 'When will you be ready to leave?'

CHAPTER 3

He travelled by train, liking the comfort, the opportunity to think. Relaxing in a window seat of an almost empty compartment Spragg studied the rugged beauty of the Grampian Mountains, the vista of the Forest of Atholl, the distant shimmer of lochs and streams running like silver thread over the wide expanses of dusky green heather. Reflected in the window his face held an odd detachment and he wondered at the passage of time which had added depth to the lines running from the corner of his eyes, those marking his cheeks. His hair was flecked with grey and the soft bulge of a second chin showed beneath the first. A battleground on which emotions had raged and left their marks.

What had attracted Myrna? His achievements? Reputation as a scholar or reputation as an admirer of the female form? Or maybe his comfortable house, the expenditure saved by giving up her lodgings?

He looked past his reflection towards the darkening scene beyond, remembering how it had happened. She had moved in as if it had been the most natural thing in the world. After the first few weeks in which her return for a hot bath and food had become a routine and then, quite simply, she had moved in.

They had eaten breakfast and it was time for her to go and he had left her while mounting the stairs to his bedroom. He had lain beneath the covers, a little tense, subconsciously aware, perhaps, that this morning would not follow the usual pattern so that when she came to join him he was ready and unsurprised.

And after, as she had lain beside him, sleeping, her lashes resting like trapped moths on the smoothness of her cheeks, he had wondered, as he had so often in the past, what it was made a woman such a splendid creation.

'Sir?' An attendant stood beside him in the aisle, a tray in his hand bearing empty paper cups and packets of biscuits. 'Coffee, sir? A snack?'

'Coffee.'

He paid and watched as the man moved down the compartment leaving the empty paper cup standing before him. Within minutes another attendant bearing a steaming pot followed the first. Seeing the signalling cup he paused.

'Black or white, sir?'

'Black. No sugar.' Spragg glanced through the window. 'Where are we?'

'Yon's the Glen Carney. You for Inverness?'

'No, Newtonmore.' A hired car could take him from there on to Laggan. 'How long before we reach it?'

'About an hour, sir. We halt a while at Drumochter to let through the express.'

An hour – he must have dozed a little thinking of Myrna.

Spragg sighed as he again studied Gulvain's letter. It had been a week since it had arrived and there had been no answer to his own announcing his intended arrival. Maybe it was still in the post. Hammond had been adamant he should leave and waste no further time. Others could have been contacted, he'd pointed out, and something had delayed the original letter; it had been dated ten days earlier than the time received. Even now the discovery could be lost to the observatory.

The train slowed and came to a halt in the brooding stillness. Framed by the windows the external scene took on an added air of mystery and Spragg found it easy to imagine ghosts moving through the heather; Picts and Caledonians who had ruled in ages past, clansmen of more recent times kilted and savage in their determination to remain free. Other ghosts too; those of men who had fought and died to protect their homes in the south and crofters who had been evicted to starve so as to clear the land for the estates of the wealthy. The Highlands had a blood-drenched history.

A jerk and the train was moving again towards the looming bulk of the Cairngorms. At Newtonmore taxis stood before the station. Spragg headed towards the first in line, jerked open the door of the rear compartment and threw in his single bag.

'Can you take me to Laggan?'

'Aye.' The old driver squinted at his fare. 'Where to in Laggan?' He blinked at the answer. 'The ald minister's hoose?'

'You know him?'

'Aye, that ah did. Mon, dinna ye ken he's deed?'

'Dead?' Hammond's voice came strongly over the phone. 'How?'

'Pneumonia and I'm not surprised. The place is as damp as a marsh. He must have been ill when he wrote the letter and that accounts for the delay. Someone must have found and posted it. My own was unopened. No phone, of course, I'm speaking from the hotel.'

'And?'

'He had something, James. I've checked his figures and diagrams as best as I can and he knew what he was doing. He managed –'

'The discovery?'

'Tentative as yet but highly probable. We'll have to check it out. I want you to tell Reilly to get all the plates taken on that area over the past few years. As many as he can find. Ask Ian to run an elimination check. Then contact all observatories owning a Schmidt and request copies of any plates they may have taken of that particular area. Then –'

'Hold on, Mal.' Hammond was sharp. 'Do you realise what all this could mean? There'll be questions asked. What can I tell them?'

'Say it has to do with our work on the Jovian moons. We're searching for any aberration in asteroidal orbits, which could give us a clue leading to the new satellite. Who knows? We may even find it. And tell Myrna –' Spragg paused, what could he tell Hammond to say?

'I understand,' said the voice on the phone. 'You miss her and look forward to seeing her again, But, Mal, it's only been three days.'

A lifetime, or so it seemed, and it wasn't yet over. Gulvain was dead and buried but his spirit lingered on and not just as a skilled amateur astronomer. The man had belonged to a fanatical Calvinistic sect and, though old, some of the fire had lingered. And his heirs, with stubborn insistence, had refused to allow him to take away any of the old man's papers or notebooks.

Which left Spragg with only one alternative to outright theft.

Back at the house, his purchases hidden beneath his coat, Spragg went to the old man's study. There he was permitted to read and make notes of Gulvain's work and, at times, be assailed by the rantings of the dead man's nephew, a gaunt and aggressive person whom he could barely understand. Fortunately, today, the man was absent and, with the door firmly closed, Spragg set to work to photograph every scrap of writing the dead man had left which he could find.

At dusk he made his last pilgrimage.

A few hundred yards from the house, housed in an old byre, Gulvain had built a small observatory, which housed the six-inch reflector he had made himself.

Gulvain had gone better than mere size. His instrument included a secondary mirror, which, by re-reflecting the image, made for a long focal length with a relatively short lattice. An aid to higher magnification as the incorporated drive mechanism was to prolonged observation; the device keeping the telescope aimed at one point in the sky so the observed stars seemed to be motionless.

But the man hadn't been interested in stars. He had searched within the Solar System for drifting masses of rock inhabiting the asteroid belt; a study that had once been Spragg's own major interest.

Now he touched the shrouded telescope, imagining Gulvain in his place, old, shivering from the cold yet firmly determined to prove something. Fighting age and stiffness and weakening eyes. Fired by his dedication and conviction of what must be.

'Professor Spragg?' The voice came from the house and he turned towards it as a woman came towards the byre. 'If you want a lift I'm leaving now.'

Janet Gulvain, Oxford educated but still with the slight lilt of the Highlands in her voice, dampened now that she was speaking to a Sassenach. Spragg moved towards her.

'Here.' He gestured with his head. 'I was saying goodbye to a really superb amateur observatory. What is to happen to the telescope?'

'It will go as a gift to grandfather's old school together with the firm hope that they will use it.'

'As they will, I'm sure.' Spragg slowed a little. 'My bag?'

'Is in the car. I saw it and guessed you'd want to catch the next train. Did I guess right, Professor?'

'Yes. And you?'

'I have things to do as yet.' As they reached the car she said, 'What did you make of his papers? I'd appreciate the truth, Professor.'

'They show a painstaking attention to detail. Aird Gulvain was a remarkable observer and a most precise recorder of what he saw.'

'A human camera?'

'In a way, yes. In the old days there was no other method they could use. Every tiny point of light had to be marked on a chart by hand. They had to be compared and checked against other charts and other seeing. Your grandfather was one of the old school.'

'Why are you so interested, Professor?' She sent the car moving down the road then, without waiting for him to answer she added, 'Is it because you think he was mad?'

'Mad? Of course not!'

'Normal, then?' She turned to look at him then concentrated again on the road. 'Old, yes, and a little absent minded and even perhaps a little senile, you agree?'

'I didn't know him.'

'I did. When I was young. That was twenty years ago now and he terrified me. You've heard of the old Biblical prophets, well he was one. Hellfire and damnation and threats of the vengeance of the Lord. I had it as a steady diet. You've met his nephew? He's nothing to what my grandfather used to be. I think he was a little insane.'

'But clever.'

'Yes, very clever, the insane often are.' She slowed as they came within sight of the station. 'But how many long for the end of the world?'

NASA had been more than helpful sending a heap of appropriate material and Spragg wondered if Irene had helped to select it. Had she touched the models of the two Voyagers? The slides taken from the transmitted films? The three-dimensional postcards of the Jovian moons? He looked at one, recognising Ganymede, and imagined Irene holding it as he held it now, looking at what he now saw.

'Mal?' Myrna had come into the room, her arms loaded with brightly coloured brochures. Her hair was a veil that she blew with sudden irritation to clear her eyes and Spragg wondered why the hell she didn't tie it back as Irene had. 'Where shall I put these?'

Like himself she was tired and irritable and resentful of the duties attendant on open days at the observatory. And now, with the Voyager promotional campaign adding extra work, her temper was short.

He said, 'I need a drink. Join me?'

'Here?'

'Why not? Get some cups and mixers and ice if you can. We need a break.'

Staff had privileges and soon Spragg lifted a paper cup filled with ginger ale, ice and whisky from his flask. 'Slarg!'

'Cheers!' Myrna returned the toast. 'You learn that up in the Highlands?'

'From television. They –' He broke off, she hadn't been born when he'd seen the programme.

'I'll be glad when today is over.' She sat, long legs covered in faded blue denim, breasts prominent beneath her uniform-like shirt. 'Do we have to mess about with this stuff?' Her gesture embraced the NASA material. 'The latest Voyagers have left the Jovian system, and are headed outward. Why make all the noise?'

'Money.' He shrugged at her expression. 'Don't kick it, my dear. It keeps us in food and drink and what comforts we enjoy. And the Voyagers aren't finished yet. There are the other major planets to be checked before they leave the Solar System for ever – perhaps in ages to come to be discovered by some alien race.'

'Who will then have the ineffable pleasure of being able to listen to some typical earth-sounds such as dogs barking, horns blowing, babies crying and a pop group!'

'Have another drink.'

Spragg poured as she held out her cup then replenished his own.

She said, 'Sean's making progress. He's persuaded Hammond to authorise the purchase of computer-time so as to check Gulvain's figures.'

Something Spragg hadn't known and he felt a quick jealousy that Reilly had taken her into his confidence. What else had they talked about?

'It isn't through yet so he didn't want to tell you,' she continued. 'But I overheard Susan talking on the phone and it's pretty definite. You know Ian's quitting?'

'I know he was thinking about it.'

'It's definite.' She held out her cup for more and he freshened her drink. 'He's got a woman in trouble and wants out.'

'He told you that?'

'When he called at the house one day while you were away. He wanted a shoulder to cry on. I let him use mine.'

'Just your shoulder?'

'That's all.' Her tone was sharp.

'You want to lend him your shoulder, that's your business. You want to lend him something else, that's your business too. Right?'

'Damned right.' She scowled into her cup. 'I'm not property, Mal, and I'm not cheap either. You I like, Ian I don't. It's as simple as that.'

The new morality was something he couldn't appreciate. A woman's body was her own and she slept around as she pleased but he didn't like it and never would. In that he was as old-fashioned as Gulvain had been and he felt a sudden urge to get back to the main problem at hand: the need to check out the potential discovery. But right now he was stuck with the duties always present on an open day at the observatory.

As usual there were questions.

'Sir!' A small boy raised a sticky hand after his simplified lecture. 'Sir, what stops the moon from falling on Earth?'

Patiently Spragg explained.

'Sir, where did the asteroids come from?'

'We can't be certain, of course, but most probably they are the remains of a planet which once orbited the sun between Mars and Jupiter.' Spragg used the pointer to touch the distorted representation of the Solar System hung against the wall behind him. 'Back in 1866 a German astronomer, Johann Daniel Titus, devised a numerical system to express the distances of the planets relative to the sun. How they were first discovered makes a fascinating story, and you will find his numerical system explained in full detail in the appropriate booklet attainable at the bookshop next to the main entrance.' Having dutifully plugged the shop he went on: 'You must remember that only the six inner planets were known in Titus's day. Now, following his table we find a correlation with every number to a planet aside from the fifth, between Mars and Jupiter. Instead at that distance we find thc asteroids. Incidentally the series is better known as Bode's Law because he wrote about it in 1772 and he was more famous than poor old Titus.' He paused to allow the dutiful chuckles to die. 'Any further questions?'

'Please, sir, when was the first asteroid discovered?'

'On 1 January 1801,' said Spragg promptly. 'It was first seen by a German physician, Heinrich Wilhelm Mattias Olbers who was born in 1758. It is named Ceres. Later he discovered two more, Pallas and Vesta, which shows what can be accomplished by an amateur. Olbers practiced astronomy as a hobby.'

'Sir –'

There were more questions and Spragg answered them mechanically, his mind on a lonely old figure at his telescope in the Highlands. An amateur as Olbers had been. Had he also left his mark on time?

Reilly thought he had.

'The man definitely found something, Mal. I've been over his figures and charts and through he was weak on math there's nothing wrong with his observations. But, to be sure, we have to run comparisons.'

'Any news on the computer-time?'

'We've got it and they're running the data now.' Reilly didn't ask how Spragg knew. 'I sent them copies of everything we have – well, almost everything. That stuff you photographed at Gulvain's had some pretty off notations. What are they?'

'Biblical references.' Spragg had worked that out on the first study of the prints. 'His granddaughter told me he was a bit of a fanatic and I guess he could have seen more through a telescope than most of us. Maybe it kept him at it.'

'And maybe it helped him to see what he wanted to see.' Reilly shrugged. 'At home we talk of the little people, what do they have in Scotland?'

'God knows.' Spragg yawned, suddenly aware of his fatigue. 'Let's not confuse things. Where's Ian?'

McGregor was in the laboratory working on his light-magnifying analogue. Myrna was leaning against the bench beside him and Spragg fought a momentary twinge of jealousy. She looked up as he approached.

'Hi, Mal. Got any of that whisky left?' She took the flask he handed to her. 'Here, Ian, it won't cure but it may help.'

'Thanks.' He drank from the bottle. 'Myrna, you're an angel. Why not come to the States as my wife? Just say the word and I'm yours.'

Spragg had the uneasy conviction the man wasn't joking. 'I'm fit, able, and potentially rich. If the beard offends you I'll shave it off.'

'And the girl in Carlisle?'

'To hell with her! I'm talking about us. Well?' For a moment there was silence then Spragg relaxed as Myrna shook her head. 'No?' McGregor shrugged. 'It seems as if you win again, Mal, but I'm keeping the Scotch as a consolation prize.' He tilted the bottle. 'Fair enough?'

'Sure. Go ahead and finish it.' Spragg looked at the mechanism on the bench. 'What's wrong with it now?'

'Bugs.'

'But you had it working.'

'I had it on test,' corrected McGregor. 'Up to a point it works fine enough but the gain is less than that obtained by an ordinary image intensifier even though the field of view is greater. I wanted to get something comparable to a Schmidt plate but with boosted magnification. And I know I can do it given the right facilities and help.'

Myrna said, 'What's the problem?'

'Bugs, as I said. Above all we need fine resolution, which means accurate components and a total absence of interference. It's easy to intensify an image – any electronics technician can do that, it's basically a matter of television, but I want more. I want to be able to take an image and both enlarge and intensify it while at the same time, filtering out all error caused by local conditions. Once I manage that all you need do is to take a sight lasting for only a fraction of time and electronics will do the rest.' He growled at the apparatus on the bench. 'But I'll never do it here. Now get the hell out and let me get on with it. I'll need something to show Rand.'

Outside darkness softened the surrounding country, turning the trees into dim shapes of mystery, the dome into an enigmatic silhouette against the sky. Somewhere an owl hooted and Myrna shivered.

'A bird of ill omen,' she said. 'So the Romans believed.'

'And you?'

'I'm not superstitious.' She stared at him, her eyes shadowed. 'Why do you ask?'

'Because I'm interested in you. I'd like to feel closer to you.' Spragg reached out and caught her by the shoulders. 'Would it be stupidly old-fashioned for me to say I love you?'

'No, Mal.' Her voice was softly gentle. 'I don't think so. Not as long as you mean it.'

Hammond said, briskly, 'Mal, you know better than to think I'm trying to rush you but we can't afford to delay any longer. Either Gulvain found something or he didn't. If he did and we don't make the announcement then we'll lose the discovery.'

'And if he didn't?'

'Then he made a mistake. An old man with bad eyes and a softening brain. It's understandable.'

'But not that easy. If we make the announcement then we're the ones responsible. We can't blame an old man for being careless.'

'Why not? He's dead.'

Spragg shook his head. 'You've been mixing with too many tycoons. They can find and use scapegoats but we can't. What you're demanding is that I put my reputation on the line. Well, forget it.'

'But when will you be sure?' Hammond paced the floor in his agitation, oblivious of the dead eyes watching him from the photographs. 'Reilly's had his computer time and checked the figures. You've taken sightings. What else do you need?'

'The Schmidt plates of the area. When they get here –'

'They won't. I didn't send for them.'

'Why the hell not?'

'I didn't want to take the chance. One hint would be enough to set the others on the trail and they've better equipment than we have. Damn it, Mal, don't you understand? It's our lives I'm fighting for. This discovery could put Althene on the map. We could get government backing once we gain the right influence. Sir Edward –'

'To hell with him!'

'Later he can roast all you want but for now we need him.' Hammond released some of his own frustration in a blaze of unexpected rage. 'You bloody academic, what do you know about it? You, locked up in your nice ivory tower with that girl, playing at being a scientist – what do you know about how the world runs? I've got to beg, beg, you understand, for money to pay your salary. To buy materials. To pay for equipment. To employ a gang of useless bastards none of whom could do a good day's work if their lives depended on it. I've got to eat food I detest, play games I abhor, be nice to people I despise and for what? So you can stand there and play Pollyanna. You and your precious reputation! Just see how much booze it'll buy once you leave here!'

'You want me to go?'

'No, I don't want you to go.' Hammond paused, breathing deeply, dabbing at his face with a scented handkerchief. The outburst had relieved his tension buy he maintained the emotional level. 'But I tell you frankly if you want to quit I won't argue. I can't work with those unwilling to cooperate with me. And I won't be threatened.'

But he could be pushed and Spragg had a shrewd idea who was doing the pushing. Sir Edward Thorne, eager for prominence, using implied threats to accelerate results. Hammond's fault, of course, he should have kept his mouth shut but, on the other hand, he could have tried a bluff that had misfired.

Now he said, more calmly, 'Mal, we've known each other too long to quarrel like this. What am I asking? Just your permission to announce that a new discovery has been made. It'll buy us time if nothing else. Even if a mistake has been made we can turn it to our advantage. An old man, dying, pleading for our help. How could we ignore him? How could we disappoint his family? A respected member of the community, a minister, a man dedicated to his hobby.'

And one safely dead.

Spragg looked at the photographs on the walls and wondered, if the men depicted could return, what they would have thought. Probably they would have sided with Hammond – they had lived in a hard and practical age. He remembered Titus, his reputation overshadowed by Bode. Of others who had lost credit which should have been his. Of Humason who had come so near to discovering Pluto, actually photographing it but not knowing what the object was.

'Mal?'

Spragg said, 'Gulvain found something but we aren't too certain as to what it is. I want to be sure.'

'But there's something there?'

'Yes. A point of light that shows no apparent movement. It isn't a star – all those in the area have been listed for years. It can't be a planet and I doubt if it is an asteroid.'

'Why?' Hammond was sharp. 'Couldn't it be one with an eccentric orbit?'

'If it's eccentric enough it can't be classed as an asteroid. No more can a comet. It could, of course, be a rogue.'

'A wanderer from interstellar space?' Hammond smiled. 'Mal, that's just what we need! Sir Edward will be delighted. Thorne,' he mused. 'Thorne – it should be worth a new spectroscopic laboratory at least. Why didn't you tell me this earlier?'

'Because there's something odd about it. Gulvain records apparent movement but we can't spot any.' He added, pointedly, 'If you'd got those plates I asked for I'd have been certain much earlier.'

'We're as certain as we need to be,' Hammond said. 'Can you tell me anything more about this object? Size? Mass? Albedo?' He shrugged as Spragg shook his head. 'Well, it doesn't matter, the important thing is to make the announcement before anyone beats us to it. No movement, though, that's odd. How do you explain it?'

'No *apparent* movement,' corrected Spragg patiently. 'Which means the thing could be just hanging there which is impossible unless it's a self-motivated object of some kind. Or, and so Gulvain believed, it is coming straight at us.' He smiled at Hammond's expression, enjoying the moment. 'That's right, James. The wrath of the Lord sent to smite the ungodly – I told you the old boy was a nut.'

CHAPTER 4

Susan Keating entered her office and, closing the door behind her, surveyed the neat array of her desk and furnishings. The desk matched her nature; items set in mathematical precision, and included an ashtray for the use of visitors who were insensitive enough to smoke, in and out trays for correspondence, a plaque engraved with her name and the record of a long-past athletic achievement.

A normal office but one on which she had set the stamp of her own personality. The carpet, won after long struggle, was the shade and pattern she had wanted. The colour of the paint, the pictures on the walls, the curtains, even the lampshade spoke of her presence. And all spoke of her success.

Straightening, she crossed to her desk and sat with a happy sigh. She checked that all was in the order she had left it and then she reached for the phone.

'Joan, get me the offices of the *Sun*.'

There was a protocol about such things. Joan, the secretary cum typist would make the connection, transfer the call and the person at the other end of the line would be suitably impressed.

A ring and the phone was in her hand.

'City desk.' The voice was bored. 'What is it?'

'I want to speak with the science editor.'

'Lady, this is the *Sun*. Can I take a message?'

'I am ringing to find out whether or not your science editor received the communication from the Althene Observatory which was dispatched yesterday. It is a communication of some importance. Will you please ask him to contact me at his earliest convenience.'

'Who should he contact?' The voice grunted as she gave her name, telephone number, and address. 'OK. I'll pass the word.'

'It is a matter of the utmost importance. It concerns a new discovery by the Observatory. A hitherto unknown planetoid in the star region –'

'Stars?' The voice sighed. 'Sorry, but we get our horoscopes from the regular source.'

'I'm not talking about horoscopes!' Susan made an effort to remain calm. 'This is a great moment in the history of astronomy. A discovery of tremendous importance. Now please make sure your science editor contacts me as soon as possible.'

A boor, she thought as she broke the connection. No respect for academic attainments and none of the deference due to a person in her position. Well, she had tried and the *Sun* could not blame her for having neglected them.

'Janet, get me the *Daily Mail*.' Susan added, 'And make sure I am speaking to the science editor.'

The *Daily Mail* was more polite. Yes, they had received the official communication. No, they did not intend making a front-page display of the news as yet. Yes, they were interested.

'Of course,' said the voice, 'this has been verified by the Royal Observatory at Herstmonceux?'

'Not as yet. The observatory has been notified, of course, but they have to fit the investigation into their programme.'

'I see.' A pause. 'Well, maybe you'll let us know when it's been done.'

The *Mirror* was almost as bad as the Sun. The *Guardian* was interested and promised to use the information if they had the room. The *Daily Telegraph* was cool, the *Times* was frigid, the *Star* couldn't have cared less.

The man she contacted at the *Express* took time to explain.

'Lady, we've got three strikes, the threat of two wars, racial violence in five cities and talk of a new election. We've almost three million unemployed and two Miss Worlds had a fight in public last night. You see the problem?'

'No.'

'Your news isn't of much interest now, is it? A dot of light in the sky – who cares?'

'It's new.'

'So was the Star of Bethlehem and you know how many were interested in that? Three. And that was a pretty big star. Important too.'

'So is Thorne.'

'Thorne?'

'The new discovery. We named it after Sir Edward Thorne who is a patron of the observatory. Sir Edward is a prominent figure in the textile trade.' She added, cunningly, 'His firms probably spend millions on advertising.'

'Not in this paper, they don't.' The voice softened. 'Sorry, but all we can give you if we use the item is a mention later in the week. You been a PRO long?'

'I'm not a Public Relations Officer, I'm a Personal Assistant.'

'I see, a shame, maybe you should get yourself a good PRO.' And then, just before ending the communication, the voice said, 'Say, why not try the locals? You're near Carlisle right? Get in touch with Sam Eagan at the *Argus*. 'Bye.'

Eagan was a round, plump man addicted to drink and strong tobacco. His suits looked as if they had been slept in and his head, now bald was rarely seen without a bettered hat bearing a stained ribbon. A reporter of the old school, his heart had never left Fleet Street even though his body, impelled by the results of certain manipulations while in pursuit of a story, had felt it diplomatic to leave the metropolis.

'Argus.' He blew smoke into the mouthpiece. 'Eagan speaking.' He listened to Susan's careful enunciation. 'Thorne? Edward Thorne?'

'That is correct. Sir Edward is –'

'I know who he is.' Among other things the man owned the *Argus*. 'How is he connected with this? I get it. Anything special about the discovery? I see. Has it been verified? When do you expect it to be? Yeah, I understand.' Eagan glanced through the window. It was a nice day for a drive and Sir Edward's involvement justified further investigation. To Susan he said, 'I'd like to make a spread of this. You know, personal interviews, photographs, plenty of human interest. Could you arrange that? You can? Good. Be with you in an hour.'

From where she lay sprawled on a blanket spread on the grass Myrna said, 'Mal, what does Rev 9:1 mean?'

'It's a biblical notation. Shorthand so you can find a place.' He reared up from his deckchair. 'Didn't you ever have religious instruction at school?'

'I skipped it.'

'Haven't you ever read the Bible?'

'No, I was too busy with text books. What does it say, Mal?'

'I don't know.'

'Find out. Haven't you a Bible?'

There was one in the house and he went to fetch it, pausing as he returned to the garden to look at the girl. She was wearing a scarlet bikini. A young and vibrant animal basking in the sun which, given time, would coat her with gold.

'Mal?'

'Coming.' He walked to his chair, conscious of his growing paunch, the wasting of his thighs. Signs of age which he would have preferred to have kept hidden but she had insisted he join her in her worship of the sun. 'You'll burn,' he warned. 'Shouldn't you be using oil?'

'Later.' She turned, the movement of her breasts catching his eyes. 'I want to get rid of this fish-belly whiteness first. What does the Bible say, Mal?'

Seating himself he turned the pages and quoted, 'And the fifth angel sounded, and I saw a star fall from heaven unto the earth; and to him was given the key of the bottomless pit.'

'And?'

Spragg continued, 'And he opened the bottomless pit; and there rose a smoke out of the pit, as the smoke of a great furnace; and the sun and the air were darkened by reason of the smoke from the pit.'

'And? Go on, Mal.'

'Read it for yourself if you're interested.' Spragg closed the Bible. 'It comes from the Revelation of St. John the Divine and depicts what is supposed to happen at the Time of Judgement.'

'The end of the world?'

'You could call it that. Fire and plague, destruction and all hell breaking loose. Starvation, flooding – you name it and it's there with all the sinners being punished and only the true and faithful saved. It used to give me nightmares when a kid. You can see why Gulvain made that notation on his papers.'

'The star which fell from heaven,' she said thoughtfully. 'If he was really around the bend he could have imagined his discovery to be the actual fulfilment of biblical prophecy. Mal, he couldn't have been serious!'

'Why not?'

'He was an educated man. An astronomer and a mathematician. He couldn't have believed that space was inhabited by angels and all that nonsense. His eyes would have told him better.'

'Would they?' Spragg looked at the clear bowl of the sky. Aside from a scud of fleecy white cloud the blueness was unmarked. 'If you had never seen anything other than the sky as it is now and I told you that there were bright points of light beyond the blue – would you believe me? Or if, at night, I told you that there were objects sending out radio waves and that these waves held regular patterns – would you accept it? Of course not. For that you need to have faith in the discoveries of others. Well, Gulvain had faith in his religion. He believed in heaven and the Bible and the things it contains. As a minister he would have had no choice but to believe, to have faith. Faith that God does exist. That the end will come. That punishment will fall on the unrighteous.'

'And that a star will be sent against us to destroy the world? Mal, you're having me on!'

'A little, yes,' he admitted. 'But it does make an odd kind of sense when you think about it. And the descriptions in Revelations are pretty graphic of what to expect if something from space should hit earth. Not a star, naturally, they had no other terms for such objects in those days. But a planetoid, perhaps, even a big meteor – maybe legends existed of what had happened way back when one had landed and John used available material.'

'Now you're going too far. I think I'll –' Her fingers reached for the fastenings of her brassiere. 'Hell! Visitors!'

A mistake, Sam Eagan was alone. He approached smiling, snapping with the miniature camera in his hand, talking as he snapped.

'Professor Spragg? Miss Keating said I would find you here. And Miss Parkin? Sunbathing, I see. A most attractive sight. Allow me to introduce myself – Sam Eagan of the *Argus*.'

'A reporter?'

'Yes, Professor, and I won't take up much of your time. It's just that your discovery is of great interest and I'd like to get a few things straightened out.

As I understand it the object could be either an asteroid, a planetoid or a new moon of Jupiter. Right?'

'We aren't sure as yet.'

'But you can make a guess. Would you call it a meteor?'

'Hardly,' said Spragg dryly. 'A meteor only becomes that after it hits the atmosphere. Before that it's a meteoroid.'

'Which is small?'

'Yes, too small to be what we've discovered.'

'Something larger, then? An asteroid?'

'Doubtful. Asteroids have been observed for years and all the large ones are known.' Spragg added, 'At a guess, I'd say it was a planetoid.'

'How far away is it?'

'We can't tell as yet. Relatively close, though. It has to be for us to be able to see it at all.'

'And heading towards us?'

'Heading towards the inner planets, yes.' Spragg did his best to mark his impatience. 'You've been given all the facts we have at this time. The object is new. It is relatively close. It is relatively large and is heading in our general direction. I'm afraid that is all I can tell you. Is there anything else?'

'No Professor.' Eagan took one last photograph. 'That is enough.'

The story broke two days later. Spragg stared at the newspaper, his hands shaking, filled with the desire to kill. All night he'd been working in the dome and now to come home to this –

'What is it, Mal?' Myrna came to stand beside him. 'That isn't the *Argus*.'

'But the story came from the bastard who called on us.' Spragg jabbed at it with a hand. 'Eagan, wasn't it? I'll teach the swine a lesson.'

Swine or not the man knew his trade. The headline screamed EARTH DOOMED! Beneath it was a photograph of herself artfully touched to emphasise her breasts. The article began:

'Today, when interviewed by our special correspondent, Professor Malcolm Spragg admitted the object he had sighted in the heavens was heading directly towards Earth. The strange new planet, which he named Thor – the Hammer of God – was discovered by chance and as yet little is known as to its nature and speed of approach. Even so, as Professor Spragg confessed, it has to be unusually large. The Professor, obviously a deeply religious man, was finding consolation in his bible when our special science corresponded called at his luxurious home in the landscaped grounds of Althene Observatory set in the delightfully unspoiled village of Ivegill some twenty miles to the south of Carlisle. Despite his outward composure his voice, at times, tended to break a little and he admitted his fear at having to keep facts to himself for the benefit of Mankind in general. The devastation that would visit the Earth once hit by this marauder from the depths of space is too awful to contemplate. The total abolition of all forms of life together with the actual rending of the crust is inevitable. The fact that the menace is so near, as Professor Spragg admitted, is cause for the greatest alarm. When pressed the Professor –'

Spragg groaned. 'Why do they print such rubbish?'

'To sell papers.' Myrna took it from him and continued reading. It was the usual mass of repetition, half-truth and biased slant of emotive words that comprised such journalistic masterpieces. The photograph of herself, designed to catch the eye and hold the attention, was an added touch. Doom and sex – the twin props of the national press displayed side by side.

'My reputation!' Spragg snatched at the paper. 'Who will ever take me seriously after this?'

'Don't worry about it.'

'How can you say that? What about yourself? Your picture spread all over the page? It makes you look a tart.'

'So what? Men like tarts.'

'It –' He broke off, conscious of their different values, the impossibility of his ever really being able to understand her indifference. Didn't it matter to her that her near-nakedness was flaunted to all? That the photograph had been taken and used without her permission? 'You could sue them,' he said. 'They had no right to print your photograph. And they had no right to lie about what I said.'

'So sue them.'

She was joking but he didn't take it like that. For a moment he glared at her then snarled, 'By God, I'll do just that. But first I'll see that bastard Eagan!'

'No, Mal! Don't be a fool! The more noise you make the more they'll like it. Can you think of anything more stupid than an outraged professor?'

'So I'm stupid now, am I?'

'For Christ's sake grow up, Mal,' she said impatiently. 'Let it die. Just don't give any more interviews. Susan will have to take care of that side of it. Forget Eagan. And forget this tripe.' She kicked at the discarded paper. 'In a couple of days it will all be forgotten.'

She was wrong.

The silly season was at hand and the public needed titivation. The story was a change from the usual run of sex-mad vicars, salubrious escort agencies and massage parlours, death-spells cast by inspired, teenaged witches, black magic rites conducted in deserted graveyards, and the tired old spate of potential disasters presented by nuclear power stations, biological laboratories, climatic changes and population explosion.

The Hammer of God beat them all.

Pacing his office, Hammond said, 'For God's sake, Mal, what came over you? Sensationalism is the last thing we want. Susan's been swamped with calls from nuts of every description. Sir Edward's having second thoughts about his support and what do you think this will do to our hopes of getting a government grant?'

'Don't blame me.'

'Who then? That reporter? Are you saying he lied?'

'He added two and two and came up with five. He twisted my words – all that crap about the end of the world! Invention!'

Hammond said, flatly, 'Susan walked with him towards your house to show him the way. She heard you ranting on about fire and damnation and the Day of Judgement.'

'For Christ's sake, man! I was reading from Revelations!'

'Eagan must have heard you.'

'And jumped at the opportunity to embroider the story. The bastard! If it hadn't been for Myrna I'd have sued!'

'It's just as well you didn't,' said Hammond dryly. 'We don't want to aggravate the situation. But things can't be left as they are. The media are after us, Mal. The more we put them off the more certain they are we are hiding something. So I want you to come out into the open. Be blunt. Tell the facts. Lie if you have to but kill this stupid rumour for all time.'

'Lie?'

'Shape the exact truth. Do you honestly believe we are in any danger? Of course you don't and it's your duty to remove any doubt from the minds of the idiots who believe all they are told. So I've arranged a television interview. I suggest you act as if you're giving a lecture but Farmer will advise you about that. He's the interviewer. Just do everything he says.'

'Like hell I will!'

'Don't be difficult, Mal. I'll be frank – I've had a request from the government. You know how important it is to avoid panic and so I promised you would kill this stupid story about a planet crashing into the earth. A planet! Where did they get that from?'

A question repeated by Stan Farmer later that day before the watchful eyes of television cameras.

He was a short man with manicured nails, over-dressed hair, cosmetic teeth and a contemptuous arrogance that Spragg found hard to swallow. But he knew his job and Spragg responded with the rehearsed answer.

'I said nothing about a planet. The word I used was "planetoid" which is a far different thing.'

'How different, Professor? Smaller?'

'Very much smaller. In fact there is no real comparison. It is almost like calling a pebble a mountain. As a matter of interest there are many such small objects in the skies.'

'And some of them actually hit us?'

'Often. Look up into the sky and you may see a trail of light. Children call them shooting stars and they are small pieces of stone and iron which have reached us from space.' Spragg, remembering his cues, gave a broad smile. 'We get hit by such meteoroids several times a day but they obviously don't do us much harm.'

'But there are other masses, aren't there, Professor? Larger ones?'

'Yes, of course, our own moon is one. But I imagine you must be referring to the Apollo-objects. There is nothing mysterious about them. They are merely asteroids that follow paths, which, at times, take them closer to the sun than our own planet. Obviously, in order to do that, they must cross out orbit. However the chance of us both being in the same place at the same time is astronomically remote.'

'You mean it couldn't happen?'

'Not in the foreseeable future.' One of the 'lies' Hammond had suggested – no one had bothered to check. 'And while we're on the subject and in case anyone gets the wrong impression these objects are also known as Earth-grazers. But a graze, in astronomical terms, is a considerable distance – far beyond the orbit of the moon, for example.'

'So we are all perfectly safe.' Farmer nodded. 'Well, Professor Spragg, you've certainly put my mind at rest. But you stated the object you discovered was coming towards us. What makes you so certain of that?'

'I said it was heading in the general direction of the sun,' Mal corrected. 'Not towards our planet. I may also have mentioned the inner planets or even the Solar System – it wasn't possible to be precise as there was no way of checking the distance.'

'Why not?'

'Imagine you are standing on a deserted road at night. It is perfectly dark and all you can see is a small gleam of light directly ahead of you. You have no idea what it is and so can have no conception of its size. It could be anything; a glow-worm, the window of a house, a flashlight, the headlamp of a car. But if, while watching it, it seems to grow larger you can assume that it is heading towards you. Of course it needn't be. The light could be a fire which merely is burning brighter.'

'Like a star that had gone nova?'

'Exactly.'

'Which is what the object you discovered could be?'

'It could be that, yes.' Inwardly Spragg winced at the damage to his reputation then hastily added, 'But remember we are moving through space all the time and that means our planet is moving from a straight-line path to the object.'

Farmer beamed, obviously convinced by the expert he was interviewing. 'Thank you, Professor, that's even better. We are moving away from the visitor – if it is a visitor – and that's an extra bonus for safety. So what would you call all the recent fuss? A storm in a teacup?'

'What else?' Spragg smiled. 'There's nothing to worry about.'

Not then and not until the end of the following month when Spragg received an invitation to visit the Observatorium der Dutschen Tautenberg.

CHAPTER 5

Sat at the dressing table, Myrna said, 'Are you taking me with you to Germany?'

'The invitation said nothing about a companion.'

'And, of course, I'm not your wife.' The sweep of the brush through her hair made a thin, spiteful sound. 'I'm just your mistress and that makes a difference.'

The brush trembled in her hand as if she fought the desire to throw it at him then lifted to attack her tresses with greater force than before. 'How long will you be gone?'

'It depends on why they have asked me to come. A few days, I guess. A week at the most.'

Rising, he moved towards her and dropped his hands to the smooth roundness of her shoulders, feeling the fine strands of hair covering the flesh, the scent of the shampoo she had used. Hair that tickled his nose and cheeks as he kissed the top of her head. Flesh which slid beneath his questing fingers as his hands dropped lower, down over her upper arms, to her waist.

Hands that caressed a statue.

He sensed her tension, the coldness that she maintained even while being touched. He kissed her again, lightly, then returned to the bed.

She said, as if nothing had happened, 'I heard from Ian yesterday.'

'Oh? How is he doing in the States?'

'Fine. It's been four weeks now and he's settled in. Rand helped him to find an apartment and he has a car and everything.'

He said, 'As long as McGregor's able to produce he'll climb. As soon as he stops he'll fall. That's the way Rand works.'

'He won't fall.' Myrna set down the brush and said, casually, 'He asked me to join him.'

'Interested?'

'I'm thinking about it. After all he did ask me to marry him.'

'No,' corrected Spragg. 'You've got that wrong. He didn't. He offered to make you his wife if that was the only way he could get you. Now, it seems you're willing to be bought. Will you be leaving before or after you get your degree?'

'You bastard! Don't you care?'

'Would it make any difference if I did?'

'It would help. I don't like to be taken for granted.'

'And you don't like to be owned.' Irritation sharpened his voice. 'Damn it, Myrna, you can't have it both ways. You want to go then you'll go but I'm not going to beg you to stay. I'm not going to give you and McGregor that to laugh over like –' He broke off. 'Never mind.'

'Like Bob and Irene? Did you beg her to stay, Mal? Did she laugh at you? Do you think she is still laughing at you?'

'Go to hell!'

'No.' She rose, tall and lovely in her newly acquired tan. 'I won't do that but I will go and dress. Why not get some rest, Mal? You look all in.'

And with reason. It had been a hard few weeks since the interview with Farmer and Spragg felt the tension of fatigue that threatened his ability to make correct decisions. More interviews had followed the first, many necessitating travel and delays. There had been a press conference in which he had been quietly made to appear a fool. In Carlisle a woman had spat in his face and called him a traitor. Hammond had been elusive and there was trouble with the telescope.

And now Myrna's threat.

Lying, eyes closed, Spragg thought about it. He had told her he loved her and had meant it – then. She had told him the same and had, probably, been equally as honest. But propinquity had worn off the bright newness and now the initial flush of passion had died, small faults were becoming more obtrusive. The way she was careless about kitchen-hygiene, for example. The scatter of garments in the bedroom. The clutter of deodorants and cosmetics in the bathroom. And, above all, the eternal jeans.

'Mal?' She was back, dressed, breasts firm against the taut fabric of her shirt. 'I'm just going into the village. Want anything?'

'No.'

'You worried about Ian?'

'No.'

'Can't you think of anything else to say?' She turned in a huff towards the door.

'Only to say that I want you.'

'Then want on.'

She looked offended but he wasn't fooled – she was woman enough to be pleased by his outright declaration.

As she left the house he leaned back, closing his eyes again, almost drifting into sleep before being jerked fully awake by the ringing of the doorbell.

'You!'

Sam Eagan smiled and lifted one hand in a gesture of peace. The other held a brown paper package. 'Keep it cool, Professor.'

'Go to hell!'

'Now why be like that? Here I come bearing gifts and you act hostile. Where's the harm in a little talk?'

'The last time we had a little talk you almost cost me my job and most probably have ruined my reputation,' snapped Spragg. 'Now crawl back into your hole before I forget I'm supposed to be civilised.'

'Why blame me for the job?' Eagan took the butt of his cigarette from the corner of his mouth and flicked it to one side. 'You're a man of the world, Professor. You know how it is. One hand washes the other, right? So I sold the story to the nationals but if I hadn't someone else would have done. And I touched on a few facts you didn't want mentioned but that's the job as I see it. To dig a little. To find out things. To make the news interesting. Have you any ice?'

'What?'

'Ice. I've some of the real stuff here.' Eagan hefted the package. 'Top-grade malt, export stock, a friend supplied me. You enjoy a good whisky? This is the best. My way of apologising. Accepted?' He beamed as Spragg, reluctantly, nodded. 'Good man! Well, let's get at it.'

As he'd promised the whisky was superb and Spragg felt both fatigue and animosity begin to vanish beneath its influence. Eagan was a louse but he was a decent louse and he'd had experience of the cut and thrust of the professional world. Anyway, there was nothing to be gained by continuing enmity.

'Slarg!' Spragg lifted his glass.

'Prost!' Eagan killed half his drink. 'Where's the girl? Out? A fine figure and a nice face. You're a lucky man, Prof.'

'Is that what you came to tell me?'

'No.' Eagan became serious. 'Listen,' he said, 'I'm a reporter and a good one. Ask anyone in the street if you want confirmation. I didn't always work for a crummy rag like the *Argus*. I just happened to make a mistake and had to pay for it.' Eagan refilled the glasses. 'Did you never make a mistake, Prof?'

'My name is Malcolm so call me Mal. That or Professor Spragg.'

'Sorry. As I was saying, Mal, didn't you ever make a mistake? Everyone does. Mine was in following a lead down the wrong alley and winding up with a story no one dared to print. Not unless they wanted to wind up in jail. Official secrets – need I say more?'

'So they censored you?'

Eagan sipped at his drink. 'It happens. I moved while I still had enough reputation to get another job but I didn't leave my brains behind. Or nose for a story.' He added, casually, 'When did you take your last observation, Mal?'

'Some time ago now, before the initial interview with Farmer. But I've been busy and –'

'Kept on the move, right?'

'Yes, but that isn't all. There's something wrong with the drive mechanism of the telescope so I can't use it anyway.'

'Convenient.'

'No, damned inconvenient. I wanted to –' Spragg broke off. 'Are you suggesting that the telescope has been deliberately sabotaged?'

'Could it have been?'

'Yes, but who would have wanted to do a thing like that? For what reason?'

'Orders, maybe?' Eagan took another sip of his drink. 'What made you give that first interview? And why did you agree to shade the truth? You were rehearsed, right? Well, what made you agree to play along? You put your reputation on the line and you must have known it.'

Spragg said, 'I agreed to the interview because it seemed a good idea to avoid any panic your story could have started.'

'Fair enough. Your idea?'

'No, Hammond's. He said he'd promised to see it done.' Spragg looked at the reporter. 'Promised someone high in authority.'

'You believed him?'

'It seemed logical. We were swamped with calls and the stories had grown out of all proportion to what I originally said. So – but what does it matter?'

'That's what I'd like to know.' Eagan took a hand-rolled cigarette from a tin, lit it, coughed and beat at his chest. 'All right, I know these things are killing me, but who wants to live forever? Now tell me if this makes sense: you made a discovery and reported it, right?'

'The Reverend Aird Gulvain made the discovery. I checked and found the object he had seen.'

'Let's leave Gulvain out of this, he isn't important. You, a noted astronomer, make a discovery and report it. What would normally happen next? Wouldn't other observatories check and verify?'

'Yes, but they need time. Observatories work to prearranged programmes and they don't like to have their schedules upset. If a new discovery is made they can't stop everything just to take a look. In any case there is always room for error; the discovery could be an old object found again as has happened several times with the asteroids.'

'From an amateur, yes,' said Eagan. 'You're a professional. They must know you would have made certain it wasn't a mistake yet they still ignore you. Why?'

'Time as I told you. And you can't really say they are ignoring me.'

'I checked with Herstmonceux and got nowhere. The Royal Observatory itself and yet, with the country in near-panic as your Director claimed, they couldn't be bothered to issue a statement. Palomar the same. Licks, Yerkes – Silence all the way. I'm curious as to why.'

The man was incredible. Spragg looked to where he sat, the battered hat pushed back on his balding head. He had taken a serious scientific discovery and made a joke out of it and now wondered why others were reluctant to get involved.

Myrna shrugged when, later, he mentioned it.

'He wants more pap to feed his public. Scandal, gossip, anything he can turn into a story. The man's a scavenger.' She sniffed at the air. 'A pity he didn't take his stink with him.'

Smoke and whisky – the fumes had lingered. Throwing open the windows, Myrna said, 'Did you tell him about the German invitation?'

'No.'

'Thank God you had that much sense. Are you still going?'

'Yes. I'll make the arrangements tomorrow.'

'For both of us?'

'No.' He didn't look at her. 'I'm going alone.'

The observatory had provided a guide. She was tall, slim, golden hair neatly framing a rounded face. Her clothing was vaguely reminiscent of a military uniform with its stark white blouse, severely cut jacket of powder blue with the pleated skirt to match falling level with her knees. Black nylon covered her legs and shoes her narrow feet. Her perfume held the scent of spring. Hilda Brandt had been an unexpected bonus. Now she paused, pointing, dull shimmers reflected from her polished nails.

'There, Herr Professor. Accommodation for the staff. It is not always convenient, you understand, for us to travel into the village.'

And little room if they did. The observatory was tucked away in an isolated region and had almost doubled the natural local population. Spragg looked at it with envy – the place put Althene to shame. The buildings were bright and clean and warm, the equipment modern, the whole installation a tribute to Teutonic thoroughness.

'There is the spectroscopic laboratory,' continued his guide. 'And there the film processing laboratory and there the projection room. For plates from the Schmidt,' she explained. 'You have seen the Schmidt?'

'Not yet.'

'You will see it tomorrow. It is the largest in the world. Larger even than the one at Palomar which has a mirror of –'

'Please.' Spragg smiled to remove offence. 'I do know these things.'

'Of course, Herr Professor. You will forgive me?'

'Anything at any time, Fraulein. Is that the Solar complex?'

'Yes, there we study the sun. You wish to see it?'

'Tomorrow, perhaps. Now I feel a little tired. If I could go to my quarters?'

He had been given accommodation at the observatory and someone with unexpected consideration had provided a bottle of schnapps, which rested together with glasses on a small tray on the desk set against one wall. As Hilda left he stepped toward it, opened the bottle and helped himself to a stiff drink. He hadn't lied about his fatigue; it had been a long journey by plane and train and later by car,

Relaxing, he looked at his accommodation. It was equivalent to that provided by a first-class-hotel; a large room fitted with a wide, double bed, a desk, chairs, a television with radio fed from a master control beside the couch, a telephone fitted with a panel of buttons. A window gave a view of the valley and the road winding down towards the village. In the growing dusk the place held a strange air of unreality as if he looked at a scene from another dimension, another time and for a long moment he studied it, imagining Teutonic knights climbing up the slopes to attack the castle in which he stood.

Finishing the drink, he felt the warmth of the spirit ease the tension of his stomach. A bathroom was attached to the chamber and he moved towards it, adjusting the flow of water into the tub before stripping and plunging in, the bottle set within arm's reach. Lying back he half-closed his eyes and let his thoughts drift as the hot water caressed his body.

He thought of Hilda, her tall, lithe slimness …

'Mal!' The voice accompanying the knocking at the door of his quarters was vaguely familiar. 'Mal, are you asleep?'

He had been on the verge of it, dozing while his mind toyed with erotic fantasies. He rose from the water and, wrapped in a towel, opened the door.

'Carl!' He smiled with genuine pleasure. 'Man, this is a surprise.'

'A pleasant one, I hope!' Carl Waldemar, a few years younger, a lot fitter and better dressed, stepped into the room. His grip was firm as their hands met and he smelt of an expensive cologne. 'Alone?'

'Yes.'

'But your Frau – sorry, I should have remembered. A long time now. But you have no other? No friend?'

Spragg thought of Myrna. 'Yes, but I didn't bring her.'

'A wise man. Why carry – what is it you say?'

'Coals to Newcastle. Did you provide the bottle?'

'Could I do less? After your hospitality to me when I was in England? You remember that night in Carlisle? And the time when that little waitress wanted to learn German?' He laughed at the memory. 'Well, I taught her a few words at least.' He raised the glass Spragg had put into his hand. 'Prost!'

'Prost!'

'I carry an apology,' said Carl as he refilled the glasses. 'Ernst Kassel is absent and so is unable to welcome you. A last-minute arrangement, you understand.'

'Nothing important, I hope?' Kassel, the Director, had sent the invitation.

'Nein. No, not that. He had to go to Berlin. To confer with those from Potsdam and the Berlin-Babelsberg.' Carl lifted his glass. 'To old places and old friends!'

'Cheers!'

Spragg leaned back in his chair. It was good to have met Carl again after so long, good that the man should remember him and have made him feel welcome. He covered his glass as again Carl lifted the bottle.

'No more for me. Keep this up and I'll be as high as a kite. Carl – what's all this about?'

'Uh?'

'The invitation didn't go into detail. Kassel just asked me to come along for mutual discussions and general observations. I came because, to be frank, it suited me to get away for a few days. I guess you've read the papers?'

'Of course.'

'Then you know what kind of a fool they made of me. The press crucified me!'

'No, Mal, not quite that.' Carl was serious. 'But you are lucky, here in Germany our press has no restraints such as yours has. So we know how to evaluate what is said and printed. Forget it. I assure you it has no bearing on your reputation.'

'All right – then why am I here. And you? Aren't you with the Hamburg-Bergedorft Sterwarte?'

'For many years now, but there we have no Schmidt. I have been here for the past month.' Carl raised a hand as Spragg opened his mouth. 'No, my friend, no more questions. Work can wait until tomorrow. Tonight a party has been arranged in your honour. You are hungry, I hope?'

'I could eat,' admitted Spragg. 'But why the party? I'm not a celebrity.'

'No?' Carl shrugged. 'Others would not agree. After all you are the one who – how do you say it? Ah, yes, you are the one who put the cat among the pigeons. So get yourself ready, my friend. Hilda will call for you.'

She had changed and now wore a long dress of some shimmering dark material that accentuated the curve of her breasts and the swell of hips and thighs. Dark stones shone dully in the golden hair and thin-strapped sandals graced the delicate feet.

'Herr Professor? Are you ready?'

'A moment.' Spragg moved into the bathroom and dashed cold weather against his face, conscious of the need to appear calm and dignified. Conscious too of the effect the girl was having on him, one enhanced by his previous erotic imaginings. 'Where are we going? Thc canteen?'

'No, the village. A room has been hired in the Gasthaus. A car will take us.'

It waited outside, long and dark and gleaming, a fit conveyance for the girl who slipped into the rear compartment after she had made sure Spragg was settled. As the driver moved the vehicle down the road he could feel the pressure of her thigh against his own, smell the sweet odour of her perfume.

'You have worked here long, Fraulein?'

'A year. I like it very much, but I shall not be here for much longer. When married I shall move to America.'

'Is your fiancé in America now?'

'No, Belgrade. He is waiting for the appointment to be verified then I shall join him at the Kitt Peak National Observatory at Tucson, Arizona. You know it?'

'I know of it but I've never been there.'

'A pity. I have photographs, of course, but it is better to have an eye-witness account.' The pressure of her thigh increased as the car swung around a curve. 'Heinrich is certain that I will like it.'

Spragg stared at his reflection in the window. 'How much further have we to go?'

'Not long now, Herr Professor. See? There lies the village.'

It nestled in the heart of the valley, small houses dominated by the looming pine-covered hills. The car halted before a timbered house with a steeply pitched roof, the eaves ornamented with elaborate carvings in time-stained wood. Inside the party was being held in a back room.

Spragg found himself with a drink in his hand surrounded by strangers all of whom in deference to his ignorance, spoke English. Carl Waldemar attended to the introductions.

'Professor Malcolm Spragg. Mal, meet Doctor Elsa Braun.'

Spragg nodded, smiling at a short, plump, red-cheeked woman with sparse grey hair and a mouth that looked as if she had just tasted a lemon. At Carl's urging he turned to beam at a group of technicians and astronomers. At a buxom wench with dark eyes and hair to match – to be told she was the niece of the landlord on duty filling glasses. At a blonde who caught his arm.

'Tell me, Professor Spragg, have you had any experience with the latest model Cominetti computer? The Z5081?'

'No.' Spragg freed his arm and tasted his drink. It was aquavite and did things to his empty stomach.

'Which model do you use at Althene?' She pursed her lips as he told her. 'You find it satisfactory?'

'No, but it's all we have, Frau – ?'

'Frieda Osten. I know of your work, Professor, and you have my admiration. Such painstaking labour.'

He looked around the room, his eyes settling on Hilda where she stood talking to a tall man with a grizzled beard. He wore a gaudy sports jacket over a polo-necked sweater with flared slacks and elevated shoes and stood very close to the girl, one hand resting on her hip, a knee almost touching her own. Heinrich? No, it couldn't be, the man was in Belgrade. An old friend, perhaps, but if she allowed such familiarity he could have wasted an opportunity while in the car.

'Professor?'

'Sorry.' He returned his attention to the woman at his side. Against Hilda she wasn't much, her face betraying wear beneath the cosmetics but she was better than nothing. 'So you're a computer expert.'

'No, I am a mathematician. A computer is simply a tool. Of course we have technicians to keep them in repair and to programme them if necessary but I am not one of them.'

'I see.' Spragg sensed that he had offended her pride. 'I must apologise for my error.'

'No need for that, Professor Spragg. You were not to know. Of course you have given us all a lot of work.'

'I have? How?'

'Surely you must be –' She broke off as Carl came thrusting his way through the crowd towards them. 'I am sorry. It is my turn to apologise. It was agreed we should not talk shop. Instead we must do something else.'

'What?'

Carl answered for her, his voice rising, booming as he pushed a fresh drink into Spragg's hand. 'What else but to follow the most sensible advice ever given? To enjoy ourselves while we still have the chance. You remember that poem you quoted that night in Carlisle?'

And, suddenly, it was back; the warm comfort of the pub and the smiling face of the young girl standing beside him.

'Gather ye rosebuds while ye may,' said Spragg, remembering. 'For time is a-flying. And the rose which blooms here today tomorrow will be dying.' He lifted his glass and drank. 'I don't know if I got it right.'

'It doesn't matter. It's good enough reason to throw a party!' Carl lifted his own glass. 'A toast, my friends. Let us eat, drink and be merry, for tomorrow –'

'We die,' said Spragg. 'So what else is new?'

CHAPTER 6

Spragg lay moaning softly. He had died and gone to Hell and had there suffered the torments of the damned. In detailed procession had come all the wasted opportunities of his life, the errors, the embarrassments. The girls who had rejected him, each refusal a wound to his ego. The child he had insisted be aborted, losing his sole chance at parenthood. The jobs refused because of his dedication to the skies. His marriage. This present trip to Germany. The party.

Spragg moaned again, feeling daylight beat against the closed lids of his eyes. Drink, of course, the initial schnapps drunk before leaving, the aquavite, the wine, the whisky, the vodka, the toasts and laughter and cheering – and there had been a poisonous green substance called vergutz which evaporated on the lips and held the kick of a rocket-engine. Hilda had served it to him, smiling as he sipped, her eyes holding all the wanton promise of Lilith.

And Carl singing and shouting as the food had been served; sucking pig with all the trimmings and cakes and bread and succulent sausages. Later there had been a display by a local troupe of dancers and, later still, the girls had circulated, mellow and smiling and deft as they escaped from groping hands. Somehow, about then, he had put his arms around Hilda and made lying promises about using his influence to help her fiancé ... then there had been the touch of chill night air and ...

Spragg turned away from the window to face the other side of the bed. Cautiously he reached out, his hand touching the warm, rounded softness of naked flesh. Hilda?

It was possible and, lying in shadowed darkness, he felt a mounting excitement. They had been close. He had made her a promise and she had been grateful enough to come to bed with him

If so it had been a waste – he couldn't remember. Details were lost but, concentrating, he vaguely remembered another in the room, a time of staggering and almost falling, of hands tugging at his clothing and then darkness followed by warmth and softness as the bed had begun to spin and Hell had opened its jaws.

Another wasted opportunity but all was not yet lost. He turned towards her, then hesitated as he saw the blonde hair spread over the pillow. The blonde hair and the smiling face of Frieda Osten.

*

Breakfast was black coffee and rolls served with butter and a conserve. He ate well, noting that sex after a debauch could have a lot to commend it. That and the clear mountain air and the shower he had taken; ice-cold water that had stung like whips and cured if it didn't kill. Now, seated in the warm comfort of the canteen, Spragg sipped at his coffee.

It had been an interesting morning. He had expected to find Hilda and the shock had thrown him but, as if understanding, Frieda had repaired the damage and carried the affair to a mutually satisfying conclusion. And had then, with quiet competence, slipped from his room as he had used the shower. Would Hilda have done that? Would Myrna? Leaving without a word, with no opportunity given for recriminations or regrets. No demands made, no promises extracted.

It was a mistake for a man to yearn after a young girl, the more so if he was of advanced years. Aside from the boost to his ego resulting from the illusion of recaptured youth and the envy of his male friends, there was little he could gain but trouble. As Shaw had said, youth was wasted on the young.

Frieda hadn't been Hilda and that was the sum of it. Did it matter what bottle he drank from as long as there was something to drink?

But it wasn't the same and no amount of philosophical meandering could make it so. He had been a fool to have left Myrna behind. Reilly would be after her with his soft, Irish charm and even Hammond could be tempted. And even if she said nothing the fact would remain, the new relationship waiting to break out again in secret meetings and arranged coincidences until, again, he would know the pain of a collapsing world.

Irene – for God's sake why had she done it? Why had she betrayed him with that bastard Arkwright?

'Professor?

'What?' Spragg blinked, starting in his chair, aware that he must have sat, dozing as his mind had drifted in the past.

'You looked a little strained.' The man was one Spragg vaguely remembered as having seen at the party. 'The schnapps, ja?'

'I guess so. I'll just take a walk to clear my head.'

Outside the air was balmy, a faint breeze carrying the scent of the trees clothing the surrounding terrain. In the distance he spotted movement; a beast of some kind running and leaving a trail of nodding fronds. Birds rose above it, wheeling before again settling to rest. A quiet, calm and peaceful scene, idyllic in its pastoral charm. Spragg stood enjoying it for a few minutes then turned and headed down the path winding around the observatory.

It led to the garden, an area cleared and set with flowers and shrubs, benches set in alcoves and obsolete astronomical instruments decorating the lawns. He halted by a quadrant and then again at a marked dial set with astrological symbols. Kepler stared at him with blind, bronze eyes, the bust set on a plinth of lichened stone, and Copernicus and Tycho faced each other frozen in a mosaic of coloured chips set in an upright concrete slab. Turning from it he saw Hilda Brandt.

She stood at the far side of the garden, searching, smiling as she saw him.

'Good morning, Herr Professor!'

'Good morning, Fraulein Brandt. Did your friend enjoy the party?'

'Friend?'

'The man you were with at the party. Tall and with a beard.'

'That's Otto. Otto Papen.' She shrugged, dismissing him. 'An old friend, but I explained that to you last night. Don't you remember? When you said that you would help Heinrich to get the appointment.'

'Yes,' he lied. 'Yes, of course. I've a friend at Kitt Peak. He could even arrange to find a place for you.'

'That would be nice.' She handed Spragg a scrap of paper. 'Heinrich's address,' she explained. 'You will need it if you are to help. I have added his telephone number and other relevant information.'

'Thanks.' Spragg tucked the paper into a pocket. 'Hilda, will you –'

'Herr Professor?'

'Nothing.' Instinct warned him not to press his luck. To ask for a date now would be to smack too much of a demanded bribe. 'We can talk about it later.' He hurried on before she could ask questions. 'Now I'd like to see the Schmidt.'

It was housed in a dome that held the attributes of a cathedral and it was the ultimate of its kind. Basically it was just a mirror, a camera and a lens, but Spragg looked at it with the respect it deserved knowing the technology that had gone into it. Light entering the upper end of the telescope tube was refracted slightly by a correcting lens and was then reflected from a spherical mirror with a short focus. The camera, placed inside the telescope at the focus of the mirror, photographed large sections of the sky without distortion at the edges of the film. It was big, the correcting lens 54 inches in diameter, the mirror 80. Beating even the one at Palomar which was 48–72.

A magnificent tool but one that could already be obsolete. Advances in electronics had made image intensifiers a relatively cheap and superior alternative and, if McGregor's analogue system could be perfected, it would put even the giant to shame.

Spragg stepped back, looking at the telescope, the dome about. It was closed now but tonight it would open and the instrument aligned. The drive would hold it aimed at the selected portion of the sky while the exposed plate recorded the received images. Tiny dots and points that burned like beacons throughout the dark immensity of the universe. Millions of stars depicted as a scatter of dusty motes.

Work they had done at Althene but there he had been forced to work with primitive equipment.

'Impressive, isn't it? But a little frightening.'

Spragg turned to see Carl Waldemar standing close. 'Frightening?'

'To study the mystery of creation and to realise that you are, in a sense, peering into the face of God. That out there, so very far away from us, could be other intelligent creatures who could be looking towards us with instruments of their own. What else is space but a great darkness from which could come all kinds of terror?'

Spragg said, dryly, 'Do you really want me to answer that? I've had enough sensationalism to last me a lifetime.'

'Of course!' Carl quickly changed the subject. 'Did you enjoy the party? I must admit I didn't think you'd be up so early.'

'Why not?' Spragg met the other's bland stare. 'You know?'

'About Frieda? Yes, but you can rely on my discretion. I am pleased for you both. She is a very accomplished woman, no?' Waldemar smiled at Spragg's expression. 'She has her doctorate and an enviable reputation in her field. She mentioned it, perhaps?'

'Only that she was a mathematician.' Spragg frowned as he strove to remember. 'That was just before you came over to join us and made that stupid toast.'

'Not so stupid, my friend.' Carl was solemn.

'I wasn't invited here just to have fun, surely?'

'No, Mal, you weren't. But Otto can explain better than I can.'

'Otto Papen?'

'Yes, he's in charge of the plate processing and examining department. You know him?'

'No,' said Spragg dryly, 'but it seems we have a mutual interest.'

His office was in a corner of the big examination chamber; a large room fitted with wide desks, lights, scanning equipment, stools on which sat figures in deep concentration. He rose as they entered, extending his hand.

'Herr Professor! I am honoured!'

He was as Spragg remembered, dressed now in a shirt and pants of dark material, sombre colours, which would normally have been relieved by the light jacket and bright cravat now hanging on a peg behind the desk. His hair, like his beard, was grizzled and Spragg realised the man must be as old if not older than himself.

His grip was firm. As he released Spragg's hand he said, 'It is not often we have the chance to entertain a celebrity. You enjoyed the party?

'Yes, but I'd rather you didn't remind me of my recent exposure in the press.'

Papen shrugged. 'The penalty of fame, I suppose, and it has to be borne with patience.' He glanced at Waldemar then back at Spragg. 'You are curious as to the invitation, of course. Naturally it has to do with your discovery. You would, perhaps, like to study the evidence?'

'You've verified? When?'

'I think, Professor Spragg,' said Papen, 'that you had better study the plates.'

They were from the Schmidt, negatives as large as newspapers, the stars depicted as black motes on the transparent film. But, from most of them, positives had been made together with enlargements of selected areas – treatments which lost definition but which clarified and exaggerated certain images. Spragg riffled though them, noting dates and regions of the sky they covered,

Papen said, 'We were following a programme of study dealing with the spiral nebulae in order to run a comparison check on distribution and magnitude. Also, in that region, are several variables and binaries of major interest.'

'Yes,' said Spragg dryly. 'I know.'

'Of course, Professor. I mention it only to explain why little interest was taken at the time in what later became most obvious. If you will study the first plate?' He grunted as Spragg set it over the illuminated surface. 'Now here, you see?'

Spragg followed the tip of the pencil-eraser Papen used a pointer

'See what?'

'Use the magnifier. Are you familiar with the region?'

'Familiar, yes, but you have far higher detail than I normally work with.' Spragg frowned as he stared through the glass. No astronomer could possibly memorise all the millions of dots that the plate revealed. To compare them one with another taken at a later date would require long and painstaking effort. But surely there was something? 'A moment! You have an earlier plate?'

He found it, set it over the other, concentrated again as he studied the superimposed images with the glass, searching the indicated region Papen had indicated. Removing the added plate he stared again then finally leaned back in his chair,

Waldemar said, quietly, 'Well, Mal, did you see it?'

A black dot, which had appeared where no dot had been before. A tiny but unmistakable disc on the negative – a minute flare on the positive, which Papen fed into a projector. One that had blossomed and died – or had apparently died.

'We missed it,' said Waldemar. 'Or rather the staff here did – I was still at Hamburg. You noticed the date?'

Five months ago and Spragg remembered what Gulvain had written in his notes. A bright flare that he had spotted and which, to him, had meant more than it had to those in the observatory. But they were not to be blamed. Such a flare could be easily missed by those looking for other objects on the plate. As it had been missed. As the significance of the minute disc had escaped immediate attention.

'It had to be close,' said Spragg. 'A nova could have looked as large and a supernova larger but neither would have died so quickly. It did die?'

'Nothing could be seen on the next plate,' said Papen. 'It diminished the urgency but a watch was maintained and, later, something was discovered.'

'Thor? And you said nothing?'

'At the time we could not be certain. There were checks to be made, computations and observations, all the usual precautions against error. Before we could be sure you had made your announcement.'

Opening his mouth and making himself a fool who saw death and destruction coming from the sky and who had rushed to cash in on his find. That, at least, was how it must have looked to the public and his colleagues. Damn Eagan! And damn Hammond for his greed and impatience!

Spragg said, 'Why didn't you announce the verification?'

'We couldn't – there are other reasons.' Papen glanced at his watch. 'I have a telephone call to make. I will order some coffee to be brought here to you, Professor. Carl, I suggest we leave Herr Spragg to study the plates.'

A challenge, Spragg knew it as they left, and felt a wry amusement at how badly they had manipulated it. Carl, obviously was here to guide him the way they wanted him to go. It was no accident he had ended in this office – if he hadn't made the suggestion it would have been arranged in some other way. But why? What was so important about a scrap of planetary rubbish way out in space?

The flare, he thought. Why had it flared? If the planetoid had an amazing high albedo, if its surface was like that of a mirror then reflection could account for the sudden blaze of brilliance as a mirror flared when struck by a beam of sunlight. But space wasn't filled with either mirrors or directed beams of brilliance so the theory was untenable. What then? If light had been reflected at all it must have come from a nearby source and there was no sign of any other spread of brilliance on the negative. But if the planetoid had hit something?

Matter, hurtling through space on opposed paths, meeting in the void. Energy could not be lost, only transformed and the speeds that would have been diminished would have resulted in an eruption of light and heat as kinetic forces were released. If one of the pieces had been relatively small and if the velocities had been high then complete vaporisation of the smaller mass could have resulted. A cloud of incandescence blooming, expanding, cooling as it expanded to fade almost as quickly as it had been created. A theory only but it would do until a better one came along.

Spragg resumed his study of the plates, checking, scanning, fitting one over the other, frowning, finally stepping from the office to gesture to an assistant.

'Have you a blink comparator?'

'Ja, Herr Professor. It is old but –'

'Get it for me, please.'

The coffee arrived as it was being installed and Spragg sipped, not tasting, setting aside the cup and turning to the sheaf of positive prints as the technicians left. They were of equal size and scale so that the bright points exactly matched those on another print. Projecting a pair of them on a screen resulted in a perfectly matched picture. But if between taking one picture and another something had moved then, by rapid alternation of the projection, the object which had moved would seem to 'blink'.

An old piece of equipment as the assistant had said but with it, back in 1930, Clyde William Tombaugh had spotted the motion of Pluto, announcing the discovery a month later on March 13th.

Now Spragg tensed as he saw the tell-tale blink.

It was small but it was there and it could not have signalled the presence of a planet or any known asteroid. It was new and was what the Reverend Aird Gulvain must have seen before writing to Althene. A check of the dates confirmed the suspicion. But what had happened afterwards?

Long hours spent in a lonely vigil cooped up in his little observatory. Chilled, aching, numbed but determined. Using every scrap of his mathematical skill to predict where the object would be, finding it, predicting again and so plotting a course.

Spragg fed more prints into the comparator. The coffee grew cold and he neither saw nor heard the girl who came to remove the cup. All his attention was on the screen, the heap of positive prints, the projected images, which, unaccountably, remained steady.

Then he remembered the television interview when he had laboriously explained the impossibility of determining the speed or mass of an object seen head-on. But since then the Earth had moved on its journey around the sun and so away from the flight-path of the stranger. Later prints would show that movement and Spragg relaxed as the images blinked. The blink became more prominent as he fed in the last of the prints.

Again stepping outside the office he gestured to the assistant, speaking quickly before the other could voice the routine salutation. 'Have you the most recent plates taken of Thor?'

'I can get them, Herr Professor.'

'Please hurry.'

Back in the office Spragg checked dates and fitted the latest print available to the illuminated viewing surface. Thor, as he had known, was no longer a small disc but a thread of brightness. The camera had been held motionless relative to the stars during its long exposure but the planetoid had been moving and had left its trail on the emulsion.

Spragg measured it with a pair of dividers. He turned as the assistant arrived with the latest plate, took it, fitted it and found the trail he had expected, measuring that too. Collating the dates he found the exact times between exposures. From the relative appearance of Thor against the star field and knowing the base-line of Earth's movement he had data to find the planetoid's distance by triangulation. Knowing the distance he could determine the size from apparent diameter. The difference in trail-length coupled with known distance would yield the velocity. Those factors added to angular observation would give the course.

Taking a point of light and giving it a name and direction, mass and speed, fitting it into a complex pattern governed by immutable rules. He had done it before and would do it again.

Rising, he straightened his back then stepped towards the door of the office. The assistant, he noticed, still lurked outside, apparently engrossed in studying a list of some kind. He looked up as Spragg stepped towards him.

'Have you finished with the plates, Herr Professor? Can I return them to the files?'

'Yes, of course. Can you tell me where I can find the mathematical department?' He saw the other frown. 'Computers,' Spragg added then, remembering, 'Doctor Frieda Osten?'

'Ja, Herr Professor, I understand. Doctor Osten. I will guide you.'

She came to meet him as they entered her domain, a cool, rustling place in which machines whispered and displays blinked. In her white coat she looked like any of the other technicians working at their places but there was an assurance in her stride and the gesture as she put out her hand.

'Professor! It is good of you to have come. You are interested in what I do, yes?'

'Yes.' He touched her hand and found it cold and wondered at her calm. 'I need your help, Doctor. The use of a computer to be exact.'

'May I ask why?' She nodded as he told her. 'I understand. But, Professor, it is not necessary. All the work has been done. Did I not tell you that you have given us a lot to do?'

'Thor?'

'What else? Take a chair, Professor,' she waved towards a desk. 'I'll have the figures for you in a moment.'

They came neat and cold and utterly impersonal and even as he began to study them Spragg felt again the odd sensation he had known twice before. The feeling of utter and complete certainty that his hand was on the future. That, like some visionary of old, he knew just what was to be. The first time he had felt it had been just prior to discovering the asteroid which had built his reputation. The second was when he had felt the irresistible impulse to leave what he was doing and to get back home where he had found Irene with Arkwright. The first time had given him fame, the second had cost him a wife and a friend, and now?

The figures gave the answer and he had a vision of implacable forces moving towards each other. Of a planet orbiting its sun and of a wanderer from space rushing blindly to a destructive rendezvous. Thor had been well-named.

Spragg leaned back, closing his eyes, feeling the papers between his hands, the figures he would check and recheck again and again. The figures which, deep in his bones, he knew did not lie.

Carl had been wrong in his toast and knew it. Eat, drink and be merry, he'd said, for tomorrow we die. Not tomorrow. The Hammer of God would strike in exactly nine months and thirteen days.

CHAPTER 7

Beneath him Myrna struggled, fighting. 'For God's sake! What the hell are you doing? Mal! Mal!'

He rolled off and swung his legs over the edge of the bed and rose to pad on naked feet towards the curtained window. It was dawn and beyond the panes a new day was coming to life. In the trees birds made their raucous sounds and, from the motorway, came the muted thunder of traffic. In the village, the town, all over England, the young would be waking eager for the new day, the lovers would be lost in passionate embraces, the old lost in dreams of past achievements.

'Mal?' Sitting up in the bed, Myrna stared at him with a puzzled expression. 'Mal, are you all right?'

He said nothing, standing before the window, drawing the curtains with a sudden gesture so that the light illuminated his naked body. His hair, she noticed, seemed thinner than before and a little fuzz on his shoulders caught the light and accentuated their slope. His waist was hardly distinguishable from chest and hips. The bluish traces of mottled veins showed on the calves and back of his knees.

A man no longer young and yet with him she had found a comfort unknown with others.

He crossed the room and, catching sight of himself in a mirror, snatched up his dressing gown. Tying the cord, he went downstairs and into the living room heading towards the low table, the bottle it carried, the glasses. The first slug burned like fire. The second lit a beacon in the pit of his stomach. The third was halfway to his mouth when Myrna stepped into the room.

'For God's sake, Mal! You'll be stoned before breakfast.'

'Would it matter?'

'I thought you had to see Hammond. The drive's been repaired and he was talking about setting up a viewing schedule.'

'To hell with him!'

'You're crazy,' she said with cold detachment. 'Ever since you came back from Germany you've been acting strange. And what kept you there so long? Three weeks and you didn't write or phone once, you could have been dead for all I knew! Now put that glass down and come and talk to me while I make some coffee.'

As he ignored her and lifted the glass to his mouth she added, sharply, 'You can't hide in a bottle. Believe me, I know.'

'How?'

She stared at him, tempted to answer, seeing again her father as she had seen him just before he died, standing in the dawn light, swaying, vomit staining his shirt, a drink in his hand. A drunk who had thrown away the last vestige of his self respect.

Then, as she made no answer, Spragg said, lightly, 'Don't worry about me, darling. I'm just taking a drink to greet the dawn.'

'I don't want you to get drunk.'

'I won't.' Spragg looked at the glass and set it down beside the bottle. 'It's a habit, I guess. The Russians like to hit the vodka and –'

'The Russians?' Myrna frowned. 'I thought you went to Germany?'

'I did, and later to Potsdam, then on to Pulkova. They've some nice equipment at the Academy of Sciences.'

'Russia? You went to Russia? But why, Mal? Why?'

'To discuss the end of the world.'

He remembered the uniforms, the flat, Mongolian faces, the hard, suspicious eyes. The guns and the men the guards had protected, those with neatly trimmed beards, some young, others old, a few who had seen too much war, too much blood. And the conferences, the endless conferences when the figures had been checked and rechecked and questions had poured through the earphones in the calm and detached voices of the translators.

Ernst Kassel had arranged it even before he had invited Spragg to Germany and Carl Waldemar had steered him the way they wanted to go. To sit and talk and tell his story. To emphasise the reality of the coming doom.

They'd known, of course. All at the observatory had known, at least those connected with the Schmidt and the computers and the communications network. Carl and Frieda and Papen and most of the rest he'd met at the party. Perhaps even Hilda, though he doubted it, her concern with her future had been too genuine. And they had all seemed too calm.

How long had the bastards known?

She said, uncertainly, 'You're teasing me aren't you?'

'Yes. I'm getting my own back for this morning.'

'You startled me. I don't like waking up like that.'

'I'm sorry.' He added, lightly, 'Did you do anything interesting while I was away? See much of Reilly, for example?'

'Of course. We've been working. Hammond set us to work checking the lines of the solar spectrum. The spectroscope doesn't need long exposures so the faulty drive didn't matter that much.'

'But it's repaired now?'

'Yes, but he's still keeping us on the same programme. It's boring but has advantages. For one thing we can live normal hours. I've even been to Carlisle a few times.'

'With Reilly?'

'He drove me. We went to the cinema and had a few drinks after in a club he knows. One night we went to a disco. It was fun.'

She didn't, he noticed, ask if he objected but it would never occur to her that he might.

'I won't go with him now you're back,' she said. 'But I saw no point in sitting around twiddling my thumbs. Are you going to report to Hammond? He probably expected to see you on your return.'

'He probably did.' Spragg glanced towards the bottle, the empty glass. 'What about that coffee?'

She made it as always, water boiled, a spoonful of powder dumped into the cup, milk added. Instant coffee, which he had never learned to like, but they had no beans and even if they had she wouldn't have known what to do with them.

Sipping, he said, casually, 'I wasn't really joking, you know. It's really going to happen. The end of the world. And soon.'

'How soon?' She blinked when he told her. 'You're mad!'

'Why do you say that? You're an astronomer. You know how implacable mathematics are when applied to the movement of spatial bodies. Thor is moving towards us. It's going to hit us. It's as simple as that!'

'Simple?' She slammed down her cup. 'What you're saying is that even if I wanted to have a baby by you I couldn't do it. There wouldn't be time. Right?'

'Right.' He wondered why she had chosen that example. 'I'm not lying, Myrna. Why the hell should I lie?'

She rose with a flash of thighs. 'There's such a thing as human error. And I remember you on the TV a few weeks ago telling everyone that such a thing couldn't possibly happen. Am I to believe you then or now? When you decide, let me know.'

She left and he heard the scurry of her movements as she dressed, the rapid thud of booted heels as she came down the stairs, the slam of the door as she left the house.

Why had she mentioned a baby?

The coffee held a sour taint and he rose and crossed to the whisky and poured and lifted the glass, sipping as he looked through the window at the brightening day. Could Myrna be pregnant? Had her anger and disbelief stemmed from a natural fear for the unborn child?

The glass empty, he went upstairs and bathed and dressed then wandered restlessly about the house, conscious of old ghosts, old memories. Irene had chosen that picture and he had laughed when she had hammered her thumb while hanging it.

Ghosts and memories from which, suddenly, he had to escape.

The distance from his house to the observatory was short but Spragg took two hours to cover it, making a long, winding detour before heading towards the dome. It was, he noticed, open, the instrument within probably aimed at the sun, which shone bright and clear in an azure sky. Easy seeing; with such a target it was hard not to get good resolution and city haze, glow and reflections had no chance against the furnace-brightness. Even vibration became a minor hazard.

The door was ajar and Spragg pushed his way inside, blinking in the relative dimness. Beyond lay the dome itself with the interior now illuminated by the sun but here in this section of the building only reflected light served to dispel the gloom. Spragg paused as he reached the little room that served to hold clothing and supply modest comforts. It was empty. He lengthened his stride as he heard Reilly's voice.

'Careful on the setting, there! And watch your step! Watch it, I said! Damn it, now it has to be done over!'

A tone he wouldn't have used to Myrna and Spragg wasn't surprised to find her absent. Reilly, standing at the drive controls, turned as he approached.

'Mal! Good to see you! How was the trip?'

'Fine. What are you doing?'

'Setting this thing for corona-photograph. Fred's giving a hand.'

Fred, a youngster from the laboratory, smiled in awed humility at the noted astronomer. 'Good to have you back, sir.'

'We'll try it again, Fred.' Reilly, intent on the job at hand, wanted to waste no time in empty greetings.

Spragg watched as the telescope moved, halted, moved again. The usual eyepiece had been removed and an arrangement of lenses and mirrors caught the magnified image of the solar disc and sent it through filters to where a glass screen rested beside the lattice. Spragg blinked as it flared with sudden brilliance, retinal images dancing, turning away as Reilly made further adjustments.

'There! That should do it. Want to look, Mal?'

The brilliance was masked now by a circle of blackness, which, covering the exact orb of the sun, allowed the flaring corona to be seen in all its majestic splendour. Great tongues and gouts of flame reared like inverted waterfalls of incandescence, taking odd shapes and proportions, falling to rise against new and more entrancing configurations.

'You've got it, Sean. Hammond order this?'

'Who else?' Reilly's voice carried his disgust. 'Make work for idiots. Right, Fred, it's all yours. Get some good pictures and you may find yourself hanging in the Royal Academy.'

'Would they consider it to be art, sir?'

'These days you could piss on porridge and they'd call it art. But let's not get ambitious. Just take some decent snaps – we can always sell prints to the visitors.'

'Would I get a royalty, sir?'

'You'll get the door if I have any more of your lip!' Reilly turned to Spragg as the youngster set to work. 'I can't really blame him. Any fool would know he's doing work which is being done a dozen times better by others.'

'But it gives him experience.'

'True.' Reilly glanced at him then led the way from the dome. Outside, he leaned back against the wall, found and lit a cigarette. 'What's with Myrna? Sick?'

'In a way, yes.'

'I'm not surprised. She's been as tense as a spring these last few days. No trouble, I hope? No? Good.' Casually, he added, 'How was it in Germany? Make any friends at the observatory?'

'A few.' Spragg remembered the other had tried to get a job there and would have a particular interest. 'I met Carl Waldemar – I think he was before your time here. And Ernst Kassel.'

'The Director?'

'Yes.' Lying, Spragg added, 'I mentioned you and he seemed interested but said they had no vacancies. But you could stand a chance later. Next year, maybe.'

'Too long to wait.' Reilly studied the tip of his cigarette. 'I've irons in the fire in the States but thanks for trying anyway. Seen Hammond yet?'

'No.'

'When you do try and find out what's going on. First the trouble with the drive and now this solar crap – hell, what more can we discover about the sun with this junk equipment? Can't you get him to put us back on the Jovian Project?'

'What more could we discover if he did?'

'Maybe nothing but at least I'd feel like an astronomer again.' Reilly dropped the cigarette and trod on it. 'Well, I'd better see how our young friend is getting on. We can't have him wasting film.'

He went back into the building, an irritated man and, thought Spragg, one shrewd enough to know that he had been lying. Well, everyone lied for social convenience and there had been no point in telling him that he'd been too busy to push his case. As Reilly had said nothing about his jaunts with Myrna. As Hammond said nothing about his delay in reporting.

'Mal! It's good to see you!' Hammond smiled, his grip firm. A mask Spragg assessed at its true value. 'Drink?'

'Why not?' Spragg glanced around the office as the Director busied himself with a bottle and glasses. Fresh flowers stood in the bowl, the windows sparkled in the sun and the wood held the scent of newly applied wax. Someone had been busy. Dowton?

'He insisted,' said Hammond when Spragg asked. 'A dedicated man – there are so few of them now. He said he wanted to feel more a part of the observatory and volunteered to polish the wood. Not strictly his job, of course, but how could I refuse? Cheers!'

Spragg lifted his glass, sipped, lowered it half-empty. Hammond was cautious with his generosity. He was also curious.

'Not much,' said Spragg when the Director asked him what had happened during his trip. 'We talked and checked some plates and I gave a talk on rogue bodies in space with particular reference to those within the solar system. Not that we have many rogues, of course, everything follows an orbit of some kind but now and again we do get the odd mass which is new.'

'Like Thor?'

'Yes.' Spragg finished his drink and stood with the glass held suggestively in his hand. 'They'd spotted it before we did.'

'And didn't announce?'

'They wanted to be sure.'

'Which shows how important it is to get in first.' Hammond ignored the empty glass. 'If I followed your advice we'd have missed the boat. As it is you, and the observatory, have achieved a measure of fame.'

Notoriety that he could have done without. Spragg said, 'Why the new Solar programme?'

'We have a commission from the Admiralty for a complete check and correlation of all coronal and sunspot activity over a three-month period. It has something to do with weather prediction.'

'Three months? What about my own work?'

'Surely, Mal, such observations are your work. Primarily you are needed here to do what has to be done. You're thinking of your discovery, perhaps? Well, surely other observatories will be studying Thor. Of course, if you feel restricted –' Hammond broke off, smiling, but the message was plain. 'You understand the situation, I am sure.'

Play along or get out and he'd made it clear. Althene now had its reputation and wouldn't want for staff. His own position could be used as a bribe or as a reward to the son of a generous patron. In fact, now, he could even be an embarrassment to the observatory. No scientific institution could afford to be associated with an apparently irresponsible glory-hound.

Pressure which Spragg recognised and which he suddenly found hilarious.

'You find it funny?' Hammond frowned as Spragg straightened, gasping for breath, tears of mirth wetting his cheeks. 'What's the matter with you, man? Are you drunk or mad, or what?'

'No, I'm sane,' said Spragg, sobering. 'Saner than I've ever been in my life before and you know why? Because nothing matters now. Nothing at all. You, your job, the observatory, your stinking little affectations – God, what a creep you are! You really think I'm going to jump when you give the word? Dance to your tune? Not on your life. Stuff you, Hammond – and your job!'

He woke from a dream in which he was a bee crawling desperately across a flat surface, legs broken, wings torn, while from high above a clenched fist descended to squash out his life. The fist vanished, the table, the dragging legs and only the buzz remained; the thin, strident hum of the doorbell.

Spragg rolled, gasping, staring at the flickering dance of coloured shadows. He lay on the floor in a gloom broken only by the swathes of coloured light, which streamed from the silent television. An empty bottle rolled under his hand and he stared at it, remembering his farewell to the Director, the walk afterwards, the return to the empty house. He had turned on the TV, killing the sound because of its inane babble, sitting to watch the mouthing of po-faced pundits as he had sipped at twelve-year old Scotch. Now it was dark and the doorbell was a dragging irritation and he swore as, painfully, he climbed to his feet.

Eagan stood outside. 'You look like hell,' he said dryly.

'I was asleep.' Spragg wiped his mouth with the back of his hand. 'Come on in. Make some tea while I have a wash.'

Upstairs Spragg studied his face. His eyes were puffed and his cheeks looked bloated. The whisky must have hit him with sudden force, he guessed. He had sprawled from the couch to the floor where he had wakened. Hours ago now and he was sober again even if he did ache all over.

'Here.' Eagan had come upstairs and now handed him a steaming cup. 'And here.' He'd found a bottle of aspirins. 'Take four, drink the tea, have a wash and I'll fix you something downstairs. Need any help?'

'No. I can manage, but thanks.'

Alone, Spragg sipped the tea and dutifully swallowed the tablets. The aspirin would take care of the head as the tea would take care of the stomach. A shower and a change and he'd be almost as good as new.

Eagan grinned as Spragg finally joined him in the kitchen. He waved to a chair and held out a tumbler half-full of assorted ingredients.

'My version of a Bombay Oyster,' said Eagan cheerfully. 'You swallow it straight down.' He waited as Spragg obeyed. 'Better?'

'I will be … What are you doing here, anyway?'

'I dropped by to see how you were getting on. I'd hoped you'd get in touch with me when you got back from Germany to put me in the picture.' Eagan took out a cigarette and lit it. Through a haze of smoke he said, quietly, 'Why the binge, Mal? Had a row with your girl?'

'That's my business, not yours.' Spragg coughed. 'Do you have to smoke that rubbish in here?'

'Sorry.' Eagan stubbed out the cigarette. 'I bumped into Myrna in town earlier,' he said casually. 'She was going into the Church of the Holy Rosary to pray and light a candle. Didn't you know she was a Catholic?'

If she was Spragg hadn't guessed it. Not once while he'd been with her had she ever spoken of attending Mass or of believing in the tenets of any faith. The act had been a gesture, he decided. A return to childish conditioning or a form of coin-in-the-fountain insurance.

'Funny how some people do without religion all their lives,' mused Eagan. 'and then, when trouble hits, they turn to God. Others, of course, hit the bottle.'

'Like me? Damn it, Eagan, what the hell are you after?'

'Answers – the truth! Why, for example, is Althene suddenly interested in the sun? Why other private observatories are busy on government contracts? Why all the big installations haven't the time to answer a simple question. I think there's a big cover-up operation going on. Take Althene – why the contract? Why else but to keep the telescope away from Thor?' Eagan was shrewd and it wasn't difficult to figure out his source of information. Dowton, of course. Spragg remembered the polished office and guessed why the man had volunteered. Bribed by Eagan he'd wanted the opportunity to snoop and report what he'd found or heard. The thought of the janitor acting the spy made him smile.

Eagan scowled. 'You find that amusing?'

'It's ludicrous! You're looking for an answer you already have.'

'Thor,' Eagan mused. 'The hullabaloo. You going to Germany. The conference – yes, the press picked it up, but no statement was issued. Thor,' he repeated. 'Mal?'

'You broke the story, remember? The Hammer of God coming to crush us all. Vengeance from the skies. The doom from outer space. Well, it's all going to happen.'

'When?'

Eagan drew in his breath when Spragg told him.

'You're thinking there could be the possibility of error,' said Spragg. 'That's what they thought at the conference. They refused to believe what they were told despite the evidence and ordered a clamp down on the news while appropriate observatories made careful checks. But no matter how you add the figures the answer comes out the same.'

'Death,' said Eagan. 'The End. There's no hope?'

'None.' Spragg added, 'If you want a drink it's in the other room.'

He watched as the other poured himself five ounces of old Scotch, refusing a similar measure.

Eagan lifted the glass. 'To life! May it be short and merry!'

'You're like Myrna,' Spragg said. 'You don't really believe you're going to die.'

'Does anyone? Go out into the streets and tell anyone you meet they've only eight months to live and they'd laugh in your face. We can't face the prospect of extinction. That's why the whole damned world is insane. We know death will come, we watch it happen, we see it – but always it happens to someone else. So we all live our lives as if they will last forever.'

'We could tell them. You did it once.'

'To sell papers,' explained Eagan patiently. 'This is different. Can you guess what would happen if people really believed everything was coming to an end in a few months' time? Whenever there's a shortage of anything people go wild. They turn to animals and grab whatever's going – what the hell would they do for life itself?'

Spragg could guess. He crossed to face the window as Eagan poured himself another drink. Outside it was raining heavily, the panes running with a shimmering waterfall, wind gushing in the trees. It would be chill and wet and yet never again might he have the chance to walk in this exact combination of circumstances. Each day now was precious for none could ever be repeated.

Spragg tensed and turned as the phone rang. Quickly he crossed the room and snatched up the instrument. 'Myrna?'

The voice was a man's. Spragg heard him out then lowered the phone.

Eagan was curious 'Something wrong?'

'No, nothing wrong. I've just been invited to America.'

CHAPTER 8

The man was tall, slim, neatly dressed, his expression masking the fact he was performing a tiresome duty. He came forward as Spragg entered the VIP lounge, hand extended, teeth displayed in a smile.

'Professor Spragg? I'm from the Embassy, Rodger Harcourt-Smythe. Welcome to Washington. Have a good flight?'

'Fine.' It had been first class all the way. 'This is Miss Parkin, my confidential assistant. You'll take care of the bags?'

'Of course.' Harcourt-Smythe beamed at Myrna.

She deserved his attention. The jeans were gone as were the boots and uniform-style shirt, all replaced by neat shoes, sheer tights, a business-like skirt, blouse and jacket. Her perfume was one of the most expensive money could buy, her hair had been set by an expert, cosmetics accentuated her golden tan. Spragg had insisted and, to his surprise, she had not objected. She was now a picture of elegance, worthy of her new position.

She returned his smile. 'Have you been here long?'

'My second year with the Embassy but before that I was attached to the liaison department of the Ministry of Defence. Your first visit?'

'Yes.'

'You must permit me to show you around. There is so much to see and enjoy here in Washington.'

Spragg said, impatiently, 'Miss Parkin will be happy to take advantage of your offer should time permit. However we are not here on holiday. You are aware of the situation?'

'Of course, Professor. You are here at the request of the American Government to take part in the scientific exposition arranged to determine the distribution and origin of the asteroids with particular reference to the Apollo-objects.' He added, a little vaguely, 'Something to do with using them as sources of minerals, I understand.'

Myrna looked from him to Spragg. 'They want to mine the asteroids?'

'An extrapolation based on the present run-down of easily available minerals here on Earth,' explained Spragg. 'The asteroids could offer an alternative supply.'

The story offered a perfect cover for what he knew would form the core of the discussions. Any genuine leaks could be explained away under the guise of speculative interest. But the mere fact that such a story had been devised and the exposition arranged was clear proof the Americans were worried.

As were the British.

Leaning back in the car Spragg remembered the short, sharp hassle he'd had with the authorities. First to gain VIP treatment, then to insist that Myrna be allowed to accompany him, then to delay his leaving until it suited them both. Concessions grudgingly conceded.

'Mal!' Myrna stared eagerly through the windows at the slender shape of the Monument rising like an ancient obelisk on the horizon. 'Do we pass the White House?'

Rodger turned from where he sat beside the driver. 'No, but you'll see it later. The White House, the Senate Building, the Jefferson Memorial – Washington is full of things to see. A pity it isn't earlier – you've missed the celebrations, but autumn has its own charm.'

Maybe, but late summer had its own hell. Spragg dabbed at his face and neck, conscious of the humidity despite the air-conditioning built into the car. He hoped the hotel selected for them had better equipment.

Rodger blinked when he fired the question. 'Your hotel, Professor? It's the Clairmont. One of the best. We have rooms reserved for visiting dignitaries and I'm sure you'll find them comfortable.'

'Rooms? Why not a suite?'

'Impossible to arrange at such short notice, Professor. But of course your rooms are adjoining.'

'And we're going there now?'

'Not exactly. The Ambassador would like a few words with you first.'

Sir Edgar Waring was an older version of the attaché. He came forward to greet them as they entered his office, smiling, nodding dismissal at Harcourt-Smythe, turning to a table bearing glasses and a decanter as the young man discreetly vanished.

'Some sherry? Or perhaps you are already Americanised and would prefer something with ice?'

'Sherry will do nicely, thank you, Sir Edgar.' Spragg lifted his own glass towards Myrna before taking a delicate sip.

Sir Edgar decided on the direct approach. 'Were you briefed in London? I mean as to your duties here?'

'Duties?' Spragg raised his eyebrows. 'I am here at the invitation of the American Government.'

'Yes, of course. They seem to regard you as some kind of expert on the catastrophe that appears to threaten us and, naturally, we were more than pleased to aid them in obtaining your services. A mutual arrangement, I trust. As you must be aware Her Majesty's Government is deeply interested in any recommendations or decisions that may be clarified at the Exposition. Especially in items which may affect the National Interest.'

'Of course.'

'I knew you would understand. We all have to pull together in times like these, what? And there is so much you could do to guide things along the correct path – a word in the right ear, a suggestion, the use of your reputation to emphasise a point. Wars are not always won on the battlefield, eh?'

'War?' Myrna looked puzzled.

'A metaphor, my dear, don't let it worry your pretty little head.' He beamed at Myrna. 'I must say Spragg is a fortunate devil to have such a charming assistant. I'm sure you will enjoy your stay in Washington. Our hosts are always hospitable – especially to a young and lovely girl.'

After Rodger had finally dropped them at their hotel and they were alone in one of the adjoining rooms Myrna said, 'God, what a fool! No wonder we lost the Empire!'

'Don't underestimate him.' Spragg watched as she kicked off her shoes and removed her jacket, skirt and blouse. 'If he wasn't clever he wouldn't have the job he does.'

'Crap!' She turned to face him, her eyes furious, and Spragg remembered the rebellious nature of his own student days. 'He's where he is because he was born to the right family, went to the right school, married the right woman and didn't step on the wrong toes. What's so clever about that?'

'He's a success in his own world which is the only way he can really be judged. At least he's learned to survive.' Then, changing the subject, he asked, 'You know why he wanted to see us, of course?'

'Sure.' Myrna sat on the edge of the bed and took off her tights, making the awkward operation seem somehow graceful. 'He wants us to act the spy. The damned fool – any reporter could tell him as much as we could.'

'Wrong. He was talking about the things that never get reported – smoke-filled-room stuff when arrangements and deals are made. From that he can assess weakness and gain advantages.' Use betrayals and bribes to make friends and create enemies – the normal tools of diplomacy. 'And you got the hint he dropped at the end?

'That I should do the Mata Hari bit? What the hell does the old fool think I am?'

She stepped past him, vanishing into the bathroom, water gushing from the shower as he reached the door.

Sitting on the edge of the tub he said, 'So you don't want to cooperate? Not even for the good of the National Interest?' He grinned as she told him what to do with it. 'Did you notice how incurious he was? The world coming to an end and he didn't seem to care a damn.'

'His class,' she shouted. 'Stiff upper lip and all that jazz. Anyway, nothing ever happens to the Establishment. They've got it made.'

'Not this time.'

'I hope not.' The sound of water died and she stepped from the shower, her body dewed with pearls, the golden skin pimpled from the final, icy deluge. She said, 'He knew all about it before we got here. He must have received the checked verification of Thor's approach direct from the Royal Astronomer himself.'

'Maybe,' agreed Spragg, 'but the Americans must have had it before that. It took time to arrange this Exposition. They must have begun to set it up as soon as they'd heard from Germany. Or,' he mused, 'they could have had prior knowledge. God knows what they've got up in space but it's more than we know about. Or one of their spy-satellites could have been adapted in some way. And if they knew then the Russians knew also.'

'Which puts us right smack in the minor league.' Myrna looked over the edge of the fluffy towel covering her nudity. 'The last to be told – so much for past glories. Well, to hell with it. What's the programme for tonight?'

'We eat then go to bed.'

'So early?'

'You're forgetting the jet-lag. We're five hours ahead of local time. Anyway I want to bone up on my notes in case I'm called on to speak tomorrow. I'm the expert, remember?' He laughed at the thought of it. 'How the hell can anyone be an expert on the end of the world?'

'You discovered Thor.'

And was here on the strength of it. The wrong man – it should have been the Reverend Aird Gulvain. He, at least, would have had all the answers.

Thomas Clottery was convinced he had one. He stood on the podium, legs straddled, head thrust forward over his notes, his voice an irritating drone.

'... so it seems incontrovertible that most of the cratering of the Moon and Mars as well as those sites clearly delineated on Earth must have been caused by an intense bombardment of matter expelled from the area of space known as the asteroidal zone. This matter was probably produced by the break-up of the planet that held an orbit between Earth and Mars in eons past. The catastrophe that destroyed it can only be a matter of speculation and for our purposes, is immaterial. The facts, however, are plain. The Moon has something like 300,000 craters of a kilometre or more. Mars, larger and closer to the asteroidal zone, should have 25 times as many craters but, in fact, appears to have only four times as many. This discrepancy is more apparent than real when it is borne in mind that the planet would have had an atmosphere and water in past ages – a combination which, aided by winds, would have erased most large and all small craters. Earth, of course, is a larger target than the Moon with 14 times the cross-sectional area and 80 times the gravity attraction. Some of these impacts must have left marks, which still remain despite the action of the elements and many of these have been mapped as highly probable sites. I mention only the Aral Sea and the Great Barringer Meteor Crater near Winslow, Arizona …'

At his side Myrna whispered, 'Mal, how can a sea be a crater?'

'It filled with water after it had been made,' he whispered back. 'There are a lot of sites like that; any coast which looks as if it is the part of a circle or any lake which looks neatly round.'

'Like Hudson's Bay or the Gulf of Mexico?'

'Yes.'

Clottery was coming to the end. After painting the picture of a tremendous explosion in space which had shattered a planet to fragments and sent those fragments hurtling against the inner worlds he ended '… seems to be obvious that the object known as Thor must be a part of the original mass which managed to avoid being drawn into the gravity well of the sun and has been following a wide-flung orbit ever since the initial holocaust.'

'Thank you, Doctor Clottery,' said the president quickly. 'A most interesting dissertation. Has anyone any questions?'

They had but they were voiced over coffee and doughnuts during the morning break.

'The man's a fool!' A thin-faced, balding professor from California left no doubt as to his feelings. 'So we have one big bang which wrecks a planet. All right – did all the stuff hit Mars, Earth and the Moon? Venus too from what we've found lately. All of it? We've checked on what was left – and why was any left? Counted what we can find in the asteroidal zone and if the planet was about Earth size, eighty per cent of it is missing. Now spray that out in a widening sphere and how much would hit and how much would miss. Give me a while and I'll tell you if I can find my goddamned calculator.'

And:

'Blew up, he said, but what made it do that in the first place? Maybe something like Thor came along and did it. So we get a kind of chain-reaction – something breaks up the planet which blasts us with debris and forms the asteroidal zone and now another comes along to do the same thing to us – say, what's the time-element in all this? Maybe we can find a pattern.'

And, more to the point:

'Who gives a damn where the thing comes from? What the hell is it going to do to us?'

Donald Lauter discussed that after lunch. He was a tall, slim, hawk-faced man, neat in his uniform, the insignia of a colonel bright on his shoulders. A military scientist attached to NASA and engaged in the space programme. One whom, Spragg guessed, would have walked on the Moon if the money hadn't run out. He stood quietly on the podium, a long pointer in his hand, waiting until all had settled.

'Your attention, thank you. Slide on, please.'

The lights dimmed as the wall behind him flared to brilliance. A crater taken from one of the orbiting vessels scanning Earth's satellite. It looked dusty, frayed, as old as time.

Lauter said, 'Note the streaks which run like rays from the edges. This is unusual and not as yet fully explained but comparison tests on simulated materials reveal they must have been created by an intensely high velocity. Next!'

Another crater, wide, deep, monstrous, peaked in the centre, the rim-wall jagged as if gnawed by rodent teeth.

'Kepler. You will note there are no rays such as are visible in the Tycho areas. Next!'

More slides, all depicting craters, giant pits driven into the lunar surface as if some lunatic had been at work with a ball-hammer, striking at random, one crater overlapping another, some with central peaks, others without, all bearing the indefinable stamp of age.

'As I mentioned comparisons have been made with various materials in order to try and emulate the appearance of the Lunar craters,' said Lauter as the screen glowed white and featureless. 'We used a base of talc and dropped various materials on it from differing heights. The results were interesting.'

The white screen blurred, steadied to show what seemed to be more lunar craters then, as the illuminated area widened, the true scale became apparent. The craters were in a box a few feet on a side, the craters were miniatures created by artifice.

'Under high-velocity impact solid materials tend to act as if they are liquid. The action of the talc proved that and these following slides, taken as water was dropped into water, shows the formation of the crater-pattern.' A click and pictures shone on the screen in rapid succession; water, a drop falling, hitting, walls rising, an inner peak forming, the whole gently subsiding, time stretched by the magic of the camera. 'Now this is film taken to show the stress and yield patterns of various substances when affected by high-velocity impact. First a boulder of granite weighing some ten tons when hit by a cannon ball weighing two pounds and travelling at fifteen hundred feet a second.'

Colours writhed on the screen as special film traced the threads of stress from the point of impact, creating a mesh of conflicting forces and energies. More film, other substances, other forces, all spelling out a story of relative strengths and weaknesses.

'As you can see the critical point is relatively low in that an applied force of small capability can result in unexpected devastation especially when applied to non-homogenous materials.' He added, dryly, 'I have no need to remind you that our planet is far from homogenous. The edges of the tectonic plates alone present an inbuilt weakness as do all volcanic sites either active or quiescent. We are also extremely vulnerable in respect of the polar ice caps. Next!'

Earth shone on the screen. Not the planet as seen from space but a Mercator projection familiar to every schoolboy, inaccurate but useful and ideal for the colonel's purpose. The pointer in his hand tapped at various regions.

'From aerial surveys it is obvious that the Earth has been struck many times in the past by masses of considerable dimensions. These impacts have left recognisable configurations, which, together with geological examination, remove any doubt as to their extra-terrestrial origin. One of the most obvious is the Barringer Crater, which has earlier been mentioned. It is roughly circular with an average diameter of over 4,000 feet. It is 570 feet deep and the bottom is filled with rubble to a depth of about 600 feet. It is surrounded by a wall of between 130 to 160 feet higher than the outside plain. Its age, as far as can be assessed, is in the region of 50,000 years. This, of course, makes it comparatively recent but not as much as the fall in Siberia in 1908 which, together with the one in 1947, also in Siberia, fortunately missed inhabited areas. The point I am making, ladies and gentlemen, is that our planet is no stranger to bombardment from space and some of the missiles have been responsible for altering our terrain. Here, for example,' the pointer moved and steadied. 'The area known as the Michigan Basin. You will note the near circle formed by the Lakes Huron and Michigan, a circle, which, if completed, would result in a crater some 300 miles in diameter. And here,' the pointer halted on the Atlantic coast of the United States. 'Kelly Crater – the arc of a circle which would be more than 1200 miles in diameter. And here we have the significant curvature of the northern boundary of the Black Sea, Lake Victoria in Africa, the Gulf of Carpentaria in Northern Australia – possible impact sites are scattered over the entire globe.'

The butt of the pointer rapped on the floor and the projection changed, the same Mercator depiction of the planet but this time the areas mentioned together with a host more were delineated with scarlet circles. More rested on the oceans.

'Submarine trenches have been plotted which could be the remains of tremendous impacts in the distant past,' continued Lauter. 'Tidal flow and currents would have eroded the original craters but their residue remains. The effect of such an impact on the nearby shores can best be imagined by considering the known effects of the tsunami following an earthquake. A wall of water would sweep from the sea and destroy everything in its path for a distance of perhaps several hundred miles. There would also be steam from the superheated water and scalding rains – an added ingredient to the normal tsunami.' The pointer rose and tapped a point on the map. 'I mentioned the Barringer Crater in detail and for a reason. According to the revised estimates the mass that caused it must have been in the region of 70 to 100 feet in diameter. Large, but it would have lost mass through atmospheric burning and we can assume that the actual size of the mass on impact was about 50 feet in diameter. A ratio, you observe, of 1 to 8. However, in the Michigan Basin, the mass responsible has been estimated at being 30 miles in diameter, which makes the enhancing ratio 1 to 10. And here,' the pointer moved to Kelly Crater, 'the object must have been in the region of 100 miles in diameter which gives us a ratio of 1 to 12.'

A pause and then with an air of finality Donald Lauter said, 'The most recent estimate of the diameter of Thor, plus or minus 10 per cent, is 550 miles.'

The dining room of the Clairmont was discreet, the classical music from the five-piece combo muted so as not to interfere with conversation. Facing him, Myrna sat toying with a steak far too large and around him, smiling, talking, engaged in the communal eating, other couples occupied about half the tables. Later all would be full but now, so early in the evening, there was time for the neatly uniformed waitresses to relax.

Myrna said, abruptly, 'Mal, I wish I hadn't come to America,' She pushed aside her plate. 'I feel numb.'

'Ill?'

'Sick. That man in there – if he was trying to scare the hell out of me he did a good job.'

Her and the others in the auditorium. Spragg remembered the silence which had followed the bald announcement, lengthening while all had made their mental computations, then the sudden extinguishing of the lights and Lauter's absence when they had brightened again. Showmanship, of course, but performed with a calculated dexterity. The rattle of figures and then, like the blast of a gun, the final shock.

Spragg said, 'You knew, Myrna. I told you.'

'You told me,' she admitted. 'But I guess I didn't want to believe you. Christ, Mal, how can you be so calm?'

Hysteria tinged her voice as she almost shouted the question and an attentive waitress took a step towards them halting to retreat as Spragg shook his head.

She took a sip of water, regaining her composure. 'Sorry.'

'No need to apologise.' Spragg recalled his own experience. First the numbness, the sick horror, the frantic rejection and then, the intellect rising above the primitive emotive need to survive, the acceptance. Or perhaps it wasn't an intellectual acceptance but a passive resignation. Death was coming, a little earlier than anticipated, but that was all. And, as a bonus, it brought freedom.

'Mal?'

'I was thinking,' he said. 'Remembering Hammond's face when I told him what he could do with his job.' He added, casually, 'That was the day Sam Eagan saw you going into church.'

'The day you told me about Thor. I didn't want to believe you. I thought you were being cruel for some reason. I – found help.' She looked at the glass of water in her hands. 'Obviously it didn't last.'

The music died, resumed after a moment, a new arrangement that tweaked at his memory. When had he heard it before? In Carlisle when he and Irene had gone on one of their little excursions? Damn it, why did he have to think of Irene?

The waitress came forward at his signal and took his order for Scotch on the rocks, glancing at Myrna who shook her head. She shook it again as he downed half the drink at a swallow.

'Trying to drown memories?'

She was too damned shrewd at times and Spragg felt the heat of a violent resentment. What he did was his business, not hers; she was the girl he slept with not the woman who shared his life. But he had no woman to share his life, not now and maybe not ever. He had only thought he had.

'Sir!' The waitress was at his side again, and this time a familiar figure stood behind her, one who stepped forward, smiling.

'Glad to have found you, Professor. Miss Parkin.' Rodger Harcourt-Smythe nodded in her direction. To Spragg he said, 'We're having a sort of function at the Embassy and Sir Edgar hopes you'll both be able to drop in. Cocktails at eight-thirty. I'll send a car.'

Spragg said, coldly, 'What if we don't choose to come?'

'Sir Edgar would be most upset.' The blue eyes were suddenly hard. 'He's the Ambassador, you know. It's almost a royal summons, what? Wouldn't do to let the side down now, would it?'

A means of making contact, nationals invited to their Embassy for drinks and snacks, time found for him to make his report. Spragg met Myrna's eyes and knew that, like himself, she was fighting the desire to laugh.

'We'll be there,' she said. 'Formal dress?'

'Just something dark, Professor and for you, my dear, something long and not too revealing.' Rodger's smile was brittle. 'No need to make all the old biddies envious, what?'

Later when they were changing and he caught sight of her tall, slender silhouette against the pale oblong of the curtained window, Spragg blurted without conscious intention, 'God, Myrna, how I love you!'

She made no reply and he wondered if she thought him a fool.

CHAPTER 9

The car was the same that had carried them from the airport and it glided through the streets of Washington, still bright but with the hint of coming dusk, the later darkness in which muggers and rapists and murderers would do their work. The secret, hidden life of the city which made a mockery of the neo-Grecian buildings, the white pillars and domes and carefully tended sward. The fester that lurked at the heart of every city, and, one day, would explode in a savage and bloody frenzy.

Myrna turned towards him, her eyes still bearing a haunted expression,

'I was thinking,' she said. 'You know a few hundred years ago all this was nothing but wilderness. Animals and a few natives living quietly in their own way. And then the Europeans came – and that particular paradise came to an end.'

'But was it ever a paradise in the first place? Those natives suffered death and disease and ignorance and the vagaries of climate. They had all the tribulations we have and many we've forgotten.'

'They were ignorant,' she admitted. 'But isn't ignorance sometimes a blessing?'

'You're thinking about Thor.'

'How can I forget it? We can't make it go away by ignoring it. That tree, that building, this car, this city even – in a few months it will all be gone.'

'A few months or a few years, what does it matter?' He strove to give her his own, detached viewpoint, the one he had had time to gain. 'When we die a universe dies with us – our own. And we all know we're going to die. The only difference is we now know just when it will happen so we have the chance to do all the things we meant to do but kept putting off to a later occasion.'

Sir Edgar greeted them as they were announced, very stiff and correct in his evening dress, medals gracing the sombre fabric with miniature touches of colour. His smile was automatic as was the touch of his hand, a dismissal and they passed on, Spragg lifting drinks from a tray carried by a waiter, passing one to Myrna, sipping at his own.

He stood with it in his hand as he surveyed the assembly. They were as he'd expected; notables, wives of influential merchants, politicians, members of other embassies, a scatter of nationals from the United Nations – the usual crowd. Rodger, beaming, pushed his way to where Myrna stood regal in a long gown of shimmering black touched with silver. More silver shone in the aureole of her hair. Both gown and jewellery had been a last-minute purchase from a shop in the Clairmont and, thought Spragg looking at her, it had been money well-spent.

'Miss Parkin! You look positively enchanting. Come and meet the Spanish Minister of War. Juan Hose Rodgego Nova De Gaia – a bit of a mouthful but he's quite nice and has an aide who acts almost human aside from his love of bullfighting. You like to watch the bulls, Miss Parkin? Or may I call you Myrna? Professor?'

'Go ahead.' Spragg waved with his empty hand. 'She's on her own time.'

And the attention and flattery and party-atmosphere would serve to banish the ghosts from her mind and enable her to laugh and enjoy her youth and beauty. As for himself there was always the anodyne of drink and he drained his glass and replenished it with another, wondering why it should taste like water and be having almost the same effect.

'Professor Malcolm Spragg! Well, I never! After all this time!'

She was short, broad, with a face lined and flaked with cosmetics, extra chins lying in steps to her jewelled throat. Her dress was too young and too tight.

'Don't you recognise me? Shelia Vaslow. We met years ago at a conference held in Paris. You read a paper on the asteroids. Afterwards we were introduced and we had some drinks and – surely you must remember!'

He said, 'Shelia! Of course! I just hadn't expected meeting you. And you've changed.' The curves now sagging mounds of ungovernable fat, things he knew better than to mention, saying instead, 'I guess we've both changed. It was a long time ago and I used to have a waist then.' He patted his paunch. 'Who would want me now?'

'Your assistant, perhaps?' Her eyes were sharp. 'She's a beautiful girl.'

'Yes, I suppose she is. Rodger seems to think so.'

'And so does every man in the room.' She sighed with envy. 'Well, Mal, have you come for the Exposition? It's in your field but do you honestly think we'll ever be able to mine the asteroids successfully? The prohibitive cost, the weight-fuel ratio, and that isn't taking into account crew problems and the need to refine in vacuo not to mention the danger of solar flares and other radiation hazards unavoidable unless extra-heavy shielding is used which again adds a greater burden on …'

Spragg smiled as her voice droned on, nodding, but not really listening.

As she paused he said, 'You've obviously given the matter a lot of thought, Shelia. Are you also attending the Exposition?'

'No. I'm working for the Air and Space museum, next to the old Smithsonian.

You must know it. They've got me creating panoramas depicting alien-world conditions.' She added. 'I had to do something after Harry died.'

'Harry?'

'My husband. You wouldn't know him. We met five years ago and he died last year. A coronary. He was attached to the museum and they offered me a job. Before that I was with the UN but Harry made me quit. He hoped for children. I guess we both did.'

A year, he thought. A year of compulsive eating to ease the hurt of her loss. Of working too hard to fill the waking hours. Did she lie awake at night wondering where she had gone wrong? Brooding over what she would do had she the chance to live her life over again?

'Shelia! I'm sorry!'

If she guessed his expression of sympathy was for more than her bereavement she gave no sign. Instead she said, unintentionally cruel, 'And you, Mal? Are you married?'

'Divorced. It didn't work out. But I'm over it.'

'That's a relief, anyway. Sometimes I think divorce is worse than death if you're in love with the one that's gone …' She shook her head then said, hopefully, 'Maybe we could get together soon. Talk over the old times and have a few drinks. Old friends shouldn't grow into strangers.'

But they already had and he was grateful to the waiter who came to discreetly pluck at his sleeve and to whisper that Sir Edgar would appreciate his company in the study.

It was a snug room lined with old books, the heavy desk an antiquarian's delight with its elaborate carving and the silver accessories that caught and reflected the light.

'You like it?' Sir Edgar had noticed his interest. 'I collect such things. I hope to recreate an office such as would have been used by my predecessor almost two hundred years ago.'

Spragg crossed the room to finger the frame of a sombre painting, to touch a brass set of scales, to move onto where a globe of the world stood on a stand at the side of the window. Idly he spun it.

'A nice collection, Sir Edgar.'

'Are you interested in old things? If so I've some maps from the sixteenth century, which might interest you and a set of duelling pistols from the seventeenth … But I forget myself. Professor Spragg, meet Charles Pyne.'

The man sitting in the deep chair nursing a glass of sherry, though in civilian dress, had the unmistakable stamp of the services. The Navy, Spragg guessed, looking at the grey eyes deep-set beneath bushy brows, the thin, no-nonsense mouth. A man who carried all the outward attributes of someone accustomed to being obeyed.

'Spragg.' He nodded, waving his free hand. 'What's it like out there?'

'Noisy.'

'Better off in here then. A busy day, I understand.'

'Sherry?' Sir Edgar lifted the decanter. He poured at Spragg's nod and handed over the delicate glass. 'I'm glad you managed to drop in, Professor. I didn't expect us to meet again so soon, but trust the Americans not to waste time.' He paused, sipping at his own sherry. 'Anything to tell me?'

'Nothing you don't already know, Sir Edgar.'

From the chair Pyne made a snorting sound then rose to pace the floor, head stooped, hands clasped behind his back. Small steps, Spragg noticed, the turns sharp, A trait learned in the confined quarters of a submarine. Halting, he snapped, 'We're not here to play games, Spragg!'

Spragg's glass rang a little as he set it down on the desk. Flatly he said, 'I'm not one of your uniformed puppets to jump when you snap your fingers, Commander. Or should it be Admiral?'

'You are impertinent, sir!'

'I don't think so. I am simply independent.' Spragg glanced at the Ambassador. 'And now, Sir Edgar, if you will excuse me?'

'Please!' Sir Edgar held his arm. 'Charles, I think you owe the Professor an apology. Professor, the Admiral – yes, Charles is an Admiral – is both tired and worried. Now pick up your drink like a good fellow.'

Gruffly Pyne said, 'I've got reason to be irritable. Still, no need to act the boor, though.'

'Professor?'

'All right, let's forget it. But what can I tell you that your other informants haven't' He added, dryly, 'I assure you there were no secret discussions or resolutions or anything affecting the National Interest. Aside, of course, from what we already know.'

'And that is?' Pyne prompted. 'You're a scientist and could be taking things which are obvious to you as being obvious to everyone. We haven't your specialised knowledge. Sir Edgar is a diplomat. He relies on advisors. Well – be one.'

Spragg said, impatiently, 'All astronomers agree Thor will hit the Earth in 226 days. The Exposition, so far, has merely verified what we already know. As far as –' He broke off as he looked at the two men's faces, their eyes.

He remembered Eagan and what he'd said. 'Tell a man he's going to die and he won't believe you'.

Pyne said, slowly, 'We get hit all the time. Dust particles, meteors – isn't there a big shower due soon?'

'The Leonids in October,' agreed Spragg. 'But we aren't talking about the same thing. Thor is 550 miles in diameter. It is heading towards us at a velocity of 5 miles a second – 18,000 miles an hour. Can't either of you imagine what will happen when it hits? Admiral, you've used guns. A .45 bullet weighs an ounce but when fired it hits with the impact of a ton. That's because of kinetic energy created and stored by motion. The faster a thing is moving the harder it is to stop and Thor is moving damned fast.'

Sir Edgar said, 'But won't the atmosphere protect us?'

'As it does against the meteoroids? No. The trails you see in the sky, the "shooting stars" are caused by tiny scraps of interstellar debris. Dust. They hit and are heated by atmospheric friction, burning as they fall and, burning, are destroyed while still in the air. A few are sometimes large enough to reach the surface and you can see many of them in museums. The largest weighs only a few tons. But this time the atmosphere is going to work against us.'

'How?'

'It's a gas and therefore it can be compressed. When Thor hits that's just what it will do. And when it does …'

The tremendous mass of the striking planetoid plunging down, the air unable to escape from beneath it because of the speed of its descent, that same air heated by compression spreading to either side below so as to form a near-solid ram, carrying the shock-wave of initial impact to flatten all beneath. A ghastly harbinger of what was to come – the colossal bulk of Thor itself slamming into the surface, turning liquid into steam, rock into liquid, splitting the crust and releasing the inner magma – killing, burning, destroying until nothing was left but the shattered debris of a broken world.

Standing at the open window of his room in the Washington hotel, Spragg looked at the massed buildings lying sweltering beneath the blanket of late-summer heat. Coloured lights glowed like land-locked stars, winking, blinking, gaudy invitations to sophisticated delights mixed with advertisements of various poisons, traffic signals, the illuminated oblongs of windows; the beacons of the sleepless, the lonely, the bored. Like mournful ghosts the wail of police sirens cut the air either to warn the criminals or to assure their victims help was on the way. From the airport, a coruscation of lights painted the clouds a dusty orange.

A man alone standing at a window watching the teeming activity of which he was not a part – an ant barely aware of the forces that affected his world. And yet, now, he sensed the interplay of powerful interests, the influences always present but rarely displayed.

Behind him he heard the opening of the connecting door, the rustle of clothing, the soft tread of feet on the thick carpet. The scent of perfume became strong in his nostrils.

Without turning he said, 'Not tired?'

Myrna halted beside him. 'No more than you are, Mal.'

He doubted it; his body was tired if his mind was not. It was three in the morning and he had drunk and talked and danced a little and smiled even as he fought the screaming desire to run and hide and pray to something larger than himself for ease and comfort. The anodyne of religion, which he had never known.

'Enjoy yourself?'

'Mostly I was bored. That damned Spaniard! The only way I could get rid of him was to tell him that I considered that anyone who enjoys the spectacle of an animal being tortured had to be mentally and morally sick. He didn't like me saying that.'

'He has his pride.'

'And regards all women as creatures created by God for the personal comfort of males. If ever there was a chauvinistic pig it's that Spaniard!'

She took a step forward and breathed deeply of the sultry air. 'Who was that woman you were talking to? The fat cow who grabbed hold of you when we parted.'

'Shelia Vaslow? We knew each other years ago. Before I was married. She never met Irene.' He added, in defence, 'She's altered a lot since then. Put on a lot of weight and I think she must have a diabetic condition.' From defence he moved to the attack. 'You seemed to be pretty engrossed with that Brazilian.'

'You noticed?' She smiled like a contented child. 'Santos is nice. He invited me to spend a week – or longer – at his home, Should I accept?'

She was playing with him, he thought, a game in which he had no interest. An aging jealous man was pathetic. He remembered her recent escort, tall, young, vital, a thick mass of dark hair and flashing teeth. To him she would be merely another conquest. But did it matter? Had it ever mattered?

She said, as if guessing his thoughts, 'Don't worry, Mal, I'm not going to become a part of his collection. That kind of man nauseates me. But I do have an invitation to visit New York. Madam Kuluva has asked me to be her guest for a few days. She is attached to the United Nations. It could be interesting.' She added, casually, 'We leave tomorrow, that is today, at noon.'

She offered no apology at not having consulted him. 'I want to see the place and I guess you'll be busy.'

'Not today. Nor tomorrow.'

'You can't be sure of that. Sir Edgar might send for you again. What happened, anyway?'

'We talked about Thor. Admiral Charles Pyne was with him.'

'A Sea Lord,' she said. 'Chief of Naval Intelligence and the man who will fire the atomic missiles if ever they have to be fired.' Seeing his expression she explained, 'I was interested in such things at University. I joined a group that wanted to stage a series of anti-nuclear demonstrations and I was involved for a while. My job was research – it's surprising what you can find out by studying the official listings. What did he want?'

'I'm not sure. My guess is that he is to report back to London on the seriousness of the situation.' Spragg looked at the city and saw the pale gleam of the dome of the Senate building in the distance. Understanding came like a kick in the groin. 'The cunning bastards!'

'Mal?'

'The Yanks! The Exposition! The whole damned thing was staged!' He felt his initial anger transform to a grudging admiration. 'I'd just thought they had arranged the Exposition to make sure we astronomers realised the true nature of the threat and could relay that information back to those in authority. It didn't occur to me to wonder why. Now I'm beginning to understand.'

She said, 'I wish I could, damn you. Mal, tell me!'

'The world's going to end,' he said. 'You know it and I know it and now every damned government must know it. Know it beyond any question of doubt. That's what the Exposition was for.' He fell silent, thinking, remembering the rows of attentive figures, the translating machines, the scheduled repetitions. A programme designed to ensure that none attending would be left in any doubt as to the true extent of the coming catastrophe. 'But why?' He demanded. 'What do the Americans hope to get out of it?'

The question every government would be asking. Myrna had another.

'How do they hope to keep the news from the public?'

'Old news is dead news,' said Spragg. 'The story will be buried or laughed off by the media or it won't be allowed to appear at all.'

'Censorship?' Myrna looked doubtful. 'Back home, yes, and in most European countries, but here in the States? You think it possible?'

'One way or another, certainly. Read the papers during the next few days and you'll see how it can be done.' He added, quietly, 'Do you really want to go to New York? I'll miss you.'

'And I'll miss you.' Her hand found his own and pressed with warm intimacy. 'But I'd like to see it, Mal. The buildings, the streets, everything.'

And it would be selfish and wrong for him to try and dissuade her. Life consisted of the sum total of experience and for him to deny her novelty would be to limit her existence.

'You go,' he said. 'Say hello to Central Park for me and don't forget to visit Staten Island. Go and enjoy yourself, Myrna – enjoy yourself!'

As the whole world should now be enjoying itself with all thoughts of future needs put aside, all doubts, all cares and worries, all rigid disciplines. Looking down at the city Myrna thought of what could be done.

'The government could open the warehouses,' she murmured. 'Free food, power, gas, liquor, transportation. Free housing. Free clothing. Freedom to do and say what anyone damn well pleased. Why not? They've paid for it. Taxed and milked and robbed and exploited all along the line. Food destroyed so as to keep up the price when the public have paid for it in the first place.

An army of bureaucrats riding like lice on the back of the populace. Politicians, civil servants, aristocrats, petty dictators – the whole stinking mess. Now, for God's sake, everyone could have a holiday. For Christ's sake, why not?'

A question he couldn't answer then or later when, after a blindly passionate coupling, she had retired to her own room to leave him lying, drained, tired and aching, to stare at the window until it began to pale with the coming of a new dawn.

CHAPTER 10

It was late when he woke. Myrna had left and Spragg ate a lonely brunch in the near-deserted dining room of the hotel. He'd bought a newspaper and read it over his coffee, amused to find screaming headlines announcing the discovery of a ring which supplied complaisant partners of either sex to Senators, Judges and visiting dignitaries. The opening shots of the smoke-screen he'd anticipated. Presented with such juicy items of tantalising filth what editor would be interested in the reports of a dry-as-dust astronomical Exposition?

Spragg left the newspaper beside his empty cup and left the dining room. He was already missing Myrna, wondering if she had left Madam Kuluva's address so he could follow her. She hadn't and he was saved from the temptation of making a nuisance of himself.

The girl at the desk said, 'If you're alone, sir, and wondering what to do then why not see the sights? We have a guided tour leaving in thirty minutes. Shall I book you a place?'

'No thank you. But you can give me a map and call a cab to drop me at the Lincoln Memorial.'

He had seen it before but it was as good a place as any to start and, after looking at the solemn, brooding figure, Spragg hesitated between visiting Arlington Cemetery or walking over the carefully tended sward towards the Washington Monument and the buildings flanking the Mall. He decided he was in no mood for the company of the dead so turned to face the soaring dome of the Capitol beyond the slender obelisk.

At length he entered the natural history museum. Spragg liked museums. Here was displayed the endless panorama of life in all its ramifications and adaptations, its blind-alleys and triumphant progression. He wandered the galleries looking at fossils, skeletons, reconstructions of plants and creatures long dead and vanished from the face of the planet. An ape-man glowered at him, a stone gripped in one hairy paw. A weapon that had been unable to save him and his kind from extinction. Another peered from beneath jutting brows but Neanderthal Man had also been unable to survive. That had been left to Homo Sapiens who stood in a simulated group, startling in his modernity.

Homo Sap – doomed to join the other relics of the past. Just another life form destined to become extinct. He, his wife, his children, everything he had known and all he had built soon to be less than dust.

'Mister?' A woman looked at Spragg as he turned, sweating. 'Is anything wrong?'

'No.' He forced a smile. 'Just a touch of vertigo, I guess. I must have overdone things a little.'

'There's a cafeteria in the building. You could get some coffee and rest up for a while.'

'Thank you – I'll do that.'

He needed something stronger than coffee. Outside the afternoon sun held all the smouldering fury of a banked furnace and he paused, squinting, staring at the buildings almost facing him across the broad, green expanse of the Mall. The Air and Space museum and he remembered that Shelia Vaslow worked there. She could have a bottle or be able to guide him to a bar. In any case she would be company of a sort.

The cathedral-like interior was refreshingly cool, galleries running around an open area in which reared the slender shapes of early rockets. Spragg passed them, riding an elevator to the upper floors, searching for someone who could guide him to the department he wanted. A guard looked blank when he asked but sent him down a passage. Another was more helpful. A woman, her face daubed with paint, her smock covered with a smeared rainbow, grinned as she invited him into her domain.

'Shelia didn't make it in today. She called up with a sick headache. I guess that reception she went to was more than she could handle. Known her long?'

'Years, but we haven't seen each other for a long time. She told me what she did here. Alien –' He frowned.

'Depictions of alien worlds. Panoramas, really, backdrops with way-out vegetation and creatures and skies.' She waved to where sheets of thin board stood against the walls, the mounds of foam, coiled plastic of various sizes, sheets and balls and oddly convoluted fragments. 'We take a load of junk, some paint, a wad of imagination and the best extrapolations we can get. That's what Shelia does – extrapolate.'

'Design?'

'In a way. You know the kind of thing – what would life be like on a planet with a white dwarf for a sun and a methane atmosphere? No one knows, really, but we try to keep things as scientifically accurate as we can. What's your line?' She nodded as he told her then said, dryly, 'I guess you don't think much of what we do here?'

'Then you guess wrong. Space needs to be understood and young minds need to be stimulated to the possibility of a broader scheme of existence. Get a kid interested and he'll want to learn more.' Spragg remembered his own early days, the brightly coloured comics, the stories, the magazines – all triggers which had fired his imagination. 'The young need something to reach out for and what better than new worlds?'

'Sure, and when they grow up they'll want to back the space programme,' she said. 'That's what this is all about really. NASA is building a lobby, which will have real muscle in a few years' time. Every kid we can hook now will be willing for us to spend his dollars when he's old enough to vote.'

'You're a cynic.'

'I'm a realist,' she corrected. 'We could have had an observatory on the Moon by now, and even a colony orbiting the Earth. We've the technical knowledge – all we need is the money. And once we get some real clout the politicians won't be able to dump us down the tubes as they did before.'

Spragg said, 'I'm sorry Shelia isn't here. Maybe I'll drop in again before I leave.'

'You want her number?' The woman scribbled on a scrap of paper. 'Here. If you can give her a boost I'd be grateful. Sometimes she gets awful low.'

She and all of us, thought Spragg as he left. The paper he slipped into a pocket, unread, forgotten as soon as his fingers had driven it from sight. Already he felt light relief that Shelia had been absent; had she been at work he would have been lumbered with her for the evening and probably longer.

He followed the signs that led him to the cafeteria. Food and drink was dispensed from a rotation carousel and he selected iced tea and a hot dog together with mustard. The food was bland, but the other visitors busy taking nourishment provided an amusing diversion. Spragg listened to a babble of French, German, some Hebrew and what he guessed to be Swedish. A party of youngsters from the south shrilled like birds and a matron, her round black face dewed with perspiration, eased her shoes off aching feet.

Leaving the cafeteria Spragg wandered the galleries looking at ancient aircraft, modern rockets, Apollo nosecones, the recently obsolete space shuttles – the history of a century compressed into an hour of fast walking. Spragg didn't walk fast. He was tired after a restless night and he had time to kill. He reached the planetarium as a performance was about to commence, paid, passed into cooled darkness and sat looking at an artificial sky. One better than most astronomers had had the good fortune ever to know; the depicted stars neatly arrayed, the bowl clear, all distracting annoyances absent.

The programme, probably to tie in with the supposed reason for the Exposition, was about the possibility of mining the asteroids and he watched as ships reached out like hungry bees to settle and return with holds stuffed with rare and precious metals.

'Albert,' murmured the mellifluous voice from the speakers. 'Discovered in 1911 it has an estimated diameter of 3 miles and its closest approach to the Earth is something like 20 million miles.' A bleak, jagged scrap of rock swelled on the dome to recede as another took its place. 'Apollo, discovered much later in 1932, smaller but it does come closer. At its nearest approach it is barely 7 million miles distant which should not be too far for mining ships to travel.' Another image. 'Vesta,' said the voice. 'One of the so-called "big four" the other three being Juno, Pallas and Ceres. These are the most promising sources of minerals and their size would make it feasible to set up permanent installations on and below their surfaces. Living quarters would be dug from the rock, sealed, supplied with air and all other essentials to normal living and viable colonies established. Pallas, for example, discovered in 1802, has a diameter of 300 miles and a surface area larger than that of France. Ceres, the largest of the known asteroids, discovered in 1801, has a diameter of 470 miles and a surface area three times larger than that of Pallas. The low gravity on these asteroids would also be an advantage. On Ceres a 180-pound man would weigh only 6. However the distances of these large masses are far greater than those of Albert and Apollo, Icarus and Hermes and …'

Spragg closed his eyes, imagination replacing the depicted scene. Ships reaching out to serve colonies which had never known what it was to stand with the wind blowing against faces or the touch of rain on the skin. Men, women and children living like moles in an artificial environment, needing suits to protect them whenever they left their quarters to venture to the surface. To stare at a naked sky and a naked sun. To be strangers to bird-song, to clouds, to rainbows, to mist, to the awesome hush before dawn, to the wonder of mountains, the poetry of seas.

But to live. To be safe against destruction by a jagged mass of rock which would smash into them and turn them into a bloody pulp and ash and broken fragments which would drift in emptiness for eternity …

He jerked awake, sweating, aware of staring eyes, conscious that he must have cried out in his tormented dream. Rising, he stumbled towards an exit, muttering apologies, thankful to get outside the darkened auditorium.

He was thirsty but not for coffee or tea. He craved a long, strong drink of whisky loaded with ice and smoothed with dry ginger ale. He wanted a cold shower and a bed to lie on and a bottle to hand. He needed to sleep and not to dream.

The stairs were to hand and he took them, running down the flights to the ground floor. The building had two main entrances and he headed for the one opposite to that he had used to gain entrance. One side of the hall was flanked by a counter and display and he slowed, coming to a halt as he recognised familiar items; the plastic assemblies of the Voyagers, the books, posters, pictures and badges of the probes which had recently passed on a new mission through the moons of Jupiter. The same items they had offered for sale at Althene and now, as then, they reminded him of Irene.

He lingered, vaguely hopeful, looking at those standing behind the counter; a tall, middle-aged man with sparse hair and gold-rimmed spectacles and two girls, both younger, with rich, coffee-coloured skins. If Irene was attached to the display she wasn't present and it had been idiotic to even imagine she could be. Her job would necessitate more than serving or talking people into buying souvenirs. Even to enquire about her would be a waste of time. Then, as Spragg turned away, he saw her.

She came towards him from the doors, sunlight behind the transparent panels haloing her with golden brilliance so that for a moment she seemed to be frozen in an icon-like depiction of grace, an illusion shattered as she took another step and halted as he called her name. 'Irene!'

Her eyes widened, moved to glance at the man behind the counter before returning to his face.

'Hello, Mal. Here for the Exposition?'

'Yes.'

'I thought you would be invited – you've earned the right.'

'By appearing on the front pages?'

'By being at the top of your profession.' She changed the subject. 'What do you think of our display?'

She hadn't changed. Her voice was still as he remembered, soft, deeply resonant, music to his ears. Her hair was a little shorter and had lost its russet sheen either because of age or artifice, but it was still thick, still framing her neatly-shaped head with a golden halo. He looked at it, at the eyes, the nose, the mouth, the lips with their familiar pout, the chin, the line of her throat. Softness met his fingers as he touched her cheek, velvet riding beneath them as he traced the line of her jaw. He lowered his trembling hand as she stepped backwards from the caress.

'I'm sorry.' He added, lamely, 'It's been a long time.'

But not long enough to dull the memory of her entrancing figure and it was still the same. The body he had known, did know, so well. Eight years, he thought bleakly, and was shaken by the waste, the criminal, stupid waste.

'You're looking tired,' she said. 'You should watch yourself at these get-togethers. You drink too much and sleep too little.'

Was she really concerned or was she just making polite noises? But how could she be indifferent? They had been married. They had been lovers. How could she think of him as a stranger?

He said, 'This is an amazing coincidence. I never thought it would happen but I'm glad it did. I've often wondered how you were getting on. How are things?

'Fine.'

'I'm glad to hear it,' he lied. 'I'm not doing too badly myself. You're looking well. You live in Washington?'

'Yes.'

'Good.' He was, he realised, babbling like an idiot. He said, more slowly, 'I'd like to take you to dinner. Tonight, perhaps? Tomorrow?'

'Sorry, Mal. I just don't think it would be a good idea for us to be together.'

He fought to calm himself. 'Just a meal together. Who could object?'

'Did I say anyone would object?' Again her eyes moved in a glance to the man behind the counter. 'I just can't see any point to it. Eight years is a long time, Mal, and when we parted it wasn't on the best of terms.'

She shouldn't have reminded him because, suddenly, it all came back. He felt again the tension, the conviction that something was wrong, the overwhelming need to drop everything and go home, only to find …

He said, quietly, 'You can learn a lot in eight years, Irene. The fact that you've made a mistake, for example. That it's stupid to cut off your nose to spite your face. Please come to dinner.'

'No.'

'I miss you,' he said. 'Surely you can spare me a little time? We have things to talk about. There are still things in the house –'

'Which no longer interest me. And now –' She broke off, looking down at the hand he had rested on her arm. 'Mal?'

Reluctantly he dropped the detaining hand. If she went now it could be to pass completely out of his life but if he tried too hard to hold her he would only drive her away. How to persuade her that she would want to see him again?

'Irene?'

Spragg turned at the sound of the strange voice at his side. The tall man with the gold-rimmed spectacles had joined them from behind the counter. 'Is everything all right?'

'Yes, Paul – I'll be with you in a moment.' To Spragg, as the man returned to his position, she said, 'Paul Sellar. A friend of mine.'

'So I see.' Spragg forced a smile. 'Close?'

'Is that any of your business?'

'No of course not.' Another mistake which he did his best to rectify. 'I'm sorry, I spoke without thinking. I must be more tired than I thought – it must be the heat.' He dabbed at his face and neck with a handkerchief. 'Let me see you again when I'm at my best. I'm staying at the Clairmont and you could come to dinner. Your friend too if you want. I won't embarrass you. We could just talk and share a few drinks and I'll tell you what's going on at the Exposition. You've heard about it?'

'Rumours only, but –'

'Think about it,' he urged, giving her no time to refuse. 'The Clairmont, remember? I'll be looking forward to hearing from you.'

He left it at that, walking directly towards the doors, not looking back and doing his best to appear casual. A cab took him to his hotel where he ordered a bottle, took a shower and then lay on the bed, sipping whisky and looking at the bright oblong of the window. As the drink took effect he relaxed, reliving their meeting.

Would she phone? Had he appeared too jealous? Should he have managed things so as to talk to her friend? Should he have spoken to her at all?

That would have been impossible. They had met and his reaction had startled him. He wanted her but, even more, he wanted her to want him. Once she did that he would have everything.

He dozed at last, waking with a start to the jangle of the phone. The window framed darkness and he fumbled before finding the instrument.

'Yes?' He listened to the voice of someone on duty downstairs, interrupting after the first few words. 'A lady to see me? Sent her up!'

It had to be Irene and he rose, dressing with feverish haste, slipping a comb through his hair as the doorbell chimed. Running to the panel he opened it.

'Good evening, Herr Professor.' Frieda Osten stood smiling at him from the passage. 'This is a surprise for you, no?'

She had arrived that morning together with Carl Waldemar and they were staying at a hotel nearby. Finding him had been simple as Carl explained.

'I knew you were in Washington and had attended the Exposition. The rest was just a matter of phoning around.' He lifted the glass in his hand. 'To a happy meeting!'

Mechanically Spragg responded to the toast. It had been Carl's idea, of course, to have sent Frieda to get him to share a dinner he didn't want and then to join a party he could have done without. But the man meant well and couldn't possible know of his chance meeting with Irene. If she called now he would be out but if she called he would know about it and could track her down.

'You look glum, my friend,' Waldemar said. 'A little lonely here in the big city? Why, when there are so many nubile young girls eager to ease your tensions for the sake of a few dollars? Or, of course –' His eyes moved to where Frieda stood at the far side of the room talking to a podgy man with a close-cropped hair style.

Spragg said, 'Carl, I'm not here alone.'

'You have a companion? That is good. Where is she?'

'She's staying with friends in New York.' Spragg caught the ironic lift of the other's eyebrows. 'She left at noon.'

'Do I know her?'

'No. She's my assistant.'

'And so she attended the Exposition with you?' Waldemar looked thoughtful. 'Which means she knows what is going to happen if she has any brains at all. How did she take it?'

'How did you?'

'At first, badly. I felt numb, sick, unable to accept what I knew to be true.

Then I got very drunk and, afterwards, things didn't seem so bad. What is the use of worrying? Thor is coming. Not all the burning candles and fervent prayers in the world can stop it. Not even joy and laughter but they, at least, ease the time of waiting.' Waldemar finished his drink. 'Let me get you another, Mal, then come and talk to Harry.'

Harry Frazer was the podgy man with Frieda. Like her he was a mathematician. Unlike her he was a trifle drunk. A state he claimed to be the best for the clear working of his mind.

'It's a matter of the synapses,' he explained after Spragg had been introduced. 'You know how the impulses jump along the nerves. Alcohol slows them down a little. Now the same thing happens in the brain. The thoughts jump too damned fast and get all mixed up but after a few drinks they slow down and you can catch and corral the bastards and detach them to jump through hoops. Catch?'

'I catch.'

'Good. That makes you one of the fraternity. You with NASA?'

'No.'

'I am. Attached to them, that is. My real line is atomics. I'm an advisor to CALNED, you've heard of them? No? Constructional Application of Limited Nuclear Devices. We haven't done much as yet but when we get the work just watch our smoke! A new Atlantic–Pacific canal cut through Mexico. Mines in the Antarctic. Deserts irrigated, mountains levelled, tunnels fashioned, bores – you name it and we'll do it. Given time we'll change the whole damned face of the planet.'

'With atomic bombs?'

'Atomic devices. They blow up, sure, but the explosion is controlled. Like dynamite. Once we lick the residue problem and get the nuts off our back who keep screaming about pollution and get a few politicians to see sense we'll be on our way. Can you realise what it would mean to Australia to have the Great Desert irrigated? To India to solve the drought problem? To Argentina to have a tunnel cut through the Andes?' Frazer looked at his glass. 'The damned thing's empty!'

Spragg refilled it and moved on to talk to others. He answered them absently, resenting the intrusion into his privacy. Waldemar came to rescue him finally, thrusting a drink into his hand, shooing away the woman who was haranguing him with her religious beliefs.

Smiling, he said, 'Well, Mal, what do you think of her?'

'Very little. She's like all Jesus-freaks – worshipping the signpost instead of following the directions. A friend of yours?'

'She came with Bud Aldcock. They arrived early and he left her here while he went off to settle some other business. You may have seen him at the Exposition – tall, thin mouth, stooped, eyes too close together. No? Well, he was there. What did you think of the Exposition? Did you find it interesting?'

'Frightening would be a better word. But they were preaching to the converted as far as I'm concerned. But it wasn't a waste of time.'

'Why?' Waldemar nodded as Spragg gave his reasons. 'You are shrewd, my friend. If the nations are to work together they must first be convinced there is no other hope of salvation. If necessary they –' He broke off, looking at Spragg. 'Is something wrong?'

'Hope – you said hope.'

'So? There is always hope.'

But not unless backed with a plan. Spragg turned to look across the room to where Harry Frazer expanded his theory of quietened synapses to a pale-faced young woman who held degrees in chemistry. To where Frieda was engaged in conversation with a physicist. To a man who had helped train pilots for the space shuttle who smiled at a female meteorologist. At the others all trained in allied skills. All attached to NASA. All, he guessed, heading for Cape Canaveral.

He said, bleakly, 'Will it work? You're thinking of blowing Thor to hell and gone with atomics. Will it work?'

'So you guessed – I wondered how long it would take you. A drink now to celebrate.' He returned with full glasses, smiling as always. 'Prost!'

'Cheers!'

'It depends on the math,' said Waldemar as they lowered their glasses. 'That and on the material available and the ships to carry it in. The Americans ran all manner of situations through their war-games and constructed analogues of almost all conceivable events. Some of the answers we can adapt to present needs, especially those concerned with logistics and the movement of men and machines. The Russians too – the project would be impossible without their cooperation, but it's mutual – they have an equal interest in survival.'

Spragg said, dryly, 'We all have an equal interest in survival.'

'Maybe, but you know what they say about equality – some are born more equal than others.' Waldemar took a sip of his vodka. 'I'm not actually in charge of the operation. It's a combined effort, naturally, but I was connected with the European conference and was asked to arrange the initial stages. Also I'm a civilian, which helps. The military are reluctant to trust each other especially those of the major powers. Well, Mal, there it is. Naturally you're involved.'

'As the scientific advisor to Sir Edgar Waring?'

'I know what you are – I suggested you be given the job. And there's more to it than you think. Don't undersell yourself – Thor is basically your baby.

That makes you important. And I need to have a friend I can trust. One who will help me celebrate afterwards if nothing else. After we've shown whoever runs this damned universe that we can't be pushed around.'

Waldemar swayed and caught at Spragg's shoulder for support. His breath reeked of whisky. 'When we've smashed the Hammer of God with the Fires of Satan. God, Mal, what a night that will be!'

CHAPTER 11

Spragg said, patiently, 'There are only three ways of dealing with Thor, to dodge, deflect or destroy. Obviously we can't dodge and the thing is far too massive to destroy. Our only hope lies in managing to deflect it in such a way that it will miss Earth instead of colliding with it.'

He looked from one to the other feeling like a schoolmaster facing intractable children: Sir Edgar, Admiral Pyne, Rodger Harcourt-Smythe, elevated to the inner councils and looking a little green, and a stranger who said little but whose eyes were never still. Peter Ogden, a recent addition to the Embassy and obviously a man of some importance.

He said, 'When you say we can't dodge, Spragg, are we to take that at face value?'

'Unless you know a way to move the Earth bodily through space, yes.'

'I wasn't thinking of the entire Earth but of the point of impact. Do you know exactly where that will be?'

'As yet, no.'

'But, once ascertained, would it be possible to change it by, for example, slowing down the advance of Thor?'

Spragg looked at the man with new interest. Not a fool, certainly, his grasp of the situation proved that. Not, apparently, a product of the usual public school system, at least he lacked the accents and ties of Eton or Harrow. A military man, perhaps, but if so one connected with intelligence.

From his chair Admiral Pyne snapped, 'Well, Spragg, would it?'

'Theoretically, yes, but in practice no.' They had assembled in the study of the Embassy and Spragg moved to where the globe stood in its frame beside the window. Spinning it he said, 'The surface of the Earth at the equator moves at a speed of approximately 1000 miles an hour. If Thor were to hit here, for example,' he rested his finger on Borneo, 'and we wanted it to hit here instead,' he moved his finger to Zaire in Central Africa, 'we would need to delay the strike by 6 hours.'

'Could the time of impact be advanced?' The suggestion came from Ogden. 'I'm not talking about it hitting a specific target, you understand, but of avoiding a certain area.'

Such as Great Britain, naturally. Spragg shook his head. 'Impossible. To do that we would have to transport explosives beyond the mass, turn, send them against it faster than its present velocity and maintain the barrage until the desired increase is attained. It simply cannot be done.'

'Then the slowing –'

'Is, as I've said, theoretical. You must bear in mind that the Earth, aside from rotation, is also moving in orbit around the sun. If we could slow Thor down sufficiently it would, of course, miss us, but the energy necessary to do that is beyond us. It would be like trying to slow down a thrown brick by shooting at it with peas. We don't have enough peas and we don't have enough time.'

And more was being wasted every moment. It was a week now since the party. Carl had gone and Frieda with him. Irene had stayed out of sight. Myrna had dropped a line to say she was going to take a look at the Niagara Falls. And still he was trying to drive sense into the blockheads!

He said, 'Gentlemen, we are faced with a cosmic threat. Thor isn't a bubble, which can be blown away. It can't be slowed. It can't be speeded. It can't be guided in any way. A pity, no doubt – Russia would probably be pleased if it hit the United States and some Americans would cheer if it were to hit Russia. Others would be happy to see it strike Africa, or India, or Australia, or China – anywhere other than on their own doorstep. But wherever it strikes the Earth is doomed. The impact will be worldwide. One entire quarter of the planetary surface will be directly affected. One quarter! Think about it.' The globe spun beneath his fingers. 'Europe and Africa – all of North America including Canada and Greenland. All China and Japan. Australia and Indonesia. South America and most of Antarctica. The axis will be disturbed, the crust – there can and will be no escape!'

Facts he had stated before with little apparent result. The inertia of planetary masses was nothing when compared to the inertia of bureaucracy.

Irritably, he said, 'This is the last time I shall explain all this. Either you believe me or not. If not there is no point in my continuing to waste my time.'

From his chair Pyne rapped, 'No need to take that attitude, Spragg. We have to be sure.'

'No one is calling you a liar,' soothed Sir Edgar. 'But certain details have to be clarified, what?' He glanced at Ogden. 'For example, do you know the exact time of impact?'

'Not as yet. Nor the time nor the place. I can give you the day but not the second.' Spragg added, bitterly, 'If you're thinking of making contingency plans to safeguard a few selected individuals forget them. When we go we all go together. There is no escape for anyone once Thor hits.'

'If it hits.' Ogden was on his feet smoothly taking charge of the situation. 'I think that is all for now, gentlemen. Obviously the Professor is a little upset and, personally, I can't blame him. Like me he could probably use a drink. Rodger? If you would be so kind?' He waited until the others had left and a tray had been set on the desk. 'Scotch or vodka?'

'Scotch.' Spragg accepted the proffered glass. 'Which department are you? MI6? Special Branch? Something I haven't heard of yet?'

'You guessed?'

'You must be here for some reason and in our modern democracy Security takes precedence even over staid diplomats. Why on earth are you wasting your time?'

'It's a job.'

'And you like doing it. Have you been watching me long?' Spragg didn't expect an answer. 'And Myrna? Is she really at Niagara Falls?'

'Yes. With Madam Kuluva – a woman with quite a reputation in certain fields. You can guess who she works for.'

'Does it matter? Myrna can only tell her what she already knows.'

'You're missing the point, Professor. It doesn't matter what you tell each other as long as you don't try to alarm the public. We're handling that pretty well at the moment as I think you'll agree.'

Spragg nodded; the papers now carried an exposé of corruption in government circles together with hints of allegations more startling than Watergate.

'You can't keep it up,' he pointed out. 'Soon anyone with a cheap pair of binoculars will be able to see Thor bright and clear if they know where to look. Later it'll be visible to the naked eye.'

'And by that time everyone will be certain that it's going to miss by a wide margin. You'll tell them that as you did before.' Ogden smiled and lifted his glass. 'How are you on imagination?'

'What?'

'Most scientists suffer from a strange blindness – they often fail to see what's under their nose. This threat, for instance. To you and to most of your colleagues it is the end. We either divert Thor or it's the finish. But what if we do manage to divert it?'

'We go on,' said Spragg. 'We survive.'

'And?' Ogden shrugged as Spragg made no answer. 'You see? That's the blindness I was talking about. Diplomats look at things in a different way and those connected with National Security –'

Spragg said, 'When a house is burning you don't argue who is to get what – you just get together to put it out.'

'You think so?' Ogden shook his head. 'Those days are long gone. Now it's a matter of greed – who is to pay for the water, the labour to carry it, the buckets?' He added, without change of tone, 'You don't seem to get on well with Admiral Pyne.'

'I just can't stand his authoritarian attitude. Just what gives him the right to give the orders?'

'He and his class?' Ogden smiled when Spragg made no answer. 'You're a bit of a rebel, aren't you? You had quite a reputation for kicking against the traces at University and you weren't too kind to Director Hammond.'

'Because I told him what to do with himself and his job? Is that a crime?'

'No, but sometimes it can be foolish.'

'The price of liberty,' said Spragg. 'Be yourself and you lose everything. So much for democracy.'

'A dream. We haven't got it and never had. It's a word used by politicians to gull fools.' Ogden shrugged at Spragg's expression. 'I'm a realist. Because I work for those who hold the reins I don't have to be deaf and dumb and blind. But, equally so, I don't have to be daft. It pays to be on the winning side. My job is to make sure we stay on it.'

'In a few months there won't be any sides.'

'If Thor hits, no,' agreed Ogden. 'But we have to take the long-term view and make plans in the event it can be deflected with the use of atomic missiles. That's why I want you to come to New York to attend the Special Emergency Session of the United Nations Security Council.'

New York? It would take him from Washington and Irene but also from the temptation of haunting the museum and NASA building in the hope of seeing her. But, on the other hand, it would take him closer to Myrna. She wouldn't stay long at Niagara Falls – what the hell was there aside from water?

He said, 'Let's get one thing clear. I'm not going to stay away from Miss Parkin. Not even if she continues to see Madam Kuluva.'

'Of course not.' Ogden was bland. 'I wouldn't even think of asking you to ignore her. And I'm certain that Madam Kuluva will see that you have the opportunity to meet. Representative Extraordinary to the UN.'

The seats were covered with red leather, the desks were of polished spruce, the carpet, like the chairs, held a sombre warmth. Little plaques; gold letters on light backgrounds, gave names and titles and country of origin. Notepads, bottles of water, ballpoint pens, completed the furnishings. At their places in the chairs the Council sat like rows of mummified corpses, earphones dangling from ears, spectacles flashing like blank windows, some apparently sleeping, all trapped in an artificial stasis of strained ritual.

Spragg leaned back, looking at the painted ceiling of the chamber, the depiction of an idealised figure pouring out a stream of good things to the clamouring masses of the world. The cost of the work would have fed a thousand for a decade – an irony that had apparently escaped those responsible for the commission. In his ears a smoothly detached voice enunciated better English than he possessed.

Since taking his place in the Council Spragg had learned something of the rules; it wasn't so much what you said but how and when you said it. The current speaker, for example, couldn't really believe in the rubbish he was saying but was saying it in order to strengthen the value of the cards in his hand. He finally came to an end to be replaced by Madam Chandi from India. Bright in her sari she spoke in English; presumably she wanted what she said to be free of all ambiguity.

Spragg yawned as once again he listened to a capsulated history of early struggles, striving, sacrifices and national destinies, all of which seemed a mandatory preliminary to the newly emerged powers. Then came the real meat of the discussion.

'... Larger powers such as the United States and Russia, which have a high nuclear capacity. My own country has few atomic plants and missiles. To place our entire capability into the common pool would be to make a sacrifice far in excess of our stronger partners. Therefore I cannot agree to operate on a basis of percentages or of yielded numbers either of which would place my country at a tremendous disadvantage. India will retain only two nuclear missiles if all other countries will follow her example.'

Spragg heard the sigh of released breath when she sat down and felt a grudging admiration for the woman's cunning. She had made a good case and if she pulled it off it would mean that India would be as strong as any other nation on the Earth in the event the Earth survived.

Israel, as usual quick to grasp the implications, next demanded the floor. Moshe Abishua, like Madam Chandi, spoke in English and didn't pull his punches. If his country was to donate all its missiles he demanded assurances from the large powers that the national boundaries, indeed the very existence of Israel itself, should be guaranteed. The boundaries he specified would increase the overall area of present dimensions by a healthy amount and would settle the West Bank, Gaza Strip, Golan Heights and the Syrian and Lebanese problem for all time. Those who stood to lose naturally objected or others did it on their behalf.

Spragg, careless of who might be watching, produced his flask, poured whisky into the glass provided and added water from the decanter. He was, he knew, offending the dignity of the assembly and upsetting all concepts of formalised procedure but he was bored and didn't care who the hell knew it. He was also more than a little afraid. This was poker as Ogden had warned him it would be but he hadn't realised then that it was suicide-poker – a game in which none could win and all were doomed to lose.

Days had slipped into weeks and, outside, the October dusk would be falling over the East River, turning the normal appearance of the man-made sewer into the enchanting mystery it had been in the time of the early settlers. A time of argument and discussion and of beating his head against brick walls. Of speaking again and again of what would happen when Thor smashed into the Earth. Of letting himself be used to aid the common good.

The house was burning – but they argued over who was to provide the water to put out the blaze. God alone knew how long it would take to thrash out the cost and who was to meet it.

He was drinking too much, he knew, but could see no reason for cutting it out. Life was full of miseries; Irene apparently lost and Myrna coming to New York a week ago to almost immediately leave again on a jaunt to Florida and the magic of Orlando. They had made brief love and he had waited for her to question him but she had surprised him by her lack of interest in what he was doing.

And Ogden, feeding him instructions, wanting reports, smiling that damned, bland smile as if the title he now carried had made him a creature of the Establishment. Which, in a way it did. It provided him with position, an expense account, good accommodation and the entry into circles that would normally have been closed.

A bell and the session ended with nothing apparently accomplished.

The girl with the pompadour hairstyle and the high, yellow boots said, 'And you can assure our readers, Professor, there is absolutely nothing to worry about?'

'Nothing at all.' Spragg lied and smiled as he lied, the result of long practice and the growing conviction that no matter what he said it wouldn't make a damned bit of difference. 'In fact it will make the most exciting spectacle anyone has ever seen.'

Thor was back in the news, deliberately so, those involved deciding it was time for the cork to be drawn from the bottle. Deciding too not only that the news should be released but how it should be handled. As Ogden had warned Spragg was in the forefront of those handing out platitudes.

Thor was real, it was coming, but it would miss by a big margin. In fact the nations acting in concert were going to reap a bonanza from the cosmic visitor. Again Spragg explained.

'As you may have been informed from the recent Exposition on the possibility of mining the asteroids the project is viable. Thor provides us with a magnificent opportunity. It will pass close which means it can be easily reached. With the calculated use of atomic devices we will split off a large section and swing it into orbit around the Earth. In a sense we will fashion a second Moon and one with several advantages over the old. It will be closer and so easier to reach and –'

'How's that, Professor?' The interruption came from a young man with an earnest face. 'Surely once we reach escape velocity it doesn't really matter how close the captured fragment will be?'

A wise guy and right. Spragg retained his smile.

'The proposed orbit will be approximately 80,000 miles as against 250,000 of our Moon. A saving that I'm sure most will think of as worth having. But more than that is the potential composition of the planetoid itself. We know that the majority of meteors are of a nickel-iron basis and so there is no reason to doubt that Thor is of the same composition. The proposed fragment will be in the region of 50 miles in diameter. A solid mass of rare and precious metal, which we can tap at our leisure. Once established in orbit our fears as to the exhaustion of raw materials will be over. Ladies? Gentlemen? If there are no more questions?'

Spragg waited until the last reporter had left the hall before making his way from the chamber towards the reception area of the hotel. As usual it was a scene of apparent chaos. Two men whom he knew to be security guards stood watching – the hotel had many UN representatives as guests. Against one wall he saw a new splash of colour where a poster had been hung that very evening. A familiar poster depicting a ebon background spattered with stars, the glow of a massive planet and, against it, the frail vanes and extensions of a Voyager.

Coincidence?

He felt the interior of his mouth go dry at the possibility that she had followed him to New York and was here at this very moment. To the receptionist he said, 'The woman who hung that poster. Where is she?'

'Sir?'

'For God's sake, man!' He found money and pressed crumpled bills into a ready hand. 'Now think. Is she staying in the hotel? Room 753. Thank you.'

He had no doubt that it would be Irene and when the door opened to his knock he stepped forward and took her in his arms.

'Mal!'

'No!' He fought her attempt to escape from his embrace. 'No, Irene, no!'

'What is it, Mal? What do you want?'

'To talk. For God's sake, Irene, can't you understand that? Just to talk.' He eased the constriction of his arms, conscious of the pounding of his heart, his rising desire. 'Why didn't you contact me in Washington?'

'There was no point.'

'Then why follow me here?'

'I didn't.' She stepped away from him, one hand lifting to adjust her hair. She was, he noted, flushed and breathing fast. 'I came to set up a display. Once it's arranged I move on. Since seeing you in Washington I've been to Chicago, Cleveland. Boston and, oh, lots of places.'

'With that man? Paul – whatever his name is?'

'Paul Sellar. We work together, yes.'

And slept together? Jealousy tore at his stomach and drummed at his brain.

He said, 'Let's leave here. We could have dinner.' Get her out before Paul could appear and ruin things. 'Please,' he urged. 'You know I hate eating alone.'

'Are you alone?'

'Of course!' Could she be jealous? 'All alone. I guess you've heard the news.'

'About Thor?' She nodded. 'The truth this time or more lies?'

'What makes you say that?'

'I was married to an astronomer once.' She gave him a rueful smile. 'Some of what he knew rubbed off. Lies, Mal?'

He nodded. 'I'll tell you the truth over dinner.'

But he didn't, conscious of those sitting close, delaying the moment until they had finished their desert and sat lingering over coffee and brandy. Conscious too that the truth was a trump card and not to be played too soon or too lightly. Irene had always been curious – now he could use that trait to his advantage.

He said, forcing himself to sound casual, 'Why not go up to my room and have a drink? We can talk there. Incidentally, I've a wonderful view.'

'So have I.'

I, not we, and his spirits soared to be as quickly flattened. Even if she didn't share a room with Paul he could be an all-night visitor.

Still striving to appear casual, he said, 'I've a lot to tell you and it's best done over cognac and champagne. Remember that time in Spain when we used to sit on the balcony at night and watch the lights way out at sea and drink sparkling white wine and local brandy?'

'And smuggle out the bottles for fear the hotel would charge us corkage.' She smiled, remembering. 'Our first real holiday together. We could hardly afford it.'

'Good times,' he said. And added, with naked sincerity, 'I miss them, Irene. The walks and the searching for bargains in little shops, the markets and the rest of it. Christ, how I miss them!' He bit at his lips, aware that he had betrayed himself. Quietly he said, 'I guess you've no taste for cognac and champagne now?'

'No, Mal – it wouldn't be the same.'

As nothing would ever be the same, he thought bleakly. Not now and not ever. Too much had happened between them and, like a fool, he had realised the value of what he had lost only after losing it. Yet he could still act in a civilised manner.

'Of course. Another drink?'

'Thank you, no.' She dabbed at her lips with a paper towel. 'But you can take me for a walk.'

CHAPTER 12

The night held magic. Even though it was late October the summer still lingered and the air held the trapped warmth of the city, relieved only slightly by the breeze from the East River. Spragg led the way, stepping along the terrace fronting the UN building, aware of the lights still glowing in the offices; lights that would burn until dawn as they burned elsewhere in other offices where real work was being done.

'The heart of the world,' she murmured, looking up at the sheer facade. 'Or it should be. Why does it take a catastrophe for people to remember their common humanity?'

And why did they so quickly forget? Spragg followed her eyes then lowered his own to where the dim bulk of a statue stood limned against the reflected glow of lights edging the water. Frozen in perpetual labour, an idealised man strove to turn a sword into a ploughshare.

'Mal?' Irene had paused and was tracing a finger over the bronze leaving a line of wetness as the tip caught and spread the patina of condensation. 'Are you ever – I mean do you ever get afraid?'

'Too often.'

'Is that why you hate to be alone?'

'Yes.' He added, 'You know?'

'Of your affairs? Of course. They're no secret, Mal, not when you've the kind of friends who love to spread gossip and stick in their knives. Don't tell me you never realised what they were like.'

He said, flatly, 'I lost all illusions concerning the value of friendship when I found Arkwright in your bed. In our bed.' He paused, trying not to remember. 'Do you remember Ian McGregor?'

'Of course. How is he?'

'He's working for Rand now. Before he left he said that you and Bob had split up.'

'He was right. It happened some time ago now. We'd drifted for years before making the final break. We just didn't get along.'

She offered no further explanation, Spragg watched intently as she stood limned against the glow of lights from the river. Brilliance caught her hair and turned it into a golden nimbus framing a face which seemed to have lost years, the lines of time erased, the scars of emotional battle voided.

'Irene! I love you! I love you!'

She sighed and moved a little closer to where he stood, halting as he lifted his hands. The magic of the night wasn't strong enough, his protestations had been too weak, the barrier between them remained.

Tasting defeat he said, quietly, 'Maybe I shouldn't have said that but I just wanted you to know. Now, I guess, you'd like to go back. I mean, if someone is waiting?'

She smiled and shook her head, reflected light dancing in her hair. 'Paul is a very happily married man. He has three children and talks about them all the time. He phones his wife every day when away from home. I doubt if the thought of being unfaithful has ever crossed his mind.'

'Three children, eh? Good for him.'

'Two boys and a girl.' Her voice held a poignant yearning. 'A nice family.'

'Yes,' said Spragg. 'Let's get back.'

He heard the scrape of shoes after they had begun their journey along the terrace and, at the same moment, caught the silhouette of a hulking shape. More sounds came from behind and he acted without thinking, pushing Irene to one side as the man ahead stepped into view, a cigarette in one brown hand.

'Gimme a light, mister?'

The old ploy of muggers, to hold the attention of the victim while the man's companion attacked from the rear. Spragg jumped to one side and felt the wind of the sap as it grazed his head and numbed his shoulder. His foot, lifting, kicked out to land on something soft. He spun as the man doubled, gasping, to see the other stagger back, screaming, hands to his eyes.

'Run!' Irene stood, an aerosol can in her hand. 'Quickly, Mal! Run!'

Their shoes thudded on the flags as they raced along the terrace, emerging in a brilliantly lit area, seeing the familiar uniforms of lounging police.

'No!' Irene caught and dragged at his arm as Spragg headed towards them. 'No, Mal, it will do no good. Those men are gone by now. We'll have to answer a lot of questions and look at endless photographs in an attempt to identify them. It will all be a waste of time.'

'The bastards! What happened?'

'I used this.' She lifted the can before slipping it back into her handbag. 'Hairspray. I always carry it.' Her tone changed as they reached an area of brighter light. 'Mal, your head! You're bleeding!'

From where she sat facing him Irene said, 'How's the head and shoulder now, Mal?'

'I'll live.' The blood had come from a graze, now patched and his padded jacket had saved him from more than a nasty bruise on the shoulder. Irene had helped to ease it, holding ice to his naked flesh, seemingly unaware of the effect of her propinquity. 'How's your drink?'

'Nice. A little too cold, perhaps.'

'That's due to the national love of ice.' Spragg held his glass between his palms, warming it. Even though he had specified it the hotel had been unable to provide unchilled champagne. 'I'll mix a brew and stand it in hot water for a while.'

He switched off the lights as he returned from the bathroom and moved towards the window, the room now illuminated only by the dusky glow from the external city. It was bright enough for him to see her profile, the halo of her hair, the lines of her body.

She said, 'You were going to talk to me, Mal. Tell me something. Have you changed your mind?'

'Perhaps.' The attack had changed things, brought them closer together, awakened in him a more tender regard. Would it be a kindness to tell her the truth? To gain time he said, 'The drink should be warmed by now. Give me your glass and I'll get you some.'

She smiled as he returned, taking the glass, sipping, nodding her approval. 'That's better. Now tell me about Thor.'

'You know?'

'I guessed. It has to be that. The first time it appeared on the news was the truth, wasn't it? It's going to hit.'

It was a relief to admit it. 'Yes.'

'When?' She sucked in her breath when he told her. 'So soon? But –'

'There's a chance,' he said quickly. At least he could relay that comfort. 'We might be able to deflect it given enough men and missiles.' And time and transport and skill – things he didn't mention. 'That's what all the stuff in the media is about – to block any awkward questions.'

'To prevent panic.' She nodded, frowning. 'Is it going to work, Mal? Can it?'

'There's a chance.'

'What kind of an answer is that? I could jump out of this window and there's a chance I might live. I could land in a load of feather mattresses or get caught up in a dangling line or something. I could even learn how to fly or –' She broke off, swallowing, her anger vanishing as quickly as it had come. 'Such a short while,' she whispered, 'So very short.'

'Six months,' he said. 'A little less. Thor will hit on April the 11th of next year.'

'Is that a Sunday?'

'I don't know. Why?'

'It would be appropriate in a way. The Sun – Sunday – but Thor isn't the sun, is it? It's the Hammer of God. But Sunday would be a good day for it to strike.' Her laugh was shaky, devoid of humour. 'I'm sorry. You must think me a fool for babbling on like that. It's the shock, I guess. It isn't every day you learn just how long you have to live.'

'There's still a chance.'

'The chance you mentioned? Do you expect me to believe it can succeed?' She shrugged at his silence. 'So that's it then. Finish. We all pack up and go home. Pick up our toys and … and …'

He waited as the tears came, wanting to hold her but resisting the temptation. This was a moment she had to face alone. Nothing he or anyone could do or say could ease that isolation. The moment of truth, he thought, how well the Spaniards had put it. The moment when nothing stood between yourself and the ultimate reality. But she would learn to live with it as he had done, as others, as those who even now were doing their best to save the world. Working even as they doubted – but anything was better than just to wait.

Taking her glass, he threw the contents out of the window, filling it with neat cognac.

'Here.' He placed it in her hand. 'Drink this. It will help.'

Like a child she obeyed. Quietly she said, 'You know, I've often wondered what I'd do if a doctor told me I had only six months to live. At first I thought I'll eat every kind of food in the world and taste every drink and see every monument and tomb and ancient building and painting and sculptor ever made. A glorified tour of the entire world. Then I thought, no, that would really accomplish nothing. It would be better to sit and read all the books I'd never had time to read before. And look at a flower, really look at it, And to get close to a pet, an animal of some kind, to try and understand the way it felt and lived. And then, at last, I thought even that was wrong. The thing to do, the only thing, would be to get close to God.'

'So as to thank Him?'

'Mal?'

'Nothing.' He shouldn't mock, she was entitled to her beliefs and what comfort they could give. 'I didn't think you were a strong believer.'

'I'm not. It's just that, at times, there is a need.' She looked at the glass in her hand. 'People shouldn't have to live alone. They should never have to do that.'

Tiny flecks of consciousness locked in individual prisons – Spragg knew all too well the pain of a solitary existence, when to be in a crowd was to be more alone than to dwell on the summit of a mountain. But Irene? As he remembered she had been sparkling and vivacious and full of gaiety. At first, anyway, when they had met and were busy discovering each other. Finding new and more entrancing facts of personality as they found new and more exciting depths of physical attraction.

She had changed – they both had changed. He said, abruptly, 'Are you happy, Irene?'

'Happy?' The glass in her hand glittered as she lifted it to sip and lower it again. 'At times perhaps. Can anyone ever be more than that? To be truly happy is to understand what the Greeks meant when they spoke of ecstasy. It's like … like …'

'Being in love?'

She said nothing, apparently lost in contemplation of her glass, the soft reflections which glowed and died to glow again in the facets of the crystal. Spragg resisted the impulse to smash it from her hand, to grab her by the shoulders, to shake her, to force her to recognise his need. Defeated, he turned away.

'Mal!'

She rose to face him and was suddenly in his arms, soft, warm, wonderful – and the universe sang in echo of his joy.

October died with masks and witches and all the baroque of Halloween. Mist drifted from the rivers to cast a kindly veil over rotting tenements and mouldering Brownstones, adding a touch of enchantment to the more ornate piles of the fashionable quarter, clothing the UN building in draperies of gossamer. On All Souls the churches droned with prayers for the departed and the stores, cleared of the grotesque paraphernalia of the festival, readied for Thanksgiving.

A time of cool evenings and pleasant days when the air held the smoke of burning leaves and the sky showed drifting masses of cloud by day and the dulled orb of the moon at night. Soon there would be snow and ice and all the discomforts of winter but, for now, it was enough to enjoy the changing face of the city.

'Look!' Irene halted before a store window, looking at the heaps of turkeys within, the jars of cranberry sauce, the pumpkins. A display model had been dressed as an old-time woodsman complete with skin cap and long rifle, 'They must have been good days,' she said. 'A man worked and slept and lived by the seasons.'

'And suffered from bad teeth, stomach ulcers, sores, vermin and vitamin-deficiency-diseases. If that man cut himself badly with that knife in his belt he could have died from infection. The good old days weren't all that good for those who had to live in them.'

'But they managed,' she said. 'It was the same for everyone and, at least, a man had a sense of freedom. If he didn't like things where he was he could get up and go.'

'I guess he could.' Spragg didn't want to argue the point. 'How about it?'

'Doing what?'

'Going to the hotel. Don't you have to phone your boss and tell him you're quitting?' He caught her expression. 'You are going to phone?'

'No.' She met his eyes, her own determined. 'Not yet. The programme has to be completed and it's only a few more weeks. To leave now would be to upset the arrangements made by others. Surely you can see that.'

'Of course, but –'

'In any case, Mal, you have your own work to take care of.'

Was she telling him that she had tried and it hadn't worked out but, damn it, they had been happy enough during the past few days. Or he had been happy and she had seemed contented enough. He trembled on the brink of asking her if it was all over, that he had failed.

Before he could speak she said, 'No, Mal, it isn't that. I just feel as if I want to be alone for a while. Finishing the programme will let me do that.'

'If that's what you want, Irene.' He managed to smile. 'I guess there's a lot I've still got to learn. But –'

'I know.' She matched his smile. 'I think we both have a lot to learn. Now I want to do some shopping at Macey's, then to the hotel, then to the museum to wrap up the display. I'll be gone before you get back from the UN.'

'To hell with them!' But it was easier to say than do. Ogden would be relying on him and Irene, he knew, would want him to attend. She had always been considerate and expected others to be the same. 'Will I see you before you leave?'

'I doubt it. You'll probably be late and there won't be time unless –' she glanced at her watch. 'I'll try. If Paul can finish up at the museum I'll come back to the hotel for a farewell drink. But I'll have to be gone by eight.'

He said, 'Must you leave so soon?'

'We've a long way to go.' She leaned forward, rising on her toes. 'Goodbye for now, Mal.'

Her kiss was the touch of a butterfly then she was gone, golden hair bright as she stepped towards the curb and hailed a cab. Spragg stood looking after it, feeling numb, shaken by the sudden turn of events. She was his wife and – no, she was not his wife. She was a woman he had met again after a lapse of years and they had spent some time together and had made love and now she was gone about her business as he must go about his.

Thoughts that gave him no comfort as he headed towards the UN building.

Lamont was speaking in his own language when he entered the chamber. Spragg sat, adjusted the earphones, listened to a spate of national pride. France was perfectly capable of taking an equal share in Operation Thor. Her technicians and scientists were equal to any in the world. Willing as she was to donate her atomic capability yet she still retained the right to fire her own missiles from her own soil. A position he wanted to make clear.

Spragg glanced around the chamber. The American met his eyes as did the Russian. Both were waiting for him to speak and he realised Ogden's strategy. Great Britain, now not so great in world affairs, would act as the middle-man.

Rising, he said, 'May I make the situation quite clear? It isn't enough that we have all agreed to pool our nuclear capability for the sake of the common good – that capability must be used with the utmost care and discretion if a successful conclusion is to be achieved. Thor is approaching us at 5 miles a second. To hit an object at a distance of millions of miles which is only a few hundred miles in diameter requires a fantastic ability as any marksman here will acknowledge. But things are not as simple as that. Thor is moving but so is the Earth; it revolves once each 24 hours. It also circles the sun at a speed of 20 miles a second. And the entire solar system is moving towards the constellation Hercules at a speed almost as great. So we are in the position of trying to hit a moving target while standing on a firing platform which not only also is moving but is moving in three vectors at the same time.'

He took a sip of water, pausing for the facts to sink in. Lecture-room experience now put to a more profitable use. The American, he noted, seemed satisfied, the Russian was frowning a little; briefed, he must be impatient at the repetition of the obvious. Raoul Lamont sat looking bland; he had probably been acting a part and was satisfied with his performance. Madam Chandi sat like a Buddha. Others rested in their chairs – people to be convinced, manipulated, threatened if the need arose.

Spragg continued, 'In view of these facts my own government, after long and careful deliberation, has reached the conclusion that it would be in the best interest of the project and of all those concerned if the nations with the greatest experience in the skills and technology needed in space flight should be the ones to manage the affair. In the light of that decision we have not only donated our entire nuclear capacity together with firm assurances that all supplies of plutonium produced in the near future will also be donated but that all our scientists and computer-capacity will be directed to the same end. We place ourselves and our destiny in the hands of those who, in the past, have not only been our allies in time of war but have shown their good intentions in many ways since those dark and dreadful days when civilisation itself stood in danger as our entire world does now.'

He sat to muted cheers. Many of the countries were only here by courtesy of charity. They had to know their bombs were Indian-gifts that were loaded with strings. Set and guarded by the nationals of those who had donated them, useless as a source of real attack or defence.

Algeria, for example, their bomb had come from Libya who had probably got it originally from Russia. If they tried to fire it they would try in vain. If they tried to take it over by force they would lose it and several square miles of terrain as its self-destruct mechanism was operated.

And others, nursing gifts from China or other self-seeking friends. Gifts which now had been placed in the common pool with promises of their return. Promises which would be ignored if Spragg knew his politics. The real power would once again lie in the hands of the original Big Five.

A man from Zaire wanted to know why the missiles couldn't be fired from within the borders of his own country.

'Have you the facilities?' Spragg asked patiently. To hurry now would be to offend and that would mean more wasted time. 'I am aware the representative from Zaire comes of a race of noted warriors and can both understand and appreciate his desire to take an active part in this battle for survival. But, sometimes, the best part we can play is to step back and let others do the work. We must use existing installations – we lack the time to build new ones. We must use existing vehicles and fuel depots and control-points. We have no choice but to take advantage of the skills of those accustomed to sending vessels into space.'

Ireland rose to back him up, Italy the same. China said nothing but sat in watchful contemplation. Sweden agreed as did Denmark that Russia and the United States should take full charge of the project. Madam Chandri objected.

She was thinking of the riches to be won if a firing point could be set up in India; the flow of money, men and supplies, the buildings left after the thing was over. A big boost to the economy and a few steps up the ladder to industrial independence.

Spragg used the same arguments he had before, this time lengthened and scattered with figures, coupled with an appeal to intelligent appreciation and ended with the hint of special consideration given for complaisance. A mistake, the next few hours were spent in market-place haggling, and it was past seven when he finally left the building. A cab took him to the hotel and he was panting as he ran into the foyer.

'Has she left? The lady in Room 755? Irene Spragg – no, Fiander.' She had reverted to her maiden name. He fumed at the slowness of the receptionist. 'Well?'

'Yes, sir, Madam Fiander left the hotel more than an hour ago. I saw her myself. She took a yellow cab but I couldn't tell you her destination.' He added, 'She left no message.'

Why hadn't she waited for him as arranged? And why, if there had been an emergency, had she left no message? The answer waited for him in his room.

'Hello, Mal,' said Myrna. 'It's been a long time.'

She lay sprawled on the bed wearing a thin robe of shimmering black edged with scarlet. Her feet were bare as, he guessed, was the rest of her beneath the robe. The thick mane of black hair was bound in a towel and her face held the scrubbed look of the freshly-bathed.

Smiling, she said, 'What's wrong, lover? You look as if you'd seen a ghost.'

One from his past, whom he had, incredibly, managed to forget. The sight of her shocked him as if he'd walked into a door. 'Why didn't you phone? Warn me you were coming?'

'I tried, no answer, so I thought I'd give you a surprise.' She added, dryly, 'It was me that got the surprise.'

He said, knowing the answer, 'How did you get in here?'

'Your wife let me in. We had quite a talk. You know, Mal, she's much younger than I'd imagined. Ten years older than me? Twelve?'

'Ten.'

'You like to get them young, don't you?'

'Never mind that. What did you talk about?'

'Things. She wanted to know what I'd been doing so I told her all about the trip to Niagara and then down to Orlando. She's been there herself. And after when I took off into the West, the Grand Canyon and the Painted Desert. Just a tourist you might say with my friend Boris paying my way. Madam Kuluva thinks the world of him. She thinks he's seduced me to the cause. Now I'm supposed to discover all your hidden secrets. Amusing, isn't it?'

Patiently he said, 'Stick to the point.'

'I will.' She reached for her bag and produced a tin and from it took a yellow-paper cigarette. Her hands, he noticed, were trembling a little. The lighter she used was new and sprang into flame as she touched a button. Blue-grey smoke roiled from the cigarette, her nose, from between her lips. 'Join me?'

He shook his head, recognising the smell, the sickly-sweet odour he had known when young and it had been the thing to smoke pot in defiance of authority. A habit he'd given up long ago.

'Do you need that stuff?'

'Need?' She looked at him, the joint forgotten. 'What is "need", Mal? I needed you, remember?'

'So much so that you left as soon as you could to go sightseeing.'

'Can't you guess what drove me? I needed things to see and people to laugh with and a way to forget. This was one.' She gestured with the reefer then, with sudden irritation, flung it to one side where it lay smouldering on the carpet until Spragg crushed it beneath his heel. 'Why, Mal? Damn you, why?'

'Why not?' He met her eyes. 'One law for you and a different one for me, is that it? You to have lovers and me to remain pure?'

She looked at her hands and clenched them to hide their trembling. 'She was more than just a casual affair, Mal. She was your wife.'

Was and maybe would be again. Then he looked at Myrna and saw what Irene must have seen, the dream of every middle-aged man such as himself. No wonder she had left so soon.

He said, tightly, 'Damn you, Myrna, tell me what you talked about!'

'You, me, and life in general. She asked how close we were and I told her. Then I told her something else. I told her I thought I was pregnant.'

'You did what!'

'Told her I thought I was pregnant. She can't have children, can she?'

He was at the side of the bed before he knew it, fists raised, feeling a raw, primitive desire to hurt, to kill. Myrna rolled as he struck at her, falling from the bed as he drove fists into the pillow. Eyes wide, she stared at his distorted face.

'Mal! For God's sake!'

He lunged towards her and tripped as his foot caught in the trailing covers, falling to hit his nose on the floor. Blood stained his lips and chin, dappled his shirt and jacket as he rose. 'You liar!' he yelled. 'You damned liar!'

'Am I?' She faced him, breathing deeply, hands lifted in a judo defence learned many years before. But now she wasn't protecting herself against a would-be rapist and, watching him, she realised there was no need for defence now. The moment of fury had passed. 'What makes you so sure?'

A question he couldn't answer. He had made love to her with the usual indifference of a man confident that she had taken all necessary precautions. Perhaps he'd had a secret wish to get her with child and so bind her closer to him. But that had been before finding Irene. Now –

'Are you?' He moved closer, careless of the blood running from his nose. 'For Christ's sake, Myrna! Are you?'

'No.'

'Then why lie to her?'

'I love you, you bastard, isn't that answer enough? We were at war.' Her voice rose. 'War, blast you. I hated her for having had you and she wanted to see me burn. So I fought dirty – is there any other way if you want to win?'

'Shut up!'

'You think you can forget me? Just throw me aside so as to make room for her?'

'Shut up, damn you!' Spragg wiped at his mouth and looked at the blood on his hand. 'Get out! Get dressed and get out! Out! Out!'

Shaking, he went into the bathroom and stripped off his ruined jacket and shirt. Filling the bowl with water he ducked his head. The bleeding was slow to stop and Myrna had gone by the time he left the bathroom. Probably to take another room, he thought, or to stay with her new-found friends. The hell with her – why couldn't she have stayed away another day?

Scotch stood on a table and he helped himself to a drink before reaching for the phone. Which museum had held the display?

He rang the desk, obtained the number, punched it and waited listening to the soft barring of the phone at the other end. Either the place was closed or no incoming calls were being received. NASA? This time someone answered.

'Yes?'

'I'm Professor Malcolm Spragg attached to the UN. I need to contact Mrs Irene Fiander on an important matter. She works for you arranging Voyager displays in museums and such. She was here in New York but has moved on. Where can I find her?'

A pause then, 'I'm sorry, mister, but the office staff has all left. Why not try again tomorrow?'

A click and his life was over. It had been over since Myrna had met Irene and hit her where it hurt the most. No matter what he said now it would be impossible to repair the damage. She would expect him to remain with his mistress and the coming child.

The liar!

Crystal shattered as he flung the glass at the wall, wishing it had landed in Myrna's face so as to ruin her scheming, deceptive beauty.

The phone demanded attention.

It was Ogden and Spragg listened as the man congratulated him on his performance at the UN. 'Now, tomorrow I want –'

'No. You don't need me and I'm sick of facing all those pimp-politicians. I'm a scientist and I want to get to work. Send me to Cape Canaveral. That's where the action is. I want to go there. I mean it.' Spragg listened, frowning, 'All right, I'll be your eyes and ears. When do I leave?'

He hung up and sat sipping from the bottle and looking at the mark his glass had made against the wall. After a while it began to look like a face, a series of faces.

Someone knocked twice at his door during the night but he ignored it both times.

CHAPTER 13

After the siren came a moment of silence, then out on the sands a giant bellowed into life. Its voice was thunder and its breath was flame; a spouting fire lengthening as it rose to challenge the sun.

From the box of the speaker the comptroller's voice held a mechanical flatness. 'Launch Charlie 4B7 a hit.'

Spragg relaxed, sharing in the victory. Another one on its way into orbit there to be robbed of its load and maybe cannibalised for materials. Or maybe not, the coding system used was meaningless to any not closely involved with the launching. Charlie could be of the series designed for re-entry, salvage and further use. As Baker could have been the now obsolete space shuttles and therefore expendable.

'Area clear!'

The area, maybe, but not the ether. Spragg frowned at the screen set before him on the desk. The original image relayed down from the International Space Station was distorted by a mass of flecks and wavering lines caused by the electronic 'noise' of the launch. Given time it would clear but it was a gamble whether or not another crew could get another launch readied before it did. Not that it mattered – his work was done.

Spragg leaned back, palming his eyes. Figures danced on his retinas, the imaginary notations made a thousand times by his subconscious even as they were forwarded to be fed into the computers. The machines could do the sums but it took eyes and a brain to determine the original elements of the equations. But to continue now with his dulled vision and concentration would be to do more harm than good. It was time for him to quit.

Rising, he went to the toilet where he washed face and hands, drying both on a paper towel as he studied his ravaged reflection in a mirror. The past weeks had left their mark. Work, he thought. Once I could take it. Now resiliency had vanished with his youth.

He made his way outside. The air struck chill after the warmed interior of the bunker. Drawing a deep breath he looked around.

Cape Canaveral was a madhouse of men and machines, a scene of frantic, nonstop activity, which had swallowed him as water does a stone. Provided with accommodation, a place to work and duties to perform he had become a part of an army fighting a war against time with progress marked by the vessels that rose into space. And, if not all his duties were concerned with astronomy, then who was he to complain?

He turned as sirens wailed to see a convoy of chemical-carriers heading to where a slender shape stood silhouetted against the sky. Adorned with flashing lights and wreathed in vapour from their frozen, liquid contents the vehicles looked like strange and alien beasts from a fevered delirium. As did the teams already cooling down the area of the recent launch. As did the others, armed and protected who stood beside ominous containers set on low-slung carriers bearing flaring symbols of universal recognition.

Unconsciously Spragg glanced up at the sky. If atomic material was being sent up then the basic programme was keeping to schedule. Or, perhaps, to save time a little was being sent up with each load. That made sense in a way, providing all precautions were being taken and he felt a sharp sympathy for those above and the work they had to do. Compared to it, Hell itself would have been a playground.

'Mal!'

Spragg turned, smiling as he saw Bud Aldcock. The man belied his appearance and had turned out to be a good companion and friend. His association with the religious fanatic had, he'd explained, been the result of a false line of logic.

'She kept preaching love, so I thought I'd give it a try. Well, maybe I moved too fast – she damned near took out an eye! Hell, no woman's worth that kind of grief.'

Now he said, 'How many is that to date, Mal?'

'God knows.' Spragg glanced towards the telemetering section of the bunkers. 'Why not ask the boys who should know?'

The section was never idle, always there were men monitoring the launches from other sites; New Mexico, the three in Russia and now, it appeared, one in China.

'They're firing from Wenchow,' explained a man with a dark face seamed with scars. 'Making good time, too, but they insist on playing it cagey. I guess they don't want us to know if they lose a few in the Pacific. The big worry is the way they're going at it. Two at a time and three launches last week. Why the hell can't they tie in with the general pattern?'

'Probably a matter of face,' said one of the others. 'I read a book about it once. It's all to do with honour or something.'

'That was before the revolution.' The dark man turned to check his screen. 'They don't put so much stock in it now. Even so –' His voice broke into a shout. 'Christ! Fred! Joe! Get on the boards! Max – get in touch with general control. The Chinese have got a wild one!'

A vessel off-course, its telemetry unbalanced or absent for the sake of fuel economy. Spragg watched as the technicians ran to their stations, voices rapping as they swept into action.

'Check the original flight plan. Find initial thrust, duration of burn, shedding of boosters if any.' A moment while voices blurred from the speakers as questions reached across the globe. 'Anyone know what a Mao is?'

'Which model? The first was a converted ICBM. They ripped out the telemetry, added boosters and settled for a small payload.' The speaker added, dryly, 'I guess they must have improved things since then.'

'Not enough.' The dark man frowned as he studied his board. 'It's heading towards sector 14.'

'That's right. Check on ETA and get hold of the poor bastard in charge of that sector and warn him trouble is on the way.'

His name was Gus Easton and he was an Angel. He had wanted to be a pilot but events had moved faster than anticipated and, suddenly, he found himself circling the Earth in free fall. Others were with him, living in a circular tin can that revolved fast enough to draw vomit down to the floor and supplied enough artificial gravity to dispense with the need for air-circulators. A bunch of raw kids, half of whom would die before they had learned how to live in their new environment. And learning, of necessity, had to be fast

They slept to wake and ride up to the long axis and pass out through the airlock to where their ships hung waiting. But first they had to suit up and check seals and tanks and radios, lifelines and reaction pistols and filters, magnetic grapnels and internal plumbing. All with good reason. It was distracting and therefore dangerous to work in a suit awash with waste products. It was hard to manoeuvre without a reaction pistol or the grapnels. It was more than hard to see with eyes seared by unshielded sunlight and impossible to breathe without air. Things they learned if they hoped to live.

Gus Easton was a veteran of nine solid weeks and was oldest in terms of experience of his bunch. That put him in charge until he died or went plain crazy when the next senior in experience would take over. It was a system that offered no hope and no reward but it was one they were stuck with. As they were stuck in space until the job was done.

'Let's get on with it.' Gus spoke into his radio. 'Let's hear you check.' He listened to the babble of a dozen voices. They were open shells fitted with powerful rocket engines, buffers, electro-magnets, lines hooks and eyes. Three men sat in each. Two of each of the three were operating hands while the third guided the craft. He was also in command of the squad. Gus was the exception in that he had delegated the driving seat to another and thus was free to concentrate on the overall situation.

Now he said over the radio, 'Right. Spread out in normal pattern. Don't move until I give the word.'

The first time in space he had almost died because he had trusted his eyes. Against the background of space things lost their relation to each other and distances became confused. Against the blue-white orb of the planet it wasn't so bad but the Earth itself held a strange and hypnotic charm. With the sun in the background things came darkened by the shields and could hit before anticipated.

And yet the environment held a strange charm and eerie majesty. Bright and harshly clear with the stars like jewels and the drifting motion of free-fall giving the impression of utter freedom of movement. A poetic image over which those on Earth could muse knowing nothing of the ache and pain of muscles and joints trying to adapt to zero gravity while subjected to sudden and relatively tremendous strains. Of the raw sores caused by the chafing of the suits. The general discomfort of life as an Angel.

'Is that it, Gus?'

'Where?' Gus narrowed his eyes as his driver pointed. 'Maybe. Keep it under observation.' Then, remembering, he added to the third man, 'You too, Sam.'

Sam Meillion, young, eager, too careless for his own good. As yet he still woke with a smile, cracked jokes, could pass urine without pain and enjoyed regular bowel-movements. Another few days, a couple of weeks, say, and that would change. He'd learn he had kidneys and that paste was a bad substitute for food. His eyes would play up and his skin get a scaly feel. He'd start to lose hair and he'd carry permanent bruises. But, if he managed to live long enough, he'd get promotion, extra pay and a medal.

'There, Gus! There!'

Hard against the blue-white swirl came a rising black shape. It lifted as if in a dream, rising, slowing as it rose, the markings now plain.

'In!' Gus rapped the order. 'Steady! Fasten and withdraw!'

Orders repeated every time they made a catch. The slowness was deceptive, relative only to themselves, but the Charlie could be a little off and to ignore the possibility was dangerous.

'Wonder what it's carrying? Candy, I hope.'

That was Hayes with his goddamned sweet tooth. He sent his ship in even as he spoke but he was both cautious and clever. He rode close, one of his crew attaching a line, the other waiting before springing abroad. A panel lifted and the others closed in.

'Any supplies?' They were getting low on water and air. They were always conscious of the air. 'Move it!' Gus let his irritation show. 'You think it's Christmas and this a gift from Daddy?'

An unwise remark and he regretted it. A thing like that could set a man off and trigger a lurking insanity. He could try and make it back home in the returning Charlie – one of the commonest ways Angels did a dutch.

'All right now,' he said, mollifying his tone. 'Let's get this stuff where it should go and get back to the sack.'

Most of it went into orbit with the rest. The supplies were taken to where the drum-like living quarters revolved like a battered beer can. The stuff in orbit would circle where it was put aside from minor drifting which could be taken care of on regular inspections. Later the engineers would come to assemble it and build what the hell it was supposed to be. Certain items, clearly marked and both small and compact, were placed well apart from each other.

'That's it!' Sam Meillion was cheerful. 'You want me to send it down, Gus?'

'Wait, I –' Gus broke off as his earphones jarred. 'Jesus Christ! We've a wild one coming up! Scatter!'

The usual response to potential danger – if one went there was no need for others to follow. Gus waited, listening, grunting as he saw the uprising shape.

'I've got it. The rest of you stand by. I'll take this one myself.'

The penalty of command as he understood it. To take on any unanticipated or unexpected danger. Hayes chuckled as the thing came closer.

'A Chinese, eh? They could have fortune cookies inside. Or some chow mein or maybe a couple of those Geisha girls.'

'Shut up!' Gus roared into his mike. 'Keep your traps shut or I'll gut you!' From his tone they knew he meant it. To his driver he said, 'Watch it now, Ken.'

'I'm watching.' The ship moved a little as gas flared from its vent. The Chinese vessel, now close, came even closer. Another touch of the controls and the ship matched velocity then edged for contact. 'How's that?'

'Too damned close!' Gus gauged distance, time, the vectors of relative motion. 'Don't hit!'

Sam Meillion decided to take a hand. The ship was within reach of the Chinese vessel, running apparently neck and neck, and there was a convenient projection. It would be a simple matter to reach out, grab hold, and bring the two craft together.

He reached out, grabbed – and the discharge of opposed electrical potentials which Gus had feared arched to fuse the gloved hand to the projection. The relative motion had been deceptive and the Chinese vessel, travelling faster, ripped the arm from the socket and spilled both air from the suit and life from the body. In effect the dead Angel had tried to form a living bridge between a railway express and a not quite as fast automobile.

'Gus!'

'He's dead!' Easton swore as the body sprayed his helmet with globules of blood. He threw it aside and it hit the driver, who, trying to avoid it, hit the controls. The vent flared into life and sent the ship slamming into the body of the strange vessel. Weakened metal yielded and exposed familiar shapes. 'Christ! Nukes!'

The detonation was a smear of light in the firmament, a touch of angry colour gone as soon as spotted. Spragg watched it from his place in the bunker and knew before the dark man spoke what must have happened.

'Easton's bought it. He tried to keep the Chinese nukes apart from the others but he couldn't manage it. A few got together and –' The flapping motions of his hands was expressive. 'Critical mass and blooie!'

'The others?'

'The rest of his Angels escaped the initial blast. We asked them if they wanted anything and they said booze and blondes.'

Consolations to men who knew they were doomed to die from the effects of the radiation that had blasted the area. The first they would get together with pills to make the ending painless, but Spragg doubted the second. Not for want of mercy or a desire to please but a woman needed food, water and air. She needed fuel to lift her and could take the place of essential warheads. And even the most willing sacrifice would hesitate knowing it would have to be a one-way trip.

On the ground, here at Canaveral, it was different. Life had taken on the peculiar aspect of a city under siege rather like the camaraderie of the war years in London when the city had been the target of Nazi bombs. People had gained something then as now. A common purpose as strong as a common misfortune. Knowing the truth, realising the importance of time, they had shed reserve. Women, in particular, had reacted in a positive manner.

Spragg left the bunker thinking of Angels. Not the kind found in religious testimony but of those so aptly named young men circling the Earth in the zero gravity of free fall. Falling, always falling and yet never to land. As Lucifer had fallen for an eternity before claiming the world as his own. Those above would not fall as long and would never be in any physical condition to claim anything but a plot of ground and a headstone. And even for that they would have to rely on the good graces of the living.

A sombre thought he could have done without. His fatigue had returned with bone-aching force and yet he knew he wouldn't be able to sleep. Not until he'd taken something to quieten the teeming activity of his mind, the figures that danced to form equations that mocked every effort they could make.

To Bud Aldcock he said, 'Coming for a drink?'

'Love to, but I'm on duty. See you later.'

A wave and he was gone and, alone, Spragg made his way to the prefabricated hut that served to provide recreation to those in his category. It was set with a bar and typical tavern games. Tables and chairs were scattered about. A pretence had been made to give visiting politicians the impression that it catered to a high level of intelligence but, basically, what the club supplied and what the scientists did was drink.

Harry Frazer waved to Spragg as he entered the hut. The man was another of those he had met at Waldemar's party but Carl himself was not to be seen and neither was Frieda. Both were probably engaged in their own ways; Carl busy with his liaison duties and Frieda tending her computers.

'Hi, Mal, have a drink?'

'Thanks – a big one.'

Harry carried the glass to a table and sat down with his own drink. 'A bad thing up there. You know about it?'

'I was in the bunker when it happened.'

'Those poor bastards!' Harry drank deeply.

Spragg took a swallow of his own drink. The hut had been decorated with scraps of green and silver, some paper-chains, bunches of dyed grass, fronds and shreds of cooking foil – all the traditional garnish of the Christmas Festival. At the far end a group of women in WAC uniform were busy setting up a wire and paper tree. Others wearing civilian clothing mingled with the scientists. One of them, a striking blonde, smiled as she looked at Spragg.

'Anne Roberts,' said Frazer. 'A nurse over at the hospital. She's off duty. A nice girl – she does her best to help out in any way she can. You're lucky. She seems to like you.'

Spragg looked at her with new interest. He knew of the new morality that many women had adopted and the advantages it gave to those who needed to relax after arduous spells of duty. As a nurse Anne would recognise the signs sooner than most. Was that why she had smiled? Did his face bear the reflection of the torment of his mind?

His eyes followed her as she moved on to stand and talk to a balding technician seated with two computer-men.

He drank and set down the empty glass and called for more then, because the bartender was busy, rose to fetch his own.

Pete blinked at his demand. 'A bottle? Hell, Professor, you know it's against the regulations to take booze out of the club.'

'Army regulations. Forget them. I'm a civilian.'

'I'm not. And this is government property. And we're all under military jurisdiction.'

'NASA too?'

'Everyone and everything.' Pete leaned forward. 'If I slip you a pint will you keep it under cover?' He grinned as Spragg nodded. 'It'll cost.'

'So you make a profit. Pass it over.' Spragg tucked the flat bottle inside his belt, loaded a couple of glasses with ice and carried them back to the table where Frazer was sitting staring gloomily at the WACs setting up the tree. 'Here, Harry! Help yourself.'

'Thanks.' Frazer poured himself a stiff drink, held it, still looking at the group. 'We go on, Mal,' he mused. 'At least some of us do.'

The lucky ones, those not drifting in space or lying in hospital wards muttering under masking bandages, bodies scarred with oozing sores. The Angels and the heroes burned by leaking chemicals, seared by the chill of frozen gases; the oxygen and hydrogen, the nitric acid vapour, the fluorine and other products of the Devil's laboratory.

The hospital was filled with the technicians who primed the vessels and those who handled the stores and equipment, men broken, bruised, crushed, blinded – sacrifices to the need for speed which forced the cutting of corners and the neglecting of safety precautions. And others who had also lost their gambles; men with falling hair and wasting blood, dead and knowing it but still aware, still able to feel. Companions of the dying Angels and from the same cause but they, at least, wouldn't die alone.

Would they end it all with a pill? Would he? Would he drink himself stupid or would he just carry on until the moment came when he couldn't lift a hand or move a muscle?

'Professor Spragg?' Anne smiled down at him as he looked up. Introducing herself she said, 'I've often wanted to meet you.'

'Why? Because I'm the original Prophet of Doom?' He was being unfair. 'Sorry, care for a drink?'

The bottle was empty and he stared at it as Frazer went to fetch drinks from the bar, setting them down to discreetly vanish. A true friend.

Anne said, 'You're thinking of those Angels, aren't you? You shouldn't.'

'No,' said Spragg. 'You're right. Let the dead bury the dead – or is it dust to dust?' He blinked as he reached for his glass. 'Are you a philosopher?'

'A nurse.'

'Well, nurse, diagnose my condition.'

'You're tired and suffering from toxin-poison due to accumulated fatigue. The tiredness is affecting your coordination and I'd take a bet your vision is blurred. You feel cold and yet have a tendency to sweat. When you close your eyes you see retinal flashes. You also experience an anxiety syndrome, affecting your mental concentration. You are beginning to doubt yourself and have a tendency to check things more than once. And you brood.'

Over Irene and why he hadn't heard from her though it would be a miracle if he did. He must ask Carl to try and locate her. Or Ogden, the man had means at his disposal and should be able to find out exactly where she was and what she was doing –

'Angels,' he said, and giggled. 'Hundreds of them riding round and round the Earth. The Americans and the French and English and Russian and Chinese and the rest, all wheeling in an eternal circle. Dead eyes watching – always watching –' He straightened meeting her watchful blue eyes. 'You forgot something in your diagnosis, nurse. You forgot to mention that I'm more than a little drunk ...'

He fell, hitting the table, sending his glass to crash on the floor. He toppled and slowly fell after it, eyes open, fully aware, seeming to drift as he fell the journey extended by a peculiar slowing of time so that he could think of a scatter of things while suspended between chair and floor; Anne, the WACs and their tree, the faces looking down at him, the crack in the ceiling of the hut, the glare of the light which was like a sun. A sun that died as he landed.

CHAPTER 14

Christmas came with a plethora of useless gifts; stones wrapped in gay paper, pens, corks, empty bottles with lewd suggestions, a dead rat – all the rubbish available which could be wrapped and handed over and laughed at when unwrapped. A distortion of the festive motive matched by the atmosphere in the club, a grim, death-house humour reminiscent of the ancient Saturnalia when the world was turned upside down and the master became the slave as the slave aped the master.

'Hail!' Pete had been elected and stood by the tree dressed in red and white finery. A bowl of punch stood on a table and he greeted each man and woman as they came to partake of the libation. 'Hail!'

Hail and farewell for we who meet today may never meet again. The unspoken meaning of the greeting and they drank and ate the little cakes and sandwiches and tried to ignore the throbbing of released giants.

Spragg had avoided the club since he had fallen down drunk to wake in his room with a throbbing head. He had remembered to eat and done his best to sleep. The following days had done little to restore his lost energy but, at least, he could close his eyes and not see the damned, dancing figures.

'Mal!' Waldemar came towards him. 'Merry Christmas!' He beamed at the terse answer. 'That's the trouble with you pagans, you have no respect for orthodox festivals.'

'Christmas is a pagan festival. The Christians stole it and adapted it to suit their own purposes.'

Waldemar shrugged, smiling. 'If you want to argue theology, my friend, you'll have to talk to the Chaplain. Me? I've other things to do.'

Entertaining certain visitors who had come to bless the occasion with their presence. Spragg had seen them when they'd been given the guided tour; stars of the entertainment world eager for free publicity.

'You don't like them?' Waldemar had seen his expression. 'Well, neither do I, but they have to be tolerated. The world goes on, Mal.'

'I know.' An election could be due and politicians had a liking for getting all the help they could in order to stay in power. The razzamatazz of show business was shared by entertainers and seekers after public office alike. 'Trouble?'

'Nothing that can't be handled with a little assistance. Are you willing to give a hand?'

Spragg looked over the crowd assembled in the hut. Frieda was absent as was Frazer, both probably with their heads together on some last-minute calculation. Bud Aldcock was standing with his head close to the dark curls of a vivacious WAC. Others with whom he had struck up an acquaintance were engrossed in their own pursuits. As good a time as any to leave.

'It won't take long,' urged Waldemar. 'They are to visit the hospital and get photographed and learn enough so to be able to make some more or less intelligent comments when questioned about Thor. You'll be free in plenty of time for dinner tonight.' He added, 'And you'll like Vivian.'

Most men liked Vivian Dawn. She had cultivated a sensuous style, an air of subtle decadence.

Smiling, she said, 'So you are the great Professor Spragg. I've heard so much about you. You must be very religious to have summoned the Hammer of God.'

'Did I?'

'That's what some people are saying. But people will say anything. They even hint that the President and I have an intimate relationship. Have you met him? A wonderful man, Mal. One of the world's greats. Tony, come and meet the Prophet of Doom.'

Tony Inch, tall, dark, swarthy, a golden chain around his neck and heavy gold rings on his fingers. He stank of masculine perfume and his clothing was the latest thing in expensive bad taste. He nodded, scowling – it was a part of his public image.

Spragg nodded back and was introduced to the rest of the party. One of them, a pop singer with sunken cheeks, said, 'Let's lay it on the line, Prof. Is this the real thing or is the public being ripped off? Come on, man, give it to us straight.'

The man was high on something or had just taken too much Christmas spirit. Spragg looked at the hovering photographers, all eager to get a few juicy shots.

'Krag, don't be rude.' The other woman in the party gripped his arm. 'He's got a thing about being robbed,' she explained. 'Ever since his first agent ran out and left him with a pile of bills and no money. But I guess we're all curious as to what's really going on. I mean, if all we need to do is to shoot atomic missiles at Thor why not do it from the ground?'

Patiently Spragg explained about the number of movement vectors involved, ending, 'Once we have completed the launching platform in space we will have eliminated the most troublesome part of the problem. We shall still be accompanying the Earth around the sun and still be affected by the galactic drift but we shall be free of the initial rotational spin together with all the problems associated with the atmosphere such as winds, storms, varying densities and so on. Think of the orbital launcher as a gun platform and you'll get a better grasp of what we need to do. Obviously the first thing is to build it.'

'Which is why you're shooting all this stuff up into orbit?'

'Yes.' Spragg remembered to smile. 'Any missiles we fired from the ground would have to fight their way up through Earth's gravity well. That takes a lot of fuel, which means a smaller load, which means, in turn, more missiles. They would have to be aimed but any deflection would be great. They would simply miss the target. So we'd have to incorporate guidance systems in their construction – telemetry. That means more weight and so more fuel and so on. But the Earth is rotating so to keep the missiles under constant supervision we'd have to relay signals via an orbiting satellite. So why not just use the satellite in the first place?'

A question unanswered. Spragg wondered if they had understood anything of what he'd been saying. Vivian surprised him.

'I follow that, Mal, but Alex here has a point.' She gestured to an attendant shadow. 'Why not just adapt ICBMs?'

'They're simply not designed for the job. Intercontinental Ballistic Missiles are like giant artillery shells. They're obsolete now as it happens but most people remember them. They're aimed, fired, they rise until their fuel is exhausted then they reach the top of their trajectory and begin to fall on the target. To make them rise higher we must provide more fuel. That means extra tanks or engines – a booster system. We might just be able to get them into orbit but they wouldn't be able to carry a load.'

'So they're useless?'

'On the contrary and it's another reason for building the launching platform. We can use them once they're in space. So we send them up and they're taken apart and adapted and fitted with warheads and made ready to go.'

'When?' Krag had been silent for too long. 'What the hell are we waiting for? If that damned rock is coming why not shoot at it now?'

'Yes, Mal,' said Vivian. 'Why not?'

She moved close to his side and he felt the soft touch of her hand on his arm and smelt her subtle perfume which hinted at depraved sophistication. 'Is there a reason you can't shoot now?'

'Distance,' said Spragg. 'Thor is small and a long way away. Relatively small, that is, but still too far to be hit.'

'Why?' The woman was shrewd. 'If we could send the Voyagers out there and aim them then why not missiles?'

He said, 'Those probes took years to reach the Jovian system. They were moving relatively slowly and there was plenty of time to relay instructions. This doesn't apply to the present situation. It is a matter of relative velocities and, well, there is really no comparison.'

'Meaning it was a dumb question?' Krag glared his anger. 'Listen, you egg-headed creep, no one is going to insult her while I'm around.'

'Then piss off!'

'What?' The sunken cheeks flushed with anger. 'Why, you –'

'Wait!' Spragg backed as the man advanced, fist raised. 'I didn't –'

He went down as bunched knuckles slammed against his jaw.

Outside the hospital a military band was determinedly playing Christmas carols as the nurse deftly treated Spragg's face. Watching her at work Carl Waldemar said, 'What the hell came over you, Mal? Why insult the man? I can understand you not liking him but to tell him that in public was stupid –'

'I know.' Spragg gingerly touched his jaw. The bone was unbroken but the flesh was bruised and a ring had lacerated the skin. 'I didn't realise I'd spoken aloud.' She had mentioned the Voyagers, which had reminded him of Irene and made him suddenly impatient with the whole stupid exercise in public relations. Well, Krag had got his publicity and Vivian her excitement.

Anne Roberts said, 'The bone must be bruised and the blow could have triggered off a delicate tooth-nerve. I'll get you something to take care of the discomfort.'

Spragg looked at Waldemar as she left the small treatment-room. Outside the band was still playing. Over the din he said, 'Any news, Carl?'

'No.'

'Damn it, man, she couldn't just vanish! Did you contact NASA?'

'Of course, but she has quit their employ.' Waldemar shook his head. 'Mal, my friend, I know what Irene means to you. But from what you told me I know how badly she has been hurt. People are like animals at such times, they want to run and hide and gain time for their injuries to heal. That, I think, is what she has done.'

'And Myrna?'

'She has left Madam Kuluva and is now under the protection of a colonel in the American Army who is giving her a conducted tour of the West Coast.' Waldemar added, delicately, 'He is far from being a young man.'

Which could explain his attraction. She had always preferred the father-figure which was probably why she had left Boris. Now she was probably living high with her reefers and drugs and drinks and stimulating experiences.

'You'll keep looking?'

'For Irene? Of course, my friend.' Waldemar rose from where he sat. 'And now I must see to our honoured guests. They should be ready to leave now. Have you a word you wish me to convey to your adversary?' He smiled as he heard it.

As he left the strains of 'Jingle Bells' played an accompaniment to the throb of Spragg's aching jaw. The nurse returned as it ended and he watched the neat movements of her body as she crossed to the faucet to fill a glass with water. He felt as if he knew her but couldn't remember having seen her before.

Approaching him, the glass in one hand, pills in the other, she said, 'Have you been drinking?'

'A little punch. No hard stuff.'

'These don't go too well with alcohol.' She placed three of the tablets in his hand. They were large; white flecked with green. Handing him the water she said, 'Get them down.'

He coughed when finally he had obeyed. 'What were they?'

'Something strong we use for special cases. I guessed you wouldn't have enjoyed an aching jaw and teeth over Christmas.'

'You were right, thanks.' He relaxed, already the pain had almost vanished. 'Can I drink later?'

'If you're careful but I'd advise you to go easy on the Scotch.'

He caught the ironic tone and stared at her, really seeing her for the first time. She looked different in uniform.

'I know you,' he said. 'Anne Roberts, isn't it? We met at the club about a week ago when –'

'You were suffering from strain and accumulated tension.'

'And I got drunk and passed out. What happened? Did you call for help and have me put to bed?' He frowned, trying to remember, but the entire incident was a blank.

'You just needed to forget, Mal. It's a common syndrome and nothing to worry about. In a sense your overloaded psyche blew a fuse in order to make you rest.' Quietly she added, 'Do you always blame yourself when anything goes wrong?'

He said, 'You're talking about guilt.'

'That accident wasn't your fault. You only announced the discovery of Thor. You didn't create it. You aren't really the Prophet of Doom announcing the coming of the Hammer of God.'

He said, tightly, 'I'm sick to the stomach with hearing that stupid title.'

'I won't use it again. I promise. Feel better now?'

'Yes.'

'Like to see where I work?'

Dutifully he followed her from the room and down the long passage to the wards and their contents of assorted misery.

Night fell with a chill wind from the sea. Inside the club the debris of earlier festivities had been cleared away and the floor readied for dancing. The bar was fully stocked. Food was heaped on platters decorated with paper-lace fringes.

Spragg found himself a glass and, remembering Anne's warning, took only beer. Sipping it he thought of the nurse, wishing she was here with him now instead of having only half-promised to join him later.

Finishing the beer, he rose to get another. Turning, he bumped into a softly yielding figure.

'Herr Professor!' Frieda dabbed at her shoulder now wet with beer. She wore a party dress of some shimmering green material and what with skilfully applied make-up and neatly dressed hair looked far younger than her age. 'Are you well?'

'I'm not drunk if that's what you mean.' Spragg found his handkerchief and wiped at the damp patch. 'Sorry about that. Can I get you something?'

'A large vodka and tonic please.'

On impulse Spragg ordered two, dumping his beer and carrying both glasses high as he edged from the bar. Frieda took hers and sipped with the delicate precision of a cat.

'I looked for you earlier,' said Spragg. 'Harry too but I guess you were both busy. Cheers!'

They drank and she said, 'Harry and I are working on flight computations. We are establishing various formulas based on a variety of load and velocity factors. As yet they are preliminary figures but will save time when we have access to more definitive data.'

'And? Surely you haven't been working all the time?'

'No.' She took another sip of her drink. 'Herr Frazer is a very accomplished man.'

In more ways than one, Spragg guessed, but kept the thought to himself. Frieda had dressed in her best for a purpose and he knew it wasn't himself.

'And you, Herr Professor? Have you anything new on our visitor?'

'A little. Velocity shows a slight increase as we anticipated. It has to be due to solar attraction but will fall as the conjunction of Mars and Jupiter takes effect. The latest determination of the diameter shows a slight increase over previous estimates – the figures are available when you want them.'

'Later.'

'Of course – I didn't mean right this minute. But Harry will need them in order to make his preliminary assessments. Is he coming to the party?'

'Yes. He will be here soon.'

And would be certain of a welcome. Thinking about it made Spragg think of Anne. Waiting for her was becoming a strain. It would be best to walk down to the hospital and see if she'd managed to get free.

Spragg finished his drink and took his leave of Frieda as she was joined by other colleagues and admirers. Outside the chill stung face and hands and he stood a moment looking at the sky. Over the sea the stars hung in brilliant splendour accentuated by the misty fuzz of nebulae smeared like glowing curtains over the secret chambers of creation. A sight that always caught at his heart.

'Mal?' The voice was low, familiar. 'Mal, is that you?'

'Anne!' He turned and stepped towards her, closing the distance between them with quick, impatient strides to catch her hands and hold them as his eyes drank her face, her hair. Her perfume was of roses and she wore a long nurse's cape beneath which something white glimmered in the starlight. 'I'm glad you could make it,' he said. 'So very glad.'

She smiled at him then looked up at the sky. 'You were watching,' she said. 'Thor?'

'It's too far away to be seen as yet.'

'But you know where it is?' She followed his arm as, releasing her hands, he pointed at the sky. 'And I could see it with a telescope?'

'Yes – if you knew just where to look.'

Anne said, 'Do you want to join the party?'

'Not really.' What he wanted was to take her, to hold her and to find what happiness he could in the circle of her arms. A wish that grew to a need even as he thought of it. 'I just want to be with you.'

'And I with you,' she said. 'So why don't we go somewhere where we can be alone?'

So this was how it happened, he thought. The direct invitation divorced of any subterfuge. 'Where?'

'I have a place –' She broke off as he shook his head. 'No?'

'No.' It would be full of the presence of others – the small things previous visitors would have left behind in a subconscious desire to stake territorial rights or to provide an excuse for a return visit. And even if the objects were out of sight the walls would know, the floor, the bed itself. 'Let's use mine.'

'Mal?' She rose a little to look down into his face. 'You asleep?'

'No.'

'Good. Feel better now?'

'Thanks to you, yes.'

'I'm glad.' Relaxing, she ran her hand over his chest. 'Man! Were you all strung up!'

A nurse – was this how it was done? To take a man on the edge of nervous breakdown and stimulate him with the sight of pain and drug him and then give him the opportunity to release all his tensions in a furious burst of sexual activity?

Turning his head, he looked into the face so close to his own. It was still beautiful but now something had been added to the eyes.

Abruptly, she said, 'When, Mal?'

'Thor?' They had been talking of his discovery. He thought he knew what she wanted to know. 'It will arrive in April. You know the date.'

'The 11th, but that's not what I meant. When will you be certain whether it's going to hit or not?'

'I'm certain now. We're going to blast it into a deflected orbit with nuclear devices. You know that.'

'I know that's what everyone keeps saying.'

'Then believe it. Thor will be turned aside. We either defect it or blast it into dust and in either case it won't be able to harm us. You have absolutely –' He broke off as she rested her hand over his mouth. 'Anne?'

'Don't lie to me, Mal, I'm too good at my job for that. Patients lie all the time. And I'm not a child. Now I'll ask you again – when? Not when Thor is due to hit but when will you be certain whether it will or not?'

'We can't be sure as yet,' he admitted. 'Maybe ten days.'

'Ten days,' she said thoughtfully. 'Call it April 1st. All Fool's Day – and God help the poor fools if Thor can't be stopped. Mal!'

Her hands had begun to tremble, her body, as like a child she moved into his arms. And now it was his turn to give comfort.

CHAPTER 15

New Year came and was over and the 100-day countdown began. As if flinching at an anticipated blow the Earth showed signs of unease; earthquakes created havoc in Turkey and China, a volcano erupted in Brazil and a tsunami inundated several islands of the Melanesian group. Items that provided up to the minute news for the media as did the spate of industrial unrest sweeping the more liberal countries.

A bell sounded the ending of the break and Spragg rose with the others as they filed from the room. It was a bleak enough place with its tables and chairs, dispensing machines serving a variety of non-alcoholic drinks and weary sandwiches and pastries, but it was a place of refuge in which all shoptalk was banned. A place to rest a while and sip apologies for coffee and tea and to pretend for a while that God was in his Heaven and all was right in the world.

In another chamber the figures were waiting.

They rested on sheaves of paper spilled from computer terminals, glowed on the displays, twined in elaborate patterns on pads but, most of all, they danced again in his mind. Endless figures, impact times and rendezvous times and the influence of solar and Lunar attraction and more.

Donald Lauter called them to order. He had recently joined the team and Spragg remembered him from when he had lectured at the Exposition. Now he stood at the end of the long table, tall and formal in his uniform, his tone quiet but penetrating. Behind him, on the wall, hung the pad of numbers they all hated to look at. Red on white and originally numbering 100 but now down to 94.

'Ladies! Gentlemen! Shall we proceed?' Lauter paused for a moment. 'As you may have learned I am now in full charge of this section of the project and would like to be given the latest developments. Naturally I have read your reports but I would like to hear from you personally. Professor Spragg? Would you care to begin?'

From where he sat Spragg said, 'Thor has displayed a slight oscillation revealed to us by a dark marking on the otherwise bright surface. The movement could be inherent in the mass, caused by gravitational influences, or more likely the result of residual forces gained from a previous impact. A flare was noted which, in a sense, signalled its arrival and this could have been caused by the impact of some small mass of debris from the asteroid belt or an unknown satellite of Jupiter. However the oscillation has no effect on either direction or velocity. Gravitational forces, which did combine to affect the velocity to a minor degree a few weeks ago have now levelled out. The alteration is minute but means that the previously estimated time of arrival must be advanced by 18 minutes 43 seconds.'

Lauter nodded his thanks. 'Doctor Osten?'

Frieda was little help. It all depended, as she pointed out, on her being given accurate data on which to work. The position of Thor was known together with its velocity. The position of Earth and the Moon also together with their speeds of motion. A relatively simple equation for her computers to solve. What wasn't so simple was to know the amount of nuclear material that would be needed to achieve the desired result, the time it should be launched, the velocity it needed to attain. A question of logistics, which Harry Frazer tried to answer.

'It's a question of maximum effectiveness,' he said after Frieda had ended. 'As yet we don't know the composition of Thor and we're only guessing when we say it's rock and nickel-iron. If it is, it's still one hell of a mass to deflect. The latest estimates put it at 585 miles in diameter and we haven't comparative figures to work with. The trick is to hit it just right and hard enough to do the job. The oscillation mentioned could help – we can time the blast so it will work in our favour. Frankly, Colonel, we can't tell you much more until you let us know how many ships you have and how much punch you can deliver. Tell us that and we'll tell you just when to leave, when to hit and when to duck.'

Lauter said, 'You'll have that information as soon as it's available. For now we need to agree on a target deadline. Any suggestions?'

The figures were familiar to them all. Thor would be 4,320,000 miles from Earth 10 days before the time of impact. To meet it at that distance missiles would have to be fired from the launching platform in good time to cover the distance before then just when depending on their velocity. There would also be a 24 second signal-delay due to the limitations of the speed of light. A long time between pressing a button and getting the desired response; double by the time it was relayed back to the operator. To allow Thor to approach closer would make the task of hitting it easier but of deflecting it harder. Somewhere there had to be an optimum time of attack.

Frazer said, 'How fast can the missiles go? I've some preliminary figures based on various fuel-load ratios but they can't be applied until we know just what is to carry which. I assume there's no standardisation?'

'You assume correctly.' Lauter was grim. 'We've had to use what we could get. We are sure of the performance of some units, of course, ours and the Russians, the British and French, but many others like the adapted ICBMs are something of a mystery. However we've a plan to take care of that. We intend to make up units of the same basic components. That means that all drives, fuel capacities and loads will be the same to the finest limits we can manage.'

'Tests?'

'We've only built one unit as yet but it shows great promise.'

Spragg said, 'Multiple units? With multiple engines?' He drew in his breath as Lauter nodded. 'That introduces a hell of a lot of variable factors. Get one Venturi out of alignment and the whole unit will be thrown off course. The guidance problem will be too great.'

Aldcock cleared his throat. 'Couldn't we do something about that? What if we sent out relay-vessels so as to cut down transmission times? Use those nearest Thor to make the final adjustments. Possible?'

'It could be done,' admitted Lauter. 'And would be if we had the time.'

But they had no time and they knew it. Even now the minutes were ticking away and tomorrow the numbers would be less on the wall and with the shrinking of time would come desperation.

'How then?' Aldcock wanted an answer. 'Mal's right in what he says about those units. One lousy jet working wrong and the thing will be useless and don't tell me the engines are fool-proof.' His voice rose a little. 'Figures. You ask for figures! Christ, we've worked on the figures until we're almost blind! What the hell are they good for without the men and machines?'

'We have them.'

'The machines?'

'The machines and the men,' said Lauter. 'Volunteers.'

They had to be that and they had to be crazy with that particular type of lunacy which makes men run into burning houses to rescue strangers or to take a chance on an unknown drug because someone had to or to do any of the million and one things which turns a man into something more than a walking, talking animal. Madmen as the Angels were, the engineers and Spragg wishing he could be one of them.

'Kamikaze,' said Aldcock. 'That bastard Lauter knew about them all the time. Letting me rave on about guidance systems and making a fool of myself. Living computers – can you beat it?'

Not with things of microchips and printed circuits and electronic blood. Not in the time available. Now flesh and bone and muscle had to take the place of snug but intricate components and men had one advantage instruments did not. They needed no 24-second response time. They would see and act with the speed of trained reflexes, which dispensed with the hampering need of thought. Young men, eager, dedicated – doomed to die and knowing it. Spragg wondered how they must feel.

Barry Dunne could have told him. Born in a black ghetto, he had used brains and physical courage to fight his way from the dead end of drink and drugs and crime to gain a degree and a place in his country's army. Later he had gained officer status and then, quite deliberately, had chosen to throw away his future.

'On your feet!' The instructor was a man of middle-height, a wide streak of grey running through dark, curly hair. His eyes were narrowed as if he'd looked too long at the sun. His left hand was missing. As the class rose he lifted it. 'Remember this. I lost it because I was stupid. I made a mistake. In space you usually make only one. That's why I'm teaching you. I'm lucky. Maybe some of it will rub off.' He paused. 'Any questions? No? Sit down!'

As they did the man beside him whispered, 'Hey, Barry, listen to that guy. What makes him so special?'

Dunne could have told him. The engineer was an engineer who'd worked with the Angels. The mistake he'd mentioned was in letting his hand get trapped and crushed between two segments of metal. The courage he hadn't spoken of had been to cut free with the help of a laser; the beam cauterising the wound as it had sealed the suit with a mess of molten metal and plastic. The luck he wanted to pass on had been to successfully ride a Charlie back down to Earth.

'You've got courage,' he said as the class settled. 'But having guts isn't enough. You're going to have to live alone in conditions you haven't dreamed of as yet. To live and work for days in the most hostile environment you can imagine. Today I'm talking about it. Tomorrow you'll start doing it. Have any of you ever worn a suit?'

A hand rose. 'I have, sir. Once when I volunteered for the Angels. They flunked me.'

'Why?'

'I couldn't breathe. They didn't give me time to adapt. I'd have managed well enough given a chance.'

'Out!' The instructor jerked his head. 'Wait in the outer room.' Thunder echoed as the man obeyed; the man-made roar of a rising vessel. As it died the instructor said, coldly, 'I'm booking that guy on a charge of wasting time. The way things are he'll get a month in the stockade. If any of you want to follow him out do it now. No charge and no penalty – just go.'

Dunne said, 'Why the difference, sir?'

'He knew he was unfit for the job but still went ahead. If you can't breathe in a suit you're no damned good for work in space. No crime and certainly nothing to be ashamed of but it has to be accepted. He wouldn't do that so I'm going to slap his wrist. Remember this. It isn't enough to be willing to die – you have to make dying worthwhile. Now let's talk about the basic components of a suit.'

He gave it to them straight using language anyone could understand, words chosen for their direct punch and register.

'You get tubes shoved up your rear and into your pecker. You want to pass water, you do it and it's collected in a bag. You want a crap and it's the same thing. You'll get cleared out before you get into the suit. You'll eat paste which contains almost no waste so there won't be any need for frequent motions.'

And there'd be bromides and amphetamines to keep them cheerful and other drugs to keep them awake and alert and some hypnotism to indoctrinate them against a last-minute change of heart. All the devices which could be thought of to turn warm-blooded, virile young men into coldly calculating machines.

Spragg watched them a couple of weeks later. Now they were suited and would remain so for increasing periods of time. In them they trained, sitting at instrument panels and moving controls to match one bright point with another. Doing it over and over until their reflexes reacted without the need for calculation or delay. Moving like the automatons they were training to become.

But they had consolation.

'I have to, Mal.' Anne stood unresisting in Spragg's arms as she explained. 'They need me so much.'

'So do I.' He tried to hold her close but felt her resistance and knew it was hopeless. She and those others like her knew their duty and would do it. As long as the volunteers needed relief they would provide it. 'Anne!'

'They have so little hope,' she whispered. 'And they are willing to die for us all.'

No hope at all and, willing or not, they would die. The very structure of their suits would see to that. A man could exist for only so long cooped up in the artificial environment and, if nothing else, their air would be limited as would their water and food. But it was more than that as Aldcock had said when he passed on the news.

'Built-in remotes, Mal! They offer to die and go ahead but still aren't trusted. They're sending out two to a unit and if one tries to change his mind they'll hit the button and blow his guts out. If that doesn't convince the survivor to play along they'll give it to him too.'

Insurance against human fragility as Anne was a reward for being a hero.

That night Spragg cried in his sleep as he dreamt of Irene.

On the 7th day before impact they saw Thor at close hand for the first time. A probe had been sent out long before and was now close to the planetoid. In the control room Spragg sat together with Aldcock, Lauter and others watching the relayed images transmitted by the television unit incorporated in the mechanism.

'Jesus!' Aldcock was impressed. 'Just look at that thing!'

Spragg was doing just that. Cameras were recording every moment and they would be played back and checked and rechecked for every scrap of obtainable information but, for now, he could sit and look and let his trained mind grasp the essentials of what the screen showed.

'It's strange,' a woman whispered 'Eerie and frighteningly alien.'

A thing that had come from the furthest reaches of the universe. Which had been warmed by the heat of unknown suns and had passed through clouds of interstellar dust. An intruder thrusting towards them like a giant fist clenched to hammer a planet into extinction.

'Albedo is fantastically high,' Spragg murmured. 'As originally suspected. The surface seems to be smoother than is normal if the composition is similar to an ordinary asteroid. Temperature?' He frowned as the man monitoring the reception gave the answer. 'So high?'

Space was an almost perfect vacuum with only drifting atoms of hydrogen and wide-spaced motes of dust found between the stars. An object moving at close to the speed of light could collect energy that would show itself in the form of heat by colliding with such debris but Thor was moving far too slowly for that. Then Spragg remembered the mysterious flare, which had caused, he thought, the dark spot on the otherwise bright surface. More evidence of a collision and the temperature level could be a sign of residual heat. Unless?

Aldcock voiced the thought. 'Could the damn thing be antimatter?'

If so they were doomed. Antimatter, the atoms set in reverse order to their own, would simply merge with and negate anything they could throw against it. Merging energy would be released in vicious flares of energy which would cancel the missiles and leave space full of flying, broken atoms, but which would leave the bulk of the planetoid intact. An imbalance that would leave Earth open to impact by the remainder.

Spragg didn't want to think of what would happen then.

'No.' Frazer shook his head as he studied the screen. 'If that was antimatter we'd have known by now. Stray atoms would be scintillating and that area is full of tiny meteors. A single hit and the flare would be unmistakable.'

'We had a flare,' said Aldcock. 'At the beginning, remember?'

'That could have been antimatter hitting Thor.' Frazer was stubborn. 'How about radiation emission?'

'It's there,' said the technician. 'But nothing too unusual.'

'Magnetic field?'

'Zero – but we're getting a pull of some kind.' He adjusted his controls. 'I've sent a signal for the probe to back off.'

Waiting, they watched as the image grew larger. The surface seemed to hold a shimmer as if composed of trillions of crystals glowing with the reflected light of the sun. Spragg watched the movement of the dark spot, measuring the oscillation. It seemed not to have changed from when he'd checked it before.

'I need information,' said Frazer. 'What's that thing made of? How can I make calculations without knowing its density? It could be ice for all we know. Hey, that'd be one for the book! The Hammer of God a bloody lollipop!'

Lauter said, sharply, 'That's enough! Concentrate on the job!'

Spragg said, trying to cool the tension, 'What was that you were saying about a pull? An attraction of some kind?'

'Just that,' said the technician. 'The probe is reacting as if it's near a respectable planetary mass. Yet a thing that size can't have a high gravitational field. It doesn't make sense.'

Not if Thor was composed of ordinary matter. Spragg leaned forward looking harder at the screen. 'Could that crystal-like coating be a patina covering lead? If so would such a mass of the heavy metal account for the pull?'

Frazer shook his head when he asked.

'Damned if I know, Mal, but the computers will give the answer. What they won't tell us is how could such a mass of pure metal be out there in the first place.' To the technician he said, 'Is this probe only equipped to scan? Hasn't it any testing apparatus?'

'Some.' The man was curt. 'It was designed to check Mercury and adapted in a hurry. We've got most of what it can relay.'

'Most? What's left?' Frazer bared his teeth at the reply. 'Aren't you a cute little fellow? Here I am beating out my brains for an analysis and your little toy is equipped to obtain a spectrogram. So why not get it?'

'I will when I'm ready. Do I tell you your job? Right. Don't tell me mine.' To Lauter he said, 'We're set when you give the word, Colonel. Where do you want me to test?'

Frazer said, quickly, 'The bulk is the more important factor. Aim anywhere but the dark patch.'

'The coating could be thin and therefore of little value,' said Lauter. The previous impact could have done some of our work for us.'

'Or left an untypical residue. Damn it, Colonel, who's the expert here? Hit the goddamn coating!'

'The patch!'

'Make up your minds!' yelled the technician. 'The probe's on its way out!'

Spragg watched as the man manipulated his controls, cursing the 3 minute signal-delay, the 6 minute total response time. On the screen the image veered, stars suddenly replacing the shimmering surface, the sudden glare of the naked sun. The probe, now rotating, was in the grip of invisible forces that negated all attempts to regain control from Earth.

'Damn!' Frazer stared at the screen, hands clenched, face contorted with rage. 'Damn! Damn! Damn!'

A frustration Spragg shared. They had left it too late. The spectrogram should have been obtained ten minutes ago while they still held the probe under their command.

'Now!' Lauter shouted as the glimmering surface came again into view. 'For Christ's sake, man, do something!'

Words weren't enough. The signal-delay made all attempts useless but the technician did his best. Grunting, he lowered his hands.

'That's it,' he said. 'If we're lucky. If I've guessed right we might get something but I warn you now the odds are against it. All we can do it wait.'

Wait as the signal flew at the speed of light towards the probe – 3 long minutes, then to wait again as long for the answering transmission to return. Wait as somewhere outside the hut, high in the air, a giant roared its fury.

'What the hell – ?' Frazer looked upwards. Like them all he had become accustomed to the sound for a regular lunch but this was different. 'Christ! It sounds like a bomb!'

It was a bomb and Spragg flung himself down as he heard the thin, shrilling whine of falling debris. Somewhere high about the complex a launch had gone wrong. The vessel had exploded, venting all its fuel in a savage gush of flame and sound, which sent the torn fragments of its construction and load hurtling to all sides to rain down like a mass of jagged shrapnel.

An accident which had been inevitable from the beginning and Spragg felt his bowels turn to water as the thin, chilling sounds came nearer, aimed directly at him so that he cringed and tried to press himself harder against the floor, to press beyond it into the ground below, the shielding dirt.

To wait, quivering, until the world collapsed in sound and fury.

CHAPTER 16

'Mal?' The face was a blur but he could see the glint of golden hair. 'Mal! Can you hear me? Mal!'

Fumes stung his nostrils and something stabbed at his arm and, suddenly, Spragg's vision cleared and he could see the woman at his side, the crisp uniform.

'Anne!'

'Of course. Who else did you expect would be here when you finally decided to wake up? How do you feel?'

'Lousy.'

'A launch missed out,' she said. 'It was heading straight out to sea when it exploded. Bits flew everywhere and the hut you were in was hit by a part of the main engine. The roof caved in and they dug you out from under it.' Pausing, she added, 'One of the tanks hit a hut in the enlisted men's sector. It still held fuel. The bulldozers are filling in the hole now.'

'The load?'

'Fuel, supplies, water, tanked air. The nuke was safe-loaded. They're looking for the segments now.'

'Anne –'

'You've nothing to worry about,' she said comfortingly. 'Some ribs broken, loss of blood, slight internal damage to lungs and liver, bruised pelvis, cracked bone in left leg, severe contusions to hips and stomach, multiple lacerations, concussion, shock and strained ligaments.'

'That all?'

'We had to remove a kidney. Don't worry – the other one is fine. All you need to do is lie there and rest for a few weeks. We've used the latest techniques and you're healing fast.'

He said, 'The others?'

Frazer, like himself, was in hospital but with relatively minor injuries. Lauter had lost an eye. Sam Harvey was in intensive care with a ruptured spleen. Aldcock had been lucky and had collected only bruises. Frieda had died on her way to the hospital.

Spragg thought about her when Anne had left and darkness signalled the coming of night. He ached but drugs had killed most of his pain and those same drugs had made him a little light-headed. The mercy of modern medicine, he thought, the things given to those who had no further hope of life and so had no fear of addiction. The least the doctors could do for those who had ruined their bodies in an effort to save the lives of those who now tended them. Drugs which, perhaps, he shouldn't have been given but which Anne had supplied.

Frieda Osten – dead. Where had she gone? What had become of all that painfully acquired knowledge? Was life nothing but an endless joke in bad taste?

If the planets are inhabited then surely Earth must be their Hell!

Who had said that? Where had he read it? When?

The greyness closed in as he tried to remember, the cloud of painless detachment filled with bright images that enfolded him and carried him to a new bright world where Irene came to him and they were young again.

A week later Spragg refused his medication. 'No.'

'Why not?' Anne stood with the tray in her hand, the syringe, the swabs and pills.

'I want to get out of here. There's work to be done –'

'And others are doing it.' She looked down at him, shaking her head. 'Your body needs rest and time to heal. Try walking now and you'll collapse. You could rip open the incision and haemorrhage. Damn it, Mal, get some sense!'

He glared at her. 'How long must I stay here?'

'Five weeks, maybe six. Just get used to it, Mal, and stop acting like a spoiled child.'

Frazer came to visit him during the third week. He limped and one cheek was puckered with an angry wound and a bandage made a turban on his head but otherwise he seemed normal.

Sitting, he said, 'You heard about Frieda?'

'Yes.'

'A marvellous woman. Gone. The goddamned waste!' One hand clenched where it rested on his knees. 'We were close, you know that? It wasn't just sex though she made that that wonderful. We thought alike and enjoyed the same things. She used to read me poetry and we played mathematical games. Hell, I was even learning German so as to be able to tell her I loved her in her own language. God, how I loved her!' Frazer blinked and looked away. After a moment he said, 'I'm sorry, Mal. I guess you don't want to hear all that.'

'It's all right, Harry. I understand.' The man had needed to talk, to get it off his chest. Spragg heaved himself up in the bed. The bruises, lacerations and contusions had mostly healed as had the broken ribs and leg but the wound in his back continued to bother him and, at times, he spat blood. 'How's it going? The work, I mean.'

'The probe was a bust as you probably know. The records were hit by the wreckage so all we have is what we saw and can remember. They've sent out another probe – a souped-up missile adapted for the job, but it won't hit for a while yet.' Frazer snorted his anger. 'The fool! Trust the military to louse things up. Lauter should have got the spectrogram while he had the chance!'

He hadn't and it was no good crying over spilt milk. The new probe would do the job. Spragg said as much and Frazer nodded reluctant agreement.

'It's a matter of time,' he said. 'We need every minute we can get. Before I can determine a firing sequence I need to know what I'm shooting at. Ice, rock, nickel-iron, lead – it makes a difference.'

But did it? Spragg thought about it after Frazer had left. The man was a specialist; a civil-engineer trained in the application of atomic power to cut channels, level hills, gouge tunnels through mountains. In such cases he would need to know the nature of the material he had to deal with. None of that applied to Thor. All that was needed was to kick the mass from its present path. Ice or iron – the basic difference lay only in the relative densities. It took less force to move a bladder filled with air than one filled with water.

That night, drugged, he dreamt of giants playing billiards using planets as balls.

The new probe reached Thor at zero minus 35. Spragg, dressed, strapped in a web of bandages, weak but grimly determined, gripped the arms of his wheelchair as Anne pushed him through the passages of the hospital and outside. She looked tired, red passion-bites showing on her neck, dark smudges circling her eyes. Spragg wondered if it was the drugs he'd been given or a sour jealousy coupled with his present inadequacy that made her seem less attractive than before.

He winced as the chair dropped over a kerb. 'That hurt!'

'Sorry.'

Like her face her voice revealed fatigue and he felt a sudden shame as he noted the thin lines meshing the corners of her eyes, the bruised appearance of her mouth. She was doing her best and who was he to blame her? Should a man be angry at the sun for shining on others than himself?

She swung the vehicle so as to avoid another minor crater. 'Things aren't what they were.'

An understatement – the installation looked as if it had been in a war. On all sides dumped and discarded containers lay in mounded confusion. The roads were scarred and pitted with the churn of wheels and tractors. Prefabricated huts stood huddled as if aware of the slums they appeared to be. Wind-blown trash had drifted against every obstruction. The air stank with the smell of burning.

As with the equipment so the men. They moved in stained uniforms, red-eyed, bearded, drugged against fatigue as they fought their battle against time. A battle that produced too many casualties as Spragg well knew. He watched sombrely as an ambulance passed them heading towards the hospital, the crude extensions which ringed it. Another man with a broken limb, acid-seared lungs, chemical burns to face or eyes, fingers missing, internal organs ruptured or a mind gone under ceaseless strain.

'Anne, will –' He broke off as a siren wailed from far across the area and cringed as, in the distance, a launch spouted fire as it headed up into the air. Another load bound for space but would it make it? Would it veer, break from control, run wild? The fear died as the flame dwindled and he looked at his hands where they gripped the arms of his chair, the knuckles gleaming white beneath the skin.

'Mal?'

'Nothing.' What was the point in asking her for a date? 'I was going to ask if this trip will take long?'

'Five minutes. Relax.'

Most were strangers but there were faces he knew; Lauter with a patch over his missing eye, Frazer, scarred but with his bandage set at a rakish angle, Aldcock who smiled and came forward to relieve Anne of the burden of the wheelchair.

'Nurse, you look marvellous! Did this crumb give you any trouble?'

Smiling, she shook her head.

'Lucky for you, Mal. This girl's a friend of mine.' Aldcock saw Spragg's expression. 'Something wrong?'

'No.' With an effort Spragg managed to control his jealousy. Aldcock had been up and capable while Spragg had been lying helpless in his bed. Well, to hell with it, he wasn't helpless now. 'Help me up out of this.'

'No, Mal!' Anne gripped his shoulder. 'You stay in the chair or I'll take you back to the hospital.' To Aldcock she said, 'See he doesn't do anything stupid. I'll come back for him or send someone for him when he's ready to return.'

'You aren't staying?'

'No. There's nothing I can do here and it's no time to slack.' Bending over the chair she kissed Spragg on the cheek and whispered, 'Be good, lover, and get well real soon. Remember, I'm waiting.'

Aldcock said as she left, 'That's a beautiful girl, Mal. You're a real, lucky bastard. You know that?'

'I know it.' Spragg inched his chair towards the end of the room, the big screen hanging against the wall. 'How long now to wait?'

Thor was as he remembered having seen it before; a huge, enigmatic lump of material, the surface glistening, marred only by the slowly oscillating patch of darker substance. The probe, he guessed, was at a greater distance, added amplification bringing the invader close. A guess verified by Lauter as he took his place beneath the screen.

'For those of you who've seen this before the probe is an adapted missile fitted with a projectile tube which can fire self-propelled thermite shells.

For those who are with us for the first time this is Thor now at a distance of approximately 15,000,000 miles. In exactly 35 days it will hit the Earth unless we are able to deflect it. The purpose of this exercise is to determine, if possible, its constituents. We shall do this by firing a thermite projectile at it and thus causing a portion of it to turn incandescent. The luminous vapour thus created will be recorded on a spectroscope. From the arrangement of the Fraunhofer Lines we shall be able to discover what kind of material forms the planetoid.'

An explanation unnecessary to the majority of those present but Spragg guessed some of the strangers must be visiting politicians or others of high influence who needed to be put in the picture.

The image on the screen wavered and blurred. The signals coming over those millions of miles of emptiness, battered by the solar wind, affected by the impact of stray atoms, the magnetic field of the Earth itself, the mess of electronic 'noise' which clothed the planet. To get reception at all was in the nature of a miracle.

And then, as another technician had reported on the previous occasion, the man said, 'We're getting a pull of some kind. Zero-magnetic field but we're getting a pull.'

Frazer said, 'Fire the projectiles! For Christ's sake, Colonel, don't let's louse up this chance too!'

A comment Lauter ignored as he snapped to the man at the board, 'Fire one projectile!'

Spragg leaned forward in his chair his eyes intent on the screen. The command would take 80 seconds to reach the probe and it would take as long again before they could be certain it had been obeyed. A long time during which the image grew larger to suddenly reveal, to one side of the dark patch, a scintillating spot of brilliance.

'Got it!' Frazer shouted his relief. 'Now try and hit the patch!'

A small target and one the projectile missed as, far to one side, another burst of radiant energy sprang into being. On companion screens rainbows flared to life; wide-banded spectrums marked with the dark Fraunhofer Lines. The spectroscopic images from each of the test-sites and, as far as Spragg could tell, identical.

'Hydrogen, iron, helium, sodium!' Aldcock read the lines as if he were reading a book. 'Cobalt, lithium, Thorium? Yes, Thorium – nothing heavy as yet. Nickel and gold.' He swore as the spectrums flickered. 'What's happening?'

The probe was beyond control. Spragg heard the sharp interplay between Lauter and the technicians as he stared at the image on the screen. It grew larger, spread to dominate the area, passed beyond it, blurred now, fuzzy, details lost as it neared too closely to the scanners, then, abruptly, was gone.

'Damn!' Aldcock glared at the blank screens. 'Well, it's no real loss. We'll have the recordings. What do you think, Harry?'

'A mix,' said Frazer. 'At least as far as I could see. Would you say it was normal, Earth-type composition?'

'Could be.'

'What kind of an answer is that?' Frazer appealed to Spragg. 'What is it, Mal?'

'I don't know and neither does Bud. The spectroscopic lines will have to be checked against known elements and even then we'll only know what is to be found on the surface. But it isn't made of ice or solid lead or iron or anything too alien. Basically it's a chunk of rock with an assortment of various elements in an unfamiliar ratio. If you want to know how it should be treated I'd suggest you handle it as you would basalt.'

An answer and Frazer was apparently satisfied with it but other questions remained. Had they done more than test the surface patina? Was the mass homogeneous? And, above all, why had both probes been affected by a tremendous attraction?

'A mascon?' Over the phone Ogden's voice echoed his bewilderment. 'What the devil's that?'

'No one knows just what a mascon is,' Spragg explained. 'The name was coined for them way back when the Apollo landings set up seismometers on the surface of the Moon. Scientists were puzzled at the quakes that happened at frequent intervals and speculated they had to be caused by lumps of highly dense matter buried far beneath the surface. With me so far?'

'Yes.'

'For a lump of matter to have a high gravitational attraction it must be incredibly dense. Both probes were pulled towards Thor when they shouldn't have been. There is no possibility of magnetic attraction. The planetoid isn't large enough to have exerted such a pull if it's merely a mass of solid rock laced with heavy elements so there has to be another explanation. I'm positive I've found it. Somewhere, buried below the surface, there has to be a mascon.'

'Which, as you admit, no one knows anything about.'

'I know it's there,' snapped Spragg angrily. 'Something has to be inside Thor for it to have exerted such an attraction. Call it a lump of neutronium if you want – God alone knows what a mascon is, but stop being a bloody fool and listen. You wanted information – well, I'm giving it to you.'

'Is it important?'

'Run out on the field,' said Spragg dryly. 'Take a kick at a football. What happens if someone's filled it with concrete during the night?' He listened. 'Yes, now you've got it. If Thor contains a mascon, and I'm certain it does, then the planetoid is of a far higher density that we'd imagined. To knock it aside is going to take all the force we've got. So if we, or anyone, has been holding anything back get on their necks and make them cough up. You understand?' His voice rose a little. 'I was at the UN, remember, and I can guess how those bastards intend to work. So get with it, man! Get with it!'

'This can be verified?'

'Yes. They know here already.'

'Then leave it with me.' Ogden added, in a softer tone, 'Sorry to hear about you getting hurt. Better now?'

'I'll live. Have you any news of Irene? No?' Spragg felt himself slump. 'Well, thanks for trying. If she should contact you – you know? Yes, of course, I'd forgotten. Do your best, eh? Thanks.'

Hanging up, he slumped against the side of the booth. No matter what happened now he'd done all in his power to do. Even to calling Ogden from an outside phone as he done before as they'd arranged before he'd come to Cape Canaveral. Cloak and dagger stuff, which he'd thought then and knew now to be utter nonsense.

He straightened, aware of watching eyes in the liquor store where he'd used the phone. The proprietor was suspicious. Spragg couldn't blame him. He must look like hell what with the drugs and hospitalisation not to mention the days of study during which he'd checked the records of both probes together with those from the space observatory. And the battle with red-tape in order to have certain tests and observations made hadn't helped either.

A horn blared from the street outside as he left the booth and headed towards the counter. 'Give me Scotch,' he ordered. Any brand.' He found money and threw notes on the counter. 'As much as the money will pay for. I'll see what my driver wants.'

He was a big, beefy man with a red face and a shock of red hair beneath his stained uniform cap. He sat behind the wheel of the army truck on which Spragg had scrounged a lift.

He said, 'Buster, I'm leaving. You coming or staying?'

'I'm waiting for a few bottles. I –' Spragg turned as the proprietor joined him at the door with his order.

'Good. Could you carry them to the truck for me, please?'

A mile down the road the driver sighed his satisfaction and handed the opened bottle back to Spragg. 'Don't get me wrong, Prof. I'm not against you egg-heads. It's just that I got word there's trouble brewing at the gate. Some nuts wanting to give us a hard time. Leave it too long and I'd have had trouble getting back in time and I've a hot date with something special. You dig?'

'Sure.' Spragg took a drink and handed back the bottle. 'Keep it.' The rest of his purchases he'd tucked about him.

'Uh, uh.' The driver grunted as he slowed a little. 'Look at the creeps!'

They were the usual crowd for whom demonstrations had become a way of life.

'You know what they want? They want us to stop work. They don't like what we're doing. The bloody fools!'

A man carried a placard adorned with a skull and the words DEFY NOT GOD! Another bore the appeal to REJOICE IN THE LORD! Spragg read THE END IS NIGH! on a placard thrust at his face. A girl with a mane of tangled hair and a face blotched with acne screamed, 'Sinners! You work for Satan!'

The driver was fuming, affected by the alcohol he'd nipped during the journey, conscious of the passage of time and the prospect of missing his date. The truck lunged forward, horn blaring, lights flashing as it roared towards the crowd blocking its path. Spragg saw grim faces, eyes suddenly terrified, a mad scramble of those with the sense to recognise their danger. A woman, more dedicated than the rest, stood with arms outstretched. A willing martyr to the cause.

Spragg switched off the ignition as a man jerked the woman to one side. The engine backfired as he again twisted the key, the report echoing like synthetic gunfire. Ahead the crowd abruptly thinned. To one side of the road a gaunt, bearded character flung a bottle that starred the windscreen with a mesh of fracture-lines. The placard at his side read GOD IS LOVE!

CHAPTER 17

The bottles Spragg had bought were for his birthday, which he celebrated a few days later. The cake bore a single candle and rested on the chest of drawers of his old room. Looking at it Waldemar said, 'One candle? Mal, my friend, I know you must be older than that.'

'I've only had one birthday – all the others were anniversaries. Come in, Harry! You too, Bud! Carl, make some room.'

Waldemar had arrived early and he dutifully moved up the bed. Spragg, as host, occupied the chair and waved at the bottles he'd set out on the floor beneath the window. Glasses and water rested next to the cake. Mixers were stacked next to a tub of ice on the floor.

Frazer said, as he handed over a bottle, 'Many happy returns, Mal. Hope you like gin.'

Aldcock said, as he handed over his own contribution, 'Why didn't you hold this shindig in the club?'

'Too many strangers.'

'The hospital then?'

'Too many nurses and doctors telling me I mustn't drink.' Spragg helped himself to whisky, soda and ice. 'They must think I'm going to live forever.'

He settled back, nursing the drink as others crowded into the room. Lauter had brought a friend, Major Judd, an expert in space medicine who favoured pungent cigars. A nurse and two WACs joined in and Spragg was appreciative when, complaining of about the heat, they removed their tunics.

Zach Cheyne thrust his head into the room and sniffed. 'Who the hell is smoking old socks? They – sorry, Major, didn't see you. Hi, Mal, how goes it?'

'I'm fine.'

'You look like death. Here, take a shot of Old Granddad, it'll warm you up.' As Spragg obeyed Cheyne said, 'I was saving that for a special occasion. I guess we're near it, uh?'

'Close, Zach, we've 22 days to go.' Spragg studied the contents of his glass. 'That's why I'm celebrating my birthday. I may not have time later on.'

'None of us will have time. How about it, Colonel? When do we launch?'

Lauter hesitated then said, 'We haven't finally decided yet.'

'We've had problems,' said the Major. 'Things we didn't expect.' He remembered the Colonel. 'I'm sorry, sir, but –'

'Go right ahead.' Lauter eased the patch covering his missing eye.

'Well, we've had trouble like I said. Accidents which shouldn't have happened and there's been some nasty incidents with the Angels. I guess you know about that?' He grunted as Cheyne nodded. 'Of course. You'd be the first to get the information. A man can't crap up there without it registering on your dials.'

'That's no longer quite true, Major. There's too many up there and we've too much to do monitoring the launches. We don't even monitor the Kamikaze.'

'Them!' Judd swallowed his drink and held out his glass for more. Frazer provided it. 'You ever wonder what makes a man want to throw away his life? Can you understand that?'

'Yes,' said Spragg. 'They call them martyrs.'

'Those who aren't committing suicide but who are sacrificing their lives for a cause.' Waldemar nodded. 'I've always thought they had to be a little crazy.'

'They are,' said Judd. 'They have to be to deny the survival instinct but the trouble is that instinct won't be denied. Once the euphoria of volunteering wears off it gains strength and begins to show itself in the form of diminished performance. The volunteer becomes prone to accidents and psychosomatic ills. He doesn't want to back out and he doesn't want to die, so anything which offers an honourable way out of the predicament is just fine.'

Waldemar said, 'I understand what you are saying, Major, but surely this was not wholly unexpected? Don't you have means at your disposal to correct the situation?'

'Of course, we have drugs and hypnotic conditioning and both have been used to maintain the state of euphoria. But to put it bluntly we can't keep the Kamikaze hanging around too long. We either use them or lose them.' Judd emptied his glass. 'Could I try some of that Old Granddad?'

'Sure.' Spragg did the honours. 'How about the suits, Major?'

'You really want to know?' Judd glanced at the WACs. 'Well, I guess they're broad-minded.' They needed to be as he went into detail as to what life was really like cooped up in a personal coffin; the stink, the itches, sores, cramps, irritations and above all the claustrophobia to which none was immune. How long could a man remain sane once convinced he was buried alive? He ended, 'So that's another problem. How long can we keep a man effective while in a suit?'

'The Angels –'

'Are only in suits for a short stretch at a time. How long do you figure the Kamikaze will have to wear them?'

Frazer said, 'Burn at 1-G for 14 minutes and we will have matched Thor's velocity. To meet the deadline we should begin shooting this time tomorrow.'

'Which means at least ten days in free fall while coasting to the rendezvous.'

Judd frowned through the smoke of his cigar. 'I wouldn't like to guess how many of them would be functional at the end of that time.'

'Would it matter?' The nurse had a pretty face but there was nothing wrong with her brain. 'Once the missiles are close will they need further guidance?'

'Unfortunately, yes.' Lauter glanced meaningfully at Spragg. 'That's one of the troubles we were talking about. Recent discoveries have aggravated the problem and we'll have to guide those missiles right up until impact.'

'Couldn't we halve the journey time?' suggested Spragg. 'Extend the burn or double the acceleration. The men should be able to stand 2-Gs.'

'They probably can,' agreed Lauter. 'I'm not so sure about the units. A longer burn is probably the best solution. We can arrange for extra fuel to be carried in bowsers accompanying the units and so maintain the thrust. It'll have to be something like that – I can't mess with the basic design at this stage.'

Spragg leaned back in the chair as the party dropped shop and concentrated on enjoyment. He felt sick and a little dizzy and his back hurt when he moved. His urine was an unhealthy colour and he wondered if his remaining kidney was functioning as it should.

Listening to the hum of conversation, the laughter from the man cuddling the WACs, the one with his arm high around the nurse, Spragg wondered what was going on in the real, political world. Waldemar could tell him and would if he insisted but it was easier to guess and, in any case, Carl was busy talking to Lauter. The big powers were now, Spragg guessed, showing their teeth. Either the small nations would cooperate to the full or, if the world survived, they would be crushed. And with the threats would come deals; all South America, Canada, Greenland and the Caribbean to the United States. Russia to spread west to the Atlantic, swallowing all Europe, the Balkans and Middle East. China to get Japan, India, Indonesia and Australia. Africa would be split and serve as the arena for future tripartite wars.

The hammer of God splitting the world in more ways than one.

'Mal?' Spragg jerked as Frazer touched his shoulder, aware that he had fallen asleep. 'You all right?'

'I'm fine.' The sleep had done him good. Spragg looked around the room. Everyone had gone aside from Frazer. 'What happened?'

'You just sat back and went quiet and we all thought you'd passed out. So we just got on with the party. Those who were lucky sneaked off with the girls and the rest of us talked shop for a while. I've stayed to make sure you're okay.'

Frazer found two glasses and loaded them with Scotch, soda and ice.

As Spragg took one he asked: 'Did they decide when to launch?'

'No, but it won't be tomorrow. Didn't you hear the discussion before you went to sleep? Lauter's waiting until they are ready upstairs.' Frazer jerked his thumb skywards. 'When they are he'll decide on the time and date.'

'Worked out your schedules?'

'A long time ago. Pick a date and time and number of missiles and I'll tell you when to send then, how fast they should go and where they should be aimed.' Finishing his drink Frazer turned towards the door. 'I'd better leave now. You sure you're OK?'

'Don't worry about me.'

Frazer paused and looked back from the passage. 'Were you really celebrating your birthday?'

'No,' said Spragg. 'My wedding anniversary.'

On zero minus 17 Earth launched its defence against Thor. It was too close and an unhappy compromise but the best which could be achieved. To increase the thrust would be to endanger the units, to launch too soon would be to risk the Kamikaze, to wait would be to let Thor come far too near.

Facts and figures, which every technician knew as did mathematician. As did Barry Dunne.

He waited in the revolving can that had been his home for the past 19 days. He was stripped and naked aside from shorts and his chocolate skin held a faint sheen of sweat. To one side lay his suit, every piece checked and rechecked by both himself and the attendant who would help him into it. He didn't talk. He didn't want company. He just wanted to sit and lean against the metal wall and let his mind drift as the grab-rope leading to the airlock drifted in the zero gravity at the centre of the can. Like he would drift when, later, mounted on his assembly, he would be thrust into space to drift for 180 hours before destruction.

He was quite calm. Even when a man sitting to his left down the can began to croon a wailing chant he didn't look in his direction. The chant was as meaningless as the soft hiss of air from the tanks of his suit, the shuffle of feet over the metal of the can, the rustle of clothing, the coughs, snorts, gasps of his fellows. Noise that had no power to register on his mind at this time. He could think of nothing, feel nothing not directly related to his mission.

And the things he had seen and heard and experienced while in space had less impact than the childhood memories of tears and laughter.

'Ready, Barry?' The attendant leaned forward a little. 'Time to go, man. Up and in your shell.'

Up and into the exoskeleton of metal and plastic and multi-layered fabric, the internal mesh and the braces and supports, the pipes fitted into the orifices of his body, the water nipple placed where his lips could find it as was the nipple dispensing the flavoured paste containing his food and drugs, and then the helmet and tanks and the air softly hissing and the mechanical voice coming from his helmet radio.

'All Kamikaze 34 through 78 report for assignment. Check in at the flashing green beacon.'

An order repeated as Barry jumped and gripped the rope and led the way towards the airlock and through it and out into space. Out to where a green jewel winked with a soft pulsation and a grotesque construction of tanks and struts and flaring Venturis and grimly menacing containers marked and starred with warning symbols waited with others to receive their human cargo.

'Askew and Clark – number 52. Elcar and Harris – number 53. Cook and Manning – number 34.'

Men drifting like wingless birds, sparkling reaction pistols wafting them on their way to reach the units which they would ride, to settle, to seat themselves, to strap in to wait.

Dunne had drawn Fred Kika, an ethnic brother, as his companion. He barely remembered the man and took his place without attempting to communicate. A silence shared by them all now that the moment had come.

'U33 – go!' A pause then, 'U34 – go!'

A stream of numbers at spaced intervals answered as engines flared to life and tongues of flame thrust the units out and away from Earth. Flame that ate the fuel even though reaching only a 1-G acceleration. A thrust that lasted less than 10 minutes.

Dunne felt the artificial gravity thrust him back against his support and held him as if he lay on his back looking up at the starry universe, the guide-screen before him displaying the dot that was his target-star. It was covered by another of a different colour and even as he watched it drifted to one site. A touch and it was back in place again only to drift to the other side. Another adjustment and the dots matched and held.

'Neat.' The voice from his direct link to his companion was soft and precise. 'You've got the touch, man. And the control too.'

'I've got it.'

And he wanted to keep it – while he did the guiding he was more than just a passenger or a safeguard in case of an emergency. Then he remembered why they were riding double, the reason they had been given.

'I'll maintain control for the first spell,' he said. 'After we refuel you can sleep if you want.'

'Maybe. Any sign of the bowser?'

Dunne stared ahead seeing nothing but the blaze of stars that filled the heavens. Automatically he checked the guide-screen and felt satisfaction when he saw the coloured dot matched to the target-star. As he looked something dark occluded a glittering point.

'There!' Kika lifted an arm as he pointed. 'See it? Over to the right and above.'

It grew as they watched, becoming a grotesque creature of the void, tanks and struts and Venturis, the whole dotted with blazing lights, a cabin that housed the crew not on watch.

Dunne turned, seeing the other units that had left with him spread before and behind and to either side. An armada coasting now, identified by the winking beacons set high above where the pilots sat. As he watched a unit jetted fire to realign itself. Another, far to one side, was obviously in some kind of trouble.

Looking back towards the bowser he saw the flare of reaction pistols as suited men streamed from the structure and an open craft containing Angels head towards the straying unit. The ether was suddenly filled with a blur of voices.

'U38 – for Christ's sake stay on course! U41 – get ready to receive Angels. Mack! Harry! Get moving or we'll lose the bastard!'

Sections drifted away from the main bulk of the bowser; tanks handled by men, impelled by open craft. They reached the drifting units and steadied, matching velocities and direction, the men working with frantic haste as they touched.

'Steady! Watch what you're doing you fool! Hold firm, damn you! Move!'

Dunne felt his own unit shift a little as the Angels made contact. They ignored both him and Kika as they freed couplings, adjusted pipes, activated the pumps that filled the empty tanks. When the task was done a man thrust his helmet against Dunne's.

'Watch the bowser. When you see the top signal-light blink red-green-red blast ahead. Burn for seven minutes precisely. Got that? Seven minutes then out and coast. Use the rest of the fuel as and when necessary to hold position. Luck!'

Then he was gone and Dunne watched the guide-screen, the now parted dots.

'What did he say?' Kika was curious. He grunted when Dunne told him. 'Top signal light, eh? You take it or shall I?'

'I'll take it. You keep watch in case some of the others come too close.'

A risk and one to be guarded against – when he fired the tubes Dunne wanted a clear stretch ahead. He watched for the signal, adjusting the controls to match the dots again as he waited. He saw red, green, red again and felt the push of his back-support as he fired the engines. A push that lasted until the overall velocity had built up 6 miles a second.

And then there was nothing left to do but wait.

Wait and keep the dots matched and try to forget the hiss of air in the helmet, the pressure of the suit and the itches and burns and cramps to come. To forget the stunning vista of the universe and the emptiness all around and most of all not to remember that this was all he would ever know for the rest of his life.

In his vision Thor began to dance and Spragg closed his eyes, seeing the movement against his closed lids, retinal flashes ringed with smaller points of fire, the flares of jetting rockets carrying men to their chosen sacrifice.

It had been something like the ritual dance of insects, he thought. The courtship flight of bees when the drones fertilise the queens then to fall and die. Or of fireflies painting elaborate pictures of light against the darkness of night as they wove minute flares of brief colour. The units had looked like that on the monitor screens as they had shifted in their elaborate saraband. It was hard to remember they had been fashioned in haste by the hands of men, each carrying a pair of heroes.

He looked again at the relay from the observatory. Thor was moving as predicted. But now tons of material were heading towards it and they would attract it with the same force as it would attract them.

But Thor, while big and heavy, was not a planet and some slight deviation could be expected. But not as yet. If at all it would come later – more figures to add to the rest, more predictions and reports to be made.

It seemed at times as if the world was nothing but a mass of dancing figures with feet drumming on his brain.

'Mal?' Frazer had stepped into his room and was looking at the screens. 'Well,' he said, 'it's done. The units are on their way. Now it's all up to the Kamikaze.'

Frazer rubbed a hand over his stubbled chin. 'We're doing it all wrong,' he said. 'We should have landed and drilled holes and set charges around the circumference and set them to blow all together so as to split the bastard in two. They would have passed over us; one section over each pole. If fragments had hit they'd have impacted ice.'

Spragg said, patiently, 'You're tired, Harry, or you wouldn't talk such crap. Drill holes – how many and how deep? A mile? Say they were a couple of miles apart you'd need something like 18,000 and as many atomic charges. And even then you'd have only ripped off the outer crust. What about the mascon?'

'If it's there.'

'It's there.' Spragg looked again at the relay. 'I guess we'd find one or more in every planet or large mass of material. They could be responsible for its formation. Drawing atoms to itself over the eons or collecting them from the formation-clouds in the beginning. We know they are in the Moon and I'll bet they are in Earth too.'

'Maybe.' Frazer shook his head. 'Holes,' he mused. 'Drilled with a laser. A mile deep and thousands of them. I guess I must be a little crazy. We couldn't have done that in a generation. Hell, we can't even do it here on Earth … I'm bushed,' he admitted. 'And you look as if you should be in bed.'

The room was as he had left it two days before, the bed still holding the imprint of his body. A hidden bottle yielded six ounces of Scotch and he nursed the drink as he lay on the bed. He should, he knew, undress and get under the covers but the effort would be too much and it was better just to lie and rest and take warming sips and let the comfort of the spirit dull his nagging aches.

'To you Reverend,' he murmured lifting his glass. 'Wherever you are.'

Destiny – who could defy it? Things happened because they must and none could know the reason. Yet Thor could provide the answer to everything. The doom promised by ancient Prophets and written in the sacred books. The punishment of God delivered by the hammer of His wrath. And against it they had only the fire of Satan. The fire and the blood of sacrifice.

Looking at the glittering stars he let his mind wander among a plethora of bright images induced by the subtle drugs in his food, the hypnotic conditioning of his mind. One that stimulated euphoria, but a conditioning that was wearing thin.

Dunne sucked air and took a sip of water and looked at the guide-screen. The dots were far apart and he hit the controls to bring them back in line. The flare from the jets thrust fingers of flame into space and he felt the unit move beneath him.

'Cut or burn!' Kika's voice was thin, edged with harsh dissonance, the words a threnody of remembered pain. Dunne listened and felt himself grow tense with sympathetic rage. Kika was his ethnic brother. His anguish was that of them both.

'Fred! Fred Kika! What's the matter with you, man? Grab hold now. You're raving!'

'My head feels funny. I keep having the same dream. Fires and men with hoods and my grandpappy nailed to the log. Cut or burn!'

'It's just a dream, Fred. Look ahead now and tell me what you see. Anything in the way we're going?'

Lights from the beacons of other units as they slowly converged. Shapes that occluded the stars and presented baroque outlines. A suited figure that waved and Dunne felt the warmth of companionship.

Kika said, breathing deeply, 'Barry, I don't want to die. I want to quit right now. To hell with the others. Let's turn this thing and head back home. I want out.'

Out of the chafing suits and personal coffins. Out of the misery they had squatted in for days now. Too many days and too much strain even for the drugs and dedication to surmount.

Back on Earth in the bunker a technician who had been monitoring the conversation waved at his superior.

'Trouble on U39. One of the pilots is acting up. Shall I – ?' He gestured towards a red button.

'How far to strike?' The officer pursed his lips at the answer. 'Give it as long as you can. Once they actually see Thor things could even out.'

Madness replaced by dedication. The urge to survive smothered by the impulse to sacrifice.

Dunne said, 'Take it easy now, Fred. We'll be remembered for all time. We're saving the world! All the kids in the kraals and those in the fields and all the brothers in the ghettos and those in school in Africa and all the other places we've heard about. Millions, billions of them. Give it time and we'll be the ones in power. But we have to give them that time.'

Time and pride and all the things they could win by his sacrifice. By his and the others now riding closer as, ahead, a mote swelled into a thing of brightness, a disc, a ball.

'There it is!' Dunne pointed. 'Thor!'

The Hammer of God bright with reflected glory and lying before them helpless to their attack. Their goal and target. Their tomb.

'No!' Kika twisted in his straps. 'I don't want to die! Let's all get together and dump everything but the fuel and ride back and –'

The words died as he died. Ending as the destructive charge incorporated in his suit exploded as the distant technician pressed the red button. Dunne heard a dull thud and saw his companion sag as he fell silent. Now his would be the task and his the glory. His name remembered for all time as the saviour of the world.

But he must keep the dots in line. The dots in line … in line … in line …

Matching them as the unit swept on, now caught in the gravitational attraction of Thor. It and those with it, a stream of units loaded with nuclear destruction, merging, riding close, heading towards the glowing orb of their target. Faster … faster … faster …

Laughing as he dissolved in flame.

CHAPTER 18

The house was just as he remembered. The lawn was ragged with the scars of winter, dead grasses lying like thin bones over the new-born green, the green itself dotted with the bright points of early flowers. The curtains, he noticed, were drawn.

The gate squealed as Spragg pushed it open, closing with a clang as his shoes rasped over the gravel of the drive. He was almost at the house when he saw the car parked on the far side.

Dropping his bag, Spragg headed towards it, hearing a rustle from the shrubbery shielding the rear of the house as he touched the bonnet. The engine was cold. He tested the doors and found them locked. The back of the vehicle was empty aside from two cans of petrol and another, sealed, of oil. Turning, Spragg headed towards the rear of the house then froze as he saw the double-eye of a shotgun aimed directly at his face.

'Hold it!' The shape behind the gun was hidden by the shrubbery.

'Who the hell are you?'

'I live here. Now just turn around and head back to the road and just keep walking or I'll blow your head off. Got it?'

'Live here? You bastard – I own this place!'

'You own it?' The voice changed. 'Spragg? Is that you, Professor?'

'It is.'

'Christ, man, you look awful!' Leaves rustled as Sam Eagan pushed his way through the shrubbery, gun lowered, eyes wide.

'I feel it.' Spragg swayed, fighting giddiness. 'Have you got a drink?'

He nursed it sitting in the chair facing the television in the living room, grateful for the fire Eagan had switched on, the pure malt doing more than the glowing bars to ease his chill. 'What are you doing here, Sam?'

'I grew tired of city life and fancied a little rest and quiet. So I packed up a few things and came out here. I didn't know where else to go.'

'And that?' Spragg looked at the shotgun.

'I borrowed it. I thought I'd find a rabbit or something.'

'In the shrubbery late in the afternoon?'

'I'm a city-dweller. How the hell would I know the best time to hunt?' Eagan took a sip of his malt whisky. 'You want me to leave?'

'No.'

'Good.' Eagan relaxed. 'There are some little luxuries in the fridge and I've put the rest of this where it will come to no harm.' He lifted his glass. 'Your health!'

'Cheers!'

Spragg felt himself relax. He was glad Eagan was here, he took the chill from an empty house and he had always liked company when he drank.

Eagan said, 'How was it, Mal? At the end, I mean.'

'It wasn't nice.'

'I heard a few things. In my job word gets around and not much stays secret. The pilots died, didn't they?'

'The Kamikaze. Yes, Sam, they all died.'

Burning like moths in a flame as they went, laughing, singing, praying, and screaming to their destruction. Spragg remembered what he had seen and heard; the echoes of murder, the ravings, the pleas from those who had weakened, the courage of those who had remained dedicated but one way or another all had died.

Sparkles in his glass evoked flashes of memory. Frazer retching. Cheyne babbling like a child with tears streaming from his eyes. Aldcock standing, beating his head against a wall, blood smearing his face.

A technician who had killed with the pressure of his red button solemnly commending the souls of the departed to God.

And the flame that had burned his eyes. The feeling when he had staggered from the bunker to lean against a wall, trembling, sweat dewing his face. Needing a drink. Needing to sleep. Needing to forget.

'Bad,' said Eagan. 'But at least you managed to get back home. Land at Prestwick?'

'Yes. I managed to hire a car and driver to bring me here.'

'You missed the big towns? You were smart. Things were getting nasty when I left Carlisle a couple of days ago. Riots, arson, looting.' Eagan poured them both fresh drinks. 'There's no reason for them to panic. They've been told over and over there's nothing to worry about. Listen.'

He pressed the television remote. Spragg looked at a bland face mouthing bland nothings. It was followed by his own in a clip taken from an early interview.

'For Christ's sake turn that crap off!'

He rose as Eagan obeyed and headed for the kitchen, A vial held the tablets he had been given and he swallowed three waiting for the drugs to diminish his pain.

'Mal?' Eagan called from the other room. 'You all right?'

'Yes.' The tablets were working,

'Want something to eat?'

'Just a sandwich.' He stepped to one side as Eagan entered the kitchen.

Spragg looked at his reflection in a mirror. His eyes were smudged with dark circles and he seemed to have lost most of his hair and the skin was meshed with lines.

'I don't wonder you didn't recognise me,' he said.

'When I heard the gate I just –'

'Decided to go hunting?'

'That's right.' Eagan's gaze was steady. He finished making the sandwiches. 'Let's go and eat.'

They ate and sat and talked and drank some more of the malt. Spragg caught himself as, dozing, he almost fell from the chair.

'I'd better get to bed. Which room are you in?'

'The spare in the front. Mal, I –' Eagan broke off as the gate squealed. Snatching up the shotgun, he moved towards the rear door. 'This could be nothing but I'd better make sure. Just sit down and relax.'

Minutes passed and then Spragg heard the sound of the door opening and footsteps as someone entered the house.

'Sam? Is that you?'

He rose as there was no answer and stepped to the door leading from the room and then froze,

'Hello, Mal,' said Irene. 'Welcome home!'

She looked a goddess, a dream as she stood illuminated by the dying light, a vagrant beam of the setting sun aureoling her hair and misting her face so that it seemed to glow. An illusion as Spragg discovered when he blinked at the smart in his eyes and found them moist with tears. But there was nothing false about the sudden weakness that gripped him, turning his legs to water so that he had to grip the jamb to prevent himself from falling.

'Mal!' She was at his side, arms firm in their support

'I'm fine.' He forced himself to straighten. 'I just didn't expect to see you. Eagan – the bastard!'

'He meant well,' she defended. 'I was here when he arrived and there seemed no harm in letting him stay. He liked you and I guess that was recommendation enough. But he couldn't know how I felt about you so he warned me you were here.'

'Warned you? With a shotgun?'

'He insists on guarding the place. Maybe he wants to feel he's earning the right to stay.' Her eyes widened as she searched his face. 'Mal, you're ill!'

'I'm all right. I was in an accident and in hospital for a while, that's all. And you?'

'Fine. Mal, are you sure?'

'I'll live as long as you – I promise. Let's sit down and have a drink and talk – Eagan?'

'He's staying outside.'

A delicacy Spragg hadn't known the man possessed but was glad he did when, later, he and Irene sat on the couch in close and warm proximity.

'I returned just after Christmas,' she explained. 'After I'd quit there seemed no point in remaining in the States and, well, I got homesick. Or perhaps I just wanted to make certain that your bitch didn't get my home.'

'Myrna lied, you know that?'

'I found out. Women of that type make enemies and some of them can be cruel. Mal, after I left did you –'

'I threw her out and tried to find you but you weren't to be found. So I joined up with Waldemar and others at Cape Canaveral. You remember Carl?' As she nodded he continued, 'He told me about Myrna, what she was doing and who with. Then, at the end, he helped to get me back home.'

'You should have brought him with you.'

'He didn't want to come. He's got ideas of his own and is staying in the States.' He added, 'Irene, I love you.'

She made no comment but her hand touched his own.

'I don't mean just want you, it goes deeper than that. I –' He swallowed. 'When I saw you it was like being shot. That's what made me stagger. It was the last thing I expected.'

But the one thing he had secretly hoped for – what else had drawn him back? Hurt, he had run like an animal to its lair. Hurt, she had done the same.

She said, 'You'd better get up to bed. A bath and a good sleep is what you need.'

'I've done enough sleeping.'

'A bath, then. It will relax you and maybe you could take a nap afterwards.' Her smile was tremulous. 'Please Mal. I don't want you to fall ill now that we're together again.'

'Are we together, Irene?'

'Yes, darling. And if that bitch tries to come between us –'

'I'll break her neck and bury her in the back garden.' Spragg kissed her gently on the cheek. 'Irene! We must never be parted again!'

Footsteps crunched on the gravel outside and a dark shadow passed over the curtains.

'Sam! He's coming back!'

'To hell with him! Irene –'

'No!' She pushed him from her. 'Later, my darling. Now go and get your bath and try to nap a while whilst I get us all something to eat.'

'We have eaten.'

'Sandwiches?' She glanced at the debris. 'I'm talking about real food. Now hurry, Mal, and don't forget to rest.'

'Which room shall I use?'

'My room,' she said. 'Our room.'

She had changed it around and cleaned it, removing all traces of Myrna.

Stripped, he bathed and sent his hand to make little waves as he soaked in the comforting water. The pills he had taken had combined with the alcohol to give a slight fuzziness to his senses.

Water splashed as he rose from the bath, little rivulets running over his torso. Dried, he padded into the bedroom and donned shirt and slacks from the bag Irene had carried upstairs. The bath had relaxed him but he was not yet ready to lie down. Instead he wandered about the chamber, looking, probing, opening the wardrobe and seeing expensive furs and gowns, racks of shoes, coats and hats. Closing the doors, he looked in the dresser and found a plethora of cosmetics, perfumes, unguents all of the best quality. Drawers held filmy lingerie. One held a small sheaf of unpaid bills.

He crossed to the window and opened the curtains to look at the dome of the observatory looming against the darkening sky. She must have been coming from it when Eagan had intercepted her to warn her of his presence. Had she been visiting old friends? Susan and even Hammond? Reilly wouldn't have known her from the old days but must have heard of her from the others. And there would be others; technicians and laboratory workers who would have made her welcome if they were still there.

Perhaps he should ask but he felt no inclination to visit the place where he had spent so many years. The curtains closed as he turned away and sprawled on the bed. Some light still filtered through where they had badly joined and he watched the glow on the ceiling, remembering other times in this very room when passion had ruled – but those times had been the product of lust, not love and, surely he could be forgiven his weaknesses.

He slept, drifting, seeing again the flame, the men dying, hearing their voices long seconds after they had been turned into ash. Knowing the sick, helpless despair.

'Mal?' Irene called to him through the closed door. 'Are you awake?'

'I am now. I'll be right down.'

Slipping on his shoes and jacket and headed downstairs. Eagan sat at one side of the table, Irene facing him at the other, the place of honour at the head reserved for himself. As he sat Spragg looked at what had been prepared, nostrils twitching to enticing smells.

'A banquet,' he said. 'Irene, this is wonderful!'

All the foods they had once yearned to taste but hadn't been able to afford now set with costly glass and silver. It was a part of what he had discovered; the expensive clothes, rare perfumes, trinkets and luxuries, which Irene had bought without regard for cost. A self-indulgence as was the food and wine.

Reading his face she said, 'Yes, Mal. Yes.'

The observatory, of course, they would know and would have told her. But Eagan?

'The truth, Mal,' he said. 'For God's sake tell us the truth. What happened out there? What went wrong?'

For answer Spragg rose and went to the big window and parted the curtain with a rasp of runners. It was there as he'd known it would be, larger now, smeared like a blood-stained thumbprint in the sky over the dome of the observatory. A sign and a portent that even now men were pointing at as they screamed their warnings of doom to come. Shouting louder than the lying newscasts, which still insisted there was nothing to fear.

'Behold the Hammer of God,' said Spragg. 'Once it was just a ball of rock and minerals a few hundred miles in diameter but we took care of that. We weren't satisfied to be crushed to death, we had to improve on the punishment of the Lord. Poetic justice – the Reverend Aird Gulvain must be laughing himself sick wherever he is. We tried to kick God's messenger in the rear and it blew off in our face.'

'Mal?'

'We sent everything we had against it,' he said, not looking at her. 'All the nuclear devices we could get into space and send on their way. The Fires of Satan with the Devils of Hell to guide them. And they did the job. They got there. They let loose with all that man-made destruction – and Thor hit back. Thorium,' he explained. 'Cobalt, strontium, lithium. Heavy metals. So we hit it and burned it and caught it alight and turned Thor into a plasma. Now we don't have a rock to worry about. We have a cloud of gas 10,000 miles wide and over 1,000,000 degrees centigrade.' He ended, bleakly, 'We've got two days.'

Spragg woke late on the morning of the second day and lay thinking of the festivities of the night before; a feast which put his homecoming meal to shame. Their last supper, the last time they would have the chance to sit and talk and eat and drink through the long hours before dawn. Then to bed and to make passionate love and to lie and talk some more but this time about the little intimate things that held lovers close.

Turning, he looked at Irene. She lay like a child with her knees bent and her face snuggled into the pillow, one hand lifted to rest below her chin. She was sweating, her skin dewed with moisture and he drew back the covers to reveal the rounded whiteness of her shoulders, the enticing lines of her back.

As he kissed them he heard the shout followed by the blast of the shotgun twice repeated.

'Mal?' Irene jerked awake. 'What was that?'

'Lie still.' Spragg slipped from the bed and dressed in shirt, pants and shoes. 'I'll see what's going on.'

Eagan met him as he ran from the house. The man was scowling, his face blotched and marked with scratches; injuries Spragg hadn't noticed before.

'What happened?'

'Kids from the village coming to see what they could find. I yelled and gave them both barrels. I wasn't aiming at them but they couldn't know that.' Eagan touched his scratched face. 'I got this from the shrubbery.'

A possibility but Spragg wondered why the man had wanted to fight his way through bushes. Why he was out in the first place when he had seemed so drunk when going to bed.

'You'd better go inside and get washed and tell Irene what happened,' said Spragg. 'Give me the gun and I'll look around.'

It was an unaccustomed burden but if Eagan had done what he shouldn't and men were after revenge they could mistake him for the other. A misjudgement, perhaps, Eagan could be as innocent as he claimed, but it did no harm to be sure and if some had the idea of raiding the house others could have the same object.

Following the road, Spragg made the familiar journey to the observatory, turning away from the main entrance and skirting the village. A man in the distance lifted a hand to shade his eyes as he stared in his direction and a woman, cleaning windows, paused until he had passed otherwise he saw no one. Returning, he circled the house and halted on a knoll to stare towards the road. Traffic was light, the normal rumble reduced to the faint whine of passing cars travelling at speed. The air held a hushed tension as if before a storm and swirling clouds covered the sky.

Irene was up when Spragg returned and watched as he settled the shotgun in a corner. She wore a thin robe, which stuck to her perspiring skin. Perfume enveloped her like a scented cloud and her hair shone like burnished gold.

'Coffee, Mal?'

'Tea. Where's Sam?'

'Upstairs. Did you notice he had blood on his shirt?'

'No. It probably came from those scratches.'

'Or someone who put up a fight.' Irene handed him a steaming cup. 'Could he have gone out after we went to bed and attacked someone in the village? A woman or girl?'

'I walked through the village,' Spragg sipped at his tea. 'No one seemed excited and if those people he shot at had come after him for having committed rape they wouldn't have given up so easily.' He added, 'But if you think he's that way inclined you're crazy to dress like that.'

The cup fell as she came into his arms and for a long moment the world was filled with scent and softness and the warm heat of demanding passion, which, somehow, changed to a fierce, protective tenderness.

After a while, Irene said, 'Shall we go for a walk?'

'If you want.'

'If Sam comes down keep him busy while I dress.'

Eagan came down as Spragg was making another cup of tea. He nodded and sat in a chair facing the big window rolling himself a cigarette. He had washed and changed and looked what he was; an aging, dissipated man.

Without looking up he said, 'When?'

'Tomorrow.'

'But you said –'

'You don't have to jump into a fire to feel the heat. There's a miniature sun out there and it's hot! Once it reaches us – before it reaches us – hell, man, use your imagination!' Spragg watched as Eagan lit the cigarette and inhaled. 'At least you won't have to worry about those things killing you.'

'Nor anything else. I didn't, you know.'

'What?'

'Rape a girl. I'll admit I had it in mind but when I got to the village I saw a man trying the same thing. She was screaming so I kicked him in the face and he got up and hit me so I hit him back. That's why I was outside with the gun. I guessed he'd come after me and he did.' Eagan added, musingly, 'I must have killed him. At least he fell down behind the shrubbery and didn't get up.'

'It doesn't matter.'

'I know. Drink?'

'No thanks. Irene and I are going out for a walk.'

'To be alone? Maybe I should be the one to go out.' Eagan blew more smoke. 'No? Then I'll just sit here and have a few drinks and do some thinking. You're certain we're all going the same way?'

'Yes.'

'Good.' Eagan looked at his hands, at the knuckles white beneath the skin. 'All of them,' he breathed. 'Every last, damned bastard!'

The inconsiderate, the uncaring, the unkind. Those who lied and stole and destroyed for the sake of destruction. The ones who loved to inflict pain. The thoughtless. The cruel. The indifferent. The bullies. The lovers of power. The ones who prated and practiced other than they preached. The hypocrites. The manipulators. The haughty, the proud, the bestial.

'It helps,' said Eagan. 'By God, it helps.' Liquid gurgled as he refilled his glass. 'Join me?'

'Just a small one.'

'You know, Mal, you live a life and at the end of it what've you got? Bad health, bad habits – and there isn't a soul who really gives a damn about what happens to you. And now it's over. Well, to hell with it.' He began to chuckle. 'Hell,' he said. 'what a joke if all along we've been on the wrong side and didn't know it. Bowing to the wrong God.' He looked at the black tablet Spragg placed on the table beside him. 'What's that?'

'An easy way out. It's what they gave to the Angels who'd been burned. It's quick – just bite and it's over.' Spragg added, bleakly, 'Don't play the hero, Sam. It isn't going to be pleasant.'

Irene was waiting when he left the room. She was dressed in a loose skirt and blouse, her legs bare as, he guessed, was the rest of her beneath the clothing. Her hair was bound with a brilliant scarf and she carried a small basket.

'Picnic things.' she explained.

They found a rolling meadow edged with trees and sat after long hours of walking to eat and drink and rest in the seclusion of shrubs sweating from the heat, which had turned spring into summer. The motorway now was quiet aside from the occasional whine of a speeding car, which made an accompaniment to the rustle and song of birds. Spragg plucked a blade of grass and studied it as if he had never seen grass before which, as he thought wryly, was near enough true as he studied the delicate tracery of fibres, the curl, the shape, the colour.

'This is so beautiful, Mal!' Irene sighed her appreciation as she lay at his side. 'It seems such a shame it all has to go.'

Burned, destroyed, seared to ash – had Eagan been right? Were they paying the penalty of failing to recognise who really ruled Earth? If the space programme had not been thwarted, if they had pressed on to take what was before them there would have been more machines, more trained men, better systems of control. They would have been able to hit Thor months ago, shattering it, spreading it through space in harmless fragments. Would God really have wanted to destroy his own? Could Satan have won had there been no interference?'

'Mal!' she whispered. 'Mal!'

They made love in the shelter of the bushes, her naked skin glowing like radiant pearls. A time of tenderness ruled by affection as he stored more memories and found a momentary forgetfulness. And afterwards they lay to look up at the branches ripe with budding leaves, delicate shades of green that veiled them from the sky.

And then to walk again, hand in hand, over the grass and along the paths, seeing no one and pleased to be alone.

It was late when they returned to the house and Spragg halted as he heard the voice then relaxed as he realised from where it came. Eagan had switched on the television and sat before it, immobile, one hand holding his glass. The voice was the usual stream of lying assurance promising all would be well and Spragg listened to it for a moment and then, with sudden rage, snatched up a bottle and sent it hurtling to smash the tube.

To Irene he said, 'I've always wanted to do that. Now go and get your shower while I sort out some music. What would you like? Bach? Mozart? The Rolling Stones?'

'Just music. Something not too solemn. How's Sam?'

'He's drunk, I guess. You go along now while I take care of him.'

Eagan was dead, his eyes open, his lips parted, a mote of black staining the lower lip. Spragg took the glass from his stiffening fingers and closed his eyes then, with an effort, heaved the man on his shoulders and carried him up the stairs to his bed. He sagged as he closed the door and leaned gasping against the wall, hearing the gush of the shower as Irene laved herself, seeing black motes and vivid flashes as he fought the pain searing his back. As the gush of water died he straightened and went back downstairs where he took a stiff drink and more pain-killing tablets. When Irene joined him dressed all in white like a virgin bride he was relaxed and smiling.

'You look beautiful,' he said. 'You are beautiful.'

'You're biased. Where's Sam?'

'In bed. He's out cold.' Spragg glanced at the music unit as the sound died. 'Well, that's it. I guess the power's failed. What shall we do now? Drink? Talk?'

'Let's go outside.'

Out into the garden there to lie side by side on the ragged grass now tinged with ugly, sombre hues. To hold hands and to feel the immensity of the universe and to know that, elsewhere, crazed humanity ran and screamed and aped the beast. But here they were alone.

'Mal, what will happen when it reaches us?'

'We burn. The air, the seas, the soil, everything. The trees will go, the grass, the ants and birds and worms and bacteria. The ground will fuse and turn into steam and the steam will be broken into atoms. When the plasma passes on the Earth will be nothing but a clinker.'

And perhaps he would have caused it with his report on the mascon. If he had kept silent, would the nations have dug so deep into their no-hope chests and used everything against the invader? Would a few bombs the less have made any difference?

'Mal,' she said. 'Mal – I'm afraid!'

He rose so as to look down at her and recognised the terror held back so long. To burn. To feel the searing touch of fire on the skin, the fat running, the blood boiling, to twist and run and scream like a living animal locked in an oven – the punishment of Hell now to be felt by all.

But not by her. Never by her.

'Here!' He produced the black tablets. 'Take one. Bite it. Quickly now you –' He sucked in his breath as her flailing hand hit his own and scattered the tablets far and wide in the ragged grass.

'Mal! Mal, for God's sake!'

He moved and found the other thing he'd obtained in the States and settled with it in his hand pointing at the back of her head. The short-barrelled revolver loaded in each of its six chambers. One shot was enough bringing instant, merciful death but he fired them all then, not wanting to see what he had done, turned to look at the sky.

The ghastly, glowing sky.

E. C. Tubb (1919–2010)

Edwin Charles Tubb was born in London in 1919, and was a prolific author of SF, fantasy and western novels, under his own name and a number of pseudonyms. He wrote hundreds of short stories and novellas for the SF magazines of the 50's, including the long-running *Galaxy Science Fiction*, and was a founding member of the British Science Fiction Association. He died in 2010.